TOM KRATMAN

THE LOTUS EATERS

SPQR

"... realistic action sequences, strong characterizations and thoughts on the philosophy of war." —*Publishers Weekly*

$7.99 U.S.
$9.99 CAN.

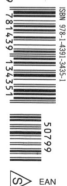

ISBN 978-1-4391-3435-1

50799

S EAN

PLACES TO GO AND
PEOPLE TO KILL

"I've got a prisoner," Cruz said into the radio. "No, I can't just kill him... Look; he's a member of a recognized belligerent force... He's got a chain of command..." Cruz looked up the trail at the bodies, tsked and said, "Well, I mean he had one... until quite recently, anyway... He's committed no war crimes of which I am aware... No, don't give me that bullshit... He was carrying his arms openly... and he... wait a minute." Cruz released his thumb from the microphone key and asked Esteban, "You did want to surrender, didn't you?"

The guerilla, rather, ex-guerilla, trouserless, on his knees with his hands bound, nodded his head so fast it was nearly a blur. If asked, he'd have said that his captor was twelve feet tall. In fact, Esteban would have towered over Cruz in another set of circumstances.

"Right," Cruz said, after keying the mike. "He's a legitimate POW under the laws of war. *I* can't just shoot him and I *can't* watch him; I've got places to go and people to kill. I want an evacuation helicopter with a jungle penetrator. NOW."

BAEN BOOKS BY TOM KRATMAN

A State of Disobedience

A Desert Called Peace
Carnifex
The Lotus Eaters
The Amazon Legion

Caliphate

Countdown: The Liberators
Countdown: M Day (forthcoming)

with John Ringo
Watch on the Rhine
Yellow Eyes
The Tuloriad

THE LOTUS EATERS

TOM KRATMAN

THE LOTUS EATERS

A Baen Books Original

Baen Publishing Enterprises
P.O. Box 1403
Riverdale, NY 10471
www.baen.com

ISBN: 978-1-4391-3435-1

Cover art by Kurt Miller

First Baen paperback printing, May 2011

Distributed by Simon & Schuster
1230 Avenue of the Americas
New York, NY 10020

Library of Congress Control Number: 2010005097

Pages by Joy Freeman (www.pagesbyjoy.com)
Printed in the United States of America

For Julia

WHAT HAS GONE BEFORE

5,000,000 BC through Anno Condita (AC) 469

Long ago, long before the appearance of man, came to Earth the aliens known by man only as the "Noahs." About them, as a species, nothing is known. Their very existence can only be surmised by the project they left behind. Somewhat like the biblical Noah, these aliens transported from Earth to another planet samples of virtually every species existing in the time period approximately five hundred thousand to five million years ago. Having transported these species, and having left behind various other, genengineered species, apparently to inhibit the development of intelligent life on the new world, the Noahs disappeared, leaving no other trace beyond a few incomprehensible and inert artifacts, and possibly the rift through which they moved from Earth to the new world.

In the year 2037 AD a robotic interstellar probe, the *Cristobal Colon*, driven by lightsail, disappeared en route to Alpha Centauri. Three years later it returned, under automated guidance, through the same rift in space into which it had disappeared. The *Colon* brought with it wonderful news of another Earthlike planet, orbiting another star. (Note, here, that not only is the other star *not* Alpha Centauri, it's not so far been proved that it is even in the same galaxy, or universe for that matter, as ours.) Moreover, implicit in its disappearance and return was the news that here, finally, was a relatively cheap means to colonize another planet.

The first colonization effort was an utter disaster, with the ship, the *Cheng Ho*, breaking down into ethnic and religious strife that annihilated almost every crewman and colonist aboard her. Thereafter, rather than risk further bloodshed by mixing colonies, the colonization effort would be run by regional supranationals such as NAFTA, the European Union, the Organization of African Unity, MERCOSUR, the Russian Empire and the Chinese Hegemony. Each of these groups was given colonization rights to a specific area on the new world, which was named—with a stunning lack of originality—"Terra Nova," or something in another tongue that meant the same thing. Most groups elected to establish national colonies within their respective mandates, some of them under the United Nations' "guidance."

With the removal from Earth of substantial numbers of the most difficult portions of the populations of Earth's various nations, the power and influence of transnational organizations such as the UN and EU increased dramatically. With the increase of transnational power, often enough expressed in corruption, even more of Earth's more difficult, ethnocentric, and traditionalist population volunteered to leave. Still others were deported forcibly. Within not much more than a century and a quarter, and much less in many cases, nations had ceased to have much meaning or importance on Earth. On the other hand, and over about the same time scale, nations had become

preeminent on Terra Nova. Moreover, because of the
way the surface of the new world had been divided,
these nations tended to reflect—if only generally—the
nations of Old Earth.

Warfare was endemic, beginning with the wars of
liberation by many of the weaker colonies to throw
off the yoke of Earth's United Nations.

In this environment Patrick Hennessey was born,
grew to manhood, and was a soldier for many years.
Some years after leaving service, Hennessey's wife,
Linda, a native of the Republic of Balboa, and their
three children were killed in a massive terrorist attack
on Hennessey's native land, the Federated States of
Columbia. The same attack likewise killed Hennessey's
uncle, the head of his extended and rather wealthy
family. As his dying testament, Uncle Bob changed his
will to leave Hennessey with control over the entire
corpus of his estate.

Half mad with grief, Hennessey, living in Balboa,
ruthlessly provoked and then mercilessly gunned down
six local supporters of the terrorists. In retaliation,
and with that same astonishing bad judgment that
had made their movement and culture remarkable
across two worlds, the terrorist organization, the Salafi
Ikhwan, attacked Balboa, killing hundreds of innocent
civilians, including many children.

With Balboa now enraged, and money from his
uncle's rather impressive estate, Hennessey began to
build a small army within the Republic. This army,
the *Legion del Cid,* was initially about the size of
a reinforced brigade though differently organized.
For reasons of internal politics, Hennessey began to
use his late wife's maiden name, Carrera. It was as

Carrera that he became well known to the world of Terra Nova.

The legion was hired out to assist the Federated States of Columbia in a war against the Republic of Sumer, a nominally Islamic but politically secular—indeed fascist—state that had been known to have supported terrorism in the past, to have used chemical weapons in the past, and to have had a significant biological warfare program. It was widely believed to have been developing nuclear weapons, as well.

Against some expectations, the *Legion del Cid* performed quite well. Equally against expectations, its greatest battle in the campaign was against a Sumeri infantry brigade led by a first-rate officer, Adnan Sada, who not only fought well but stayed within the customs, rules, and laws of war.

Impressed with the legion's performance (even while loathing the openly brutal ways it had of enforcing the laws of war), and needing foreign troops badly, the War Department of the Federated States offered Carrera a long-term employment contract. Impressed with Sada, and with some of the profits from the contract with the Federated States, Carrera likewise offered to not only hire, but substantially increase, Sada's military force. Accepting the offer, and loyal to his salt, Sada revealed seven nuclear weapons to Carrera, three of which were functional and the rest restorable. These Carrera quietly removed, telling no one except a very few, *very* close subordinates.

The former government of Sumer had a cadre and arms for an insurgency in place before the Federated States and its allies invaded. In Carrera's area of responsibility, this insurgency, while bloody, was contained through the help of Sada's men and Carrera's ruthlessness. In the rest of the country, however, the unwise demobilization of the former armed forces of the Republic of Sumer left so many young men unemployed that the insurgency grew to nearly unmanageable levels. Eventually, Carrera's area of responsibility was changed and he was forced to undertake a difficult campaign against a city, Pumbadeta, held by the rebels. He surrounded and starved the city, forcing women and children to remain within it until he was certain that every dog, cat and rat had been eaten. Only then did he permit the women and children to leave. His clear intention was to kill every male in Pumbadeta capable of sprouting a beard.

After the departure of the noncombatants, Carrera's legion continued the blockade until the civilians within the town rebelled against the rebels. Having a rare change of heart, Carrera aided the townsmen against the insurgents to take the town. Thereafter nearly every insurgent found within Pumbadeta was executed, along with several members of the press sympathetic to the rebels. The few insurgents he—temporarily—spared were sent to a surface ship for *rigorous* interrogation.

With the war in Sumer winding down, the Federated States, now under Progressive rather than Federalist leadership, unwisely fired Carrera and his legions. And, as should have been predicted, the terrorist money and recruits that had formerly been sent to Sumer, where the Salafi cause was lost, were instead redirected to Pashtia, where it still had a chance. The campaign in Pashtia then began to flow against the Federated States and its unwilling allies of the Tauran Union.

More than a little bitter at having his contract

violated and being let go on short notice, Carrera exacted an exorbitant price from the Federated States before he would commit his forces to the war in Pashtia. That price being paid, however, and in gold, he didn't stint but waged a major—and typically ruthless—campaign to restore the situation in Pashtia, which had deteriorated badly under Tauran interference and faint support.

Ultimately, Carrera got wind of a major meeting taking place across the nearby border with Kashmir between the chief of the United Earth Peace Fleet and the emir of the terrorists, the Salafi *Ikhwan*. He attacked, and in the attack and its aftermath killed thousands, captured hundreds, and seized a dozen more nuclear weapons, gifts of the UEPF to their terrorist allies. One of these weapons Carrera delivered to the capital of the major terrorist supporting state of Yithrab. When detonated, this weapon not only killed the entire clan of the chief of the Salafi *Ikhwan*, but also at *least* a million citizens of that city. In the process, he framed the Salafis for the detonation.

That destruction, seemingly at the hand of an Allah grown weary of terrorism, along with the death or capture and execution of the core of the Salafi movement in the attack across the Pashtian-Kashmiri border, effectively ended the terrorist war on Terra Nova.

The price to Carrera had also been heavy. With the end of the war with the terrorists, and having had more revenge against the murderers of his family than any man ought desire, he collapsed.

Unfortunately, he is still needed by his adopted home of Balboa.

CHAPTER ONE

How is Man to be well-governed? How is he to govern himself? Many approaches have been tried and many more proposed. Some of these have been, in the words of a philosopher of Old Earth whom we know of only as R.A.H., "weird in the extreme." None have worked; none have lasted. All have ultimately failed and usually in the most disastrous ways imaginable.

It must be admitted, as we begin our inquiry, that it may be that there is no answer. Possibly Man cannot be well governed, or not for very long. Possibly he cannot govern himself very well for very long, either.

And yet, there may be a clue in the words of another philosopher of the home world, the man we know of as Sherlock Holmes (which is probably a pseudonym). Perhaps, just perhaps, if we can eliminate the impossible, what will then remain, however improbable, might be the answer.

Let us, then, begin our inquiry.

> —Jorge y Marqueli Mendoza, *Historia y Filosofia Moral*, Legionary Press, Balboa, Terra Nova, copyright AC 468

Anno Condita 470
United Earth Peace Fleet *Spirit of Peace*

Against the tapestry of stars, the ship, its lightsail furled, spun on its own long axis. Below, likewise spinning, though at right angles to the ship, was the blue, green, and white world of Terra Nova. Between the world and the stars, past the ship's geosynchronous orbit, whirled the moons Hecate, Eris, and Bellona.

Inside the ship, on the low gravity observation deck, through a thick, transparent viewing port, Captain and High Admiral *pro tem* Marguerite Wallenstein searched for familiar constellations, mostly hidden in the bright sea of stars.

Eyes squinting, Marguerite managed to pick out the first of the five stars that formed the fangs of the constellation Smilodon. The head, however, was beyond her ability to perceive among the mass, even with those five to guide her. After a while, she gave up on the rest of Smilodon and began to search for the Leaping Maiden. This one was easier to see with the naked eye, situated as it was to the galactic north, in a field less dense with stars.

This is a waste of time, Wallenstein half-chided herself. *But for the nonce it's easier than thinking.* For the moment, thinking was sending her blood pressure up and giving her a sick feeling in the pit of her stomach.

A leggy, blue-eyed blonde who had missed beauty by an almost imperceptible fraction, Wallenstein was, despite appearances, well over a century old. The extra years and youth were the gift of Old Earth's anti-agathic medicine . . . that, and her position within the second highest of the home world's six castes.

In her hand, resting on her thigh, Wallenstein grasped a paper copy of a message received just that day via courier drone. The paper ordered her home for "consultations."

Still, I must think. What the fuck do they want of me, back on Earth? wondered Wallenstein. *What could the Consensus ask of me there that they would not just as well ask me via courier? I don't like this. Does the Consensus suspect I had a hand in the disappearance of my predecessor? Do they know I did? Do they know I helped one of the barbarians below to capture him and the marchioness of Amnesty? Do they know about the nukes? If they do, if they know any of that, I'll be going home to a quick court-martial, a quicker trip back to space, and an even quicker trip out an air lock sans suit.*

But it's not like I have a choice. They've already designated my stand-in. If I don't go, Battaglia will certainly have me arrested and that trip out the air lock will come even sooner.

Elder gods, if we knew of even one more world, I'd just take my ship there, colonize it, and set up in business for myself.

Sadly, we don't. It's Old Earth and New, and the rift that joins them, and that's it.

I can't even mutiny here. Senior in the Fleet I may be, but unlike most of the ships' captains I'm not in the peerage. A mutiny would have me and Peace and maybe a couple of others against the rest. That's a losing proposition, too. My own crew would space me if I tried it.

Her eyes continued their quest, searching now for the Pentagram, yet another of the constellations familiar here and unknown back home. Even while she searched, though, her mind decided. *Nothing for it but to go back home. There, maybe, I have a chance to survive. Maybe even I'll have a chance to prosper.*

Wallenstein turned her vision from space to the planet below. Her eyes focused on the area where the continents of Southern Columbia and Colombia del Norte joined. The narrow isthmus there was cloud covered now, as was much of the sea to its north.

If I thought it would work, she mused, *I'd consider asking Carrera for asylum. But since he hasn't answered my calls since that one day . . . no, home it is.*

Wallenstein sighed, thinking, *But who can I trust to keep an eye on things here for me?* Mentally, she ticked off the names of the fleet's captains, before finally settling on, *The count of Wuxi. Not only are we friends, but he's one of the few Class Ones who hasn't let that status go completely to his head. More importantly, he absolutely* loathes *Battaglia. Yes, Bruce can at least give me good intelligence when I return. If I return.*

The sick feeling in Wallenstein's stomach grew more acute with that thought. She turned her view back to that narrow isthmus. *And, speaking of Balboa and Carrera, I think maybe I need to have a meeting with General Janier before I leave, to advise him to cool it until I come back. If I do.*

Casa Linda, Republic of Balboa, Terra Nova

Lightning flashed over the wide *Mar Furioso* to the north, briefly illuminating the crested waves. Sometimes it struck down to the sea below. At others it seemed to dance from cloud to cloud, never touching down. Still other flashes were diffused behind heavy blankets of storm clouds, causing large portions of the angry sky briefly to glow.

Underneath the fiery display, surface vessels struggled through the waves, some on their way to the Transitway to the west, others having just left it, and still others merely paralleling the coast on their trek between Southern Columbia and Colombia del Norte, the twin continents joined at the narrow Isthmus of Balboa.

A couple of miles from the frothy surf, on the marble-railed back balcony of a grand old stone-built house, situated on a steep hill overlooking the sea, the lightning likewise lit two eyes. They were strange eyes and, to some, frightening. They watched the lightning as they watched the struggles of the ships at sea. They watched as if curious but not involved.

A primitive bird, extinct on its homeworld, landed on the balcony's railing in an effort to get under cover from the lashing rain. Half a moment later another bolt lit sky and eyes. Its light reflected from the eyes, making them seem as if they lit up of their own accord. The bird may have been primitive; it was not stupid. One look at the glowing eyes convinced it, *Better to brave the storm than to sit here with* those.

❖   ❖   ❖

Patricio Carrera blinked two or three times against the bright blinding flash. *Funny,* he thought, *for a half second there I thought I saw a trixie. Maybe I'm sicker in the head than I'd realized. Maybe...*

Ah, never mind. Not important.

Little seemed very important to Carrera, of late. Little had, since he'd collapsed the year prior, a result of a combination of overwork and overwhelming guilt at having become at least a candidate for the title of "Greatest Single One Day Mass Murderer in Human History." This wasn't a title he wanted, though he thought it was one he might well deserve.

Carrera looked down at his hands, thinking, first, *Miserable dainty things,* and then, *How can I defile my wife with the touch of hands so stained with blood?*

Besides that questionable title, Carrera had many others: The Blue Jinn... *Carnifex*—the Butcher. Most still referred to him by his military title: *Dux Bellorum,* in Latin, or *Duque,* for short, in Latin's daughter, Spanish. And no one had ever so much as suggested that he resign his title and position as commander of the *Legion del Cid.*

Though I should, he thought. *That, or find a way to force myself to take up once more the duties that are plainly mine.*

Lightning flashed again, in the distance. It was another shot of ribbon lightning, which again lit from behind the clouds across the sky.

That's what Hajar looked like... almost... in the last second before the fireball destroyed the camera I watched by. What did the people see—ninety-nine percent of whom, or more, were utterly innocent, I am sure—in that last second before the fire engulfed them? Poor sorry bastards.

But did I have a choice, really? A valid one, I mean? The Salafi Ikhwan intended to nuke not one but a dozen cities. Yes, I captured their nukes before they could. But they could have gotten more . . . probably . . . eventually. And they'd have used them if they had them, of that there is no doubt at all.

Now? Now they've no support. I nuked Hajar but they took the blame. And virtually everyone in the Moslem quarter of this world counts that as Allah's doing, his ultimate statement and command that terrorism is wrong. More practically, not one country in the world is loony enough, now, to give them shelter, on the chance they might bring in a nuke and allow it to detonate. A reputation for incompetence has hurt them more than any reputation for frightfulness.

I saved tens of millions of people, maybe. I killed a million, though, maybe more, for a certainty. And my hands still drip with blood. And I can't bring myself to touch my wife.

She was fairly tall for a woman of any race, but remarkably so for a woman of Balboa. In her stocking feet, Lourdes Nuñez Cordoba de Carrera, wife of Patricio Carrera, stood five feet, nine inches. In heels, which she usually avoided, she towered over her man.

Like her husband's, Lourdes' eyes, too, were rare. In his case it was the color, and the dark blue circles about the irises that gave them a frighteningly penetrating quality . . . that, and their odd habit of seeming to glow under certain lights at certain angles. In hers, a gentle and beautiful golden-brown, it was the sheer

size and shape that excited men and made women
cringe with envy.

Those huge and lovely golden-brown orbs remained
open, though the woman lay abed. Hand tucked
between pillow and cheek, Lourdes stared at the
strobe-lit French doors that led to the covered balcony connecting her husband's office and library with
their bedroom.

I'd wish he'd come to bed, the woman thought,
feeling frustration well mixed with anger and despair,
*but, then, what would be the point? All he'd do is
lie as far to his side of the bed as possible, and then
turn away. And if he actually did sleep? Then the
screaming would begin.*

*He thinks I can't guess at Hajar. Why do men think—
how* can *they think—that there are any secrets from
wives? I hear the name of the city; I hear him mutter
his plea for forgiveness. I see the tears on his cheeks.*

*But he never talks about it, when he talks at all.
Does he think I wouldn't understand? It was* war. *My
people were in danger. All* people *were endangered.
Worst of all, my children were targets. Does he think
I would prefer any number of strangers over my own
son, Hamilcar, or my little girl, Julia?*

*Silly man. Come to me and, for a while, at least,
I will make you forget. Come to me and give me
another son.*

In his own room, on the same floor, Hamilcar
Carrera, eight years of age, stirred. His eyes opened
and focused on the ceiling, onto which a home planetarium, the best model made on Terra Nova, painted
stars. The planetarium was a gift of the boy's father.

Instantly, sensing that their charge was stirring, the turbaned Pashtun who slept on the floor to either side of the boy, guarding him as if he were a god, were on their feet. They had weapons in hand as their eyes searched for the threat.

"It's nothing, Karim, nothing, Mardanzai," the boy assured his followers as he sat up. The Pashtun did not relax for an instant. "The thunder awakened me," Hamilcar explained further. Not that the guards needed explanations, oh, no. If it was their lord's will to awaken and walk, then it was their merest duty to follow and protect.

"Where is my father?" Hamilcar asked.

"I saw him on the balcony, lord," Karim answered.

"I will go to him, then," the boy said, sitting up and placing his feet on the throw rug beside his bed. "He shouldn't be left alone too long."

"I sent two men to watch over him after I saw he was awake," Karim said. "Alena, the witch, insists we watch over those you love, lord, as we watch over you." The boy nodded his thanks. He'd long since given up trying to break the guards of their form of address.

He was about to leave when a series of cautionary coughs from the Pashtun reminded him. Nodding again, the boy turned and walked to a corner of his room, taking in hand his rifle, a handmade gift of the Balboa Arms Corporation, over in Arraijan, in honor of the boy's eighth birthday. The rifle was a full caliber F-26, but specially lightened and shortened and with a muzzle brake to reduce recoil. Likewise were the pistol grip and foregrip carved to fit an eight-year-old's hand. Under the black paint the Pashtun had laid on to reduce shine, the thing was ornately inscribed.

Hamilcar checked the rifle to ensure it was loaded, then padded out the door and down the corridor to his father's office from which a glass-paned doorway led to the balcony. The two guards, joined immediately by two others who had stood alert at the boy's door, followed.

Ciudad Balboa, Republic of Balboa, Terra Nova

Caridad Cruz followed her own husband from the bedroom to the living room. She found him there, seated in his chair, admiring his sole badge of rank, his centurion's baton.

"And they say we women are vain," Cara said to Ricardo, smiling and shaking her head.

Cruz looked up, his heart suddenly warming at the sight of his short, brown and still very pretty wife. "Men are just as vain, no doubt about it, *queridisima esposa*," he admitted, lowering his baton to his lap and smiling at her. "We're just as vain, only in different ways."

The centurion was as brown as his wife, and, at about five-seven, not all that much taller. She found him handsome and assumed everyone else did, too.

Cara glanced about the walls of the living room. On two wooden pegs driven into one wall rested Ricardo's rifle, an F-26. Below it, on similar pegs, was his very first rifle, a simpler and cruder Samsonov, purchased for a very nominal price from the legion in which her husband served, as a memento of that service and of his first campaign. On the opposite wall hung his battle-scarred and stained lorica, the silk and liquid metal body armor he had worn for years. Cara tried to keep the thing clean. *But not too clean. I love the smell of my man.*

On a third wall hung Ricardo's decorations. She'd heard the citations read off for some of them, those awarded formally when he was home from the wars. The knowledge of the things her husband had done both filled her with pride and chilled her to the marrow. She never read the citations themselves, lest that refreshed knowledge drive her to try, once again, to talk Ricardo out of the legion. She'd done that before. He'd acquiesced, too. The loss of purpose had nearly killed him.

He must be free to do the work he loves, she reminded herself, glancing over the wall holding the awards. *He must be free if, for no other reason, because when he's miserable,* I'm *miserable.*

And, too, it's not like I'm ashamed when other women come over, and have to pass under his corona civilis *to come into the house. I like their envy of the courage of my man. Is that so wrong?*

"What's wrong, Ricardo?" she asked. "Did the thunder awaken you?"

Cruz shook his head. "No . . . I never really got to sleep." Seeing that that wasn't really an answer to her question, he added, "Things are not right with the legion since the *Duque* had to . . . take a sabbatical. It worries me. We are not the kind of force that deals well with inaction."

"But the war is over," she said. "We won."

"One war is over," Ricardo corrected, picking up the baton again to admire it. "There will be others." He seemed very certain of that.

Please let it not be so, God, the wife silently prayed, even as she knew the prayer was futile. For there *would* be other wars, and her man *would* fight in them. It was the way of the world just as it was the way of Ricardo Cruz. Between the Santandern guerillas infesting Balboa's province of La Palma, the Tauran Union troops occupying the Transitway, the old government cowering in the old section of *Ciudad* Balboa under Tauran Union protection, and the drugs passing daily through the country, there *would* be war.

Cara shivered at the thought. "Any word on the *Duque*?" she asked, changing the subject slightly.

"No, none. I'm tempted sometimes to ask you to presume on your friendship with Lourdes..."

"I can't. She has enough troubles."

"I know," he agreed.

Headquarters, Tauran Union Security Force– Balboa, Building 59, Fort Muddville, Transitway Area, Balboa

No matter what that Old Earth bimbo told me before she left, I know I could take these peasants out now. So thought an elegantly slender man dressed, perhaps absurdly, in the reproduction blue velvet uniform of a marshal of the army of Napoleon. Impatiently and repeatedly, General Janier, Army of the Republic of Gaul, slapped his unawarded marshal's baton into the palm of his left hand. The baton, like the uniform, was reproduction. Fake or not, both captured something of the spirit of the man, as did his hawklike, pugnacious nose.

Not that Janier had much of the republican sentiment of a Lannes or the family fidelity of a Davout

(Janier's mistress lay asleep nearby in a suite of offices he'd had converted to an apartment for her) or the stoic loyalty of a MacDonald. He had some of the sheer courage of a Ney. And he had the one thing virtually all of Napoleon's marshals had shared: love of glory.

And why shouldn't I? I am related to half of them and descended from more than one.

Sad, sad it is; to be a man of my inclinations and breeding, and be saddled with the wretches who rule the Tauran Union. Pacifist swine. Eunuchs, the lot of them.

A flash in the distance lit Janier's sneering face. In this case, the flash came not from the more distant lightning, but from an explosion somewhere across the Transitway, at Balboa's premier training facility, the Imperial Range Complex, nestled in the corner formed by *Lago* Chagres and the Transitway, rather, that portion of it called the "Gallardo Trench." The legion and the Tauran Union troops shared the complex, not always amicably.

Mine, preparing to fight theirs, or theirs, preparing to fight mine, I wonder. No matter. No one is going to fight anyone right now. With their leader incapacitated, the locals won't start anything—more's the pity—and with my political masters unwilling to fund me or give me the troops I need, I can't start anything. That Wallenstein woman was wasting her time telling me not to do something I can't do anyway.

Still, this is all a house of cards. I sit athwart the Transitway. Ultimately, the Balboans—the ones in power—won't accept that state of affairs. The Balboans who will accept it rule over a tiny corner of the country and dream of ruling it all again. And why should they not dream? There's little for them to steal where they are. And theft is in their very genes.

The general ceased slapping his baton into his palm. He shook his head. *As is crime, generally. Even now, they fund themselves—they think I don't know, the fools—by assisting in the drug trade and taking their cut.*

Well, if they're criminals, at least they're good at it. They cover their tracks well. All the pressure to stop the trade, all the pressure coming from the Federated States, falls on those who have nothing to do with it. And them, the peasant Parilla and his defunct renegade Carrera? They can't deal with the real problem because that real problem is guarded by us and guaranteed by the Federated States.

A house of cards; let one thing come loose and it will all crumble.

On the other hand, the sinister hand, if it all crumbles while the Balboans—the enemy Balboans—are ready and I am not, I just might lose. No glory, no name, no place in the history books. Simple defeat and a footnote to avoid my example. That is intolerable.

Perhaps things will improve when the permanent high admiral of the United Earth Peace Fleet comes to us, be it Wallenstein or someone else. At least the filth in the Tauran Parliament will listen to him or, if Wallenstein's appointment becomes permanent, her.

SS *Hildegard Mises*, *Lago Chagres*, Balboa Transitway, Balboa, Terra Nova

A dozen or so miles to the southeast of Janier's head-quarters there was a ship anchored in the lake, rocking violently in the wind-driven waves. It was well guarded at all times, though the guards only changed at night.

It hadn't moved in at least a year. Someday, it would, but only to get rid of the last traces of evidence when it was finally sunk into a deep ocean trench.

Whether the ship would have any people aboard when it went down was a matter of some speculation for the group of guards who manned it in rotation. They reported to Carrera's chief of intelligence, Omar Fernandez, and he was noted for tying up loose ends neatly.

Loose ends?

There was an evil-looking, weasel-faced man waiting in one of the ship's offices when former High Admiral Martin Robinson and the Marchioness of Amnesty, Lucretia Arbeit, were escorted in. Both of the Old Earthers bowed deeply and respectfully to the man. They'd long since had their arrogance beaten out of them.

"I have a little problem," said Legate Omar Fernandez, his weasel face splitting in an unpleasant grin.

"A problem, sir?" asked Robinson worriedly. Arbeit merely shivered in place. Though both measured their years in centuries, and both, as Class Ones and members of the Peerage, had received the best anti-aging therapy Old Earth could offer, still both looked to have aged like cheese left in the sun, all wrinkled and hard and dry. This despite neither of them having been subjected to real torture in many months. Indeed, they'd been *wrung* dry long ago.

"A couple of problems, really," Fernandez said, his eyes flickering once at Arbeit, and then a second time, at Robinson. "One is that we haven't been able to get your old shuttle working again. I don't suppose you know anything about the flight computer?"

Robinson gulped. "No, sir. It wasn't anything in my training. I can fly one but..."

Arbeit shivered still more; her naval rank came from her civil position. She didn't even know how to fly one.

"Pity," Fernandez said, in a voice that seemed to contain real regret. "Well, there goes one reason to keep you both alive."

Arbeit crumpled to her knees then, bending until her face rested on the floor and weeping as softly as she was able. Fernandez felt a certain pity for the woman. Had he known her life story; he'd have felt nothing but disgust. *He* tortured. He didn't generally enjoy it.

"Are there other reasons?" Robinson asked hopefully. "Could there be?"

Fernandez shrugged. "Possibly. Much depends on whether or not the two of you, or either of you alone, have seen the error of your old ways and decided to join our cause for the betterment of humanity.

"You see," Fernandez continued, "we're getting rid of this ship and what it represents. It should have been done a while ago, but...well, never mind.

"The current storm is expected to last another three days. The ship sails in the morning out into the Shimmering Sea, where a terrible accident will take place. The crew and your guards, of course, will be evacuated in time...since they're mine."

Arbeit heard. She had the sudden image of herself chained in her cell below decks as the waters arose and the rats scurried across her body and face and then the bubbles began leaking from her nose and—

She screamed, once, a very long and drawn out,

"Nnnooo . . ." before she began to vomit with fear onto the floor.

Robinson was more composed, if only slightly. "Please, Legate," he begged, getting to his knees and clasping hands together, "tell me whatever I can do to help. Anything. *Anything!*"

Arbeit didn't have words. Even so, the pleading look she gave Fernandez as she raised her vomit-dripping chin from the floor echoed Robinson's words, "Anything."

Casa Linda, Republic of Balboa, Terra Nova

I wish there were something I could do, Lourdes mentally sighed. *Anything, really, to bring my husband back. It's so lonely, despite Artemisia, Alena, and the kids. I need my man again.*

An unpleasant thought intruded. *What if I am the one holding him back? I mean, I thought I was doing the right thing when I chased off Xavier Jimenez with one of Patricio's guns . . . but what if he needs the work and the purpose more than the rest? I just don't know . . . I just don't know.*

Carrera heard nothing, what with the lashing rain, the driving winds, the thunder and the pounding of the surf below. Still, he became aware slowly of a presence or, rather, several of them on the balcony with him. One, he felt, in the chair next to but slightly behind his own, was very small.

"Hello, Ham," he said, over the natural roars surrounding them.

"Dad," the boy answered.

"What are you doing up?"

"Thunder woke me...my guards said you were out here...didn't think you should be alone."

"You know," Carrera said, "for an eight-year-old, you're a pretty bright kid."

"Chip off the old block," the boy answered, as if by rote. "But, really, Dad, you shouldn't be alone up here."

"Maybe not," the father half conceded.

"I like the storms, too," Hamilcar said. "Or, at least, I'm drawn to them."

"'Chip off the old block,'" Carrera echoed, adding, more softly, "and in more ways than that."

The boy looked out over the trees to the sea. A flash of lightning showed fierce waves. "Will our boat be in any danger?" he asked. The boat he referred to was the family yacht, at fifty-four feet nothing too extravagant compared to what could have been purchased. Rarely used, and then more often by Carrera's staff than by anyone else, the boat rested in a small harbor at the base of the steep slope that led from the *casa* to the sea.

"It'll be fine," his father answered.

Carrera pointed out to sea and said, "Wait for the lightning again and you'll see a yacht down there, a big one, struggling against the waves."

Hamilcar looked to where his father was pointing. Lightning flashed again and he saw it, as not much more than a big speck. "What kind of idiot takes a yacht out on a night like this?" he asked. "Drug runners?"

"It's possible," Carrera answered. "But we can't know and I hope we're not sending a small patrol boat out to intercept in this shit.

"Even so, 'it's pleasant, when the sea is harsh and the waves are dashing about, to watch from the shore the struggles of another.'"

Around his father the boy could curse. "That's actually bullshit, Dad. I know you, because I'm like you. You want to be out there, fighting with the sea."

CHAPTER TWO

For something which has, from time to time, been alleged to be a mere invention, war is remarkable for having been independently invented in all times, in virtually all cultures, and by all races. The trivial exceptions do nothing except to prove the rule. Nor is the phenomenon unique to mankind; lower animals, some of them, wage war, even though they invent nothing.

In short, the allegation of invention is nonsense; war is part of us, part of having the will to live and prosper, the desire to cause our genes, our classes, our countries, and our cultures to live and prosper, the heart to fight, the courage to risk ... even to die, and the intelligence or instinct to organize, the better to do those things. Any other position is, in the universe in which mankind lives, wishful thinking at its worst.

—Jorge y Marqueli Mendoza, *Historia y Filosofia Moral,* Legionary Press, Balboa, Terra Nova, copyright AC 468

Anno Condita 470
Anno Domini 2524
Observation Deck, UEPF Starship *Spirit of*
***Peace*, Solar System**

To an outside observer, had there been any, the ship
would have appeared brighter than day. Some of this
was the reflection of direct sunlight from the ship,
but still more was the reflection of that sunlight off
of the huge sail that propelled the ship between the
jump points and braked it at the end of the journey.
In contrast, Earth ahead of it was mostly swathed in
night, only one thin crescent to the right side lit by
the sun, and a larger area to the left lit by the moon's
reflection. A corona of sunlight framed the sphere,
except for a small part covered by the moon.

On the night side, the side from which the *Peace*
approached, a few cities and resorts of the elites could
be seen by their artificial glow. Outside of those, at
this distance, not even major continents and oceans
were visible except through image enhancement.

At least none of the cities are burning, thought
Captain Marguerite Wallenstein as she watched the
approach from the observation deck. As subsequent
messages had made clear, once *Peace* passed the rift,
one of the reasons she'd been recalled to Old Earth
was precisely that; that the reverted areas, those areas
over which the Consensus, Earth's high governing body
and the successor to the old UN Security Council,
had lost control, were growing even as the barbarians
within them grew more aggressive.

Relaxing back into the seat reserved for the high

admiral of the United Earth Peace Fleet, a position the captain hoped to assume very soon and permanently, Wallenstein crossed long, shapely legs while her fingers unconsciously toyed with her mid-length blond hair. One might have thought her to be perhaps twenty-five years of age, and a young looking twenty-five at that. In fact, she was several times that, courtesy of the anti-agathic treatments that were Old Earth's last scientific breakthrough and the right only of the upper castes, Class Ones and Twos, who replaced themselves but slowly and were critical to the management of the planet. Even at that, Class Twos didn't get the full treatment and could only be expected to live about two and a half centuries. Class Ones? Not one who had received the full treatment had yet died of natural causes.

Wallenstein was only a Class Two, something she also hoped to rectify with this trip.

Tall, generally slender, and even svelte, Marguerite Wallenstein, captain and admiral *pro tem*, was not quite a beauty, with a nose a bit too large and eyes that, while of a very lovely blue, were just slightly too small. Despite these minor flaws, however, she managed to exude an earthy sensuality that, coupled with a willingness to use her body to get ahead, had seen her through difficult times in the UEPF. Indeed, that eager willingness had seen her to her present, exalted, permanent rank.

For any superiors who might have been less than enchanted with her nose or eyes, Wallenstein's breasts were simply magnificent, which magnificence had been considerably aided by low, shipboard gravity. Hard work and genetic predisposition had seen to the maintenance of a narrow waist and shapely rear, ship's gravity notwithstanding. For that matter, she could have had her nose and eyes surgically altered. Why she hadn't remained a mystery even to herself. Perhaps it was simple pride.

A speaker mounted to the wall of the observation deck announced, "Incoming intelligence update, Admiral."

Unseen by the officer, Wallenstein nodded and said, "Record for my later review."

She doubted the update contained anything new. Mentally Wallenstein ticked off the areas lost that she knew of. *Southern South America... lost... Buenos Aires sacked and burned, and the new front line of civilization is Montevideo. Canada, at least most of it, is under glaciers. The Great Plains between the Rockies and the Mississippi? Held by horse-riding nomads ethnically mixed between what used to be called "Native Americans," blacks, Asians, and whites, but culturally more similar to Genghis Khan's Mongols... those, or Attila's Huns. Southeastern Asia has revolted, restored Roman Catholicism, and massacred the punitive force the Consensus dispatched. And outside of Cape Town, Southern Africa is in anarchy. Northern Europe is ice. Revolts brewing in Central America...*

She almost shivered in anticipation. It was pretty clear at this point that the Consensus did *not* intend to space her. *The bastards need me now, all right. I wonder if I could get away with...*

Wallenstein's reveries were interrupted by a call from the observation deck's speaker, "Final approach run impending... shorten sail... stand by for braking... Admiral to the bridge..."

Balboa, Terra Nova

On the surface of a different world than the one approached by Wallenstein's *Spirit of Peace*, in a small and normally fairly insignificant country, a huge bridge, the Bridge of the Columbias, was packed on both sides, with traffic slowed to a crawl where it wasn't halted outright. Stuck in that traffic, with the tropical sun beating on the roof of his vehicle and threatening to overwhelm the air conditioning, Legate Xavier Jimenez, 4th Legion, Commanding, fumed.

I hate driving through the Transitway Area.

Jimenez was a physical oddity. Hair and features, but for color, were basically Caucasian, and more than handsome Caucasian, at that. His skin, though, was a high gloss anthracite. The coloration and the good looks ran in the family. So did a great many less genetic attributes, notable among these a fierce patriotism.

It's not bad enough that, after nearly a century of colonialist occupation, the old government brought in a different group of colonialists to secure their own persons at the expense of the country. Oh no, to add injury to insult, the Tauran Union troops, nearly twelve thousand of them, who provide that security, sometimes, and for no obvious reason, cut off traffic into and through the Transitway, stopping and searching cars and their drivers and passengers as if Balboa were somehow Tauran territory. Bastards.

The Transitway Area itself was a slice right through the middle of the country, smaller in some areas than it had been during the previous occupation, but encompassing now in practice certain sections of the capital, *Ciudad* Balboa, that had never been under colonial administration since the ouster of Old Earth's United Nations, about four centuries prior.

Jimenez fumed about that, too. *Sure, the country was under threat, and sure, we had to take the legions we'd created off to the war. But did we really have to bring in the stinking Taurans for local security? The gringos were obnoxious enough, but they couldn't hold a candle to the Gauls ... or the Anglians. And then the gringos had to broker a peace deal ...*

Mentally, Jimenez spat. Still, he was honest enough to admit to himself, *On the other hand, there was going to be a civil war with the old government and its supporters once Parilla was elected president. And the old government didn't have a lot of choice, either, since a prominent part of Parilla's platform was trying the lot of them for corruption.*

And, of course, the Federated States had a strong interest in the Transitway. Hell, the whole world does. But those interests don't trump ours.

The Federated States, the gringos (which epithet had followed them across the galaxy, just as "Frogs" had followed the Gauls), had paid for the Transitway, had secured it for the better part of a century, and still took a proprietary interest. It was that interest, and the threat of a local civil war, that had impelled them to broker a deal whereby the old government would retreat to, and hold sovereignty over, a portion of the capital, the Taurans would stay to guarantee the safety of that government and the Transitway, and Jimenez, Parilla, Carrera, and the legions would fume.

The Transitway itself was an above-sea-level canal connecting both of Terra Nova's two major oceans. It was not only a money and time saver for the roughly fourteen thousand merchant ships a year that used it; it also allowed the Federated States Navy to switch warships from one ocean to the other more or less overnight. That ability allowed it to dominate both oceans, since none of the other players on Terra Nova cared to spend enough to match the entire Federated States Navy. Indeed, the rest of the planet combined didn't care to spend enough to match the FSN.

(For that matter, had the Federated States decided to convert the wet navy to a space navy, which it was very close to being able to do, technologically, there was nothing even United Earth could have done short of nuclear war to prevent them from dominating local space as well.)

At the moment, from his temporarily halted vehicle, Jimenez glanced right and looked down from the Bridge of the Columbias at the Transitway's northern mouth just as two moderately large and apparently rusty ships passed each other, one heading out into the *Mar Furioso*, Terra Nova's largest ocean, and the other heading inland to pass through the locks on its way to the Shimmering Sea.

"Makes no sense to me, Legate," Jimenez's driver, Pedro Rico, said. "I mean, it isn't like we couldn't cut them off from sea, land, and air if we wanted to. What's there? Maybe twelve thousand of them; better'n fifty fucking thousand of us. Closer to a hundred and fifty if we called up the reservists."

"It's more complex than that, Rico," Jimenez answered. He was a pretty egalitarian sort and didn't mind—rather enjoyed, actually—conversing with the enlisted legionaries. In this particular case though, he *couldn't* speak freely.

The problem, son, Jimenez thought, *is that Patricio set us up for a particular kind of war, in which the timing was critical. We don't even know for sure what that timing was supposed to be, since he kept it all—well, most of it—in his head.*

Which is precisely why we're going to see the son of a bitch. We need him, now as never before, and he's got to snap out of it.

To snap Carrera out of it was something easier said than done. He'd always been a pretty tough sort, so everyone agreed, but the combination of ten years of the continuous strain of command in war, first in Sumer and then in Pashtia, to say nothing of the various peripheral campaigns on land and sea he'd sponsored, coupled with having the blood of over a million innocents on his hands (though *very* few people knew about that), had effectively broken him the year before.

For five local months, a full half of a Terra Novan year, the man had not said a word, but simply stared off into space. He'd eat if someone fed him, otherwise not. Even if he wouldn't speak, he'd still screamed regularly at night. The old nightmares he'd suffered were gone, but now he had a brand new set of them.

His wife—his second wife; the first was dead along with the three children she'd borne Carrera—made it nearly her entire life to nurse her husband back to health. In this she'd been notably successful, at least in comparison to the state he'd been in when he'd returned to her, catatonic from, among other things, his nuclear demolition of the Yithrabi city of Hajar.

On Terra Nova no one outside of Carrera's immediate circle knew about that nuclear attack. At least one person off world, the current commander *pro tem* of the United Earth Peace Fleet, knew. Or thought she did, which amounted to the same thing.

Truth be told, few on the planet even suspected. It was much easier to believe that the Salafi *Ikhwan*, the terrorist scourge of the planet, had somehow gotten hold of a large nuke, which nuke they had inadvertently set off in the compound where it had been stored, which compound just happened to be the family holding of their late leader.

"Think it'll work this time, boss?" Rico asked. This was not the first time they'd driven to the *Casa* Linda, always at least in part to try to swing Patricio around.

"It has to, Pedro," Jimenez answered. "If I have to have you put a gun to his wife's head while I beat some sense through his own thick skull, it has to."

There's no more time for him to convalesce. I wish there were; he needs it. But there isn't and so he can't have it.

"Yeah," Rico half agreed. "But what if the bitch meets us at the front door with a submachine gun again?"

Spaceport Rome, Province of Italy, United Earth

Two armed guards rode in seats behind Wallenstein as her shuttle descended to the Eternal City.

Rome, much restored, spread out beneath them as that shuttlecraft broke through the clouds. Marguerite resisted the urge to press her face to the porthole of the little craft. After all, the guards were lowers, Class Fours, she thought, and they would be watching. Even so, her head twisted, her chin dropped, and her eyes searched out the landmarks she had not seen in more than a decade, even since her last trip home to convey the late—*I hope the bastard is "late"... though Carrera never expressly promised me to kill him*—High Admiral Martin Robinson to his new command around the alien star.

Just as Geneva was the bureaucratic locus of United Earth, so was Rome its emotional heart. Indeed, nearly half of Old Earth's half million Class Ones made the city their home. Why this should be so, Wallenstein was not quite sure. Perhaps it was the more pleasant weather, especially as more northerly Europe, like Canada, was in the grip of a little ice age. *Little, they call it... but it seems to go on and on and has since the early twenty-first century.* Perhaps it was a harkening back to the glories of the Roman Empire.

Wallenstein slowly shook her head. *But I think it has more to do with the emotional satisfaction of having triumphed over a stifling Christianity and taken the Vatican for ourselves. Certainly, when the last pope was burned by the* Ara Pacis, *we at least half-intended to show that we were the power in the world... and Christianity was dead.*

Of course, Christianity is demonstrably not *dead on Terra Nova, though it is rather arguable how Christian it is. And it wasn't just Christianity we wanted to extirpate here; all the Abrahamic religions had to go, except for Islam, which had earned itself a place.*

Marguerite shivered, unconsciously, in fear for her planet. *At least it wasn't very "Christian" of Carrera to nuke an Islamic city in revenge for his first wife and their children. I wonder what he'll do if and when he finds out that Martin was at least partially responsible for that. Can a couple of hundred light years be space enough to shield Old Earth from a vindictiveness of that magnitude?*

Casa Linda, Balboa, Terra Nova

A great black shape stood in the open doorway to the *casa*, framed by two of the guards the legion still kept on Carrera's person and residence, part of the couple of hundred in and around the house. The guards were Pashtun Scouts in the legion's employ. From their point of view they were actually there to guard Carrera's son, Hamilcar, whom some of them, or perhaps all of them, had decided was the avatar of God. They could hardly do that without at the same time guarding Carrera, Lourdes, and the other, from their point of view only semi-divine child, the toddling girl, Julia.

The black shape was Sergeant Major John McNamara. Though considerably older, old enough to have retired from the Federated States Army a dozen years before, and though considerably less good looking, Mac was otherwise a near twin for Jimenez. Both were tall, black, whippet thin, and simply *mean* looking. Appearances, moreover, were not the only points of relation. McNamara was married to Jimenez's niece, Artemisia, about four decades his junior and pregnant with their second child.

A former Miss Balboa, even pregnant, Arti still turned heads and made younger men groan with desire.

"He's inside," Mac said. "I got Arti to take away Lourdes' submachine gun. She wouldn't shoot a pregnant woman...though she just might have shot me. They're together now in the kitchen with Tribune Cano's wife, Alena."

Speaking English, his native tongue, McNamara had a lilting Maiden Islands accent and a tendency to mispronounce the diphthong "th." Speaking Spanish, as they were now, he was accentless.

Under the cover of returning the salutes of the guards on the door, Jimenez affected not to notice the sigh of relief breathed by his driver, Rico, at the news that Lourdes had been disarmed and was, so to speak, being watched.

"Have you talked to him?" Jimenez asked.

Mac shook his head. "I figured it would be better if we double-teamed him *while* Lourdes is out of the picture."

Jimenez nodded slowly. While neither man had any doubt that he was much smarter than McNamara, likewise neither had any doubt that the sergeant major general of the legion was much the wiser, much the better at handling men, much the more "people smart."

"Where's Patricio?" Jimenez asked.

"Up on the back porch, drinking." Mac switched to English to mutter, "He does too fockin' much o' t'at."

"Let's go up and chat, then, shall we?"

"I'll grab anot'er bottle and some glasses," Mac replied, still in English. Then, switching to Spanish, he said, "Rico, you can park the car around back. You know your way to the guards' mess, right? Hope you like Pashtian food."

"I got used to it, Sergeant Major," the driver answered.

Rome, Province of Italy, United Earth

Old Earth transportation was, for the most part, fairly conventional. The styles might have excited comment on Terra Nova; the mechanics would not have. The big difference was that, at least on the reasonably prosperous parts of the other world, private conveyance was common. On Old Earth, it was the perquisite of the high and mighty.

"The SecGen wanted to chat with you before you made your presentation to the Consensus the day after tomorrow," said Wallenstein's escort, another Class Two named Moore, as their car sped through Rome's uncrowded streets. "He told the Admiralty to stuff it, that they could see you after important matters were taken care of."

In appearance, Moore seemed a near brother to the captain. Albeit a bit taller, he was likewise blond and blue-eyed, as were most of Old Earth's ruling class.

"Can it wait until tomorrow?" she asked. "Gravity aboard ship is less than here and I find I'm very tired."

"He assumed that," Moore answered. "You're set to meet tomorrow, over lunch."

Lunch with the SecGen? Wallenstein mused. *Or*

*am I supposed to lunch the SecGen? Well, whatever
the market will bear. I'll bring kneepads in a satchel,
just in case.*

"How did he take the news of the loss of the high
admiral and the marchioness of Amnesty?" Marguerite
asked. *Note: I didn't say "deaths"; I said "loss."*

Moore sighed. "Rather hard, actually. He and the
marchioness were very close."

"Did he . . . ?" Wallenstein let the question trail off.

"Yes," Moore answered. "The entire Consensus
accepted your version of events." He knew from her
tone that Wallenstein had been worried about that.

Now Marguerite sighed, and hers was with relief.
If there had been any suspicion that she had turned
the high admiral and Lucretia Arbeit, the marchioness, over to the Terra Novans, she'd have been for
the chop, she was quite sure.

*Fortunately, the only people who know that are
myself and another Class Two who wants a caste lift.
Oh, and Carrera back on Terra Nova . . . but he's not
likely to tell anyone.*

Casa Linda, Balboa, Terra Nova

Carrera didn't look up as McNamara and Jimenez
took seats to ether side of him around a small wooden
table on a largish balcony that overlooked the *Mar
Furioso*. Indeed, he didn't acknowledge their presence
until Mac placed another bottle of whiskey, along with
two glasses, next to the nearly drained bottle sitting
by the ice bucket in the middle of the table. At that,
Carrera only said; "Welcome."

Jimenez thought, *It's funny; despite the gray hair, he actually looks younger than he has in years.*

Mac filled the silence that followed Carrera's one word by taking the open bottle and pouring what was left, half and half, into the two glasses he'd brought from the bar.

"Lotsa history made right here," Mac commented, as he transferred ice from the bucket to the glasses.

Eyes still affixed on the ocean in the distance, Carrera said, "That's *so* lame, Top. You couldn't come up with a better opening line than that?"

"Man's got to play the hand he was dealt, sir," McNamara said, while plinking ice into his own glass.

"I suppose," Carrera conceded. He turned his eyes from the ocean to McNamara's dark, seamed face. "Hey, you wouldn't happen to have a cigarette, would you? Lourdes won't buy me any. I haven't felt up to driving in a while. And she's threatened all the help with death if they give me one."

Tobacco on Terra Nova had been infected with a local virus that tended to make it much less carcinogenic than was the case on Earth. Even so, it couldn't precisely be called *good* for anyone.

"Sure, boss," the grizzled older man said, reaching into a pocket and pulling out a pack of Carrera's preferred brand, Tecumsehs, imported from First Landing in the Federated States, and a lighter. These he slid across the table.

"You're not drunk," Jimenez said in surprise, gesturing at the now empty bottle.

Carrera shook his head. "I sip. But that bottle's been on that table for over a week, ten days maybe. I find if I get drunk that I feel things I don't want to feel any more, remember things I'd just as soon forget.

"Not that I don't remember them in my dreams, mind you."

Rome, Province of Italy

For reasons known only to himself, Moore directed the driver of the vehicle to pass by the *Ara Pacis,* Augustus's Altar of Peace and the holiest spot on all of United Earth. Here the last vestiges of open Christianity had died—been *burned*, rather—and one couldn't get more holy than that.

"I don't mind that it's a bit out of the way," he informed the Class Four driver.

"Yes, lord," the driver answered.

"What's with the ribbons around the heads? They're kind of attractive. Should I wear one to keep in style?" Marguerite asked, once she noticed that about one in twenty of the people they passed on the street wore them.

Moore snickered, "The diadems? No, I don't think so. They've become something of a fashion statement by the children of the Class Ones. From our point of view, it saves trouble by telling us lowly Class Twos exactly whom we must bow and scrape to. There's a color and ornament coding to it I can brief you on later.

"It isn't just the children, actually," Moore amended. "Some fairly older Class Ones have taken to wearing them, too, the last couple of years. The SecGen, however, has not."

Whatever the Class Four driver thought of the

subject of diadems or fashion statements, he kept it to himself.

"*Ara Pacis* coming up on the left, lord," the driver announced, slowing his vehicle to a crawl. The Altar itself had been modified some centuries prior, with a matching white marble roof having been placed over it, and overhanging the sculptures on the sides. Along with the roof two narrow sets of marble steps led off, at right angles to the steps that led inside. The building that had once housed it and protected it from the air pollution was gone. With so few cars and so little industry operating, it was no longer needed.

Moore didn't bother to look right away. Marguerite, however, did, and was surprised—perhaps better said, shocked—to see rivulets of red running down the Altar's creamy marble sides. She looked up and saw five muscular men in outlandish garments, all gold and feathers, two of them holding a sixth who was naked but for a loin cloth.

"It's an Azteca day," Moore explained, though the bare words explained little. "Those come only a few times a year." He added, "Some objected, of course, to using the Altar of Peace for human sacrifice. On the other hand, the Azteca have or influence a significant block of votes within the Consensus. And the Orthodox Druids were on their side since they wanted to have burnings and hangings here."

Marguerite gulped as she watched the sixth, near naked, man forced down to the stone roof and flipped over. A black, jagged obsidian knife, the hilt wrapped in cloth, in the hand of one of the other five, flashed down. Out came a dripping heart, probably still beating, which was held aloft. As the heart was squeezed out and then tossed over the side of the altar, she looked away. Even so, however repulsive the scene, it was still fascinating. She turned her eyes back to the Altar.

"Just thought you might find it interesting," Moore said.

"Where do the victims come from?" Wallenstein asked.

Moore shrugged, saying, "Some are political pris-oners from Central America. It's been in a state of near rebellion for years. Some, too, supposedly, are genuine volunteers."

The next victim was a beautiful, young, brown-skinned girl. She wept and screamed and struggled pitifully with the larger men dragging her to her death. Even through the sealed windows of the vehicle Wallenstein heard the girl's screams. She heard, too, when they were abruptly cut off.

"The Azteca insist it's a necessary terror against the lowers," Moore said, just as the car left the area and drove off. "And if you think this is a bit much, you ought to go to The Burning Man this year."

Casa Linda, Balboa, Terra Nova

"The problem, gentlemen," Carrera said, "is that I am *terrified* of taking command again."

"Terrified?" Jimenez asked. "You?"

"Yes . . . terrified . . . for my soul."

He held up both his hands, thinking, as he always did, *miserable, dainty things.* "See these. These are the hands of the greatest one-day-mass-murderer in the history of our planet and the second greatest in the history of the human race. I'd had *friends* in Hajar ... children I'd held in my lap. And I murdered them." He shook his head. "Somebody who can do that? He's got no business being in command of anything."

"T'at may be true," McNamara said in English, "t'e first part, anyway. But it ain't t'e whole trut'. You know what, boss? T'em fockin' Yit'rabis ain't had no more truck with t'e Salafi mot'erfockers since Hajar. T'ey ain't had no money to give t'em cause t'ey had to spend it decontaminating and rebuildin' t'eir fockin' capital city. T'ey ain't had no sympat'y for t'e mot'erfockers, neit'er, since t'e Yit'rabis are *sure* it was t'e hand of God t'at set off t'at bomb. So maybe, yes, you killed a million people. But maybe, too, you saved ten or twenty million of 'em."

Carrera nodded slowly before answering, "The one is speculation. We know for sure about the other, though."

Jimenez snorted. "So we have to be sure about things before we can act, do we, Patricio? Fine. Let me tell you about some things we can be sure of. We can be sure of them because *you* set them up, and what you didn't set up you allowed. One of those things is that *my* country—I would have said *our* country but you've abandoned it—is bisected by a foreign occupier. Another is that a chunk of it is ruled by as vile a cabal of self-seeking corruption as ever went unhanged. We've got fifty thousand regulars under arms, and twice that in reservists, willing and eager to fight to free that occupied portion."

Jimenez stood angrily, jabbing his finger in Carrera's direction. "This is no speculation, Patricio. There's a war coming and it's *your* fault. You can't duck it. There are people going to fight that war because *you* formed them and *you* trained them. You can't duck that, either.

"Your soul, friend?" Jimenez sneered. "Screw your soul; you've got *responsibilities*."

Carrera sighed, then lifted and sipped at his drink. "You're a bastard; you know that, Xavier?"

"He's just been a bastard lately," Lourdes said to Artemisia, sitting across the wooden kitchen table from her. "Grouchy...inconsiderate. Cold to me and to the kids and being cold to the kids tears my heart out."

Sitting next to the two, the green-eyed, light-skinned Alena stifled a *harrumph*. Being cold to Hamilcar, Iskandr to her, who was to her mind and by her upbringing an avatar of God, was just beyond the pale. Even so, Alena was one of those odd people whose guesses were so good that she might as well have had second sight, if, indeed, she didn't have it. She had a very good idea of why the *Duque* was so distant.

"Sex?" the younger and far more statuesquely built black woman suggested. Artemisia was inarguably the prettier of the two, as well, if not by much. Even so, Lourdes had eyes so large and so beautifully shaped they ought to have been against the law...of God if not of man.

"Oh, Arti..." Tears sprang to Lourdes' eyes. "He hasn't touched me since he came back from the war."

"Another woman?"

Lourdes dashed away the tears. Sniffling, though trying not to, she answered, "No, no, it's not that. He's barely left the house and never left the grounds since he came back."

"He sure ain't been trying to hammer my old ass," offered the cook, preparing dinner twenty-five feet behind the two.

At that, Lourdes couldn't help but laugh, even as her fingers continued to brush at her eyes. "Thanks, Tina," she said, adding sardonically, "you've no idea how much better that makes me feel."

"Well," Arti boasted, "over sixty or not, Mac's a randy goat. So I doubt Patricio is too old for sex."

"Mac has you for inspiration," Lourdes answered. Lovely eyes downcast, she added, "Patricio only has me."

Artemisia snorted. "Only you, eh? I would *kill* for your eyes, your lips, and your ass. To say nothing of your legs. No, honey, it isn't that any man would find you unattractive, still less Patricio. I think it must be something else."

For the nonce, Alena kept her own counsel.

"I feel unclean, you know," Carrera said. "Ever since Hajar I've felt dirty and unworthy of my wife or the kids she gave me."

"Did you ever tell her that?" asked McNamara, reverting once again to Spanish.

Carrera shook his head. "She doesn't know about Hajar. Not that I gave the order to destroy it, I mean. And if I told her, I'm afraid she'd feel the same way I do, that she'd feel I was unclean. I don't think I could take that."

"He thinks I don't know about the destruction of Hajar," Lourdes whispered, low enough that the cook couldn't hear. Alena caught her breath.

Artemisia leaned in and cocked her head to one side, whispering back, "What about Hajar?"

"He did it. He's never said so, but . . . as if a man could keep from screaming during nightmares, or a wife not be able to figure what he was screaming about."

"He did," Alena confirmed.

"John never told me," Arti said, slowly. Turning to Alena she asked, "How do you know?"

"I rarely know how I know," the Pashtun woman answered. "Nonetheless, I know."

"I shouldn't have said anything either. Arti, you can't tell anyone. Ever. Not *anyone*. Nor you, Alena."

Both the black woman and the Pashtun looked scandalized, if for different reasons. Artemisia said, "Me? Tell someone we nuked a city? And maybe get ourselves nuked in return? Oh, no, Lourdes. That secret is safe with me."

"I don't talk much," Alena added, "and anything that might bring a risk to Iskandr? That's simply *impossible*." The Pashtun woman looked scandalized at the very thought.

Lourdes shook her head. "Whatever are you going to do when you have children of your own, Alena?"

That might not have been a sore point with another woman. With Alena, raised in a culture that placed a very high value on female fertility, it was an embarrassment. Nor was it lack of trying. As much as she knew, she simply didn't know why she hadn't yet conceived.

Nonetheless, she answered, "Raise them to serve my lord, Iskandr."

Rome, Province of Italy, United Earth

Though Moore had politely offered to bed her, Wallenstein had begged off, citing fatigue and the need for rest. He'd taken it quite well, she thought, but then sex was the cheapest and freest commodity on Old Earth.

She'd claimed the need for rest, but she wasn't resting. From a balcony of her guest quarters, overlooking the brown-flowing Tiber and the Mausoleum of Augustus on the other side, Marguerite stared in the direction of the *Ara Pacis*.

I wonder if that was the secret we'd never admit to, that war is a constant and the only choice you have is war between outsiders and war against your own. Funny that they never discussed this at the academy.

And so we have peace, here, on Old Earth. If, by "peace," we mean a constant series of insurrections, a vast secret police apparatus to quell the lowers, terror in the form of human sacrifice for any of the lowers that raise their heads from the muck... beautiful young girls being dragged off to have their hearts cut out to terrorize the families of beautiful young girls.

Oh, and a ruling class that's taken to wearing the emblems of demigodhood to let the rest of us know our places. That must be very important to "peace," as well.

Could I change any of it? If I get permanent command of the Peace Fleet and get myself raised to Class One, I mean? I am inclined to doubt. After all, the direction we're heading is all down. Ten years ago there was a little trouble in the outlying provinces. Now rebellion is open in many of them, simmering just below the surface in others. Ten years ago there were no human sacrifices. Now the Orthodox Druids—thank whoever may be listening that I am Reformed—hang and burn men to propitiate the gods. Now the Azteca cut out the hearts...

Marguerite turned away from the balcony and its

view of mausoleum and ancient flood. Sitting down on a broad sofa in the suite's salon, she drew her knees up under her chin and wrapped her arms around her shins.

On the other hand, these simpering nancies of the First Class are weak. Weak! Martin was among the best of the lot and I was a lot more capable than he was. Give me enough time, and as a Class One I'll have all the time in the world, and put me in a position to elevate some other Class Twos—that Moore fellow seemed unhappy enough at the current set up—and maybe, just maybe, I can reform this planet. Make me a Class One, give me those assistants, and leave me in command of the Peace Fleet and what would the diadem wearers have to stop me with?

Which still doesn't answer the question: What does one do to reform a planet gone so rotten? But, again, as a Class One, I'll have all the time in the world to figure out the answer to that.

If, that is, I can stop the barbarians on Terra Nova from springing out of their hole like Temujin's hordes and upsetting everything here before we can right ourselves.

That's my advantage over Martin. He could only think of a way to make Terra Nova cease being a threat to us as we are. That's why he had to be so absolute. I, on the other hand, can think of a way to make us something Terra Nova will not be a lethal threat to . . . given the power and given the time.

Wallenstein looked around at her temporary quarters, which went way past adequate and even opulent all the way to decadent. *And there are some perks to the effort.*

Casa Linda, Balboa, Terra Nova

"We've kept Quarters One open for you, on the *Isla Real*," McNamara said.

Jimenez snorted. "We'd have had a mutiny if we tried to fill them." More seriously, he added, "Really, Patricio; we've been able to keep things going as well as we have in good part because we could tell the troops you would be back. That's been getting pretty threadbare for a while now."

"I've missed the boys," Carrera admitted with a sigh that sounded as if it were of longing. "But you might as well have turned the quarters over to the commander of the Training Legion. And your own, as well."

"Why's that?" Mac asked.

"Because we're going to have to move the legions and tercios—yes, almost all of them—from the *Isla Real* to the mainland."

"We're?" Jimenez asked.

Carrera sighed once again. "Yes. 'We're.'" *Bastards.*

"And I'll need to talk to Raul . . . and the leaders of the legislature. I'm not taking sole responsibility for the shit that I do anymore, if only because I don't quite trust my own judgment anymore."

CHAPTER THREE

Valid moral judgment is not a question of saying, "Wouldn't it be nice?" or observing, "Isn't it so awful?" and then insisting that the universe be or cease to be whatever the speaker thinks would be nice, tomorrow, or is bad, today. Valid moral judgment must also be realistic judgment. It does not become so merely for taking a favored fantasy and insisting it is reality. And yet so many, throughout human history, have done just that.

—Jorge y Marqueli Mendoza, *Historia y Filosofia Moral*, Legionary Press, Balboa, Terra Nova, copyright AC 468

Furiocentro Convention Center, Balboa City, Terra Nova

Nearly everyone who really mattered in the legion was there: Four thousand officers, six thousand optios, centurions, and sergeants major, about four thousand warrants, and as many junior noncoms as could be spared from their day-to-day duties. Even the schools had been shut down for two days to allow the cadres and some senior students to attend, while key civilians who worked for the legion had also been dragged in.

The Golden Eagle of the overarching *Legion del Cid*, plus those of the legions, themselves, First through Fourth, also golden, stood in a rank on an elevated dais, legionary eagles flanking the sacred eagle of the entire legion. Ahead of those, and slightly lower, were sixteen silver eagles. Ten of these belonged to the ten tercios, or regiments. Then there were the eagles for the *classis*, the fleet, and the *ala*, the aviation regiment. The two for the training units, initial entry and leader and specialist training, stood alongside that of the Opposing Force Tercio, composed mostly of highly combat experienced expatriate Volgan paratroopers. Technically the Volgans were not part of the legion, their official contract being with the Foreign Military Training Group. Some of the Volgans were now citizens of the Republic, others not. Lastly, on the left as the eagles faced, was the eagle for the *Tercio de Cadetes*, the elite youth regiment, itself nearly twelve thousand strong, in six schools, and not counting the adult cadres for those schools.

The place was stuffed to roughly twice its capacity; there were no chairs as there hadn't been room. (All the chairs sat outside under tarps.) Moving everyone to the Center, too, had been a logistic task of no little magnitude, involving use of busses, airplanes, airships, hovercraft, helicopters, Balboa's one useable train line and, in a few cases, privately owned vehicles and even movement by foot.

Every military man and woman present wore either undress Class B khakis or the mostly green, pixilated tiger-striped, slant-pocketed battle dress worn by the legion when at home in Balboa. Mufti-clad civilians were present, most of them either propagandists for Professor Ruiz's propaganda group, operating out of the university, or scientists and researchers from *Obras Zorilleras*, the legion's research and development arm.

Standing in the back, behind closed doors, Raul Parilla, *Presidente de la Republica*, and Patricio Carrera waited with McNamara.

Parilla, short and stocky, with brown skin highlighted by steel-gray hair, wore mufti, as befitted a civil chief magistrate. Conversely, Mac and Carrera wore their battle dress, Mac carrying his badge of rank, the baton of the sergeant major general of the legion, while Carrera's battle dress carried only his name, his service, and, on his collar, two small pin-on eagles surrounded by wreaths for his rank. He didn't even bother with the gold-buckled leather belt that most senior legates wore. The trappings of rank and power had never meant much to Patricio Carrera.

"You look nervous, Patricio," Raul said.

Carrera grunted and gave a curt nod. "Simple explanation: I *am* nervous. I *loathe* speaking in public. Always have."

"That's not quite true, you know," Parilla corrected. "I've seen you warm to your audience and your subject before. What you hate is *waiting* to speak in public, fearing you won't do very well. Though why this should be, I don't know."

"He's right," Mac added. "And on that note, gentlemen, if you'll permit, I'll go announce you."

Headquarters, Tauran Union Security Force– Balboa, Building 59, Fort Muddville, Transitway Area, Balboa

"Malcoeur, you fat, slimy toad," shouted General Janier, the Tauran Union commander in Balboa. Tall and slender, handsome after a fashion but for an unfortunately large nose, the general was again dressed in his favorite costume, a replica of that of a marshal of Janier's hero, Napoleon.

"Oui, mon general?" the toady answered as he filled the lower half of the door to Janier's officer with his wide and short bulk. They called the Gauls "Frogs," and in Malceour's case, the description was apt, from his wide bulk to his shortened, froglike, pug face. The toady, a Tauran Union—which is to say Gallic—Army major, served as the great man's aide de camp.

"What is this meeting the locals are holding? Why was I not informed? Twenty thousand of them show up on our doorstep and I wasn't informed!"

"We had no warning, *mon general*. Apparently the word went out late last night and—voila!—they were suddenly here."

Janier gave Malcoeur a suspicious look. Was it possible the toad was enjoying his commander's discomfiture? *No, impossible;* so Janier thought.

"Nonsense, you fat fool," the general said. "This is an army of uncultured, uncivilized barbarians, people without tradition or experience or higher military education. They do not simply give orders and move. Even *we* could not assemble such a force so quickly."

We *likely could not*, agreed the aide silently. *But they seem to be able to. One suspects there are standing orders and plans in place to move like that, though we do not have adequate access to their plans and operations department. And we would have informed you a bit sooner, except that you were busy fucking your mistress in the apartment you carved out for her from military offices, just down the hall.*

Malcoeur was an ass-licker, so all on the staff agreed, but he was an ass-licker who could still *think*. And he *was* enjoying Janier's feeling like a fool.

"Go and fetch me the G-2"—the intelligence officer for the Tauran Union forces in the Transitway—"and bring the miscreant to me by the scruff of his neck," Janier ordered. "I am confident that after we have a little chat he will not in the future be so remiss."

Rome, Province of Italy, Old Earth

Almost, *almost*, Marguerite felt confident enough of her position to skip proskynesis before the SecGen. But, *no, this is too important to both the Earth and myself to let pique and arrogance get in the way.*

Moore stood beside her at the grand door to the former papal apartment. The two waited while the *majordomo* announced, "Captain and Admiral *pro tem* Marguerite Wallenstein, Class Two, for an audience with the Secretary General."

Moore said, "I'll be waiting when you've finished, Marguerite."

Clutching a valise in one hand, Marguerite nodded and advanced alone. She showed more confidence than she truly felt. The soft, plush rug underfoot muffled the sound of her high, black uniform boots. At a spot on the carpet about a dozen meters from the SecGen's large and ornate desk, Wallenstein placed the valise down and dropped to her knees. Leaning forward, she then placed both hands on the carpet ahead of her. Keeping eye contact until the last second, Wallenstein then bent and kissed the carpet three times, on the last kiss leaving her forehead to the floor. She straightened out until her breasts and belly were flush to the carpet and stayed that way.

"Arise, my child," the SecGen called. As gracefully as possible, under the circumstances, Wallenstein did. When she did, she was able to note certain things about the SecGen. He was young in appearance, very young. *Well, you would expect that from the very best anti-agathics,* she thought. *Such as are available to Class Ones,* she added, with bitterness in her mind. She thought he must have had extensive plastic surgery, too. *No man could be that . . .* pretty. *Not naturally.* Lastly, and most oddly, the SecGen shimmered, as if his skin had been freshly dusted with gold. *Which it probably has been,* she thought.

"Come closer, Captain," the SecGen said. Marguerite felt her stomach sink.

If he's using my permanent rank then maybe I won't be prorogued into the Admiralty. Shit.

The SecGen made a subtle but imperious gesture with his left hand. Marguerite thought she heard the door closing behind her and suddenly felt as if the *majordomo* had left her alone with the SecGen.

"My dear friend, the marchioness of Amnesty, wrote to me of what wonderful command of your tongue

you had," the SecGen said, twisting his chair to one
side. "Before we discuss weightier matters, show me."

Furiocentro Convention Center, Balboa City

Jorge Mendoza, warrant officer, and Ricardo Cruz,
Senior Centurion, saw each other, recognized each
other, and immediately pushed through the ranks
of the men to wrap each other in grand bear hugs,
pounding each other on their backs. Cruz was careful not to knock Mendoza over. Jorge's legs, both of
them, were made of artificial carbon fibers, enhanced
with computer control. Mendoza and Cruz had been
pretty tight for some years now, ever since Jorge,
though blind at the time, insisted on joining in a
political street battle at Cruz's side. Guts like that,
Cruz tended to appreciate.

"Jorge!" exclaimed Cruz, "I haven't seen you since—"

"Not since you were in the senior centurion's course
and took my class in *Historia y Filosofia Moral*,"
Mendoza supplied.

"It was a good class," Cruz complemented. "I got
a lot out of it."

"Thanks, Ricardo. I appreciate that. I had—"

Mendoza was interrupted by a familiar voice, McNamara's. "Gentlemen, the President of the Republic and
the Commander of the Legion."

The enormous room hushed to a deathly stillness as
every man braced to attention. The stillness was soon
broken by the sounds of Carrera's and McNamara's
boots, tap-tap-tapping down the stone walkway. Parilla's
softer civilian shoes made no comparable sound.

A murmur began right at the inner corners of the mass of humanity where the stone walkway divided them. It spread from there, across the rear rank and down toward the front like a wave. Too, like a wave, or perhaps a tsunami, the volume grew as more and more of the legionaries heard and passed on, "He's really come back to us. Our *Dux Bellorum* has returned."

Discipline held until Carrera, Parilla, and Mac were almost two thirds of the way to the stage on which rested a podium and the gold and silver eagles. At that point a junior centurion along the central aisle twisted and looked over his shoulder and said to himself, *To hell with it; I'm going to shake the commander's hand.*

The centurion broke ranks and stood right in Carrera's path with his hand outstretched. "Welcome back, sir," he said.

Another commander might have been angry. Carrera was . . . more than touched. Tears glistening in his eyes, he took the centurion's hand in a firm grip, pumping it and saying, "Thank you. It's good to be back."

At that point, the thing became a near riot, with legionaries jostling and pushing to get close to the man who had led them to victory through two wars and a police action of sorts on three continents. Even McNamara's voice couldn't get the men back into order until Carrera had shaken five hundred or more hands, and endured more back-slapping than was, strictly speaking, healthy or safe.

In the end, Mac had to use his size and presence— he towered over the average legionary—to force his way past the throng, up onto the stage and to the microphone.

"Enough, you bastards," he said, the words reverberating from the walls. "Cease and desist. You'll kill the man and here we've just gotten him back."

Headquarters, Tauran Union Security Force–Balboa, Building 59, Fort Muddville, Transitway Area, Balboa

The G-2's name tag read "de Villepin." He entered Janier's office confidently. And why not? He was at least as politically well connected as the general and could do at least as much damage to Janier as the latter could do to him, rank notwithstanding. Moreover, Janier knew it. His words—"by the scruff of the neck"—had been for his toady Malcoeur's benefit. And Malcoeur had basically shrugged that off.

Before Janier could say a word, de Villepin raised a hand and said, "I didn't worry about telling you, or order that your time with your mistress be interrupted, because, however large it may be—and yes, it's almost twice the size of our little pocket division—it's not equipped to attack anybody. I have people inside, besides.

"More importantly, the reason for the assembly is that their old commander, Carrera, is back. I had thought, we had all thought, he'd retired. Apparently this is not the case. The assembly is likely his little way of announcing he's back and in charge."

"You say you have your people inside?" Janier asked.

"Well . . . people who work for me, about eleven of them, if every one managed to attend." De Villepin smiled sardonically. "Technically and legally, I suppose they're Carrera's people. I'll have an admittedly incomplete report by tomorrow evening at the latest. More details will follow as more of my spies check in. It may be a week or so."

"So late?" Janier asked.

"If they aren't careful, Carrera's intelligence organization will catch them." De Villepin added, ruefully, "That ferret-faced bastard, Fernandez, is pretty good at what he does...and has methods available to him that are not permitted to me...usually. What would happen to my people if he caught them would not be strictly in accordance with the World League's Charter of Human Rights."

"Whatever it takes, then." Janier agreed, with a shrug.

Rome, Province of Italy, Old Earth

Though she'd come prepared, in more ways than one, to do whatever it took to secure her ends, Wallenstein balked, for the first time in a long life. It surprised no one more than herself, too. Still, memories of servicing her "betters" since she'd been a teenager had risen to the surface. So, too, had memories of being betrayed and abandoned by those "betters," once they'd had their fill of her. *I've prostituted myself for well over a century and what do I have to show for it? Nothing? No, not nothing, but not enough, either. And enough is enough. Diadems are enough. Teenagers being cut up on the* Ara Pacis *is enough. Enough!* The confusion, uncertainty, and indecision on her face was replaced with a steely hard determination.

"No," Marguerite said to the SecGen. "You don't

need me for that and doing it would say nothing positive about my ability to deal with the problems you and yours have created and let fester. You want your cock sucked; ring the bell for the *majordomo*. I've had enough of you Class Ones and your puerile obsessions with your genitalia."

Without bothering with a departing proskynesis, Marguerite turned on her heels and began walking, head proudly erect, to pick up her valise.

"Stop," the SecGen commanded. Unseen, he smiled, the smile possibly having an element of satisfaction to it. "Have a seat. You are, of course, right. I don't need you for your mouth but for your mind. You're also right that we have problems of our own making."

Wallenstein did stop. Her chin raised in anger. "I have conditions," she said, without turning.

"Let us discuss them, then," the SecGen agreed. "And you may assume that whatever may happen with the general meeting with the Consensus tomorrow, my word will carry."

Furiocentro Convention Center, Balboa City

Carrera, a bit battered perhaps but beaming all the same, ascended the stage and walked to the podium with its microphone. He already knew, from McNamara's command to the boys to "cease and fucking desist," that the volume was properly adjusted anyway.

Well, you'd expect little things like that to go right with a good organization.

"Without belaboring the obvious," Carrera began, "It's good to be back. I'm ... I'm truly sorry it took so long." He shook his head slightly. "I'm not going to give you any explanations. That's not because you don't deserve them; it's that there aren't—"

A warrant officer near the front shouted out, "We don't need any explanations, sir. It's enough that you *are* back."

Carrera smiled, half shyly. "Thank you, then, again, for that. So let's get to the meat of it; where do we go from here and why?

"The why should be obvious; our base, our *country,* is under occupation, both by foreigners and by an illegal rump of a corrupt government that those foreigners protect. To get rid of them requires at least the threat of war, and possibly the actuality. They know this, and so we can and must assume that they, too, are preparing for war.

"We've got three things," Carrera continued. "We've got a home base—or most of one—with a government that cares for us. We've got twenty-four regular line combat cohorts in the ground elements, plus another eighteen drilling reserve cohorts, mixed infantry, mechanized, and *cazadores*, and individual reservists enough to fill twice that. We've got supporting arms for all of those, generally in plenty though we are short in some areas, notably artillery and air. And . . . we've got enough money, over eighty billion Federated States drachmas, to make every regular in the legion here or elsewhere wealthy for *several* lives, let alone one."

He gave a shrug and waved a hand deprecatingly. "I don't want the money. I never have, for its own sake. As far as I'm concerned, you could split it up among yourselves. But there's one big problem. I could give you the money, but I couldn't then give

you a safe place to raise a family. I couldn't keep the
United Earth Peace Fleet off your backs. I couldn't
get rid of the Tauran Union, which has occupied the
most important and valuable chunk of Balboa, or the
rump of a false government that shelters under the
Taurans' greedy claws. I couldn't get rid of the stinking
Kosmos"—cosmopolitan progressives—"that insist every
form of decay is progress and do everything they can
to hasten that decay. I couldn't keep them from taking
it all away from you and giving it to their"—Carrera
sneered—"no doubt deserving selves."

Carrera scratched beside his nose as his lips formed
the tiniest of smiles. Rhetorically, he asked, "You all
already knew all that, right?

"That, however," he continued, "does not mean that
you are not going to be *earning* more money. Note
where the emphasis was in that last sentence. 'Earning.' You're going to earn it because we are going
to change the force radically. To expand it, yes—and
that's how you are going to be earning more money,
as you advance in rank much faster than any other
soldiers on the planet—but also to change it.

"Our days of providing a regular force so that we
could rent ourselves out to foreigners to fight their
wars for them are, for a while, at least, over. Our days
of concentrating on counterinsurgency are over, too.
Our first fight, in Sumer, a decade ago, has more to
say about our future than any number of operations
we have undertaken since.

"There is one possible exception to that," Carrera
said. "We might—it is at least within the realm of the
possible, and we are mutually bound by treaty—have
to send troops to support President Sada and the

Republic of Sumer against Farsia. Even that is only a partial exception, as a fight with Farsia would be heads-up, conventional combat. Conversely, though, we have a finger on at least one good legion from Sumer that will come to us at need. If you doubt that, let me remind you that in Pashtia, Sada sent us everything he could spare, and then some."

Headquarters, Tauran Union Security Force– Balboa, Building 59, Fort Muddville, Transitway Area, Balboa

"What *are* we going to do," de Villepin asked, "if the subject of the meeting is war between those legions and ourselves? I mean, a few years ago when they had almost everybody deployed to Pashtia we could have taken them with only minor reinforcement from Taurus, nothing that couldn't have been flown in over the course of a few days. Now that they're all back they could walk in with a rock in each hand and still beat the shit out of us."

"Nonsense," Janier insisted. "We are still a first rate, professional, and, above all, *Tauran* force facing amateurs who've been lucky in only fighting third raters to date. Though, yes, it will be harder now." The general sneered. In the light of day the doubts and fears he'd entertained several nights previously seemed ephemeral and silly. "If the bastard Columbians hadn't interfered I'd have done just that, too, beaten these peasants like I owned them."

De Villepin didn't correct Janier, but did think, *That's probably true, though the casualties they'd have inflicted*

*on our forces in Pashtia in revenge would have been
disastrous and politically insupportable. And neither of
us can afford to lose our political support. Which we
would if we fought a war on behalf of those who support us and lost it ... or suffered too many casualties.*

Rome, Province of Italy, Old Earth

The SecGen tugged at one altogether too perfect ear.
"The last time we got involved in a war, directly, on
the ground of Terra Nova, we had our asses handed
to us. It was too far and too hard to support. And
the guerillas impossible to eradicate."

"That's true," Wallenstein conceded. "But it's not
as if we sent very good people to fight that war. We
were still consolidating our hold here and simply didn't
have the quality to spare."

"I don't have it now, either," the SecGen said.
"You've seen the streets of Rome, the strutting para-
sites living off of the achievements of their elders,
sporting their diadems, and simply assuming that this
way of life is eternal, without any need for sacrifice.
Moore, I know, showed you the *Ara Pacis* and the ...
sacrifices. I *have* no worthwhile Class Ones to send
you, Admiral. The few of them that are both capable
and trustworthy I need here."

"I'll make do with good Class Twos and Threes," Wallenstein answered. She was surprised, shocked really,
that the SecGen saw Earth pretty much as she did. He
likely didn't see his entire Class the way she did, though.

*I wouldn't take any Class Ones if you offered them.
Well, I'd prefer not to, anyway.* "And I intend to use

locals to do our campaigning for us. There are many there who would prefer to see the enlightened rule of United Earth."

"That hasn't worked out that well so far," the SecGen said.

Wallenstein nodded. "Martin was, perhaps, overly ambitious," she answered.

Furiocentro Convention Center, Balboa City, Balboa, Terra Nova

"The program is ambitious," Carrera admitted. "But it is not, as a practical matter, more ambitious than the one that brought us from an idea, to a staff, to a small legion, to two small ones, to two larger ones, to four of them, plus supporting arms.

"The very short version of this is that every current legion is going to become a corps. A fifth corps will be created from tidbits taken from here and there. Every tercio will become a legion, plus several legions will have to be created almost from scratch. Every existing cohort will have to expand to the size of a tercio and reconfigure itself to be an organization for heads-up, conventional combat. I mean serious bloodletting.

"Some—many—of the units are going to have to shift large cadres to form still others.

"We are going to be buying or building or rebuilding tanks and planes and ships and guns as never before. We need trucks and helicopters and armored personnel carriers galore. Uniforms. Rifles. Radios. Machine Guns. Mortars . . . ammunition."

Carrera stopped to pour himself a drink of water,

wishing deep down that it were whiskey, before continuing with, "The biggest change will be in personnel management. We're not going to be a regular force anymore. In fact, the regulars will be pretty much limited to you people here, and those who couldn't attend but who have at least earned stripes. You will provide a cadre for units four times bigger than the cadres you provide. The difference will be made up of reservists, men and women we've sent to training, kept with the colors for a year or so to assimilate and socialize them, and then released to civil life . . . to partly civil life. Between you and the reservists, you will form the core for units, again, four times larger, with the difference being made up of militia. The difference between reservists and militia will be ability. The militia will be average, everyday Juans. The reservists will be those with some of that special spark that all or at least most of you have. Overall, the ratio will be one regular to three reservists to twelve militia.

"Generally speaking, you will all hold two ranks, permanent and full mobilization. You'll wear and be paid at your full mobilization rank when you are, in fact, mobilized and when your units are called up for training.

"Yes, that means the twenty-four or so thousand people we have on their second or subsequent enlistment, or who are lifers, will form the leadership for a force of about ninety-six thousand, not quite three percent of the country, while that ninety-six thousand will provide the leadership for a full force of nearly four hundred thousand, or about eleven percent of the country.

"Yesss . . . that's right, all you squad and section leaders. Get used to the idea of being first centurion to a maniple . . . *soon*. Signifers and junior tribunes"—which

in most armies would have been called "second-" or
"first lieutenants"—"I *sure* hope you've been keeping
up with your studies; you're going to be commanding
cohorts before the signifier half of you even have to
begin shaving regularly. Senior tribunes?"—captains
and majors in other armies—"There are eagles in your
future . . . that, or relief for cause."

Headquarters, Tauran Union Security Force–Balboa, Building 59, Fort Muddville, Transitway Area, Balboa

In his ornate office, behind his massive desk made
of hand-carved Terra Novan silverwood, Janier contemplated the series of gold-embroidered eagles on
the blue material of the sleeves of his reproduction
marshal's uniform.

How sad, he thought, *to be born into the wrong
time. Seven centuries ago and I could have marched
with the emperor; made my name at Marengo, Auster-
litz, Jena-Auerstadt. Now, all I can do is try to make
my name in* Balboa . . . *which is hardly the same thing.
Life is* so *unfair.*

*Still, it could be worse. I have good troops, great
power. The weather is pleasant and the surroundings
more civilized than in, say, Middle Uhuru. At least my
mistress here is approximately white.*

The general breathed a deep sigh pregnant with
frustration. *I could take the rest of this country if my
political masters would allow me to and support me in
it. At least, now I could. It's simply a question of iso-
lating that force out on the* Isla Real *by navy and air,*

and we have the assets to do both back in Taurus, then grabbing Parilla's government, the one that presides over the rest of Balboa. Yes, there are a hundred thousand enemy reservists, but they can be handled with their leadership stuck out on the island. And even the island must surrender when the food runs out.

There are, of course, those distressing rumors that the Legion del Cid has nuclear weapons. But I don't see them using them on their own base country. The things aren't terribly useful, anyway; and didn't the Yithrabi terrorists prove that when they set one off by accident in their own capital?

Capital . . . capital . . . I can see myself marching proudly through the capital after I have won the war here. I can see myself at the helm of Gaul, tugging its strings, while Gaul tugs the Tauran Union's strings, the TU runs the World League, and the World League shits on the damned Columbians of the Federated States.

Of course, the trick will be to make sure that United Earth is not in a position to pull my strings. Well . . . half the trick, anyway. I still need to find a way to convince the TU to support me.

I wonder if the Balboans, themselves, wouldn't assist in that. That would be a help.

Rome, Province of Italy, Old Earth

Marguerite breathed a small sigh of relief when the SecGen agreed, "I can shave a little more off the top for maintenance of the Peace Fleet. But you have to understand; my position depends in good part on *not* asking too much in the way of sacrifices, and on giving the people that matter what they want. Why, after all, do you suppose I let the Azteca and the Orthodox Druids get away with their insanities?" The SecGen uttered a curse. "Why, oh, *why* can't those morons be like the caliph of Rome, on the other side of the Vatican? He, at least, is a sensible man, an atheist."

Wallenstein ignored that. As a member in good standing of the Reformed Druidic faith, she didn't really approve of the caliph or his cynical manipulation of his diminishing faithful. Changing the subject back, she said, "If you can't provide what the fleet needs quickly—"

"—I can't—"

"—Then we'll have to bring it forward in packets." Marguerite chewed on her lower lip for a time, thinking hard. "I really need to keep the Peace Fleet on station around Terra Nova...hmmm..."

Marguerite's eyes brightened. "Well, the colonization fleet is still in orbit around the moon."

"No one's looked to those ships in *centuries,* Marguerite," the SecGen said.

"I know," she nodded. "But things in space, at least the things that aren't being used, don't deteriorate much. Those ships will probably work still. Besides, we don't need all of them, just enough to run a regular shuttle service to the Peace Fleet. I can do some juggling of personnel in the Peace Fleet to man a shuttle service...even enough to bring the colonization ships back on line." She laughed, a trifle bitterly. "Why not? I've got ships around TN operating off skeleton crews to reduce the wear and tear on life support. I've others that are half-cannibalized. I have those crews doing make-work on Atlantis Base because there's no place in space to put them."

"Well," the SecGen said, "as you get your fleet running again you will run short of people."

"No," she shook her head. "That won't be a problem. It isn't going to happen so fast that we can't train new people."

Furiocentro Convention Center, Balboa City

"Training is going to be a problem," Carrera said. "Reservists and militia will be cheaper than regulars, with reservists serving only seventy-five days a year and militia thirty or so. That's still expensive and still more troops out in the field than we have training areas for, despite the major maneuver areas at *Lago Sombrero*, the Guarasi 'Desert,' and Fort Cameron. We also need to bring about thirty to thirty-five thousand new people to the colors a year for the foreseeable future. And *they're* going to have to do their initial training on the *Isla Real*, the only place we have facilities for it. Obviously, there's not room out there for you and them both.

"So you and your units are going to be moving to casernes on the mainland. Which we have to build. Which we have to find and buy land for. Which is also going to be expensive as hell.

"Fortunately, *Presidente* Parilla—" Carrera gave a nod to Raul, sitting between McNamara and Fernandez, the Intel chief, in the front row—"has offered to let us use, more or less permanently and more or less without restrictions, a great deal of the nationally owned land to establish major training areas.

"This will, I imagine, piss off the world's environmentally conscious and sensitive class to no end."

Carrera's tone and smile said all that needed to be said about his deep and abiding lack of concern for the sentiments of those environmentalists. Oh, yes, he had set aside some funding for the preservation of the endangered trixies, but that was more personal than environmental in motive.

"And you have to be wondering where all the extra troops are going to come from. We already have some substantial numbers of legionaries from every state in *Colombia Latina*. In fact, we take in a couple of thousand Spanish-speaking foreigners a year and have almost since we started, eleven years ago. Those numbers have to go up. A lot. As do the numbers we take in from Balboa itself.

"And at this point, I'd like to ask the president to the stand to explain some legal and political changes. *Presidente* Parilla?"

Carrera came to attention as soon as Parilla stood. Following his cue, all the military types present did likewise, while the civilians, such as there were, simply shut up and stood a bit straighter.

Fernandez, sitting next to Parilla's vacated chair, fumed, *He's giving too much away. There are half a dozen people here on the Tauran Union's payroll that I know of. How many more are there that I have no clue to?*

On the plus side, I'll find out about at least a couple more that I don't currently know about when they go scurrying to inform their masters of what's been said here. That's something, I suppose.

Fernandez was right to be worried, if only because intelligence and counterintelligence was his job. For that matter, supervision of covert direct action, a euphemism for assassination and sabotage, was also his bailiwick. He was rather good at his job, too, due to a combination of practical experience, sheer ruthlessness, and—this was the general opinion of those in a position to know—brainpower.

And then, too, if there are half a dozen people here on the enemy's payroll, I've a dozen in his key offices on mine. Those, and the commander of the Castilian battalion who feeds me information simply because he hates the Tauran Union and wants his country out of it. It's fair, I suppose. Except that I know Rocaberti has spies in our force, more than a few of them, and I've never managed to get a spy right on his immediate staff. Not for lack of trying, either. But blood counts and they're all his relations, to one degree or another.

But, Patricio, you need to make the enemy work for his information. Everything you give him for free leaves him free to devote resources to finding more.

Carrera, standing on the stage while Parilla made his way up it, stole a glance at the space the president had vacated. In particular, he looked at Fernandez's ferretlike face. *I know exactly what you're thinking, Omar. Too much information, given too freely. "Make the enemy work for his intelligence," isn't that what you've been nagging me over for better than ten years? That's not the right calculation. We also need our own people not to have to work for information they need to support the mission.*

It's an arguable point, I admit, and one with, perhaps, no truly satisfactory answer. But, besides that we need our own people on board, there are at least two other factors. One is that intelligence freely given can also misdirect. In other words, the more the TU looks at the main force, the more they see it as adequately powerful, the less inclined they'll be to look for other things that go beyond adequately powerful.

The other thing is that I have not given anyone, not even you, my ferret-faced friend, all the information.

Rome, Province of Italy, Old Earth

Wallenstein had had months to think on the voyage from new Earth to Old. She'd put those months to good use.

"Why are you so convinced that this Carrera person and the petty little fiefdom he occupies have to go, Marguerite?" The SecGen drummed his fingers on the marble inlay of his ornate desk, a thousand-year-old relic dug out the Vatican's cellars. The finger drumming made her nervous.

Best not to mention the nukes, she thought, *since I had a small part in them. Fortunately, I don't have to mention them.*

"He upsets things," she answered. "He's an unpredictable factor that is controlled by no one, listens to no one, and can be deterred or bribed by nothing."

"Are you *sure* he can be bribed by nothing?" the SecGen asked. "Near immortality is no small thing. Would he cooperate with us for that?"

She shook her head in doubt. "From what I can gather he already has the only kinds of immortality that might matter to him: children and a belief in the Christian god. Those, and that he's already going

into the history books, if that matters to him. Plus...
well..."

"Go on," the SecGen urged.

"I think he makes us the most useful kind of enemy,"
Wallenstein answered.

"Please explain."

"As a practical matter, our kind of people never
could have taken and held power here on Earth if
Terra Nova hadn't been there as both a draw, initially,
and a dumping ground, later, for those who would
have resisted us. The discovery of the rift and then
of the other planet are what changed the political and
philosophical make up here on Earth.

"That can't happen there. There is no other rift
with a useful planet at the other end—at least none
that's ever been found—and so there is no place to
send away the kind of people we sent to Terra Nova.
Without that kind of demographic change—or engineering, there towards the end—we lose. At least our
kind of people lose."

I say "our kind of people," Wallenstein thought,
but they're really not my *kind of people.*

"So, in any case, our experience here on Earth is
nonanalagous and we need another way."

"Which is?"

"Our natural allies on Terra Nova need to establish
their credentials by a series of decisive acts. They're
not, mostly, very competent to do those. They can't
even do a half decent job of humanitarian intervention, let alone run a war."

"And that's where you come in?" the SecGen asked.

"That's where I come in," she agreed, with a deep
nod. "Not that I'm in the same military class as this

Carrera; honestly, I'm not. But with the Fleet restored, and sufficient other forms of aid to our allies on Terra Nova, I can still stymie him, report his every move, keep him from pulling the kind of clever, sneaky things he's been specializing in for ten years.

"And I'll need to build him up, in the public eye, as a kind of monster. That way, when our people on TN triumph, slay the monster, they will have credibility to spare."

"Do you so hate this Carrera?" the SecGen asked.

Wallenstein suppressed a slight shiver. "Oh, Your Excellency," she said, "I don't hate him at all."

The SecGen noticed the shiver and raised a single, quizzical eyebrow.

Furiocentro Convention Center, Balboa City

Parilla cocked his head, raised one eyebrow, and cast his gaze over the throng until they quieted. Even after they had, he waited until Carrera had taken a seat before he began to speak.

"What I'm going to say is as much political as military, or arguably more so. My friend, Patricio, spoke of three tiers that will compose the legion. Arguably there will be seven . . . I mean six."

"Don't even mention *the cadets, Raul,"* Carrera had warned.

Sorry, Patricio. Parilla looked apologetically at Carrera, sitting in his vacated seat in the front row.

"Besides the regulars, reservists, and militia, there are also those who could have come to the colors but did not. Some of those can be expected to volunteer when the abstract threat of war changes to actual or imminent war. After those are people who may never spend a day in uniform but who can still be put to work as civilians, digging trenches if they've no other skill.

"Lastly are groups like the police, the Young Scouts, firefighters; all of whom have some training, a chain of command, and a sense of civic duty, and all of whom can supplement the rest in critical ways."

"And please don't *mention the hidden reserves,"* Patricio had also said.

I didn't. Besides, I doubt you've told me about all of them.

"Between them, these can produce the force *Duque* Carrera requires to defend the country . . . from anything or anyone.

"All that said, Balboa itself is split, and not just by the former government cowering in its enclave in Old Balboa City and the Taurans who bestraddle the Transitway. Even though the legion has adopted Balboa—no surprise since you're eighty-three percent Balboan—and my government has adopted the legion—also no surprise since you're all that stands between us and the stinking Taurans—we still exist in two separate worlds. The only junction between those worlds are myself and the few members of the Legislative Assembly who have served in the legion. And even that junction is emotional rather than legal."

Parilla reached a hand toward his lower lip and tapped it contemplatively with his fingers. He shrugged his shoulders as if to say, *Oh, well, may as well get on with it.*

"No sense in dilly-dallying; we're bringing the legion

into the government as a second legislative body, which we shall call the "Senate." The Senate will be co-equal with the current assembly and will have complete power over the legion and its assets. Initially, since I am a veteran of the legion, I will serve as president of the Senate or—what was that you wanted to call the office, Patricio? *Princeps Senatus?* The rest of the initial body of the Senate will be chosen, one per cohort, later one per tercio, from the discharged veterans of those cohorts and tercios. Still later, as the centuriate assembly which will elect members to the Senate is formed, you may choose someone else."

Not that, under the circumstances, that is very likely, very soon.

Seated in the front, Carrera thought, *Yes. Precisely because I no longer trust my moral judgment. Not that it was ever all that good.*

CHAPTER FOUR

Both Heaven and Hell are absolute dictatorships; the only difference is the being in charge. A similar rule applies to human government. A democratic government over a society composed of decent, law-abiding, civic-minded and civically virtuous people can bring prosperity, security, all the good things in life. Conversely, a democratic government in a society gone rotten, or one where only family and blood count, or where it is every man for himself, can create a Hell on Earth. A monarchy may be decent and stable, as Anglia's was for many centuries, or it can be the nightmare of work-to-death camps in Volga under the Red Tsars. Indeed, people may be freest of all under a monarchy like Anglia's, or they may be utter slaves to the whims of Volga's autocrats. An aristocracy may rule well and provide great benefit to everyone, aristocrat and common, alike. Equally, it may be a corrupt oligarchy that loots the society for its own benefit. The questions then, always, and for every possible form of government, are: "What is the quality of

those in charge and how can we select them for
virtue and maintain them in virtue?"

—Jorge y Marqueli Mendoza, *Historia y
Filosofia Moral*, Legionary Press, Balboa,
Terra Nova, copyright AC 468

Anno Condita 470
Main Parade Field, Legates' Row, *Isla Real*,
Balboa, Terra Nova

The plane was a high winged monoplane with a great
deal of glass to it. Called a "Cricket," it performed,
more cheaply, a number of tasks within the legion that
most armies used helicopters for. The scout/command
and control plane's engine droned loudly as it made a
steep descent to the parade field fronting Quarters One.
Looking down, Carrera shook his head ruefully. He put
his mouth to Lourdes' ear and said, "I'm getting old."

"How's that, Patricio?" the woman asked.

In answer, he grimaced and put his right index
finger near the window, jabbing it downward three
times. Lourdes looked out and saw a sea of humanity,
partially pixel-clad and in at least equal measure in
civilian, dry season white, packing the parade field.
The troops and their families had thoughtfully left a
rectangular open area, just slightly larger than required
to land a Cricket. She looked and smiled, pleased that
the people still loved her husband as she did.

"So much for coming here unannounced," Carrera
said.

"But how . . . I mean, you told hardly anyone. We
didn't even bring any *bags*." Which wasn't strictly true.

Carrera had a carry-on and Lourdes a small trunk. But from her point of view that *was* no baggage.

He shook his head. "Grapevine. Rumor control. One of the centurions at the *casa* paying back a favor to an old friend on the island. Or, most probably, all three."

Which is why "secret, unannounced Annual General Inspections" are never secret or unannounced.

"It's very hard to keep a secret these days," he added, "if people don't think it *should* be kept or owe favors to or need favors from people who don't want it kept."

Lourdes looked suddenly guilty. "Well . . . I *did* tell Artemisia that we were coming. *Someone*, after all, had to make sure Quarters One was ready."

Again, Carrera shook his head. "She didn't spread the word. Arti *can* keep a secret."

Lourdes briefly considered nukes and destroyed cities and mass murder and thought, *Lord, I hope so, her and Alena . . . well, about Alena, at least, I have no doubts whatsoever. I'd be jealous of her, I think, and her relationship to Hamilcar, if I weren't so completely sure that if a meg were coming for Ham, the fish would have to eat* through *Alena to get to my boy . . . and she'd be prying its teeth loose from the inside while kicking its gut into jelly the whole time it was swimming.*

As the plane practically auto-hovered over the landing spot—there was enough of a head wind for the thing almost to take off on its own—Carrera glanced over the assembly. He saw that it was not just people, soldiers and their families, but that someone had arranged an honor guard in legionary dress whites, set up a public address system, and had a limousine on station. He turned his head slowly, looking for someone senior he could tear a new asshole in for ruining his planned, private landing.

But, *no, no one above a junior centurion that I can see. And I'm not going to chew one of them out for being . . . well . . . for being polite, I suppose. And it is kind of thoughtful.*

I hope to hell they aren't really expecting a speech.

"That was a very nice little speech," Lourdes said, as the two walked from the limousine to the open doorway of Quarters One. Artemisia stood in the doorway. "Especially since you weren't planning on giving one."

"I didn't say a word to anyone except my uncle Xavier and Mac," Arti announced, loudly. "And they wouldn't have told."

Xavier wouldn't, Carrera silently agreed. *Mac? I'm not so sure. Though I* am *sure that if it was the sergeant major he'd have covered his tracks well enough that I'd never find out even if I tried. So why bother? Hell with it.*

As Carrera and Lourdes began to ascend the steps to the wide, columned, wraparound porch, they heard a hellish screech, which screech was soon followed by a brightly feathered head bearing remarkably intelligent eyes.

"*Jinfeng!*" Carrera exclaimed, stopping and bending down to skritch the blue, green, red, and gold reptilian bird atop its head. This particular bird had been the pet of—though perhaps *companion to* was closer to correct—Carrera's late wife, Linda.

The bird pulled its head back as if to say, *You don't visit in years. You don't write. You don't call. Harrumph!*

"I'm sorry, *Jinfeng,*" Carrera said, apologetically.

He kept his hand outstretched while saying, "I wasn't well for a while."

Bright the bird may have been, about as much so as a grey parrot. Still, it wasn't bright enough to understand the words. It understood the tone well enough, though...well enough to give one last indignant screech and a halfhearted snap that deliberately missed the fingers before moving its head into Carrera's reach.

"I've been feeding them," Artemisia said.

"Them?" Carrera asked.

Arti didn't have to answer. While *Jinfeng* was being well skritched, three more heads suddenly popped out of the bushes and offered their own screeches.

"*Jinfeng!* You're a mother!"

The very existence of the Noahs was surmised from three factors, a handful of artifacts, the Rift itself, and the very strange variety of life on Terra Nova.

That life came, broadly speaking, from several sources. One source was Terra Nova itself, though little of the planet's naturally evolved life had survived the introduction of other, more highly evolved life. Little of it, too, was commercially valuable, though Terra Novan olives—a gray, wrinkled skinned, plum sized, and highly astringent stoned fruit—were. Likewise, chorley was a native grain obtained from a low, sunflowerlike plant that made an excellent, buttery bread. Too, there were various forms of peppers, from Joan of Arc to Holy Shit to Satan Triumphant, which spiced up, literally, Terra Novan cuisine.

(Actually, no one could really *eat* Satan Triumphant in anything except the most dilute trace amounts, but it had found commercial value as a vesicant, a blister

agent, during the planet's Great Global War that had
ended sixty-one years before. It was also used occasionally as a food preservative. This was touchy, though,
as the slightest trace too much of Satan Triumphant,
and the food would be completely preserved. Not
only would bugs not touch it, neither would people.)

Then there was the alien, and possibly genengineered, life. Almost all of that was dangerous. There
were the septic mouthed, nocturnally predatory,
winged reptiles called "*antaniae*," or moonbats, with
their nightly cries of "*mnnbt, mnnbt, mnnbt.*" Among
humans, these were dangerous mostly to children,
especially small children, and the old and weak. The
moonbats were predators of a particularly nasty sort.
Venomless, their bite would begin an infection that
only heroic measures could defeat, and then only
if caught in time. Otherwise, the victim would suc-
cumb to the infection, more moonbats gathering as
it weakened, until the combination of numbers and
weakness allowed the vile creatures to descend and
feed on the still-living victim. *Antaniae* were especially
fond of eating the eyes and brains of the very young.

Besides the *antaniae*, there were at least three
species of plant life deadly to man, the tranzitrees,
the progressivines, and the bolshiberries. All of these,
pleasant to gaze upon and sweet to eat, produced a
toxin not dissimilar in its effects to *C. botulinum*. This
toxin was particularly insidious in that it affected only
higher forms of life. Thus, domestic herd animals
could, if not carefully kept from doing so, consume
the fruit of those plants, build up the toxin in their
systems, and deliver highly fatal doses to man.

It was surmised that both the *antaniae* and the

deadly plants had been genengineered expressly to be dangerous to intelligent life. Certainly, casualties among early settlers to the planet had been horrific enough, as evidenced by such place names as Desperation Bay, in Lansing State, in the Federated States, Gagandie, in Wellington (a city founded and christened by Australian thought-criminals whose country on Old Earth had not been given a settlement area of its own), and *Ni Hoi Thlee*, in Zhong Guo.

With the arrival of man had come all of man's domestic animals and food crops, from horses to goats and from wheat to blueberries. Additionally, many species endangered on Old Earth had found, or been given, a home and a new lease on life on Terra Nova.

However, when men had first come, they had discovered that Terra Nova had already had an abundance of life so endangered that it had already become extinct on Old Earth. This accounted for the presence of *Jinfeng's* subspecies of archaeopteryx, or "trixies," as well as beasts of land and sea from sabertooth tiger to carcharodon megalodon.

"What happened to the father?" Carrera asked. Breeding *Jinfeng* had been a pet project for some years; he'd even imported several males to the *Isla Real* for her to choose from.

"You know males," Arti said sardonically. "Once he'd had his fun he bugged off. I think he hangs around the solar tower. At least, I've seen *Jinfeng* winging it in that direction, from time to time, the shameless little hussy."

And did you *get the holes in the wall fixed that you and Mac made, thumping the bed against it?* Carrera wondered, raising one eyebrow and grinning. Arti knew well enough what he was thinking and ignored grin and quizzical eyebrow, both.

The solar tower, more properly the solar chimney, was an extremely tall reinforced concrete structure with an enormous circular greenhouse off center and down slope from its base, towering three-quarters of a kilometer above the island's dominant terrain feature, Hill 287. An enormous circular concrete tunnel running up the slope of the hill connected the greenhouse with the base of the tower. Heated air running through the thing turned turbines that provided all the island's power needs, and to excess, for the fifty-thousand men and women of the legion plus the families. The top of the tower was perpetually shrouded in mist.

There were several others in the Republic of Balboa, all built at legion expense and to legion profit, that provided whatever of the nation's electric needs the hydroelectric dams did not. Moreover, the towers sold their electricity eastwards towards neighboring Santa Josefina. Carrera had never given orders to cut electric power either to the Tauran occupied Transitway or the rump government in Old Balboa City. Though he'd never explained it to anyone, his rationale had been, *If I cut them off now, it will inconvenience them for a while and at the same time cause them to make themselves invulnerable to my cutting the electricity off at a later, more critical date.*

"He also comes by here, sometimes," Arti continued, "mostly for free eats. At least, I *think* the one that comes by here is the father."

Casa Linda, Balboa

Two turbaned guards stood outside the conference room. Two others were within. There were always that many, or more, for when the boy slept two of them slept on thin cushions to either side of his bed while two more stood awake and watching, arms in hand, their pale green, gray, and blue eyes barely blinking.

They did other things, too, those guards. Hamilcar Carrera-Nuñez, eldest child of Patricio and Lourdes, was already a crack shot, could fight with fist, dagger, or lance, at least within his weight class, or even a bit above it, and could ride like the wind. The guards seemed to take a personal pride in passing on the lessons learned by their tribe of nearly three thousand years of combat on two planets.

Despite the guards' surpassing paranoia where his safety was concerned, Hamilcar was not in the conference room for safety's sake. Rather, he had learned to hijack the computer to play wargames from the legion's educational programs on the conference room's big Kurosawa screen. On that screen now, thousands of electronic shadows were dying as a young student of the art of war swung in his flanks onto the opposing exposed flanks and smashed his cavalry into the computer enemy's rear.

It's a lot better, now, thought Hamilcar. *Much, much better since Dad snapped out of it. Mmm... mostly snapped out of it,* the boy corrected. *I can hear when he screams at night no less than Mom can. And she doesn't really* know*, not the way I do, why he screams. After all, I was there.*

Poor Dad; when I'm a little older I'll be able to take some of the burden away.

Hamilcar knew, because his father had discussed it with him, that within a year, a year and a half at most, he would be going to Pashtia on his own—or, rather, with his company of guards—to grow some in ways the local schools could never teach. He suspected that it had more to do with getting him someplace comparatively safe than it did with furthering his education. Not that Pashtia was precisely safe, or perhaps ever would be. But there he would be guarded by hundreds, really thousands, of fanatics, every one of whom from the chief down to the least little girl milking a goat would eagerly die to prevent anything from happening to "Iskandr, avatar of God."

"Which is nonsense," the boy muttered aloud, his fingers sending a recall command to his light cavalry. "I'm not an avatar of any god. I'm just eight years old. With maybe some skills and knacks. And a slight resemblance to a nearly three-thousand-year-old image on a gold plate in a dusty cave somewhere in Pashtia."

On the big screen, trapped shadows, nearly eighty thousand of them, continued to die.

Isla Real, Balboa, Terra Nova

From the island, the sea today might as well have been an expanse of blue painted glass with waves drawn on. Close in, one could see that the waves were real enough, but very gentle. They rolled in to a smooth, sandy beach, dominated by a hill with a couple of natural caves in its face.

"We could butcher them down there," said Aleksandr Sitnikov, late of the Red Tsar's Fifth Guards Tank Regiment, as he pointed from the shallow cave mouth down to the beaches to the north, northeast, and northwest.

Carrera nodded but said, looking around the shallow cave, "I expected you would have made more progress than you have, Aleksandr."

The short and balding Volgan looked sheepish. (All Volgan tankers were short, though baldness was optional.) "I know," he said. "And I'm sorry. But I ran out of money last year and Esterhazy"—the legion's Sachsen-born comptroller—"wouldn't shit me any more money without your *express* order."

Carrera thought, *Query to self: Despite what was intended to be a training program that developed vast individual initiative, did my behavior the last couple of years before I cracked make people defensive and rob them of initiative? Ask Mac and Xavier; no one else will answer honestly. If so, how do I fix it?*

He nodded his understanding, agreeing, "Fair enough. Not your fault. The money will be forthcoming. Can you finish preparing the island for defense within three years?"

Sitnikov could remember a time when Carrera had been so worn out with the struggle, so tired, that he'd have lashed out viciously over any failing. *The rest did him good, I think. Which is good for me, too.*

"It will cost more," the Volgan answered. "The old rule still applies: You can have it quick or good or cheap; pick any two. And, of course, some preparations cannot be completed, per your guidance, until war is impending or has already begun."

Sitnikov's face then took on an uncharacteristically mulish cast. "And besides that, I've got the problem of running the cadets. They're a goddamned *division* all on their own, Patricio. I've been juggling the two for years, probably to the detriment of both. You really need someone to do both, separately."

"I know," Carrera agreed. "And I am sorely tempted to make that someone Esterhazy, who is not only a trained engineer but also the fucker who should have taken the initiative and given you the money." He sighed. "But if I did, who would be comptroller?"

"That, happily, is *your* problem. I didn't sign on with you to specialize in personnel management."

"You didn't sign on to run herd on teenagers or design a system of fortifications, either," Carrera answered drily, "but you never bitched about either one."

"Actually," Sitnikov corrected, "I signed on to teach your first troops to operate White Eagle tanks. You just bribed me into staying on for the cadets and this island."

"Mere details."

"Hmmm...details...tanks... I've got a demonstration for you, if you're up to it."

"Demonstration of what?" Carrera asked.

"Bunkers, actually," the Volgan answered. "If I didn't have the money to build them all, I did have enough to build some of the prototypes we first discussed and to test a few of the designs."

"Best put these in," Sitnikov said, taking a pair of earplugs from a pocket and handing them to Carrera. He took another set out, rolled them in his fingers to collapse them to narrow cylinders, then stuck those in his own ear canals. Carrera did similarly.

In front of them a Jaguar II (formerly "White Eagle") tank sat with the tank commander's upper torso sticking out of the turret. Sitnikov gave the tank commander, or TC, a thumbs up. Immediately the tank commander dropped down into the turret, hurriedly closing the hatch behind him.

Sitnikov shouted, "This is going to "

KABOOMMM!

"—sting."

Before the last word was out, indeed, before the concussion from the muzzle had dissipated, a concrete bunker downrange was blocked from view by the evil, black smoke of a good-sized explosion. Eight seconds later, after the turret had traversed a few degrees, the same thing happened to a second bunker, then, another eight seconds later, a third . . . a fourth . . . a fifth . . . a sixth.

"Jesus, I hate those things," Carrera muttered, completely unheard by anyone but himself. "Sting" was something of an understatement. The Volgans made great guns, of tremendous power and range for their weight and complexity. A major downside, however, was that the muzzle blast from those guns was somewhat incompatible with maintaining human health.

The TC of the tank emerged and made an all clear signal. Sitnikov nudged Carrera's arm, even as he dug into his own ears to pull out the plugs. "Come, let me show you." The Volgan picked up a box and began to walk toward the still smoke-obscured bunkers.

"The concrete we use," Sitnikov explained, "is special. For fill we use coral we blast out of the reefs around the islands. Remarkably strong stuff, that is. Plus the cement is very high quality, as good as made anywhere on the planet."

Carrera nodded. It was no legend that, during the Great Global War, bunkers made of such material had taken direct hits from sixteen-inch naval guns and very large aerially delivered bombs and survived intact.

The Volgan continued, "While we may have to face a substantial aerial bombardment, heavy-weight naval gunfire is a thing of the past. I think *we* carry the largest naval guns on Terra Nova today, in our Kurita-class cruiser, and they're only six inchers. Still, what will resist a sixteen-inch shell is likely to resist a thousand-kilogram bomb as well."

"Not a deep penetrator," Carrera pointed out.

"A penetrator of any size," Sitnikov countered, "would rarely or never be used on a bunker containing at most three men and a machine gun or light cannon."

Carrera nodded. "True enough."

"And after I show you these, I have something else to show you in reference to bunkers a deep penetrator might be worth expending on."

"What's in the box?" Carrera asked.

"Toys and garbage," Sitnikov answered cryptically.

The range had been short. Thus, each of the six bunkers had taken a direct and well-placed hit from the tank's main gun. The hits were, however well-placed, off center.

"There's no point in testing for what happens if a major round hits the firing aperture," Sitnikov explained. "In that case the crew dies. We're more interested in what happens when a gun hits any other part of the bunker."

The Volgan led the way around to the back of the bunker, to its entrance.

"This first one shows what happens when a tungsten or depleted uranium long-rod penetrator hits anything but the firing aperture or hits at an angle that drives it through the bulk of the shelter. And it's...ugly."

Carrera looked through the entrance. Inside, lit only by daylight, the butchered carcasses of three pigs lay on the concrete floor. *No,* Carrera thought, *they're not all dead.*

One of the pigs, still breathing, lifted its head and looked at Carrera hopelessly before laying its head down again and expiring. Air escaping from punctured lungs turned pig's blood into a red froth.

Ignoring the iron-coppery stench of porcine blood, Carrera looked at one wall, where a long, deep furrow of concrete had been blasted out, leaving the rebar exposed. He nodded, not needing an explanation for what had happened. *The penetrator, when passing through the concrete, simply forced displaced concrete out the most convenient side, explosively.*

"The next one," Sitnikov said, pointing and leading the way, "is a high-explosive plastic, or HEP, hit."

Here, Carrera saw, the outside surface of the bunker was deeply pitted and cratered over an area of about a foot and a half in diameter. Walking to the back and, again, peering through the entrance, he saw something similar to what had been in the interior of the first bunker. This included three dead pigs—mercifully they *were* dead by this time—as well as a large, fairly round gap of exposed rebar.

"The exterior explosion sends a shockwave through the concrete. As the shockwave bounces back from the inner face, that face detaches . . . explosively."

"I understand."

"The next," the Volgan said, walking on, still carrying his box of toys and garbage, "was a simple high-explosive round on a superquick fuse." At the bunker Sitnikov opened a steel door. "We only closed it for this one and the last," the Volgan explained, "to get a good simulation of concussion. It didn't matter for the others."

Carrera said nothing but looked through the open portal and saw three . . . *living pigs*.

"Straight concrete," Sitnikov said, "and the concussion gets transmitted pretty much in full. This stuff . . . well, what we've done to it, *plus* the peculiar qualities of the coral fill, and . . . well, you can see for yourself."

Carrera's face grew mildly contemplative as he considered the stunned, staggering, but still living pigs. "What were you planning on doing with our porcine brothers?" he asked.

"Back to the farm?"

"No," Carrera shook head. "Seems kind of cruel . . . maybe even double jeopardy. I think they ought be retired for 'service to the legion.'"

"Your pigs," Sitnikov shrugged. He walked to the next bunker. "Now it gets interesting. Look for yourself."

Carrera saw that, curiously, there was a wire mesh over the open portal and that behind the mesh were stunned but otherwise healthy porkers. He looked inside and saw no exposed rebar. He walked around front and confirmed that, yes, there was a pitted crater about where there had been one on the first bunker. For the moment, he withheld comment.

"This next one," Sitnikov said, pointing, "was another tungsten penetrator. You'll find the pigs are mostly healthy enough."

Carrera walked over and looked again through wire mesh. As the Volgan had predicted, those pigs weren't even stunned.

"All right, what's the trick?"

Now Sitnikov placed his box on the ground and opened it. From it he withdrew a number of two- to three-inch colored plastic shapes, a tetrahedron, a square, a pyramid, a cube, a sphere. These he placed on the ground, then reached in again and set beside them a small, plastic soft drink bottle.

"Those are the tricks," he said. "For the last two bunkers, plus the one you haven't seen yet, we placed these more or less randomly in with the concrete as we poured. They have the effect of breaking up the shock wave from HEP, of providing space where concrete can go when displaced by a penetrator, and of muting the concussion from a hit or near miss with high explosive."

Carrera mused on the concept for a half a minute, then pronounced, "Clever . . . but I've got some questions," Carrera said.

"Shoot, boss."

"What the hell are these projections of concrete all around the base of the bunkers?"

"The technical term is 'rafts.' Basically, they help keep the bunker from flipping over from a near miss from a big shell or bomb."

"Are the plastic fillers expensive?"

Sitnikov shook his head. "Cheaper than the concrete they displace."

"What's the cost of a bunker?" Carrera asked.

"About five hundred legionary drachma for the base structure, exclusive of NBC filters, electrification, labor for camouflaging, and such."

"And you want to put *how* many up?"

"We still haven't finished completely surveying the island for defense. Right now, my best guess is that we need about fifty-four hundred of these, plus maybe another six hundred that will cost several times more to house redundant tank turrets, plus thirteen—twelve more, plus one we've already built—underground shelters of very large size that will cost considerably more than the other six thousand, together, plus..."

"Show me."

The elevator fell and fell, lifting stomachs mouthward. To reach it, Sitnikov had driven into a tunnel that led right into the side of Hill 287.

"We put up the first one," he explained, "in part by using the budget you gave McNamara to build a secure facility for the precious metal. He and I had a little chat and agreed that we could kill two birds with one stone. So you have your secure vault, and you also have a very deep and strong fortification."

"How many floors down is it?" Carrera asked.

"It's more than fifty meters from the surface, though still above sea level. There are twelve floors, each with about four hundred square meters of working and living space. You could house a cohort in it, more or less comfortably. Though this one is modified from the base design in order to serve as a command and control station, with service support and a small infirmary.

"We can put up to six, including this one, under this hill," Sitnikov continued, as the elevator slowed

to a stop. "Here, they'll be safe enough from a direct
hit even from the really deep penetrators the FSC is
developing. Well . . . provided it's not a nuke, anyway.

"Should some enemy try the other approach, an
offset hit to create a camouflet, a large hole beside
the bunker to collapse the foundation, we've left a
considerable space between the bunker and the rock
of the hill and reinforced that space. The other locations, and those are driven by tactical considerations
that we can't do a lot to change, need something else."

As the elevator doors opened to a sparse, Spartan,
concrete-walled emptiness, Sitnikov took a one-drachma
coin from a pants pocket, and a pen from his breast
pocket. He held the coin out between thumb and
forefinger, parallel to the floor.

"Imagine," the Volgan said, "that this is a steel, about
two inches thick and a bit less than two feet around.
Call it a 'shield.'" He showed his pen held in the fingers of the other hand. "Now imagine this is a deep
penetrator." He moved the point of the pen to the coin.
"When the penetrator hits the shield, it will either hit
it so near the edge it simply rips through, or it will hit
further in and pick up the shield, or it will hit more or
less in the center. In the latter case, the shield, being
bigger than the penetrator, will have more resistance to
the rock or concrete and so reduce the depth of penetration. In the middle case, where it hits between the
edge and the center, it will cause the penetrator to . . .
tack, basically . . . to shift from coming straight down to
coming in partially on its side. This, too, will change
the cross section and reduce penetration. For the first
case, where it just rips through, we need to have more
than one layer of shields."

"I recall *Obras Zorilleras* sending me a message telling me something about this technique," Carrera said. "Cost?"

"Not cheap, particularly," Sitnikov answered, with a shrug. "Though we are looking into using reformed and realloyed scrap to cut costs.

"In any case, that is how we're planning on securing the big shelters that have to go someplace else."

"Won't work," Carrera said. "The explosion will rip off the layer of shields and the next bomb that comes in will go right through."

"*Might* not work," the Volgan conceded. "But we'll have a couple of things working for us."

"Such as?"

"Bombs like that are expensive and rare. Nobody has an excess. They're also expensive in terms of operational costs; planes, because they're doing that, can't do anything else for a while. People also have acquired a lot of faith in them, such that they're disinclined to question whether or not a hit was a kill.

"Somebody drops one of those bombs on a shelter, they're going to get all the signature, smoke, and debris that would indicate a kill. Why should they question that?"

"They still might," Carrera insisted.

"Yes, they might," Sitnikov conceded. "But we can't do anything about that and this is our best shot."

"Fair enough, then."

"And besides, we might have some chance of replacing the shields in between a strike and a repeat." Seeing that Carrera looked highly dubious of that, Sitnikov amended, "Well . . . a *chance*, as I said.

"And I've something else to show you."

❖   ❖   ❖

Carrera whistled. It really was a lovely thing Sitnikov had wanted him to see.

"My boys made it in sections," Sitnikov said, explaining the fifteen-by-twenty-five-meter terrain model that filled up over half of the shelter's bottom deck. "Then we moved it here and modified it."

The model showed the rough, curved-tailed, tadpole shape of the *Isla Real,* plus a fair amount of the surrounding water. From each side two strips of blue-painted "water" leading almost to the island were marked "Mined." There were crude, wooden ship models on each side of each strip. In addition, arcs were drawn in the blue and marked with artillery calibers: "122mm . . . 152mm . . . 160mm . . . 180mm . . . 180mm ERRB."

"It isn't my job," Sitnikov said, "to worry about the geostrategic endgame. That's your problem. Mine—half of mine, anyway—has been to design the defense of this island and the closure of the Transitway."

Sitnikov walked to a corner and picked up a very long pointer. When he returned, he set the edge of the pointer on the gap between the naval minefields and the island. "These minefields, as long as they're not cleared, close the Transitway. Note we left gaps within artillery range so that *we* can let through whomever we might wish to." The pointer moved to the wooden ship models. "We don't need anything too very special to lay the mines. Any old ships will do. They simply need to have the mines on board, a means for hauling them to the top deck, a crew to arm them and push them over the side, and maybe someone to record where they were dropped. The mines will have to be on activation timers. There are four ship models because we think we can lay these barrages in about three days, using four.

"The mines can conceivably be cleared, of course. No obstacle is worth much unless covered by observation and fire." The pointer began to touch on various turreted fixtures, all around the perimeter of the model. "These are to be taken from the turrets of the Suvarov-class cruisers you never restored."

"Those are only six-inch guns," Carrera objected. "They won't range the extremes of the minefields, and any fortifications to cover those extremes, being landbound or close to land, are vulnerable."

Sitnikov gave an evil grin. "They don't have to cover them. The things won't even be manned, except for skeleton crews to traverse the turrets and *look* threatening. Instead,"—the pointer shifted to a set of what were obviously models of ammunition bunkers behind the turrets—"each of these will hold an eighteen-centimeter gun which will fire reduced bore, sabot shells, with laser guidance packages, the laser beams doing the painting coming from"—the pointer made a circular motion around the top of Hill 287—"here and a few dozen other likely spots. OZ ran the math, and a lengthened 122mm shell, surrounded by a sabot, fired from a 180mm gun will range over eighty kilometers. This will allow coverage of both mine barrages as well as, by the way, any amphib ships or combatants engaged in trying to take the island."

"Those guns will only unmask, though, for a major push. For individual mineclearers, we'll put in some fixed torpedo firing installations, spaced around the island." The evil grim returned. "Mineclearers are notoriously slow."

Carrera nodded his head up and down sl... so to clear the Transitway the enemy would clear the mines. To clear the mines he needs t... rid of our guns and torpedoes. To do that he has to clear the island..."

"And to do that," Sitnikov finished, "he must land. If he lands, he bleeds. He bleeds *oceans*."

Carrera noticed several other ship models around the island. "What are those for?" he asked.

"Those are derelicts," Sitnikov answered. "We'll take older freighters and outfit them for fighting positions. Then we'll anchor them, unmanned, around the island, in shallow water, at all the best beaches. We'll make them look as if they're carrying supplies for the defense. Maybe even, they will. An enemy, if he attacks them, will sink them, but in shallow water. If he doesn't attack them, *we'll* sink them during an attack. Then we can shunt infantry out to take up the fighting positions. They'll make a landing a bloody endeavor."

Carrera had a sudden image of infantry wading through the water to get to a beach while an unseen machine gun *behind* them chopped them down. "Good thought," he agreed. "Best for the people in the derelict ships not to use tracers, though."

"Well, of *course*," Sitnikov said.

"Have you worked up a table of organization and equipment for the defense?" Carrera asked.

"Yes. In broad terms it will take a standard infantry legion—new form, not the old hexagonal counterguerilla organization—reinforced with another infantry tercio, a coastal artillery tercio, a fixed fortified defense tercio, some extra air defense, engineer, and other support

.roops. In all, about twenty-four thousand men. If we have to defend the island from an invasion emanating from the mainland, you would have to add quite a bit to that."

"Doable," was Carrera's judgment. He thought for a while, then said, "Leave me here and go round up the commander of the Training Legion. Bring him to me."

"Any particular reason you want him?"

"Two of them," Carrera answered. "It's a good news-bad news kind of thing. First, I'm going to promote him to Legate III. Then, we're going to show him this model, you're going to brief him, I'm going to brief him on how to turn the Eighth Training Legion into the Eighth Infantry Legion, quickly, at need. And then I'm going to send you back to the cadets and stick *him* with preparing this defense.

"And Sitnikov? Hurry, please. I have to meet Siegel after dinner at the *casa*. After that, later this evening, I am meeting with select committees from the new Senate and from the Legislative Assembly."

CHAPTER FIVE

The military mind, and the force those minds create, is innately rapacious, security obsessed, and covetous of power. That said, the civilian political mind is likewise rapacious and covetous of power, and may well be security obsessed. All this can be more or less tolerable. Woe to the state and people, however, that fall under the sway of civilians who are security indifferent . . .

The military mind is rapacious, but that rapacity has limits. It may force life to subordinate itself to the practical needs of war; it will rarely or never, on its own, force life to subordinate itself to mere fantasy or high sounding theory . . .

The need for civilian control over the military is not, in any case, based on any presumption that the civilian mind is, on average, wiser or more creative or more moral than the military mind. Indeed, human history provides no unambiguous evidence to support any such proposition. Rather, the moral imperative of civilian control is based on two related factors. One is that, will they, nil they, civilians *will* be affected, *will* suffer, from the decision to go to war. This, if nothing else, entitles them to a say in some form, though that say may be no more than the *option* to have a say, with conditions. The second is that, without adequate civilian support, every serious war effort that is not immediately successful is ultimately doomed to failure. Failure in war is, of course, the height of immorality.

In any case, civilian control of the military does not mean that those who never served are best suited to exercise control. Rather, those who have never served are not clearly morally fit to control the military. Neither are those who have enjoyed it and made it a life. Conversely, those who have served and, duty done, left service, have shown a willingness to do that which they do not like, for the common good . . .

> —Jorge y Marqueli Mendoza, *Historia y Filosofia Moral*, Legionary Press, Balboa, Terra Nova, copyright AC 468

Casa Linda, Balboa, Terra Nova

Carrera still used the *casa* for business, and would eventually return to it full time, once the legions had finished deploying from the island to the mainland.

"Sig" Siegel caught him on the upper back balcony of the house, the balcony that looked out over the sea. Carrera was yawning so deeply that he wasn't aware of Sig's arrival until Siegel gave forth an artificial cough.

Carrera stifled the yawn and looked up at the slightly portly teddy bear look-alike. "Oh, sorry, Sig," he said.

"You all right, boss?" Sig asked, his voice full of concern.

Carrera nodded. "For certain values of 'all right,'

I am. I'm just tired all the time. You would think
a year of fucking off and doing nothing would have
been rest enough, but..." He let that sentence die,
incomplete, then said, "The funny thing is I'm slightly
less tired since I got back to work."

Siegel noticed a four-pointed sort of jack Carrera
was twirling in the fingers of the hand he had not
used to stifle the yawn. "Caltrops?" Sig asked. "Is that
what this is about, boss? Caltrops?"

Carrera tossed the thing, casually, to the table top,
next to a closed notebook atop which was a manila file
folder. One sharply pointed arm ended up oriented
directly upward. Given the shape defined by the points,
it was the only possible orientation.

"That, and a few other things I want you to take
charge of."

"I'm listening, boss."

"We need something to erect a wide area, instant
obstacle. Scatterable mines are out, since the Tauros
watch sales of those closely. Besides, I'm not at all sure
that scatterable mines can't be remotely sensed, given
a sophisticated enough set of sensors." Carrera's eyes
shot upward, toward the United Earth Peace Fleet.

"We suffer from a serious dearth of reliable allies,
Sig," Carrera said, conversationally. "I trust Sada in
Sumer. Pashtia is sort of"—Carrera stuck out one
hand over the table, palm down, and wriggled it—
"reliable. I don't trust the Federated States past any
given election. And the Taurans are, of course, the
enemy. Zhong Guo might be.

"Our ability to do things in secret here in Balboa,"
he continued, "is limited; too many eyes on us. Other
states in Colombia del Norte and Uhuru are overrun

with Kosmos who stick their unwelcome noses into everything. Our Volgan contacts are good for some things, not so good for others, and we always have to wonder who's reporting what to whom.

"On the other hand, sometimes the enemy of my enemy really is my friend."

About that Siegel said nothing.

"I've made a deal with Cochin," Carrera said, "to provide us with labor, some manufacturing ability, and testing grounds. What I want you to do is to go there. Make contracts to produce these things, tens of millions of them. Then run some experiments to perfect a way to spread them over a considerable area in massive numbers."

Carrera moved the file folder to one side and opened the notebook, reorienting the latter to show Siegel a sketch drawing of a barrel stuffed with caltrops, with a linear-shaped charge to cut the top from the barrel and an explosive base to expel the contents. The caption on the sketch said, "Briar Patch."

Siegel looked it over and exclaimed, "That's a very cool idea, sir. But there are some problems."

"More, maybe, than you imagine," Carrera said. "These things are going to have to be stored, some of them in the open, for anything up to years. And in one of the wettest countries on the planet."

"That's what I meant," Sig explained. "A high explosive for a projecting charge will damage the contents. And low explosives tend to ruin themselves over time by absorbing water."

"Right. Figure it out."

"Why not hand this to *Obras Zorilleras* to develop?" Sig asked.

"Fernandez tells me there's at least one informer in OZ, but probably only one."

"Oh. Oh, fuck."

"It's not that big a deal," Carrera said, with an indifferent shrug. "Better one we know about than one we don't. But some things, really secret things, we can't send through OZ anymore."

Siegel nodded. "You said three projects, boss."

"Right. Actually, I said, 'A few more.' Here's another one." Carrera flipped the page to a different sketch, this one captioned, "Sarissa."

"I want you to develop a barrage balloon, to be used in mass, and suitable for making it very hazardous for jet aircraft to overfly an area without going to a height that makes them vulnerable to air defense. Also, I want you to develop a very large fuel-air-explosive mine that can be preemplaced, but not filled until needed. And it has to be able to be remotely detonated"—again Carrera's eyes shot upwards—"and not by radio means." The sketch for that said, "Volcano."

"The last thing I want is prepackaged light artillery. Kuralski has rounded up some seven hundred 85mm guns, surplus from the Great Global War and in pretty good—actually depot rebuild—shape. Apparently they've been...umm...'lost' from the Volgans' books. I want half of them, a decent load of ammunition for each, plus fire control equipment, packaged for long-term storage in shipping containers and put on ships. The rest will be shipped here openly."

Again, Carrera showed Siegel a diagram. "I don't have a name for this project," he said. "The Volgan 180mm started as a naval gun and was turned into a heavy field piece. I've put our friends in Volga to work designing and building a railroad carriage. In some ways it's the simplest thing. We're going to take receipt of thirty-two of them, openly, that we'll mount in the old bunkers the Federated States left behind. I need you to receive sixty-four of these, secretly, break them down into shipping containers, and send them to the *Isla Real*. Don't sweat ammunition; that's coming separately."

"Sig, these are your babies. Go to Cochin. You don't speak the language, I know, but you do speak French, and all the educated Cochinese do as well. Make whatever contacts you need, pay whatever bribes you must, buy whatever talent and materials are required. Get me those five things. I'll send ships to pick them up when you have a worthwhile load.

"While you're at it, nose around for any redundant military supplies and equipment we might be able to get cheap. In particular I am interested in aircraft."

Siegel looked confused and torn. "Can I bring my wife?"

Sadly, Carrera picked up the manila folder and passed it over. "These are transcripts of some phone calls. Also some events in your wife's recent history. She's been passing on information, too, Sig. To the Tauros. And, yes, Fernandez confirms you didn't know."

Carrera sounded like he meant it when he said, "I'm sorry."

"Sig looked terribly upset when he left, Patricio," Lourdes said.

Carrera didn't answer except to bite his lower lip and nod.

"You're not going to tell me about it?"

Still biting, he shook his head, "No."

Lourdes sighed sadly and began to turn away.

"It's personal to Sig," Carrera explained, hurriedly. "I've no right to tell anyone, not even you. If it were... Lourdes, please sit down."

Carrera hesitated. This was going to be hard...*hard*.

"Lourdes, how much have you guessed about why I collapsed?" he asked.

"You mean besides the obvious, like burning both ends of the candle for ten years?"

"Yes, besides that."

She smiled slightly. "Well, let's see. What am I supposed to make of it when you ask, in your sleep, 'Would you prefer, Mustafa, that I obliterate Makkah al Jedidah and the New Kaaba?' Or when you say, 'Cheer up, old man. You still have one son left: Me'? Patricio, I *know* you nuked Hajar."

"Oh."

"Oh."

"And your feelings on that?"

"I sometimes think of men like Adnan Sada and women like his wife, Ruqaya, and think, 'They could have been my friends, too, those people Patricio killed.' But then I think, 'could have been is not the same thing as *were*.' And I think, 'how many people that *are* my friends have been saved because you terrified the Yithrabis into ceasing their support of the Salafi *Ikhwan*?'"

"It wasn't just adults like Adnan and Ruqaya I murdered," Carrera said. "There were children in that city, maybe half a million of them." He looked down at the hands he loathed. Holding them out, he said, "There's the blood of half a million kids on these hands, Lourdes."

"And *my* children and the children of my friends, to include Adnan's and Ruqaya's, are safer because of it."

Lourdes stood up and walked the step and a half to the stone railing around the balcony. "Patricio, if you're asking me for absolution, I can't give it. I'm not only not a priest, I'm not even Catholic. But if you're asking me if I understand that you did what you had to do, that the world is a safer and perhaps better place because of it, then, yes, I do understand that."

"That's not exactly what I'm asking," he said. "I'm asking if..."

She turned around, placing her shapely posterior against the stone and folding her arms across her chest. "Of *course* I still love you, you idiot."

Carrera's head sank onto his chest. "Thank you for that, my love," he said, softly.

Lourdes walked to the side of his chair and took his head in her hands, pressing it to her abdomen below her breasts. She said nothing but contented herself with stroking his hair and his cheek. After a time Carrera consulted his watch.

"It's a bit over an hour before the select committees get here," he said. He stood up and took her hand. "Let's go to bed."

Carrera looked, oh, a *lot* better on leaving the bedroom he shared with Lourdes than he had for a long time. For her part, he thought the smile on her face might have to be surgically relaxed. Sighing contentedly, he closed the door behind him and walked briskly, with more energy than he'd felt in seeming *ages,* down the broad steps, around a corner, and down a narrower set into the basement.

Carrera's first thought, as he entered the conference room in the basement, was, *I should have held this somewhere else. But where? No place off the island is as secure.* The reason he thought that was . . .

"Gentlemen . . . ladies . . . *please.* You are not supposed to stand at attention for me anymore." Carrera's voice went low and he sounded wistful as he added, "That's not the purpose of this at all. Now, if you would *please* take your seats."

Parilla, the only one present who had not stood to attention, tried, mostly unsuccessfully to contain a wry, *I told you so* smile. Whether that smile was directed at Carrera, at the Senatorial Select Committee, or at the legislators who had followed the senators' lead wasn't entirely clear.

The group was almost entirely male. There were two women from the Legislative Assembly, true, but even some of the legislators tended to be ex-legionaries, hence typically male, since many had run on Parilla's presidential ticket and been elected on his coattails. Of those, most had volunteered for the select committee. On the other hand, the initial Senate had been handpicked from legion veterans. Those were mostly male and, of the women who had passed through the legion, none had really had the chance to shine.

Where "shine," thought Carrera, *equals the opportunity to lose eyes and limbs. In any case, they haven't had the chance . . . yet.*

His eyes swept over the small assembly, counting human appendages. Of the twelve senators of the select committee, there were only nineteen arms, seventeen legs, and twenty-one eyes. *I sure hope none of them lost their balls,* too. Their average age was a bit over thirty-five, a deliberate effort on the part of Parilla and Carrera, who had done the hand selecting, to make the Senate as mature as possible, given the constraint that the legion was mostly young.

After the committee members had taken seats, Carrera took his own. "Senators," he began, rather than *Conscript Fathers*, which had been his first instinct. They really were too young for that title, in any event, even though they had been conscripted. Then, nodding at Parilla, he continued, "*Princeps Senatus* and President, legislators, I've *asked* you here"—Carrera put a very strong emphasis on the word, "asked"—"because we are facing a war, a very hard war, and there are things I am no longer willing to take on, myself, things I no longer trust my own judgment with."

"You want us to be your conscience?" asked one of the senators, a dark skinned ex-legionary turned farmer by the name of Robles.

"That among other things," Carrera answered.

"*Duque*, that will never work," Robles said. "We all know you and we all know you *well*. Listening to others is not your strong point. At least, it isn't if you don't have to. And you *don't* play well with others. I remember a certain bridge in Sumer."

Carrera smiled shyly at the memory. Once, during the invasion of Sumer, ten years prior, Carrera had bombed a bridge out of existence under the very noses of his allies, and for not much more reason than to avoid the difficulty of actually having to coordinate with those allies.

He forced the smile away and nodded. "I know. I'm just going to have to learn."

Robles looked very doubtful. Still, he shrugged his doubt off for the moment. Maybe, just maybe, Carrera could change. *But*—

"And what happens, *Duque*," Robles asked, "when you want to do something and we say, 'No'?"

In answer, Carrera took a folder from atop the table and opened it. Inside was a sheaf of white paper, stapled at one corner. He signed at the bottom of the first page, flipped that and signed the next, then the next, until he reached the last page, which he signed in the middle. Wordlessly, he slid the packet over to Robles, who began to read.

"Holy fucking shit!" the senator exclaimed before he was halfway through.

"What is it?" asked one of the legislators, Marissa Correa. The short and stout woman's light brown eyes flashed with curiosity.

Robles didn't answer immediately. He quickly scanned the rest of the package and then slid it in turn to Correa. "He's just turned over nearly everything— seventy or seventy-five percent anyway—to the Senate."

"Yes," Carrera said. "Everything but a quarter of the general fund, my family trust, which I have no right to give away, this house, Quarters One on the *Isla Real*—I think I want to retire there—and a discretionary fund sufficient to provide at least a few hundred, and possibly as much as five hundred, million a year. It's closer to seventy than seventy-five percent, once you take account of the exemptions."

Carrera's finger pointed at the agreement. "And now, Ms. Correa, if you would turn to the last page and sign, as a witness and as a promise that you will not reveal anything of security interest to the country or the legion, and then pass the thing around, we can get on with this."

"My God," Robles said, "you're really serious."

"Very," Carrera agreed. "If I don't listen, and can't convince you, you can now fire me. Or make it impossible to support the legion unless I resign, which amounts to the same thing. Actually, you can fire me for any reason or no reason. My only job security is that I don't know that there's really anyone to replace me if you do. Jimenez, maybe, but he wouldn't take the job.

"Ah . . . and there is one caveat," Carrera added. "I will still track the money, and if I find any of it going astray I will drop a word in the right ear, and the people responsible will be killed. You can try me for murder afterwards, but they'll still be dead. Similarly, if any of the Senate don't voluntarily step down or if they don't fight for election or reelection when their time comes, they're toast."

"Don't worry about that, *Duque*," Robles said. "Just drop that word in *my* ear. I'll kill 'em myself."

Carrera's lips tightened even as his eyes turned Heavenward. *I wish I could tell you about one other important thing. You see, we're already a small nuclear power. If you read that . . . that contract carefully, you'll see that, in effect, I turned release authority over to the president. And I hope and pray we never have to use them. Again.*

But I can't tell you because, even though you're all handpicked and vetted, that must *be kept quiet or the Federated States will come down on us like a ton of bricks.*

Back in their bedroom, after the select committees had left, Lourdes was still glowing from an altogether too long delayed session of serious lovemaking.

"You are looking awfully happy, Patricio," she said,

"for a man who just gave away over seventy-five billion in Federated States drachma."

"Closer to a hundred and fifty billion if you count the value of everything, land, equipment, buildings, and such," he corrected. "Not to mention the pension fund and the value of trained men over untrained. Are you sorry I did?"

"No," she said without the slightest hesitation. "It's a small price if it makes you happy again."

Carrera leered meaningfully. "You know what would really make me happy again?"

She leered right back. "I can think of a couple of possibilities," she said, while ostentatiously running her tongue over her lips. "Why don't you sit on the side of the bed and we'll try one of them?"

Prey Nokor, Cochin, Terra Nova

"Nokor," Sig said, as his eyes opened wide to the sun streaming in through the blind over the window. The mattress of the bed on which he lay was lumpy, but at least the linen was clean.

"Shit, still in Nokor."

A former colony of the Gauls, and then of the Red Tsars, Cochin had all the decay—physical, economic, and moral—that one might associate with either of those two bits of history, or with suffering a major civil war in recent memory. Because the Cochinese had endured all three, the decay was not just trebled but cubed.

Proof of that decay, over and above the lumpy mattress, occupied a fraction of that mattress in the form of a fifteen- or sixteen-year-old Cochinese hooker who was effectively owned by the house. At least Sig hoped she was only fifteen or sixteen. This was not from any perverse preference for very young girls, but merely because a hooker of that age was most likely to *be* just a hooker, rather than a spy for either Cochinese Intelligence or the Secret Police.

The girl's name was Han. She'd told a more than half drunken Siegel, down in the hotel bar, that it meant "moral." She'd told him, moreover, in French and then laughed her cute little rear end off.

"Moral? Me? Isn't that just *too* funny?"

Sig had shrugged it off. "We all sell ourselves, Han," he'd said. "Some of us even get a fair price."

It had been an ugly scene with Siegel's soon to be ex-wife, shortly before he'd departed Balboa. It was uglier still when he'd called Fernandez, who had come immediately with an escort of military police. These had handcuffed her, forced her to sign some papers, and then escorted her to the airport with her passport stamped to prevent readmission to the country.

As Carrera had, Fernandez said, "I'm sorry, Sig."

"Don't be," Siegel had answered. "Right now I'm too pissed off to be hurt. Besides, I'm going to the land of the two-drachma blow job. It could be worse.

"Would it have been better, do you think," Siegel inquired, "to have kept her on and fed her disinformation?"

Fernandez shrugged. "Close question. If we don't bust the occasional spy, the Tauros, who are not necessarily stupid, will assume we *choose* not to bust any. They might assume then that we know about all of them. This could make it problematic to feed disinformation when we want to. Then, too, busting one validates the perceived secrecy of the rest. We've even had it happen that we busted one—that one we shot—and fear from that caused two more to panic, do something dumb, and reveal themselves.

"Better, I think, to take one into custody occasionally. And, too," Fernandez added, "you're one of us and if you want the bitch out of the country and an *in absentia divorce*, I think we owe it to you to help. Patricio agreed. Besides, you don't need any distractions, where you're going and what you'll be doing there."

Distractions? Sig thought, while Han, straddling his loins, performed a slow corkscrew. *Now this is a distraction. The best kind. Except that I need a distraction from the distraction, or it will be over much, much too soon.*

"Hey, Han," he asked, "how much to rent you from the house . . . as a *translator?*"

The girl didn't miss a beat . . . or a twist. "Five million Cochinese Bac a day," she answered. "Or six Federated States drachma."

Must delay . . .

"And of that, how much do you get to keep?" Sig asked.

"In FSD? Two," she answered, switching from a corkscrew to a slow and graceful up and down. "One of which goes to my debt."

Always the way, isn't it, then? Someone else gets most of the girl's profit. Oh, Jesus that's . . . MUST DELAY.

"And how much . . . to just buy your contract . . . from the . . . proprietor?"

The girl immediately stopped moving. She looked

very worried. It was a trick, often enough, to wait for
a girl nearly to pay off her contract and then resell
the rights to her, which resale price was inevitably
added to her debt.

Sig understood this. "No, no. I'll *give* you your
contract back once my business here is done."

That was much better, much less worrisome. She
resumed her gentle, rhythmic movements, saying,
"About eight hundred FSD, free and clear. How long
will you be here?"

That was actually about twice her price; a girl has
to watch out for herself.

Sig answered, "A few years."

Oh, Lord Buddha, the girl thought. *A few years
to be* free.

*God, I hate this place. It isn't even the stink from
the rice paddies. But whatever Tsarist Marxism in its
Cochinese mutation may have been, pretty to look
at, it is not.*

Dan Kuralski, Sig, and Han were in a warehouse
quite close to the riverside docks that made Prey
Nokor an inland port. Inland from the river, past the
city center, the newer parts of the city grew from the
ground like rancid, gray, concrete mushrooms.

Kuralski, who had thought it advisable to see to
the offloading of this first shipment of guns, thought
he knew what Sig was thinking.

"If it makes you any happier," he said to Sig,
"Volga's about as bad...except for the rice paddies,
of course; they're in a league by themselves. On the
other hand, Volga has some water and air pollution
problems you don't have here."

Between the warehouse and the dock, but nearer to the former, a shipping container rocked on large forklift carrying it along a less than smooth road. The rocking grew worse until, finally, the thing upended, falling completely off the forklift's tongues.

Han scowled and walked away, toward the forklift, without a word. When she reached it, she scrambled her four-foot-eleven frame up the side of the lift to the driver's station. There she proceeded to berate the shrinking, cringing, embarrassed driver until his head hung in utter humiliation.

"Who's she?" Kuralski asked.

Sig answered, "Han? She's my . . . ummm . . . administrative assistant and translator."

"Yes, I am sure," Kuralski said, grinning. "What did you pay for her?"

"Eight hundred FSD," Sig answered, "for her contract. Plus a salary of thirty-two FSD a month. If I'd known how valuable she was, I'd have paid ten times that."

"You mean you would have billed it to Pat?"

"Well . . . duh."

Han returned, still scowling. In French, which Kuralski didn't speak, she said, "Stupidmotherfucking-refugeefromareeducationcamp! Pigfuckingdumbbastard! Shiteater!"

"Thanks, Han," said a beaming Siegel. "I couldn't do this without you."

"What's she think you're actually *doing*?" Kuralski asked.

"She thinks I'm smuggling arms to some revolutionary movement in Uhuru or Colombia del Norte."

Kuralski shrugged. "Works for me."

✧   ✧   ✧

Later that afternoon, after the last of the guns were offloaded and transshipped into the warehouse, Sig oversaw the repackaging of a light artillery piece. He read from the data plate, *Serial Number: 12543.* Glancing over the manifest, Sig checked the gun off. He watched as a crew of Cochinese slave workers he was renting from a reeducation camp moved the gun by hand into a shipping container, then braced it from several angles with precut lumber. The container was on its side. Shells, three hundred and seventy-five boxes of two shells each, were fitted around the gun and bracing. Then more lumber was used to fix them in place. Sight, aiming stakes, field telephone and wire, gunner's swab and worm, camouflage net and about fifteen other items almost completed the package. Then more precut sections of lumber were added. When the workers were done, Sig closed the container and placed a metal railroad seal on the door. The crew then replaced the atmosphere with an inert gas.

One down. Twenty-three more to go. This week. Sig signaled for a forklift to move the filled container to a fenced yard by the docks.

Gia Lai, Cochin

One of the nice things about Cochin, as a place to test explosives, was that there was so much unexploded ordnance lying around, which ordnance the Cochinese Army made some effort to clear, that surface explosions, even fairly large ones, were so common as to not incite commentary. Or even to be noticed.

Sig wondered, *Do you suppose that was in Carrera's mind when he selected this place for testing? Hmmm...might have been.*

Sig swatted away a mosquito as he and a Cochinese sapper, Sergeant Tranh, a combat engineer whose commander was being paid twenty FSD a week for the use of him, primed a plastic barrel with blasting cap and fuse. Siegel watched the sapper carefully tap the cap, held in his right hand, one wrist slapping against the other to knock out any dirt which might be in the cap and which could interfere with detonation. Tranh then inserted the fuse, about six feet in length, into the cap. He then turned the cap, fuse inserted, until the cap's opening was pointed away from him. Lastly, he crimped the cap to hold the fuse in place.

In French, Siegel said, "Okay, Tranh. Set the igniter and prepare to pull." The little Cochinese inserted the other length of fuse into a pull igniter and turned a knob to screw the fuse in tight. He looked up at Siegel for the word to go. Siegel looked at his watch and nodded. The Cochinese shouted a warning, three times, and pulled the small metal ring at the end of the igniter opposite the fuse. Smoke began to curl upward. Then the two retired to a bunker nearby where Han already waited. Siegel consulted his watch once they were safe inside.

It had not proven possible yet for Sig to obtain anywhere near enough caltrops for even a single test. Oh, he could have had ten thousand made by hand. But they'd have been nonstandard, of variable strength, size, and weight, and thus useless for testing purposes. Arrangements for some limited manufacture of enough caltrops to run several more tests were still being made.

Sig was also working with a local sewage treatment plant to process shit into a kind of plastic for mass manufacture of the scatterable obstacles. A few bribes to the commander of a local combat engineer battalion who had given Sig the use of Sapper Tranh had provided several tons of both high and low explosive.

The test "caltrop projector," therefore, had only a loose packing of gravel in place of the caltrops. For this test Siegel only wished to find out whether or not a linear shaped charge could be used to cut the top off of the barrel just prior to the main bursting charge, a plasticized ammonium nitrate mix, sending the payload up and out. Siegel didn't have the physics to predetermine how much explosive was required to spread eight or ten thousand very light and un-aerodynamic caltrops around an area several hundred meters in radius. He intended to experiment until he found out. He mused, from time to time, on the question of whether a clever sergeant—or rather a bunch of clever sergeants—weren't more cost effective than a highbrow scientist...or even a number of them.

As the seconds hand on Siegel's watch swung round, he hunched himself lower into the bunker, Tranh following suit. The sapper reached out one hand to push Han's head lower.

It's hardly the first time a man ever pushed my head down, the girl thought. *This one, at least, means me well by it.*

Then a half-pound of RDX based linear shaped charge and twenty-eight pounds of ammonium nitrate-based explosive rocked the earth. A pattering of silver-painted gravel flew up and then fell on and around Siegel's bunker.

Headquarters, 4th Corps, Cristobal, Balboa

A silver-draped Christmas tree from uplands in the eastern part of the country could be seen from the street. James Soult glanced at it only briefly before he parked the staff car at the curb to let Carrera disembark. That human fireplug, Mitchell, bearing a submachine gun, was already on the sidewalk with his eyes searching for trouble before Carrera's feet touched the pavement.

A sentry called the building to attention as Carrera walked through the main doors. Carrera wished the man a Merry Christmas and continued on to Jimenez's office. He found Jimenez hunched over his desk, a sheaf of paper spread out before him.

Jimenez stood to attention when he realized Carrera was present. "How can I help you, sir?"

That, in itself, was odd. Normally Carrera and Jimenez were on a first name basis on any occasion that didn't absolutely require formality.

"Nothing, Xavier," Carrera shook his head. "I just had nothing better to do for the morning and thought I'd stop by and see how your troops are doing."

"The corps grows, Patricio," the lean black answered. "I, on the other hand, am not doing so well."

Carrera had started to ask the problem when he glanced down at the papers scattered across Jimenez's desk. He picked one up, scanned it, glanced at the return address "The *Estado Mayor*'s Ib wants to know how many of your machine guns are functional? Why? It's too trivial a concern for national level staff."

"I don't know," Jimenez answered, shrugging. "I

just answer the mail. And, frankly, I and my staff have fallen behind. We've been in the field training. Sorry."

Carrera's fingers continued sorting through the mess on Jimenez's desk, looking over the paperwork. "What? The II shop wants to know what percentage of potential recruits pass their physical. The provost wants a list of crime statistics from the Fourth Corps?" He read another: "They want to know how many people attend Sunday services in the regimental chapels?! That's absurd!"

Carrera replaced the papers on Jimenez's desk and thought, *And I've a sneaking hunch it's my fault for not being there to prevent this sort of nonsense. It wasn't enough, apparently, just to keep staffs small so that people couldn't create the demand for this kind of crap. It has to be killed at the source.*

Jimenez shrugged once more. "It's been getting worse lately, too. Ah, Patricio; it's not like it was when we were getting ready for the war. Those were good days, damned good. Just train, train, train and to hell with paperwork."

Carrera nodded, then asked, "Got anything to drink, Xavier?"

"Rum and coke? Wouldn't mind one myself."

"It'll do." Carrera took a seat as Jimenez rang for an orderly. A couple of flies buzzed above the top of Jimenez's desk. Carrera glanced at the flies with a certain interest.

As he waited for the drinks to arrive, a muttering Carrera looked over each demand for information littering Jimenez's desk. He looked back at the flies, now buzzing near a window. Finally he spoke. "Xavier, don't answer any of this shit. Still, I want you to do one more report. Nobody's asked for it, and I really don't want the information. But make up a flypaper report."

"A flypaper report?" Jimenez looked incredulous.

"Oh, yes," Carrera grinned. "A flypaper report. Direct it to the attention of the acting chief of the *Estado Mayor*. Put down the number of rolls of flypaper used, where they were placed, how high, how many flies were caught by placement, Throw in anything you can think of that might conceivably have a bearing on that critically important question: the efficacy of flypaper. Then send it up with an letter of apology for being late."

"Apology? Late? But no one's asked for a 'flypaper report' until now."

"I know." Carrera smiled knowingly. "Now let's have those drinks. And Merry Christmas."

CHAPTER SIX

Besides failing to account for the cost of a given good, it is a great moral and logical fallacy of the universe, or at least upon the two planets of it which know Man, to measure good and evil only by their intensity and scope and never by their duration. War is the greatest of evils, so might Man (or at least cosmopolitan progressive, or Kosmo, Man) say, and so might he say, too, that we must never wage war even against the greatest oppression. And yet wars inevitably end while oppression goes on and on (and typically ends, if it ends, in war anyway).

War, however, is only the obvious extreme case. Consider reproductive rights. Surely a woman has a right to her own body to do with as she pleases. This is a certain, plain, obvious, and irrefutable good. But just as surely, the children of the women who do not feel that way will soon outnumber the children of the women who do. Those children will learn and carry the values of their parents, as will their children. Also, they will vote. And then expansive, liberal reproductive rights will democratically disappear to join with the children never born to the women most dedicated to those rights. Thus will a generation or two of free reproductive

rights for women be followed by one hundred or
one thousand generations that scorn them. Thus,
the plain, certain, irrefutable and obvious good
is *meaningless,* because it cannot last, because it
destroys itself as it destroys the conditions which
permitted it.

So, too, unlimited democracy . . .

—Jorge y Marqueli Mendoza, *Historia y
    Filosofia Moral,* Legionary Press, Balboa,
    Terra Nova, copyright AC 468

Anno Condita 470–471
Casa Linda, Balboa, Terra Nova

The tree was decorated, the stockings hung, and
Hamilcar's Pashtun guards had even managed to figure
out where the exterior lights went. (Also, since the
lights would have tended to silhouette them, they'd
figured out that they'd better double the number of
guards and push them out, away from the house. As
Lourdes said, "Paranoia, thou art a Pashtun. Thank
goodness.") Now, as the clock neared midnight, Carrera
and Lourdes had *Casa* Linda mostly to themselves but
for the guards outside and the ones keeping watch
over Hamilcar upstairs.

As midnight struck, Carrera walked to a console and
removed a small box, the kind that would contain a
necklace. He handed the box to Lourdes. She opened
it to find a string of pearls, large and perfect, shining
pink and iridescent in the subdued light. Lourdes made
a happy sound, reached up to kiss Carrera heavily,
and ran to where she had hidden her gift to Carrera.

Lourdes' gift was in a box, about three feet long—or a bit more, and four inches on a side. When Carrera had removed the paper he found that the box was wooden. He removed the lid to discover a sword, old and, from the inscription, Spanish.

Lourdes said, "I had to send all the way to Taurus to find it for you. It is from the sixteenth century on Old Earth. The dealer told me it wasn't the sword of anyone famous. But he believed and showed me why he believed that it once belonged to a conquistador. I thought it would go well with your collection. I hope you like it."

Carrera took the sword from its box. He drew the blade from the scabbard. It was very well preserved, he saw, for something nearly a millennium old and made of steel. The lights from the tree gleamed along the shimmering metal of the blade. Carrera made an appreciative sound. "It's wonderful, Lourdes. You understand, though, it's too rare for me to carry around."

Holding the sword to catch the light better, Carrera saw small flakes of rust and that the blade was, in a few places, pitted. This was no surprise. He said softly, to no one in particular:

> "How dull it is, to pause, to make an end,
> To rust unburnished, not to shine in use,
> As though to breathe were life."

By his tone, and his eye, Lourdes knew he was pleased. She paused, took a deep breath. "I have another present for you, Patricio. I hope you like it as well. But you can't have it for a while."

Carrera raised a quizzical eyebrow.

"I'm going to have another baby...in about seven months."

"Really?" he asked, then, smiling broadly, said, "Cool."

"Well," she said, eyes sparkling and lips turning wicked, "it's not like you've left me with my legs together too often lately."

"Just making up for lost time."

University of Balboa, *Ciudad* Balboa

The university was rapidly becoming as split an entity as the country that supported it. True enough, most of the facilities were here on the main campus, in what many were beginning to call "Free Balboa," as opposed to "occupied Balboa." Even so, that portion which was in the Transitway Area, plus the few buildings in the small portion of the city owned by the rump government of Rocaberti and his cronies, had pretty much ceased responding to anything emanating from the University Rectory.

Professor Ruiz, de facto propaganda minister for the legion and the rest of the country, at the moment not only did not but *could* not care a bit about the split in the country or the split in the university. *He* was nursing a splitting headache, courtesy of the New Year's party held by his department the night before.

Still, work had to go on, even on Terra Novan New Year's Day. Work, in this case, consisted of reviewing a series of two-minute-long commercials for the legion's junior military academies.

This was a tough one, Ruiz thought, through the

pounding in his head. *We couldn't show the military side of the cadet program . . . too likely to frighten away parents. Besides, Carrera was explicit that that was to be downplayed. So all we have is some martial music, staged pictures of fourteen- and fifteen-year-olds dressed up in gray fatigues while attending class, and a few shots of kids marching in parade. Still, though, the legion is so tightly woven into the fabric of the country by now that all they need is a reminder, I think. And for that, these commercials will do well enough.*

Not many miles from where Professor Ruiz underwent his ordeal by hangover, a poor boy from a poor family sat through an interview. The boy's parents and his own teacher conversed while trying to find a way to pay for the boy's continued education. The family was named Porras; the boy went by Julio. He was a handsome kid, if a bit on the skinny side. Porras's family had not always been so poor.

Although education was free in the Republic of Balboa, the uniforms and books required were not. The Porras family had been able, by scrimping and saving, to send Julio's three older siblings to school properly attired. But Julio's younger brothers and sister also needed school clothing, and the father was without a steady source of income. There just wasn't enough money.

The teacher said, "*Señor* and *Señora* Porras, I wish I could help. But I have only a teacher's salary. It isn't too generous. Julio is my best student, my best by far. And a good boy, too."

Not a tremendous fan of the military, less still of

military education, the teacher was reluctant to suggest to the boy's parents that he try to go to one of the new schools the legion had started.

Still, the teacher thought, *for a bright boy like this even a military school would be better than nothing.*

"There is a possibility. I don't know how you would feel about it. Maybe you should ask Julio. There are schools run by the *Legion del Cid* that provide everything... books, uniforms, room and board. I understand there's even a small stipend for the boys, though I'm sure it's nothing lavish. But you must understand, this will be a military school. It is intended to educate young men so that they can volunteer for and serve in the legion upon graduation."

Julio's father asked, "Will the boys be soldiers as soon as they enroll?"

"No, I understand they will receive some military training, mostly as an exercise in character building. But they are not supposed to be a part of the legion until after they graduate. Even then, I've heard, it will be up to them whether they actually join or not."

The teacher turned to Julio. "Would you like to go to that school, son? It will be difficult."

Julio, who knew better than anyone the struggle his parents faced every day just to feed him, assented without a second thought. *"Madre, Padre,* I would like to go to one of these schools. Very much."

The mother asked, "Do you think Julio can get into this school, señor? Will he be far from home?"

The teacher reached into his desk and pulled out a piece of paper. "It lists here the desirable qualities the school is looking for. Grades? No problem there. Extracurricular activities and leadership? Julio has captained our soccer team, and won the school prize for a writing competition. Teacher's recommendation? If you are truly willing to let him go, I will give him as good a recommendation as anyone will receive. I think he should be able to get in. As for being far from home, I understand that the legion assigns boys where it has an opening, without much regard for where they may live."

The father asked the last question. "How soon must Julio leave for the school?"

"This paper says initial cadet training begins on the thirty-first of this month. We have until the fourteenth to have Julio's application in."

Ciudad, Intersection *Via Santa Josefina* and *Via Belisario Carrera,* Balboa, Terra Nova

Drivers honked with gleeful abandon. Honking right back, Mitchell used the greater mass and intimidation power of his rather beat-up vehicle to force his way through traffic to a spot not far from an office building's door. Wordlessly, Carrera got out. Equally wordlessly, Mitch drove off and turned the corner.

The sign on the door said, "Balboa Yacht Corporation, S. A." The sign was a bit of misdirection. Not only did the BYC have little to do with yachts, it rarely had much to do with the sea, though there had been at least one significant exception to this.

BYC was a front, a wing of *Obras Zorilleras,* or "OZ," the legion's research and development arm. More specifically, it was that section that dealt with the aerial combat and the air defense of the legion

and the Republic. Moreover, it dealt with them in
their material, tactical, and systemic aspects, all three.

BYC was a front in more ways than one. The door
with the sign did lead to a suite of offices that could,
for example, tell the prospective yacht purchaser,
"Oh, no, *señor*, we are much too busy—Julio, you
lazy swine, did you finish the drawings for the duke
of Belgravia?—as I was saying, *señor*, we could not
hope to—Marissa, you wretch, I said get in touch with
Borchadt Marine Engines *now!*—Where was I, *señor*?"
and keep that up indefinitely or until the prospective
buyer walked off in disgust.

Of course, there was no need to do that with
Carrera. He nodded as he passed by on his way to
a small office. That office, in turn, served as a cover
for the door that led to the *real* BYC suite. The real
BYC suite was normally entered from an alley off of
a completely different street.

The offices were plain, if not bare. There was
little decoration on the off-white painted walls. The
desks and chairs were functional, but no more than
that. There was but a single telephone in the suite.
Of its computers, all but one were sealed off from
the outside world.

"Miguel," Carrera said to Legate Lanza, chief of
the legion's *ala*, or air wing, as he emerged from the
front put on by BYC.

"*Duque*," Lanza nodded back. Balding, his waist
thickening, a bit stoop-shouldered and generally showing his age, Lanza was dressed in mufti, gray trousers
and an embroidered silk, short-sleeved, *guayabera*
dress shirt.

Carrera asked, "What have you got for me?" In truth, he'd made his plans so far in a partial vacuum. It could all fall apart if there proved no way to nullify his likely enemy's air power. That knowledge, rather, that *uncertainty*, was a frequent cold spot in the pit of his stomach.

"A concept," Lanza answered, "and some recommendations. You know our people here?"

Carrera shook his head. "I know some of them, but go ahead and do the introductions anyway."

"This way then, boss." Lanza inclined his head and turned away towards a hallway.

The group was small and entirely composed of ex-Volgans, ex-Jagelonians, and a single ex-Sachsen. All but one were pilots. Of the pilots, two had subspecialized in military intelligence.

"*Duque*," began one of the latter, a compact Volgan who went by the name of Grishkin, "let us begin by telling you what we think you are going to face if it comes to war between you and the Tauran Union, or war between you and the Tauran Union allied with Zhong Guo. We are assuming in this that the Federated States will not support you. If they would, you need not worry about an air threat at all."

"That's about the way I see it," Carrera agreed, running fingers through his hair. "Go on; worst case it."

"Very well," said Grishkin. "Basically you are looking at an aerial assault from as many as five medium aircraft carriers, three Tauran and two Zhong. In all, that's only about three hundred aircraft, only about two hundred and forty of them combat aircraft. You could, conceivably, handle this if you're willing to spend the money and devote the personnel to the problem."

"But it won't just be aircraft carriers, correct?"

Grishkin nodded. "We think not, *Duque*. We think that, if it came to a general war, you can count on the Taurans paying any price to gain access to air bases in Santa Josefina to your east. Moreover, since the collapse of the Volgan Empire, Cienfuegos to your south has become an economic basket case. Mere sharing of language and culture will not be enough to prevent the Cienfuegans from opening their legs to Taurus and giving them whatever they want. And you must assume that Maracaibo, being itself a new Tsarist-Marxist state, will ally with the TU happily and eagerly."

Carrera nodded. This was nothing too far off from what he had considered on his own. Moreover, he had at least a partial solution.

"Assume," he said, "that I can redirect sufficient of our foreign-born legionaries to their home countries to punish any nearby Latin state badly, with an insurrection, for opening themselves to the TU."

"Except for—"

"Yes," Carrera cut him off. "Except for Cienfuegos. I have no appreciable number of volunteers from there. They're a closed society, so infiltration would be very difficult. Basically, I've no useful connections, no good way to punish them, yet, for what amounts to cultural treason. I'm working on that."

"I'm sure," Grishkin shrugged. "That still means you're going to be facing up to twelve hundred sorties a day, from the east, from the west, from the south, and from the sea to the north and south. That's a lot of God damned ordnance dropped on your head, *Duque*."

"Look," Carrera said, waving one hand, brusquely, "I already *know* it's going to hurt. Give me something I can work with to cut down on that pain. Give me something I can use to get some maneuver time and space to defeat a landing or landings."

"There is a way," Grishkin answered, for the first time smiling.

"I'm listening."

Grishkin looked at one of his compatriots. "Fuck-offski," he said, "you're up.

"My name is Yakubovski," the latter reminded. His face was completely devoid of humor, grimmer than cancer, in fact. "They make a little joke and call me, 'Yabukovski.' In effect, that means, 'Fuckoffski.'" The Volgan gave an evil smile. "I'll get them all, later, in my own way.

"There are basically two ways an air force can come at you, *Duque*," Yakubovski said, "en masse and by what is sometimes called a 'conveyor belt.' They much prefer the latter. Indeed, just assembling the former, gathering and organizing a major strike, is so wasteful of fuel—which cuts into ordnance carried, wears out the planes so badly—while they're hanging around waiting for the rest of the strike package to assemble, uses up so much time, and is so hard to coordinate, that air forces will usually only do it to establish initial air superiority or supremacy, or to support a major effort on the ground.

"The conveyor belt, on the other hand," Yakubovski continued, "has none of those flaws. Small strike packages are quickly assembled and easily controlled. They do not overstrain fuel and ordnance units on their way out, or maintenance units when they return. Airfields are orderly and efficient. Aerial refueling is easy. Conversely, aerial refueling of up to twelve hundred aircraft in a few hours is impossible for the TU. Even the Federated States cannot handle so much.

"However, the conveyor belt has its own flaws. It cannot be used efficiently *until* air superiority or, in preference, air supremacy is established. If one tries, one finds that an altogether inefficient mix of aircraft must be used, fully a third of them equipped not for ground attack but for aerial combat. Still others must carry munitions for suppression of air defense."

Yakubovski stopped speaking for a moment, searching Carrera's face for a glimmer of understanding. The latter, on the other hand, kept his face blank while leaning back in his chair and staring upwards at the junction of off-white painted wall and white hung ceiling.

After perhaps a minute's quiet, Carrera asked, "You're trying to tell me that if I can maintain the ability to engage and destroy small strike packages... Hmmm, define small."

Yakubovski didn't miss a beat. "About fifty or sixty aircraft, maybe half of them strike aircraft."

"Okay. If I can meet and defeat something that size, then they'll have to go to larger, less efficient strike packages, that are also less deadly on a per aircraft basis?"

"Yes, which for all the reasons mentioned, plus the difficulty of planning and coordinating a major strike, will not come all that often."

Carrera lowered his head, closed his eyes and held

up one finger for silence. He pictured, in his mind's
eye, a major air raid coming in to Balboa...

"So I need to be able to defeat a raid of sixty
aircraft?" he mused.

"Something like that," the Volgan agreed. "If you're
willing, it might be well to plan for twice that. In
fact, we have."

"What does that take?"

"Besides the barrage balloons you are calling 'Project
Sarissa,' and the lavish air defense suite you are building, either two hundred or so fairly modern fighters
or three to four times that in obsolete fighters with
some improved capabilities. We recommend the latter."

"Why?"

Grishkin answered. "Partly it's cost, *Duque*. Two
hundred modern fighters, on their own, without even
counting training and maintenance, will cost more
billions than you can lightly afford. Six or seven or
eight hundred obsolete fighters cost...well," Grishkin
handed Carrera an advertisement, torn from a news-
paper printed on yellow paper.

"You're shitting me," Carrera said. "Under twenty-
five thousand FSD for a depot rebuilt Artem-Mikhail
82 Mosaic-D? That's a typo, right? They left off a
zero or two?"

"No, *Duque*, it's not a typo. In fact, it's practically
an attempt at piracy. Larceny, anyway. I ran down—I
have my contacts, after all—the original source for
the aircraft and the markup in that advertisement
has been quite high. For that price we can get the
aircraft, several replacement engines, and spare parts
for years of operations. And for a few hundred thousand FSD each, we can upgrade the things to where

they would have a reasonable chance of killing TU fighters and strike aircraft at about two for five. If you are willing to risk men in training, we might get that up to three for five."

"They'll bomb the shit out of our airfields and we'll never get a plane off," Carrera objected.

Grishkin laughed and wagged a finger. "Oh, no, *Duque*. The AM-82 is *very* rough-field capable. Moreover, we can get true vertical takeoff for them, or at least for some of them, in the form of a Zero Length Launch system. This is basically a trailer mount with a blast shield and some rocket assisted take off, or RATO, bottles mounted to the plane. They've been done. They work. Nobody's ever really used them because guided missiles took over. In your case, and Balboa's, they might make more sense."

Carrera shrugged. *Maybe.* Air war was not really his forte.

"Explain to me how *you* see an air war developing," he said.

Grishkin pointed. "Fuckoffski, you're up again."

Yakubovski stood and said, "Still using the TU as a template, *Duque*, the first attack will probably come en masse. Your air defense artillery would unmask, briefly, but shut down, run, and hide as soon as the individual systems and batteries have any reasonable excuse to. The TU would then pound a lot of empty jungle. Oh, sure, they'll hit legitimate targets, too. We aren't saying this will be easy.

"After a day or two of that, maybe three at the most, the TU would declare 'air supremacy' or make some such meaningless public relations point.

"At that point, expect the TU to go to the more

efficient conveyor belt type of operation. After putting up with that for a few days, you unmask your air defense, lift your aircraft, and attack with very heavy odds in your favor to engage a smallish TU strike package. Hurt it badly, even if it hurts you, too.

"The TU then has to revert to larger, all capacity, aerial task forces. The legion hides for a while.

"After a bit, you could expect the TU to again declare 'air supremacy' and go back to conveyor belt operations. Once again, the legion hits a small raid and hurts it.

"At about that point they'll try to get clever and do small raids but with a larger air-to-air group waiting to ambush. You ignore all such attacks until the larger group is not in evidence. Small fishing boats, coast watchers, and spies, plus whatever technical intelligence you can develop, will be important here. The effect is still virtual attrition on the TU, since planes not bombing are . . . well . . . not bombing, which is fine."

Yakubovski sighed. "I know, we all know, you've never told us your end game. Still, a blind man could see that, if you can drive out the TU and if the TU later lands, you must attack and crush that landing. Now imagine you can time it so that your artillery prep for that counterattack begins just as a TU air raid is departing."

"The TU's going to say, 'Oh, shit,' and start trying to assemble a major strike package. But the ground pounders are going to be screaming bloody murder for support. Politically, that will force the TU air forces to start scrambling and trying to assemble whatever can be assembled to help the ground pounders. Then your AM-82s lift. Your barrage balloons lift. Your

ADA unmasks. The TU comes in, but in small groups and facing something truly awful, old planes, but a lot of them, and with good weapons, and a *thick* air defense umbrella.

"You're going to pay, of course. We're undecided about whether the air force you must build will be annihilated, or just butchered. The smart money is on annihilated. But you can get the time, through expending their lives and planes, to fight and win a battle on the ground."

Carrera looked questioningly at Lanza. His return look as much as said, *They convinced me, boss. Though the idea of my boys being sacrificial lambs is not something I'm too comfortable with.*

"How far along in planning are you?" Carrera asked.

"Very far," Lanza answered. "Costs, tables of organization and equipment, training programs, instructor requirements, land usage, facilities . . . give us the money and we can start tomorrow. The boys have even done the redesign work to bring the Mosaic almost into our day and age."

"Something still bugs me," Carrera said. "Two things, really. I don't understand: Why so cheap and why so many?"

Grishkin shrugged, answering, "For the latter question, the Red Tsar never threw anything away and neither did his allies and clients. For the first question . . . basically, nobody wants them anymore so their value is reduced to not much more than the metal . . . and even metal prices are down. Everyone's looking for the most modern planes, whether or not they can maintain them and whether or not they've got the training system and the social system to procure sufficiently high quality human material for pilots. Over much of our world, it's a prestige thing, mostly, a way to keep the sons of the ruling classes amused and give them more reason to strut and better ways to talk girls into bed.

"The average air force, in the world, is nothing but an expensive indulgence. There are only a few air forces that even matter. One of those, sadly for you, is the Tauran Union's."

"Yeah...no shit." Carrera hesitated, perhaps only due to an innate conservatism, before agreeing, "Fine. Lanza, get your cost estimates to the *Estado Mayor*. We're going to go for it.

"And God help the poor kids who will, I have no doubt, volunteer in droves for this."

Carrera looked genuinely happy as he slunk out the entrance to the real offices of BYC, into the trashy alley, and then into the nondescript car driven by Mitchell and guarded by Soult. The latter two shared a look that said, *Dunno why but it can't be bad.*

"*Estado Mayor* building, Mitch," Carrera said.

"Sure thing, boss," Mitchell said, turning the key and bringing the engine to life. "Umm...boss, if you don't mind my asking, why so chipper? It just ain't like you."

"Two reasons," Carrera answered. "One is I've got a little more hope of survival than I did have. The other is I'm going to cut a little cancer out of the system at the *Estado Mayor*. Meanwhile, ignore me for a bit. I have to work myself into a fury."

El Estado Mayor, Balboa City, Balboa, Terra Nova

There were over a hundred senior officers and noncoms present. Of those, only two, Jimenez and McNamara, knew what was the occasion for the assembly. Even Jimenez's chief of staff and sergeant major hadn't been told by their commander. As for Mac, *Letting out the word about the boss going to the island so he can have a proper reception is one thing. But this… this really* needs *to be a surprise.*

Legate Pigna of the Seventh Legion, recruited and based in the east by the border with Santa Josefina, thought if anyone knew what was up, it would be Carrera's sergeant major-general. He walked over and asked Mac directly.

"No clue, sir," McNamara lied, then retrieved his integrity by adding, "which means I know exactly, but am forbidden to say. I'd tell you if I could."

Mac actually rather liked the Seventh Legion commander, both at a personal and a professional level. He considered Pigna somewhere around the bottom of the top third of legion commanders and knew Carrera shared approximately the same opinion. Moreover, the Balboan legate looked like a soldier, from narrow waist to broad shoulders to strong chin to pencil thin mustache. If the man was a trifle ambitious, and Mac thought he was, that ambition tended to come out in the form of pushing the troops hard. This, the sergeant major didn't disapprove of. He wore a high decoration for bravery at his neck, the *Cruz de Coraje en Oro con Escudo,* so Mac couldn't fault him on his combat performance either. If Pigna had any flaw, in the sergeant major's opinion, it was perhaps that he had a trifle too much personal pride.

Pigna sighed. "I hate being surprised."

"I understand, sir." *And I wish I could warn you that this is going to be a really unpleasant surprise, too.*

Jimenez's voice sounded off, "Gentlemen, the *Duque*, commanding."

I so *wish,* thought Jimenez, while braced at attention, *that I had never taught Patricio to smile while chewing ass. It's unnerving, being on the receiving end.*

Carrera had been chewing for a while by now, and the tongue lashing showed no sign of flagging.

"I thought," he sneered, "that you were all soldiers... real soldiers... not neversufficientlytobedamned *pimps*! Not bendoverandgreaseyourass *whores* for bureaucracy!"

A good ass chewing is a rehearsed operation. Carrera had spent *days* rehearsing this one.

Present, besides Carrera, were the five corps commanders, thirty-two commanders of legions and sublegions so far designated, the chiefs of staff and sergeants-major for all of those, plus six members of the primary legion staff, including the acting chief, standing in for Kuralski. McNamara was there, too, but he stood behind Carrera, immune to and exempt from the ass chewing.

Kuralski himself had been sent one of those letters that sometimes drives the recipient's blood pressure up into the Never Never land of apoplexy and cerebral stroke.

Pounding his fist on a table with each syllable, Carrera continued, "I turn my back on you for one miserable year and you revert to pencil pushing bureaucrats?" The pounding ceased and his voice took on almost the quality off weeping. "God! God! God! Where did I fail? How could I have been so wrong about you all?"

It could be worse, Jimenez thought, philosophically. *Napoleon, back on Old Earth, used to beat his marshals over the head with a stick.*

From the table Carrera picked up the top copy of a sheaf of papers perhaps a quarter of an inch thick. "Suarez," he said, reverting to a facial and verbal sneer. He crumpled the paper into a tight ball and threw it directly into the face of the Second Corps commander. "Pussy."

The next name he...well... "read" wouldn't be quite accurate. "Cursed," perhaps, would be closer. "Brown."

Aaron Brown, a short black legate who had been, before being recruited by Carrera, a tanker with the Army of the Federated States, steeled himself for the coming blow. Not that a sheet of crumpled paper would hurt, except deep inside.

Nor did it, when it struck him square on the nose... except deep inside.

"Chin, you *stupid*..."

Only the corps and legion commanders were blessed with a paper projectile to the nose. All the other flypaper reports Carrera saved for the acting chief of staff.

"And you...you wretch of a pencil pusher!" Carrera crumpled a flypaper report and threw it into the acting chief's face. He continued crumpling and throwing as he screamed, "Who cares about your silly fucking reports?" Another report struck the chief's face. "Who needs them?" And another. "Who told you to have your fucking staff suck my commanders away from training their units? Are you some kind of fucking Tauran saboteur?" Carrera reached up and ripped the legate's insignia from the chief's shoulders.

"Get out! Get out now. You are retired effective today."

No doubt about it, Jimenez thought. *The son of a bitch is good at what he does.*

"Obviously I have made a number of serious mistakes," Carrera said, his voice growing terribly calm. "I made you legates and put you in command of legions and corps, or made you my key staff, because I thought you had enough courage to stand up to the inevitable bureaucracy. Or, at least," he looked directly at the bent back of the departing acting chief, "not to make the bullshit grow."

Carrera sighed, as if brokenhearted. "Where I am going to find *real* officers, now... men of talent and courage..."

That was just a little too much. "We're *sorry*, sir," Brown said. "It just sort of... grew on us."

Carrera stopped in mid-tirade. He nodded slowly and said, "All right. Enough then. Don't let it happen again. Don't just let the bureaucrats nail you to your desks with endless demands for information.

"You are all on probation. You have disappointed me... badly. If you let the administrative shit the staff has been laying on you distract you from training your men, you have let them, and the legion, and the *country* down... badly. In the future, *try* to remember that your duty is to prepare for war, not to shuffle paper.

"Except for Jimenez and McNamara, dismissed."

✧   ✧   ✧

After the others had left, Jimenez said, "I didn't deserve that. Neither did the others."

Carrera cheerily agreed. There wasn't a sign of anger on his face now. "I know, Xavier. If anyone's, the fault was mine for letting administration get out of hand."

"So why the ass chewing?"

"Because I'd already chewed my own ass and, after that little session, the next time someone starts asking for useless information, your brother commanders will tell that person to take a flying fuck for himself. Besides, I've been thinking about dumping the acting chief for a while. This way, more people benefit from the lesson."

McNamara shook his head, doubtfully. In his accented English he said, "I t'ink you were maybe a little *too* hard on t'em, boss. T'ere's such a t'ing as overacting."

"It's possible," Carrera agreed, still cheerily. "But they're big boys. They'll get over it."

Jimenez shook his head. "The acting chief won't. You *fired* him. He wasn't a bad sort, you know."

"You want him in *your* corps?" Carrera asked.

"I didn't say that."

"Well then—"

"—but now that you mention it I do have a place for him."

"As? Besides 'Assistant Corps Vector Control Officer,' I mean."

Jimenez thought upon that for a minute or so. "He was a better commander than a staff weenie. He never wanted to *be* a staff weenie, not even chief of staff. I think he could be a decent to good tercio commander."

"What tercio?" Carrera asked.

Jimenez already had the answer for that. "Forty-fourth Artillery, Fourth Legion. We're really running short of competent artillerymen, you know."

"Fine," Carrera said. "But let him stew for a few days first, so that he appreciates the grace."

"I wouldn't wait t'at long, boss," McNamara said. "Whatever his faults, and t'ey were many, the old acting chief was pretty damned dedicated. He's going to take t'is *hard.* Maybe even terminally hard."

"You really think?" Carrera asked.

Hmmm. I suppose it's possible.

"Okay, Mac," he said, then turning to Jimenez he added, "Xavier, invite him to dinner. Tell him you are *going* to work on me to rescind my order and to get him a slot. That will give him a lot of well deserved suffering along with a reason not to decorate the wall. "Fair enough?" he asked.

"Yes, sir," Mac said. "T'ank you. I t'ink t'at's t'e right t'hing."

"It's fair, Patricio," Jimenez agreed.

All but two of the dismissed officers and noncoms looked downcast. Of those two, one, Arosemena, the former acting chief of staff, looked borderline suicidal, he was so upset. The other, Legate Pigna, kept his face carefully blank. Inside, though, Pigna was seething.

How dare that bastard gringo, how dare he insult me to my face? Humiliate me in public? Heap scorn on me and all these men? This is an insult that can only be washed out in blood.

EXCURSUS

"Government of Balboa," from *Global Affairs Magazine*, Volume 121, Issue of 10/474 AC

Balboans self describe their state as a "Timocratic Republic," where "Timocratic" is taken to mean "the rule of virtue," as opposed to the rule of wealth, which has all too often been presumed, despite copious evidence to the contrary, to be virtuous. Balboa is more properly said to be a mixture of a popular republic and a limited military near-dictatorship, existing side by side but with the better funded, more aggressive military branch gradually taking over more and more of the functioning of the country, even as it becomes less dictatorial. That process continues as of this writing.

In structure, the government of Balboa appears conventional, with three branches, executive—consisting of the president, two vice-presidents, a cabinet and sundry executive agencies; legislative—with both Senate and Legislative Assembly; and judicial—consisting of a national level Supreme Court and lower, provincial, and district courts.

In terms of domestic politics, the geography of the country is profoundly subdivided. The bulk of the state is split into two parts, eastern and western, by

the existence of the Tauran Union-occupied, World
League-mandated, Transitway Area, running approximately through the center. Of the remainder, a fair
chunk of the capital, *Ciudad* Balboa, is under the sway
of the previous government as a result of an order,
intended to prevent civil war, from the Federated
States of Columbia.

The bulk of the state, the Republic of Balboa, proper,
is further subdivided in two ways. Conventionally, it
consists of eleven provinces, ranging from *Valle de las
Lunas* in the east to *La Palma* in the west. Although
provinces sometimes have a considerable emotional
pull on their inhabitants, politically they do not mean
much in Balboa. They have no degree of individual
sovereignty, no independent police or militia, nor any
right to make province-specific laws. Even provincial
governors are appointed by the national government.

The military division of the country is the more
profound one. In the year 470 AC, the Senate, initially
an appointed lawmaking body composed entirely of
military veterans (though gradually becoming an elected
body, still composed entirely of military veterans and
elected by veterans), divided the national geography
into several overlaying and overlapping grids, which
grids paid absolutely no attention to existing provincial
or district lines. These grids, the exact boundaries of
which fluctuate slightly, are regimental.

One grid layer is composed of combat regiments,
of which it is believed there are about forty. Parallel
to that is another grid that defines combat support
regiments—artillery, combat engineers, air defense
artillery, military police, and the like. Parallel to those
is a grid layer of headquarters and service support

regiments. There are further grids for the air and naval arms, as well as for certain unique regiments, such as the *Tercio Amazona* (qv), which is female, the *Tercio Gorgidas* (qv), which is male homosexual, the *Tercio Socrates* (qv), for the elderly, and the *Tercio Santa Cecilia* (qv), for the handicapped. Which grid a given citizen belongs to, if he or she belongs to one, is determined at the time of their voluntary enlistment into the armed forces of Balboa, the *Legion del Cid*. It is believed that age, health, sex, and, where applicable, sexual orientation are the primary factors in assigning a prospective recruit to a layer of the grid and a regiment.

A Balboan may or may not have a deep emotional attachment to his district or province. If he is an immigrant, as many are, of late, he probably has *no* attachment to his district or province. His devotion to his regiment, however, if he belongs to one, is profound. His regiment has recruited and trained him, given him the most exciting years of his life, and paid for his education after service. It may well have fronted the loan for his house, his farm or his business. It may have *built* his house.

If he is married, the odds are good that the reception was held in the regimental hall, of which there are about one hundred and fifty scattered about the country, and the ceremony itself presided over by the regimental chaplain. His young children may be educated at a regimental school or attend a regimental summer camp. He and his family likely receive primary medical care, at low cost, at a regimental clinic. He drinks with his regiment. He goes fishing with his regimental comrades, at the regimental fishing

hole. He shops for food and clothing at the tax-free
regimental exchange or commissary or at the larger
exchanges at legion or corps level. When he takes
his wife or girlfriend to dinner, it is probably at that
same low-cost but not inelegant regimental hall he
was or will be married in, surrounded by the tokens
of glory he helped earn, and of which he is a part.
Moreover, his regiment is his primary political representation, via the Senate, elected by the regimental
centuriate assemblies.

CHAPTER SEVEN

There have been few revolutions in human history that have worked out generally for the benefit of those on whose behalf the revolutions were ostensibly launched. The first Red Tsar of Volga, for example, launched his revolution with the stated aim of uplifting the workers and peasants. (Though, in fact, his greater aim was rationalizing war production and asserting a more general societal control to serve the needs of the Great Global War.) The effect, in any case, of the Red Tsar's revolution was, at the lowest socioeconomic levels, to return those same workers and peasants to the state of serfdom from which they had previously escaped. At higher levels, on the other hand, the Red Tsar merely substituted or supplemented his then-existing nobility with a new nobility uplifted from Volga's previous middle and professional classes, the very same people who had, for their own interests, fallen in behind him in his revolutionary bid.

Observation of this phenomenon is not restricted to our planet and goes back not merely to Old Earth, but to *ancient* Old Earth. For his play, *The Assemblywomen*, for example, Athenian playwright Aristophanes has his proletarian heroine, Praxagora, respond to the question, "But who will till the soil?" with the simple answer, "The slaves."

Indeed, what we can tell from the scattered stories that have come down to us, from those who came to our planet at the very end of the wave of immigration, is that on Old Earth the largely peaceful revolution that gave that planet a world government also had the effect of reducing more than ninety percent of humanity there to a state of servitude.

—Jorge y Marqueli Mendoza, *Historia y Filosofia Moral,* Legionary Press, Balboa, Terra Nova, copyright AC 468

Anno Domini 2524
UEPF *Spirit of Peace,* Earth orbit

Despite her new and exalted caste and rank, Class One and marchioness, vice Lucretia Arbeit, of Amnesty, Wallenstein wore no fashionable diadem. And when she saw her senior staff and shuttle deck crew in full proskynesis on the deck—

She didn't have to feign fury. Marguerite *was* furious. "Get up! Get up, dammit! I'm no stinking, head in the clouds idiot. I don't need to be fooled into an unreal sense of my own importance. I'm not so deep down convinced that I'm a walking turd that I *need* this kind of reassurance that I'm not. On your feet!"

Sheepishly, hesitatingly, the staff and deck crew stood. First to stand was Khan, the male chief of Intelligence. At Wallenstein's command he first raised his face from the cold metal deck and stole a glance to see if she seemed serious. It seemed she did. Khan pushed his upper torso off the deck and rocked back. After tapping his wife, Khan from Sociology, he grasped her arm in one hand and pulled her up along with himself.

Around them, others likewise arose from their postures of submission and humiliation. There was a clear correlation between caste and speed with which the crew obeyed the now high admiral's command. Indeed, it wasn't until Wallenstein walked down the shuttle's ramp and stormed across the deck to where the mostly Class Three, Four, and Five deck crew lay, and said, "Yes, that means *everybody*," that those lessers began to get to their feet.

"Staff meeting in half an hour," Wallenstein announced, turning and walking off toward the hatch that led from the shuttle deck.

There have always been classes and castes, thought Marguerite, alone in the admiral's quarters. *There will always be classes and castes. And those who cry out against the injustice of it all only want to displace those at the top and put themselves there. At least, that's the way to read it from the results they get. And can't people be presumed to really desire what they actually achieve? At least when they do so well by it?*

She quickly skinned out of the dress uniform, all black and silver, she'd worn for the trip up from Earth, replacing it with a more comfortable shipboard undress uniform. This was still the black of space, but of a softer material and a more yielding cut. And, best of all, it lacked the stiff high collar that some fashion maven had inflicted on the Peace Fleet centuries before. She didn't bother to hang the dress uniform up, tossing it instead over the desk across which the former high admiral had so often used her body. Housekeeping wasn't her job.

All right then, she thought, running a finger up a seam to seal the garment to her hips, *so it's unavoidable. Is this such a bad thing? Isn't it most important that the Earth be well governed? Isn't displacing a class gone rotten and replacing it with a better one the only way to achieve that?*

She stopped dressing for a moment to apply her new rank insignia, silver crossed batons surrounded by a wreath, to her old uniform. Eventually, so she supposed, she'd pick an aide de camp or two to handle things like that for her.

"Odd, really," she said aloud, as she finished affixing the rank to her collar herself. "I thought it would feel better to do this. Somehow, it doesn't feel like anything. Then, too, I didn't feel as much as I expected to when the secretary general publically elevated me to Class One and enfeoffed me with Amnesty."

Wallenstein laughed at herself and her circumstance, then said, "*Sic transit gloria mundi.*" Thus flees the glory of the world.

On the other hand, she thought, tugging on her tunic, *the tithes that go with Amnesty will also help with the fleet. I do so hope Mr. Brown can get a good price on Cygnus House, too. I couldn't continue to own it anyway, not after I saw and smelled that sick, twisted bitch's dungeon.*

Boots went on last, calf length and supple black leather to match the undress uniform. With those,

Wallenstein stood and walked to the mirror on one wall of the admiral's quarters.

"Best I can do." She sighed, though she was, in fact, still the attractive woman she'd been since *becoming* a woman. "And now, to meet my *public*."

"Gentlebeings, the high admiral," the adjutant announced as the oval hatchway to the ship's conference room sphinctered open and Wallenstein walked in. The hatch closed behind her as soon as it sensed she was past. Each officer present pushed their chairs back from the massive Terra Novan silverwood conference table and stood immediately to attention. With a nod, Wallenstein walked between the staff's chairs and the room's iridescent ironwood-paneled walls.

Even before taking her own seat, she ordered, "Seats."

Just as they had when ordered out from proskynesis, the crew hesitated.

Wallenstein glared. "I said, 'seats,' dammit. I don't have time . . . *we* don't have time for meaningless formalities. Sit!"

Marguerite didn't wait to see if the staff obeyed. Rather, she swung her chair almost one hundred and eighty degrees to face the large Kurosawa viewscreen on one wall of the conference room. Not far from that was the hatch leading to the admiral's bridge, a feature so far little used.

"Computer," she said. "View of the boneyard." Instantly the screen went from blank to filled with rank upon rank of ghost ships, their lightsails furled, the dark side of the moon visible on one corner of the screen.

"We're going there," Wallenstein announced. "We're going to get several of those running. Six, I think, right now, enough for a resupply every four to six months, indefinitely. They are going to become our lifeline to Earth. Don't bother asking where the credit is coming from; suffice to say that His Excellency, the SecGen, has approved a considerable increase to the fleet's budget and a major reallocation of industrial and personnel resources to our support.

"This ship," she continued, before anyone could even register surprise, "is going to be skimmed for cadre to command those transports. The rest of the crews will be coming from the academy and from weeding out some likely prospects from Fleet Base, both on Earth and on Luna. Those, and eventually the crews that were beached on Atlantis Base because we cannibalized their ships. The new commanders will have to train their crews themselves and with a minimum cadre.

"Job One, however, will be restoring the ships we need to full functionality. That should help with the training. Hopefully, we'll be able to restore one or two, then head back to Terra Nova ourselves, leaving stay-behinds to finish the restoration on the rest.

"Our first target for restoration will be the *Jean Monnet*. It's almost the newest ship out there. It was the last mothballed. And its maintenance records indicate that it is likely in the best shape of the lot.

"Oh, one more thing. I have no intention of burning up in a defective shuttle. We're going to be taking every shuttle we can cram aboard the *Peace*, plus every shuttle we can cram aboard the first few of our restored ships, plus all the parts we can loot."

UEPF *Spirit of Peace*, Luna Starship Holding and Storage Area

A large cargo shuttle, recovered from one of the abandoned transports, was having obvious difficulty maneuvering to dock at that transport. The shuttle, Marguerite saw from the manifest, was carrying one hundred and twelve newly graduated midshipmen and cadets from the Fleet Academy, along with about ninety tons of Class Fours and Fives for scut work.

The problem, Marguerite thought, watching from the observation deck of *Peace* as the shuttle applied reverse thrust and backed off for a second attempt, *is half that none of my people are used to dealing with the unusual or the unexpected. There's no surprise there and maybe not any blame either. After all, the Fleet spent centuries in orbit about Terra Nova and in all that time there were precisely two unusual events. At least only two that made it into the records. The other half is that I just don't have enough qualified people, for all my brave talk to the SecGen.*

She watched further as the shuttle missed its second attempt, pulling up this time and barely missing a collision with the edge of the open bay.

Marguerite shook her head with disgust. Reaching over to a small box mounted next to the large, clear viewing port, she pressed a button and said, "Operations. Here's a general rule for you. Write it into the SOP, as a matter of fact. WE DON'T HAVE TIME TO TRAIN PEOPLE RIGHT NOW ON THE FINER POINTS OF—ELDER GODS PRESERVE

ME!—DOCKING WITH A STATIONARY, NON-
ROTATING SHIP. Have the comp take over docking
on shuttle flight"—she glanced down at the manifest—
"number one seven two.

"Training we'll have time for when we've got a full
recovery crew aboard the *Jean Monnet*. Until then,
priority is personnel and materials. Got it?"

"Aye, Aye, High Admiral," answered the voice from
the box. Before the box went silent again, Wallenstein
heard a different voice commanding, "Shuttle One
Seven Two, Shuttle One Seven Two. Halt in place
and get your butterfingered hands *off* the controls.
We are taking over your docking from here."

One problem I didn't anticipate, thought Marguerite, alone in the high admiral's quarters, *was that I
can't get laid! For all my planning, I just completely
missed that little inconvenience.*

*It was never a problem before, not since I took com-
mand of the flagship. Here, there was always a high
admiral to fuck . . . or whatever. Now, I'm in charge
and the only way to have sex is to use a subordinate.
Even if I were willing to do to someone aboard what's
been done to me for so long—and I'm not—how the
hell does someone take me seriously after they've seen
me panting like a dog in heat or moaning all the
idiocies people do in the throes of passion? How do
they even look at my face without remembering the
last time they saw a dick growing out of it?*

*Might not be such an issue with a woman, I sup-
pose, but that is not my actual preference. Besides, the
only one I find really attractive is Khan and she's a
submissive. And, in bed, I prefer to be the submissive,*

*as a relief from having to be in charge all the rest
of the time. Fuck.*

I foresee a miserable *decade or two ahead.*

*Hmmm...bring a boy toy up? It's permitted but...
no...that's contemptible. Then everyone would imagine
seeing a dick growing out of my mouth but would not
associate the dick with a real man.*

Misery, misery.

"High admiral on the bridge," the junior watch
officer announced as Wallenstein stepped out of the
elevator and through the oval hatchway.

She looked grumpy. No one knew why and few
thought they could make even an educated guess.
After all, hadn't the strange woman dispensed with
the hallowed tradition of proskynesis? Who knew what
other bizarrenesses lurked in her feverish brain. She'd
never been so hard to figure out when she'd been a
mere, non-ennobled captain.

"Report," Marguerite ordered, taking her seat and
then listening with only half an ear and a quarter of a
brain as the watch officer went through the daily log.

Note to self, she thought. *This is not my job. Captain
for the* Spirit of Peace: *Appoint, soonest. But who?
My old exec isn't up to command and knows it.*

"High Admiral, this completes my report," the watch
officer said, finally.

Wallenstein nodded. She looked up to determine
that the relief was already on station, then tilted her
head toward the hatchway and said, "Dismissed." She
stood, saying, "I'll be in my day cabin if I'm needed."
Even though I really should *be down in the admiral's
bridge, planning for the future.*

✧   ✧   ✧

"Call from His Excellency, the secretary general, High Admiral," the intercom announced. "I am piping it through to you now."

"*Only* to me," Wallenstein ordered.

"Of course, High Admiral," the intercom announced.

"My dear Marchioness," the SecGen greeted as his face appeared on Marguerite's viewscreen.

"Your Excellency," she returned.

"I've been thinking about your personnel problems and I believe I have a partial solution for you."

"Indeed?" Wallenstein tried and, so she supposed, likely failed, to sound enthusiastic.

The SecGen's face split in an I've-got-just-the-car-for-you grin. "Why, indeed, yes. I have a nephew, the earl of Care, a wonderful boy, of the very best breeding. He's always been enthusiastic about space. He's in the Academy's class of 2526 but, I thought, given his flawless parentage and the precedent you've set with graduating the Class of 2525 early, that he'd be just perfect to command the *Spirit of Peace*. And the boy could hardly hope for a better mentor than yourself."

"A spy, you mean." Marguerite kept her face carefully blank.

"A spy," the SecGen happily agreed. He then added, somewhat ruefully, "Marguerite, he's the price I have to pay to keep your little program going. Be thankful I was able to come up with someone in my own family. The World Food Organization faction wanted to put up the count of TransIsthmia, Julio Castro-Nyere. I was only able to beg off by citing to the growing troubles there."

Marguerite sighed and said, "I appreciate your intervention, Your Excellency, but have you any idea just how troublesome an untrained captain command-ing my flagship will be to me?"

"I do, actually," the SecGen agreed, nodding shal-lowly on the screen. "Some idea, anyway. Have *you* any idea how troublesome Count Castro-Nyere or one of his children would be to you?"

Wallenstein smiled thinly. "Since you put it that way, Your Excellency, I look forward to the assignment of the earl of Care as Commanding Officer, UEPF *Spirit of Peace*, with enthusiasm."

"I knew you would understand . . . Marguerite, Rich-ard's not a bad boy; trust me on that. And remember, we didn't make the world, we just have to deal with it."

No, she thought. *We didn't make it; our great-great-grandparents did. The bastards.*

"Not a bad boy," Wallenstein thought, eyes closed and body leaning back in her chair. *I wonder what "not a bad boy" means in a day when diadems are the latest fashion statement and our ruling class gath-ers about a monument to peace to watch young girls have their hearts torn out while the cameras transmit the lesson to the masses. Does he restrict himself to pulling the wings from flies? Is that what "not a bad boy" means in this enlightened age?*

On the other hand, based on intelligence reports from TransIsthmia, Count Castro-Nyere would never content himself with pulling the wings from mere flies. That is one sick branch of the human family tree, arguably even worse than my predecessor as marchioness of Amnesty.

Briefly, Marguerite indulged in a daydream of a future in which she could return to Old Earth, triumphant and vengeful, weeding the ruling class out with a fine tooth comb and elevating to power decent Class Twos and—who knew?—perhaps even some worthy Threes.

But I won't cut their hearts out, she thought. *The Earth has plenty of rope and plenty of trees. Those will be good enough.*

Wallenstein's face suddenly brightened. *Well . . . let's suppose Richard, earl of Care is a right bastard. So what? I'm high admiral, after all. If I must, I'll just space the little wretch once we're under way.*

In the shadow of the moon, *Jean Monnet*'s sail began to unfurl as gas was released into the inflatable ring about its perimeter. Had anyone bothered to dig into the records they would have discovered that the orbit that kept the ghost fleet on the dark side of the moon had been chosen for the boneyard *precisely* so that the sails could be inspected without the worry of the sun's light pushing the ships out of orbit. The little light reflected from the Earth, at the current angle, was not expected to be a problem for the duration of the exercise.

The hull of the *Monnet* was lit now, in places, both from navigation lights and, emanating from the interior through portholes, light from recovered and repowered cabins. There was still no gravity inside, a situation that in some ways aided but more generally interfered with recovery efforts. Neither would there be any gravity, barring only the moon's insignificant tug, until the crew was certain enough of *Monnet*'s structural integrity to begin to spin her up. And, should they discover that there *were* problems with the hull, that spin-up would not take place until the ship was maneuvered to the only site in the solar system capable of dealing with such problems, the toroidal shipyard just sunward from the system's asteroid belt.

And if we've got to use the shipyard, Marguerite thought, *we're just screwed. At least with* Monnet. *I picked this one because it seemed likely to be our best and easiest recovery. I don't have—Earth doesn't have the skilled space workers to do a serious repair anymore. I'm hoping that these repairs will go some ways towards fixing that lack.*

The sail continued to spread as the filling gas forced the sail's ring further and further outward. It was really quite magnificent in its way, as much so as wind filling the sails of wet navy ships had been in an earlier day. Whatever the *Monnet's* sail lacked in ruffle and snap, moreover, it more than made up for in size. It was simply huge, even staggeringly huge. Looked at from the side, it utterly dwarfed the ship it was designed to propel, even though that elongated, egg-shaped ship was approximately the size of an old style, wet navy super carrier.

United Earth Colonization Service (UECS) Ship *Jean Monnet*, AD 2524

You can't hear *the crack of a flapping sail,* thought the *Peace's* chief engineer, Commander McFarland, detached to command the *Monnet* until he could train a replacement. *You can't hear it, but you can feel it.*

That was true enough. As the sail's ring filled and it stretched out, it also stretched the thousands of filaments—the *sheets*—that bound it to the ship, sending a vibration even through that massive vessel, through the bearing that connected the bridge to that vessel, and through the captain's chair to which McFarland was strapped in the absence of gravity. Since, even when under way, the bridge of the *Monnet* contra-rotated against the spin of the main hull, there was never any gravity there anyway.

Others would go out later, in shuttles, to inspect the forward side of the sail. From where the engineer—no, the *captain*, now—stood, however, things looked—

"She's nearly as good as the day she was launched, Skipper," said one of bridge crew. "Ninety-seven percent of the sheets show up as solid. We've enough in ship's stores to replace those which aren't."

McFarland nodded, then keyed his intercom for his propulsion section. "Your crew ready to get in their EVA suits and inspect the inside of the sail, Mr. Buthelezi?" he asked.

Came the answer, "As ready as they're going to be, Skipper. They're already suited and lined up at the mast locks."

"Very good," McFarland said. "Do it."

In the very beginning, centuries past, it had been determined that lightships would require a mast to support the sail and for the sail to rest against when furled. Moreover, since the ships' primary means of both propulsion and braking would be the light of a sun, either there would have to be two sails, or the entire ship would have to rotate to set the sail for braking, which would require reaction mass, or the mast and sail would have to rotate around the ship, which would require structural mass, machinery and, in a word, complications. It had been a very close call at the time. Nonetheless, the consensus had finally settled upon a rotating mast as being no more difficult to build and, in operation, somewhat cheaper.

Rumors that the decision was driven more by the particulars of ownership of the consortium that would build the rotating machinery were, of course, ruthlessly suppressed.

It was up this hollow mast, devoid of gravity but for the trivial tug of Luna, far below, that Buthelezi and two dozen suited midshipmen pulled themselves, hand over hand, through hard vacuum. Behind them, behind the closed hatch of the air lock, another group of twenty-five was already preparing to take their places.

EVA work was both tiring and dangerous.

UEPF *Spirit of Peace*, Luna Starship Holding and Storage Area

At this distance even image intensification couldn't make the boys and girls inspecting and repairing *Monnet*'s sail anything more than dots that occasionally sparked as they used their suits' backpack maneuver units to move across and above the inner surface of the sail.

Wallenstein found that she actually cared about these boys and girls. *And why not? They're* my *people. And they're so damned eager to please they almost make me think the system has a chance. Elder gods, was I ever so innocent?*

While Class One parents had not just pulled strings

but formed circle and weighed anchors to keep their precious little darlings from being graduated early and dragged off, Class Twos had tended to see the early graduation as an opportunity. It was an absolute fact that, excepting only Richard, earl of Care, not one Class One middie was scheduled to join Wallenstein's fleet and not one young Class Two or Three had objected to joining.

Marguerite listened, smiling, to the chatter over the radio as the midshipmen found little rips in the fabric of the sail and swooped down to seal the rips with strips of tape specially made for the purpose some long ago day. They didn't find many such rips. That there were rips at all was a result of orbiting astral debris that could even puncture the hull of a ship. Indeed, that had been the major job in bringing the *Monnet* back on line, finding and fixing hundreds of leaks, large and small, in the hull from strikes from fast moving particles, some of them no larger than grains of sand.

On the other hand, Wallenstein thought, *it's not as if there are all that many children of Class Ones anyway, or that all that many of those attend the academy. And my Twos and Threes are at least the real children of real people.*

Thinking about children—and the middies were, compared to her own century and a half, little more than children—started Marguerite to thinking of other children, younger ones, on a different planet. She'd been able to push it from her mind, for the most part, for decades. But ever since she'd seen the sacrifice at the *Ara Pacis*, everything she'd tried to suppress had come flooding back.

And I helped raise money for explosives to blow innocent people up, she mentally sighed. *How many incarnations is that going to—rightly and justifiably— cost me?*

Time to make an appointment with the chaplain, I think.

It has sometimes been said that, after Saint Patrick came to Ireland, the Catholics moved right in and took over from the druids with hardly a ripple, adopting many of the mannerisms and customs of the druids, the better to spread their own faith. It surprised no one, then, that when Christianity was suppressed by United Earth, the druids in many places came back and took over from the priests, again with nary a ripple, and in turn adopting and adapting many Catholic customs. One of these was *confession*.

"Bless me, Druid, for I have sinned," said Wallenstein, sitting opposite the chaplain, approximately lotus-style, on the floor of her quarters.

"Speak to me of this," the druid answered. The chaplain sat at the opposite corner from Marguerite. "Hold nothing back, for the Elder God or Gods, however many or few there be, will know if you do."

Marguerite took a deep breath before answering, "I am a murderess, or—if I remember my Fleet Law class correctly—at least an accessory before the fact to murder, many times over. Back on Terra Nova, while the war on the Islamics was raging, I arranged for many pseudokidnappings, the ransoms of which went to buy arms and explosives for the killing of innocents."

The druid nodded, his artificially grayed beard

rustling on the robes over his chest as he did. "The Elder God or Gods knew this. What else?"

"I am almost as guilty of attempted megacide, though at least there I was foiled."

"And?" the druid asked.

She shook her head. "That's all I think, all that was past my duty in any event. Oh..."

"Yes?"

"I betrayed the former high admiral, Martin Robinson, to his enemies, partially in revenge and partially so that I could take over his position.

"And that's really all. Except..."

"Go on."

"I arranged victims from among the lowers for the former marchioness of Amnesty to torture in her sexual games." Marguerite gulped as her eyes grew wide. "Oh, gods, I'm going to be reincarnated as a toad, aren't I?"

Marguerite thought she saw a thin smile on the druid's face, but the beard concealed so much of that she couldn't be sure.

"Quite possibly," he answered. "And that might be a best case." The druid's face grew dark as he added, *sotto voce,* "Though for all that, I can hardly say you've done anything worse than have my orthodox brethren, of late."

"What was that, Chaplain?"

"Nothing," the druid said. "Just thinking aloud."

Wallenstein suspected she knew what her chaplain had muttered.

"You have a serious problem, Marguerite," the druid said.

"I *know* that, Druid. Why do you suppose I asked to confess?"

The smile shone through the beard now, without doubt or question. "Oh, maybe because it's been *decades*," the druid observed.

"No, that's not it," Wallenstein insisted. "Then again, I'm not sure what it is."

That's a lie, a little voice whispered in Marguerite's head. *It's that after being used for well over a century you finally realized that you were being used, and to no good end for anyone except those who used you. And you know it, just as you know that you were complicit in your own degradation, and for unworthy goals.*

But I have no need to tell him *that.*

Don't you? the little voice insisted.

No. Not for what I plan.

Suit yourself. You will anyway.

Yes, and isn't that a nice change?

"Well," said the druid, "it doesn't really matter. Ours is a religion somewhat short on mandatory ritual. As least, we of the Reformed Druidic faith are short on mandatory ritual."

The druid smiled again, asking, "Have you never thought about our religion, Marguerite? I mean really *thought* about it? How is it that a faith that was essentially extirpated by the seventh century found a rebirth in the seventeenth? And what of what was lost in those thousand years? What of what was lost between when Vespasian overran the Isle of Wight and when Suetonius Paulus destroyed our center at Anglesey?"

"It's never really been my job to think about it," Marguerite answered. "My mother was a priestess and so she raised me in it."

"The answer is simple, in any event," the druid

said. "It doesn't matter in the slightest," he shrugged. "It doesn't matter because our faith really isn't about gods anymore, if it ever was. Rather, it speaks to human needs. The God or gods—oh, yes, I believe he or she or they exist—can fend for themselves and hardly need us.

"Instead, we are a philosophy, a philosophy concerned with people living well, and reasonably virtuously. The religious aspects are tacked on tatters and scavenged rags, not even good whole cloth. And none of that matters because we are not about God or gods, but about people.

"It is our *reason* that leads us to the religious convictions we have. It is our reason that leads us to reject the notion of Heaven and Hell and substitute for them reincarnation, something theologically almost indistinct from the old Catholic notion of Purgatory, just as our reason and our understanding of people has caused us to adopt the old Catholic sacrament of confession, along with much of the pomp and ceremony.

"You asked to confess because you have a cancer in your soul and need a way to excise it. I would answer you that by confessing you have in goodly part already excised it. I would say to you too that, just as one can never cross the same river twice, so you, too, have changed and are hardly the same person who did the things that are eating at your soul. Finally, I would say to you that to be whole and pure again, you must do some great good for your people, or indeed *all* people."

Razona Market, Brcko, Bosnia Province, Old Earth

"Some great good," mused Wallenstein. *How hard it is to do a "great good." Even so, I can still do some little ones.*

The newly ennobled high admiral, escorted by a half dozen Marines, moved through the market on foot. She stopped here and there to inspect the merchandise, sometimes pulling a chin down to check teeth. The hawkers came up to her at each stop she made. Some had the girls and boys bow. Others tapped the goods with short whips to make them turn to display their wares.

One girl in particular caught Marguerite's attention. She was a lovely little brown creature, perhaps fourteen years of age or a bit more.

"Where are you from, child?" the high admiral asked.

"TransIsthmia, Your Highness," the girl answered.

"How did you end up here?" Wallenstein asked.

The vendor supplied the answer. "She's a rebel brat, sold by Count Castro-Nyere. If she isn't sold quick, a buyer from the Orthodox Druids has expressed an interest."

Marguerite nodded. "And your name?" she asked.

"Whatever you want to call me," the child said, casting a fearful look at her owner and vendor.

"I want to call you what those whom you grew up with called you."

"Esmeralda, then, Your Highness."

Wallenstein nodded and began to turn away.

"You worthless little twat," the vendor said, frustrated

at the apparently lost sale. The frustration was all the
worse because he hadn't a clue how the wretched
bitch had screwed it up. He raised a scream from the
girl when he struck her across her budding breasts
with his short whip. He raised his arm to strike his
property again. Before the blow could land, the vendor
felt his wrist held in a firm grasp. Turning, he saw
the blond woman in the black uniform, a wicked grin
splitting her face and her fingers wrapped around his
whip hand.

"That will be *quite* enough," Marguerite announced.
She released the hand and then turned to one of her
Marines. "Call in the troops," she ordered.

The Marine spoke into his communicator. Almost
immediately the air was split with the sonic boom of
a dozen or more shuttles. These landed and began
disgorging troops to surround the largest and oldest
slave market on the Continent. Indeed, it was so old
it had actually been established by the long since
defunct United States of America.

Turning back to the vendor, Marguerite said, "Fetch
me the owner of this place, and any vendors who wish
to make a claim for recompense on their . . . property . . . before I seize it for service to the Fleet by the
authority of the secretary general of the Consensus."

CHAPTER EIGHT

The perception of a left right political spectrum has survived for seven centuries and spread across two planets. There are sound reasons for this, despite the fact that it is not perfectly descriptive. One reason is that the core of political differences is the varying perception of the nature of man, at those perceptions' extremes: Perfectible by breeding (right), perfectible by training and education (left), neither perfectible nor even all that changeable by either (center). A second reason is that the existence of one extreme tends to organize people along the other. Perhaps better said, the two extremes tend to organize each other. Moreover, they tend to drag people away from the center, or to make those who remain in the center very quiet . . .

Take the typical X-Y graph that purports to describe the true nature of the political spectrum, one that, perhaps, posits an X axis that describes the attitude to planned social progress or attitude to human reason, while the Y axis describes the attitude to government or attitude to power. If one plots out a given sample of people one will find that two corners of the graph are uninhabited. There is no one who is both sane and not a moron who has a very positive attitude towards government (except insofar as such a person may be personally dependent upon a government meal ticket) and a very negative attitude to planned social progress, or vice versa. Instead, in plotting a sample, one gets a fairly narrow oval, running from lower left to upper right. Turn that graph clockwise forty-five degrees and look at it again. Yes, it now describes left-right again, with minor up and down differences, which differences are irrelevant when compared to the major right-left differences and which are, again, overcome by the mutual and hostile organization driven by the extremes...

> —Jorge y Marqueli Mendoza, *Historia y Filosofia Moral,* Legionary Press, Balboa, Terra Nova, copyright AC 468

Anno Condita 471
Isla Real, Balboa, Terra Nova

There were secrets well kept and then there were rumors of secrets not so well kept. One of the latter was that the legion had captured a UEPF shuttle in Pashtia some years before. The rumor was, in fact, quite true, though never admitted to.

"Unfortunately, Patricio, we can't get it to so much as hover, let alone fly," Lanza said to Carrera, the both of them deep in the bowels of Hill 287 in a specially constructed hangar.

"Why not?" Carrera asked.

Lanza sneered. "It's partly a function of the fact that your ham-fisted ground pounders shot it up. But what little damage that didn't do was done when you had *infantrymen*— Boss, what the *fuck* were you thinking? *Infantrymen?* They can break *anvils!*—take the goddamned thing apart before you loaded it out."

"Best we could do on short notice." Carrera shrugged. "Besides, it looks fine."

"Oh, sure," Lanza agreed. "We got the body put back together. Sortakindamaybealmost. We even got the enginoo to work. But you know what? You can't fly it without the computer and the right program, and the computer was *toasted*. Just toasted. We can't even make up a simulation to *train* somebody to fly it."

"Well, don't *cry* about it," Carrera said. "What do you need to make it work?"

Lanza shrugged. "A new flight computer? At least the goddamned *manual* for the wrecked one."

"No manual in the thing?"

"No, lots of manuals in the thing. On Old Earth microdisc. Which, admittedly, we have been able to read. But none of them tell us how to fix the blasted flight computer. Apparently it's an 'echelons above God' level of maintenance."

For just a fleeting moment Carrera thought about a UEPF communications device sitting in an electromagnetic proof safe at the *Casa* Linda. *No,* he thought. *That UEPF captain with the sexy voice knows about a lot of what I have. But she doesn't, I don't think, know about this. Besides, the only things she'd take in trade are my nukes, and those I'm not about to give up. And even if I would, I not only need this thing to fly, I need her not to know about it. Which she would if I asked to trade for a replacement flight comp.*

Carrera looked over the smooth lines of the dead

shuttle. It was actually quite a pretty craft, a large wing itself with smaller, variable geometry wings for control when in atmosphere. The repair crew had even repainted the symbol of United Earth, a distorted drawing of the home planet in white, surrounded by a wreath, and with abstract lines superimposed for latitude and longitude.

"We *think* the IFF"—Identification, Friend or Foe—"still works," Lanza offered. "Though the codes have got to be out of date."

"Why do you think so?" Carrera asked.

"Just that it had no obvious damage and when we took it into the secure vault and powered it up we got a satisfying light display. 'Best we could do,'" he echoed.

"I asked Fernandez already," Lanza said. "He says his 'special intelligence source' has dried up. At least temporarily. He also said he was doing *his* best."

Hmmm, Carrera wondered. *What's the best I could do? Hmmm . . . haven't used her in years, but maybe, just maybe, Harriet might be of some help. On the other hand, can I really trust Harriet, even if she can help and is willing to? Have to think about that one.*

"Is there anything the Federated States might have that would help you?" he asked Lanza.

"A Lob mainframe computer, maybe," the aviator admitted. "Maybe somebody *really* good at recovering data from a fucked up . . ." Lanza stopped momentarily, plainly puzzled. "I was about to say 'hard drive,' but the fucking thing doesn't *have* a hard drive, at least not what we generally mean by the term."

"Keep working on it," Carrera said. "Let me see what I can do."

BdL *Dos Lindas*, Naval Harbor, *Isla Real*

Aircraft took off and landed in steady streams from the airfield at one end of the arc of land that made up the tail of the tadpole-shaped island. A very few ignored the airstrip, landing or taking off from the ship anchored in the harbor that the tail formed.

The ship was old and, more than any warship afloat on Terra Nova, battle scarred. The worst of the scarring was on her portside rear quarter, where she'd once been the recipient of an antishipping missile that had nearly destroyed her . . . and had destroyed many, many of her crew.

To one side of that scar, enclosed in clear polycarbonate, an ancient sword—at least the core of it was ancient—that had made the trip from Japan on Old Earth to Yamato on New was welded to the hull. Likewise inside the polycarbonate was the shadow of a small man, the hand of the shadow touching the hilt, the *tsuka*, of the sword.

That was the holiest spot on a ship that every man of the crew considered generally holy.

Above the polycarbonate case, welded sword, and thin shadow was a flight deck, roughly seven hundred feet in length. Along one side of the flight deck a mix of light attack, reconnaissance, and rotary wing aircraft were lined up. As the ship was under blackout they were only visible at a distance as shadows, back-illuminated by the lights of the fleet base, itself on the northern edge of the island by the bay.

Above the flight deck, in the superstructure on the port side amidships, Legate Roderigo Fosa, commander of the *classis*, or fleet, trusted his own eyes more than any technological marvels. Below, the bridge crew watched radar and sonar screens as well as the closed circuit, light amplifying televisions that showed both the surrounding waters and the crew working the flight deck.

Further down in the bowels of the ship a different crew kept track of the movements of the fleet, which fleet consisted of one heavy cruiser, the *Barco de la Legion Tadeo Kurita*, mounting twelve six-inch, long-range guns in four triple turrets, three corvettes, equipped for air defense and antisubmarine work, two patrol boats, and several service ships carrying everything from parts to petrol, from beans to bullets.

It was a nice little fleet and, if it was small compared to some, well—

"It's still the size of the fight in the ship," muttered Fosa, "not the size of the ship—or fleet—in the fight."

Not that the ship was heading to a fight. Oh, no. It was ostensibly headed to an antidrug patrol, in support of and in concert with the Federated States Navy and Air Force.

"And I'll perform that mission," Fosa muttered, even as he contemplated the *real* mission, the stealth mission.

There are three primary factors that affect an aircraft's radar cross section. These are size, materials, and shape. Although it is the least important factor, if two aircraft have exactly the same materials and shape, but are of different size, the larger will have a greater radar cross section. For shape, the important things are to have no sharp edges, no flat surfaces pointed toward the radar. For materials, there are tricks that can be used. The first trick is, construction wise, the tougher. Radar "notices" the change in density of an object in the air. To the extent that that difference is tiny, radar is apt not to notice. The second trick is to make the aircraft "lossy," a chemical property referring to the conductivity of a material. Lossy materials convert radar energy to heat. In the case of the Condor auxiliary propelled gliders developed by the legion, lossiness had been achieved by use of a spun carbon fiber and resin shell.

The heat was, of course, itself a problem and had been on Old Earth for over five centuries. Even on Terra Nova, thermal imagers had made it possible to detect even fairly faint heat differences at considerable distance.

Without knowing the real capabilities of all their potential enemies, the legion had assumed the worst, made a virtue of a vice, and created what was probably the stealthiest aircraft, if one of the lowest performing ones, on the planet. Outside of that spun carbon fiber and resin shell, they had built up a thick layer of one of the best insulating materials known to man, polyurethane foam. That foam was fairly dense toward the shell, but became increasingly less dense as one moved outward from the shell. Indeed, the "dielectric constant" of the things was, where foam met air, no more than 1.01, which is to say one percent more dense than the air surrounding.

Moreover, since overkill was one of the legion's core values, within that foam was embedded a very large number of very tiny concave-convex chips. These, arriving at their final position within the aircraft randomly, tended to reflect and diffuse whatever radar energy

they met, or collect and then diffuse that energy…
and in directions as random as their own random
placement. Objects on the glider that could not be
made of carbon fiber or polyurethane had been more
carefully designed—no randomness permitted—to
be most likely to direct radar energy away from any
transmitter. For propulsion the Condor had a pusher
propeller, smoothly polished and made of the same
carbon fiber-resin material as its shell. Heat from the
engine was further dissipated by being mixed with
cold air and released from dozens of small vents on
the upper portions of the wings.

It had been just such a glider—albeit one under
self-guidance—that Carrera had used to carry the bomb
that destroyed the Yithrabi city of Hajar, effectively
closing out the war with the Salafi *Ikhwan*.

"This is just a recon mission, Montoya. You understand that?"

Warrant Officer Rafael Montoya, tall, brown, and
skinny, nodded his answer to Fosa, then added, "Yes,
sir, I know that. And the sooner it's over the better."

"Well, we won't be in position for you to launch
for three or four days. Sleep well beforehand."

Montoya laughed, white teeth shining in his brown
face. "Skipper, if you were going to recon someplace,
someplace where you had absolutely *no* idea about the
defensive capabilities, the sensors, the weapons, the
rules of engagement…tell me, sir, how well would
you sleep for the few days before?"

Fosa did not smile, but then he rarely did. "Warrant Officer Montoya," he said, "if you find that you
cannot sleep at least eight hours in every twenty-four

until you launch, let me know and I will have you drugged to sleep. And the rest of the time, except when eating or defecating, I expect you to be in a flight simulator."

"Aye, aye, sir," Montoya answered. Fosa wasn't the kind of man to argue with.

Fosa turned a glaring eye to the warrant. "Mr. Montoya, you have your orders and yet you are still here. Now run along, like a good lad, and follow them, while I continue with the ostensible counter-drug mission that is our excuse to get you to where you can launch."

Headquarters, Tauran Union Security Force–Balboa, Building 59, Fort Muddville, Transitway Area, Balboa

"No, *mon general*," said de Villepin, the intelligence officer. "I don't think—"

Janier held up one hand to silence his G-2. The general's eyes tracked a buzzing annoyance winding low over his desk.

Someone had let a fly in through an open door. It was an unavoidable incident of life in the tropics, and as annoying as it was unavoidable. Screens on the windows could only keep down the numbers, even as they ensured that those flies that got in couldn't leave. This was what flypaper was for.

Janier sneered at the fly. He then picked up his telephone and punched in the number for his chief medical officer. "Kouchner, you filthy swine! The flypaper report you showed me said we had the fly problem under control! Why, then, is there a fly in my office?"

Janier slammed the phone down, apparently without waiting for an answer, and shouted out, "Malcoeur, you toad, get in here."

When the short, tubby, frog-faced major made his appearance, Janier said, "You are a toad, descended from toads." His finger lanced out at the buzz. "Follow your genes and catch that fly."

As Malcoeur scurried off to find a flyswatter, Janier said to de Villepin, "Continue."

The intel officer sighed. "As I was saying, no, *mon general*, I don't think we can use the drug trade to entice the Federated States into invading Balboa again, joining us in invading, or in supporting our invading Balboa. The ties are too close for that. Worse, the Federated States under its current regime is almost as casualty averse as our political 'masters.' And, if nothing else, the Balboans would make them bleed a great deal. Just as they will make us bleed unless we are very, very clever.

"We *can*, however, use the allegations of drug trafficking to confuse the Federated States, to make them ambivalent about both Balboa and the partition they inflicted on us some years ago in the interests of peace."

The conference room, though large, was empty but for Janier and de Villepin . . . and the fly. Air conditioners hummed at two of the windows. It was as well they were working, since Janier was wearing his favorite uniform, the reproduction blue velvet and gold-embroidered informal dress uniform of a marshal of Napoleonic France. Hundreds of golden oak leaves covered the facings, the collar, the shoulders, and ran down each sleeve. But for the air conditioning, the combination of velvet and beastly-uncomfortable, stiff, high collar would have made the thing life threatening in Balboa's tropical clime.

Idly, Janier tapped his likewise reproduction marshal's baton, with its thirty-two gold eagles, on the broad, wooden conference table.

"Do you think that will work?" Janier asked, "Do you really think it will work when, if anyone is trafficking in drugs, it is our allies in the old government, cowering in fear in their little quarter and desperate for money?"

De Villepin nodded. "*Mon general*, it is *precisely* because the rump government is involved in the trade that I am most confident that they can arrange to make it look as if it is Parilla and *his* government, aided in every particular by the *Legion del Cid*, that is running the whole enterprise."

Janier stopped tapping the table with his baton, raising the thing to rest against his shoulder and cheek. "It *is* elegant, I admit."

The baton began to tap again, this time against the Gallic general's cheek. He chewed on his lower lip while slowly nodding. Plainly he was weighing the pros and cons of de Villepin's plan.

"All we really need," the general finally said, "is to get the Federated States or one of the TU's high courts to take out drug trafficking charges against either Parilla or Carrera. Both would be nice but either will do. At that point, the FSC's hands are tied while ours will be left free." Tap. Tap. Chew. Chew. Tap. Chew. Mull. Ponder . . .

"Do it. Set it up. As quickly as possible." Janier mused a bit more. "It would really be a help, you know, if somehow we could split the enemy's ranks so that it looked as if he were falling apart, and we and our clients of the old government would have to step in for the sake of law and order."

De Villepin answered, "Well, it's still a bit uncertain, but now that you mention it ..."

BdL *Dos Lindas, Mar Furioso,* Terra Nova

The ship was moving fast enough to cause spray to rise and wet the bronze figurehead that graced the bow under the flight deck. There was a popular theory that the ship's name, *"Dos Lindas,"* came from the figurehead's two perfect breasts. The setting sun, reflected from the waves, danced and played over the bronze of the figurehead, making it seem a thing not merely alive but divine. That an artificial rainbow from the spray framed the bronze only added to the illusion of divinity.

Higher than the figurehead, and much farther back, on and around the rear elevator that connected the hangar deck with the flight deck, a well-rehearsed deck crew worked under an awning preparing an auxiliary-powered glider for flight. Above the deck, on the fenced open space atop the conning tower, Legate Fosa and Warrant Officer Montoya watched final preparations.

"Remember," Fosa cautioned Montoya, though his eyes remained fixed on the glider, "your job isn't really to map a bloody thing. If this works, we'll be sending more missions out to recon the place. You have only to get there, overfly the island, and see if they notice you."

"I'll know that they'll have noticed me when they blast me out of the sky, right?" Montoya chided. He, too, had eyes only for his aircraft.

"We'd prefer that didn't happen," Fosa answered, still serious as cancer. "Now what do you do if they do notice you and happen to shoot your ass down? Assuming you live, of course."

"I push the button on my global locating system that will change its settings to make it appear to have malfunctioned," Montoya answered without hesitation. "I try to ditch at sea, and swim ashore. Thereafter, I try to avoid capture. If captured, I insist I was on a counter-drug reconnaissance mission, suffered a malfunction, and was blown off my patrol route. The prevailing winds will support that story. I tell them I tried to avoid capture because people who shoot down an aircraft engaged in legitimate law enforcement mission are unlikely to treat the pilot of that aircraft too very well."

"Very good," Fosa answered. "Now go do it."

The two turned to face each other, Montoya tossing off a typically ragged Air *Ala* salute, which salute Fosa returned with the comment, "Fucking aviator slobs. Git!"

The sun was just down. None of the moons had yet risen. In the darkness, with a headwind of eleven knots and the carrier doing another eighteen, takeoff wasn't a question of speed to become airborne. It was a question of the deck crew removing the lashings that held the Condor to its cradle on the flight deck and jumping back. Montoya's Condor, with its fifty feet of wingspan, instantly lifted above the flight deck.

It was then that he gave a little gas to the engine, just enough to stay well above the flight deck as it moved out from underneath him. This was a little tricky as the sheer bulk of the *Dos Lindas*, moving underneath, displaced enough air to tug at the broad-winged glider, pulling it downward.

Despite the turbulence, Montoya kept well above the flight deck until the carrier was safely away. Although he kept his aircraft aloft easily enough, the pilot's spirits sank as the carrier left him to his mission. Indeed, seeing through his night vision goggles as the stern of the ship rapidly moved away gave Montoya one of the loneliest feelings he'd ever had in a life that had had its share of loneliness.

"Nothing for it, though," he said to himself, pulling his stick back and to the left to turn toward the southern coast of the western triangle of Colombia del Norte. It was there that he would find the updrafts from breezes blowing across the *Mar Furioso* and up the great chain of mountains they called the *Atacamas*. Those, if taken both ways, would extend his fuel to the UEPF lodgment on Atlantis Island and, "God willing, back again."

It was over a hundred and fifty miles before the Condor would cross the coast.

Two hours, near enough, Montoya thought. *And, if I learned nothing else during* Cazador *School, it was, "don't sleep when you're tired; sleep when you can."*

Montoya's fingers played over his control panel, setting a wake-up call for an hour and a half and confirming his preprogrammed flight plan. The autopilot then took over, throttling down the engine to a speed of seventy knots and settling in to a flight altitude of one hundred meters over the sea. The pilot released the stick as soon as he felt the autopilot take control. Tossing his head to move the night vision goggles, or NVGs, up on their frame, he then settled back, crossing his arms over his chest.

Gonna be a looong flight, was Montoya's last thought before sleep took him for, at least, a short time.

Before the third wake-up *ping*, Montoya's hand was reaching for his stick even as he tossed his head down to reposition his NVGs. His left hand sought out and found the on switch for the goggles, twisting a quarter turn clockwise to turn them on.

"I wasn't sleeping, Sergeant," the pilot said automatically.

The moon Bellona was up by this time. In its light, never so bright as Old Earth's one moon, he saw the mass of the *Atacama* range rising to the north before him. The coastline was fainter, but still perceivable in the grainy, greenish glow of the goggles.

As soon as the autopilot sensed Montoya's hand on the stick it relinquished control. He nudged the stick back and gave a little more gas to the engine to gain optimum altitude to enter the mountain wave of uplifting air.

Montoya glanced around in an attempt to find a lenticular, or lens shaped, cloud that would mark a particularly good updraft. Unsurprisingly, the goggles weren't quite up to seeing that, even though they were the best Haarlem-produced NVGs money could buy.

No matter, he thought. *There are the mountains*

and I know the wind blows to the north. There will
be a mountain wave to carry me up.

The engine had been killed to save fuel that would
be needed later. Under the natural power of the
mountain wave, Montoya corkscrewed upward at
several kilometers an hour. His ears popped repeatedly as he twisted his head and worked his jaw to
equalize pressure.

At about forty-five hundred meters above sea level
another series of warning *pings* sounded to advise
Montoya to don his oxygen mask. This was a pressure
demand system, one that would provide overpressure
of oxygen to allow the glider to ascend about ten
thousand meters while still keeping the pilot conscious.

He'd drilled it more than a thousand times in his
career as an aviator. Even using his left hand, the mask
was on his face and affixed to his helmet in seconds.
Oxygen flow started immediately and automatically
thereafter, some of the gas being forced out of the
tight-fitting mask by the overpressure.

The global locating system, or GLS, consisted of
twenty-four satellites, some of them geosynchronous,
in orbit above the planet. It was one of three such
systems in orbit (or, arguably, four if one counted the
ships of United Earth Peace Fleet, which could do
GLS duty at need), but was far and away the most
complete and the best (again, excepting the UEPF).

In effect, the system worked by sending out sig-
nals from each satellite, which signals amounted to,
"This is Satellite X. At the tone the time will be..."
By comparing the times to the known positions of

the satellites, a receiver could calculate position on the surface, height above the surface, and, if moving, direction to a very high degree of accuracy.

When Montoya's Condor reached fourteen thousand meters, his navigation system informed him: *pingping-ping*. Pulling his stick over and forward, he ceased his corkscrew upward and began the roughly thousand-kilometer-long, slow, shallow dive that would take his craft east northeast to where he expected to pick up another mountain wave to gain more altitude. Along the way, he would continue to receive uplift from air rising to pass over the *Atacama* range.

He'd packed his own rations for the trip, carefully setting aside anything with even a hint of beans or, worse still, peppers. He'd kept the small bottles of high test rum because, heated flight suit or not—

"God, it is fucking *cold* up here."

Tapping the Condor back into autopilot mode, Montoya removed his clumsy gloves and tore open a pouch of "mystery meat." It wasn't "mystery meat" because the cockpit was so dark he couldn't see the labeling on the pouch. It was "mystery meat" because no one really knew what its origin was.

The thing was about half frozen, frozen enough, in any event, that his spoon was useless. He squeezed the bottom of the pouch with his right hand to force the semi-solid chunk upwards. Then, pulling the oxygen mask away with his left hand, he bent his head and drove his teeth through the slab.

"Oh, yummy," Montoya sneered into his mask, while chewing. "Note to self: Word with the *Duque*, first opportunity. Not good."

Once the meat chunk was but an unpleasant memory, Montoya reached down for another pouch. He could feel the texture of the next one through the foil wrapping.

"Tortilla, fried, chorley and corn, mixed," he recited from memory. "How grand."

Actually, the tortilla, a half-inch-thick, yellow patty, wasn't bad. It wasn't home cooking, no, but it wasn't bad.

After those two, Montoya's fingers did a little searching through the container under his legs. Soon they came to something he really did want, a small plastic bottle he knew from memory was labeled, "Rum, legionary, 50 ml, 160 proof, product of *Distilleria Legionario,* Arraijan, Balboa."

After that, he slept, dreaming of a girl who was considerably warmer than the frozen cockpit that was his reality.

The sun had risen, set, risen again, and was now setting as Montoya heeled over to leave the *Atacamas* behind. His altitude was just over fourteen thousand meters. That alone would be enough to reach the UEPF's island of Atlantis, but it would not be enough to reach it, overfly it, and return.

Montoya turned a hand crank to elevate the Condor's small propeller. Once it was in position, and the warning light shone "locked," he pressed the starter.

Nothing.

He pressed the starter again.

Still nothing.

"Fuck. This is going to cost a little time and fuel. Assuming, of course, that it works. Well . . . it usually works."

Taking his hand off the starter button but leaving the throttle open, Montoya nosed his Condor over into a steeper dive. He felt the pressure on his posterior lessen. As the thing picked up speed, the propeller also began to turn more rapidly. It took several minutes and several thousand feet before Montoya felt the jolt of the small engine starting and then the mild, steady vibration of the motor turning on its own.

With the engine still running Montoya turned the glider back, wandering back toward the mountain range to regain some of the altitude he had lost.

The mind wanders sometimes. In the uneventful portions of his flight, Montoya's mind wandered, too.

Long flight . . . slow flight . . . nothing to see but my instruments and the clouds. Alone . . . as usual.

I can't say I've never had any luck with the women. I just never had any luck that lasted. Wonder if I'll ever meet the right girl.

Gisela was nice . . . but too hot tempered. Jocasta . . . well . . . who wants to share. Yelena Samsonova had beautiful eyes but when she turned, so did they. Besides, she was three inches taller than me; more in heels. We looked silly together. Still . . . those eyes . . .

I wish I could find a nice girl like Caridad, Cruz's wife. Sadly, she has no unmarried sisters. Or maybe a little jewel like Marqueli Mendoza. Ah, but such women are rare . . . rare.

I don't even remember how many women I've had. More than fifty? No, closer to one hundred. And the ones I wanted to keep didn't want me . . . and the ones who wanted me I didn't want to keep.

I think the fault must be in me somehow. . . .

✧   ✧   ✧

Fernandez, whose project this was, and the people who worked for him, including one section of *Obras Zorilleras*, had thought about the problem quite a lot: At what range is it even possible for the UEPF on Atlantis to pick up electrical signals from the glider's instrumentation or the tiny amount of radio energy created by the spark plugs in the motor? Ultimately, they'd had to admit, they had not a clue. Their best guess was worthless.

"But," had argued one of the OZ people, "we know the UE routinely lets aircraft and airships pass to within about two hundred and fifty kilometers. We also know that at two hundred and ten they engage without warning. Maybe that's the effective range of their weapons, true. But, just as likely, maybe that's the effective range of their sensors."

It was the best guess they had, from the best brains available.

And time to stop thinking about girls. Even if they are the most pleasant subject of contemplation . . . especially when one does not know how much longer the pleasure will even be available.

The sun was sinking again into the horizon, casting long rays out across the azure sea. Montoya could not help himself from glancing at it. And why not? It might be his last sunset.

At what the GLS told him was two hundred and sixty kilometers out from Atlantis, the pilot killed the engine and cranked it down into the fuselage of the glider. This took several minutes. He then killed every electrical instrument aboard, including his navigational system and the GLS receiver. At that point he was left with a pressure-driven, sensitive altimeter that didn't use any power, a magnetic compass with a glowing needle, and his NVGs, without which he was unlikely even to be able to see the island. Even those being turned on was considered a risk.

"'An acceptable risk,'" Montoya quoted. "I wonder if they'll kill me with lasers like the ones on the *Dos Lindas*, or if they'll use missiles, if the earthpigs use anything so primitive. Or maybe they'll just scramble some kind of aircraft we have not a clue to and shoot me down. Or—and isn't this a happy thought?—I can be the very first pilot shot down by a charged particle beam in the history of this world. Or maybe—"

"Or maybe," Montoya said aloud as he slid over the island at eight thousand feet, "just maybe they can't see me at all."

For reasons more instinctive than intellectual, the pilot had had a very rough mental time of it as he'd crossed the island's shore. Surely *that* would be the point at which they would absolutely engage. But no, nothing happened. He'd crossed the shore, then turned to the right and followed the coast for nearly an hour before he spotted what had to be, by its lights, the major city or base on the island. He'd glided over that too and still, "Nothing. By God, it works. It *works*!"

He'd had one bad moment, when he came too near to what was apparently the island's major, or perhaps only, air *cum* space base. There was heavy traffic that passed within a few kilometers or so, UEPF shuttles heading down to ground or off into space. Montoya couldn't help snickering over the UEPF's ignorance.

"And on that happy note, I'm out of here. Fernandez needs to know that the earthpigs can't see Condors. That's a helluva lot more important than joyriding the clouds is."

There was a chain of low mountains that ran through the center of the island, north-northeast to center to south. Though nothing so impressive as the *Atacama* range, Montoya was fairly sure he could find a mountain wave to raise his craft for the return journey.

CHAPTER NINE

We live in an age of institutionalized fraud. Virtually *every* age in human history has been an age of institutionalized fraud. Whether it be the fraud of the divine right of kings, the fraud of superior genetics, the fraud of the malleability and perfectibility of man, the fraud that freedom comes without a hefty price, the fraud of the dictatorship of the proletariat, the fraud of the possibility of taxing the rich without them passing the tax on to the middle class and poor...the list of frauds is endless. To expand upon the Old Earther, Rousseau, man may be born free and live everywhere in chains, but more importantly he is born innocent and is everywhere made a fool of. His chains are constructed of his foolishness.

To a great extent man wants to be fooled; indeed, he insists upon it. In his entertainment he will demand that the most trivial things bring the most profound and certain changes for the good. He will reject the politicians who even *attempt* to speak truth to him, and embrace most warmly those who lie best. He will insist upon the existence of the free lunch. He will rarely understand that those who shout, "Power to the people," really mean, "Power to those who shout, 'Power to the people.'" Those who "speak truth to power" are much more likely to be uttering lies to those whose only power is to cast a vote.

And still, amidst all this fraud, there are things that are real, things that are true. A mother's love for her child, or a husband's for his child and his wife; these are almost always real. That honor, integrity, and courage are the only things one truly owns is true. The penalty a people ultimately pays for submitting to fraud is real. That political power grows from the barrel of a gun is true. The concrete of a bunker and the steel of a cannon; those are real.

—Jorge y Marqueli Mendoza, *Historia y Filosofia Moral,* Legionary Press, Balboa, Terra Nova, copyright AC 468

Anno Condita 471
Headquarters, Twenty-Second Tercio (ex-351st Tsarist Guards Airborne)
Centro de Entrenamiento Legionario, Fort Cameron, Balboa, Terra Nova

The little convoy consisted of a wheeled armored car in the front, with another taking up the rear, a truck carrying a score of fierce-visaged, turbaned riflemen, and a single armored Phaeton sedan carrying Carrera, a gravid Lourdes, and their eldest, Hamilcar. As the sedan came to a halt in front of the brown and green painted, arched metal building that served as the headquarters for the Twenty-Second Tercio, ex-Volgan Colonel, now Legate, Ivan Samsonov stood on the wooden steps fronting the Quonset hut and rendered a

hand salute. The legate's wife, Irena Samsonova, stood
by one side, his adjutant by the other. Irena was a
stout woman, kindly faced, and dressed in a simple
white, knee length frock suitable for the climate. Of
Legate Samsonov's daughter, Yelena, there was no sign.

The turbaned Pashtians were out of the truck and
surrounding the convoy before Mitchell even had
turned off the sedan's engine. Carrera emerged, too,
and held the door for Hamilkar and Lourdes. She
looked radiant despite, or perhaps because of, the
prominent bulge in her midsection.

Carrera stuck his head in the sedan's still open
door and said, "Mitch, we'll be a while. Why don't
you take a break and try some Volgan food?"

Mitchell was easily bright enough to break that
code: *Nose around and check on everything from
morale to hygiene.*

"Roger that, boss," the warrant answered.

A company of Volgan paratroops sang a martial
song as they marched by the headquarters. Carrera
could make out the syllables but couldn't understand
the words. To him it sounded like:

Put' dalyok u nas s toboyu,
Veselej, soldat, glyadi!
V'yotsya, v'yotsya znam'a polkovoye,
Komandiry vperedi.

Soldaty v put', v put', v put'!
A dlya tebya, rodnaya,
Est' pochta polevaya.
Proshaj! Truba zov'ot,
Soldaty—v pohod!

The Pashtians of Hamilcar's guard and the Volgans had a history of cutting each others' throats. Carrera glanced from singing paratroopers to glaring riflemen and decided, *No, probably not today.*

Catchy tune, Carrera thought. *I'll have to have Samsonov have it translated into Spanish.* He also observed that the Volgan troops were not acne-faced young conscripts. They looked older, more mature, more confident; professionals, as advertised. As opposing forces for the legion's training center, the Volgans of the company passing by wore the dark, Sachsen-designed *tarnung,* or camouflage, uniforms. Others wore different uniforms at different times. Samsonov himself wore the legionary pixilated tiger stripes in jungle colors. The Twenty-Second was one of only three regiments on Terra Nova with its own costume department, the others being Fernandez's intelligence Tercio and the Fourteenth Cazador Tercio. Not particularly tall, the Volgan commander gave the impression of vast solidity and strength, topped by a round head, itself fronted by a face that looked both highly sincere and very intelligent.

Noting Carrera's interest in the passing company, Samsonov asked, "You like singing, *Duque*?"

Carrera nodded, "Yes, Ivan, for its own sake and as a weapon of war both."

"Yes, well, they not that good. Someday you come, hear regiment's chorus. They are good."

"I'll do that," Carrera agreed, while thinking, *If I can find time to wipe my ass, anyway.* "As a matter of fact, if the chorus, or even a part of it, is available, I wonder if your lovely wife wouldn't escort Lourdes..."

"Excellent idea," Samsonov agreed, smiling broadly. He said something to his adjutant in their own tongue, causing the adjutant to nod briskly, then turn on his heels and enter the building behind.

He didn't have to say anything to Irena; she understood the English her husband and Carrera shared well enough. She floated off the steps with a grace and fluidity surprising in a woman of her solidity.

As Irena took Lourdes by the arm and began to lead her off, Hamilcar cast a glance at his chief of guards. *Protect my mother.* At the guard chief's word, a quarter of the twenty guards immediately fell out of their perimeter and formed around Lourdes and Irena.

Carrera watched only for a moment, to make sure Lourdes was comfortable, before turning his attention back to Samsonov and asking, "By the way, what does the song mean?"

Samsonov stopped and thought for a moment. "It means ... 'The march before us with you is long ... soldier take livelier look ... regimental banner whips and twists ... commanders are up front. Soldiers on march'—that chorus—'And for you your own field mail is waiting but ... Listen? ... no, Hark!', maybe Hark ... 'trumpet calls ... and soldiers march on.'"

"Have one of your people send a copy to Professor Ruiz, would you? Along with some trooper with a good voice to sing it for him."

"Certainly, *Duque,*" the Volgan agreed. "And now, breakfast, yes? Men eat better here than they used to. And we don't have to grow food ourselves. So when they get fat, I have more time available to work fat off. It more than evens out." Samsonov called something into the headquarters and positioned himself by Carrera's left side.

Carrera walked with head cocked, hands clasped

behind his back. "Tell me about your regiment's capabilities, please. And with no fluff; if you can't do something, I need to know."

Samsonov shrugged, "As you wish. We were one of better parachute infantry regiments of former Tsarist Army. You know this. Possibly we are best. Towards end, with your help, we could pay and feed men when rest of division going to scrap heap. Many good men transfer over to us from other regiments in 117th Guards Airborne Division before we leave *Rodina*. NCOs, *Praporschiks*—you would say 'warrant officers'—and officers; most have much combat experience. Some older ones fought in Pashtia. Others on borders during break up of empire. Most other ranks too. All volunteers. Many long service troops. I am prejudiced, I know, but I think we are better than same number from FSC 39th Airborne Division, maybe not so good as FSC Rangers. . . . Then again, maybe."

Carrera nodded. "Pay?" he asked.

"Very good, by Volgan standards. My privates' five hundred and twenty-five Federated States drachma a month is five or six times as much as mid-level manager in Volga now. This part of reason morale is high. Plenty to send home, plenty to have good time here when not on duty."

"Problems?"

"Still we have no Orthodox chaplain. Many men do not care. More do."

"I am looking into that. Kuralski has some prospects. He's had a hard time finding one to suit. Thought he had one, but that priest wanted to be made a tribune."

Samsonov did not understand. "So make tribune."

"No," Carrera shook his head emphatically. "I don't

generally commission lawyers, doctors, pilots...specialists like those can be, should be, warrant officers or enlisted. Only leaders of men get commissioned. No commissioned chaplains unless they go through the same route as other officer candidates. I don't suppose your regiment had a combat experienced Orthodox priest?"

Samsonov snorted. "In Tsar's Army? Hah! Psalm singers stayed behind while men went out to fight."

"Thought not. We'll keep trying."

Seeing that Samsonov was content with that, Carrera changed the subject. "Ivan, what kinds of missions are your men capable of? I don't mean being an opposing force to train my troops. What kinds of combat operations can you do?" Carrera looked down at Hamilcar and added, "You can speak freely in front of my son."

Samsonov answered, "We can do air parachute drops to seize vital targets: airports, bridges, chokepoints. Airmobile operations also, if someone else provide helicopters and aircraft. We get helicopters?"

Carrera nodded. "Working on that, too."

"We do also most typical antiguerrilla missions: ambush, raid, reconnoiter, counterterror. I don't usually care for counterterror, bad for discipline."

Carrera knew that counterterror meant to the Volgans pretty much what it had meant to himself and the legion in Sumer and Pashtia. It meant not just destroying terrorists so much as inflicting greater terror than terrorists on the same target population: hangings, burnings, mutilation, massacre. Never, officially, rape but that had happened, too. Which often led to more hangings, of course.

"How about amphibious landings?"

"Difficult. That was mission of naval infantry. Perhaps we could if beachhead not contested." The Volgan considered that for a moment more, then amended, "Probably we could, with a little practice."

"Would your men fight for Balboa?"

The Volgan hesitated. *He said he wanted an honest answer, but can this one* take *an honest answer?* Deciding that Carrera likely could, he said, "Realistically, no. They do not think of themselves as mercenaries. Even though they—we—are. They don't know any more of Balboa than jungle they are training in. Those . . . and bars and brothels. But they fight for me. And if good reason, I will fight for you. Do not expect suicide mission from me. My regiment is my country; I must preserve it above all. Is most important consideration. But I would be willing to undertake some real operations. It would be good for regiment. They get . . . soft . . . without some fighting."

Carrera was content with that for now. Reaching the mess hall, Samsonov called the mess to attention and led the way to the officers' area. Carrera did not really approve of interrupting the troops' meal, nor of the fact that he, Hamilcar, and Samsonov sat down without waiting in line. An orderly brought them their meals: kasha—a sort of porridge with meat or fish, meat in this case—bread, butter and jam, Balboan sausage, hard-boiled eggs, some kind of pastry, and glasses of hot tea. At a glance and nod from Samsonov, another Volgan officer, also sitting for breakfast, hurriedly finished and left. The officer hid his distaste at passing between two of Hamilcar's Pashtians on his way out. There was one more Volgan there; a youngish looking

tribune whose name tag read "Chapayev." The boy ate
mechanically, with no real interest in his food, as if
greatly preoccupied with some difficult problem. Oddly,
Samsonov didn't indicate that Chapayev should leave.

Carrera dipped a spoon into the kasha, trying to
hide a lack of enthusiasm. Again he changed the
subject. "How goes your training?"

Samsonov pointed at the tribune. "Victor, tell the
Duque how training goes in your company."

Chapayev gulped before answering. "My Spanish
is...atrocity. *Casus Belli,* all on own. I try."

Nodding, as if searching for words and discovering
that, perhaps, he had enough, if only just, Chapayev
continued, "Is great problem, learning be like Tauran
infantry. Some have many drill...no...drills. We, too.
Others...none."

"That's so," answered Carrera. "Also, it's hard to be
what you're not. I understand that. Also, I don't want
you to lose everything you already have, just for a little
more accurate presentation of the various Tauran forces.

"Tell me, how are you training for helicopter missions without helicopters?" That question was directed
at Samsonov, who answered that his troops were doing
most of their work on mock-ups, maps, blackboards.

"Fine for now. Kuralski is working on recruiting
more helicopter pilots for your detachment of IM-71s
when they arrive."

"What did you think of the Volgans, Ham?" Carrera
asked as the convoy sped over the gravel road in the
jungle-striped, fast diminishing light.

"Besides that some of my Pashtians hate the Volgans'
guts, Dad, they seemed pretty decent."

The father looked directly at the boy, raising one eyebrow.

"Oh. You wanted an *assessment*. Okay, Dad. Morale seems high, probably because however shitty—"

"Hamilcar!"

"Sorry, Mom." The boy sniffed, then turned his attention back to his father. "However poor their living conditions now, they're a lot better than they were back in Volga. They seem disciplined, Dad, maybe a little *too* disciplined. And they put too much into appearances. Lots of painted rocks and tree trunks at *Fuerte* Cameron. They know they're an elite group and like that a lot. Proud, I think. From the demonstrations Legate Samsonov gave us, they seem pretty sharp on the attack."

"They rehearsed all that, you know," Carrera said. "Don't take it at face value."

The boy nodded. "I figured they probably did, Dad. Even so, they couldn't have done so well, even with rehearsals, if they weren't pretty good to begin with. I mean, that mortar fire was *close* to their assault line."

"Good," Carrera said, closing his eyes and leaning his head back against the Phaeton's cushions. "Very good."

He felt Lourdes stiffen suddenly, next to him.

"Are you all right, hon?" he asked, sitting up and opening his eyes.

She twitched again, as if half in surprise and half in pain. A literally expectant smile lit her face. "I'm fine, Patricio, but could we perhaps go to the hospital rather than home?"

"Mom," Hamilcar asked, "are you going to have the baby now? Cool."

✧   ✧   ✧

Ah, good, thought Victor Chapayev, as he pulled up his e-mail and saw that he had a message from his wife, Veronica Chapayeva, back in St. Nicholasburg, in Volga. In Balboa he lived the life of an aesthete, sending most of his pay home to maintain her. No whores for Chapayev. Little vodka either. He worked, he studied, he wrote her every day. Indeed, it was in good part the tribune's dedication that had caused Samsonov to elevate him to a company command (as an official part of the Foreign Military Training Group, the Twenty-Second still organized by battalions and companies rather than by cohorts and maniples) rather rapidly.

Chapayev stifled a yawn. It had been a long day with his company, commencing with physical training at six in the morning and just ending now, well after sundown, after the after action review that followed the day's training mission.

Opening the e-mail, Chapayev scanned the short missive. It was even shorter than usual, a bare five sentences: *I miss you. I love you. When are you coming home? My mother is ill. I need more money.*

Chapayev shook his head, thinking, *My little Veronica, you never were much for the literary.* He fired off a quick response, though at that it was still longer and more thoughtful than the message he'd received, then opened up his bank account and made a transfer of a couple of hundred FSD to the joint account he held with his wife.

That transaction completed, Victor shut down his computer and walked to the radio. Turning it on to the only station in Balboa that played classical music, he sat beside it, closed his eyes, and indulged his only real interest besides his wife and his job. With the stars rising, and the murmur of the *antaniae* outside—*mnnbt, mnnbt, mnnbt*—Chapayev closed his eyes and let the music take him to sleep.

Hospital Ancon, *Cerro* Gorgia, *Ciudad* Balboa, Terra Nova

Lourdes awakened without her baby and almost immediately began to panic. Then her husband walked into the room, smiling while holding a tiny child cradled in his arms, with Hamilcar and her eldest girl, Julia, on either side.

"Ah, you're up," Carrera said. "Good, because this little darling is in need of lunch. Which, as it happens, you're extremely well equipped to provide."

"Not that well equipped," Lourdes said, looking down at her chest. "Well . . . maybe a little better equipped than I am normally."

"Well enough equipped for *my* complete satisfaction," Carrera replied. "Though my preferences have to take second place for now, since she's the baby and she wants to be fed."

He leaned down, kissed his wife atop her head, and passed to her her newborn. Lourdes took the baby and began to undo her top to present her breast. "What are we going to call her?"

Carrera rocked his head from side to side. "Even though *I* did all the really important work, I think you get to choose. Mother's privilege, let's say."

"Hmmm." *Hamilcar's position is secure. Julia has her*

father more or less wrapped around her finger. This one
will need a little something extra to compete, I think.

"Then we'll call her 'Linda,'" Lourdes said.

For just a moment before affixing herself to her
mother, the baby made a gurgling, happy sound.

Carrera sighed. "Linda it is, then, by popular acclaim.
I suppose—"

He never quite finished the thought, as the skyline
outside Lourdes' hospital room was suddenly lit with
fireworks.

"What the—?"

"Mac passed on that you had dropped another one,"
he said. "The troops are celebrating. Noisily."

Lago Sombrero Ammunition Supply Point (ASP), Balboa, Terra Nova

The facility was soundless but for the roar of a powerful engine and the cries of the *antaniae*. Under a
moonless, overcast sky, beneath a long metal shed
that blocked out all overhead view, and surrounded
by earthen walls that covered the bunker entrance
from ground observation, one uniformed man guided
another in driving a blacked out, unnumbered Ocelot
infantry fighting vehicle *cum* armored gun system
down a ramp and through wide-spread bunker doors.
Only when the doors were sealed tight did the first
man turn on a light to guide the vehicle to park in
its proper place. Under the light, the bunker walls
seemed moist, with mold growing in the corners.

"Jesus Christ, Centurion! What is all this?" asked
the driver after he'd dismounted.

"Officially, it's bunker number 17, *Lago Sombrero* Ammunition Supply Point," answered the centurion.

"No, no. I mean 'what is *all* this.'" The driver spread his arms wide to take in the dozen armored vehicles, two of them tanks, that the bunker held.

"Oh...that." The centurion gave a friendly smile. "This is a hide for equipment, one of many here at *Lago Sombrero* and some other places. What does it look like?"

"Like a hide, I suppose. Let me rephrase. Why are we hiding equipment here?"

The centurion shook his head. "Because one never knows when a tercio's worth of armor no one knows about may come in handy."

"Who knows about this?"

"Me, the First Legion commander, the Penonome Military Academy commander, *Duque* Carrera and a few of the staff, and now, you."

"I don't think I want to know anything about any of this, Centurion."

"Too late, son. I needed help moving all this shit. Fernandez's group came up with your name as the most closed-mouthed man in the First Legion. So here you are. We'll be filling up the rest of the non-ammunition bunkers a vehicle or two at a time for the next couple of years. We also have to come in from time to time to check the vehicles out. Then, too, we have a list of supplies that need storing here. I suppose it goes almost without saying that this has to be our little secret, right?"

"How do I get into these things?"

"Just lucky, son," the centurion answered, "just lucky.

"Look, don't sweat it," the centurion added. "It's all

really simple. Every month or so, just before a time when the weather and light conditions are going to be just right, and we know there are no recon satellites or UEPF ships overhead, a new track or two, sometimes maybe three or four, will be delivered to the First Legion. They'll duly issue it and pull in an older track to go in to the depot for rebuild. Except that about fifty percent of the time the 'old' track will have just come out of rebuild, in which case it comes here. And then we prep it for long term storage. Speaking of which, go over to that cabinet and pull out the plastic wrap inside. Then get us a tank of nitrogen from the cabinet next to the first one."

"Nitrogen? Why nitrogen?" The soldier sounded nervous.

"Didn't you ever have any chemistry in school? I said nitrogen, not nitroglycerin. It's not dangerous. We just use it to replace the air around the tracks—after we seal them in the plastic—so they don't rust away."

"Where did you learn to do this, Centurion?"

"Out of a book, boy. Well . . . that and a course run out on the *Isla Real*."

Executive Complex, *Ciudad* Balboa, Balboa, Terra Nova

Despite the high wall that surrounded the complex, the sounds of traffic could be heard even within the president's office. Parilla was pretty much deaf to those; what attention he had to spare was focused on listening for the sound of a Cricket, bringing Carrera in for a meeting.

The subject of which is not going to please friend Patricio, Parilla thought. *But when he gave up control of most of the money to the Senate he also assigned responsibility to the Senate. And they're taking their responsibilities seriously, seriously enough to say, "Halt, we're going broke!"*

The rest of his attention span Parilla gave over to reading a book, his reading glasses perched between the bridge and the end of his nose, while he waited for Carrera to show at his office. The government comptroller, *Señor* Dorado, was already seated.

One side effect of the Federated States' mandated repartition of the country was that the old executive offices had fallen inside the border of the enclave granted to the old government. Thus, while Parilla's government had physical control of the Legislative Assembly complex, there had actually been no place for the president to sit.

For a short while, during the time Carrera had first convalesced on the *Isla Real*, Parilla had made do with the *Casa* Linda and its outbuildings. That was, however, pretty damned suboptimal what with most of the population of the country being on the other side of the Tauran Union-controlled Transitway.

For another half a year, near enough, the president, cabinet and executive department had sat in various rented office spaces. This, too, had been something less than ideal, as getting the cabinet together for face-to-face communication was, given *Ciudad* Balboa's appalling traffic, always a time consuming and problematic activity.

Thus, in the time since Parilla had taken office,

much effort and no little amount of cash had gone into creating a new executive complex containing mansions for Parilla and his two vice presidents plus the cabinet officials, along with executive office buildings for all the major agencies, and barracks space for a cohort of guards. There was even a set of quarters for Carrera, as de facto chief of defense, though he and Lourdes had never moved in and had no intention of ever moving in.

When Carrera arrived at the receptionist area fronting Parilla's office he was greeted by a statuesque, slightly olive skinned, and intensely attractive brunette in her late twenties—Parilla's secretary and, so it was rumored, one of the old dictator Piña's many former mistresses. That the woman would have been a mere girl in her early teens at that time only made the rumor the more credible. The receptionist, Lucilla, stood and announced Carrera's arrival into an intercom, then walked—or, rather, swayed while moving forward—to open the door to Parilla's office. Turning the knob, she bent down just enough for Carrera to get an eyeful of most enchanting cleavage. She smiled at him as she straightened back up. It was a smile of interest and a statement of availability.

"I'm starting to get on in years, Luci," Carrera said. "Someday you are going to give me a heart attack doing that."

The woman answered, one eyebrow lifting for emphasis, "From that or from something else, *Duque*." Her smile grew into an invitation.

Carrera just shook his head, a regretful grin on his face. Thinking of Lourdes, he said, "I don't mind dying, dear, but I do have my preferences as to how. A knife in the back while I sleep is very low on that list."

Inclining her head and shrugging her shoulders, and incidentally jiggling her breasts, the woman just gave Carrera a look of something very like sympathy. *You don't know what you're missing.*

Power corrupts. Luci had been around power since her mid teens, about the time her breasts reached their full development. She was, in many ways, as corrupt as a human being could possibly be...and she liked corruption, too. Unnoticed by Carrera, Luci returned to her desk, picked up a phone and began to dial a number.

Parilla was already walking from his desk to the door to greet Carrera. He, too, took in a good eyeful of some of Balboa's loveliest scenery before closing the door behind Carrera and leading him to the small conference table that graced the office. The comptroller was already seated. He stood for the president and Carrera.

After a very brief period of small talk the accountant opened his briefcase and extracted a series of thick folders.

With a dramatic, even melodramatic air, Dorado said, "Without either a substantial drop in expenditures—or some large increase in revenues—the government will be bankrupt within five years."

Carrera stared at the accountant as if he were quite mad. Unfazed, Dorado continued.

"Numbers do not lie. With current defense expenditures hovering above two and a half billion per year, and expenditures growing as they are, we simply cannot meet the defense plan past that time. We will actually begin to feel shortages well before that. And if there is an economic downturn globally, even the admittedly huge sum you've turned over to senatorial control will drain away like dirty dishwater."

Parilla raised an eyebrow in Carrera's general direction.

Carrera shrugged. "It doesn't matter. We'll be at war with the Tauran Union within five years. After that, a little thing like bankruptcy hardly matters."

"Sure," Parilla agreed. "But what if we're *not* at war with the Taurans within that time? What if they can delay things for ten years?"

"Then we have a problem," Carrera admitted. "But, Raul, *now* is the time to be buying equipment. *Now* is the time to be buying shipping, or getting it under long-term lease, anyway. *Now* is the time to be bringing young boys and even girls into the legions, before the population bubble disappears. Our women used to be the most fertile on the planet. That's changed and I don't know if it's ever going back to the way it was."

Staring Carrera directly in the face, Dorado said, "Of all your programs, only those run by Professor Ruiz are not ruinously expensive. Even then, his radio, television, films, music, and translations of military works don't quite break even, even with foreign sales. Of course, since you directed that the Military Museum, which falls under Ruiz's department, not charge more than a quarter drachma for entrance, that's a loser. I have given the money from the anticrime campaign over to the professor to keep his department running."

Carrera perked with interest. "Money from the anticrime campaign?"

"Yes, *Duque*," Dorado said. "We've had to sell

seized property at distress sale prices, but still there was cash, some gold, seized bank accounts, a couple of yachts, one small merchant vessel, some residential property. It made us about two million last month. Of course, if the campaign is ultimately successful, you can expect that source of funds to dry up too."

Carrera leaned back in his chair, covering his eyes and rubbing his eyebrows with his fingertips. *Victims of our own success. I suppose I am pushing expansion faster than I should. But I've only so much time. Where do I get more money? A lot more.*

To Parilla he said, "I'll look into finding some other sources of funds. Or maybe let Esterhazy"—the legion's comptroller and investment officer—"run a little wild."

Isla Real, Balboa, Terra Nova

Carrera had come out of his post-Hajar funk with a base suitable for a small corps of about fifty thousand. That amount of barracks space, recreation facilities, housing areas, hospitals, and the like was more than adequate for the number of new trainees the legion had to take on annually, roughly thirty-six thousand. Indeed, it was about three or four times more than was actually required, since thirty-six thousand annually meant about twelve to fourteen thousand at any given time, plus a few thousand regulars in professional development courses. That excess didn't even include the dependent housing areas, most of which were unneeded now that only a small percentage of the population, the regular cadre, was even allowed to have families on the island. Centurions and optios were living in spacious quarters formerly reserved for tribunes and legates.

There were still several myriad jobs to be done before the *Isla Real* and the other islands of the chain could serve to guard the northern approaches to the capital and the Transitway. There was, for example, already one dual pier for offloading supply ships. For an island fortress with a good expectation of being bombed viciously in the not too distant future, one double pier could not be enough.

There was already an all-weather, hard surfaced, asphalt ring road that roughly paralleled the island's coast, connecting tercio casernes with ranges, training areas, and the more complete facilities of the main post, to the north, by the tadpole's tail. That asphalt could be expected to be turned into craters interspersed with boulders under a sustained, intensive aerial attack. Thus, both a parallel system of easily repaired dirt roads and a half-subterranean, narrow gauge railway were under construction.

During Balboa's long wet season, roughly eight thousand tons of water fell on every square kilometer of the island...*every*...*day*. The drainage system they had was adequate for peacetime purposes. It would crumble under sustained aerial assault, making defensive positions untenable, providing vastly expanded breeding grounds for insects, and potentially opening up any defenders to the triple scourges of malaria, yellow, and dengue fever.

Thus, the drainage system, too, was being revetted, backed up, supplemented, and—for some lines—moved underground.

Sitnikov had actually given Carrera only a truncated

version of the fortification plan. There was much he had not covered. For example, eventually there would be just under three hundred kilometers of one-meter culvert and tunnels of varying dimensions connecting various positions within the defense plan.

The Volgan tanker had demonstrated the types of bunkers to be built, but hadn't gone into their deployment in any depth. For example, the centerpieces for the defense were to be thirteen forts, each dominating a piece of key terrain or a probable landing site. Those forts would typically consist of fifty to sixty of the type of heavy bunkers Sitnikov had demonstrated, but those bunkers would be connected by tunnels, trenches, and culverts, draw their air from remote intake sites, and have very deep and strong shelters for their garrisons. Redundant tank turrets, emplaced in concrete, would also cover any bunkers that could not be covered by the limited firing arcs of other bunkers.

Then there were the sixteen hundred positions to be built for armored vehicle hides; some seven per actual vehicle. Artillery and mortars needed an additional four hundred and sixty real firing positions, as well as several times that in plausible fakes.

The nearby islands of Santa Josefina and Pablo Gutierrez were slated for similar treatment.

The general layout of the defensive scheme was that the big island would be divided into several areas. Nearest the coast would be a triple defensive line. Each of those three lines was to consist of platoon battle positions that would have three-hundred-sixty-degree security, thus preventing more than a couple of kilometers from being rolled up once a penetration was made.

That was known as the coastal defense area, although it did not, generally speaking, cover the actual coast so much as it restricted it. Snipers, mines, obstacles, and a few concrete mounted tank turrets would actually see to waterfront defense, though delay was a better word, of the first few hundred meters inland from the high tide waterline.

Behind the coastal defense area was the artillery area. It, like the coastal defense area, was somewhat arbitrarily named. Infantry would also be present, as would support troops who could serve as second and third line infantry in a pinch. The artillery area would contain the redundant Suvarov-class cruiser turrets allocated to the *Isla Real*, as well as bunkers—many disguised as ammunition bunkers for the cruiser turrets—for fifty-four 180mm guns. There were also six battalions of 160mm mortars—eighteen batteries— intended for the island. Given the presumed enemy air superiority, most of the time, at least, each of these batteries needed seven alternate positions.

Behind the artillery area, in a dense ring about Hill 287, was the core area. This was to contain most of the deepest and strongest shelters, plus a thick glaze of defensive bunkers, and would serve as the nexus for power distribution (two small Hakunetsusha nuclear reactors were intended to back up the island's existing solar chimney which was expected to last mere minutes after the initiation of hostilities), and transportation of troops and supplies.

"Full employment's a wonderful thing," said Sam Cheatham to Carrera, as they watched one of Cheatham's larger crews creating a new company-sized fortress on the island. Cheatham was the CEO of the Balboa Foundation and Wall Company, S.A. In some ledgers this corporation was also known as the Seventieth Engineer Tercio, *Legion del Cid,* just as Cheatham appeared on some rosters as "Legate Samuel Cheatham."

"How far along are you with this one, Sam?" Carrera asked.

The engineer shrugged, saying, "About a quarter done, though the thing won't really be ready until the concrete's had some time to cure.

"Come on down, let me show you how the boys work."

BFW had organized itself into several teams for the effort. The first, or "survey," team found and marked the site for the fort's bunkers, shelters, and tunnels according to the master plan. It also marked the direction in which the bunkers were to be able to fire. Following the survey team, an "access" team made sure that the construction equipment and materials would be able to get close enough to the planned site.

Sometimes the access team needed to do nothing; trees in triple canopy jungle grew rather far apart. At other times the team had to cut a tree or a few trees, lay some steel planking, gravel or light asphalt, or build a trough from the nearest convenient point to the bunker site.

An excavation team did such digging as the bunkers, the shelters, and the culverts and tunnels that would lead to them required. Where needed they also put in temporary supplements to the main drainage system. The excavators were careful to preserve the topsoil and any vegetation separately before digging deeper. There was no ecological motive in this; they simply wanted the soil and plant life for natural, self-replenishing camouflage.

Some excavators used heavy digging equipment. Other excavation was done by hand by some hundreds of healthy and strong criminal prisoners—politicals were not used on the works—serving sentences of less than fifteen years. These earned two days of "good time" for every day of adequate performance. The work was hard, but since the food was rather better than a prison's mess, because a small stipend was paid, and because of the chance to live something closer to a normal life, convicted criminals tried very hard to get on the program. Another inducement, not much mentioned, was occasional access to a small brothel integral to the temporary prison camp. Female criminals—again not politicals—gained the same benefits as the male laborers for service in the brothel. As with the excavators, only volunteers were accepted for service in the brothel and health was an absolute requirement.

Looks were not, but then again, criminals didn't really deserve the best.

"We reached bedrock with this one," Cheatham explained in a loud voice, pointing into a hole. "We don't always."

Over the noise of the jackhammers scoring the bedrock to allow rock to displace in the event of a subsurface burst from a penetrating bomb, Carrera asked, shouting, "What if you can't reach bedrock?"

"In those cases," Cheatham answered, "the excavators bore anywhere from three to seven holes down to bedrock and set up concrete pylons to support the base of the bunker. Sometimes the bunker has to be built on a sort of concrete 'raft' to prevent it sinking into the ground or being displaced by a near miss from a bomb."

Carrera nodded. "Ah, yes, Sitnikov mentioned the rafts to me once."

A substantial team of tunnelers, these from Balboa Exploratory Mining, a wholly owned subsidiary of Balboa Foundation and Wall (and also known as 4th Cohort (Heavy Construction), Seventieth Engineer Tercio) had dug space for the two-hundred-and-forty-man shelter inside of the hill the fort was intended to dominate. This was more than the strength of a normal infantry maniple but it was assumed that the fort might well be cut off and have to be self-sufficient for a period of time until relieved. It would be manned by a very overstrength company.

The tunnel to the shelter was some eight hundred and thirty meters long, with its entrance toward the center of the island. The tunnel entrance, too, had outlying bunkers to cover it, which bunkers could only be reached from culverts leading off from the tunnel.

"Who are they?" Carrera asked, still shouting over the jackhammers below.

"The 'Rebars,'" Cheatham shouted back. "The 'Rebar and Mold Detachment.' Concrete hasn't much tensile strength on its own. They put in the rebar lattice—reinforcing iron rods—that give tensile strength to the concrete."

Cheatham pointed to a different crew, sweating, straining, grunting, and cursing for every meter gained, as they rolled precast concrete culverts to the site and laid and joined them in the trench behind a bunker's hole.

"We use from twenty to seventy meters of culvert to join each bunker to either the central shelter or a tunnel. We mostly cut and cover those. See those old plastic soft drink bottles?"

Carrera, tired of shouting, nodded.

"They keep their shape and they don't degrade under environmental stress. We put them around the culverts to provide a bit of space for earth displaced by bombardment. It ain't perfect but we think it will help."

Away from the central shelter, the BFW carpentry department (Bravo Maniple, 2nd Cohort) built—or rather, since the parts were manufactured at a central site near the cantonment area and then moved, rebuilt—the wooden interior mold to a fighting bunker. That was heavy plywood, mostly, with strong wooden beams at the corners and edges. Heavier logs formed a roof that would absorb spalling if the shelter took a direct hit on top from a bomb large enough to break pieces from the interior face of the concrete. A thick layer of synthetic rubber was glued to the interior of the plywood mold to help reduce the concussive effects of incoming high explosives.

A steel mold was erected around the rebar. It was perpendicular to the ground on the sides. Several other mold sections, which formed a dome when joined over the main construction, were set up nearby. The overall site engineer—in the corporation's military configuration he was a tribune—returned during the molding and rebaring phase to direct the placement of the flattish trapezoidal shapes that defined the firing ports so that they would cover the maximum possible terrain while providing the minimum possible target. The sometime tribune had to slither through the rebar, snakelike, to get behind the trapezoidal mold in order to orient it just right.

The Rebars also installed the pipes that would allow grenades to be dropped from the inside of the design to the revetted ditch that would be left in front of it. They emplaced the double-curved pipe that would provide an air vent—doubly curved with a drainage pipe that led outside to prevent inflammables being poured down it into the bunker. Fixtures for steel shutters were added in this phase of construction along with the pintle that would hold and guide the cradle for the bunker's eventual main weapon.

"Come on," Cheatham shouted, "they're ready to pour that one."

That one, Carrera saw, was a major fighting bunker.

The molds were in place, covering the lattice of rebar that would reinforce the structure. A trough led to them from a cement truck just off of the road. At a signal from the engineer foreman (who also happened to be a reserve centurion; go figure) the truck driver wrenched a lever. Cement, good quality Portland with a partially coral aggregate and reinforcing aramid fibers for added tensile strength, began to flow down the trough, helped by engineers with paddles.

"We put in an additive," Cheatham explained, in a somewhat softer voice now that they'd left the jackhammers behind. "It helps the concrete flow."

The first concrete filled the floor and sealed around the culvert that, along with the bunker, would later be covered by earth. The culvert led to another excavation, deeper and wider. The first truck was empty before the area defined by the molds was more than one sixth filled.

When the first truck had pulled out, empty, another pulled into position to dump its six cubic meters. Then came a third, fourth, and fifth through ninth. During the pour of the sixth, seventh, and eighth trucks the construction crew added sections of dome mold and threw in an assortment of shaped pieces of plastic, of an average dimension of two inches on a side.

"Good job, boys," said the foreman of the crew. "Back to the truck. We can fill three or four more before nightfall."

"It'll be a couple of days," Cheatham said as he escorted Carrera back to his vehicle, "but that bunker is now the responsibility of the 'Recovery' team. They'll wait until the concrete's set sufficiently for the molds to be taken down, then pass the molds on back to the 'Rebars.' The interior mold, the treated plywood, we leave in place.

"After that, a couple of days after, the 'General Labor Group' comes in to put more hollow plastic cubes and soda bottles around the sides and then fill the dirt back in over the bunker and the cubes and culvert. They also do the recamouflaging with the foliage we stripped off in the beginning."

"Remind me," Carrera said, a look on his face composed half of wonder . . . and half of financial desperation, "remind me of just how much concrete we are going to be using."

"This fort will take seventy-two hundred cubic meters," Cheatham answered, without hesitation. "Some forts will take a bit less, others, somewhat more. More than ten times what goes into the forts is going into the entire program. If you want a big figure, that's one hundred and five thousand truckloads of concrete. If you want a little one, it's only going to equal a cube about one hundred and ten meters on a side.

"Of course, that's still about what went into the Maginot Line, six centuries ago, on Old Earth. And," Cheatham added, "we have some advantages over that system of fortifications. We can't be flanked."

CHAPTER TEN

Along with all the other illusions and frauds of human existence, there have been and are the millennial philosophies, those reform movements who promise us a paradise in this life, if only we would X or Y or Z. There are at least three common problems with these philosophies. One is the Year Zero problem. Another is the assumption of a closed system problem. The third, related to the second, is the illusion, perhaps better said, *de*lusion, of the possibility of permanence.

It is the last, the delusion of permanence, that allows the millennialist to avoid the need to realistically define and measure good and evil not merely by their intensity and scope, but also by their practical duration. Assuming permanence, an infinity of good results, allows the millennialist to accept, even to advocate, *any* and *every* practical amount of evil because, measured on the scale of a presumed infinity, any good, however trivial, must outweigh any evil, however vile, done to achieve it. Kill twenty million. Nay, kill two hundred million. Even these levels of atrocity cannot compete with even a tiny permanent improvement in the lot of mankind. That this is intellectually sloppy bothers the millennialist not at all.

Of course, nothing is permanent without being in a closed system. Millennialist philosophies are illegitimate for that reason alone.

The Year Zero problem, the problem that society and custom are as they are and will carry their effects over into the future, can, of course, be overcome . . . provided one is able to identify and willing to kill everyone whose values are conditioned by having, unfortunately, been born prior to the millennialist turning back of the clock to some presumed, and mythical, Golden Age. Unfortunately, even were it possible, this leaves alive only people with no values whatsoever.

> —Jorge y Marqueli Mendoza, *Historia y Filosofia Moral,* Legionary Press, Balboa, Terra Nova, copyright AC 468

Anno Condita 471
Hotel *Rustico,* San Antonio, Balboa, Terra Nova

The town was situated in the caldera of a long dormant volcano. Because of that volcanic soil, the caldera was lush and green beyond the power of mere words to describe. Mathematics could describe it after a fashion. Simply multiply the greenest thing imaginable by something approaching infinity. That would have been a fair approximation.

The hotel itself was almost snug up against the sheer western side of the caldera. This area was, if anything, greener still, except where it was an explosion of flowers. Too high up for mosquitoes, the place was almost supernaturally healthy. Some of this health may have derived from the sheer joy of being there.

Many well-to-do Balboans kept holiday places there, some, like the hotel and its name, quite rustic, others nearer to palaces. Legate Pigna, for example, of the Seventh Legion, kept a place there, as did several twigs of the Rocaberti family tree. For that matter, so did Arias, the senior man of those police still loyal to the old government and President Rocaberti. It had, in fact, been the policeman who, upon hearing of the mass ass chewing delivered by Carrera to all his senior leaders and staff, had found and sounded out Pigna before inviting him to this meeting.

"Oh, take the idiotic fake mustache off," said one of the men gathered in the back room of the Hotel *Rustico*. "It's not like any of us don't know who you are, Pigna. It's not like everybody who is anybody in Balboa doesn't know everyone else who is anybody."

Pigna glared down at the speaker, one of the rump president's nephews, a young but very fat man he knew only by sight. That clan tended to run to fat, anyway, and as far as he was concerned, they all looked alike. He was about to reply when he heard a group of Cadets or perhaps Young Scouts marching by the front of the hotel singing:

> "... *together with the legions then,*
> *Rise up together with the legions then.*
>
> *In the morning we rise early*
> *Long before the break of dawn,*

Trixies screeching in the jungle,
Moonbats scurrying from the sun.

Now assemble, mis compadres.
Gather, boys, and muster, men,
Hand to hand with butt and bayonet,
Let their blood across the homeland run.

And you are welcome, Balboenses.
Side by side we'll make our stand
Hand to hand with butt and bayonet.
We'll rise up together with the legions
　　then..."

"*That,*" said one of the men present—Pigna assumed he was foreign, probably Tauran, Gallic, from his accent, "is a chilling thing to hear from the throats of barely post-pubescent teenagers. I'm de Villepin, by the way."

"Your children don't sing songs like that in Gaul?" Pigna asked.

De Villepin shook his head, confirming his origins. "No . . . not anymore. The bureaucrats would have apoplexy. There they sing about peace and love, the Family of Man, and glories of the Tauran Union."

"It's aimed at you, you know," Pigna said. "They're raising a generation here that, with the best of democratic motivations, wants to rip out your throats and drink the blood."

"We know," de Villepin replied. "It is . . . worrisome. It is even worrisome to my . . . superior, General Janier. We must put an end to it before that generation grows to manhood."

"Never mind all that," said another of the men present. Pigna recognized him as the old head of the police, one of the Arias brood, now reduced to lording it over the couple of companies of police left to the old president in the old city. "We all know what the problem is and why we're here. We have to put a stop to all this . . . this . . . madness."

"It would be better if you could do that for yourselves," said de Villepin. "Oh, yes, we would help behind the scenes. But still, in the long run, it is best if you take the initiative."

"With what?" said the policeman. "I've got less than five hundred men that I control and no more than that number that would go along with me in the hope of restoring old times again."

"Ah," said Pigna, "but I have over four thousand. And by the time I am in a position to do anything it will be closer to ten thousand."

"In a position?" de Villepin enquired.

Pigna sighed. "On the scale of the force being created my one *legion* doesn't count for much. Applied in the right place, it could count for a lot. But I can't just mobilize it and move it. We'd be intercepted and destroyed on the road or in the air. On the other hand, in about a year or fifteen months we'll do our annual training at the *Centro de Entrenamiento Nacional*, at Fort Cameron, not all that far from here. That would put us in a position to seize certain key facilities."

"You've been giving this some thought," Arias accused.

Pigna didn't deny it, but did say, "Enough to know that I can't do it alone. I can possibly hoodwink my men into seizing President Parilla, for example, if I told them it was Carrera's order, but they would never, not in a million years for a billion drachma, seize Carrera. I can get them to, say, take over the television and radio stations and seal the City off from traffic. They would not attack other regiments in the legion unprovoked."

He looked very pointedly at de Villepin and added, "Any plainly Tauran activity, any attack made openly, would shatter the illusion I would create for those men and lose me control over them."

De Villepin nodded agreement. This one *had* been giving it some thought.

"We can probably restrict our activities to the fairly clandestine," the Gallic intelligence chief agreed. "Say, using a commando group to take Carrera and sundry other of the legion's highest ranking men. And perhaps Parilla if we decide that would be best."

"The corps commanders and General Staff," Pigna said. "Get them and I'm a fair shot for first among equals. If my legion is in a position of control, I would *be* first among equals."

"I doubt we could keep such a vast enterprise secret, or hide our involvement long before being discovered," the Gaul objected.

"Block the road from the City to *Valle de las Lunas* and you would take more than half out of the picture, at least for a while. And, if you chose the right place and right method of blocking, it could be many days before anyone discovers your involvement."

This, de Villepin considered. "Perhaps," he conceded. "It would help if we could somehow convince the Federated States that we were acting in their interest in doing all this." He mused, "Perhaps a bit of lawfare would be in order."

Belalcázar, Santander, Terra Nova

The place was by no means upscale. Waitresses bantered with customers, cooks shouted out for orders to be picked up, flies buzzed lazily from table to table. In this restaurant of no great name or reputation, two men who took some pains to *have* neither name nor reputation sat over coffee. One was an assistant to one of the members of the increasingly powerful Belalcázar Drug Cartel; the other a specialist in moving drugs from Santander, where they were grown and processed, to Southern Columbia and Taurus where they were avidly consumed. Neither felt any guilt at being in the drug trade. Either, if asked about guilt, would probably have answered that drugs were a South Columbian and Tauran problem; that, even if the trade from Santander stopped, those who craved the drugs and those who profited from the craving would simply look to new sources and new—even homemade—drugs.

After several hours of conversation the two men reached across the table to shake hands. The deal was struck. Seven tons of nearly pure *"huánuco"* paste (in fact, an extract of the leaves of a primitive plant, apparently brought to Terra Nova by the Noahs, that might or might not have been an ancestor to or relative of the terrestrial coca plant but which at least produced a very similar alkaloid) would leave Santander within the week to travel through Balboa on their way to the Federated States, Secordia, and the Tauran Union.

Aduana (Customs), Herrera International Airport, *Ciudad* Balboa, Terra Nova

As with many public servants in the less developed parts of Terra Nova, *Señor* Donati was much underpaid. As with nearly all of those, he supplemented his income, where possible, through a mixture of cash for favors. Sometimes these were trivial, both the favors and the cash. Sometimes they could be quite substantial.

Chief of the main airport's customs office, Mr. Donati was well placed for both the doing of great favors and the receipt of great rewards. He was at the moment engaged in the former, in anticipation of the latter.

And it's so easy, he thought, quietly filling out the necessary forms to insure the easy passage of several crates of what he assumed were drugs. The crates were due in on a flight from Belalcázar later this afternoon. Twenty thousand drachma were already in the chief's wife's account; fair payment for little more than looking the other way and approving and amending a few forms. The payment had started considerably larger. But, of course, the chief had not been able to keep everything the Santanderns had given him. Some few thousands went to his men in the *Aduana*. Rather more went to certain high-ranking people in the rump government of the Republic, which still had considerable influence among the civil police and customs service.

In particular, thought Donati, *the office of the president—the old president—always insists on its cut.*

Still, what Donati had been able to keep made quite a tidy sum. Certainly in Balboan terms it did.

Almost as valuable as the money given directly, the

Santanderns had also given the customs chief a bagged kilo of nearly pure stuff. This was neatly stowed in the chief's briefcase. He would turn it over to a street dealer this evening for many thousand drachma more.

And none of that had to be shared.

Executive Complex, *Ciudad* Balboa, Terra Nova

The Honorable Thomas Wallis, Ambassador to the Republic of Balboa from the Federated States of Columbia, shared few of the values of his more enlightened kindred. Wallis was an ordinarily friendly faced, medium-height, slightly heavyset man, who wore his suit somewhat uncomfortably. There were reasons for that, as there were for the lack of shared values, as there were reasons why *he* had been made ambassador, to the complete surprise of himself and everyone else.

The reason for the lack of comfort when wearing a suit, and for the rest, was that Wallis had been a career soldier before entering his country's foreign service. Surprise or not, given how badly the Federated States had needed the troops of the legion for the campaigns in Sumer and Pashtia, and given how few career soldiers it had in its ranks, Wallis had been a natural. Parilla and Carrera could *talk* to him, with confidence that what they said would be understood, and that their concerns would find a sympathetic ear.

"Ambassador," Carrera began, ". . . Tom, I don't know what you and the Federated States want from us. We're already doing everything possible to stop the trade through or near Balboa. The *classis* is engaged almost entirely in drug suppression."

"Which the Federated States pays for," Wallis corrected.

"Which the Federated States pays most, but not all, of the operating costs for," Carrera further corrected. "Which is a drop in the bucket, anyway, compared to salaries, food, wear and tear on the ships..."

"Which you would have to pay for anyway," Wallis finished.

"Which we would have to pay for anyway," Carrera conceded, with a sigh. "But that doesn't change that we're still doing everything we can."

"And yet the drugs still get through," Wallis said.

Parilla suppressed a sneer, not so much at Wallis as at the policies of his country. Still, he said, "They wouldn't if you hadn't split our country."

"The Tauran Union is *not* running drugs," Wallis insisted.

"No, they're not," Parilla agreed, with a shake of his old, gray head. "At least so far as I *know*, they're not. But the stinking corrupt oligarchs you people insisted have a safe base in the capital *are* running the drugs."

Wallis inclined his head, skeptically. "Can you prove that?"

"We're working on it," Carrera answered.

"Right. And you know what the rump government says?"

"I can imagine," Parilla said. "But they're lying sacks of shit."

"*I* could stop the drug trade," Carrera said, a wicked, nasty tone in his voice. "I could stop it *easily*."

Don't go there, Patricio, thought Parilla. Though his friend was a lot better, a lot more human, these ten or twelve local months, there was still a monster lurking inside him, Parilla believed, which monster could emerge without warning. He sensed that monster's presence now.

"*I'd* just take all the drugs we seize in a year," Carrera continued. "Then I'd poison them—I might have to go to Volga for a suitable poison, something with a delayed effect, and then sell them to distributors in the Federated States and Tauran Union. No living drug users; no drug problem."

He sighed and Parilla sensed the monster retreating.

"Fortunately or unfortunately, though, I've given up the power to do that."

Fortunately, Wallis thought. *Because whether that would solve the problem or not, it would likely be considered an act of war.*

"Will the Federated States support us if we take measures against the rump government?" Parilla asked.

Wallis shook his head. "In the absence of overwhelming proof that they're guilty, probably not. Even with that proof, many in my government would not believe it. And even if they did believe it, the Tauran Union would not let you take serious measures against their charges. There *is* a minority in the FSC—a large minority—that would like you to simply disappear."

"And *still* you expect us to do something about this beyond what we're doing," Carrera said. "Well, fine, but you won't like *that* either."

Wallis answered, "The way you might be inclined to do it? Probably not. But Pat, it's not like the Federated States isn't willing to foot the bill in exchange for a little control. And we'll help you with any intelligence we have."

❖   ❖   ❖

Later, after Wallis had left, Parilla asked with exasperation, "Why, Patricio? Why the hell do you feel compelled to say things like that?"

"Because it's the truth." Carrera shrugged. "When the Federated States invaded this country all those years ago—and remember, I was part of that invasion—we killed *your* people, now *my* people, because of a problem that originated in the Federated States. I didn't care too much about that at the time, but I do now. It was wrong and it was *useless*. The sheer fact that Wallis has a reason to come and bitch at us now shows us how useless it was.

"I mean, *really*, Raul; the sheer *arrogance* of the bastards, blaming Balboa for their own *weakness*." Carrera practically spat out the last word.

When Patricio goes native, Parilla thought, *he really goes native.*

"I need to talk to the full Senate," Carrera said.

And when he says he's going to subordinate himself to something he keeps his word . . . even if he has to wrap himself in chains to do it.

"I'll set it up." Parilla chewed on the inside of his cheek for a few moments, eyes darting upwards as he pulled up a mental calendar. "They're not meeting in full session for about four days. Will that do?"

"That would be fine. Thanks, Raul."

Parilla nodded briskly, then asked, "Just out of curiosity, what do you want from the Senate, and since I preside over it, me?"

"We need to do something ostentatious to keep the FSC at least neutral."

Parilla coughed. "Ostentatious?"

"Yes," Carrera agreed. "Ostentatious. An official declaration of war would be 'ostentatious.'"

Curia (Senate House), *Ciudad* Balboa, Balboa, Terra Nova

Whereas the Legislative Assembly building which predated the partition of the country was large, modern, and ostentatious to the point of tackiness, the building in which the one hundred and forty odd senators plus Parilla met was, if anything, understated. Its exterior walls were of dressed but unpolished granite from the quarries on the other side of the Transitway. A portico projected about thirty feet out from the main roof, held up by four columns of the same material as the walls. A single broad stone staircase the width of the building led down from the base of the columns to street level.

Flanked by guards, Carrera walked up those stairs, to the platform upon which rested the columns, to the bronze doors that guarded the main entrance.

"Guards stay outside, Jamie," Carrera said to Soult... who plainly didn't like the order. Soult nodded acceptance, even so, and posted the guards around the door.

At the door was a liveried servant of the Senate. Carrera announced himself to the servant formally, "*Dux Bellorum* Patricio Carrera requests audience with the Senate of the Republic." He then took out and handed over his service pistol.

This the senatorial servant tucked into his belt before he turned away to make the announcement. Carrera thought, *If these fuckers stand at attention when I*

come into the chamber I will kill *them.* He then asked
himself, *Hmmm, why is that? Answer: Because I need
them to be a* check *on me, not a rubber stamp, not
a collection of subordinates.*

Parilla, sitting in a curule chair, wondered, *Will
these people understand what I've explained to them,
that they must not treat Patricio as their boss for his
sake? I hope so. We can't put on him, or let him take
upon himself, all the moral burden. Not anymore. If
we do, we'll crush him. And if we crush him, lose
the use of him, we'll lose our country permanently.*

The senators didn't rise, though plainly enough some
of them weren't comfortable with remaining seated. In
any case, instead Carrera gave a polite half bow and
began to speak. "Thank you, President Parilla, gentlemen of the Senate, for agreeing to listen to me today."

Again, *almost,* Carrera began his speech with the
words, *Conscript Fathers.* Since however, he actually
had more or less conscripted the Senate, he thought
better of it. Besides, his speech, while intended to
affect the senate, had for form's sake to appear to
be aimed primarily at Parilla.

"It has been pointed out to me," Carrera said,
"that the Federated States of Columbia is in a war.
It has also been pointed out to me that we, here in
the Republic, are *de jure* neutrals in that war. Indeed,
we patrol, partially at our own expense and partially
at the expense of the FSC, in order to maintain our
neutrality in that war, by keeping those prosecuting
that war *out* of our territory.

"That war is their war on the illegal trafficking in

drugs. Besides the Federated States on the one hand, and their cobelligerents, the Tauran Union, on the other, the other parties are a mix of criminals, social revolutionary guerillas turned criminal, and even some persons"—Carrera didn't mention the rump government by name, but deliberately looked in the general direction of the old Presidential Palace to make the point—"within the Republic."

Carrera swept fierce eyes across the senator-filled pews. "Our neutrality is being violated. Not only are drugs passing through our porous borders and coasts, the paramilitary arm of some of the drug-trafficking organizations has set up housekeeping to the west, on the border where our province of La Palma touches Santander. They cross that border, into our territory, regularly and with impunity."

He looked directly at Parilla. "It must stop, *Señor Presidente*. If it does not, the Federated States, the Tauran Union, for that matter, would be within their rights to violate our compromised sovereignty . . . in self defense."

Parilla thought, *Which, if you think about it, would accord with what we suspect of Tauran Union plans perfectly.*

"What do you ask of us, *Duque*?" asked Parilla, leaning forward in his chair.

"We must make war," Carrera answered, "with the specific goals of reestablishing our neutrality. I think it would be better, for a number of reasons, if we did that openly, through a legitimate declaration."

Parilla nodded gravely, then looked to his left and then his right. "Senators, have you questions for the *Duque*?" he asked. When no hands came up Parilla glared, letting his baleful eye land on certain senators in turn. *You people are* paid *to ask questions. You had better have some.*

One hand immediately shot up.

"Senator Robles," Parilla said, "you are recognized."

"Thank you, Mr. President," the dark-skinned ex-legionary said. Turning to Carrera, Robles asked, "Whom, specifically, *Duque*, do you intend to target?"

"Initially, Senator, the guerillas *cum* narco-traffickers in La Palma Province, the gangs within the Republic that I have reason to believe are their adjuncts, and the seaborne smugglers."

"Not the producers and wholesale suppliers then?"

Carrera hesitated for a moment before answering, "I'd like to. Oh, Senators, you have no idea how much I'd like to." *If for no other reason than to ensure that the FSC remains at least neutral.* "But they are all in other countries, especially Santander and Atzlan. Attacking them would be invading people who ought to be our friends and who have more, much more, trouble from narco-traffic than we do."

"If we authorized you to attack them," Robles continued, "could you?"

"Unquestionably," Carrera answered, without a trace of hesitation. "Though not immediately. It would take some preparation." *Like a few hours' worth, which would not be enough time for anyone here to warn anyone there if we've made a mistake in selecting any of you.*

Robles sat down. Another hand went up.

"Senator Higuera has the floor," Parilla announced.

"What is the cost and how do we pay it?" Higuera asked.

"The cost is speculative at this point in time, Senator," Carrera answered. "We have it on good authority that the Federated States will pay all operational costs, as they do for our air and maritime patrols."

"Fair enough, for now," Higuera agreed, taking his seat.

"Senator Atencio," Parilla said, seeing a third hand.

Atencio, Carrera knew, was an attorney who had signed on with the legion early, for the initial campaign in Sumer, before taking his discharge and resuming his law practice. He'd worked in the Judge Advocate section, Carrera recalled, before casualties in the Sumerian city of Ninewah had required he be reassigned to leading an infantry section, then to command of a century.

And not badly, thought Carrera, looking at the *Cruz de Coraje en Oro* hanging from Atencio's neck above his tie.

"Rules of engagement, *Duque*?" Atencio asked.

"Wartime rules, Senator," Carrera answered, then added, "I had hoped to treat them as prisoners of war before turning them over to the National Police."

"Won't work, *Duque*, and you know it won't. The police are rife with corruption."

"Shall I try them and shoot them under military law then, Senator?"

"I will support such legislation," Atencio answered, "*if* we decide on war." He looked around the chamber and asked, loudly, "Will my colleagues?"

Seeing they would, Atencio sat down.

"Senator Cornejo?"

"They will retaliate, *Duque*," that Senator said. "Are you prepared for that? Are you willing to accept those casualties? Remember, in Santander those filth have brought governments down, murdered thousands, intimidated, bribed . . . undermined society from top to bottom."

"To terrorize us?" Carrera asked. "*I* can do terror. If *you* authorize it."

Cornejo laughed, being joined by dozens then scores more. "Oh, we know you can, *Duque*. We *know* you can."

Carrera emerged from the *Curia* with his face set in a grim smile.

"How did it go, boss?" Soult asked.

"Pretty well, Jamie. Do me a favor; get Jimenez and Suarez on the line and . . . Fernandez, Fosa, and Lanza. And Kuralski, since he's back on duty. Tell them it's a go. They lift at three in the morning. I have to go back in and hammer out some details. Notably, how to get the Legislative Assembly to approve using law of war rules within our territory."

"Then we *are* going to war again, boss?"

"Yes, Jamie," Carrera answered.

"About time."

The telephone rang next to Senior Centurion Ricardo Cruz. Cruz knew he could sleep through incoming artillery fire; he'd done it, after all, and more than once. A ringing phone, on the other hand, might mean an alert. *That,* he could never sleep through.

He picked up the phone. "Cruz," he announced sleepily.

"Cruz, you lazy bastard," said the voice on the other end. Ricardo recognized it as coming from his cohort's sergeant major, "Scarface" Arredondo. "Come on over. Free rum!"

That opened Cruz's eyes. "No shit? Free rum?"

"It's what I said, isn't it?" Scarface answered.

"Be right over," Ricardo said, replacing the phone on its hook. Next to him, his wife, Cara, stirred.

"Free rum?" she asked, then, seeing his nod, said, "*Mierde*," before laying her head back on the pillow and pulling the covers over her face. She didn't want her husband to see her cry.

Headquarters, Tauran Union Security Force–Balboa, Building 59, Fort Muddville, Transitway Area, Balboa

"*Merde*," said de Villepin. Shit.

The air in Janier's headquarters could only be described as panic-stricken. It was after duty hours; the staff had had to be recalled. Oddly enough, Janier had been found at home in bed with his *wife*.

Better, for once, thought de Villepin, *that he should have been with his mistress.*

One of the watch officers announced, "Fort Williams reports that helicopters are lifting—no, they don't know to where—and reservists are reporting in to their units . . . I've got eyewitness accounts of Suarez's corps, that's LdC Second Corps, moving their Cazador regiment to link up with the Balboans' *classis* . . . More reservists reporting in all over the city . . . No report of First Mechanized Legion . . ."

Janier, dressed in standard Gallic battle dress rather than his blue velvet monument to a bygone age, listened carefully. Worry grew inside the Gaul. *This is completely unprovoked. What the hell are they doing? What the hell are they planning? Should I roll the troops I have? Call for help from the TU? No, no sense in that; they can't get here in anything like quick fashion. And why wasn't I—*

He glared at his G-2, de Villepin. "Why the fuck wasn't I warned?"

"Because *we* had no warning, General. This was completely out of the blue." The G-2 shook his head in wonder. "Whoever thought they could mobilize so quickly? I didn't." De Villepin looked down at the carpeted floor, softly adding, "Who thought they could mobilize so secretly? Even for the previous exercise, that meeting they held of the leadership, I had a little warning a bit over a day out."

A Sachsen officer seconded to Janier's headquarters stuck his head in the door to the command post. "There's an officer here from the legion who wishes to speak with the general," the Sachsen announced.

De Villepin looked at Janier, who gulped first, then forced calm into his face and voice and said, "By all means. Show him to my office."

The Balboan officer was in battle dress. He had a pistol hanging from a shoulder holster, the shoulder holster being in brown leather. On his collar were pinned subdued rank insignia for a senior tribune, that much Janier could see for himself. How senior he didn't know, as he really had never thought it particularly important to study the small details of his adversary.

"My commander and my president wish me to

inform you that this mobilization is not aimed at you or your forces," said the senior tribune. Janier was startled to see the name "Carrera" above the tribune's right pocket.

"He's my brother-in-law," David Carrera explained. "He says to inform you that this mobilization is not aimed at you. He also says to inform you that it would be very easy to adjust his aim. Lastly, he says, do not mobilize your forces or he *will* adjust his aim."

Merde, thought Janier.

Later, after David Carrera had left, Janier called his logistics, intelligence, and operations officers into his office. The toad, Malcoeur, was excluded since there were no flies to be caught.

"Gentlemen," Janier said, civil among his social peers, "the fact of the Balboan mobilization, the speed and secrecy of the thing, makes me think we need something more here."

"We don't have room for any more ground troops," said the Log officer. "All the barracks are stuffed to overflowing and putting troops, long term, in tents is both expensive and unhealthy."

"Would it be sufficient to bring in another squadron or two of air?" de Villepin asked.

"No," answered the logistician. "Half the barracks at the air base are full of ground troops, too, and even were they not, the base is in range of more artillery than I care to contemplate. We'd just be giving the Balboans more targets with no commensurate increase to our power."

Operations poked a tongue into teeth turned yellow from smoking. His face indicated he was searching for an answer that was almost at the tip of his tongue. Janier looked at that face expectantly. His operations officer was handpicked, and came with rather a good reputation.

"The *Charlemagne*," ops said, suddenly. "Same airpower as a squadron... or rather more, really. No need for barracks. Nuclear powered so no fuel expense. And it's something the Balboans really don't have a good way to strike at."

"They do have an aircraft carrier," de Villepin objected. It was not stated very forcefully.

The ops officer shrugged. "They've got an old carrier, converted to a coastal raider, with a fair defensive suite, true, but with no high performance aircraft. It is not a match for *Charlemagne*, not nearly."

Janier nodded. The Gallic carrier would be a help. "Inquire," he said. "Paint a dire picture. Get me in a position where I do not have to worry about the shit the Balboans pull."

De Villepin looked museful for a moment. "Speaking of pulling shit," he said, "this might be a good way to bring in the commandos we need to assist *our* Balboans in their little project, without tipping anyone's hand. And, then too, the *Charlemagne* would be extremely useful in ensuring that no troops come from *Isla Real* to the mainland during those events."

Cruz Residence, *Ciudad* Balboa, Terra Nova

I am so tired of this shit, thought Cara, as she leaned against the doorframe of the house she shared with Cruz and watched her husband's back recede into faint light of the streetlamp. Cruz had his rucksack slung over one shoulder and his rifle gripped in the opposite hand. He placed both in the trunk, then walked to the automobile's door. He stopped to wave, once, and then opened the door and sat down, closing the door behind him. The car started with a muffled roar.

Cara Cruz sighed and shook her head. *How many times have I seen you off like this, standing alone in a doorway? I wish I understood what it is that calls to you. I wish I understood the smile you try to hide when going on active service.*

Of course I don't understand those things, not for a minute. All I understand is that there is a call, that you do love your work... and that I love you, you bastard.

Oh... and I understand that you know I'll be waiting here for you when you come home. Please come home.

BdL *Dos Lindas, Puerto* Jaquelina de Coco, La Palma Province, Balboa, Terra Nova

The early morning sun lit the sea, but only lightly upon the top and the edges of the coastal jungle. Centurion Ricardo Cruz rested his hands on the chain railing to one side of the ship's stern, looking at the shore as the ship made way parallel to it. Near his feet rested his pack and rifle. Around him, likewise seated on the deck, rested the men of his platoon.

It wasn't much of a port, Cruz thought. And, he surmised, it could never do as a homeport for a major warship. It didn't have much of an airstrip. It was not much of a town. Indeed, if one took and weighed every building in the town, plus the weight of the asphalt on the airstrip, and the two rock jetties that defined the port, the light aircraft carrier laying two miles off shore would still have outweighed the entirety of what was on land.

"No, it isn't much," Cruz mused. "And yet it is still ours, and no foreigners may walk in and take it from us."

I wish I could tell you, Cara, that that's the reason I'm here. But that would be a lie. The fact is that I love it, the action, I mean, and that I need it.

Cruz sensed the presence of another standing nearby. He turned to look and saw one of the swabbies of the *classis*.

"Centurion Cruz?" the sailor asked.

"Yes."

"I'm to lead you to the helicopters scheduled to take you in."

"Lead on, then, sailor," said Cruz, turning away from the shore and towards his men. "On your feet, boys."

Fosa, too, was quite unimpressed with the sleepy, mostly ramshackle town. "On the other hand," he mused from his bridge, watching his Yakamov helicopters boarding and launching chalk after chalk of foot soldiers to deposit them in and around the town and further into the jungle, "it does have some buildings; it does have an all weather airstrip, and—even if the port isn't up to sheltering the *Dos Lindas* or the *Tadeo Kurita*—it can still deal with small merchies, the escorts, and landing craft. So it's good enough for our purposes."

Suarez, standing to one side of Fosa, nodded. He

also looked at a chart which showed how much of his force, a mere fraction of one infantry legion, was ashore. With a single tick mark on the chart from one of Fosa's sailors, Suarez stood to attention, saluted and said, "I relieve you, sir." That tick mark indicated that half of Suarez's force was now ashore.

It's a small enough force to begin with, Suarez thought, *given the size of the area we have to reestablish control over.*

Fosa returned the salute and answered, "I stand relieved, sir." From that moment on, until and unless the fleet retired, operational control of both had passed to the land force commander, just as it had previously resided with Fosa, the commander of the naval force.

"Good luck, *compadre,*" Fosa added. "We'll support from here as we're able."

As if to punctuate that statement the four triple six-inch turrets of the BdL *Tadeo Kurita* rotated slightly. The center gun of number two then spoke in anger, flames and smoke shooting out over the water. Even as stunned or dead fish began floating to the surface, the entire ship barked out a twelve-gun broadside.

"Seems your boys have made contact with *somebody,*" Fosa observed.

Frente Nacional Liberacion Santerdereño (FNLS) Camp Twenty-seven, La Palma Province, Balboa, Terra Nova

If the town of *Puerto* Jaquelina de Coco wasn't much, FNLS Camp Twenty-seven, twenty odd miles to the south of it, was even less than that. At least Jaquelina had one paved road and some rooftops of solid material. The camp had mud and more mud, with open latrines dug none too deep and far too close to the well, some half-falling-apart *bohios* roofed with rotting leaves, hammocks strung between trees, and altogether too many flies and mosquitoes. That latter, especially, droned in swarms outside the nets slung by the denizens of Camp Twenty-seven as protection against them.

On the plus side, thought one of those denizens, "guerilla fighter" Esteban Escobar, as he glanced about at the surrounding squalor, *the work load ain't much. And there's pussy.*

The sun barely penetrated through the thick canopy overhead. Still, the mottled shadow hid little of the camp from those, just awakening, who inhabited it.

Esteban had once been a rather bright student at the national university in Santander's capital, a "dull middle-class grind," as some of his classmates had called him. Then he'd fallen in with a very pretty and very radical girl from the upper classes. She'd made certain introductions, first to her body, then to some illicit substances, and then finally to some friends. He'd left school—*Well, why not? My grades were going to shit in favor of sex anyway*—and joined the Movement.

His life as a guerilla had started out poorly and gone downhill from there. First there'd been the Army of Santander, hunting him and his comrades like vermin through the mountainous jungles. And they'd gotten progressively better at it, too. Even that wasn't the worst of it, though. The worst had been the things the police had done to break the guerillas' support networks in the towns and cities.

Little food, no money. And pussy—even, maybe

*especially, upper-class pussy—will only carry you so
far,* Esteban mused, swinging slowly from side to side
in his hammock. Absently, the guerilla's hand reached
up lightly to caress a small crucifix hung about his
neck. With so many Catholic priests in support of the
Movement, it was perhaps the only Tsarist-Marxist
inspired guerilla group on Terra Nova where the rank
and file were required to keep their religion.

There was a buzz in his ear. Esteban let go the
crucifix and swatted at a mosquito that had found a
hole in the netting he'd spread over his "bed." *Dammit. Missed the little bastard.*

In a quest for survival, Esteban and his "company"—
never more than about sixty-five fighters anyway—had
moved on. They'd had to move forward because the
"liberated zone" the government had temporarily granted
the FNLS as part of a ceasefire arrangement was already
at carrying capacity. There'd been no going back.

And wasn't that fucking brilliant, the guerilla thought.
*Vigilantes everywhere, within days of our showing up.
Fucking* Autodefensas!

In time, after many fights, few of them victorious,
the guerilla band, now reduced to thirty-seven, found
itself on the Balboa-Santander *frontera*, with no place
to go but into Balboa.

And here we "prosper." The jefes *back in Santander
send us processed drugs; we send them on; we get
a cut of the take. All in the interests of the people's
struggle against oppression, of course.*

*And all of which buys us some worn out, tumble
down huts, a shitty well, some muddy trails... and
some food and an occasional piece of ass from the
locals.* Viva la Revolucion!

"*La Revolucion,*" Esteban mentally sneered. *What is the revolution? Some upper-class pussy? A jefe smelling faintly of cologne that comes by every half year to lecture us on the dialectic? Running drugs to keep that jefe in style in Belalcázar? A priest who pretends to be a Catholic? Chinga la Revolucion. The revolution is nothing but taking the drugs to Puerto Jaquelina and transshipping them to some assholes in* Ciudad *Balboa.*

I want to go back home and start school again. I'm tired of this shit.

I want—what the fuck was that?

The aircraft—a Turbo-Finch Avenger—was basically a modified crop duster; armored, upengined, with thirteen hardpoints for ordnance and a fair electronics suite. They were cheap; they were tough; they were highly maneuverable. They also, with their comparatively fuel-sipping turboprop engine, had a very impressive range and loiter time. The one hanging over Esteban Escobar and his unwashed comrades had taken off from the military strip on the *Isla Real* some hours ago.

"Well, that's that," said Montoya into his radio, just after dropping the last of his original load of four electromagnetic pulse bombs and gunning the engine of his Turbo-Finch to get the hell out of range of the bomb before it fried all his electronics and left him at a very unpleasant "one with nature."

A voice answered; Montoya thought it might be the commander of the Air *Ala*, Lanza, himself, but couldn't be sure for all the static.

"Well done, Rafael. Head to the strip at *Puerto* Jaquelina de Coco. They're not ready to refuel and rearm you yet but they can receive you well enough. And the carrier's choppering in some fuel pods and ammunition pallets as they can."

"Beats a carrier landing," Montoya answered. "I'll be along."

Several kilometers behind and below Montoya's aircraft, a bright flash and somewhat muffled boom told of an EMP bomb doing its bit to fry every radio and satellite phono within a fairly large circle on the ground.

Lightning? Thunder? Esteban listened carefully for a while over the sounds of the jungle and its creatures. *No. Thunder and lightning aren't generally accompanied by the sound of an aircraft engine . . . or . . .* —he listened more carefully still—*maybe two or three of them. That I can* hear. *And . . . helicopters? Time to wake the* jefe, *I think. And I think maybe we're in neck-deep shit.*

God, I love *this shit*, Senior Centurion Ricardo Cruz thought to himself as he led his platoon through a neck-deep swamp twenty miles southeast of *Puerto* Jaquelina de Coco. Cruz, average height for a Balboan, which is to say, medium short, helmeted, dressed in pixilated jungle tiger stripes, sloshed along as quietly as possible, his F-26 rifle held above his head.

The platoon had been choppered in to a spot over the jungle onto which had been dropped a tree landing platform. This platform, basically a hexagon of pipes with six longer pipes leading from it to a larger hexagon, the whole connected by wires the better to catch on the foliage, and topped by chain link fencing, allowed helicopter-borne infantry to land atop the jungle rather than try to find a large enough landing zone. The men descended from the TLP by ladders hooked to the sides and let down through the thick canopies.

Cruz had had to rush and bully the men to get them off the helicopters and onto the uncertainly swaying platform, then do it all over again to get them moving down the ladders.

Well . . . reservists, most of them. One has to make allowances.

Now they moved as quickly as practical in a race to ambush a trail junction that intelligence insisted was regularly used by the denizens of several guerilla camps.

CHAPTER ELEVEN

The closed system problem itself consists of two related parts, belief in the practicality of social and technological stasis, even while insisting on material and/or moral betterment, and the unwillingness to accept that there are exterior issues beyond the control of the millennialist, which issues are beyond control *precisely* because they are exterior.

The easy assumption of social and technological stasis, of course, fails, again *precisely* because it is merely an easy and thoughtless assumption. And once it begins to fail, the millennialists, who cannot admit that their sophomoric fantasies are just that, turn to the secret police, the propaganda ministry, and thought control to enforce stasis.

Millennialists also, be they Ayn Rand, from Old Earth, or the Red Tsar, from New, or the cosmopolitan progressives, from both, also live under the implicit delusion that the universe stops at the end of their reach. Where was Rand's answer to the problem of national defense or of public health (by which we mean plague prevention, not socialized medicine)? She had none but wishful thinking. How did the Red Tsars imagine they would keep out the ephemeral information that led to the downfall of the Volgan Empire? Oh, yes, they could keep people from leaving the empire with barbed wire, walls, mines, machine guns, and dogs. But they could not keep information *out,* however hard they tried. The latter fact, acting on people imprisoned behind those walls and machine guns, was sure to cause an explosion. As for the Kosmos, even leaving aside the majority who appear to be nothing but unutterably corrupt and sanctimonious hypocrites, what is their answer to those who do not accept Cosmopolitan Progressivism and are aggressive about it? They have none. Or none they will admit to.

—Jorge y Marqueli Mendoza, *Historia y Filosofia Moral*, Legionary Press, Balboa, Terra Nova, copyright AC 468

Anno Condita 471
La Palma Province, Balboa, Terra Nova

Throughout the night Cruz's troops had sloshed through the swamp to the distant flash and muffled sounds of artillery. Now, with the water having receded to about ankle level, the sun was up and the damned mosquitoes were *feasting.* Worse, the platoon couldn't use any repellent; that might drive off the bugs but could also warn off the quarry. No one on Terra Nova had yet come up with an insect repellent that didn't stink. True, they had antihistamine pills for the swelling and itching. They also had to hope their inoculations and malaria pills were sufficient to ward off disease. Yellow fever was a disease particularly awful to contemplate.

Cruz didn't have a junior officer to train yet, and perhaps never would. For all the legion's rapid expansion, they kept to the rule: No more than three percent commissioned. Indeed, by the time he could expect the platoon to have an officer, it would probably have expanded to a maniple, of which he'd be first centurion, with two or three officers and seven or eight more optios and centurions.

On the other hand, not having an officer, in an armed force that didn't have a fetish for paperwork (for which function officers were, admittedly, useful) suited Centurion Cruz just fine.

Oh, all right! I suppose officers have other uses. But I don't need one for this.

Ahead, the point of the platoon, two men from second squad both raised a single fist overhead as they went to one knee. Water rippled outward in tiny waves from where the knees displaced it. All the rest of the platoon, except for Cruz, did likewise, in a wave running from front to rear. The centurion hunched over and walked forward to the point, perhaps a little awkwardly under his thirty-kilogram pack.

At the point, one of the scouts, holding middle and index finger together, pointed down slope to what appeared to be the junction of three trails, two leading east toward Balboa City and the Transitway, one leading west toward the Santander border. Cruz, laying his F-26 down carefully with the rifle's foregrip across his boot, pulled out his GLS receiver and map.

After about thirty seconds' worth of study, Cruz nodded, half to himself and half to the men on point. One finger went up, which Cruz rotated rapidly in a circle: *Squad leaders to me.*

While awaiting his immediate subordinates, Cruz cleared away some leaves and began drawing in the damp earth. His finger traced out the three trails, a river the map marked as being a bit farther on, and positions for his subordinates. Once those arrived, he began giving instructions in a soft voice.

For most of the men, this was a first combat mission.

Up to me to make sure it isn't a last *combat mission,* thought the centurion.

Esteban was the first one out of Camp Twenty-seven. This was more due to the fortuitous accident of being the first to warn the *jefe* than to any organization on the part of the *jefe* or his men. Organization was not actually a FNLS strong point anyway.

It was as well that he was the first one out. Before half the group had left, while the tail of the column was still forming, the camp had been suddenly drenched with a deluge of fire. With trees rising up and then collapsing to the jungle floor, with huts expanding out to their molecular components, and with the cries of butchered men and women somehow rising above the roar of the shells, Esteban and his comrades—such as remained—did what any sane men might do when faced with a power they *could not* resist. They ran.

The ambush on the trail leading to the Santander border was "V" shaped, where the apex of the V was at an angle of ninety degrees. At that apex, two M-26s, the light machine gun version of Balboa's F-26, aimed up the trail. The integral scopes for the machine guns were rotated off to the right side; for this kind of beaten zone in this kind of light, human eyesight, unaugmented, was superior to the highest practical technology.

Each arm of the V was composed of one squad. The third squad to the platoon Cruz had sent swinging out and westward, in two parts, to warn of the approach of others, to seal off the kill zone and "pick up the spare," and to act as security outposts for when Cruz and the platoon sprang their first ambush and then raced westward to set up two more.

Cruz, too, was at the apex of the V, his rifle set to one side and twin detonators for directional mines clutched in his hands. He glanced left at a nervous-seeming M-26 gunner. The gunner, Castillo, a short, stocky militiaman with about four months of initial entry training and maybe eight weekend drills, eighteen years old and scared shitless, felt rather than saw his centurion's gaze. Sheepishly, Castillo looked back at Cruz and forced a smile out, then discovered he felt the better for it. The gunner resumed peering through his sight. He didn't say a word, though he did think, *Thanks, Centurion. If you don't* look *worried, I guess I don't have to be.*

Thank God I got out of that camp in time, thought Esteban, still leading the remnants of his group and still moving at as fast a walk as his legs would support. Every now and again, when his path wasn't blocked by vines or the sparse undergrowth that popped up wherever a fallen jungle tree had opened a space for sunlight, Esteban looked behind him.

At least I've still got my chingadera *rifle!*

Not all did. Especially had those towards the rear,

the ones most nearly swept up in the flood of shellfire that had deluged Camp Twenty-seven, dropped theirs. Perhaps some had dropped the arms in shock. Perhaps others merely wanted to shed the weight to increase their speed. It didn't matter. Of the two thirds of the group that had escaped the shelling, over a third were weaponless.

"Jesus," Castillo whispered, hugging his face tighter to the stock of his machine gun while easing his finger off the trigger guard and onto the trigger. "Half the sorry bastards don't even have guns."

"Rifles," Cruz absently corrected. "And so what?" He tightened his fingers slightly on the detonators.

Directional antipersonnel mines—something like what would have been called "claymores" or "MONs" on another world, in another time—could in theory scour an ambush's kill zone free of life on their own. After all, each had about seven hundred ball bearings or small cylinders encased in plastic resin, those fronting a highly brissant explosive that should have shattered them into seven hundred projectiles, which seven hundred should have spread out and swept the ground more or less evenly.

Theory was one thing. In practice, some went into the ground and others too high into the air. Some stayed in groups of five or ten or twenty, nearly certain death should they hit something living and then split up, but considerably less likely to hit anything. And then there's the sheer malicious *chance* factor with explosives. They do odd things.

✧   ✧   ✧

Esteban saw the blossoming black and orange flowers before he felt a thing. It seemed to him that the first thing he felt was the displaced air from the passage of a zillion homicidal bees. Then he felt the explosions, rattling his brain as they pounded his body.

Shocked senseless, his fingers loosened on their own, letting his rifle slip to the ground. He was also distantly aware of something running down his legs toward the ground. Even with that, though, he was too shocked to feel any sense of shame.

Even before the chain of explosions had pummeled his body, Esteban saw flashes from the undergrowth. Only then did he become aware of the screams of his comrades, scythed down behind him.

Cruz couldn't see *shit* through the smoke from the mines and the dirt they kicked up. No surprise there; one rarely could. Instead, he trusted to chance for sixty long seconds while the rifles and machine guns swept across the kill zone. Some of them, at least, *should* have been able to see something. Cruz went by those sounds, by his own sense of timing, and by when the moans and screams of his platoon's victims let up. Then he blew a whistle and charged forward with the assault team, through the smoke . . . and right into Esteban Escobar, standing in utter shock in a place so obvious that every man of Cruz's platoon must have thought that either someone else was surely covering it or that no one could have survived the mines.

Cruz hit a block that hadn't been there when he'd set up the ambush, and which he had, not unreasonably, assumed would not be there after he fired off the mines. Thus, he wasn't even remotely expecting it and both he and the guerilla went down in a tumble.

Not being shocked shitless, as a single whiff told him the guerilla was, Cruz was the first on his feet. He aimed from the hip and was about to cut down the other, even as the men of his assault team worked through the supine forms laid out bleeding on the trail, when he noticed a small gold cross around the guerilla's neck. That stayed his finger from the light trigger of his F-26. From the cross Cruz looked up at terror-filled eyes, tears beginning to well, and said, "Ah, fuckit."

"I've got a prisoner," Cruz said into the radio. "No, I can't just kill him . . . Look; he's a member of a recognized belligerent force . . . He's got a chain of command . . ." Cruz looked up the trail at the bodies, tsked and said, "Well, I mean he *had* one . . . until quite recently, anyway . . . He's committed no war crimes of which I am aware . . . No, don't give me that bullshit . . . He was carrying his arms openly . . . and he . . . wait a minute." Cruz released his thumb from the microphone key and asked Esteban, "You *did* want to surrender, didn't you?"

The guerilla, rather, ex-guerilla, trouserless, on his knees with his hands bound, nodded his head so fast it was nearly a blur. If asked, he'd have said that his captor was twelve feet tall. In fact, Esteban would have towered over Cruz in another set of circumstances.

"Right," Cruz said, after keying the mike. "He's a legitimate POW under the laws of war. *I* can't just shoot him and I *can't* watch him; I've got places to go and people to kill. I want an evacuation helicopter with a jungle penetrator. NOW."

✧   ✧   ✧

"Blllaugh!"

Esteban had rarely even *seen* a helicopter before, let alone ridden in one...let alone ridden in one flying nap of the earth. Between looking out the side porthole and seeing trees *above* the helicopter, being lifted away from his seat when the thing dropped like a rock and pressed into it when it rose like a balloon, and generally having his stomach do the—

"Blllaugh!"

He had a new set of trousers, Balboan camouflage, given him by a sympathetic crew chief. That same crew chief who now held the back of Esteban's head and forced his face into the bag to catch the vomit laughed. Still, even amplified by his own misery, the sound didn't seem to the POW to be terribly malicious. Then again it was hard to hear between the sound of the engine, the steady *thrump-thrump-thrump* of the nearly invisible blades and the regular—

"Blllaugh!"

The crew chief shouted into Esteban's ear, "No shame, son, no shame. A lot of people get affected like that." Esteban wanted to say thanks but—

"Blllaugh!"

—instead he just nodded—weakly—that he'd heard. The paper of the bag ruffled his face while the aroma of his own vomit assaulted his nose.

"We'd fly a little higher and flatter but the intel types say you guys might have some shoulder-fired missiles." The crew chief shrugged. *What can you do?*

The guerilla thought about that. *We just* might, *too. Rumor control said so and—*

"Blllaugh!"

Oh, God, maybe that would be better.

Estado Mayor, Balboa City, Balboa, Terra Nova

As soon as the helicopter had set down on a square concrete pad surrounded by close-cropped grass, the crew chief had pulled a black bag over Esteban's head.

"Sorry," the crew chief had said. "Orders."

Immediately thereafter the door had been whipped open and two sets of hands had roughly and expeditiously pulled the POW out of the chopper, forced him to bend over slightly, and hustled him to a waiting vehicle. That vehicle sped away. Miraculously, or so Esteban thought, his stomach had settled down the instant the helicopter had landed.

When the sedan stopped, mere minutes later, two more sets of hands—or perhaps they were the same; Esteban couldn't be sure—dragged him out and then backwards to somewhere he knew not. He was dumped, unceremoniously, into a hard chair. In all, the entire process from landing to seating had taken perhaps five minutes.

A voice said, "Remove his mask."

Esteban was still shaking like a leaf in a strong wind when the black bag was removed from his head. He hadn't a clue what awaited. Torture? Death?

Probably both and in that order.

Once his eyes readjusted to the light, the prisoner saw a small, slight, and weasel-faced little man standing before him with a very uncommitted expression on his face.

"I'm Legate Fernandez," the man said, "and I understand you surrendered to our men. I have a few questions for you."

✧   ✧   ✧

"I don't know, *señor*," Esteban said, shaking his head. He was nervous, understandably so. "Someone in the *aduana*, that's all my *jefe* ever said. I never went with him to deliver the goods."

The one called "Fernandez" sighed. "That doesn't help much, Esteban. Work with me here. Did your *jefe* ever say anything about him or how he operates? A physical description maybe?"

The prisoner shrugged. "He called him 'a gold-toothed motherfucker.'"

Fernandez shook his own head. "Gold teeth, son, are not particularly rare around here."

Esteban licked his lips nervously. *Torture and death. Torture and death.*

"The *jefe* called his contact a *chumbo* once."

"A prick? The world is full of pricks."

"No, no, *señor*. In Santander a *chumbo* is a prick. But I think my *jefe* was using local slang for a *chumbo*, a black man."

The POW could see from Fernandez's scowl that this, too, was not very helpful. *The Balboans have black folk just like we do. Shit. Torture and death. Torture and death.* He stretched for something, anything that might be useful.

Esteban offered, doubtfully and nervously, "He . . . the *jefe*, I mean . . . he always said that payment was a mix of money and usually a single bag of the stuff, sometimes two, for his contact."

Fernandez tilted his head sideways even as his mouth formed a little quizzical expression. After a few moments' thought, he straightened his head and said, "Please, work with me here, Esteban; if a shipment's just gone through—you said these were big shipments?

"*Si, señor,*" the Santandern agreed. "Often more than a ton. Twenty tons, once. I know because I helped load it."

"Okay. So a shipment that size gets cut by ninety percent or more before being sold on the streets of the Federated States or the Tauran Union, right?"

"*Si, señor,* that's my understanding."

Fernandez stopped speaking long enough to go to his desk and make a telephone call. He asked a few questions, got a few answers, said, "Thanks. Goodbye," and hung up.

"That was an acquaintance of mine," Fernandez said, "at the Federated States Drug Interdiction Team at their embassy. He says that a big shipment usually depresses prices in the FSC and TU. See, the dealers have a hard time hanging on to a large inventory and so they sell as quickly as they can. It's a supply-demand issue, much complicated by a the-police-are-looking-for-this-shit issue."

Esteban nodded, eager to please and avoid *Torture and death. Torture and death.*

"Now," Fernandez mused, "if I had a small quantity of something, would I want to transship it on to someplace where the price was depressed?"

Esteban shook his head vigorously, *no.*

"So think I," the legate agreed. He seemed almost genial, too. "Especially if there's a substantial number of just plain rich folks locally I could sell it to. But to whom would I sell it, and how would I get my product to market?"

Before Esteban could even formulate an answer,

Fernandez touched an intercom and said, "Come get the prisoner."

Oh, God. Torture and death. Torture and death.

Two fierce looking guards came in. Fernandez told them, "Take this man to a holding cell. Feed him if he'll eat. Treat him well. He's been most cooperative."

As Esteban was led away he heard Fernandez speaking into a telephone again. "Patricio," he heard the legale ask, "just how far do your war powers extend? No, I don't mean outside of the country, actually."

Old Balboa City, Balboa, Terra Nova

The neighborhood was old and picturesque, built upon the charred remains of the original settlement in the then United Nations-supervised colony of Balboa.

Up the narrow, cobblestoned street, between the close-packed rows of five-story mansions, most of them converted to upscale apartments or condominiums, walked a young man of perhaps twenty to twenty-five years. That young man was slight of build; light complexioned and prosperously dressed. He walked from the area of the Old City toward a neighborhood that was everything the Old City was not . . . everything bad, that is.

Rats scampered quickly and furtively across garbage strewn streets, leery of the *antaniae* that clustered on leaky roofs. From glassless, unscreened windows came the sounds of tuberculoid coughing and wailing babies. Even so, far worse than the moonbats and the rats were the human filth that preyed on the *barrio*'s inhabitants.

This was the city's open social sewer. And despite Legate Sam Cheatham's comment to Carrera, full employment—*honest* work for everyone—had not quite yet come to Balboa.

The young man continued to walk, pretending not to notice the nondescript, aged automobile that passed him on the street every few minutes. The vehicle's four occupants, as well, tried not to observe the young man too obviously.

As the young man turned a corner, a hand from an unseen assailant reached out to grab him by the back of his collar. He felt the point of a knife pressed against his back.

"What have we here? A *rabiblanco* coming home from visiting his sweetheart. Empty your pockets, *white ass*."

The young man did as he was told, but in doing so he dropped a handful of loose change, apparently from nervousness. A fist lanced out at the pit of his stomach. The young man bent over, reflexively. Another blow knocked him to the ground. A shutter in an upper story apartment closed at the sound.

Kicks followed. Unnoticed by the assailants, the same nondescript car that had shadowed the young man pulled serenely past his prostrate form. The car stopped. Three men, armed and masked, emerged from the car and closed on the scene of the crime. The beating of the young man stopped when the leader of the street toughs felt the cold metal of a pistol silencer press against his neck. All four of the thugs were forced to lie down by two of the men from the car. "On your bellies, assholes." The third helped the young man back to his feet.

"Are you okay, Corporal?" asked the third man from the car.

"Sure," answered Corporal Enrique Velasquez, of the Tenth Infantry Tercio. "The cocksuckers didn't have time to hurt me badly." He dabbed a handkerchief at some blood dripping from his face even so.

One of the two men from the car who still guarded the thugs said, "You were bait this time. So you get to finish the job, except for the two that higher needs. Those are the rules." He handed a silenced pistol to Velasquez, who thanked him politely.

Then Velasquez walked up to where the muggers lay parallel on the ground. He shot the first two, once each, in the back of the head. The pistol made a soft *pffft*, quieter even than the working of the pistol's steel slide as it leapt back and forth to strip, catch, and feed a new cartridge. The expended cartridge flew up and to the right before hitting the ground with a soft ring. Blood and brains splattered the sidewalk, even as the smell of shit, not all of it from the dead, wafted up.

The same automobile that had brought the three rescuers to the scene returned, the driver stopping his vehicle and opening the trunk. Velasquez and another lifted the two corpses one at a time and dumped them in the trunk, even as the remaining two legionaries taped the still living thugs securely. These, too, were then dumped in the trunk atop the bodies.

"Okay," said the sergeant. "Let's drop off the garbage at the city dump. After that, we'll turn the survivors over to our contact."

An old woman peeped out from her window. "Chico," she asked Velasquez, "is it safe to come outside?"

"Only for a little while, *abuela*. But soon it will be safe all the time."

Estado Mayor, Ciudad Balboa, Balboa, Terra Nova

One had to give Fernandez his due. Given a new mission, he moved faster than anyone had a real right to expect, starting with giving the operation a name, *Nube Oscura* or Dark Cloud, to arranging funding, to recruiting a few score reliable troops for the effort.

He didn't entirely trust the Civil Police for work like this; they were still too close to the old ways and the old government. Moreover, there was more than sufficient reason to believe they were, in too many parts, corrupt.

Starting from scratch, Fernandez mused in his windowless basement office, *and given orders to move quickly…well, we've had a good beginning. Fifty-seven criminals killed, half of them saved for interrogation before being executed. Illegal? So what? They volunteered to be outside the law when they broke the law. And, moreover, when they caused my country to be threatened with another gringo invasion they become my personal enemies as well as the enemies of all right-thinking Balboans. In short, fuck 'em.*

A good beginning, he repeated the thought. *That's given us the next tier up, the gang leaders. From there…*

Aduana, Herrera International Airport, *Ciudad* Balboa, Terra Nova

They waited until the crowd from the last airship to land had dispersed before walking forward.

Corporal Velasquez, like his senior, *Sargento* Lopez,

wore civilian clothes, slacks and *guayaberas*, embroidered shirts that took the place of suits for much of Balboa's population most of the time.

"*Señor* Donati?" asked Lopez.

"Yes," the *aduana* chief answered, impatiently, "I'm Donati."

"Then you must come with us."

Subbasement, *Estado Mayor, Ciudad* Balboa, 471 AC

The entire facility had the smell of disinfectant, much like a hospital. Like a hospital, too, the whole place was rather quiet, all subdued voices and muffled mechanical sounds. Under the artificial lighting, and with that pungent stink in his nostrils, a bound and gagged Donati shuffled down the corridor under the direction of his guards. He thought he had caught a glimpse of his wife being led off down a corridor crossing the one he followed. That was worrying enough to cause his heart to sink. Who knew what she might divulge?

One guard put a hand on Donati's shoulder, stopping him in front of a metal door unmarked save for a room number. The other guard opened the door and said, "Enter."

The room inside was lit, with one desk and a hardback chair in front of it. At the desk sat a swarthy, somewhat overweight sort, in the uniform of the legion, making an entry into a page in a file folder. Without looking up, the swarthy one made a motion that the guards should seat Donati, which they did, roughly.

Donati thought there was something about the man at the desk to mark him as foreign, but couldn't quite put his finger on it. That man continued to write for several minutes before closing the folder and looking up.

"My name is Mahamda," the man said, in accented Spanish, "Warrant Officer Achmed al Mahamda. I am a recent immigrant to Balboa. From Sumer. You are going to tell me everything I want to know about the drug trade, how it works, who are the players, where are the facilities, what are the routes, how much money is involved, where it is, and how to confiscate it.

"You're going to want to lie to me. Don't."

EXCURSUS

"Government of Balboa," from *Global Affairs Magazine*, Volume 121, Issue of 10/473 AC

Each tercio, or regiment, of the *Legion del Cid*, the armed force of the Republic of Balboa, sends to the Senate one senator who serves for an eight-year term, with one quarter of all senators being reelected—or not, as the case may be—every two years. Senators are elected by their regimental centuriate assembly, composed of the discharged veterans of the regiment.

Upon graduation from initial entry training, all newly minted soldiers are assigned to a political century, an arbitrary grouping of exactly one hundred. (That is to say, *officially* it is arbitrary. In practice, wealthier and better educated people appear to be deliberately scattered among the centuries not only to reduce their political influence but to force those wealthier and more influential types to watch out for their century-brothers.) Soldiers killed in initial entry training are also counted, and their names enrolled in the other centuries being filled at the time of graduation.

That is one type, one might call it the "post-revolutionary" type, of century. The other type consists of those who were soldiers prior to the "revolution," which is to say prior to the election of Raul Parilla as president of the Republic and prior to the establishment of the Senate. These, plus their dead comrades, of which there were very many, were formed into political centuries shortly after the Parilla assumed power.

No one is ever added to or dropped from a century's rolls. No one votes within his century until formally discharged from the legion. No century ceases to exist, or loses its voting power, until the last member has died. This has not yet happened.

Biennially, all the centuries of a tercio meet, together, at the tercio's main cantonment area or on the grounds of the regimental club, whichever is most convenient. There, six classes of decision are made by the voting members of a century. The first of these is for the political centurion, a position of some local honor and thus avidly sought. The political centurion directs the century in its voting, runs administration for the next two years, oversees the century's Health, Welfare, and Mutual Aid Fund (managed by *Banco* de la Legion, S.A.), tallies the vote and, in the ultimate extremity, leads the century in combat.

The second decision is whom the century shall support in the political campaign for the National Legislative Assembly, before which campaign the centuriate assembly is invariably set to meet. The second decision is only the century's preference, as the final decision of support is determined by the full regiment's centuriate assembly. Support in this case means two things: A) Members of the regiment are honor bound to vote for the candidate selected, as a group, even though votes for election to the National Assembly are individually tallied by secret ballot and B) the members of the regiment, indeed the entire regimental organization, will canvas aggressively for that candidate. In practice this has meant that not only do the veterans of the nation's armed forces absolutely control the Senate, but that they also exercise de facto control of the legislative assembly, given that the purely civilian populace tends to scatter its own vote. Nothing requires that the civilians do this, of course. It should go without saying, but we'll say it anyway, that no regimental centuriate assembly has ever yet endorsed a non-veteran for public office. Note that the veterans never win every seat in the Legislative Assembly. They have never yet failed to take over half.

Third, in presidential election years, the century votes for whom the entire national centuriate assembly shall support for the offices of the President and Vice Presidents of the Republic, the President also being Commander in Chief of the Legion and *Princeps Senatus*. There is currently a constitutional amendment pending to make this office completely the purview of the centuriate assembly.

The fourth decision concerns the regiment's senator. This is decided by a majority vote of the centuries. It is entirely possible, and sometimes happens, for this to be a minority popular vote.

It is also worth mentioning that regiments are of different sizes, different annual intakes, and have varying numbers of political centuries. Senators do not vote their own persons in senatorial deliberations; they vote the number of centuries in their particular regiments.

Fifth, in addition to regimental senators, there are also another five percent at-large seats which are open only to persons who have earned high awards for valor in action, the *Cruz de Coraje en Oro con Escudo y Espadas* or higher. In practice, this level of award is so rare that these could conceivably become lifetime seats were Balboa ever to have a lengthy period of peace. These at-large seats are voted on by all the political centuries of all the regiments, with those half dozen or so candidates garnering the most centuries being seated.

As an aside, there is a theoretical third class of senator, composed of ex-presidents who have completed a second term without being impeached. These seats are to be for life.

Both valor seats and for-life seats vote the average number of centuries for the rest of the Senate, i.e. total number of political centuries divided by the number of regimental senators.

The sixth class of decisions made by the centuriate assemblies is called ratification. In the ratification process *any* century may, by popular vote, call for any law or treaty passed by the Senate, or any decision of the National Supreme Court, to be subject to ratification. If said law or decision is not ratified by at least one third of all centuries, they are rendered null and void. Since the legislative system is bicameral, nullification of the Senate's passage of a law also nullifies the bicameral passage of the law. This, because it is something of a pain for the centuries, is rarely used, though it has happened and laws have been nullified and decisions overturned because of it.

❖   ❖   ❖

A word should be said here about minority representation. The typical, average regiment, because women only enter the legion at about twenty-three percent of the rate of men, is predominantly male, said males being typically nationalistic, conservative, heterosexual, and more or less religious and patriarchal. Nothing has been done to ensure atheist or internationalist proportional political representation, but there are four "special" regiments, the *Tercio Gorgidas*, the *Tercio Amazona*, the *Tercio Santa Cecilia*, and the *Tercio Socrates* that are set aside for gays, women—both lesbian and heterosexual—the handicapped, and those very aged who elect to serve in some capacity in their sunset years. (These four regiments are the only regiments into which someone can permanently transfer after accession into a different regiment, though such transfers are voluntary and rare.) If nothing else, this gives each of those groups a distinct voice and the *opportunity* to barter their votes for fair treatment, beyond which perhaps no political system dependent upon consent of an empowered majority can really go.

Finally, we must address two peculiarities of Balboa's political system: 1) its structural traditionalism and conservatism—so at odds with its partial but widespread socialism—and 2) that, as a practical matter, the dead keep their vote, if not indefinitely, then often long after they have died. The latter is reinforcement for the former.

Consider: War, which is perhaps the Balboans' major export industry in the form of high priced auxiliaries, typically reduces the numbers, hence the political power, of those who have no objection to waging it.

Under the Balboan system, while those individual numbers may be reduced, the political power of the class that feels that way remains at full strength, since the centuries in which those people were joined vote at full strength on their behalf, even after death.

Consider: People tend to grow more conservative with age. The fact that members of centuries are not replaced means that those centuries grow older and more conservative even as their strength of numbers lessens. This weights the Balboan political process, more or less heavily, in favor of conservatism and traditional values.

Consider: The entire gamut of philosophies we tend to think of as Liberalism, Internationalism, Cosmopolitanism, Tsarist-Marxism, Progressivism, Humanitarianism, etc. have as one of their major values one form or another of antimilitarism. These people, and Balboa has something approaching its share, tend not to join the legion, not to be accessed into political centuries, to be barred from most public offices (though some do squeak through into the Legislative Assembly), and thus to be effectively politically disenfranchised, even though they may retain the right to vote for the Legislative Assembly.

CHAPTER TWELVE

The inevitable transition from left wing progressivism to oppressive hereditary aristocracy, on Old Earth, was already written plain in the nature of what was then called the "Transnational Progressive Movement," on that world, then, or "Cosmopolitan Progressive," now, on ours.

It was and is written plain in the extraordinary care these people take to ensure the well being of themselves and their children. Are they part of a fund-starved organization seeking to do good? This is no reason not to have human servants at their meetings to pour the water. Neither is it a reason for them not to be paid at the very highest rates prevailing anywhere. Less still is it a reason not to ensure that their children are funded to the best possible schools. And, take it as a given, they really *need* to live in the best their city of residence has to offer. And all at the expense of their underfunded organizations.

It was and is to be seen in the grandiose titles and honors these people granted and grant themselves; "High" this and "Plenipotentiary" that, "Extraordinary" that and "Grand" this . . . "Your Excellency" and "Eminence."

It was and is clear in the favors they do for each other, and each other's children, as it is in the bounties they salt away for those children.

Indeed, it is seen in the broad harm they do humanity, even as they claim the good. For what does it matter if they ruin mankind, so long as the servants pour the water, the pay is high, their own children are cared for, their titles resound, and they have enough graft to pay for that First Landing mansion?

> —Jorge y Marqueli Mendoza, *Historia y Filosofia Moral*, Legionary Press, Balboa, Terra Nova, copyright AC 468

Anno Domini 2524
Anno Condita 471
UEPF *Spirit of Peace*, Luna Starship Holding and Storage Area

High Admiral Wallenstein felt the shuttle bay doors slam shut through the metal under her feet. She couldn't hear them at all. The shuttle itself, on the outside a twin for the partially restored one in a subterranean workshop in the *Isla Real* on Terra Nova, was already resting on the deck before the bay was sealed against the vacuum.

Marguerite intended to meet the new captain, Richard, earl of Care, on the shuttle deck. She didn't have to; indeed it was somewhat contrary to normal protocol. She was there because she absolutely didn't want the crew engaging in proskynesis and the only way to make sure that didn't happen was to be there, issue the order, and ensure it was carried out herself.

Debarking for the earl and new captain had to wait until the air was returned to the shuttle deck and the reception committee had filed out and formed up. A recorded bosun's pipe sounded, the crew—other than Marguerite—came to attention, the hatch to the shuttle opened, and Richard, earl of Care, stepped out.

Elder gods, Marguerite thought, *he looks . . . scared. Oh, sure, he's trying to hide it but you can see that he's hiding it. Who would have thought? After being raised with all the arrogance of the First Class?*

Richard stepped down to the deck, faced Marguerite, and made a half bow. She returned about a tenth of it, doing little more than inclining her head. The earl of Care then straightened, made a typically stiff cadet's salute and announced, "Richard, earl of Care, reports to the High Admiral of the Peace Fleet."

Marguerite returned the salute, and this she did fully, said, "Follow me," and without a glance backwards, walked off the flight deck and through the hatchway.

Richard, earl of Care, noticed the lovely brown girl tidying up Wallenstein's office as soon as he entered the room. She curtseyed and went back to her work until the high admiral said, "Thank you, Esmeralda. We'll be fine for now."

"Can I get you anything, my lady?" the ex-slavegirl asked. Like the other four hundred and seventeen slaves commandeered by the high admiral, she'd been freed and given a choice. Since the choice was join the fleet or go back home—to TransIsthmia, in her case—she, like every one of the others, had chosen the fleet. Still, if she hadn't had all the choice imaginable, at least she was a genuine member of the crew, with pay and a degree of dignity and self worth. Wallenstein hoped those things might make up for the many, many indignities Esmeralda had suffered in her short life.

Taking a seat by a small conference table, rather than at her desk, Marguerite told the girl, "If you would inform the cook that I and the earl of Care will be dining here, my dear, I'd appreciate it."

"Certainly, High Admiral," Esmeralda answered before leaving.

Once the girl was gone, Marguerite asked, "Why the hell are you here, son?"

"My lady," said Richard, earl of Care, "I don't really know *why* I'm here. All I know is that my uncle commanded and I had to obey." The boy looked both pained and embarrassed as he admitted, "High Admiral, I haven't the *first* clue about commanding a starship. Among the Class Ones at the Academy I wasn't even particularly high ranking, either in leadership *or* in academics."

Meaning he couldn't afford to pay the bribes, thought Wallenstein, *couldn't afford to or wouldn't. I wonder which it is.*

She asked.

Richard gave a little sigh. His eyes rolled up toward the ceiling of the high admiral's quarters. "My lady, while some feoffs are still quite flush, Care is not. And for reasons I don't fully understand, my parents decided on having *two* children, of which I am the younger. My elder brother received the Grand Duchy of Microsoft, which is comparatively well off. With the tithes from Care, my father was able to buy me a spot at the Academy, but that was all."

Hmmm. Other motivation for the SecGen: Take care of an impoverished relative? Possibly. But that's not important right now.

Wallenstein ordered aloud, "Computer, Academy records, complete, Richard, earl of Care." Those appeared on her viewscreen within the space of a few seconds.

"But I thought those were—"

"I'm the high admiral now. I can get whatever information I want that the fleet has," she explained. Richard suddenly looked *very* embarrassed.

Wallenstein forced a small smile from her face as she read. *Four hundred and thirty-seven demerits. And that's after walking off an even larger number. Peer evaluations . . . bad from Class Ones . . . but generally good to very good from the Class Twos and Threes. Interesting. And no one who gets a C minus in "Appreciation of pre-Islamic Art in sub-Saharan Africa" but an A in "20th Century Music" can be all bad. Maybe, just maybe, I can work with this. But first a few questions.*

"You didn't seem too taken aback," she observed, "about the lack of proskynesis. Why?"

Richard snorted. "My lady, I know my peers. They don't deserve proskynesis. Neither do I. Neither does anyone."

Oh, I can probably *work with this.*

"What do you think about your new responsibilities as captain of a starship?"

The boy didn't even hesitate in answering, "That I'm utterly unfit for them. Not necessarily unsuited;

about that I just don't know. But I am unfit for them as I am now."

Yes, I can work with this.

"What do *you* think you need to become fit...?"

Esmeralda knew she wasn't really fit to be the high admiral's cabin girl. For one thing, she hadn't been aboard ship nearly long enough to become used to the reduced gravity. Nor did she really know any of the protocol. On the plus side, she could at least find her way to the galley and to the small cabin Wallenstein had assigned her as quarters.

For that matter, other than for her capture in Trans-Isthmia and shipment to Razona Market, she hadn't been a slave long enough, or profoundly enough, to really understand it. She'd been raped, of course, by her guards and the vendor. But that was to be expected. Nor was it anything new; she'd been raped with some regularity for the last couple of years by the household troops of Count Castro-Nyere. She didn't like it, not even remotely, but it was something one got used to, especially when every girl of her class could expect it, and no one attached any particular shame to it.

On the other hand, she'd had a strong feeling that being a slave, had that status continued, would have been awful indeed. And that's assuming she hadn't been stuffed into a wicker basket and burned alive by the Orthodox Druids as her former owner and vendor had indicated would happen if she failed to find a buyer.

Now? Well, she wasn't precisely free. But she was well clothed, well fed, free from the threat of rape, and was even paid a cabin girl's stipend.

Life could be a lot worse, Esmeralda thought as she scurried between the admiral's quarters and galley, *than it is aboard this starship. And the high admiral has never made any demands on me for any service my parents wouldn't have approved of. That I never expected when she brought me away from the market.*

Starships were their own best flight simulators. Ideally, a captain would practice with his own bridge crew on his own ship. Unfortunately—

We can't do that, thought Marguerite, as she drilled Richard for approximately the twelfth time on procedures for deploying the sail. *For one thing, for better or worse, and until and unless I decide to space him, he is the captain. As such, I need him to be effective. Put him on the bridge and show the crew he knows nothing and I'll have to space him to avert a mutiny. For another, we don't need to actually go anywhere right now. So . . . we use the simulator with only myself in attendance.*

"That was a little *better*," she said. "But we'll do it again even so. And this time, Captain, *do* try to remember to empty the fill ring and draw in the lines *before* you give the order to rotate sail."

Richard looked at the simulated ruin of the sail in the viewscreen, then hung his head, ashamed. "I'll try to do better, High Admiral," he whispered.

Odd, Wallenstein thought. *I feel sorry for the boy. Do I actually rather like him? Maternal instincts, so long held in check, resurfacing? Elder gods, wouldn't that be funny? Me, feeling something beyond contempt for a Class One? Then again, the boy's not a normal Class One, is he? No, he's actually pretty human.*

And, thinking of Class Ones, I do wonder what that inbred idiot I had to leave in charge of the fleet is doing in my absence.

Gods! It was so hard to leave the fleet in that dolt's care. Not that I had any choice.

UEPF *Spirit of Harmony,* in orbit over Terra Nova

It has been said, and often repeated, that military and naval officers fell into one of four categories: A) active and intelligent, who made good staff officers, B) lazy and intelligent, who made good commanders because they, being lazy, would always find an easier way, C) lazy and stupid, who could be put to good use by clever staff officers and commanders, and D) active and stupid, who should be shot for the improvement of the breed.

It should be noted that, in a command context, stupid is a fairly relative term; many people, though more than ordinarily bright, are still far too stupid.

Harmony was not Battaglia's ship. Rather, that worthy normally commanded UEPF *Spirit of Brotherhood*. Still, he was in charge; he was responsible.

"He wants to count widgets," the captain of *Harmony* said to his exec. "Widgets and flight line and azimuth cores. He also wants to inspect whatchamacallit maintenance and framistat compliance. Likewise dingas calibration and our ship's ever-critical frobnis program. Similarly, oojamafrip orientation."

"*Sirrr?*" the exec asked. "Sir, I have not the first frigging clue what you're talking about."

"Neither do I," the captain said, with a shrug. "Neither does he. Neither does anyone. What the earl of Pksoi really wants is to fill up his time by wasting ours."

"Ahhh. I'll get right on it, sir. I'll have the crew polishing widgets and calibrating dingases in no time."

The captain smiled. "See that you do. And don't forget the oojamafrip orientation."

"Oh, yes, sir," the exoo agreed, false enthusiasm shining in her face. "Very important to orient our oojamafrips. Or it would be if we had any . . . whatever they may be."

The skipper chewed his lower lip for a few moments, thinking very dark thoughts, and then added, "Remember, we've only got to put up with this shit until Wallenstein gets back."

"If the Consensus doesn't space her, sir."

"Well . . . yeah."

"But, sir, what if they *do*?"

Did ever a man talk so much and say so little, wondered *Harmony*'s skipper as Battaglia droned on, and on, and on, for the third hour of his little post inspection pep talk. *"Vanguard of order and peace" . . . yeah . . . that's gonna resonate. "Inadequate maintenance"? Get my crew some fucking spares, asshole. "Ration accountability"? What the fuck; do you think they're selling the shit dirtside? Dropping it in containers? Getting the payment exactly how? Oh, elder gods, spare me the attentions of the First Class.*

Gods; what if the Consensus really does space Wallenstein?

UEPF *Spirit of Peace*, Lunar Starship Holding and Storage Area

High Admiral Marguerite Wallenstein stood in the light. There was minimal gravity in this chamber, perhaps fifteen percent of Earth normal. She held onto a rail with one hand. In the simulation room, Richard, earl of Care, sat in the silent darkness of a virtual reality helmet that completely enclosed his head. Moreover, he sat on a complex gimbaled chair. Wallenstein hit a button, beginning the disaster response program called, for reasons lost to antiquity, the "*Kobayashi Maru.*"

The exercise was *supposed* to be disconcerting. Some very fine minds, psychologists' minds, had gone into making it so, back in the days when the Peace Fleet had mattered to more than a few.

It began with sensory deprivation. All sound was cut off by the helmet. The comparative lack of gravity made the command chair, and the straps that held Richard to it, something less than real. The stars, or, rather, their images, swirled before his eyes, making it seem as if he were tumbling, end over end, lost and alone. Richard felt nausea begin to rise. He tried to focus on one star alone, in an effort to keep the nausea at bay. It didn't work; they were clustered too close together to blot out the rest.

A voice began to drone in Richard's ears, explaining the situation. He knew he was supposed to pay close attention but with his rising gorge he was barely able to make out the general scenario.

He did catch a few things, "...first ship to transit...

new star system ... disaster ... no relief or rescue possible ..."

It was sufficient for the program that Richard's vital signs show nausea. It wasn't strictly necessary that he actually vomit. Accordingly, as soon as he'd reached the necessary threshold, the stars cut out, being replaced by lifelike images of the bridge crew—rather, *a* bridge crew from sometime back in the twenty-third century going about their daily business. Past the bridge crew were several viewing screens. In one of them Saturn receded in the distance. Various well-lit diagrams of his ship stood spaced along the walls.

Richard felt the tiniest shudder in his command chair, even as the images likewise moved slightly in his view. He didn't notice it, but several sections of the diagram changed color subtly.

One of the female crew clasped a hand to one ear. "Captain," she announced, "meteoroid strike amidships. Belts fifty-eight through sixty, decks ... Zulu through ... Victor report minor air loss."

Richard hesitated for a moment; the nausea was still with him.

The crewwoman asked, "Shall I seal off the affected sections, Captain? Shall I dispatch damage control?"

Fuck me to tears, Richard thought. *The high admiral will have my ass for lunch for that.*

"Aye, away damage control parties to the area of the penetration." Richard took a quick glance at the diagram. "Negative on sealing the area."

"Aye, aye, sir. Damage control parties away."

"Casualties?" Richard asked.

"None reported, Captain."

✦   ✦   ✦

"Skipper, this is Damage Control Alfa. We've found the hull breach. Sealing it now."

"How large is the breach?" Richard asked.

"Two millimeters, no more," the program answered. "We've leaked a little air but nothing dangerous."

Richard turned his head toward life support, the VR helmet changing scene with the turn. "How do we stand on reserve oxygen?"

"Reserve storage is more than adequate to compensate for the loss, Captain," the program answered, in a man's voice. It then added, "Carbon dioxide filtration and separation continues without degradation."

Okay. Well enough, thought Marguerite. *The boy didn't overreact. Of course, he hasn't yet asked the right questions . . .*

His command chair definitely shuddered. And this time it was non-trivial.

"Meteoroid strike, Captain," the same female simulacrum said. "Stern, belts ninety-four through ninety-seven; it has passed through all decks. Captain, there are casualties. The ship has taken on a four mil yaw."

Fuck.

"Damage control?" Richard asked.

"Aye, Damage Control here, Skipper. I've dispatched a team."

"Good," Richard said, then asked of the bridge crewwoman, "Can we get visual on the damaged sections?"

"On screen now, Skipper."

Apparently power was at least partly out in the most recently struck section. The cameras had to operate off of light enhancement. This was perhaps just as well as the first image the viewscreen caught was of the remains of a crewman, sliced in two and then explosively decompressed. Parts of his torso had gone fairly flat while his inner organs floated outside. The two pieces of the late crewman rotated, one clockwise, the other counter. The grainy green image was at least some insulation from what would, in living color, probably have been another nausea inducing experience.

"Skipper," Damage Control added, "we're not going to be able to get in there until that team suits up."

"How long?" Richard asked.

"Be at least a quarter of an hour," Damage Control answered.

At least the strike wasn't near either of the reactors, the captain thought.

And you still *haven't asked the right question. Tsk.* For a moment Marguerite contemplated giving the boy a hint. *But, no, let him figure it out for himself.*

"Meteoroid strike, Captain. Deck seventy-four, belt X-ray, compartment one-eleven. External cameras show it slicing the hull but not entering the ship. No casualties."

"Elder gods, where in the hell are they coming from?"

"Bingo," Marguerite said aloud. In his VR helmet there was no chance of Richard hearing. "That was the right question."

"I've got nothing forward, Captain," the crewwoman answered. "Nothing on radar, lidar, or visual."

"Then look *behind*," Richard commanded.

The simulation was good enough for the crew-woman's face to acquire an expression of horror. She turned back away and began manipulating the controls in front of her. A flip of the switch, just before she faced back toward Richard, changed the viewscreen from slowly orbiting entrails to an outline of the ship. The diagram shrank in scale until a cloud of *something* appeared on the lower right side of the screen. A dotted line, marked with time hacks, showed the ship's course. Another showed the course of the meteoroid cloud. They intersected.

"I ran back the orientation of the spinning decks in time, Captain. All three strikes came from the direction of that cloud."

The simulated crewwoman turned again back toward her panel and the viewscreen. She exclaimed aloud, with a strong note of panic, "Lord Buddha, we're going to die!"

The program could be used both with or without a human moderator. It was preferred to use such a moderator, because machine intelligence had never proved worth a damn in analyzing or reacting to the nuances of human emotion, or the speech which either moderated it or exacerbated it. A human might get it wrong; a machine was certain to.

Wallenstein listened very carefully to every syllable Richard uttered.

"Calm down," she heard Richard snap. "Give me some options."

Not bad, Marguerite thought. *Sure, he's got a little fear in his own voice. If it were completely absent that would scare me—or any sensible member of the crew—more, since that would mean he was an idiot. Not bad.*

"I'm sorry, Captain," the simulated crewwoman said. Subtle hints—the drape of shoulders, the angle of head, and the few expressions he could see—told Richard he'd said approximately the right thing.

"'Options,' I said." Richard paused for a moment and then added, "Think before you give them to me. In the interim, sound Red Alert, General Quarters, and Don Suits."

A siren wailed through the notional ship. Lights flashed. The simulacra on the bridge began reaching into nearby compartments and pulling on their emergency suits. These were unarmored but would at least keep air in. The computer could not simulate Richard putting on a suit, but, after a short period of time, changed his image to show the outlines of a clear facemask even while the VR suit pressurized in places to simulate the feel of a emergency suit.

The chair shuddered once again, then began to spin. Even though the image painted on Richard's eyes stayed approximately the same, barring only that several crewmembers who were still unstrapped while putting on their suits were thrown violently across the bridge, the combination of spin and unchanging view rekindled his nausea.

Fuck. "Where was that?" he demanded.

"We've lost the mast, sir, though the sail's hanging on by the stays! Medical team to the bridge!"

There was another shudder in the chair, followed by spinning in the vertical plane.

"Another strike amidships, Captain!

How many more *of these?* Richard wondered. That sparked another thought.

"Activate the alternative bridge. XO to the alternate bridge. XO to the alternate bridge."

"I've got some options for you, Captain," Operations said. "But they're not good options."

Life support announced, "Captain, that last strike missed Reactor Number Two, but it's taken out the cooling system."

"Captain, we've just rotated into the remains of the mast."

"Captain, sick bay has taken a hit."

"Captain, inspection shows the keel tube is bent and rotation of exterior decks must halt. She's ripping herself apart, Skipper."

At that the gimbaled chair began a purely random rotation, even as the speakers in the helmet began to blare out the sounds of screeching metal and composites, being torn apart.

"Option One, Skipper, is to..."

Disasters were coming at him fast and furious now, with still new disasters springing up from old ones. Was there an urgent repair that needed to be made? Was one of the damage control teams annihilated? *Why, oh why, didn't I have them suit up after the first hit?* Reactor overheating? *I should have ordered one of them shut down to reduce the chances of a critical hit.* Worse, some of his regrets were mutually exclusive or contradictory. Power outages? *Thank the elder gods I kept both reactors going; what if I'd shut down Number One?*

Richard was simply too busy at the moment to suspect the truth, that the simulation program was *designed* to keep him behind the command power curve, to throw him decisions and disasters faster than he could keep up with them, however quickly and even however wisely he might have decided, to do so the faster, the faster he moved.

In the end, it didn't matter what he did. Reactor Number Two went critical and, next thing, he found himself once again slowly spinning, alone with the simulated stars.

This time, right into his helmet, he did vomit.

Wallenstein wrinkled her nose at the vile aroma arising from the helmet as she removed it from Richard's head.

She pushed it as far from her nose as she could, then carried it to a stand against one wall. There she picked up a towel that she carried back and handed to Richard.

"Actually, you didn't do badly," she said.

He answered, while wiping his face with the towel, "I lost my ship."

"Everyone loses his ship," she assured him. "*Everyone*. That's not the point."

"Then what *is* the point?" he asked, dropping the foul towel.

"To see who panics, who turns into a gibbering monkey, who becomes abusive. On those grounds, you did pretty well."

"Not well enough to be worthy of actually commanding the ship."

Again, Richard's basic decency, so rare in a natural

born Class One, and humility, which was much rarer, struck her.

"You will be," she assured him. Moreover, she was surprised to discover, she believed it was true. *And that's important, not least because I'm not going to have time to hold your hand once I get back and have to deal with that idiot, Battaglia.*

CHAPTER THIRTEEN

Democracy, it has been said, can only exist until the voting populace discovers it can vote itself largesse from the public coffers. Though it is less often said, it also happens that the voting populace discovers— indeed it is educated to the notion—that it has the power to radically expand the size of those coffers, seemingly the better to vote themselves largesse.

How quickly this happens depends on many factors. A relatively classless society is relatively immune, for so long as it remains relatively classless. There are several reasons for this. Large among these reasons is that, without great disparities in wealth being shoved into people's faces, they feel little envy. Less emotionally, without some apparent concentration of wealth to be tapped, people will tend to see government redistribution schemes as little more than an exercise in taking money from their pockets, peeling off a large percentage for government overhead and then returning that much reduced sum back to their own, now sadly emptier, pockets.

Never mind that even in societies with great inequalities in wealth it works much the same, as the poor use the government to take from the rich, and the rich use the fact of ownership over property, and the ability to set prices (which price setting is driven by the common tax, acting in lieu of a conspiracy), to take it right back from the poor. People tend to want to believe the illusion that this does not happen or, at least, need not, even though their own lot never improves, long-term, under such a regime. Thus they demand that the government take ever more from the rich, which causes the rich to take ever more from the poor, with only the government itself gaining any advantage whatsoever, as it takes an increasing cut of an increasing share.

This continues, at least, until the taxation gets to the point that it begins to hurt the economy. After that, government takes an increasing share of a decreasing pot.

> —Jorge y Marqueli Mendoza, *Historia y Filosofia Moral*, Legionary Press, Balboa, Terra Nova, copyright AC 468

Anno Condita 471
Presidential Palace, Old Balboa, Republic of Balboa, Terra Nova

The government which had been electorally defeated by Raul Parilla, running with the support of the legion, the same government which had been kept alive by the Tauran Union and the Federated States, didn't control much of the country. It owned some of the police. It had most of the old city, which was but a fraction of the new, and not the largest fraction at that. It had some government buildings, the national cathedral, a museum, a few monuments, an opera house, and some very nice urban residential areas along with some wretched ones. Also it had the Presidential Palace, a sort of Venetian palazzo, complete with courtyard, and even some trixies. Wire mesh over the courtyard kept the trixies in and the *antaniae* out. Neither species was very happy about that.

"I want him dead! I want the *hijo de puta* dead!" The patriarch of the Rocaberti family fairly shrieked at his nephew, Belisario Endara-Rocaberti. Belisario had been named for the republic's greatest hero, Belisario Carrera, multi-great grandfather-in-law of Patricio Carrera. No one, least of all Belisario himself, thought he quite deserved the name. Frankly, at five feet six inches and with a girth of two thirds of that, he just didn't look the part. Nor was he, as he'd have cheerfully told anyone, the stuff of which heroes were made. Sometimes women found that honesty charming. Other times, for some women, his not inconsiderable wealth and prominent family name were more attractive.

Still, he had his virtues. Realism was one of them. Young Endara-Rocaberti walked to his uncle's second floor office window and drew the curtains.

"Do you remember whose statue is out there, uncle?" he asked.

The pseudo-president scowled, his jowls trembling with rage. "Of course I know. Your namesake. The peasant bastard."

"Not just *my* namesake," Endara-Rocaberti corrected. "My mother and father just gave me the first name. That's not too uncommon, really. But your great enemy, your *dangerous* enemy, has the last name."

"He's no blood of the original."

"No, he's not," the nephew agreed, shaking his head. "He's worse for us. He gave up his own country and citizenship. He adopted the name of the clan he married into, the real Carrera clan. He became one of the people and as one of the people he's defended the people. Uncle, he's *popular*, he's *dangerously* popular."

"Fine. Now tell me something I don't know," the rump president said bitterly.

Belisario Endara-Rocaberti remained silent.

Forcing himself back to a degree of calm, the eldest of the family continued, "Two days ago Donati at the *Aduana* disappears. This morning several hundred kilos of uncut, prime *huánuco* was seized. Uncut, I tell you! And it's all the doing of that motherfucker Parilla and his dog with the pilfered name, Carrera. Whatever it takes, however you have to do it, make those two disappear. And soon.

"On the plus side, at least Donati didn't tell them anything of the major stash in the city."

Belisario chewed on his lower lip for some moments before answering. "I have a warning, Uncle. I can find the men to do this. Our friends in Santander will probably be willing to help. Or perhaps the Taurans. But such a thing would not be without risk. How do you suppose they got Donati to talk so quickly? How do you suppose they *got* to Donati so quickly? Parilla and Carrera, especially Carrera, are men of complete ruthlessness. If we try and fail the penalty will be great. I think you should wait until Pigna is ready and in position."

"No. Just get rid of them and let me worry about the risks."

"I shall try, Uncle. On your head be it." *Except it won't. It will be on* all *our heads.*

Unscheduled legion flight from Herrera Airport to Santa Catalina Island, Balboa, Terra Nova

While the ex-president had gotten some of the police, Parilla had most of them, most of the country, *and* the prison system. The police had come with all their virtues and vices intact.

The small cargo aircraft that served, among other things, to transfer serious criminals from the mainland to Balboa's shark-encircled prison colony on Santa Catalina Island, turned slightly southward. The passengers leaned against the movement.

"Over water now, Tribune," the pilot of the aircraft said.

"We'll wait a few minutes, then, Sergeant," the police tribune answered. In pre-Parilla days he'd have been a senior lieutenant. Now the police had adopted the same rank structure as the legion.

After that short time had passed, the tribune jerked open the passenger door, stuck his head out, and looked below. A rush of sound and air entered the aircraft, causing the prisoners, including ex-customs supervisor Donati, to shiver with more than cold. Looking back the tribune saw that already the land was several miles behind.

Pulling his head and shoulders back into the airplane he turned his gaze to the regular passengers— all of them convicted of serious crimes; the brutal prison colony on Santa Catalina was not for mere pickpockets—and nodded with satisfaction. The prisoners, fourteen of them, were bound, hand and foot. Their eyes were either shut tight, or opened wide in pleading terror. The tribune took another look outside. He made a gesture with his thumb.

The sergeant and another policeman walked over to the prisoner next to *Señor* Donati. As they walked the swaying deck their hands traced along the walls of the cabin for balance. Reaching down, the two policemen picked up Donati's neighbor, who began to thrash in their grip. They carried him, despite his struggling, to the door.

The tribune read the prisoner's sentence sheet aloud, almost shouting to be heard over the engines and the air rushing past the door. "For participation in *narcotrafico* you have been sentenced to fifteen years at hard labor on Santa Catalina. Sadly, you seem to have escaped." He reached over to pick up a weighted chain. This he hung from the prisoner's bonds, wrapping one chain around the other and fastening them with a loose knot. The prisoner sagged, helpless and hopeless, weeping like a baby.

With a sneer, the tribune tilted his head toward the plane's door. The sergeant grabbed overhead handholds for stability and placed one foot in the small of the prisoner's back. The last Donati saw of his recent neighbor was his back and the back of his legs, feet flailing, as he made an unplanned and unscheduled exit from the aircraft.

The tribune made as if spitting out the door and turned back, walking towards Donati.

"Wait! Wait!" Donati shrieked. "I know more. I know much more. I can tell you where the stuff is stockpiled."

Bingo, thought the tribune, turning away from and passing over Donati to grab the next in line.

By the time the aircraft reached Santa Catalina

only seven men—the three policemen, the flight crew, and a cowering Donati—remained aboard. The others would be entered on the prison colony rolls for a few months, then be reported as missing. Given the currents, and the presence of sharks around the island, no one would ever even bother to look for the "escapees." It was all very clean and above board.

It also tended to keep costs down.

Presidential Palace, Old Balboa, Republic of Balboa, Terra Nova

In an abandoned four-story building, once a mansion and now fallen on hard times, standing not so very far away from the Presidential Palace, a group of not quite fifty of the five hundred odd police who had remained loyal to the old regime practiced hostage rescue under the tutelage of some of General Janier's commandos. The money for the exercise, indeed for the entire training program, came from Janier's office. The commander of the group, one Moises Rocaberti, was another of the old president's nephews. In many ways, Moises was the preferred among those nephews. The sounds of firing, albeit blank firing, and of the simulators used, echoed across the pigeon-infested squares of the old city.

"It's not as bad as all that, Uncle," Endara-Rocaberti said, trying his best to ignore the sounds of firing. "After all, if the . . . other . . . government seized several tons of the stuff, that will just drive up the price generally. I doubt we'll lose that much, overall. Certainly the demand won't go down."

"Oh, the demand will skyrocket," the rump president

agreed. "The problem is that that demand will be filled, if at all, by stockpiles already south of us, in Atzlan, the FSC and the Tauran Union. We'll get none of it and as soon as we and our friends on this end replace our stocks—and that's going to take *months,* the price will drop. Like a lead brick. No, nephew, this is disastrous."

The nephew sighed. He found himself doing that a lot lately, when in discussion with his uncle. "Maybe it's time to pull up stakes and leave, Uncle, to sell what we can and get out. Maybe we could sell our interest to Parilla, give him this corner of the Republic. Surely he'd prefer a nice clean monetary arrangement to a war."

Rocaberti, senior, shook his head dismally. "We're not the ones he's facing; the Taurans are. We could leave and he's still got a fight on his hands with them. It doesn't change Parilla's position in the slightest. So why should he pay? On the other hand, we can stay and, if he loses to the Taurans, we get our old position back."

"I spoke to some of the Taurans on Janier's staff," Endara-Rocaberti said. "You know, in relation to the little project you set me to? They're worried, badly worried."

"You didn't tell them about our plans for Parilla and Carrera, did you?" the rump president asked.

"Oh, no," Endara assured his uncle. "I just wanted to see what the general air was about their headquarters and ask maybe about being put in touch with one or another of their private military groups."

"I thought," the uncle said, "that you were going to the Santanderns for help."

"I did. I am. But they tell me they don't really have the system in place or the skills for this kind of thing. Set a bomb off in a crowded market? Sure. Kidnap an unguarded journalist or judge? Easy. But both Carrera and Parilla are *hard* targets. I thought that maybe a private contractor from the Tauran Union, coupled with some muscle from Santander, might be just the ticket."

"And?"

"And," the nephew continued, "I've got two . . . mmm . . . two specialists from a Gallic firm—one of them is actually a gringo—flying to Santander next week to link up with the Belalcázar cartel. Five or six weeks after that they'll be ready. Then we bring them into the country. I've made arrangements for that, for a place for them to stay hidden while we await an opportunity. I have my own sources to identify when such an opportunity may arise."

The ex-president nodded, gratified. "You have done well, nephew."

Endara-Rocaberti rocked his head from side to side, signifying a mix of agreement and disagreement. "I've done well enough in preparing something we probably shouldn't do, Uncle. Before I give the final word to proceed, I wish you would think very seriously about the risks of what we've embarked on. And wait for Pigna and his Seventh Legion to be at Fort Cameron."

"No."

Headquarters, Tauran Union Security Force–Balboa, Building 59, Fort Muddville, Transitway Area, Balboa

"What do you mean we should 'de-escalate'?" Janier asked of his intelligence operator, de Villepin. For a change, Janier was again wearing Gallic battledress rather than his blue velvet atrocity.

"I mean, *mon general*, that the Balboans are raising and equipping forces at a rate that is rapidly making them unassailable by us here. Already I am not convinced we can win. In a year? I think we cannot win. In two years? I shudder. Moreover, there is a chance, a good chance, that the disaffected legion commander I told you about may well solve our problems for us if we'll just be patient, as he is being patient."

De Villepin continued, "Fact: they've recently purchased something on the order of *six hundred* jet fighters. At least that's all we know about. Are those fighters obsolete? Yes. But they're still six hundred. Worse, they're being upgraded, perhaps substantially. Fact: they've reorganized into a four—maybe five—corps force of what may be eleven divisions, or perhaps twelve, and a number of independent regiments. Are those corps and divisions full strength? No. But they *will* be. Fact, and this is in many ways the most disturbing thing of all: they are building fortifications as if *they* believe they can defeat any initial attack here and would then have to face a larger attack later. Clearly *they* think they can defeat that first attack or they wouldn't waste the money and effort they've committed to digging in."

"They're living in a dream world," Janier countered. "Along with your 'facts,' have you not noticed they are mere militia, peasant rabble, at best?"

"An arguable point, 'at best,' *mon general*. The cadre for that peasant rabble are all long service regulars, with a decent, even enviable, combat record. And that cadre recently took some of that peasant rabble into the deepest darkest jungle in the world and routed out some thousands of the guerillas that infested it. Quickly, too."

"I know all this," Janier said. "This is why our plan is

to take out that cadre first, leaving the rabble leaderless. What flaw do you see in that?"

"Assuming we have to, if Pigna fails us, none, in principle," de Villepin conceded. "Which does not mean that there is not a flaw, or that the Balboans will accommodate us. Or that that task does not become more complex with each passing year.

"There is something that troubles me, though," de Villepin said, "something that goes to core principles. I think you are basing your estimate of what will happen if we can take out the leadership on what would happen in the Tauran Union."

"Accurate enough," Janier agreed.

"Well . . . back home, the bureaucrats who rule us have spent decades indoctrinating the young to obedience, accommodation, and faith in the group, in the Consensus, and in following customs and mores, rather than in the prowess of the individual."

"Which gives us the obedient cannon fodder on which our military strength rests," Janier said.

"Just as a thought," de Villepin mused, "what would it mean if the young of this place are educated to place primacy on individual initiative?"

"Then they'll have built a castle on a foundation of sand," Janier said.

Puerto Lindo, Balboa, Terra Nova

After all these centuries the great stone castles and their ancient guns still kept watch over the normally sleepy port and its town. It was a little less sleepy, this day, than usual as the bay was about to be witness to the most complex technological effort the legion had yet undertaken. (Indeed, it was so complex that most of the workers and all of the design staff were expatriates, mostly Volgans, on contract to the legion. It would be many years, decades even, before the native educational system was up to so high a level of technology.)

The first Meg-class submarine should have been ready two years prior. The sad fact was that it was only now that a seaworthy version was ready for trial runs and depth tests. That submarine, SdL-1, *Submarino de la Legion 1*, christened the *Megalodon*, rocked gently in the sheltered harbor, tied to a bumpered pier and surrounded by some of the ex-Volgan warships and sundry merchant carriers purchased by the legion in years past but never restored to full operating condition. Not far away from where the sub lay at anchor a construction crew was building a sub pen, while yet another crew laid a special, double-tracked rail line from the factory down to the rising shelter.

One at a time those old Volgan ships were being towed to the *Isla Real* and sunk or dismantled for fixed positions or cut up locally for scrap. Some of the scrap went into fortifications, both on the island and along the south side of the Gatun River, or for ammunition production. A great many artillery and mortar shells could be made from ten or twenty thousand tons of steel ship. Indeed, a great many—millions, in fact—*were* being made from old steel ships.

And precisely none of that steel went into the production of the *Meg.* In fact, the submarine was about ninety-four percent engineering plastic, by volume, exclusive of any water in the ballast tanks. That had

been much of the problem with production of this
first test model. Prior to the *Meg*, the largest plastic
casting machine on the planet of Terra Nova had been
able to cast a cylinder no more than four and a half
meters in diameter. *Meg*'s pressure hull was made
up of cylindrical and hemispheric sections, milled,
machined, and heat bonded together, of six meters in
diameter. Thus, the shipyard had had to have designed
and built a plastic casting apparatus from scratch.
Worse, the only company that had seemed capable
of doing so was in Anglia. As a practical province of
the Tauran Union, deprived of its own foreign policy,
Anglia had balked at providing military technology
to Balboa, however much the military nature of the
project had been disguised.

Ultimately, in order to get approval for the project,
they'd had to declare the Meg class to be for drug
interdiction, then redesign it to have external torpedo
tubes, with the torpedoes to be carried inside the tubes,
in distilled water, between the pressure hull and the
smooth, teardrop-shaped exterior fairing. With that,
Balboa had been able to claim, "How can this thing
be an offensive weapon? It doesn't even have torpedo
tubes. No, no; it's for police work... and research."
(Which was, at least for this first model, and at least
for the time being, true.) This, along with some not
insubstantial bribes (and the assistance of some very
anti-TU Anglians), had finally secured permission for
the creation and export of the casting apparatus.

The power source had been another nontrivial problem. Nuclear? There had been two practical possibilities,
a pebble bed modular reactor or a very small nuclear
reactor developed by the Hakunetsusha Corporation, in

Yamato. The former, however, was too large while the latter depended on convection cooling that would have been problematic in a submarine intended to operate and maneuver much like an airplane or glider. (On the other hand, some of the Hakunetsusha reactors had been ordered for emergency power supply to the *Isla Real* and the Gatun Line. There was, obviously enough, a serious disconnect between what various government bureaucracies and treaty regimes *thought* were militarily significant technologies, and what really *were* militarily significant technologies. In fact, *everything* was militarily significant, down to and including machinery for canning food.)

Failing nuclear, the designers had had to come up with some other air independent propulsion, or AIP, system. None of the Taurans, naturally enough, had wanted to sell their systems. Ultimately the choice had come down to molten carbonate fuel cells or solid oxide fuel cells. The latter had won out, primarily because the concept permitted shapes more suitable for application in a smallish—at thirty-six meters in length, within the pressure hull—submarine.

The *fact* of the prototype's existence couldn't be hidden in the long run. What Carrera and Fernandez hoped was that the *number* and capabilities of the final design could be hidden.

But, thought Carrera, standing on the dock to wish good luck to the test crew, *if this one just disappears into the ocean there won't be any more to keep hidden. We couldn't afford the waste.*

Two years lost, he mourned. *Two years. There was a time, just before I broke down, I might have shot one of the engineers to inspire the rest. Now I've fenced myself around with chains to keep me from doing any such thing. That's tactically moral, I'm sure. But is it strategically immoral to possibly lose having an important weapon in time to be of use? No matter. Even if I had shot one of them, that would still not have guaranteed that they could have completed the job any faster. And it just might have guaranteed we'd never have the subs. Better to be a civilized man. As much as I can be, anyway.*

The seventeen sailors on the test crew, along with Miguel Quijana, the captain of the second boat, the *Orca*, still being assembled, were all graduates of the legion's Cazador School. They waited expectantly in two ranks. Carrera rarely had patience for the kind of formality that suggested. He put his arms out at about shoulder height and beckoned with his fingers for the men to cluster around. They didn't need to be told a second time. They immediately broke ranks and formed a small semi-circle around their *Duque*.

Carrera looked at the first sub's captain, Chief Warrant Officer Chu. He was formerly a "yacht" skipper under Project Q, which had done so much to crush the Islamic pirates of Xamar during the war against the Salafis. Chu had been hand selected by Carrera and the *classis* commander, Roderigo Fosa, for this first submarine because he was one of the most mule-headed, determined squids in the *classis*. Chu, along with thirty-three others, had spent the last year detached from the legion and floating around the world, often literally, their roles rotating between unpaid "volunteers" to various civilian undersea research projects and "Officer Under Instruction" with three different submarines in the Volgan Navy, plus one each in the navies of Yamato and Zion. A couple of them had also spent some time understudying at the plant of the solid oxide fuel cell manufacturer, in the Federated States.

"You and your boys ready, Captain?" Carrera asked.

With a small smile the warrant answered, "As much as we're going to be without some hands on, *Duque*."

Carrera nodded his head slowly. *I understand that.* To the crew as a whole he said, "Boys, I can't tell you everything that this is about. I can only tell you that it's important, maybe as important as anything we're doing to defend ourselves."

From their expressions, Carrera knew what the sailors were thinking. *Tell us something we didn't know. If this weren't important, you wouldn't have shown up. For that matter, neither would we.*

They'd all been down on submarines before. What none of the crew had ever experienced, however, was diving in a submarine that had never been on a dive before. They were sweating, and it wasn't just from the heat of the surface they were about to leave.

Standing in the stubby conning tower, or sail, Chu's first order, before ordering the boat's water jets engaged was, "Engage the clicker."

The *Meg* was an immensely quiet boat. It was more nearly undetectable by active sonar than any submarine of which the legion was aware—or for that matter, of which the Imperial Navy of Yamato or the Navy of the Volgan Republic were aware. It had an extraordinarily low magnetic and electronic signature. It didn't put out much heat. The "clicker" was to advertise the sub's presence by simulating the

sound of an imperfectly cut gear in the jet propulsion units, said units being presumably inadequately
isolated. *Click ... click ... click*. Except that the clicking was so fast, consistent with what it was trying to
simulate, that it came out as more of a whine except
at *very* low speeds.

As long as they think they can find us by that,
thought Chu, *they'll be most unlikely to look for a
better way*.

Carrera knew about the "clicker"—the idea had,
after all, originated with *Obras Zorilleras* and been
pushed by Fernandez's crowd—but he couldn't hope
to hear it as the submarine eased away from the dock
and began heading out of port, its impellor pumps
churning the water slightly behind it.

There were other sailors at the dock. Likewise,
off in the distance he could see some cadets from
the Sergeant Juan Malvegui Military Academy peep-
ing out through the battlements of the old fort on
which the academy was situated, trying for a glance
at their ultimate military commander. Carrera knew
they were there.

*And I swear to You, God, if these people weren't
watching I'd get on my knees and pray for that crew.
As is, they'd think I'd gone soft. Will You accept the
wish for the reality? Best I can do under the circumstances. Watch out for them anyway, will Ya? And
please don't blame them for Hajar. That was all me.*

Miguel Quijana didn't get on his knees to pray for
the crew of the *Meg*, either. He did, however, cross
himself as the sub moved off.

Carrera noted that. *Interesting character, Quijana,* he thought. *I hope we didn't make a mistake.*

The other sub skipper had been the subject of considerable discussion between Carrera, on the one hand, and Fosa, on the other. As Quijana was the only survivor of the patrol boat *Santisima Trinidad,* self-sacrificed to save the flagship, the *Dos Lindas,* when it was attacked in the Straits of Nicobar during the legion's pirate suppression campaign, Fosa felt he owed Quijana something. Carrera, on the other hand, had had significant doubts about the boy.

"No, Rod," Carrera had said, "I *do* believe him when he says that his captain booted him off the boat just before slamming it into the side of the suicide ship that was coming for you. That's not the problem. The problem is that some people *don't* believe it, that he knows some don't, and that he might be inclined to, shall we say, 'reckless' behavior to *prove* he didn't desert his ship. And that worries me."

"There've been fights, you know," Fosa had added.

"And I won't deny," he'd admitted, "that the doubts eat at the boy's gut. But I know him. I took him on as an orderly after the *Trinidad* was lost. He's not the reckless sort. Give him a chance, Patricio. He deserves it."

The tree-shrouded island at the mouth of the harbor was passing to starboard. Chu ordered a slight change in direction to the west, following the "research vessel" that would accompany the sub on the surface, in case things went wrong. Just as the *Meg* was about to put the island between itself and the docks, the captain looked behind.

He's still standing there, watching us. Odd…very odd. What does he think; that he'll be able to pull us up by sheer will if we have a hull breach or engine failure? Well, knowing the bastard, he probably does.

Once outside the protection of the island and the harbor, the waves, which had been practically nonexistent, picked up noticeably.

"Well, no time like now to check the basic seal between hull and sail," Chu muttered. Still maintaining his spot in the conning tower, he ordered, "Bring her down to two meters."

What did that Volgan bastard say was the difference between a leak and a flood? Oh, I remember: "You find a leak; flooding finds YOU." Or the Yamatans? "If you find water coming in and suddenly smell the overpowering stench of shit, Chu-san? That's a flood. Surface, if possible, and then change trousers."

Assholes, the lot of 'em. But what great guys.

Some of the Volgans who had trained Chu's boys had had odd senses of humor. Prior to one particularly deep dive they'd stretched out a piece of thin blue cord from one side of the pressure hull to the other and tied both ends down, at a little below waist height. By the time the Volgan submarine had reached apogee, the string was touching the floor, that's how much the surrounding pressure had compressed the hull.

One of *Meg's* crew, Guillermo Aleman, had done the same across the control room. The string was still taut, of course, the boat was practically on the surface. Yet it was a reminder to everyone of just how far down they intended, eventually, to go.

In theory, using the thickness and type of plastic

that had gone into the construction of *Meg*, a spherical diving chamber could submerge to about twenty-four hundred meters before collapsing. The sub, however, was not spherical but cylindrical and it was believed they could do no more than a fraction of that depth safely. They couldn't have done even that fraction if the boat had been driven by a shaft running through the hull, rather than the six externally-mounted, electrically-driven impellor pumps it used. These breached the hull only in the form of leads cast right into the sections concerned.

But only a tenth of theoretical depth for today, Chu thought, as he descended a ladder and then reached overhead to pull the hatch shut behind him. He dogged the hatch, thinking, *A tenth and we'll call ourselves lucky.*

The boat's exec—another senior warrant, though junior to Chu—evacuated Chu's chair as soon as he saw the senior's boots. Chu sat, leaning onto the arm of the chair and cupping his mouth and chin in one hand.

Chu said, "Chief of Watch report rig for dive."

It was a tiny crew; the boat's exec, Junior Warrant Officer Ibarra, served as Chief of the Watch for the nonce. Indeed, the crew and sub were so comparatively small that the usual procedures were quite truncated and simplified.

The XO glanced at the buoyancy compensation panel and reported, "I have a straight board, Captain."

A straight board meant that there were no illuminated circles, indicating open hatches. Had there been such, instead of a series of dashes forming a straight line, there would have been one or more circles, indicating an undesired opening.

"Dive the boat. Make your depth twenty meters."

"Aye, Captain, twenty—two zero—meters," answered Ibarra.

From the diving station another submariner said, "Make my depth twenty meters, aye, sir." Another, beside the diving station, added, "Chilling the rubbers, aye, sir." A third said, "Helm, fifteen degree down angle on planes. Making my depth twenty meters."

The exec said, without facing Chu, "Forward group admitting ballast, Captain . . . aft group admitting ballast."

They could feel the boat sinking, a feeling that was not yet remotely comfortable. Automatically, the crew leveled the boat as it reached its depth. As the boat leveled off at the depth ordered, Chu again thought of odd foreigners with odder senses of humor. "Check for leaks," he said.

The *Meg* had an odd—really a unique—method of flooding and evacuating its ballast tanks. Like the pressure hull, these were cylindrical. Basically, the boat took advantage of the very low boiling temperature of ammonia. The ammonia was kept inside of flexible tubing made of fluorocarbon elastomer with a seven hundred and fifty angstrom thick layer of sputtered aluminum, followed by a five hundred angstrom layer of silicon monoxide with an aerogel insulation layer. Heating elements inside the tubes—called "rubbers" by the sailors and designers, both—heated the ammonia into a gas, which expanded the "rubbers" and forced out the water. To dive, the ammonia was allowed to chill to a liquid rather than heated to a gas. Chilling was really only a factor when quite near the surface, and then only if the water was warm.

✧　　✧　　✧

"Engineering, no leaks, Skipper...Power room, no leaks, Captain...Forward sonar chamber; she's dry as a bone..."

So far, so good, thought Chu. "Make your depth fifty meters."

Quijana sat apart from Carrera. Whether this was because he was shy, because he had an exaggerated notion of the importance of rank, or for some other reason, Carrera didn't know.

Quite possibly he's embarrassed to still be alive when his shipmates are dead, Carrera thought. *Should I invite him over and make it clear...or at least hint...that I don't think he deserted his boat?* He thought about that for long minutes before finally deciding, *No, it would be too obvious that that was what I was doing. Which would embarrass the poor shit even more.*

He thinks I am a coward, Quijana thought to himself, seated at the edge of the dock above the water, his legs dangling free over the edge. *How could he not? How could he not when I, alone of all my crew, survived the battle in the Nicobar Straits?*

And, too, was I not relieved when Pedraz booted me over the side? I know I was, even if I'll only admit it to God. Are you a coward, Miguel? Or are you just afraid that you are? Didn't you volunteer for submarine duty precisely to prove to yourself that you're a man? You know you did.

I remember that day. I see and feel it in my dreams, the smoke and the flying tracers, Pedraz's boot in my ass. Then sinking in the water and struggling up to the surface. A last glimpse of the Trinidad, *engines smoking, as it charged for the enemy's hull. And then the blast, a plume of smoke and debris, the shock wave that knocked me senseless until I was picked up by the* Agustin.

And so I've done everything I can to convince myself, not others but myself, that I am as good as any other man, as brave.

But has it worked? No, not entirely. I still wonder. Perhaps I always will.

The sun was beginning to set in the west when Carrera, still sitting at the dock, became aware of the presence of some small number of others behind him. He wasn't sure how he knew, but those presences seemed small. He turned and saw half a dozen boys from the nearby military academy, standing quietly with trays of food. They all looked pretty thin to Carrera.

"We didn't want to disturb you, sir," said one of the boys; his nametag read, "Porras." "But we saw you out here waiting pretty much all day and...well... we scrounged you and your driver and guards some food. From the mess. The mess sergeant said it would be all right."

Carrera nodded his head at the boy, then at his companions. "Thank you, gentlemen. I appreciate that. And...I think I have been remiss. I should have thought to feed the men with me."

That last was true enough for the purpose, but wasn't all the truth. In fact, Lourdes and Mitchell's wife had packed a lunch for the small group; they'd just not been especially interested in eating it, given the miserably wet *Puerto Lindo* heat.

"Would you boys care to join me?" Carrera asked.

"Oh, no sir...we couldn't, sir...we haven't got perm—"

"Ahem," Carrera said, "I'm sure your commandant won't object. As a matter of fact, consider it an order."

Porras answered for the group. "As long as you put it that way, *Duque*—"

"I do."

"—we'd be pleased to join you."

"Good, and while we're at it," his voice changed to a shout, "Captain Quijana, join us if you will."

"Oh, no, sir," said Porras, around a half a sandwich. "This place is *great*. It's hard, yeah, but it's still great. Always enough to eat. No cost to my parents. They don't even have to *clothe* me. And the money saved sure goes a long way back home. And we get to *train*. With *weapons*."

Carrera nodded while thinking, *I* hate *poverty. Unfortunately, you can't just pull people out of it without ruining them. The most you can do is help them help themselves. And even that's tricky.*

One of the boys added, "My parents have more money than Julio's, *Duque*, but he's basically right. This is a good education, better than my parents could have afforded for me."

Well that's something *in my favor*, Carrera thought. *I wonder how far it will carry me given that I'm going to use these boys like expendable property.*

One of the boys pointed out toward the island at the mouth of the harbor. "*Duque*," the boy said, "look; the submarine's returning."

"Thank God," Quijana whispered.

CHAPTER FOURTEEN

One factor that tends to bring this mutual looting about more quickly is the presence of an enfranchised, more or less large, but distinct minority within a generally pluralistic society. This happens quite without reference to race or culture; it is the minority status that drives the event. Perhaps better said, the minority status, because all minorities are or feel they are under threat in one way or another, tends to drive those members to vote as fairly cohesive blocks to defend their perceived interests, even as elites move to exploit those fears for their own ends.

Even where the minorities are relatively wealthy and influential themselves, often governments find they must buy off, rather, *seem* to be buying off, the population at large to distract attention from programs designed for the benefit of those minorities.

Moreover, we see in the Tauran Union a sincere attempt to create a state composed of nothing but minorities, even as we see a blizzard of currency fly from place to place, interest group to interest group, with the government taking, as usual, its enormous cut.

—Jorge y Marqueli Mendoza, *Historia y Filosofia Moral,* Legionary Press, Balboa, Terra Nova, copyright AC 468

Anno Condita 471
Restaurante MarBella, *Ciudad* Balboa, Balboa, Terra Nova

The restaurant was small, clean, and perhaps a little quaint. Moreover, it looked out over the sea to the north. Over the mud flats exposed by the receded tide, seagulls whirled and dived in the warm wet air. Past the seagulls, an airship soared majestically just below the clouds, carrying passengers and cargo from Colombia del Norte to the Federated States to the south. On the open air veranda, the proprietors had cleared away all the customers, seating them inside.

Alone but for his guards, Carrera waited for a man self-described as an "Emissary of Peace" from a group that claimed to wish nothing but prosperity for and cordial relations with Parilla, Carrera, and Balboa. Carrera had chosen the MarBella as the meeting place because it served, as far as he was concerned, the very best corvina—a particularly savory type of fish—in the Republic.

Soult and Sergeant Major McNamara entered the veranda, followed by a quite light skinned Santandern wearing an expensive looking Tuscan suit. Mitchell followed the Santandern.

The sergeant major pointed out Carrera, then

gathered up Soult and Mitchell and sat a table nearer the entrance.

Carrera watched the Santandern approach. *Odd, really; he doesn't look like a particularly bad sort. Just a regular working stiff, seems like. Maybe a little better fed and better dressed than most. Hmmm...who was that Old Earth philosopher who talked about "the banality of evil"? Maybe this one's a good husband and father? Oh, well, no matter.*

The Santandern was a lawyer by the name of Guzman. Guzman officially worked for the former law firm of the rump president of Balboa, Rocaberti. Unofficially he thought of himself as the Counsel General of the *Huánuco* Processors, Shippers, and Vendors Free State. Guzman didn't much like what he did. He didn't even much like himself. But he had a family to support and debts to pay.

The lawyer looked Carrera over carefully as he approached his table. *Another brainless soldier?* he wondered. *Corrupt? Somehow I think...not.* Wordlessly, Carrera motioned for Guzman to sit. As the lawyer sat, he thought, *Too dainty a hand to go with his reputation. A Napoleon, making up for a physical defect with aggression? Possibly.*

Carrera brusquely asked, "Why are you here and what do you, or the people you represent, want?"

None of my contacts informed me that the bastard was rude, Guzman thought. *Or maybe he doesn't think he is being rude. Be flexible.*

Guzman decided to go directly to the point. "I am here to offer you—you and General Parilla—a substantial amount of money for you to stop hindering the people I represent."

"Indeed?" Carrera lifted an eyebrow. "Santander, Atzlan, or both?"

"Both, actually, although I normally answer to someone in Santander."

"And your offer...your *principal's* offer?"

A waitress approached. Guzman shut up and pretended to peruse his menu. "What's good?" he asked.

"Most anything, really," Carrera answered. "I'm having the *corvina al ajillo*."

Guzman closed his menu and said to the waitress, "That sounds fine."

The lawyer had come prepared to bargain. He began low. "Three million drachma per month, each, to you and General Parilla, for you to stop interfering with our business."

Carrera just laughed, surprisingly mildly. "You insult me, *señor*."

Well, thought the Santandern, *that's a nice start. No screaming rage; just staking out a bargaining position.*

"Very well, then. I'll double it to six million."

"I don't think so."

"Well, what *do* you want?" Guzman asked.

"I want the shit kept out of Balboa and its territorial waters. Where it goes I couldn't care less about, as long as it doesn't come through here or to here. Moreover, I want you to get control of any, shall we say, 'random elements,' and force them to the same rule."

Guzman snorted. "You want us to take on the guerillas? That would be even more expensive than bribes. How about ten million? One hundred and twenty million a year."

The waitress returned, bearing their plates. These

she set down in front of each man, and the garlicky smell of the dish rose into their nostrils.

It's almost *tempting,* thought Carrera. *Even Parilla might want to go for it. We could buy a lot of training, a lot of equipment, and a lot of caring for our people with that much. But the cost is far too high. How many low level bureaucrats will be corrupted with bribes if we took them, even if we didn't keep them? How many soldiers and policemen will start getting in the habit of looking the other way? It isn't that I care a shit what happens to drug addicts in the Tauran Union or the Federated States, except insofar as I think the planet would be better off without them. I didn't care about them even before I came here. But this would be just a sort of moral disease in Balboa. Besides, even if I were a whore, we'd still have to haggle over my price.*

The lawyer tried hard to read Carrera's face. It was, after all, a good part of his job to read what people were thinking from their expressions. *If I up it by another million or two now, he'll go for it.*

Guzman decided on two. "*Duque* Carrera, for your cooperation I am prepared to offer you twelve million . . . each . . . every month . . . to both yourself and *Presidente* Parilla. Of course, for that amount, we would require a certain degree of active assistance."

Carrera frowned, shook his head, and answered, "Eat. Your food's getting cold."

Something in the tone suggested to Guzman the phrase, "And the condemned ate a hearty last meal." He suddenly lost his appetite and placed his knife and fork down on the plate with finality.

"Not hungry?" Carrera enquired, his voice full of

false concern. "What a pity." Carrera beckoned to McNamara. The tall, slender, well aged black sergeant major took long strides to the table."

"Sergeant Major, Mr. Guzman seems to have lost his appetite. Arrest him, please, and deliver him to Legate Fernandez for questioning."

The Santandern immediately blanched.

McNamara hesitated, thinking, *We just got him back. We've got him nicely cocooned in...well, for lack of a better term, "righteousness." It isn't worth throwing that away for whatever little advantage we might get from destroying this Santandern.*

The sergeant major's expression must have told. Carrera asked, "You disapprove?"

"Sir...I t'ink t'at's a really bad idea. Sir, whet'er he represents an official country or not, he's still a diplomat. Wrong not to let him go, sir. Bad precedent. Even if he is a scum-sucking lawyer."

Carrera took in a half breath, then bit off a retort. *If Mac says it's wrong,* he thought, *then there's a good chance that it's wrong.* He rocked his head from side to side a few times in indecision. Finally he admitted, "I suppose you're right, Sergeant Major. Please escort Mr. Guzman to the airport; he has an airship to catch. And Mr. Guzman? Don't come back to Balboa uninvited; I won't be responsible for your safety. And tell your people to keep their shit out of my country."

On a whim, Carrera reached up and took from around his neck a golden crucifix on a chain. "Give this to your masters," he said, handing it to Guzman.

Belalcázar, Santander, Terra Nova

Even in an organization as egalitarian and nontradi-
tional as the unofficially named "*Huánuco* Processors,
Shippers, and Vendors Free State" there were some
members who were a little more equal than others.
Jorge Joven was one among them. Indeed, his only
true peer in the organization was Pedro Estevez. It
was Estevez whom Belisario Endara had dealt with
in preparing a team to get rid of Parilla and Carrera.
All three sat now, along with Guzman, in a secure
room, heavily and not too tastefully decorated, in the
basement of Joven's palatial, isolated mansion, in the
hills overlooking the city.

"Son of a bitch," cursed Estevez. "Offer him money...
a decent offer you said it was, right, Guzman?"

"*Si, padron*," the lawyer confirmed. "A huge amount,
twelve million FSD monthly."

"And he won't take *that*? He's a mad dog, then,
and mad dogs need shooting."

Endara sighed, conscious that he'd been doing
a lot of that lately. "A mad dog he may be, Pedro,
but he is more of a rabid mad dog. Very dangerous,
too dangerous to fuck with lightly, as I have tried to
explain to my uncle."

"That was my impression, *padron*," Guzman confirmed to Estevez. "If his assistant hadn't talked him
out of it, I'd be in prison now."

"Oh, no," Endara said. "I assure you, you would
never have made it to prison." Endara's look grew
contemplative. "You know, it's odd that he let you go.
It's really not his style at all."

"So I gathered," the lawyer agreed. "Indeed, I am so sure I was within inches of doom that I've paid to have a special mass said for his tall black."

"Was that Jimenez or McNamara?" Endara asked.

"I don't know. He called the man 'sergeant major.'"

"Ah. That would be Sergeant Major General McNamara. Tough old man who manages to keep a very young and very beautiful wife very happy. He's one of the four or five people who actually have any personal control over Carrera."

"Well, no one is going to need to control the son of a bitch once he's dead," Estevez said.

"I was rather hoping you would talk my uncle out of this," Endara said, shaking his head, "since he won't listen to me on the subject."

Estevez nodded, seriously, even judicially. "And so I would have if this man had not insulted me and mine," Escobedo's head tilted toward Joven, "by refusing our very generous offer."

At the word, "generous," Guzman remembered something. He bent over and reached into his briefcase and withdrew from it a golden crucifix on a chain. This he handed to Escobedo with the words, "Carrera said to give this to you."

"What?" Escobedo raged. "Is he trying to tell me to make my peace with God?"

"No . . . no," said Endara, who knew a great deal about Carrera. "I think Carrera meant something rather different."

Once Estevez and Joven had heard just what Endara thought Carrera had meant by sending a crucifix, both their anger and their intentions expanded radically.

Federated States Embassy, *Ciudad* Balboa

Ambassador Tom Wallis came around from behind his
desk to shake Carrera's and Fernandez's hands, then
McNamara's. He then gestured to introduce them to
another man, this one with a plainly cultured tan, heavily
muscled, blue eyed, blond, tall, and gringo. Sunglasses
hung suavely from the gringo's pocket, and—to blend in
with the locals—he wore a *guayabera* which successfully
failed to hide a Bertinelli high-fashion holster.

"This is Mr. Keith, gentlemen," Wallis said.

"Gavin Keith," the gringo added.

Carrera disliked Keith instinctively. He thought of
a piece of advice once given by a Federated States
Marine Corps acquaintance on how to find a "Sea
Lion," the FS Navy's underwater recon and demolitions
commandos: *"Go to the nearest high water mark and
follow it until you come to the bodybuilder, lying in
a lawn chair, catching rays, wearing sunglasses, and
stylin' with a PM-6 submachine gun."*

"You used to be a Sea Lion, didn't you?" Carrera
asked, suppressing a smile.

"Team Six out of Big River," Keith answered. "How'd
you know?"

"Just a lucky guess," Carrera answered.

If Keith suspected that he was somehow the butt
of a private joke, his self image couldn't permit further inquiry.

Wallis also suspected that some sort of criticism
had been passed. He decided to change the subject.
"Mr. Keith's organization has some information that
might be useful to you. In fact, it might be critical."

"What's that?" Carrera asked. "And what organization?" *Who knows; maybe the muscles haven't cut off the blood supply to the brain in this case.*

"I'm with DITF," Keith answered, "the Drug Interdiction Task Force. We've got people inside the Belalcázar organization. We think you're going to get hit, soon and hard."

Carrera raised an eyebrow. "Do you mean me, personally, or do you mean my family and friends? Or Balboa, generally?"

"All of the above," Keith answered. "We've got no details, not yet, anyway. We're working on it. There is one thing, though..."

"Yes?"

"They've got shoulder-fired surface-to-air missiles available. If I were you I wouldn't take any aircraft anywhere anytime soon."

Fernandez frowned, nodded, and then admitted, "I've got nothing, no sources whatsoever, among the narcotraffickers, Patricio. Only when we grab one... and this report of light SAMs sounds... plausible, certainly.

"Is it just the Santander people or is Atzlan involved, too?" Fernandez asked.

"Atzlan is... interested," Keith said, "but, so far as we can tell, not involved. They're on the other side of the supply chain. What you're doing here doesn't affect them that much, if at all."

And it doesn't hurt, thought Fernandez, *that I had my wet work people, especially Khalid, exterminate one group of the bastards some time ago. Hmmm. Maybe it's time to put Khalid back to work again; he's my best. But in Santander this time.*

Hmmm. Wet work? Have to work on Patricio myself to get him to agree, these days.

Police Headquarters, *Ciudad* Balboa, Balboa

The afternoon sun cast long shadows from the trees lining the main thoroughfare on both sides. Striped by those shadows, a dirty white van, old and badly used, pulled into a parking space next to the former headquarters for the Transitway Area Police. The building itself, less than forty feet from where the van parked, was a one story, light brown painted, stucco structure. A group of policemen and women, numbering perhaps twenty-five, stood on the grass fronting the building. Another police officer, this one wearing sergeant's stripes, read aloud from his clipboard the duty instructions for the night shift.

A young police officer, Emilio Alvarez, half ran from a side door of the police station to his car parked a few hundred meters away, opposite the Balboa Knights of Pius V hall. As he passed, Alvarez took little notice of the T-shirted passenger exiting the van. Like all new members of the police force inducted of late, Alvarez was a member of the Reserves, in his case of the Tenth Infantry Tercio. He hastily tucked a fatigue shirt in as he rushed to be on time for his weekend drill.

Amidst a cacophony of fruitlessly honking horns and mostly good-natured cursing, Alvarez crossed the street, weaving his way through crawling "rush hour" traffic. On reaching his automobile, he bent slightly to unlock the door. Opening the door, he looked up to see two men, one of whom he thought he had just seen getting out of a white van, cross the street at a very fast walk. The men broke into a fast run.

Afterwards, Alvarez was to remember everything which followed in remarkable detail: the approach of two running men toward his car, the way the desk sergeant turned to look at the van, the small puff of smoke that escaped from underneath it, the blinding flash, and then the bodies—and parts of bodies—of the night shift being smashed into the crumbling wall of the police station.

Alvarez was thrown to the ground by the blast. He rolled over to his belly and then arose to all fours. Paying no attention to the cuts on his face and—where his own car's windows had shattered—his chest, Alvarez drew his sidearm and rushed into the street. Now he really did notice the two men, one in a dirty white T-shirt, the other in a cheap looking *guayabera*, that arose from the asphalt, swearing about something. Whatever it was they were cursing, Alvarez was too deafened by the blast to hear. It didn't matter.

One of the two bombers, the one in the *guayabera*, began to reach under his shirt for a gun. Alvarez quickly took a firing stance. The gunman put both his hands into the air, followed by his companion a moment later.

A female Tauran Union corporal, Gallic by birth, and shapely enough even through her battledress, had also survived the blast. She rushed over to where Alvarez had the two bombers covered. Seeing another uniform, Alvarez beckoned the corporal over with one hand, the other keeping the pistol steady-aimed on the bombers. He handed over his pistol and said, "Watch these two. Kill them if they make a move."

The languages were just close enough. The Gallic corporal nodded, angrily, then took the pistol and held it on the bombers. Alvarez raced for the ruins of the police station. On the way he passed dozens of dead; men, women, and children. Still others cried or screamed. He left those for what aid the other survivors could give them. He had to get to the police station.

When he reached the smoking yard in front of the station, Alvarez began to throw up. He had seen dead people before, but never so many in one place, never so many so completely ruined. Fighting his nausea, Alvarez returned to the wounded on the streets. There he could still do some good.

Estado Mayor, Ciudad Balboa, Balboa, Terra Nova

As reports rushed in—a bombing in Cristobal, another two in *Ciudad* Balboa, a fifth in *Ciudad* Cervantes to the east—Fernandez gently held a framed portrait of his daughter, his only child, killed years before by a terrorist's bomb.

What a terrible world we live in, child. I would have thought—though I should not have thought it—that those days were past. Silly me.

The reports of casualties were fragmentary, at best. Even so, there were well over a hundred known dead, and possibly as many as twice that. Of wounded there may have been a thousand. Among the dead were half a dozen elderly tourists from the Federated States, killed while dining at a small and quaint restaurant overlooking the sea. This, of course, had the Federated States enraged.

Fernandez placed the portrait back down on his desk, then stood. His normally ferretlike face twisted into a hate-filled sneer. "Revenge," he said aloud, then repeated, "Revenge."

Casa Linda, Balboa, Terra Nova

The boy stood in front of his father's grand desk, hands clutched behind his back and head thrust forward. A sea breeze wafted through the window, bringing with it the not unpleasant aroma of the salt sea to the north. Outside birds chirped in the trees below the balcony. Closer still, on that balcony, a half dozen trixies, plus one, took turns grooming each other.

"What now, Dad?" Hamilcar asked.

"Now we bring the war to them in ways they probably never even imagined," Carrera answered.

The boy frowned slightly. "Did you know this would happen?" he asked.

Carrera sighed, chewing his lower lip and looking up towards the ceiling of his office. His face scrunched of its own accord. "I knew *something* like this would happen. That's not really your question though, is it?"

The boy shook his head. "No. I really want to know why it's worth it."

"It's complex," Carrera said. The boy looked directly at his father as if to ask, *Do you think I'm not bright enough, even at nine years old, to understand?*

The father understood the unstated question. "All right, then," he said. "We are going to war with the

Taurans in anywhere from one to three years. We can win that war, provided the Federated States stays at least neutral. To make them stay neutral, we have to deal with their concerns. Of those, a big one is the drug trade."

"But you've told me before that that problem is entirely of their own making, entirely their own fault."

"And I told you the truth, Son," Carrera answered. "But the mere fact that it is their own fault has very little to do with whether they accept that it's their own fault. They don't. They won't. Maybe, even, they *can't*. I don't think they can, anyway." Carrera sneered. "After all, how can they blame the innocent, rich, white stock broker who feeds several thousand drachma a week up his nose when there's a guilty, brown, and dirt-poor *huánuco* grower iniquitously cultivating the stuff to feed his starving family?"

"Huh?"

Carrera laughed bitterly. "Never mind. Just accept that people often not only don't think logically, they often can't, and that certain forms of government often make this worse. Accept it, because it's our reality. Just as it's our reality that we are the most powerful of tiny states on this planet, but are still tiny for all that."

"All right," the boy agreed. "So you accepted that some of our people would be killed?"

"Acceptance is perhaps not the right word, Son, implying it was a happy compromise. Let's say I understood it would happen, or at least could, and I was prepared to fight it, mitigate it, and retaliate for it."

Hamilcar's eyes narrowed. "That's bullshit, Dad," he said.

"All right then," Carrera said. "Call it 'acceptance,' if you insist, so that we could prevail in an inevitable war—at least I *think* it's inevitable—to recapture all of our country."

"Hard on the people who were killed, Dad," the boy observed. "Some of them were my age . . . or even younger."

"How many would be killed to no purpose if we fight the war that is coming and lose?"

"More, I suppose."

"More and to no good," Carrera said. "And on the subject of people your age being killed, your mother and I are agreed; you are leaving the country sooner than we'd planned."

The boy's eyes narrowed again, even as his little shoulders stiffened. "It's wrong to send your own family out of a danger you've helped bring on everyone else, Dad."

The father nodded slowly and deeply, agreeing, "Yes, it would be wrong. But I'm not sending you away to protect my son. I'm sending you away to preserve my replacement."

Hamilcar thought about that for a moment. It made sense and was possibly even the right thing to do. "Where are you sending me?" he asked.

"You, and your Pashtun guards, and Alena, and her husband, Tribune Cano, are heading back to Alena's people. They will preserve you. And possibly teach you some things you need to know."

"All right then," the boy agreed. While his mother would cheerfully have sent him out of harm's way because he was her son, his father, he knew, would never shame him that way. "Since you're heading east tomorrow, Dad," Hamilcar asked, "and since I'm leaving soon, can I go with you?"

"I wish," Carrera said. "But no, I have to preserve my replacement. Besides, the first part of the day I have to meet with Parilla. You'd be bored to death."

The boy looked crestfallen, enough so that Carrera added, "But in a few days there is a ceremony of sorts I want you to undertake before you go."

Carrera Family Cemetery, Cochea, Balboa

Flames arose from torches on the green. The flickering flames cast shadows across the grass. The torches were there partly for their light, partly for the smoke that helped drive off the mosquitoes. Mostly, though, they used torches for the sense of visual drama they lent the proceedings.

Lourdes had not been invited. "Love, in this one thing, you cannot be witness," Carrera had told her.

Her eldest was there, the boy Hamilcar Carrera-Nuñez. The boy was wide eyed, half at the spectacle and half at being led kindly by the hand by his father. They walked along a path marked with the flaming torches towards the marble obelisk that marked the grave—though it was more memorial than grave, really—of his dead half-siblings and their mother, Linda.

Before moving to the memorial Carrera had shown the boy pictures of Linda and their children, explaining their names and telling him stories about them in life. He'd also told the boy how they'd been murdered.

"That's why I spent so much time away from home, Son," the father explained, "hunting down the men responsible."

"I understand, Dad," the boy said.

Perhaps he did, too. He was a bright lad, extremely so. Carrera expected great things of him. *Kid will likely be tall, too, given that his mother's 5'9".*

Around the obelisk were several close friends: Kuralski, Soult and Mitchell, as well as Parilla. Jimenez, McNamara and Fernandez were in Pashtia. Those present were uniformed and stood at parade rest as Carrera led the boy forward by the hand.

Soult brought out a Bible, which he handed to Carrera. Releasing Hamilcar's little hand, the father knelt down beside him, holding out the book and saying, "Place your left hand on this and raise your right. Now repeat after me."

"I, Hamilcar Carrera-Nuñez..."

"I, Hamilcar Carrera-Nuñez..."

"...swear upon the altar of Almighty God..."

"...swear upon the altar of Almighty God..."

"...undying enmity and hate...to the murderers of my brother and sisters...and the murderers of their mother, my countrywoman...and to the murderers of all my country folk...and to those that have aided them...and those that have hidden them...and those who have made excuses for them...and those that have funded them...and those who have lied for them...wherever and whoever they may be...and whoever may arise to take their places. I swear that I will not rest until my fallen blood is avenged and my future blood is safe. So help me, God."

"Very good, Son," Carrera said, handing the Bible back to Soult and ruffling Hamilcar's hair affectionately. "Now we are going to have dinner with my friends, back at the house. The day after tomorrow we go back to getting ready for the next war."

Executive Mansion, Hamilton, FD, Federated States of Columbia

"God," muttered the president. "God, but I would like to teach those people a lesson."

About a couple of hundred slaughtered Balboans the Progressive Party, currently in power in the Federated States, cared not very much. Half a dozen murdered citizens, however, and their friends and relatives, to say nothing of a fickle press baying for blood, were of considerable concern.

The president of the Federated States of Columbia, Karl Schumann, was sufficiently concerned with that problem that he hardly paid any attention to the zaftig intern kneeling between his legs with her raven-tressed head bobbing. Ordinarily, the president would not have been able to think clearly while the intern was so engaged. Under the circumstances, he had no trouble thinking but considerable trouble concentrating on her efforts.

The Office of Strategic Intelligence, Justice and State tell me the Santanderns are responsible. The Joint Chiefs are not so certain some radical group in Balboa didn't do it. Me; I think it was the Santanderns, the drug running Santanderns.

What do I do? Tell the Army to go after the drug lords with special operations people? We don't know which one to go after, which one gave the orders. We don't even know which cartel. Bomb them? Same problem. And if they are this ruthless outside of Santander, what's to stop them from coming after me? The Secret Service reminds me daily, in word and deed, that I am

*vulnerable. And the drug lords' resources are certainly
adequate to get me if I provoked them.*

In that last it was possible that Schumann was giving the cartels too much credit. Then again, possibly
he wasn't, either.

*No. I'll just let make a statement. People will forget
in time. They always forget in time. It was only six
of our own killed. Hell, they were probably Federal-
ists, anyway.*

*Yeah, yeah, that's the ticket; ride it out. And think-
ing of riding it out . . .*

"Honey," the President of the Federated States said,
"head's nice and all, but I'd rather you shuck out of
your skirt and panties and get on all fours."

Executive Complex, *Ciudad* Balboa, Balboa, Terra Nova

Parilla's secretary, Luci, turned her office chair and
crossed her legs to reveal as much thigh as possible. It was an automatic gesture, as well as a
needless one. Few men bothered to look at her legs
when there was such a bounty of breast to catch
the eye.

Carrera forced his own eyes away, sighing as he
often did when passing through the president's door.
*I wonder if she even thinks about it, or if it's all
genetic autopilot. Hmmm . . . I wonder if Parilla's
fucking her. He's an awfully young old man and a
man is, after all, only as old as the woman he feels.*

Mitchell stayed behind in the anteroom as his
chief went in to consult with the president, the door

clicking shut behind him. It was one of the perks of driving or guarding Carrera; flirting with the president's secretary.

Just flirting though, Mitchell thought. *Chica's enough woman for me.*

Even so, Mitchell sat on the corner of Luci's desk, making small talk and taking in as much of two of Balboa's greatest natural wonders as possible.

"Where to today, Mitch?" Luci asked, with a friendly but not necessarily inviting smile. Not that she'd have minded having a go of it with the stocky aide, but he'd shown long since that he wasn't available for anything but admiring the scenery.

"Enough admiring the scenery," Carrera said, his face mock serious. Mitchell was only slightly less mocking when he braced to attention and sounded off with a "Yessir" that would have been loud in a much larger space than the anteroom.

Luci rolled her eyes. She knew that the display was as a much a show as she routinely put on herself. Carrera waved goodbye casually as he and Mitchell headed out the door and toward the elevators. Luci then stood, closed the door behind them, and turned to make sure Parilla's door was shut as well. Only then did she pick up the telephone.

Highway *InterColombiana,* Nata, Balboa, Terra Nova

Randy Whitley replaced the hotel room phone on the receiver. He then stood, picked up a small satchel

that had been resting on the bed, and went to collect his people.

Had he but known it, Mr. Keith had a former comrade on the other side. He probably would not have
been surprised. The drug lords had recruited a number
of foreign-born *mercenaries*, or, as they preferred to
think of themselves, "contract professionals." Like most
mercenaries in the modern age, these were veterans
of various nations' special operations units. Generally
speaking, such men were attracted by the money available from contract work, that and the excitement.

For a dozen times more than he had ever made
as a Sea Lion or a Legionnaire with the Gallic armed
forces, former Petty Officer 2nd Class Whitley had
attempted to train a group of former thugs to something roughly analogous to Sea Lion tactical standards.
Neither tactics nor training, however, were actually
Sea Lion strong suits. Whitley himself was a walking
advertisement for what really were Sea Lion strong
suits. He had muscles on his muscles, arms the size
of legs and legs the size of trees.

Five of the men he had trained, plus Whitley himself,
had waited in and around this sleepy town bisected by
the Pan-Columbian Highway for over a week. Two,
including Whitley, now sat in a rented automobile. Two
others pretended to pray in the small Nata Catholic
church; the same church, so said a bronze plaque on the
white painted wall, where Belisario Carrera had once
prayed for victory in his war with Old Earth.

To the man with him in the car Whitley said, "Go
across the street to the telephone booth. Pretend to
make a call."

The Santandern nodded and left, crossing the

street nervously, carrying his weapon in a small black satchel. He'd free the firearm once he was in the telephone booth.

The remaining two men crouched by the road to either side of the town, east and west, to warn Whitely of Carrera's approach.

Trees whizzed by as the big Phaeton 560 ESL tore up the highway, east toward *Ciudad* Cervantes. Carrera sat up in the front of the big auto, rolling his hands together, chewing his lip, and fuming. The news had come from his brother-in-law, David Carrera, via cell phone just as the Phaeton crossed over the Bridge of the Colombias. One of the dead had turned out to be a cousin of his late wife. *A nice girl,* he remembered. *Bastards!* He was in a killing rage.

There were two guards in back. Mitchell drove. He'd seen his chief in this kind of mood before. *No sense in chatting to distract him,* Mitchell thought, *not when he's like this.*

Both men, driver and passenger, glanced to the side frequently and regularly. Likewise did the guards. Even so, their attention tended to stay on the road to their front and the buildings and trees to either side. Thus, they missed the man who watched them pass, stepped out, and said something into a radio.

Randy Whitley, former Federated States Navy Sea Lion, Gallic Legionnaire, and current private contractor, said, "Roger," into the small radio and tucked it back into a shirt pocket. Whitley than returned his right hand to the pistol grip of the RGL, Rocket Grenade Launcher, he carried and whistled at the Santandern in the telephone booth across the street, who pretended to be talking into the telephone. Another whistle alerted two similarly armed, olive skinned assassins at the front of the church.

Whitley sighed. *Damned shitty work for someone who set out to do good in the world. But a man's got to eat, and ever since the drawdown under the progressives, contract work's been the only way to do that.*

Sure wish I'd had more time to work with these assholes. Nobody understands; it ain't all just knowing how to shoot.

Farther on by half a kilometer a lone man stepped out of a telephone booth and into the road. He raised a weapon. Mitchell saw it before Carrera did.

"Oh, fuck!" Mitchell said. He reached an arm over and pushed Carrera down onto the seat. Then, ducking low himself and screaming something mindless, he aimed the car at the gunman and floored the gas.

You fucking idiot, Whitley cursed to himself as one of his men—the one in the phone booth—stepped into the roadway and raised his PM-6 to a hip firing position.

Buy 'em books, send 'em to school, and what do they show for it? Nothin'.

The submachine gun was silenced. Whitley saw rather than heard the muzzle rise and flash as a stream of bullets tore out of it toward the Phaeton. Many of the bullets impacted on the radiator. Others smashed the windshield. At the last split second the gunman jumped out of the way. The car clipped his leg at about mid thigh, snapping it, and threw him, spinning while screaming, some distance away.

✧   ✧   ✧

The Phaeton careened out of control and smashed into a telephone pole. Carrera was thrown forward into the dash. He gasped aloud—"ahhh, Gggoddd!"—at an awful pain he felt in his right shoulder. Briefly stunned, he shook his head to clear it. That hurt, too. Pain or not, he then reached under the seat and pulled out one of the weapons kept there—a Pound submachine gun, along with several magazines. Shouting something to Mitchell and the guards, Carrera opened the door and rolled out, then crawled to a position in front of the caved-in grill and next to the telephone pole.

Whitley aimed his RGL at the car and let fly. The backblast smashed shop and home windows behind him. The rocket impacted on the rear passenger door, killing the two guards and causing the rear of the Phaeton to explode in flames. Whitley dropped the rocket launcher, drew a pistol, and walked forward to finish the job. Two men by the church, who hadn't so far done anything to help Whitley's ambush, ran up the street to join him. The original gunman lay screaming in the road. The two lookout men had their own transportation. They were only to fire if Carrera's vehicle had made it through the main ambush and tried to exit town. Since it hadn't, they followed their instructions and rode off separately.

"Keep both sides of the street covered," Whitley ordered. The two unused gunmen complied.

Carrera heard the order and thought, *I'm* so *dead.*

Private Hector Pitti, Sixth Mechanized Tercio, was new to the legion, and only a militiaman to boot. His rank was as low as it got without being an outright recruit. Still, he was proud of his military status, proud enough that his F-26 rifle hung over his *lorica* in a place of honor in his living-*cum*-dining room *cum* kitchen. A full magazine sat on a narrow shelf right underneath the firearm.

Pitti heard no shots. Moreover, the sound of a crashing auto was nothing remarkable anywhere along the InterColombiana. But when the rocket grenade launcher fired, and its backblast shattered the windows over the kitchen sink, Pitti thought that it was about time to take his rifle from the pegs that held it. There was no time to don his body armor, the *lorica*.

With hands still shaking from the blast, he did so. He held the rifle in one hand while the other fumbled with the protective tape that sealed the ammunition in the magazine. That wasn't working too well until Pitti swung the magazine under one armpit to hold it. Cursing, he fumbled with the tape until thumb and forefinger managed to grasp it. A quick pull and the tape came off of the mouth of the magazine. He dropped the tape, then lifted his arm, releasing the magazine and catching it with his hand. Slamming it into the F-26's magazine well, he was already jacking the bolt as his feet carried him to the shattered window.

Carrera would probably have been dead, too, had not one of the reservists of the town—*got to get that man's name!*—stuck his issue rifle out of his front window to fire at Whitley. It was a hurried shot. The militiaman missed.

Still, shocked at the unexpected fire and the bullets cracking the air nearby, the former Sea Lion dove to his belly. "Motherfucker! Where did that come from?"

Whitley slithered around on the gravel as he scanned for the source of the fire.

That distraction was all Carrera needed. Rolling over from his covered position next to the car, Carrera winced as his right shoulder temporarily took the weight of his torso. He fired two short bursts at Whitley, the bolt chattering and the bullets making little sonic booms, lower in pitch than those from the F-26. One or more likely, given Whitley's size—several of the Pound's bullets connected; Whitley spun and then fell to his rear end, torso still upright. He made no sound beyond a surprised "oomph." The assassin seemed confused when he looked down at his red stained, ruined midsection.

Rising to a crouch and aiming over the Phaeton's hood, using it to support his aim, Carrera turned on the other two. These were just now rising from where they'd taken cover at the unexpected shots. Surprised anyone was left from the Phaeton after the RGL had struck it, they fired from the hip. Carrera, conversely, took the time to aim. His metal-shrouded pin sight lined up on the upper torso of one of the gunmen. He stroked the trigger, lightly, and was rewarded by the image of the gunman's chest rippling under the impact. A late round, driven high by muzzle climb, hit the assassin's head, exploding it like an overripe melon.

Good thing the Pound is low recoil, Carrera thought absently, as his sight traversed to the last remaining assassin. *Otherwise, I wouldn't hit shit. Ouch.*

The bullets from the still spraying and last standing assassin struck the hood of the Phaeton, as well as the tires. Air rushed even as metal gave way and chips of paint flew.

Again Carrera's finger stroked the trigger, then twice again in rapid succession. The last assassin fell with satisfying screams of pain.

Carrera rose to a crouch and duckwalked forward, stopping once to change magazines. He donated another burst each to the two olive skinned gunmen, then turned back to the white one.

Still looking dazed and confused, the ex-Sea Lion tried to focus his eyes on the uniformed man in front of him.

"It was just business," Randy Whitley said, in English, as if that explained everything.

"So is this," Carrera answered, placing the smoking muzzle against Whitley's forehead. He squeezed the trigger again, causing the contract professional's head to disintegrate in a spray of blood and bits of brain and skull.

The militiaman who had spontaneously fired in Carrera's support ran out with his rifle at port arms. That he looked like a soldier, despite his working-man's clothes, was all that kept Carrera from firing on him as well.

"*Señor*, you are bleeding," the militiaman said.

Carrera ignored that. Pointing to the broken-legged gunman lying on the ground, he said, "Guard him, soldier!" Then Carrera ran to the driver's side of the Phaeton to see to Mitchell and his guards. It was not pretty. Flames licked around the guards' bodies, as hair and uniform material added their stench to the smell of cooking pork.

Carrera's heart sank as his bile rose. "Oh, hell. Ah, shit, Mitch! What am I going to tell your wife and kids?" Carrera looked only once to be sure. Mitchell was dead, the back of his head missing where a bullet had forced his brain out of it. He put a hand on Mitchell's blood-stained shirt and began quietly to cry, even as he pulled his friend's corpse away from the fire. The people who had begun to gather now that the shooting was over looked wonderingly at the soldier who stood leaning against the car, head hung in sorrow.

He stood that way, weeping, for only a few minutes before hurt changed to a cold, inhuman fury. Carrera turned around and walked to the broken-legged gunman. By the submachine gun lying several meters away, Carrera knew that the militiaman had searched and disarmed the gunman. He told the militiaman, "Get me an iron bar or a big stick."

"*Si, señor*, I have a crowbar in my house."

"Perfect."

When the militiaman returned with the crowbar, Carrera turned over his Pound SMG, took the crowbar and slapped his left palm several times. He ignored the pain emanating from his injured shoulder. Some pains can overwhelm others. He said to the gunman, "You killed my friend."

Two swings and the Santandern's knees shattered. Carrera then bent down and, putting the crowbar on the ground, grabbed each leg in turn and twisted it. The gunman arched his back and shrieked. When he tried to bend over to reach his crushed knees, Carrera let him. Then he picked up the crowbar and broke each forearm. Several distinct blows so destroyed the Santandern's arms that his hands flopped uselessly in the breeze. The Santandern fainted. Carrera sent the militiaman for smelling salts.

While he waited, Carrera lit a cigarette. Two police in a squad car arrived on the scene, followed by an ambulance. The policemen took a fire extinguisher to smother the flames, while one of them hauled out the bodies of the two guards in the back seat. When the ambulance crew went for the Santandern lying motionless on the road, Carrera waved them away. "See what you can do for my men," he said, even though he knew there was nothing that could be done.

The stretcher bearers looked at Carrera's uniform and insignia of rank. They left the Santandern where he lay.

The smelling salts not arriving quickly, Carrera borrowed two ampoules from the ambulance. These he crushed and held under the Santandern's nose. The gunman choked and sputtered, then began to moan. The militiaman returned without the salts.

With a kindly voice, Carrera told the militiaman, "Thank you. It's all right. I don't need them anymore. And thank you, too, for saving my life. That was quick thinking, Private . . . ?"

"Pitti, *señor*. Private Hector. Sixth Mechanized Infantry Tercio."

"Again, thank you, *Corporal* Pitti," Carrera said. Pitti's eyes widened.

Once the Santandern was again wide awake and shrieking, Carrera placed himself on the man's left side and methodically broke all of his right side ribs, moving each blow up a bit higher than the one before. Some took more than one blow before he felt the rib give way. Then Carrera walked around to the gunman's right side. The militiaman and the police winced with each blow, but could not leave until dismissed. As a practical matter, given who and what Carrera was in Balboa, they couldn't object either. Most of the eye-witnesses left when the first of the gunman's bones was driven through his skin, blood spurting across the asphalt, and he began to scream like a young girl. Once, when the Santandern almost stopped reacting to the pain, Carrera took the crowbar by the hooked end, jammed the other end into the assassin's abdomen, dug around, twisted twice, and pulled. At the sight of the greasy-looking, bluish intestine, the older of the two policemen promptly threw up next to the yellow-painted squad car. The Santandern screamed anew, then turned his head to one side and vomited as well. Flies began to settle on the loop of intestine almost as soon as it appeared.

It took the Santandern almost thirty agonized minutes to die. When Carrera finally grew tired, and became aware once more of the pain in his shoulder, he stood over the Santandern, took a last look at Mitchell, still lying beside the smoldering Phaeton, and brought his crowbar down, again and again, until the man's head was a shapeless lump, brains leaking out onto the roadway for the ants.

When the beating was done, Carrera walked over to Whitley's body and pulled out his own penis to urinate on the corpse.

That done, he reclothed himself and turned to the policemen. "See if there's any ID on the gringo-looking one. Photograph his corpse and print him. Get a blood sample. Then feed them all to the dogs!" he ordered, in a voice that permitted no questioning. Turning, he asked of the ambulance crew, "Could you do something about my shoulder? I think it's broken."

❖   ❖   ❖

Crouching under a table at a small roadside café about a hundred and fifty meters down the road, Endara witnessed the entire incident, including the beating. He left the scene before he could be questioned by the police. Thereafter, telling his uncle, the rump president, that he was seriously underestimating the nature of the opposition, Endara began to make arrangements to leave Balboa for healthier climes. When he arrived in Santa Josefina, a week later, he claimed to be a political refugee.

Raul Parilla never found out why his receptionist left for parts unknown following the attempt on Carrera's life. However, she and Endara were often seen together in the nightclubs and restaurants of the capital of Santa Josefina.

Mitchell was buried with honors in a small part of the *Casa* Linda grounds Carrera set aside as a cemetery. His wife, Chica, great with child, and Lourdes held each other and wept while the priest went through the ceremony. Carrera just stood with one of his hands clenched behind his back in pain and fury. The other arm was immobilized by the cast that held the shoulder. The sergeant major and the rest of Carrera's personal staff made up the pallbearer detail and firing squad.

Within three days of Mitchell's murder a diplomatic pouch containing weapons and munitions, along with some fifteen new embassy personnel, arrived in the Balboan embassy in Santander. Within a few days of that, three Balboans of the Fourteenth Tercio (*Operaciones Especiales*) were dead, as were eleven bodyguards of various cartel members in Belalcázar.

No drug lords were killed, unfortunately. However,

all took to their most suburban palaces for protection. The remaining nine unwounded Fourteenth Tercio men began gathering intelligence on those same palaces. They also, with the replacements for the wounded and dead, undertook some more sanguine operations.

As the drug war spread to Santander, it waned somewhat in Balboa. Although Carrera's marksmanship and rage had made certain that no useful intelligence would be forthcoming from those who had tried to kill him, there were still the two bombers captured by Alvarez.

Cut off from support by Endara's desertion, the remaining six Santanderns hid out in a *pensión* in Balboa City. There they might have remained in safety had not one of them used the word *chumbo* to indicate his male appendage to a visiting whore, along with instructions as to what he wanted her to do with it. In Balboan slang *chumbo* meant a black man. In Santander it meant penis.

Looking for the substantial reward offered for information leading to the capture of the bombers and assassins, the de la Plata-born hooker had recognized the word as one used by the more numerous Santandern hookers in Balboa. She had gone straight to the police after collecting her earnings. In the ensuing firefight, four policemen were hit, three mortally, and all but one of the Santanderns shot to death. That one, after being delivered to Fernandez, had cause to regret not being killed.

CHAPTER FIFTEEN

Political revolutions *fail*. It is in their nature. That is to say, a revolution, any revolution, will tend to fail unless it isn't really a revolution at all, but a recognition of a preexisting fact. To actually change anything profoundly, quickly, and lastingly is simply too hard.

This does not mean, of course, that the *revolutionaries* will fail. They may, indeed, take power. They very often manage to do quite well for themselves. Very often, indeed, they manage to do pretty well by their great-great-grandchildren. And yet still the revolution itself will have failed.

Between Old Earth and New, we have seen dozens of failed revolutions: France, 1789 AD, got rid of its king and nobility well enough ... and had an emperor and a new nobility within fifteen years. No Marxist revolution, whether Leninist or Tsarist, has managed to last more than about seventy-five Old Earth years. How many peoples of once-colonized states have awakened a few years after their revolutions wishing the colonialists were back? Even here in Balboa, Belisario Carrera's revolution, in the early days, got rid of the Old Earthers, but morphed into a corrupt oligarchy of our own within a couple of generations.

And the successes? One can count them on the fingers of one hand. And in each case, be it the plebes seceding from the patricians in ancient Rome, the Athenian demes demanding power in return for their service in the fleet, or the American colonists, two factors stand clear: Those revolutions were limited in what they sought to achieve, and they recognized an already established state of facts. Thus, even those examples beg the question of whether they were revolutions at all in anything but name.

> —Jorge y Marqueli Mendoza, *Historia y Filosofia Moral,* Legionary Press, Balboa, Terra Nova, copyright AC 468

Anno Condita 471
Punta Cocoli Airfield, *Isla Real,* Balboa, Terra Nova

Two Nabakov-21 jet transports awaited the party on the airfield, their engines turning the air over the concrete of the strip into a couple of blotches of wavering haze. Within the haze, surrounded by it, two double lines of sweating Pashtun along with a dozen Balboan tutors boarded, along with their families. The Pashtun wore the pixilated desert battledress of the legion but with turbans atop their heads. The tack for the horses they would pick up in Pashtia. The impedimenta—personal baggage, tentage and supplies—was already aboard and strapped down under netting.

"Now listen to me carefully," said Carrera to Tribune Cano, wagging a finger a few inches in front of the latter's nose, "I don't care if these people think Hamilcar is Jesus Christ himself, let alone a reincarnation of Alexander. There will be *no* bowing and scraping. None."

Carrera had to use his left index finger; his right arm was still immobilized.

"Easier to order than to enforce, *Duque*," said Alena, Cano's Pashtun wife, standing at her husband's side. "He *is* Iskandr, the avatar of God."

Carrera smiled then, thinking, *Never underestimate the benefits of a classical education.*

"Indeed," he said. "Let us suppose for the moment that that is so. Was Iskandr, the boy, told that he was a god? Did his people do proskynesis? Was he spoiled?"

Alena's smooth brow wrinkled. "Well . . . no, not so far as we know, anyway. His godhood wasn't made manifest until God himself spoke to him at the place called Siwah."

"Right. Has this happened, to the best of your knowledge, with Hamilcar, my dear?"

Wrinkled brow was joined by pursed lips. "Ummm . . . no," she forced out.

"Does it not then occur to you that that is the way it must happen, that the boy not be treated as a god until God himself decrees it?"

Brow and lips were then joined by narrowing eyes. "Perhaps."

Carrera looked from Alena to Cano and back again, while saying, "No perhaps about it. You will not ruin my boy. Though there is something . . . if I could speak with your wife privately, Tribune . . ."

I will not weep, Lourdes ordered herself. *I will not; I will not; I will not! I will . . .*

"Mom, stop crying," Hamilcar said. "You're embarrassing me."

"You don't understand," she sniffed. "You are my son. You are my life. Seeing you go is like having a piece of me cut away." The mother dropped to her knees on the scorching concrete and wrapped her arms around the boy.

"No, I understand," he whispered, "But you bore all of me in a small part of you. You, on the other hand, from beginning to now, are the only home I've ever known. I am *sooo* going to miss you, mother.

"But if you cry anymore you're going to make me cry too... and the guards will be upset if I do that."

Hamilcar, seated between Cano and Alena, crawled over Alena's lap to put his face to the window. He wanted one last glimpse of his mother. Yes, Alena was almost a mother to him and had been since they'd first met. Yet a boy could only have one real mother.

"Iskandr," Alena said, close to the boy's ear (for whatever name his worldly parents had given him, to her he was and only could be Iskandr), "Iskandr, it will be all right. You will like my people... your people, as you will like your new home."

"I know," he answered. "I already do. I always have. It still hurts."

"I know, my Iskandr," Alena said, reaching up to stroke the boy's hair. "But you will get over it. Your destiny demands it."

As the plane carrying Hamilcar gunned engines and began to taxi down the runway, Lourdes wailed aloud into Carrera's shoulder, "My baby, my baby!"

He held her tight with one arm, stroking her hair gently with the hand of the other. *Weep, Lourdes, weep. I would join you if I could. I can't and so you must cry for the both of us.*

Headquarters, 7th Legion, Gutierrez Caserne, *Ciudad* Cervantes, Balboa, Terra Nova

Pigna replaced the telephone back onto the receiver atop his desk. The receiver sat next to a large-scale map of Balboa City. On the other side of it was a small portable computer, one of two computers on the desk.

Being the commander of a reserve unit, Pigna mused, *may not be an all-day job, but it is an every day job. Worse, it seems like the decisions I get asked for are the most trivial imaginable. I'd rather be commander of a regular tercio than of a legion of reservists.*

On the plus side, though, it leaves me with a lot of free time. And since I have to do all *the detailed planning for this myself...*

Pigna returned to the spreadsheet displayed on his computer screen. Using the control device two worlds had called "mouse" he selected a unit from one column, cut it from there, and pasted it beside another column. Thus was Second Cohort, Forty-Seventh Artillery Tercio tasked with securing the Bridge of the Colombias over the Transitway. Beside that entry, Pigna typed, "Self mobile by prime movers and auxiliary engines on the guns from Fort Cameron to the Bridge."

Pigna turned his attention back to the map. Again, he selected a unit...

Fort Cameron, Balboa, Terra Nova

They used Samsonov's regiment's conference room. Maps were tacked to walls and spread across the large central table. The chairs were stacked against one wall. Outside, guards were posted just out of earshot. The place had been swept and then swept again for listening devices.

In theory they were assembled to discuss expansion plans for the *Centro de Entrenamiento Nacional*. In fact, Carrera's staff and key commanders were there to work out the details for a major hit.

Carrera was of an age now when healing was slow, hard, and imperfect. His shoulder ached and probably would, at least when the weather changed, for life. This was the opinion of his doctor, at least.

"The problem, gentlemen," Carrera said, ignoring the pain, "is that I want to hit the bastards hard, but I don't want to alienate Santander when we do. In fact, I really want to pin the whole thing on the Federated States."

"Neat trick, if you can pull it off," said Dan Kuralski dubiously. He removed his broad-brimmed hat to scratch as his bald pate. "Frankly, I doubt we can."

"We can," Carrera insisted. "I've made arrangements for us to host two of the Federated States Army's three Ranger battalions at the right time, along with a small group of aircraft. That's unusual enough to divert eyes to them. Moreover, we'll be keeping them more or less out of the way, and our aircraft, especially helicopters, will make a larger than usual number of sorties in support. Arguably, it will all look like troop movements."

"That's why you want use my people?" Samsonov asked, his Volgan accent thick. "We all white? Well . . . almost all white."

"Yes," Carrera confirmed. "I'll want you to go in sterile, but that will also suggest an FSC attack."

"Why, *Duque*?" asked Lanza, head of the legion's aviation division, or *ala*. "I mean, why pretend it's the FSC doing the attack you want?"

"It's complex," Carrera said. "But, short version: Assuming war with the Tauran Union at some point in the not too distant future, I don't want Santander annoyed enough with us that their government feels compelled to support the TU, or allow it to base there."

"Fair enough," Lanza agreed.

"You can't use me then," Fosa, head of the *classis*, or fleet, said. "We're too obviously yours."

Carrera nodded his head deeply. "We can't use the *Dos Lindas* or the *Kurita*," he agreed, "nor even any of the corvettes or patrol craft, at least directly. That doesn't mean we can't use some of your sailors or the hidden reserve."

"Have to stop playing opposing force for a while," Samsonov counseled.

"I know," Carrera agreed. "Kuralski is working out a scheme to have units going through your training center operate against other, main force, units."

"*Trying* to work out that scheme," Kuralski corrected.

"You'll succeed, I am sure," Carrera said.

"Month to train?" Samsonov asked.

"Sure. Rather, six weeks. The FSA Rangers will be here then. In any case, I'm more interested in hitting at the right time than at any particular set time. We've got to look for a confluence of tidal and weather factors, plus eyes-on-target knowledge that the targets are home. The first two are givens, since our weather is fairly stable that time of year, and the last two are under our control."

"Can do, then," the Volgan said. "If someone else bring to fight. *And* we get to train together for while. Must first talk men into it. You join us tonight at regimental dinner?"

"If you think it will help," Carrera answered.

"Could hurt?"

"No, probably not. If this is family, too, I'll send for Lourdes and Mitchell's wife."

"Might help."

Carrera gave Samsonov a curious, raised eyebrow look. "You were planning a formal regimental officers' dinner for this evening? Odd sense of timing."

"Could see coming," Samsonov answered, with a shrug. "You got whole legion, practically, disassembled to rebuild bigger. What you haven't is off in jungle in La Palma. Mine only force still whole that not already in jungle hunting guerillas."

Lourdes had been reluctant even to broach the subject with Mitchell's wife, Chica, thinking, *It's just too soon for her to be going to a social event.*

Still, at Carrera's insistence, his wife had explained it. Chica had had exactly one question. "Will it help get revenge for my husband and the father of my children?"

"Maybe," Lourdes had admitted. "That's what Patricio told me he intends, anyway."

The corners of Chica's mouth turned up in a wintery smile. "Then I'm going. I'm *definitely* going."

❖　　❖　　❖

Bagpipes, thought Carrera, *are an odd thing to hear at a Volgan dinner. Bagpipes being accompanied by balalaikas and jackbooted dancers stomping atop tables is altogether too weird.*

Carrera kept his face carefully blank. *Oh, well, at least they cleaned their boots, given the food out, and all.*

Samsonov leaned over and, over the screeching, said into Carrera's ear, "We borrow pipers from Second Infantry Tercio. Down in jungle, they not need anyway. Cost me two pallets of good vodka even so."

"Why don't you start your own band?" Carrera asked.

"Working. Slow. The Jagelonians have pipes, but different, not so loud...forceful. We have...a dozen men working on learning. Someday. Not yet ready."

"Fair enough," Carrera agreed. "Do me a favor though."

"What that?"

"If...when you do get your pipe band going, please don't have them pipe in the haggis. As a matter of fact, please don't *have* haggis." *Not if you want me to show up again.*

"Haggis start on dare," Samsonov said. "We paratroopers...we crazy; we not stupid."

At a subtle signal from the pipe major—it was, in fact, too subtle for Carrera to catch—the pipers, who had been marching around between the tables and the walls of Samsonov's regimental officers' club, suddenly stopped their marching. The dancers ceased their stomping, jumping, and somersaulting, then bowed as one, jumped off of the tables, formed up and marched off to the tune of the pipes. The pipers, too, formed up behind the dancers and marched off through the main door, their music fading as they went.

"We emotional people," Samsonov said. "Sentimental. Watch."

"Watch what?" Carrera asked.

"Evil capitalist term: Salesmanship," the Volgan answered.

"Aren't you concerned about security leaks? I mean, Fernandez has never caught one from among your people, but it only stands to reason . . ."

"We have leaks," Samsonov answered. "Many of them. But the leaks are to State Security back in Volga, not to people you want us to attack and destroy."

"And VSS has nobody involved in crime?" Carrera asked, dubiously.

"Many, but not this kind of crime . . . well, drug running, yes, but opium, not huánuco. If we take down the Santanderns, is, from VSS point of view . . . eliminating competitor product . . . and competitor. Now watch." Samsonov twisted around and said to one of his younger officers, "Menshikov, translate for the *Duque*."

Carrera listened with, at best, half an ear to Menshikov's translation. Instead, his attention was entirely on Samsonov and the faces of the officers and warrant officers—*praporschiks*—the regimental commander was addressing.

Those seemed rapt as their commander recited the history of the organization from its earliest days as one of the Tsar's Guards regiments, then through the Great Global War wherein the unit—so Menshikov translated—was transformed into paratroopers and suffered roughly two thousand percent casualties over the course of the conflict, to the disastrous incursion into Pashtia, and the fall of the Red Tsar whose ancestor had brought Tsarist-Marxism to Volga to aid in the GGW.

Many Volgan heads shook or nodded as Samsonov described the misery for the Army and all its formations after the fall of the Red Tsar. Menshikov didn't bother translating that word for word, instead explaining: "No pay...no money for fuel...no training... we had to grow our own food and we weren't very good at it. Nor was the land near our base good soil. Cold barracks."

"Of course," the translator added, "that was just for our regiment. Others had it worse. Half those people out there are from other regiments that joined ours after you hired us."

Smiles broke out across the sea of round Volgan faces as Samsonov made the comparison between the unhappy past and the regiment's comfortable present. "We were starving. Now I worry I'll have to put you all on diets. We were unpaid, poverty stricken. Now? Our pay for our lowest private is better than a middle manager makes in Volga. We don't have to wrap ourselves in shoddy blankets and shiver in our quarters through the long and bitter winter. And best of all, now we have the money, the fuel, the equipment and the ammunition to train to be what we are called to be, among the finest, most elite, soldiers on the planet."

Samsonov pointed at Carrera. "Thank this man for that," he said, then waited for several minutes while the other Volgans stood as a man and applauded Carrera. For his part, Carrera just nodded and returned a shy smile.

"And how many of you," the Volgan continued, once the applause had died down and the men had returned to their seats, "have married into this, our new home?" Dozens of hands shot up. "And how many still have feelings for our old home, for the holy soil of Volga, fertilized from one end to the other with our blood?" All the hands shot up.

"This is right and proper. But you know what, comrades? Both our homes are under threat. And that threat is real."

Samsonov gestured again towards Carrera. "This man you were just praising was almost killed by that threat recently. His man *was* killed. And that man, *Praporschik* Mitchell, was *our* comrade."

Chica, seated on the other side of Lourdes from Carrera, started when her husband's name was mentioned. Still, she held her blond head proudly erect, fighting back her tears.

"See his wife," Samsonov said, gesturing with an open palm toward Chica. "Brave, is she not, to be sitting here dry-eyed and asking for our help with her beloved husband's body barely cold in its grave?"

Chica hadn't a clue about the words. The tone, however, was clear. It was also too much. She buried her head in Lourdes' shoulder and began quietly to weep. Several of the Volgans could be seen, as well, dabbing at their own eyes.

Smiling coldly, Samsonov asked, "So . . . comrades, will we put up with this? Will we let our new home be corrupted? Will we let their filthy substances pollute our old motherland? Will we let the death of a comrade go unavenged? Will we be unfaithful to our salt?"

"NYET!"

"Will you fight with me then, for our new home and our old, for justice and right, to secure a decent place for our children to grow up?"

"*DA!*"

"Very good. Meeting for battalion and company commanders tomorrow, following physical training. In the interim, drink up."

Samsonov sat down again, next to Carrera. "Piece of cake," he said.

While the core of the mission was to be the Twenty-Second Tercio of Volgan paratroopers, there were jobs for both the *classis*, the fleet, and Lanza's aviation *ala*.

The *classis* would not be using any of its major combatants, neither the battle-scarred light aircraft carrier, the *Dos Lindas*, nor its one serviceable heavy cruiser, the *Tadeo Kurita*. Even the corvettes and patrol boats were barred from direct participation, as being too easily and obviously traceable to Balboa and the *Legion del Cid*. Instead, they would maintain something like their normal drug interdiction picket line.

Sailors from those ships, however, would be used. They would man the ostensibly civilian vessels the legion had procured over the years against just such a contingency. These included the S.S. *Mare Superum*. Like much of Carrera's armed force, the *Mare Superum* was part of the hidden reserve. Normally it carried paying passengers around the islands near the *Isla Real*, and along the coasts of Balboa, San Jose, and Santander. Nonetheless, every crewman aboard was either an active duty sailor, a reservist, or a militia member of the legion. Of late, the ship had spent most of its time sailing the eastern coast of Santander.

Besides the *Mare Superum* was the research vessel reconfigured to carry commandos, the S.S. *Francisco Pizarro*. There was also the command, control, and communications ship for the exercise, the Motor Yacht *Phidippides*. Last was the three-thousand-ton bulk tanker, *Porfirio Porras* (no relation to cadet Porras). Along with pumps and fuel adequate for the helicopter detachment, *Porras* carried a helipad disassembled and stowed under tarps on the deck. In addition, three largish hovercraft would set up a refueling and rearming base at the airstrip at *Puerto* Jaquelina de Coco.

Lanza's contribution consisted of thirty-eight IM-71 helicopters, some of them configured as gunships and most of them sporting auxiliary fuel tanks, a dozen Turbo-Finch strike aircraft, and fifteen Nabakov turboprops, several of those also configured as gunships, along with a half dozen Cricket scout planes. Additionally, a half-dozen rough-strip-capable fighters would base out of Jaquelina de Coco, to drive off any attempt at an intercept from the Santandern Air Force. The air and ground crews were the very best Lanza could provide, supplemented by Samsonov's hand-picked Volgan aviators.

Life is a lot better here than in Volga, thought Pritkin, Samsonov's chief aviator, *but it was getting a little dull.*

Pritkin was a proud holder of the Order of Saint Ilyich (for the Red Tsars had wisely enslaved the Church to the cause of revolution, rather than oppressing it), earned for bringing his helicopter in, over and over again, to a wind- and fire-swept hilltop in Pashtia to bring out several score Volgan wounded. Some of the older and more senior men of the Twenty-Second, in fact, owed their lives to him, though the action had cost Pritkin most of his crew in dead and wounded. Because of that long-ago action, Samsonov had hunted the aviator down to recruit him for the regiment in Balboa.

The tall, rail thin aviator's cornflower-blue eyes looked out from underneath the stubby brim of his flight helmet to the little, jungle-shrouded, postage-stamp pickup zone, or PZ, where a company of paratroopers awaited him and the other five IM-71s of his flight.

Pushing left pedal and easing his stick forward, Pritkin did a single pass to the right of the PZ, glancing left to eyeball the length and breadth of the thing. One pass was enough. Pritkin pressed his throat mike and announced to the infantry waiting below, "No fucking way I'm getting six birds in there. Two is possible. You need to reconfigure to load two at a time."

The answer came back, "Fuck . . . roger . . . figures. Give us five minutes."

"We'll be around," Pritkin said. "Call when ready. Don't dawdle; we've enough fuel but hardly an abundance."

Jaquelina de Coco, La Palma Province, Balboa, Terra Nova

Under the noonday sun, in three hovercraft, half of Pritkin's refueling platoon plus an MP platoon for security prepared to land and set up their fuel point by the town's dirt-improved-with-perforated-steel-planking airstrip. They, like all the men of the task force, wore Federated States Army issue battle dress, or close copies thereto, and aramid fiber helmets.

Centurion Ricardo Cruz, returned with his platoon for a brief break from jungle patrols, watched the unloading and set-up with considerable interest. In fact, he was interested enough to stop writing his letter home, and given how he felt about his wife, Cara, that was very interested indeed.

Odd, Cruz thought. *Those are clearly our hovercraft. Just as clearly the uniforms, weapons, and accoutrements are* not *ours. And those troops? They're way too white. And . . . ah, there's one I recognize from my last trip through Fort Cameron. They're Volgans . . . and they look interestingly serious. But why dressed up like Federated States troops?*

Castillo, the machine gunner, seated on the grass nearby, was watching even as Cruz was. "What the hell is all that, Centurion?" the gunner asked.

"None of our business, I suspect," Cruz answered. He pointed, "And neither are those half dozen jet fighters winging in from the east."

Fort Cameron, Balboa, Terra Nova

Language was the big, obvious problem. There were three in use in the force: Russian, Spanish, and, as a *lingua franca,* English. Among one group the languages were Spanish for boat crews, Volgan for the troops the boats carried. The commander of ground troops spoke English as did both the boat captains. The aircraft supporting spoke Spanish or Russian. Another group had Spanish- and English-speaking transport and gunship pilots and Volgan ground troops. For these a few translators were assigned. After weeks of work and practice the kinks had been worked out, mostly.

The date to launch had been fixed by the confluence of natural factors, tide, moons, and weather, plus the pattern of movements of the human targets. Beginning at midnight, two days prior, Fort Cameron had been disconnected from the rest of the world. MPs at all usual exits to the post had been doubled and roving patrols swept the perimeter roads. Samsonov's officers confiscated all cell phones and removed all telephone transmitters except for the main number which led to the Intelligence Officer's desk. Fortunately, of those troops lucky enough to have had time to find romance with young Balboan women, most had settled down quickly into married life. Their women were on the friendly side of the wire and had been educated of late to keep quiet. Thus, the number of "Can I please speak to my boyfriend?" calls was minimal. For those there were, the regimental intelligence officer, the Ic, simply answered in Russian, rude sounding Russian at that, and then hung up.

Ordinarily, the closure of a post would be a noticeable event. Samsonov had foreseen this, and ordered the place sealed for a couple of days a week ever since receiving his orders from Carrera. Thus, it had become nothing too remarkable.

What was somewhat unusual were the nearly forty helicopters—enough to carry almost a thousand fully combat equipped men—lined up on the post parade field, all of them sporting auxiliary fuel tanks and many with machine gun and rocket pods attached. Equally odd, for sheer numbers, were the fifteen Nabakov

turboprop transports and the dozen armed attack
aircraft, all forming a fan of sorts at one end of the
post's short airfield. As far as the bulk of the Volgan
paratroopers knew, the assembly of aircraft was only to
support another training mission. Nor should they have
thought differently. They carried only blank ammunition
in their magazine pouches; they'd been issued no grenades, of either the hand- or rocket-launched varieties.

Indeed, only company commanders and above knew
of the real mission. What the soldiers might have
guessed none but themselves knew.

"I'm tired of these silly training problems," said
Sergeant Pavel Martinson, a dark skinned Kazakh
of partially Nordic extraction. He pulled off his F.S.
Army model aramid fiber helmet to rub at the sore
spot on the top of his head formed by the pressure of
the nylon ring that held the headstraps of his helmet
together. "Three fucking opposing force rotations in
as many months and still we train in between."

"Training mission, you silly twit?" answered his platoon leader, *Praporschik*—or Warrant Officer—Ustinov.
"You weren't with us in Pashtia, were you?"

"No, I didn't come to the regiment until two years
ago."

"Hmmm. Not your fault. See the 'strong man' over
there?" Ustinov used Samsonov's nickname. "See the
look on his face? That semi-saintly glow that says,
'Urrah! Soon we get to go kill something!' This is no
training mission. We're going to hit someone. Soon.
And put your goddamned helmet back on."

Even as Ustinov and Martinson spoke, the first
loaded helicopter made its appearance over the barracks

that surrounded the parade field. Soon others began taking off and turning toward the sea and the airfield on the *Isla Real*. Then the first of the Nabakov transports gunned its dual engines and began to roll down the strip.

Isla Real, Balboa, Terra Nova

"Ballsy. No doubt about it. I'm glad I tagged along when the regiment left for here." Martinson, like many young men around the world, thought going to battle to be a fine idea.

Ustinov swelled with pride; what troops felt for their colonel they felt for the regiment. And so, in a way, they felt for him. "Oh, yes. It has been too long since last we did our jobs. This will be a good exercise. Now come on, boy. The company commander has rehearsals for us all night."

Two miles from *Punta Cocoli*, on the *Isla Real*, the Balboan skipper of the S.S. *Mare Superum* cursed at his deck hands. "Come on, dammit, make the rope fast."

The small launch made fast, several Volgans scrambled up the rope ladder that was hung over the side. The senior Volgan reported, "Tribune Shershavin, Captain."

"Welcome aboard, Tribune. Take a few moments to store your gear. Then meet me on the bridge." The captain pointed out the staircase that led upward. "My crew will see to your men."

Beyond where Shershavin stood, the captain saw another ten small boats crawling over the sea toward his ship. Beyond them, an approximately equal number closed on the S.S. *Francisco Pizarro*, anchored a mile away. The *Pizarro* was a research vessel reconfigured as a light troop carrier. Between the *Mare Superum* and the *Pizarro* were two more ships, one the Motor Yacht *Phidippides*, the other the 3000 ton bulk tanker *Porfirio Porras*. The troopships would weigh anchor and sail at intervals, but before first light. *Phidippides* was the command ship for the exercise.

As Shershavin's men climbed the ropes, a flotilla of four patrol boats sped by, heading south, their bows rising and slamming back to the foamy blue. The waves from the PTs' passage rocked the rubber boats, making the climb aboard more difficult for the Volgans.

Two IM-71s, the lead flown by Pritkin's XO, Tribune III Pavlov, lifted up from the island. The helicopters carried in their bellies a load of tiny toe-popping "butterfly" antipersonnel mines, mixed in with some larger ones. The toe-poppers were fairly harmless until sensitized by impact on the ground. There were more than ten thousand of each in the two choppers. For larger mines, each chopper carried a smaller number of magnetically fused antiarmor jobs. Per Carrera's specific instructions some of the mines had been painted with a red glow-in-the-dark paint. The idea was to dissuade people from trying to clear or run through the obstacles. They couldn't be dissuaded by what they couldn't see or didn't know about.

This was a most critical part of the operation. Pavlov had been warned that he must succeed. The helos turned south to their rendezvous with the *Porfirio Porras*.

❖   ❖   ❖

Carrera and Samsonov watched Twelfth Company and the Scout Platoon loading their eight helicopters. Carrera stood straight; he had had enough healing time by now to hide any vestige of his injured shoulder. Extras choppers stood by in case some of the primaries should fail.

By 20:55 hours, with the sun long since set, it was time for Samsonov to board. He asked Carrera for a last time, "Will you not please listen to reason, *Duque*? There is no need for you to go on this."

"Yes there is, Legate," Carrera insisted. "Personal satisfaction."

With a frustrated wave of his arms, Samsonov gave up. He signaled for Menshikov. In Volgan, he said, "Menshikov, stay with the *Duque*. Translate. Keep him from doing anything silly and getting hurt." Then, shaking his head at the silliness of a colonel-general equivalent going on a small unit raid, Samsonov boarded.

Menshikov said to Carrera, "Samsonov has assigned me as your translator. And guard."

Carrera waved to the lead helicopter as it took off to follow the path to the *Porfirio Porras*.

"Come on, then, Menshikov. Let's see to our own transportation." Together, they sprinted for the eight Nabakovs that would take Number Fifteen Company to its objective.

Pushing their way past the camouflage-painted men of Fifteenth Company's mortar platoon waiting to board the last Nabakov, Carrera and Menshikov ran forward, avoiding the invisible propellers, to the second bird.

The Commander of Fifteenth Company saluted and said something to Carrera in Volgan.

Menshikov translated, "The company commander apologizes for his poor Spanish, says it's nice to see you again, and also says, 'Welcome aboard, sir.' He says, too, 'Today we get even for your soldier.'"

Carrera almost exhausted his own Volgan in answering directly *"Da!"* Then, to himself, in English, he whispered, "For Mitchell and others as well."

Chapayev, the commander of Fifteenth Company, saluted again and ran to board the first Nabakov in line. The commander had little idea of that airplane's specific history. It was the very same plane that had dropped Cazador Sergeant Robles and his team to their doom in Sumer, a decade before. In this case, it was being piloted by Miguel Lanza himself.

As Lanza had explained it to Carrera, "This is the longest, the toughest, the most problematic sub-mission we've got going. With all due respect, boss, you're nuts if you think I'm not flying lead bird."

The Volgan tribune took his seat, the one by the door that would enable him to be first out of the plane.

The roar of the twin engines increased. The Nabakov began to taxi down the runway. At ninety-second intervals the remaining eight Nabakovs, one of them a gunship, sped down the strip and lifted off into the darkness. The last of them was gone by 21:15 hours, local.

Belalcázar, Santander, Terra Nova

Señor Estevez sat on an imported leather couch sipping brandy. A great fire raged in the grand marble fireplace opposite, a guard against the mountain's cool night air. Estevez stared into the flames and contemplated the future.

I think it was a mistake to try to coerce the Balboans, a mistake to let my anger get the better of me. Oh, yes, we killed some police officers ... and more civilians. All that has done is to make them tighten up their internal security laws. That, and give them more sources of intelligence on us.

And now? Now I cannot even go outside my own estates. People who look and sound just like our own, waiting to kill us, using diplomatic access to get into Santander which we can't, usually, use to get people into Balboa. And they are at least as ruthless as we are ... at least. Why, just last month they blew up Rodriguez's mistress and the two children. Before that, they found and kidnapped Chavez's uncle and sent him back in a dozen pieces. Now all of us are stuck behind walls, with everyone we care about stuck with us. And I am so tired of my wife and mistresses fighting with each other.

Coco Point, *Isla Real*, Balboa, Terra Nova

"Fuck it!" Samsonov's XO, Koniev, shouted into the microphone of the flight helmet he wore. So far the helicopters had performed well, lifting off with no problem, with none returning to base. Such fortune could not possibly last. This, the last lift of the mission, with ten helicopters, had a problem. Number Two bird, it seemed, had developed engine trouble.

"Fuck it!" Koniev repeated. "Get the troops off and put them on Number One spare." The pilot of the

XO's helicopter spoke briefly into his microphone. At one end of the Pickup Zone another chopper lifted into the air and moved to within one hundred meters of the defective IM-71. Troops, pushed and prodded by shouting NCOs and officers, began to debark from the bad helicopter and to run across the PZ to the newer arrival. The spare took off twelve minutes late and turned west toward La Palma province. Since it would refuel at La Palma, there was no problem with expending some extra fuel for the extra speed to catch up with the main group.

Federated States Airborne Command and Control Ship (ACCS), 257 miles east of Santander, Terra Nova

For many purposes, and especially in a highly permissive environment, an airship was superior for command and control and as a radar platform to a heavier-than-air aircraft. It could linger, or loiter, could carry a much larger and heavier suite of sensors and defensive armaments, and was much, much cheaper to operate. Thus, it was an airship, operating far at sea where there was no possibility of an enemy fighter, which kept track of possible drug smuggling operations by air and sea.

The command and control module for the ship, as opposed to the pilots' station, was more or less centrally located. Being well inside, the module was lit. Within, seated in front of banks of computer terminals, more than two dozen members of the Federated States Air Force tracked everything inside of five hundred miles, air, surface, or in space. While the ACCS couldn't track a submarine at depth, it was perfectly capable of picking up the just-under-the-water submersibles occasionally used by the narco-traffickers.

A lieutenant at one of the radar terminals announced, "Sir, those radar sightings are still increasing."

The chief of the C and C module, a colonel of the Federated States Air Force, stepped over to where he could see the radar screen. "Show me what you've got," he said.

The lieutenant on duty used a plastic pointer to illustrate, tapping one icon on his screen after another. "Here, sir, we've got two groups heading west from this island north of Balboa City. It looks like there are eight or nine in the first group, maybe just one in the second. Speed says helicopters; they're flying low, almost skimming the waves. Then there's a string of nine flying generally north. They started off from the same place as the first group. Speed is one hundred eighty-five knots. Transports of some kind. Here, too," the lieutenant pointed to another group of glowing green fuzzballs on his screen, "we've got eight or nine, also flying low and slow. Helicopters heading north."

"Any ID?"

"No, sir. We queried. If those birds are carrying transponders they've got them turned off." A new dot appeared on screen over the *Isla Real*. It was quickly joined by another, and then two more. The lieutenant said, "Those are faster. Maybe C-31s."

The colonel pondered. He was a man who read the newspapers almost religiously, so he was aware that F.S. citizens had been killed in Balboa within the last few months. *No ID,* he thought. *Good formations. One bird separated from the rest—that's a command and control bird. I think I'm seeing Schumann hitting back. But why weren't we notified, at least? Hmm. Fucking Drug Interdiction pukes. Fucking Spec Ops bastards.*

The senior put a hand on the junior's shoulder. "Son, you don't see anything. Understand?"

The radar officer did not understand at first. His eyes looked for some kind of explanation in his colonel's face. All they found was a knowing smile. Gradually, a glow of comprehension spread across the lieutenant's face.

The senior inclined his head, made an off-center nod, and grinned broadly. *Who says lieutenants are stupid?* He then winked and continued, "You didn't see anything, but let's keep on watching whatever it is you don't see, shall we?"

UEPF *Spirit of Brotherhood,* in orbit around Terra Nova

The bridge crew, eyes fixed on their stations and their instruments, didn't see Battaglia, duke of Pksoi, chewing on his right forefinger nervously.

I should have been told already, the duke fretted, *that Wallenstein's been spaced. There's been plenty of time for a court-martial by now. A messenger drone should have popped the rift and broadcast months ago. But . . . nothing. I suspect I'd better get used to the idea she's returning to command. Dammit.*

Seated to Battaglia's fore, the intelligence desk officer announced, "Captain, we've got some unusual activity around the Isthmus of Balboa and the Republic of

Santander. A lot of troops moving by air. Some naval activity, too. The numbers aren't so unusual, sir, but they're crossing from Balboa into Santander and that *is* unusual."

"We're not over Balboa," Battaglia said.

"No, sir," agreed intel. "We're getting this from *Spirit of Harmony*, which is in orbit over that part of the world."

"Identities of the parties?" the Duke of Pksoi asked.

"No idea, captain. *Harmony*'s too far out for image identification and there's nothing in the clear on the EM spectrum."

"Have them send down a skimmer for a closer look," Battaglia said.

"Aye, sir . . . Sir, *Harmony* says it will be a while."

S.S. *Porfirio Porras*, 120 miles east of Nuqui, Santander

As they had rehearsed over a score of times in the last few weeks, the combined Volgan and Balboan crew erected the homemade wood and aluminum landing pad over the forward deck. At first there had been serious language problems. The captain of the ship had then decided to let the Balboans set the pad up on their own. This they had been able to do, but never quickly enough. So with hand signals and some translations, the refueling crews from Pritkin's squadron had been reintegrated into the helipad crew. It had taken many, *many* repetitions, but the combined crews had learned to set up the helipad at acceptable speed.

"Pad's up, Skipper. Fuel lines are ready."

The captain consulted his watch. "Thirty minutes, First. No smoking anywhere aboard ship. Remove the central radar nets. Secure them well; we don't want a helicopter sucking one up into its engine. Put the guide on the pad and stand by."

"Aye, sir."

Jaquelina de Coco, La Palma, Balboa, Terra Nova

"Only nine birds, sir," announced the platoon centurion leading the half of the refueling platoon that had come here by hovercraft.

Terrence Johnson, acting as Carrera's eyes-on-the-ground for a critical juncture in the mission, looked across the river mouth through his night vision goggles. *There's the last one.* "There's another one coming, Centurion. No change to the plan."

"Sir!"

S.S. *Porfirio Porras,* 120 miles east of Nuqui, Santander

The steady wop-wop-wop of the rotors and the whine of the jet engines carried far and well across the ocean surface. At the sound, a man standing above the deck on a wood and aluminum frame lit two infrared flashlights with conical projections. The helicopters split up. One came in low and slow, shifting to the hand signals of the guide. The others began to circle the *Porras*, keeping low and a good distance away.

Six men, all carefully avoiding the tail rotor spinning

invisibly in the darkness, clambered over the side of
the helipad to tie down the chopper's landing wheels
against the rocking of the ship. The guide crouched
low as two more men, Volgans, dragged a nozzled fuel
line across the pad to the waiting helicopter. After a
time of steady *glug-glug-glug* the pilot signaled the
chief of the "ground" crew that his bird was full. The
wheels were untied and then the guide signaled the
chopper to take off. Its engine whined as the wheels,
now released, lifted from the pad. That helicopter
slithered off to one side and headed away, barely
missing the head of one of the fuel crew. It then
assumed a slow, fuel conserving course for Santander.
Another one left off circling to line itself up for a
landing. By 22:30 hours the second had departed and
the next bird, of eight remaining, had taken up station
to refuel for the rest of the journey.

Federated States Airborne Command and Control Ship (ACCS), 225 miles east of Santander, Terra Nova

The senior officer aboard returned to the working
deck from using the toilet. His radar officer told
him, "Sir, I've got a surface contact. Not large. It
appeared about fifteen minutes ago. Suddenly, like it
rose from the sea."

*Oh, that makes sense. A submarine with a landing
pad attached to refuel the helicopters. The modification
must have taken a while.* Then the colonel realized
it *had* been months since the president had sworn
revenge. *Bastard Schumann may get my vote after all.*

Altitude 4200 feet over the *Isla Real,* Balboa, Terra Nova

Montoya, his course of fighter pilot instruction interrupted by the call for this mission, spoke briefly into
his radio. Changing frequencies many thousands of
times per second, the radios were almost undetectable
and almost unjammable.

Under the Turbo-Finches hung an assortment of
two-hundred-and-fifty- and five-hundred-pound bombs,
along with rocket pods on the wings, and two napalm
canisters each. An auxiliary fuel tank hung directly
underneath each airplane.

Without verbally responding to Montoya, all four
aircraft turned to the same heading and speed and
headed generally north.

S.S. *Mare Superum,* five miles northeast of Buenaventura, Santander, Terra Nova

"All stop. Drop anchors," ordered the ship's captain.
A few hundred meters behind, the *Francisco Pizarro*
also slowed to halt. The captain turned to Shershavin.
Pointing to the glow in the distance, he said, "Tribune,
there is the town. Begin landing your men.

Shershavin saluted and left the bridge. At a gesture, the men of Number Fourteen Company, minus
its first platoon—even now awaiting the lift from La
Palma, began to push rope nets and rubber boats with
small muffled engines over the side of the ship away
from the land. The troops lowered themselves down,

hand over hand, into the rubber boats and then cast off. Small muffled engines went *pfft-pfft-pfft* behind them. In the lead boat, Shershavin guided the rest around the ship's hull and toward the shore. As the major made the turn under the blunt bow, he turned his attention and his night vision goggles toward the *Pizarro*. There, too, small boats were moving to the land to join in the assault.

La Palma, Balboa, Terra Nova

"Move over, Tribune, I'm coming with you." Johnson tossed his load carrying equipment to the floor of the helicopter. Then he climbed in and took a seat on that floor. As the helicopter lifted into the air, causing the old familiar sensation of increased weight, Johnson thought, *Damn, I love this shit. All we need are Wagner and some loud speakers.*

Federated States Airborne Command and Control Ship (ACCS), 210 miles east of Santander, Terra Nova

The radar officer tapped his screen to point at the various elements of the unfolding drama. "Sir, both groups, the one from the mainland and the one by the submarine, are moving out again. Ah, we've lost the mainland group, I'd guess they're flying nap of the earth. And we've got . . . one, two, four, call it seven more birds leaving the island, middlin' fast. Oops, there goes the, uh, sub, I suppose . . . it's disappeared, sir. We've also got two more pairs of helicopters, holding station off the west coast."

Unseen now by the ACCS, S.S. *Porfirio Porras* (Atzlan registry), hidden under its nets and its refueling mission completed, set sail for Balboa.

"And, sir . . . I've got something odd on screen. It's a recon skimmer, I think, coming from the Earthpig fleet."

The colonel smiled. "They think they can fuck with us, do they? Weapons!"

"Here, sir."

"Warm up the defensive laser. Wait for my command; but when that thing gets close we're going to burn it out of the sky."

MY *Phidippides*, 25 miles west of *Punta* Marielena, Santander, Terra Nova

In the sealed cabin, illuminated only by bluish-green lights and the glow of radios, a soldier plotted the known or presumed positions of the nine distinct forces en route to targets in Santander. Over the next two minutes single code words received over the radios sent the troop back to his plotting board to confirm or change the locations. Samsonov's Ia, or operations officer, made a quick analysis of the various forces' location and schedule. He was authorized only to make major changes for major problems. There weren't any. He made a single radio call out. "Code Cathedral, repeat, Code Cathedral." No changes.

Various locations in Santander, Terra Nova

Johnson and a Volgan tribune crouched just over the pilots of the lead helicopter of their flight. To either side of the line of birds, steep jungle-covered mountains reached for the sky. A large stream ran between the mountains. In the grainy green view of Johnson's goggles was the light of a town, Bordero, Santander, about ten miles ahead.

The nearby city of San Lorenzo was much too bright to look at directly with the goggles.

Seventy miles east of Johnson, the first of five Turbo-Finches crossed from the water to a hook-shaped spit of land jutting out into the *Mar Furioso* from Santander. The lead pilot checked his GLS and the map strapped to his leg. *Punta Martes. Right on time.* The Finches changed course and began to pick up altitude to get over the mountains that shielded San Lorenzo.

"Santa Juanita River below, sir," said a helicopter pilot to Samsonov, who was standing just behind him. Samsonov strained to make out the river through the little bit of clear view available to him. Satisfied that he had seen enough to be sure, he turned and walked back, using the troop seat frames as handholds against the bucking of the helicopter as it followed the contours of the jungle-covered hills and valleys. Samsonov sat and leaned over to the next man in line. "Pass it down. Thirty minutes."

✧   ✧   ✧

Miles to the south-southeast, Warrant Officer Montoya glanced out the left side of the plane at the sleepy fishing village of Baudo Arriba. *Good. Right on time. Practice pays.*

A light rain spattered the ocean surface. Engine shut off for the last few meters to reduce noise, a small rubber boat slowed as it neared the shore. Shershavin leapt out of the boat and into the shallow water. Two other men jumped from the same boat, grabbed the line, and towed it to shore at as much of a run as they could manage in two feet of foaming surf. To either side other boats touched in and their occupants disembarked. Shershavin looked ahead at a small but steep hill on which stood a well-lighted mansion. He knew that the men of Thirteenth Company were dismounting perhaps a mile away, on the other side of town. Their target was similar, but on a lower hill. The mortar platoon began to set up their guns on the shoreline, aiming stakes forward and left at twenty-five meter intervals. Troops carrying silenced submachine guns in the lead, Number Fourteen Company went into the jungle and up the slope. Shershavin called on the radio for a check up from his two supporting Finches, now crossing a few miles west of Cabo Caminando. The difference in speeds between the amphibious force and its air support, as compared with the other three forces, had caused Samsonov to give Shershavin alone the right to use his radio with some freedom.

If Carrera wasn't airsick, it was only by the grace of God that he wasn't. After two trips up and down over two different mountain ranges, some of the boys aboard the Nabakov were not so lucky.

Shit, Carrera cursed, *it always seems you miss something*.

The somethings missing were sufficient air sickness bags. Having no choice but to puke on the floor, the sick soldiers had covered it with vile smelling vomit. Carrera forced himself to choke back a spurt of his own. Almost retching, he went forward to the flight deck for some minor relief. He saw the navigator *cum* copilot give a thumbs up signal to the pilot. The town of El Dorado, Santander, continued to sleep as a stream of aircraft flew by, low, overhead.

CHAPTER SIXTEEN

No society can truly be called civilized which is unable to deal with barbarians, of both the external and the home-grown varieties. This is so unless one cares implicitly to define "civilized" as "that which is comfortable but weak, unwilling to defend itself, and in the last stages of life before descending into barbarism."

Of course, since good and evil must be measured by duration as well as scope and intensity, and since such a "civilization" has no prospect of having much more duration, that "civilization" is hardly worth defending anyway. That said, should the people of such a civilization *choose* to defend it, its probable duration and thus its intrinsic value will increase in proportion, just as those decrease when the people reach a consensus *not* to defend their society.

But what then is civilization? Arts and letters? Education? Public Order? Rule in accordance with law? Trade? Specialization of function? Urbanization? Public works and roads? Ports?

Civilization shows all of those things, yet it is more than any of them, singly or in combination. At core, civilization is a system of society which permits something near the maximum number of

people, for any given geographic area, to enjoy the
maximum feasible quality of life, for the longest
possible societal duration.
> —Jorge y Marqueli Mendoza, *Historia y
> Filosofia Moral,* Legionary Press, Balboa,
> Terra Nova, copyright AC 468

Anno Condita 471
Belalcázar Air Force Base, Santander,
Terra Nova

In his headphones Pavlov heard from the base below,
"Unidentified aircraft! Unidentified aircraft! Move
away from the flight line and parking areas or you
will be engaged!"

Pavlov ignored the calls except to mutter, "With
what?" Reducing power to the main rotor, he allowed
the chopper to descend to only one hundred and
twenty feet above the ground. That was high enough to
provide enough fall to arm the mines his bird carried,
and also high enough not to worry about sucking any
trash that might be blown skyward into the engine.

Pavlov looked left and saw that his wingman had
likewise descended and was even now slowly moving
along and above the taxiway. From the rear of the wing
helicopter, through the open clamshell doors, a deluge
of little mines, some of them glowing, descended to
the concrete.

It was seeing the glowing mines hit and then bounce
up off of the concrete that made Pavlov think, *I have
entered the world of the surreal*.

Pavlov, himself, went for the one of the aircraft

parking areas showing plain in his goggles. A lone guard below fired his rifle at the bird, the muzzle flash plain in the gloom.

"Ignore that," the pilot cautioned his door gunner. He pretended he hadn't heard the gunner's return comment. At the fighter jet parking area, Pavlov swung stick and played with his pedals to produce a sort of aerial ballet overhead, the chopper twirling and swinging and shifting from side to side. The Santandern jet below was deluged with toe popping mines. The helicopter moved on to the next. Unheard by the crew, sirens wailed out a warning, rousing the base from its slumbers. More rifles were fired at the IM-71s. These, too, were ignored as the choppers continued their work of making the only nearby Santandern air base temporarily unusable. As each helicopter finished its mining, it turned its attention to the radar dishes, several civil and one military. Machine guns sparked, colanderizing the radar dishes with fire.

Well, thought the crew chief, *we weren't told a thing about* not *shooting up the radar.*

Federated States Airborne Command and Control Ship (ACCS), 205 miles east of Santander, Terra Nova

The radar officer cursed with surprise. "Motherfucker! Sir, three pairs of fast movers just popped over the mountains east of Balboa City. No identification." The lieutenant made a quick speed check. "Yes, sir. Definitely jets. Course suggests they came from somewhere in the Shimmering Sea."

The lieutenant colonel stifled a curse of his own. *Goddamned Navy. By what right do they cut us out?*

"And, sir? That recon skimmer—at least I think it's a recon skimmer—from the UEPF will be in range in twelve minutes."

Weapons added, "I'm tracking it, sir. We can down it on your command."

The colonel thought, *This operation has to originate at echelons above God. No way I can get permission to fire in any timely fashion. Well . . . I'm an officer of the Federated States. I see my countrymen in action. I see a threat. I am duty bound to take out that threat, if it's within my capabilities.*

That will sound great at my court-martial, won't it? Ah, screw the court-martial.

"Fire as soon as they're in range, Mister."

Hacienda of *Señor* Estevez, Belalcázar, Santander, Terra Nova

Unable to sleep for all his worries, Estevez tossed and turned on his king-sized mattress. His wife, plump beyond her years, snored softly beside him. *I would so much rather be in bed with Gabriela, or—better still—Isabel.* But domestic peace was important. He couldn't sleep with either of his mistresses in his own home.

An unusual sound roused Estevez. He rolled to his back and sat straight up. *Helicopters? Police come to arrest me? But what's that screech?*

Whatever the sounds were, they couldn't be good. Estevez roused his plump wife. "Marta," he insisted, "get up and gather the children! Quickly, woman! Go! Get to the basement. I'll join you when I can." As the wife rose and began to rub the sleep from her eyes, Estevez ran out of the bedroom, pulling on a robe and shouting for his guards.

From five thousand feet overhead, Montoya turned on his siren, banked his plane over and began a dive. He felt himself pushed back into his seat so hard that he thought he could feel the stitching through his flight suit.

Flicking on the radio he announced his call sign for the mission and "Diving to the attack." A voice answered, "Roger," with a strong Volgan accent.

Montoya saw the target hacienda and his personal target, a large barnlike structure a few hundred meters from the main building. Intelligence had identified this as a barracks for guards.

At twenty-one hundred feet, two blackish ovoid shapes, each a two-hundred-and-fifty-pound bomb, fell away from beneath Montoya's aircraft. He felt the Finch balloon slightly as its load was reduced.

"Bombs away," he announced to himself, pulling the stick back into the pit of his stomach. Whatever pressure he'd felt in the dive was nothing compared to the force pulling him down into his seat as he fought to pull out of the dive.

Far below, the helicopters began very slowly to approach the lawn around the hacienda.

The shriek coming from somewhere above wouldn't have been so bad if Francisco Estevez had ever heard its like before. He hadn't. It might have been tolerable if some of his comrades had, and they'd been able to reassure him. They were running around like chickens with their heads cut off. It might have been acceptable if he'd been a trained soldier. He was a tyro, recruited to his cousin's guard force to provide a sinecure to a relative. In short, Francisco was completely unprepared for the attack, mentally, morally, and as a matter of training. It was about the limit of his ability to join the dozens of other armed men racing from their barnlike barracks to the main house.

As Francisco fumbled with loading a magazine into his rifle while trying to run across the manicured lawn to his assigned position, he saw his elder brother. "What's going on?" he shouted out.

"Who the fuck knows? Just get to your position."

Twin explosions, so close together as to be almost indistinguishable, rocked the world behind Francisco. A wall of hardened air slapped his back. He was slammed forward and down, first to his knees, then to all fours, then to his belly. The metal receiver of his rifle punched into his stomach.

Francisco felt, more than heard or saw, pieces of flying metal and wood tear the air around him. Lifting off the ground and twisting his head, Francisco saw that the barn was gone, it its place an expanding cloud, black and angry, that threatened to engulf him. Francisco shook his head to clear it. This was a mistake, he found, as pain and nausea shot through him.

Half deafened, still Francisco heard or felt someone screaming close by. Through the dark and acrid smoke he crawled toward the sound. Though it was only a few feet, it seemed like miles. A legless man, bones showing and blood spurting, thrashed the ground. One leg, still shod and covered in denim, lay nearby. He turned the over the body of the screaming, legless man.

"Oh, no. Oh, *Hermano*, what will I tell mother?"

The siren shriek overhead returned. It was followed by more explosions, closer to the *hacienda*. Then there were many more explosions, smaller ones. A rocket passed over Francisco's head. He never heard whether it exploded or not.

Heavy machine gun fire, each burst like a series of fists against a wall, passed by him. Bright tracer lines burned themselves into his retinas. He turned his head in panic as the steady *whop, whop, whop* of helicopter blades cutting the air assailed him. Like a cornered rabbit, Francisco looked frantically around for an escape. He heard more helicopters to his right and his left, explosions to his front. Picking his brother up on his shoulder, Estevez began to run to what had been his rear.

As two helicopters broke off from the main body to drop off the platoon that would seal off escape, the other four, landing on line, began to disgorge the rest of Twelfth Company across the lawn. Those armed with rockets and machine guns fired forward to cover the paratroops' exit.

"Look at that!" cried the copilot of the rightmost bird. The goggled pilot turned his head to see a Santandern struggling with a load on his shoulders across the ruins of a large wood building. *Orders are orders: "Maximum feasible frightfulness*," thought the pilot as he swung the IM-71 over slightly to bring its guns to bear. He pressed the firing button, causing the helicopter to shake with the recoil. Fifty-one caliber bullets, one in

five a bright green streak, lashed the ground around
the target. The image in the pilot's goggles flared.

Dirt, dust, and splinters of wood kicked up around
Francisco Estevez. Two projectiles, at least, found him,
passing through his lower torso. Both hips smashed to
red ruin, he was bowled over, his load flying. Francisco landed in agony, his blood staining the green
grass beneath him.

For a few moments he lay there in shock. Then,
dimly, he remember his brother who had to be somewhere nearby. Francisco forced his arms to lift his
upper body from the ground. Dragging his useless
legs behind him, he pulled himself on his hands and
elbows to where his brother had been flung.

The tracer-caused flare in the night vision goggled
lessened. "One's still alive," said the copilot. "You
know the orders."

A second burst followed, longer than the first. The
Estevez brothers, distant relatives of Señor Estevez,
died side by side, Francisco's hands still trying to pull
his elder brother to safety.

The helicopters had each a single side door, mounted
on the left, and rear clamshells. With the chopper
bucking from the rotor wash kicked up from the
ground, the crew kicked open the clamshells even as
Samsonov jumped out of the side door to the ground.
Automatically, the legate of the Twenty-Second rolled
and came to a prone firing position, eyes searching
frantically for threats and targets.

The more heavily laden radio telephone operator, or

RTO, jumped after Samsonov. Because the helicopter was slowly moving forward, however, the RTO landed closer to the target than his commander had. He crawled back toward Samsonov, taking a position to the left rear of the legate. Samsonov shot an inquiring glance at the RTO, which was answered with a smile.

"Almost as much fun as Pashtia, sir," said the RTO.

Samsonov raised an eyebrow. "Boy," he shouted, "you're not old enough to have seen Pashtia."

"True, sir," the RTO agreed, unabashed. "But every-fucking-body *talks* about it enough that it sure as shit *seems* like I was there. Sounds like it was fun, too."

Samsonov shook his head and shouted, "This is all just a job, boy, just a job."

While Samsonov and the RTO exited the narrow side door, the bulk of the helicopter load had begun pouring in a double file out the back, through the clamshells. Warrant Officer Ustinov bent low, fearful of walking his head into the rotor spinning overhead. He was followed by Martinson.

Even before the platoon finished forming, Samsonov was the first to rise. RTO in tow, he began shouting into his microphone.

Someone was listening. Ustinov saw his company commander off to his left. The tribune arose, blowing a whistle and hand signaling for his platoons to begin moving up. The tribune had one arm curled overhead, the other pointing a rifle toward the hacienda. In the center of the Twelfth Company, soldiers of the weapons platoon serving as riflemen did short rushes to form a rough line. Light fire, so far overhead it must have been unaimed, came from the direction of the target building. No Volgans were hit.

Ustinov and Martinson, still crouched low to avoid the helicopter's spinning rotor, moved up as well, pushing and prodding their platoon to get on line. The chopper gave off a differently pitched whine, lifted a few meters higher, and then, tail boom up and nose down, moved closer to the hacienda. At a certain point the chopper leveled off again. Its guns began firing steadily at the house. With troops behind it, rockets were, for the moment, right out.

To his right front Ustinov saw a line of tracers reach out twice toward the ruins of some large building, then return fire to the house. To Ustinov's left, far past the company commander, two more helicopters swung over after dropping off the platoon charged with sealing off the far side of the main building. They then added their fires at right angles to those of the helicopters that had dropped off the bulk of Twelfth Company.

Somewhere ahead someone was screaming. Whether it was a woman, which it sounded to be, or a man so badly hurt as to scream like a woman, none of the Volgans could tell. Martinson thought it was a man, and muttered, "I wish someone would put that poor bastard out of his misery."

Ustinov heard a siren wail coming above and to his front, and moving right to left. This was joined and then overwhelmed by a sound like a huge sail being ripped in half by a giant. That was the rattle of multiple, wing-mounted heavy machine guns, firing together. More tracers, red unlike the Volgan's green ones, spattered the area immediately around the house. The cacophony of screams, half pain and half terror, increased.

Turning briefly to look behind him, Ustinov saw Samsonov, now standing upright, calmly walking forward and still speaking into his radio. *Well, he never was much of a one for taking cover,* thought the *praporschik.*

The siren returned, this time moving left to right. Rockets exploded against the hacienda walls, ripping off stucco and shattering glass. Ustinov listened to his radio for a moment, then shouted for his platoon to advance at a walk. Several score Volgan paratroopers stood up and began to trot forward, the steady crackle of their rifle fire preceding them, beating down any possible opposition. Helicopters pulled away and moved to a nearby landing area to await the recall. The Volgan advance slowed only once, to allow the men to fix bayonets.

When the company was about sixty-five or seventy meters from the hacienda, the commander gave the preparatory command, "Into the assault." Ustinov echoed it. The commander then shouted, "Forward!" With a tremendous cry of *"Urrah!"* the Volgans began to run toward the house, spraying fire from the hip.

The sound coming from their assailants was terror incarnate. Bombs and bullets might kill, but that "Urrah!" was the sound of cold steel and shrieking death.

"Surrender, *señor*. We *must* surrender!" shouted Estevez's deputy, Ernesto, over the firing.

Estevez risked a glance out of a shattered window. He saw a scene from Hell, if Hell were lit by tracers and flares. There was a line of—*What? Soldiers? They look like no police I've ever seen*—running forward. Some paused briefly to use their bayonets on any live bodies or corpses lying on the ground. A burst of fire, probably unaimed, drove Estevez back down behind the cover of the solid wall.

He told his deputy, "About a hundred men, big and white. Gringos." *I should have told that young fool to stay away from the Columbians. Oh, well, a gringo jail is better than dead.*

Still, he hung his head in indecision. After a minute's thought, Estevez spoke again. "Ernesto, tie that doily to the end of your rifle. Here, give it to me." Estevez then pushed the end of the rifle out the window shouting, in English, "We give up. Don't shoot." From downstairs came the blast of grenades. The house shook.

My God; what if they're not very interested in prisoners? Then Estevez remembered a small gift sent to him from Balboa and realized, *My God, what if they* are *interested in prisoners?*

Buenaventura, Santander, Terra Nova

Rabble. Just damned rabble, thought Shershavin. He stood on an open patio outside the target house. From inside the house came the sounds of grenades and automatic weapons fire. At each blast and burst the growing crowd of prisoners shuddered. Shershavin looked them over. There were about twenty-five men, two women, one old, one quite young and pretty, as well as a couple of children. The women and children, along with some of the men, cried unceasingly. They never noticed when the firing stopped.

The movement up the hill from the beach had been easy. It was made easier still by the fact that all of the drug lord's "soldiers"—Shershavin sneered at the misuse of the word—had taken shelter against the rain. Most of these had never known what had killed them. His unit was in position for an assault a full twelve minutes before the Finch assigned to support him was to begin its dive. Shershavin had called on the radio to tell the bomber to hold off until further notice. Then Shershavin had sent two teams of two men to take out the guards. This they had done, silenced submachine guns coughing. So, when the airstrike on the target on the other side of town had begun, and the rest of this hacienda's guards had spilled out, they had been met by a scythe of fire from Fifteenth Company's men, already in position around all the exits. The unused Finch had been sent off to support the other half of the company. The mortars by the beach had also been directed to give their support to the other men attacking the other target.

A knot of Volgans pushed three men out onto the patio for Shershavin's inspection. The squad leader reported, "This is the last of them, sir. Found them hiding out in a shelter. Quite fancy it was, too, sir. Like the Red Tsar's own winter palace."

Shershavin consulted his target folder. Yes, there was the picture. "*Señor* Cortez, I presume?"

When the drug lord attempted to deny, Shershavin simply said, "Don't bother. Now, tell me, who is important to you in this group?"

Cortez just glared.

"I see. Well, everyone you don't identify as important dies anyway. It's up to you." Shershavin shrugged, "All the same to me, really."

Not losing his hate-filled expression, Cortez pointed

and answered, "These two are my deputy and accountant. None of the others...you bastard."

Shershavin ordered the guards' squad to take Cortez and the other two to the boat. As they were pushed ahead at bayonet point, some of the other Volgans began to push the male adults still left back toward the house.

Shershavin walked to the remainder, the two women and the children. Leaning down and taking firm control of the older woman's chin, he pointed south and said, "Go. Take other woman and children with you. Now."

At the beach, Cortez asked, "What will happen to the others? My wife and my two mistresses?"

Shershavin didn't answer, but simply looked at his watch, counting, "Five...four...three..."

His counting was interrupted by the half-muffled sound of massed automatic weapons fire and screaming. Some of the screaming sounded distinctly feminine.

"Must have a word with that platoon's commander about the importance of precise timing," said Shershavin, to no one in particular.

Cortez gulped. "You bastards!"

"The price of acts of war which fail to follow the laws of war is reprisal," the Volgan answered. "You should have thought of that."

Later, bound and in a rubber boat heading out to a near rendezvous at sea, Cortez looked back and saw a red glow from the hill his former residence had dominated. The glow soon became a tower of flames, shooting high into the sky.

Florencia, Santander, Terra Nova

The Nabakov NA-23, along with several of its siblings, circled high above and out of convenient earshot of the town. The town itself, if one could call a place a "town" that had a population of nearly one hundred and forty thousand, was crammed into a narrow valley, at one end of a bad road. It glowed faintly. Most of the shacks of the place lacked electricity. Even for those dwellings that had electrical service, bulbs were generally too expensive to be used wastefully.

Still, the town glowed enough to mark its existence. It didn't matter, in any case. For Carrera and the Volgans he accompanied, the town's sole reason for existence was to mark a reference point for the guerrilla camp situated some miles away.

"Over there, *Duque*," said one of the Balboan pilots, pointing to where a rough airstrip had been hacked from a flat area running along one side of an otherwise steep ridge.

Carrera saw nothing until he lifted his own night vision goggles to his eyes. Then it was clear, or clear enough, in any case. Even as Carrera watched, a single Nabakov approached the rude airstrip for an unscheduled landing.

Several months prior, two men had been captured by a young Balboan policeman and reservist after those men had detonated a bomb, killing two dozen police and more than twice as many innocent bystanders. Those men had been *rigorously* questioned by

Warrant Officer Mahamda, one of Fernandez's chief
interrogators.

One of the captives, very early on in his interrogation, had spit on Fernandez and vowed that FNLS, the
Frente Nacional Liberacion Santerdereño, which was the
main Santandern guerrilla group, would avenge him.

Fernandez had not been especially bothered by
the spit; it was understandable if foolish. Moreover, a
crushed testicle had been more than adequate revenge.
Still, he had been extremely intrigued by the idea of
a Tsarist-Marxist group dealing with drugs and drug
dealers for profit. Interrogation had been intensified.
Eventually, as Mahamda had discovered, FNLS, cut
off from Volgan and Cienfuegan aid, had been thrown
back on its own resources. These had been slim
indeed. Just to survive, FNLS had had to do business
with Belalcázar and even distant Atzlan. Sometimes
the guerrillas provided some combat capability and
occasional contract terrorism to various drug dealers.
At other times, they provided training for the drug
lords' personal guards. More importantly, the guerrillas
had carved out their own niche in the drug world,
primarily moving *huánuco* leaves and semi-refined
paste from the wild highlands to the urban producers
for further refinement and distribution.

With some effort and a little electricity—and this
had eventually caused one of the prisoners to die of
cardiac arrest—Mahamda had been able to pinpoint
the exact location of the FNLS headquarters for drug
shipments.

It had all been rather tricky, really. Unlike most
pairs Mahamda had dealt with in his long career as
an interrogator, the two captive guerrillas had had a

prepared story. Almost they'd succeeded in fooling the Sumeri émigré. Ultimately, it was the completeness of that story that had aroused Mahamda's further suspicions. He'd continued the torture, asking a series of seemingly innocuous but detailed questions, things unrelated to either the bombing or the FNLS that the captives were unlikely to have agreed on beforehand. Mahamda had asked things like, "What is your partner's place of birth?" or "His preferred brand of rum?" or "Are both of Juan's parents still alive?" Anguish had followed all nonmatching answers until the men had been *trained* to tell the truth for terror of the consequences of being caught in a lie.

The information gained having been brought to Carrera, he had duly entered an FNLS headquarters on his target list. As with every other target on the list, the headquarters was reconnoitered in advance, both by air and by a four man team from Fourteenth Cazador Tercio. The latter had penetrated the general area only with great difficulty, but had still managed to return with photos and detailed sketches. Another overflight, only a few days prior, had reported no obvious changes.

Continuing to scan with his goggles, Carrera confirmed the scouts' report. The local FNLS headquarters was in an expansive villa, a complex rather than a single house, surrounded by a low wall, reinforced with earthen bunkers. It stood some five miles southeast of the town of Florencia, up a tortuous mountain road. The wall was itself protected by a broad barbed-wire fence. Nearby, less than a kilometer away, in fact, a fourteen-hundred-meter dirt airstrip had been laboriously carved out of the mountainside. There was a refueling station on the strip. Usually only a few guards were present. A dirt road led from the strip through jungle and wire to the villa's gate. Per instructions, the recon team had not attempted to get past the wall.

Mahamda had managed to extract an estimate of the number of guerillas in the camp and their weaponry. Those admissions by the captives had been confirmed by both aerial and ground recon. The latter had also confirmed that these were not mere bandits but well-armed men with something like real training. East of the villa and farther up the slope was a rifle range, reported as being frequently used. The ground recon team had also reported explosions, some single, some double, which they were reasonably certain were both demolitions and heavy weapons training in progress. The comings and goings of groups of armed men suggested to both air and ground recon that there were other units in the general area, but neither recon element had been able to pinpoint the precise location of any of them. They were able to confirm that none were within three or four miles of the villa.

The tactical problem was a difficult one. Other powers might have been content to drop a number of guided bombs. The legion had those, and could have delivered them easily enough. The difficulty there was that bombs, even precision guided ones, were not all that effective; not effective enough, in any case, when the objective isn't mere punishment, but massacre. That meant troops had to be landed, and landing troops in the face of one's own aerial bombardment was...somewhat dangerous.

It had been a close question and neither Carrera nor Samsonov was entirely confident they'd picked the right answer.

Faced with a more serious fight than generally expected, Carrera had asked Samsonov which was his best rifle company. Samsonov had answered, without hesitation, "Number Fifteen. I put all men that transferred from Division Recon Battalion into Fifteenth Company. Good boys. Company commander, Chapayev, is young, but talented officer. You met him once."

When, in planning, the question had arisen as to the wisdom of jumping from the NA-23s to assault the villa, Samsonov had objected. "In mountains? No. Too high, air too thin, men will fall too fast. Besides, most of us are not trained for parachuting into trees."

Those were sound objections. "Assault landing?" Carrera had asked.

"Think best," Samsonov had answered. "One plane to secure strip, then others follow."

"Hmmm," Carrera had wondered aloud, "how do we keep the local guards from shooting up the plane as it lands?"

"That is only question of deciding which Kosmo humanitarian activist organization works most closely with Santandern guerillas," Samsonov had answered. "Maybe Red Cross."

Thus, instead of jumping, one plane would go in first, marked with the insignia of the Red Cross, to secure the landing strip and fuel facilities.

✧   ✧   ✧

That first, falsely-marked plane landed with only the airfield guards to witness. The guards hadn't been expecting a flight, but in any guerilla movement coordination and information sharing tends to be problematic. Still, the guards began to walk over to enquire as soon as the plane rolled to a stop.

A side door flew open. From it emerged four Balboans from the Fourteenth Tercio, all dressed in mufti. Two of the Balboans called out greetings in Spanish and walked toward the three guards running to meet them. The two others, doing a fair imitation of the universal "pee pee dance," trotted to the far side of the airfield as if to relieve themselves. Half disappearing below the lip of the airstrip, the latter two made motions as if loosening their clothes. Instead of penises, however, silenced Pound submachine guns were pulled out. The eyes of those two followed their comrades closely as those comrades neared the FNLS guards.

"What the fuck are you guys doing here now?" the chief of the Santandern guards asked. "I've got no word of any flight coming in and I know for a fact we don't have enough leaf or paste on hand to justify using one of these to take out what we do have.

The Balboan shook his head. "Ain't that just like the fucking Committee?" he asked. "Nobody tells nobody nothin'. We're carrying shit in, not bringing it out."

"Shit?" the Santandern asked.

"Serious shit," the Balboan said. "Ammunition, some guns—some *heavy* guns—mortar shells, explosives, and a couple of crates worth of uniforms and field gear." All of which was, technically, true. So what if the uniforms weren't actually *in* crates? They would have filled a couple of crates easily enough.

"No shit?"

"No shit. Estevez, over in Belalcázar, made a deal with the Committee. He provides the shit; you guys smash the Balboan Embassy."

"Ohhh. That makes some sense then." The FNLS guard leader agreed. "Need help unloading it?"

The entire time the two parties, Cazadors and airfield guards, had been walking closer to each other. At a range of under six foot the two Balboans drew silenced, large caliber pistols, with cartridges loaded down to be subsonic. The Santanderns barely had time to register shock and surprise before the muzzles flashed and their heads and chests were ruined by bullets that broke up upon hitting flesh or bone to create great swaths of destruction inside human bodies.

The senior of the *pistoleros* spoke a code word into a small radio masquerading as an earpiece. At the word, the second pair of Balboans ran to the little shack that housed the rest of the guards. Civilized men, they tried the door to the shack first and found it open. Gripping their silenced Pound submachine guns, the Balboans walked in and began methodically spraying the reclining men inside. They killed them all, quickly and silently, then went from body to body, shooting each one in the head, once, to make sure.

Meanwhile, back at the Nabakov, the rear ramp dropped and Chapayev's men bustled out and then ran to take positions around the airfield. The Balboans, leaving responsibility for the field to the Volgans, had returned to the Nabakov to await Carrera's arrival. Even without orders from their commander, they intended to wait for Carrera and guard him when he landed.

Crouching by the ramp, under the light of the

moons Eris and Bellona, Chapayev saw the Cazadors approach. He kept his rifle on them until they were close enough to recognize. Then he rested his rifle and picked up the radio transmitter to order the rest of the company in.

Overhead and at a distance, the gunnery officer of the one supporting Nabakov modified to the gunship role scanned the ground through his thermal cameras. The gunner's face was lit green by the glow of his screen. To Chapayev, through an interpreter, he reported, "No armed men outside the villa walls. There are three lying down on the strip—"

"Those are dead," Chapayev interrupted.

"I figured that, Tribune. I see your men forming perimeter around the strip—"

"Forget the strip. We control that."

"Fair enough," the gunner agreed. "Besides, those infrared chemical lights your men are placing are making the thing a little confusing.

"The villa's got a dozen men I can see manning the walls. The whole thing's surrounded by bunkers I can't see into, though I can tell you that at least some of them—mostly the corner ones—are manned."

"Give me the numbers of the ones you're sure are manned," Chapayev said. The gunner began calling them off while the Volgan made notes on his sketch of the place. By the time the gunner had finished his report, the first of the main body of troop-carrying Nabakovs was reversing thrust on the airstrip, raising a cloud of dirt large and thick enough to blot out the hurtling moons overhead.

❖   ❖   ❖

Carrera was in the first main body Nabakov to land. Before beginning his descent, the pilot had peremptorily ordered him back to his seat and to buckle in.

"This is going to suck like you wouldn't believe, *Duque*," the pilot had shouted back, as Carrera buckled himself in, in the forward-most, starboard-side seat next to Menshikov. "Would be hard to control it with your body plastered across the windscreen."

Carrera felt a sudden drop as the pilot reduced power to the propellers. Next came a lurching bounce as the first wheel touched down, followed by another. Carrera was forced to his right, and Menshikov against him, as the pilot reversed thrust on the propellers to slow the plane. Whether the pilot screwed up the timing, or a landing wheel had found a soft spot, or the great god Murphy had touched the plane with his evil finger, the thing began slewing its tail to the right. That was bad enough, but when Carrera twisted his head to look out the small porthole window he saw through a great cloud of dust that the right side wing seemed to be trying to dig itself into the dirt of the airstrip.

We're going to die, Carrera thought. *The wing will dig in; the plane will flip; we'll flip and then slide upside down until we crash into the first one. Then it's fire and death.*

Well, with luck we won't survive until the fire.

Goodbye, Lourdes. I'm going to miss you.

Up in the cockpit the pilot fought frantically with his controls. He managed to get the plane pointed in the right direction, only to discover that he'd overcompensated as the tail began to swing to the left.

Fuck! Fuck! Fuck! We're gonna die. And I can't see shit!

The moons' light glowed off of the cloud of dust, provided just enough illumination for Chapayev to see the front of the incoming plane, wreathed in dust and twisting left and right as the pilot fought for control.

That's the Duque's *plane. Samsonov will kill me if it crashes.*

It could have gone either way. As it went, the left side landing wheel hit another soft spot. This was just enough to nudge the plane to an inclination the pilot could deal with. Slightly. Sort of. In the few seconds of proper orientation the plane slowed a little. This gave the pilot a little more control over the wild swinging of the fuselage. A little more control helped him slow the plane a bit more and reduce the oscillation. That gave him...

"I think I shit myself," the pilot said to his copilot.

"No 'think' about it," the copilot answered. "I *did* shit myself."

Both men, trembling like leaves in a strong wind, peered through the windscreen and the thinning cloud of dust at the first plane to have landed, sitting no more than a dozen meters to their front.

Behind them, the paratroopers and Carrera bustled out of the side door. There wasn't time to fuck with lowering the ramp.

As his feet hit the soft ground, Carrera was met by a pale Chapayev and four civilian-clad Balboan Cazadors.

Carrera's first words to the Volgan were, "I don't know if the pilot fucked up or if the airstrip is fucked up. No matter. I want these planes bunched at the other end of the strip, and manually turned around to face where they came from. Now! Before another goddamned Nabakov tries to land!"

CHAPTER SEVENTEEN

Civilization is not coequal with aesthetics, however many people who consider themselves civilized may tacitly insist that it is a matter of aesthetics and nothing but. Nor must what we like to think of as civilized conduct be universal or eternal. Indeed, there has never been any such civilization except in the sophomoric pipedreams of the willfully ignorant.

Aztec priests cut the living hearts from captives. The Aztecs were highly civilized. Old Rome's Crassus crucified over six thousand rebellious slaves along Rome's Appian Way. Rome, too, was civilized.

On the frontiers of that Old Earth empire, or along those of the Chinese empire, when facing the barbarians, barbaric conduct was the required norm. Inside those empires, when dealing with their home grown barbarians and criminals, barbaric punishments were the preferred norm.

On our own planet, when faced with the barbarism of fanatical Salafi nomads, those nomads were treated as barbarically as they had treated others.

This is not a flaw of civilization, nor even a feature. It is a necessary precondition for the maintenance of civilization. Civilization must meet barbarism and either convert it, destroy it, contain it, or terrorize it into submission or withdrawal. This is so, among other reasons, because barbarism is the natural state of mankind, the state to which man gravitates on his own and has the hardest time rising from.

—Jorge y Marqueli Mendoza, *Historia y Filosofia Moral*, Legionary Press, Balboa, Terra Nova, copyright AC 468

Anno Condita 471
Florencia, Santander, Terra Nova

Female mosquitoes buzzed outside the protective net, slamming themselves repeatedly into the gauze, following their instinctive drive to obtain a blood meal for the fertilization of their eggs. Farther away, fearful of approaching the camp, *antaniae*, Terra Nova's genengineered winged reptiles, cooed softly. *Mnnbt, mnnbt, mnnbt.* Through the torn screen of a glassless window, the diffuse moonlight of Eris and Bellona illuminated the sweat-sheened breasts of a young, sleeping girl.

Comandante Victorio rested his head on one arm, admiring the sleeping form next to him, breasts bare to his gaze in the night's heat and glowing with the moons' light filtering through the windows.

So young, so idealistic, so pretty, thought Victorio. *Above all, so easy to convince that even* this *was for the revolution.* He smiled at the remembrance of the first seduction of Elpidia, the sleeping girl.

Victorio had himself been just so naive and idealistic. That, however, had been many years ago. Recruited by FNLS as a university student in Belalcázar, two

dozen years before, Victorio had been enthralled by
the by then well-established Cienfuegan Revolution,
as he had been by the more recent and still tenuous
victory for the Cause in Cocibolca, east of Balboa.

At first, before his broader talents were recognized,
Victorio had been used as a rabble rouser, leading many
student protests. Then, after a period of observation,
testing, and review, once it was known that his ideo-
logical purity was unquestionable and his leadership
ability high, he had been transferred to a field unit
of the movement.

Twenty-one years in the bush, Victorio mentally
snorted. *Twenty-one years and those peasant pigs
never rallied to us. Twenty-one wasted years, while
the government hunted us like rabbits. Bastards! Using
us for little more than training aids for officer cadets.
Aiaiai... and we had been so close for a while, too.*

Victorio tore his eyes from Elpidia's gently rising
breasts and lay his own head back on his thin pillow.

*And then the Red Tsar was lynched in St. Nicho-
lasburg. Soon Cienfuegos could afford no more aid.
Annam began cozying up to the imperialists. Cocibolca
couldn't hold.*

*We tried to use drugs to continue to finance the
revolution. The cartels fought us, and we lost. Well,
almost lost. Too many heroes who, it turned out, could
be bought. More ruthlessness than the Army showed;
the cartels went after families. Finally, at great cost,
we have our own little piece of the trade. And, of
course, the odd paid mission from the cartels.*

*Oh, we still spout talk of revolution, ushering in
the rule of the people, all that bullshit. Some of the
young ones, like this little thing with her breasts so*

provocatively exposed, still believe. Not me, not any longer. I am happy with enough to be able to eat regularly for a change, and to have a place to sleep out of the rain. Everything else is just icing.

Victorio rolled over to go to sleep. As he did he heard a commotion from beyond the wall. He listened carefully for a moment. The watch was saying something about airplanes. The guerilla chieftain cursed softly, then arose to investigate. The girl, thus awakened, began to rise, herself, before her lover pushed her back gently to the bed.

"It's probably nothing," he told her. "Rest."

At the leather-hinged door Victorio stopped momentarily to listen. He heard no airplanes, precisely, though there was what he thought might be the sound of an unfamiliar engine. *Well, they've probably already landed. They? No, more likely one; these mountain walls do odd things to sounds.*

Victorio walked briskly, his Volgan-designed rifle held in one hand, to the building that in a regular army would have been called something like the "orderly room."

The FNLS was short on military formality and didn't feel it was much of a failing. The group leader of the guard simply nodded his head in recognition at the *jefe* and said, "One plane, anyway, landed up at the strip. Its engines have never stopped so we can't tell for sure if more followed."

"The guards?" Victorio asked.

"No answer, but the odds aren't bad they're just doped to the gills . . . or drunk."

The *jefe* sighed. *Yes, those are the odds.*
Man the perimeter or grab what leaf and paste we

*have and run? I think ... it's early to run, and we'd
lose too much if we left the* huánuco *behind.* To the
group leader he said, "Send a patrol, half a dozen
men, to the airfield. For the rest, hundred percent
alert; man the perimeter."

"You think it's serious?"

Victorio shook his head in negation. "No, I think
it's probably someone who landed at the wrong strip
by mistake. But it could be the police or it could be
something else. Hmmm ... are the mortars still out?"

"*Si, jefe.*"

"Tell them to stand by for my call. We may need
their support."

Technically, the Nabakov gunship was an "ANA-23,"
rather than an "NA-23." The extra A was for "Attack."
It carried, besides one high velocity 40mm automatic
cannon, a brace of 23mm Volgan guns and, in its latest configuration, four .50 caliber machine guns in a
single quad mount. All fired out the port side. They
had a limited traverse controlled from the gunner's
station. For greater changes in aiming, the plane had
to align itself.

The gunner was actually the crewman with the
greatest intelligence collection capability, as he had
the main screen to the thermal cameras used in target
acquisition and aiming.

As the Fifteenth Company began to move off from
the mountain-carved airstrip, the gunner called Carrera, now known to be on the ground.

"*Duque*, we've got major activity down below. I
see ... call it seventy, give or take a few, people running
all over the target area. Might be more; it's hard to

keep track. They're lining up in groups before moving. I think you've been heard, over."

"Roger. Figures. We had some unforeseen problems on the strip. Does it look like they're trying to evacuate?"

"Negative, *Duque*," the aerial gunner said.

"Roger. Stand by." Carrera ran forward to Chapayev, Menshikov following close behind. The Fourteenth Cazador Tercio bodyguards kept their position surrounding Carrera.

Through Menshikov, Carrera said to Chapayev, "Tribune, I just heard from the gunship. They know we're here. We knew they might hear us coming in. It's your operation, but my suggestion is to drop the sneaky shit and move like hell onto the objective. I can have the gunship start pounding now."

It took Chapayev perhaps all of five seconds to decide. "*Da*. Thank you, *Duque*. We do that."

Chapayev began to shout to his platoons to move out smartly, while his forward observer notified the mortar section to begin working over the villa. Carrera notified the gunship to engage.

"*Si, señor. Solo un minuto*." It was seconds rather than minutes before the sky lit up with the muzzle flash and tracer burn of four .50 caliber heavy machine guns, water cooled, pouring down a stream of lead onto the villa compound. The eighteen hundred-plus rounds per minute were so close together that each shot blended into the next to create a sound like a zipper being pulled closed dangerously fast. Carrera's party joined Fifteenth Company in sprinting through the widely spaced trees for the villa, the whole party guiding on the gunship's tracers.

❖   ❖   ❖

The FNLS were hardly a professional force. The patrol ordered out by Victorio was just leaving the main gate to the compound as the point of Chapayev's company reached the edge of the forest surrounding the villa and nearest the gate. The Volgans tended to be literal and, often enough, excessively obedient to their orders. Rather than set up a hasty ambush to catch the patrol in the open, the point element of Fifteenth Company opened fire immediately. They were rewarded with a couple of hits, but no more than that, before the rest of the patrol scurried back inside the compound, frantically closing the gate behind them. Inside, the survivors hid in the shadow of the surrounding wall, fearful of entering into the open where a storm of fire from something on high was drenching the place with a leaden sleet.

From the headquarters window *Comandante* Victorio took one look at the stream of tracers coming down from above, then another at the scared-shitless patrol being driven in through the gate, and said to himself, "We're fucked. Those aren't police, less still some flight that got misoriented and landed at the wrong strip. Those are the goddamned gringos."

But do we run or do we fight it out? He tried to envision how the gringos had gotten to him. *Jumping? No, the Cienfuegans said you don't parachute onto mountain ranges, generally. They must have landed. Now how many planes could land on that strip at one time? Not that many. I think we're facing equal odds, give or take. Sure, they've got that fucking airplane overhead but that can't stick around forever. It could maybe follow us, though, if we try to get away through the jungle. That's an unsavory prospect. I think we fight it out here, maybe try to get away in the day after the gunship goes away. Or even if it stays, it will have a harder time finding us in the jungle heat. At least that's what the Cienfuegans said. Besides, we have some friends not so very far away.*

So if we're going to fight it out . . .

A shell impacting near the headquarters reminded Victorio that he wasn't without some support of his own.

But where to use it? There's a good chance we could take out any planes on the airstrip. That, however, won't do a damned thing to help us here, now.

"Get hold of the mortar platoon on the radio," he said. "Tell them I want fire on the woods nearest the main gate."

As the Volgan point man reached the edge of the forest that marked the cleared area around the villa, he went to one knee and took cover behind a tree. Chapayev took cover a few meters behind him, using his voice to direct his platoons into assault positions to right and left.

As those men were moving, each heard the odd screech of incoming fire. For many, it was a first. Still, enough of the *praporschiki* had served in Pashtia and on the borders during the breakup of the Volgan Empire to know. Chapayev and his men went to ground automatically as the first of several mortar shells exploded in the trees overhead. A Volgan screamed for a medic. As more shells landed the cry for help spread. The Santanderns' mortars were joined by increasing, and increasingly effective, rifle and machine gun fire, as the defenders fought back from their bunkers. Green tracers skipped among the trees.

The paratroopers returned the Santandern fire without noticeable effect. Volgan medics, oblivious to the incoming mortar rounds, ran from position to position, picking up the badly wounded and carrying or dragging them to the rear, where the company's senior medic had set up an ad hoc aid station. Many wounded men refused to be pulled back, shaking off the medics and continuing to return fire.

Chapayev's Forward Observer, or FO, called the Fifteenth Company mortar section to order a cease fire. When, after about two minutes, the incoming rounds failed to stop he knew it wasn't Volgan mortar fire cutting into the company. He ordered a resumption of firing on the compound, then stuck his head around a tree to adjust the firing. A bullet, flying low, passed through the FO's head, spattering brains over his radio operator, just behind. The RTO pulled the FO's body back to cover, then took his place and continued observing.

Carrera shouted into his radio for the gunship to find and silence the FNLS mortars. Aerial support fire abruptly ceased, even as a more powerful whine from the sky told that the plane was moving off. With the gunship gone, the defenders' fire increased.

Victorio felt his confidence in his chances surge with the first angry, orange-red blossoming of fire in the tree line. That confidence momentarily soared as the fire from overhead cut out.

"Right on," congratulated the guerrilla leader, into the radio. "Keep it up."

Victorio stepped outside, still sheltering as much as possible from the incoming mortar fire, and began pushing his fighters to their positions.

After he had seen the last of his guerillas to the walls and bunkers, Victorio stepped over the inert form of a girl with a rifle. She lay on her back clothed with only a camouflage shirt, and that unbuttoned and in disarray. Her legs were bent at the knees, foot under her, and legs obscenely spread. Victorio closed her legs with a booted foot, but gently. The girl's body was torn by two huge holes from which blood oozed. By the villa's lights, and the moons', he could see she was his partner of the night before. *I will mourn you later, my little dear one.* He ran to the southeastern bunker, to direct the fighting from there.

As the gunship flew, the crew for the 40mm, swaying on their feet from the maneuvering, frantically changed their ammunition mix to what the gunnery officer had called for, "shake and bake." This was mixed high explosive and white phosphorus, the former to break apart anything flammable and the latter to set it alight. It was exceptionally good for fuel, and not a bad mix for wood-packed ammunition.

"Gun up!" the chief of the forty announced into his microphone.

"Roger," the gunner answered, while peering at his green screen.

"There they are," he announced finally. "I can see the mortar barrels glow in the thermal sight."

Tracking by the glowing barrels became superfluous as the flash from the mortars' rapid fire gave away their position to the thermal imager. The pilot of the ANA-23 answered his gunnery officer with, "I'm lining up for a sweep. Take them out. We'll fire as she bears."

"Roger."

The gunner had one screen for target identification linked to his main thermal sight. There was another, a linked computer touch-sensitive screen, for engagement. He tapped the latter screen for the target, then tapped the button to create a firing solution. The gunnery computer then took note of the target, analyzed its location, the aircraft location, the aircraft speed, altitude, and direction, and a mix of meteorological data, and automatically adjusted the 40mm gun's elevation, training it slightly forward at the same time. A caret appeared on the gunner's screen, as well as on the pilot's. In addition, the pilot's screen received instructions on orienting the aircraft. The target spot remained lit after the gunner had removed his finger. That glowing spot moved inexorably closer to the targeting caret.

KaWhoomfKaWhoomfKaWhoomfKaWhoomf! Though mounted at the ANA-23's center of gravity, the high velocity forty packed a massive wallop. The entire airframe shook with the recoil. As quickly as one four-round magazine was expended, the gun crew slapped in another. In all, sixteen rounds were fired, twelve high explosive and four white phosphorus, before the aircraft had moved beyond the ability of the gun to train.

Fortunately, sometime between rounds nine and eleven, a fuel tank on the ground had been ruptured.

Since round twelve was both right on target and white phosphorus...

The pilot looked out his left side window and grinned with satisfaction. "I *love* my job," he said.

The copilot, on the other hand, said nothing. Instead, he whistled as a very large explosion rent the jungle below. This explosion led to several more, even more spectacular than the first, as whatever ammunition the mortar men below had unpacked went up with the fuel.

The series of explosions, so much louder than the distant *crump, crump, crump* of the mortars firing, told Victorio that his mortar support was no more and that his little command would soon again be under intense fire from above. Almost he gave in to despair. Perhaps, even, he would have, had not a radio call come in from an adjacent unit of the movement.

"We've been training in your area and can come to your aid in about half an hour," the woman on the other end of the radio said.

That was tempting but... *maybe there's a better way. I thought it best not to use the mortars on the aircraft. But the enemy to my front couldn't have responded to a mortar attack even if he'd wanted to. He can, on the other hand, respond to a ground attack and he just might.*

"How far from our airstrip?" Victorio asked.

"Closer," the woman answered. Victorio thought he recognized the voice as coming from *Comandante* Ingrid, a fiercely dedicated fighter who he knew slightly from meetings at infrequent conferences. "Maybe fifteen minutes... no... ten. Ten if we accept some risk."

"If you want to help, go for the airfield," Victorio advised. "The gringos have it. But be warned; there is some kind of aerial platform, a gunship, roaming overhead. It just took out my mortars."

"We saw it," Ingrid spat back, her voice full of fury at the imperialists. "We can spread out to reduce its effectiveness. Unfortunately, we can't retake the airfield if we're spread out too much."

"I don't need you to retake it," Victorio said. "It will be enough if you distract the gunship away from my base and cause them to break off the attack here."

"Done."

If I believed in God, Victorio thought, *I'd thank Him for putting Ingrid's band near enough to help. Since I don't, despite Father Castaño's sermonizing, I'll just be grateful to fate.*

The gunner was just tapping in a new targeting command for the villa when the ANA-23 received a frantic call from the airfield, the call punctuated by single shots and longer bursts coming through clear across the airwaves.

"We've got a group of guerrillas," the platoon commander below said. "Strength unknown; they're hitting us from below. We think they're working their way around our flanks—"

The transmission was drowned out by a long burst of fire. The ground commander repeated, "They're working their way around our flanks to get higher. I'm sending out half a section to each flank. Watch out for them. Right now the aircraft are safe enough, but if they get to the lip of the field or, worse still, above us, it's going to be a long damned walk home."

Carrera had apparently been following the conversation. His voice came over the ANA-23's radio. "Concur. Secure the field."

Carrera, sensibly prone behind a thick trunk, shook his head with admiration as he watched Tribune Chapayev walk the firing line as if unafraid. Carrera couldn't make out one word in fifty of the tribune's running diatribe.

But no matter. The words aren't important; the tone and the heart behind them are.

Of course, the better question is how we ended up this way. Too ambitious? Poor planning? Maybe. On the other hand, what we planned did get a group of first class soldiers to the enemy, while giving him little useful warning that we were coming. It does have the motherfuckers pinned to their compound. And casualty-free perfection is not the goal; destroying the bastards is the goal. If we can still do that, the plan and execution will have been good enough.

If . . .

"Keep up the fire, boys," Chapayev shouted over the rattle from his soldiers' rifles and machine guns, and the incoming *zing* of the enemy's fire. "Beat their fucking heads down."

A machine gun nearby went silent suddenly and stayed that way a moment too long for comfort. The Volgan began to trot over when he felt a tremendous blow to the calf of one leg. The force of the hit spun him, twisting his legs around each other and depositing him on the damp ground.

The leg was too close for Chapayev's night vision

goggles to focus on. He felt for the wound, wincing as his finger found a long but, as far as he could tell, not terribly deep gash. Blood poured around his questing fingers but at least it didn't gush.

Moments after the tribune was hit, a medic flopped to the ground at his side, asking, "Are you hit, sir?"

"A little," the Volgan answered, voice quavering slightly. "Not bad. Can you bind it up?"

"I can, sir, but if you don't get your head down, or at least behind some cover, I'm not sure what would be the point."

Carrera saw the Volgan struck down. He began to rise to go to the man's aid when he saw, briefly and faintly in the strobelike light of the firefight, the red cross of a medic's arm as the medic beat him to it. Moments later, with the medic's help, Chapayev got himself sitting up with his back to a tree that stood between him and the enemy.

Despite the action, a small portion of Carrera's mind continued to calculate, coldly, rationally. *We've got to pick up the tempo here,* he thought. Telling his little guard detachment, "Follow me," the *Duque* began to crawl forward.

A few minutes later he heard a now-familiar voice. Chapayev was once more on his feet, limping back and forth along the tree line encouraging his men. Carrera, bodyguards in tow, crawled up to a tree in the rough center of the company line. At what looked to be about two and a half kilometers in the distance, he saw the stream of fire that said the gunship was engaging the enemy below the airfield.

Fuck. Can't pull back with the guerrillas still alive.

They'll pursue and eat us for breakfast. Can't send any troops to help the airfield. We've got to hold there, win here, then go back and win there.

As Chapayev limped by, he was hit again and sent spinning. Carrera crawled over and dragged the Volgan behind the cover of a tree. Once Chapayev was close enough that his face could be seen by the light of the muzzle flashes, it was obvious the man couldn't command the company any longer.

Carrera twisted his body to face Menshikov. "Tell him he's done enough."

As he translated, Menshikov saw what Carrera had seen, that Chapayev's face had gone a ghastly white with loss of blood. *We're so fucked,* the Volgan translator thought.

Carrera risked a look around the tree. Not too far away, close enough to make with a surprise rush, there was a shallow draw that led past the villa. Farther on there looked to be a drainage ditch that also led near to the southeastern bunker. The steady stream of tracers lancing out from it said that was the bunker that was doing the most to keep the Volgans down.

If we could take out that bunker...

"Shit. I don't speak Volgan . . . Menshikov, take charge of the company. Keep them firing. I'm going up that ditch."

Still with his bodyguards in tow, Carrera crawled along behind the Volgan firing line until he reached a point he judged to be nearest the ditch he had seen. Bullets smacked the trees overhead, sending chips of bark and wood flying.

On the way he crawled over the body of a dead Volgan paratrooper. Next to the corpse was what appeared to be, and on inspection turned out to be, a satchel charge. *There is a God,* Carrera thought.

Pulling the charge's strap over one shoulder, Carrera made a check of his own Pound submachine gun and made ready to rush for the ditch.

Seeing the tensing in his *Duque's* body, one of the Balboan Cazadors grabbed his web gear to hold him back.

Carrera lurched forward only to fall on his face. With a snarl, he turned on the Cazador. "Son, whatever your legate told you, I guarantee he won't do anything worse to you if I'm killed than I will if you don't get your fucking hands off my belt." The Balboan let go.

Now freed of the restraining hand, Carrera rushed for the cover ahead. The Balboan who had grabbed Carrera's belt followed, as did the other three. The last of the group was hit two meters from the edge of the depression, machine gun fire spinning him around and leaving him in the dirt. The man moaned with pain until a second, unnecessary burst made sure he was dead.

Finally understanding where Carrera was headed, Menshikov directed the Volgan fire to suppress any Santandern position that could see into the ditch. Bullets pockmarked select places on the wall ahead.

Victorio, now crouched in the bunker he had chosen to command the fight from, had often wished, in his younger days, to cross swords with the gringos and defeat them. And now, at long last, it looked like—

"We're holding the sons of bitches. We're holding them."

One of the guerilla fighters shook his head and said, "*Comandante,* we've got company."

The guerilla then raised a rifle to shoot at Carrera's head as it peeked over the top of the ditch. One of the Volgans back with the company fired at the head. The Volgan missed, but the fire caused the guerilla, too, to miss by inches. That near miss spattered dirt and caused Carrera to duck his head again.

Menshikov saw Carrera's position near the bunker. He passed the word: "Fix bayonets!" Fire from along the tree line slackened temporarily in a sort of a ripple as word was passed from man to man and each man took his rifle off his shoulder to comply. Then, bayonets attached, the fire resumed. Menshikov sent one squad, reduced now to five men, to crawl up the same ditch to support Carrera and his guards.

Spitting out dirt from the near miss, Carrera automatically checked his trouser leg cargo pockets for grenades. *Double fuck. Of course I don't have any. I'm the next fucking thing to a fucking general officer. We don't carry grenades. We're not smart enough.* He asked his escort if they had any. No, they were in civvies; there'd been no place to hide any hand grenades.

Okay. Have to use the satchel charge, then my bayonet—understandably, the denim-and-*guayabera*-dressed Balboans didn't have those either—*to cut the wire.* He pulled his Volgan-designed bayonet and scabbard from his belt, drew the bayonet, and affixed it to the scabbard to form wire cutters. These he handed to one of the Balboans.

While Volgan fire snapped overhead, keeping the

bunkers' occupants' heads down, Carrera grabbed the straps of the satchel charge and swung it experimentally to make sure it would clear the sides of the ditch. Then, keeping his grip in the same place, he used his free hand to pull the igniter. With a pop, the igniter sparked and caught the fuse alight. A thin stream of smoke began to rise from where the internal heat bubbled and split the plastic around the fuse.

There really wasn't time to think now. Where he might otherwise have hesitated about sticking his head up amid all the fire, now Carrera had but one thought: To get rid of the satchel-encased catastrophe before it blew up in his face. He swung the charge around three times, then lifted up on the fourth and released it to fly toward the bunker.

He barely beat to the dirt the bullets that sought his life.

Victorio saw Carrera's sparking bomb fly to a landing that had to be near the main firing port for his bunker. He began to order one of his men out to throw it back, then realized that he was the only one unoccupied. He dropped his rifle and ran out the back of the bunker, then turned and lunged the six feet to the satchel. Bullets from the attackers' firing line across the clearing kicked up dirt at his feet. As he stooped to pick up the smoking bundle, one of the Volgan's bullets found him. He felt one leg jerk as he fell. Again he tried to throw the bomb away, even if only a little. He was hit again, this time in the chest. Victorio coughed blood as he made a final attempt to get rid of the damned bomb.

I'm sorry, friends. I can't. Too weak.

The explosion stunned Carrera and his men. Dirt and rocks showered down on them. Again risking a look over the ditch, Carrera saw a tangle of logs, dirt, and sandbags where the blast had partly knocked in one side of the bunker. He directed the Balboan with the wire cutters to begin working through the wire, one other to watch over him. Then he and the remaining guard began to fire their weapons down the line of Santandern bunkers, suppressing them.

A sound to his right caused Carrera to turn and almost to fire up the ditch. Then he saw the familiar shape of a gringo helmet. His finger eased from the trigger. With hand gestures, he told the Volgans to start clearing the bunker line from the south to the north. Fortunately, they *did* have grenades.

In the distance, short bursts from the ANA-23's various guns told that the fight at and for the airfield was still ongoing.

A burst of fire from above raised screams from a small assault group a bare fifty meters away, causing *Comandante* Ingrid to shudder. Ambushing a patrol from, or overrunning an outpost of, the Santandern Army was one kind of thing. They were just men, like her own, and could be killed. But Ingrid was now realizing that the gunship overhead was a wholly different order of threat. She couldn't kill it; she couldn't even engage it to any effect. And it could *see*. The screams that followed nearly every burst from overhead told her the damned thing could see well, even through the jungle cover.

Run? She asked herself. *Do I run and leave Victorio to his fate?* Can *I even run or will that flying*

*monster pursue? No... no. So I stay here and die...
or I run and die...or...maybe...*

"Fix bayonets," the female guerilla commander
ordered into her radio. "Wait for my command, but
we're going to charge them...get in among them where
that airplane can't fire for fear of hitting its own."

Even as she heard her little command group fixing bayonets behind her, Ingrid heard one of them
mutter, "Oh, shit."

"Shit," said Lanza, as the perimeter around the
airfield suddenly exploded with flashing muzzles and
the strobe-image of soldiers locked in battle, hand
to hand and bayonet to bayonet. Still sitting in his
command pilot's chair, Lanza flicked on his radio's
transmit button and ordered, "All copilots will remain
with their aircraft. All other aircrew will take up small
arms and assemble on me. NOW!"

Bloody good thing, Lanza thought, unbuckling himself from his pilot's seat then grabbing a submachine
gun on his way out, *that Carrera insists everyone is
an infantryman first and foremost.*

"*Duque,*" announced the gunship over the radio,
"We can't support the airfield anymore. Ours are all
mixed up with theirs. We can see it on the thermals
and it's nothing but bayonet and rifle butt all over
the place."

"Roger," Carrera answered. "Come on back here
and support the bulk of the company. We're pretty
mixed up here, too, but it looks like we're going to
win here and I don't want any of the fuckers escaping."

"Wilco, *Duque.*"

Sitting back against the walls of the ditch, Carrera contemplated the tattered remains of the Santandern who had tried to throw away the satchel charge. *You were a brave son of a bitch, I'll give you that*. He took a deep breath, rolled over and began to add his fire to that of the paratroopers.

CHAPTER EIGHTEEN

Other factors in the fall of civilizations concern separation of the elites and denial by those elites of goods and services required or desired by the larger, non-elite portion of the civilization. The separation is not merely physical, though it is usually that, too. As important, the separation becomes one of lack of accountability of the elites to the masses.

Consider who typically forms the elite: Unelected judges, politicians often gerrymandered into lifetime seats, hidden—hence safe—bureaucrats, unpoliced journalists with agendas that bear no particular correlation to advancing the truth, hereditary aristocrats, the denationalized and greedy rich, self-appointed activists, entertainers judged alone on their ability to make the unreal seem real, etc. None of these are truly accountable to those over whom they exercise power and influence. . . .

Take it as a given throughout human history: lack of accountability leads, invariably, to irresponsibility. Irresponsibility in those who wield power, be they elites or—in the rare genuine democracy—the masses, is disaster.

> —Jorge y Marqueli Mendoza, *Historia y Filosofia Moral*, Legionary Press, Balboa, Terra Nova, copyright AC 468

Presidential Palace, Santa Fe, Santander, Terra Nova

Fountains splashed peacefully into long reflecting pools framing the paved walkway from street to palace. The walkway led to a classical revival front, four sets of double Corinthian columns—though the leaves were styled after the native tranzitree, not the acanthus— holding up an entablature, itself surmounted by a low, triangular tympanum. Long wings led out to either side of the entrance. In one wing, in one room, slept the president of the Republic of Santander.

The aide hesitated before waking his sleeping chief. Still, the news was so frightful . . .

"*Señor Presidente*, please, you must rise."

The president of Santander rolled over and sat up, rubbing sleep from his eyes. "What is it, Rivera?"

"Señor, our cities in the east are being attacked."

The president was wide awake instantly. "Who? What? Where? How many? Maracaibo? The FNLS?"

"No, *señor*," Rivera answered, as his president pulled on shirt and trousers. "Not Maracaibo and certainly not the *Frente*. Beyond that, we don't know who, not for certain. We do know that four air attacks were launched against places in Belalcázar, and five more against Santiago. There are estates burning all over the suburbs. Buenaventura was hit with one or two; reports are confused. And Florencia, also. There are reports of attacks on the ground in some of the same places."

The president started, added up two and two, and came up with, "Those gringo bastards."

"*Sí, señor,* probably the gringos," Rivera agreed. "And probably going after the cartels."

"Bastards," the president repeated, then thought, *But what do I do? They are a friendly nation, sort of. And if they are going after the cartels, as Rivera says, they are doing me a favor, in the short and medium term, at least.* He bent his head down over his desk, deeply worried. *In the immediate term, however, they have violated Santander's sovereignty, which I am sworn to uphold. In the long term, I can't just ignore this or come next election, I will pay for it.*

"Rivera, get me the Chief of the Air Force."

There was a delay while the aide dialed the nearest air base, on the outskirts of Santa Fe, which was also the headquarters for the national air force. The Air Force Chief of Staff came on line, sounding half asleep.

"Villareal speaking."

"General, this is the President. I want you to get some fighters in the air and send them east. There are forces attacking several of our cities. I want you to force some of them, at least, to the ground where they can be arrested."

Villarreal's voice was replete with exasperation, but none of it seemed directed at the president. "*Señor Presidente,*" he said, "I have just been made aware of this. These people have attacked the base and airport at Santiago, as well as others. The runway and taxiways are shut down with mines. The radar is out, all of it. We have no effective coverage of the eastern part of the country. I am trying now to get two fighters from here into the air. I have also tried to call the airship the Federated States keeps off our east coast. Maybe they'll tell our planes where to look once they are in the air."

The president sighed. Soldiers could be so stupid sometimes. "Villareal, who do you think is attacking us? The trixies of the mountains? The UEPF? Balboa, perhaps?"

"Oh...I see, *señor*. Well, then you must realize that any pilots I send up I am sending to their deaths. We have good boys, but we can't match the planes or the ordnance of the Federated States Air Force."

"I know, General. But we have to try, for dignity's sake, if nothing else."

"Yes, *señor*. I will have two fighters in the air within thirty minutes. They are fueled but they must be armed."

Santandern Air Force Base, Santa Fe, Santander, Terra Nova

Captain Hartmann and Lieutenant San Martin shook hands and separated, each climbing the short ladders to their cockpits. Hartmann's grandparents had come to Santander from Sachsen after the Great Global War. They had done well in manufactures, being counted among Santander's legitimate rich before the 440s. San Martin's family was older money, landed gentry from the first wave of settlement from Old Earth. The two were, in fact, brothers-in-law, having married the younger sisters of their squadron commander.

San Martin waved to Hartmann as the former's canopy closed down. Hartmann returned the wave then added power to begin to taxi out towards the runway. By agreement, Hartmann was to sweep north, first to Florencia, then southeast toward Buenaventura.

Meanwhile San Martin was to go east to Belalcázar, initially, then farther east to the sea. The two pilots were agreed that they would force down one of the intruders or die trying.

Engines whining, San Martin followed Hartmann out onto the runway. With a roar his jets pushed him back into his seat as they pushed his Illusion jet fighter into the sky.

Federated States Airborne Command and Control Ship (ACCS), 271 miles east of Santander, Terra Nova

The defensive laser mounted on the airship cracked once, loudly, causing the weapons and radar officers to cheer. "That recon skimmer is toast, sir," Weapons announced.

The lieutenant on the radar frowned, checked, rechecked, and then said, "Sir, the Santanderns are sending up their air force . . . well . . . some of it."

When the senior officer aboard walked near to hunch over the radar screen, the lieutenant pointed out two blips as they arose and then separated over Santa Fe. "It isn't much, sir," the lieutenant said, "but it could put a crimp in operations."

Oh, dear. The colonel walked across the deck to the communication station. He told the commo officer to set a radio for a broad spectrum transmission, without encryption. "Okay, all you people out there. I know who you are, and you know who I am. What you probably don't know is that there are two bogies up looking for you." The colonel read off the course, altitude, and speed of the two Santandern craft. "Just trying to lend a helping hand. Good luck and Godspeed. Out."

MY *Phidippides*, *Mar Furioso*, Terra Nova

Little by little the operation was winding down as the troops of the Twenty-Second finished up—rather, fin- ished *off*—the remainder of the opposition, reboarded helicopters and ships, and began to return home. The chief of operations watched the plotter move symbols across the map, marking the progress.

A radio operator reported, "Sir, two more Finches safely landed at Jaquelina de Coco. Refueling now to return to Cameron. The last four report across the border and twelve minutes out from Jaquelina. The Belalcázar force is boarded and in the air . . . they're a couple of minutes late."

Still watching the map, Samsonov's chief of ops dis- missed the Turbo-Finches from his mind and returned his attention to the map. He concentrated on the twin lines being plotted from Santa Fe marking the progress of the Santandern fighters. Next to the lines, times were written in based on the speed reported by the ACCS. The Santandern planes hadn't been spotted as of yet by any of the six Mosaic fighters in the air and under the regiment's control. He expected radar sightings from the Mosaics as the Santanderns crossed the *cordillera* that ran like a spine parallel to Santander's east coast. Ops was worried. The orders were to avoid engaging regular Santandern forces . . . unless they were effectively engaging an element of the assault force. The Santandern jets could do that.

"Move the Mosaics west to take positions closer to the coast."

"Sir, Santiago Force is in the air and heading home." The RTO held the headset tighter to his ear and listened closely. After a moment he announced, "Sir, Santiago Two Bravo reports transmission trouble in its number two bird. They don't think they'll make it home on their own. Santiago Two Alfa has left them behind."

Again, the regimental operations officer consulted the map. He leafed through an annex to his copy of the operations order, then picked up a microphone. "Santiago Two Bravo, Santiago Two Bravo, this is Marathon, over."

Warbling and distorted as were all radio transmissions from helicopters, the response came back "Marathon, this is Santiago Two Bravo, over."

"Santiago, Marathon. You have two rafts aboard. I want you to head for Checkpoint Papa"—Ops referred to a spot in the ocean where the water was several thousand feet deep—"then ditch. Repeat, get the troops out and ditch your bird. I'm sending a boat for you. I'll also send two helicopters from the reserve." The ops officer looked up at a chart of call signs. "Your rescue birds will answer to Marathon Two Romeo, the boat is Shepherd . . . ah . . . three." Ops hesitated, then resumed. "Santiago, if you can't make it to Checkpoint Papa, you have got to get as far out over the water as you can. Remember, you've got a potential hostile coming in on your tail. Do not let him get you over land."

"Marathon, this is Santiago, Wilco, over."

Ops tapped his lips with his fingers for a moment before he ordered, "Send two of the Mosaics to cover

Santiago Two Bravo." Then, turning back to the map, he put a finger on Florencia and cursed silently.

Florencia, Santander, Terra Nova

Another moon had risen, adding a bit of light to the confusion at the mountain-carved airstrip. Under that light, Carrera found Lanza sitting cross-legged and staring at a corpse. It took a moment to realize the corpse had breasts. He sat down next to his air chief. "Are you all right, Miguel?" he asked.

Lanza nodded. "I didn't know it was a woman; I swear I didn't," he said. "I just saw someone with a bayoneted rifle and so I fired."

"If it's any consolation," Carrera said, "I had everyone down at the guerilla base shot, female or not."

"It isn't any," Lanza said. "It's different when you do it up close and personal."

"I suppose," Carrera conceded. "Are you okay to fly?"

Lanza nodded.

"Good. Then get back to your plane and get ready to fly us home."

Menshikov strained to help a medic lift the last nonambulatory casualty onto the third Nabakov in line. Two others, also full of wounded men, seized documents, and captured computers had already taken off over the mountains, hugging the trees. The wounded Volgan moaned, then coughed. The stretcher disappeared into the door, scraping the soldier's arm as the stretcher was twisted and dragged. Carrera ran up to join Menshikov and said, "I just talked to the gunship.

We've got company coming. One jet, presumed a fighter, is about twelve minutes out."

Menshikov looked at the now closing door to the Nabakov. "If we don't head straight back to the medical facilities in Balboa we'll lose some of the wounded, sir."

That hurt. These men had fought for him, and to let them just die . . .

Carrera pushed away the humanitarian thought. There was no room for such sentiments, under the circumstances. "I know," he said, "but most of the worst off are already gone." He pulled out his map. "If we head north and cross the Cajamarca border we can stick low to the ground. That pilot will lose us from his radar—might never even see us—if we stay low enough. We can then head out over water. The pilots tell me the fuel will last till we get back to Balboa, if barely."

"Yes, sir. I'll give the orders for the security team to pull back now, if you'll tell the gunship to cover us till we're gone."

"Right . . . Tribune?"

"Yes, sir?"

"Good job."

Menshikov answered, "Thank you, sir." He thought about the dead and the wounded and asked, "Was it worth it, sir?"

Carrera chewed at his lip and said, "I think so."

Santander's Illusion fighters were less than state of the art. Where a more modern jet might have told Hartmann his location, in his plane Hartmann had to use a map and do some figuring. Ahead, his radar showed seven targets, then six, then five as the planes twisted around behind the mountain range where Santander's western *cordillera* split off from the central.

As more targets disappeared from his screen, Hartmann was faced with a decision; pursue or follow the plan and head to Santiago. *I can probably catch up to the targets ahead before they reach Cajamarca, but I might never see them in the trees and hills. Best to follow the plan and head to Santiago.*

A few miles short of where the FNL3 villa burned, Hartmann veered towards Santiago.

Carrera breathed a sigh of relief as he felt the Nabakov level out after its long descent down the mountainside. Menshikov and the surviving bodyguards had insisted that Carrera be on this airplane, to get him out of the country as quickly as possible.

This was a different airplane than he had boarded at Coco Point but it stank of vomit as much as Number Two had. To the vomit were added the coppery smell of blood and the stench from some poor trooper's ripped gut. Medics moved around, as best they could in the twisting, turning transport, to help the wounded. Some of the injured had been assessed as "expectant" by the Volgan field medics. That meant they were expected to die. The nylon benches and floor were therefore full of those too badly hurt to spend much effort on and those too lightly hurt to need much. Carrera, deprived of Menshikov's services as translator, went from troop to troop offering what comforting sounds he could.

One of the troopers, listed as "expectant" and deathly pale under the red interior light, spoke fair Spanish. As Carrera shook his hand and thanked him, the Volgan pulled his ear close and asked, "Got a drink, sir?"

"Gimme a second." Carrera caught a medic's attention, said a few words, and took the small bottle of vodka the medic passed over. He unscrewed the cap, leaned down, and said, "Soldiers first," as he handed the bottle over.

The Volgan paratrooper took the bottle, raised it to his lips and took a long pull before passing it back. Carrera likewise took a drink and then began to hand the bottle back to the Volgan. He stopped when he realized the soldier had stopped breathing.

Santiago, Santander, Terra Nova

Hartmann didn't need any highly advanced navigational gear to find Santiago. Standing high above the city's lights, up on the commanding mountains to the east, four huge bonfires sent smoke, sparks, and flames to the sky. Hartmann checked his radar as he circled the city. No targets, nothing flying at all. He straightened out from his turn and set course to fly to Buenaventura. As he departed the area he radioed to Santiago Air Force Base, thousands of feet below.

"When can you people put up something to join me?" Hartmann asked.

The control tower answered, "Hours after daylight. The bastards skimmed by us just before one in the morning. Two helicopters; model unknown. They dropped thousands of these little damned mines on all the taxiways, the parking area, and the runway. Mixed in with those were some antivehicular mines. A bunch of them were painted with some red glow-in-the-dark paint. More weren't. We found out all the mines weren't painted when one of our people went out to try to sweep the way clear with a push broom. He stepped on one that wasn't painted. It smashed his foot. Anyway, at first light we'll begin to clear the base. Sorry. And, no, we can't refuel you either. Bastards."

Hours after first light, thought Hartmann, *too late. I guess it's still up to me.*

MY *Phidippides*, *Mar Furioso*, Terra Nova

"Sir, *Mare Superum* and *Pizarro* are out of Buenaventura waters and splitting up."

"What about Santiago Two Bravo?"

"They've made water, but they say their bird won't go much farther."

"Marathon Two Romeo, rescue?"

"They've gone past Checkpoint Papa and are flying a back azimuth toward Santiago Two Bravo."

"Tell Marathon Two Romeo to set their altitude above Santiago Two Bravo's. No sense in finding each other the hard way."

"Sir! Also, sir, the Mosaics have radar contact on one bogie, heading from Santiago to Buenaventura. They are moving to intercept."

"Tell them to warn the other guy off. They are not to kill anybody they can avoid killing."

Buenaventura, Santander, Terra Nova

Hartmann didn't even bother to check his position as he passed over the town. He had a radar contact, moving maybe a hundred knots, dead ahead of him. He aimed his Illusion straight at the contact and closed. Hartmann never even noticed the two small ships, one sailing north, one sailing south, that he overflew on his way.

Missile range, thought Hartmann, when he'd closed some. *Guns or missiles? The orders were to force them down to arrest them, not produce a railroad car full of bodies. Guns it is.*

Hartmann heard his threat warning radar chiming out danger. He chose to ignore it. The target—it had to be a helicopter—was only miles away. And there was another one—no, two!—closing on the first, moving faster and at higher altitude.

By the moonlight Hartmann saw his target. Yes, it *was* a helicopter. Lining his sights up ahead of the bird, he fired a short burst across its bow.

When the line of tracer fire shot past the front of the crippled helicopter, the pilot had instinctively shied from it, veering sharply right. Men in the back of the helicopter shouted their alarm. Overhead and behind the flight position the transmission ground out a sound of gradually disintegrating metal gears.

The pilot told his copilot, "I'm going to hold her in this position as long as I can. Get back, dump the life rafts, and get the men out. Have them leave their equipment aboard. I'll exit before the bitch sinks." When the copilot hesitated the pilot shrieked, "Go on, damn you! I'm a better swimmer than you are."

The copilot thought about continuing to protest. The look on the pilot's face made him think better of it. He unbuckled and crawled back to the troop compartment.

✧   ✧   ✧

Out at sea, in the blue-green light of the *Phidip-pides'* operations center, the ops crew heard the radio blast out, "Marathon, this is Four! The bogie just fired at the helicopter!"

"Can you take him out, Four?"

"Roger!"

"Do it!"

Amid hellish confusion—though at least there was no screaming—the troops in the back of the helicopter stripped off their gear, dropped their weapons and radios, and dived out the left side door to where, hopefully, two small rubber rafts floated. The copilot had been first out—someone had to insure the boats inflated. The crew chief pushed the others out one after another, then joined them in the darkness. When the pilot, head turned rearward, saw the crew chief go he pushed his stick over to get the helicopter as far as possible from the struggling men. Sparks and smoke came from the engine compartment.

Hartmann forced his head back forward as he made a high-"G" turn. He knew that there was another jet out there somewhere close. His radar warning buzzer told him so. Nonetheless, he lined up on the stricken helicopter to fire again. If he couldn't force it back to shore, he'd give the sea plenty of bodies to eventually wash ashore for evidence.

Hartmann's thumb reached for the firing button. He flicked off the safety cover and began to press. Before the guns fired he felt something strike his aircraft and then the unmistakable feel of an airframe coming apart around him. What had hit him was a mere conjecture until he saw a second missile streak by.

"Chingada," Hartmann said as he released his stick and reached down for the ejection lever.

"Mosaic Four has fired, sir! Two missiles. She reports one hit. The bogie has lost its engine.... Four reports an ejection ... he thinks.

Federated States Airborne Command and Control Ship (ACCS), 210 miles east of Santander, Terra Nova

The work deck exploded in cheers when the radar officer reported the Santandern as downed. *Never,* thought the colonel, *never have I been so proud of my country as I am today.*

Life Raft One, Santiago Two Bravo, *Mar Furioso*, Terra Nova

Clinging to the side of the raft, the copilot watched the helicopter turn over on one side and fall to the water. The spinning blades cut the water even as the increased resistance of the water tore the blades apart. He thought he saw, but couldn't be sure, his pilot trying to exit the side door as the helicopter took water and sank from sight.

Above him the copilot saw twin streaks and either a single or a double explosion; he couldn't be sure. The sonic boom he had heard as he had entered the water ended suddenly. From miles away came the sound of something hitting the waves, hard and fast.

The copilot scanned the skies around him. A different sounding sonic boom passed overhead, heading southeast. In the moonlight, the copilot thought he saw a parachute. This was confirmed when he did see the flashing of a strobe light, perhaps a mile away, or a bit less, the jet pilot's rescue beacon.

A few minutes after the last sonic boom had died away, the copilot heard the welcome sound of helicopter rotors, two, he thought, rapidly nearing. He activated his own strobe.

"Marathon, this is Two Romeo. We're on station and the other chopper is picking up the troops now. But Marathon, we've got a problem."

From many miles distant, Ops asked, "What?"

"The Santandern pilot," answered the rescue chopper's pilot. "He's in the water. I doubt they'll find him anytime soon, if at all."

Ops considered. *Twin problems. We want to leave the Santanderns in doubt as to who is responsible and we want to keep their military and noncombatant—or at least non-Cartel—losses to a minimum.*

"I admit to being a little stumped. Any suggestions, Two Romeo?"

"Nobody's going to mistake me for a Balboan. Not once they hear me speak Spanish. And my English isn't bad either. I can swim. While my copilot maintains a hover, I'll pull him out, cover his eyes, and give him a choice he can't refuse. Then we drop him off somewhere not too convenient. I'll be the only one he sees."

"Move out and draw fire, Romeo."

✧   ✧   ✧

Hartmann's automatically inflating life vest kept him afloat. The pilot's seat was sinking somewhere deep below him. Idly floating on his back, he wondered, *Will the sharks get me first? There are megalodon in these waters. That would be quick if not exactly painless. Or will the vest leak so that I drown? Or maybe a storm comes up? Whatever it might be, there's essentially no chance that my own air-sea rescue will find me.*

Oh, oh, what's this? Ah, the invaders. They'll just machine gun me from a distance, I think. Adios, Patria.

To the Santandern's surprise, the helicopter didn't go into a hover at a reasonable distance away, where reasonable was defined as "good to shoot fish in a barrel from." Instead, it kept coming closer until it was almost exactly overhead, at a distance of about twenty feet. He saw a shape emerge from the side of the chopper, then felt his body begin to rock as a great spout of water shot up beside him.

The Volgan pilot surfaced, moments later, near Hartmann. The Santandern waved. "Nice of you to drop in."

"You speak English?" the Volgan shouted to be heard over the chopper. It was few enough words that a foreigner was unlikely to pick up the Volgan accent.

"Flight school in the Federated States," answered Hartmann succinctly.

"Good. But we can speak Spanish. Now, we can do this one of three ways. I can take you back with me and no one you know will see you any time in the next half century or so. Or, we can leave you here and maybe you'll be found and maybe you won't."

"You said three ways," Hartmann reminded. There was also a fourth way, as both men knew. The Volgan— or gringo, as Hartmann thought—had the good taste not to mention it.

"It's up to you. But we can take you back and drop you off."

"And the catch?"

"You've got to swear to me that you won't say who we are."

"Be serious. I've got to say something."

"Fine. Tell them we were men from outer space, Cajamarcans. Make something up."

Hartmann felt his arm. He was pretty sure it was broken. He knew he wouldn't last out here very long. Shock and exposure would get him if nothing else. And Santander's Air Rescue Service was next to nonexistent. "I agree."

The Volgan waved to the helicopter to throw a rope. This he tied under Hartmann's arms. The rescue crew pulled him up by main strength, the helicopter having no winch attached. The rope was returned. Then the helicopter turned east towards Santander before heading for home.

San Martin had focused on Hartmann's radio beacon as it activated. He had had no luck chasing down any of his sightings. They had all either lost themselves in the trees and hills, or had crossed over into Balboa before he could intercept. He picked up a radar contact, a helicopter that seemed to be hovering over the approximate location of Hartmann's beacon. San Martin was about to use his IFF, Identification Friend of Foe, when the helicopter turned east toward

Santander. *Oh, it's one of ours.* San Martin told himself that he would never again have a bad word to say about Santander's helicopter units. San Martin turned back toward Santa Fe.

CHAPTER NINETEEN

Elites of today favor coddling the criminal class. The elites, then, will deny the common people arms necessary for self defense. This is easy for the new aristocracy; they live in gated communities, with armed guards, and as far from criminal elements as possible. They will also deny the commoners the social good resulting from the putting to death of the wicked. The elites don't suffer from this; their gated communities and their guards make them fairly immune to crime.

Are your public schools a ruin? Never mind; you and your children don't count. Jobs gone? Electrical service spotty? Public transportation unreliable? News full of lies? Not to worry; the elites are well taken care of, behind their walls. And fear not for your elite, neo-aristocratic rulers' children. Those children will attend good private schools even as the elites subject yours to a system that, imposed by foreigners, would be a crime against humanity, an act of war.

But then, the elites *are* foreigners; even if they— purely notionally—share your citizenship, they have renounced all of its meaning. And the people owe them nothing, not even their lives. They are at war with you. You should fight back.

Without mercy.

> —Jorge y Marqueli Mendoza, *Historia y Filosofia Moral,* Legionary Press, Balboa, Terra Nova, copyright AC 468

Anno Condita 471
Executive Mansion, Hamilton, FD, Federated States of Columbia, Terra Nova

"Turn that shit off," said the President, Karl Schumann. A flunky picked up the remote to turn off a television that seemed to have nothing on it but antigringo protests from Atzlan to la Plata.

The president, watched by his press secretary, the secretary of state, the Chairman of the Joint Chiefs of Staff, the attorney general, and a few others, paced vigorously from wall to wall.

"General," Schumann asked, "are you absolutely certain we didn't do it? The President of Santander is positive that we did."

JCS suppressed a highly amused smile, answering, "Mr. President, we know exactly who did do it. The ACCS we have on patrol over the Santander coast recorded the whole thing as it happened, even though they didn't quite understand what was happening. The Balboans did it. I don't know all the details, but they did it. And they set it up to pin it on us."

"But ... *why*?"

"My guess," answered the JCS, "is that they didn't want to piss off the Santanderns because they've got all the enemies they need already. And, too, it isn't like we haven't been pressuring them to do something about the drug trade, or as if they don't have good reasons to keep drugs out of Balboa."

"What's the ambassador down there say?" Schumann asked of State.

"Ambassador Wallis says the Balboans won't admit a thing to him. They refuse to discuss it. Which is screwy, because if it was them, then they know it couldn't have been us."

"It wasn't us," JCS reiterated.

The secretary of state gave JCS a look which as much as said, *So you say.*

Schumann returned to his desk and sat down. "In any event," he said, "Santander, the whole of Columbia, thinks we did do it. There were protests today in every capital. The Santanderns are showing helmets, our kind of helmets, all over the news. They claim we shot down one of their planes and shot up an airfield. Their president is threatening to shut down diplomatic relations and kick us completely out of the country."

State shook his head. "Not a chance, Mr. President. They need us."

"Mr. President," said JCS, "we can prove to the Santanderns that the Balboans did it. We'll just release them the tapes of the whole incident." The general screwed up his face. "But then, they wouldn't necessarily believe we couldn't—didn't—fabricate the whole thing, would they?"

The press secretary bent down and whispered something softly in the president's ear. The president's eyes grew wide and he said, "Ladies and gentlemen, if you leave me alone for a few minutes to confer..."

When the room was cleared the president of the Federated States asked, "No shit?"

"It's true, Karl. Your polls are soaring. Everyone in this country thinks you did it, and they're just tickled pink by it. And you *need* this. The people are happy the country's getting even with someone, and don't really give a shit if it's not the real guilty party."

"But what about all the civilians killed, kids even?"

"Just the cost of doing business. Besides, they were just foreigners. Nobody cares."

"And if Balboa decides to take credit?"

"They won't. First, because now no one would believe them. Second, they'll be too late once you've said we did it. Third, because, as the general said, Balboa probably doesn't want Santander pissed at them. Santander is, after all, ten times bigger than Balboa is. Last, if they wanted to take credit, they would have done so already."

The president reached a decision. "Bring in the others."

"Mr. President, you're live."

Schumann looked into the camera, his sincerest-seeming expression writ plain on his face. "My fellow Columbians. I would like to announce that a raid was conducted against certain members of Santander's drug cartels who were implicated in the recent criminal attacks in the Republic of Balboa in which Federated States citizens lost their lives."

"Naturally, I will not divulge any details of the mission. Operational secrets will be preserved in my Administration. But let this be a lesson to those who would resort to terror, wherever they may be. You cannot run far enough or fast enough. You cannot hide well enough. The forces of justice will overtake you."

As the president fielded questions, the press secretary marveled, *What a master. And he didn't even have to lie, exactly.*

Santa Fe, Santander, Terra Nova

Of the roughly one dozen drug lords attacked, all had been killed or, more commonly, captured, along with sundry accountants, assistants, wives, and mistresses. No one in Santander actually knew how many of each there had been. In any case, the losses did not, by any means, mean the end of the cartels. The money to be made was a magnet, one that pulled in greed as a normal magnet attracted iron. There were always new people to step up, nor had all of the old been targeted. At best, one could say that the efficiency of the remainder and the replacements might be somewhat less than that of those lost.

Or might not have, too.

That remainder, and the replacements, met with Guzman in one of the ornate-to-the-point-of-tacky palaces that had been spared assault.

Guzman contemplatively held a golden crucifix on a golden chain. "This," he whispered, "is proof positive of who was behind the attacks. The Balboan, Carrera, gave it to me. I gave it to Escobedo. It has returned to me again via the Balboan Embassy."

"Having gone to all the trouble of pinning this on the gringos, why should they let us know who really did it?" asked one of the remaining drug lords, *Señor* Ochoa.

"So we learn the lesson," Guzman answered.

"Lesson?"

"Yes...don't fuck with them. They gave me a more explicit message along with the cross. They want me, and one of you gentlemen, to go to Balboa. They promise safe conduct."

Ochoa attempted a sneer, but found he didn't have the heart to pull it off. "Or what?" he asked.

"Or else the attacks continue until we are all dead. Along with our families. I was told we have a week, no more."

Isla Santa Catalina, Balboa, Terra Nova

Carrera, Fernandez, Menshikov, the sergeant major, Soult, and a dozen guards from Fernandez's department were waiting at the small landing strip when Ochoa and Guzman arrived by legion plane. Most of the party looked quite somber and serious. Fernandez was the exception; his people now had enough captured documents, laptops, and prisoners to keep them busy for years.

The Santanderns were received coolly but politely, and then led to a lunch under a wide canopy. Carrera was somewhat surprised that Ochoa looked, if anything, more the legitimate businessman even than Guzman.

"I had nothing to do with the attacks on your country," Ochoa began.

Carrera looked at Fernandez who answered, with a shrug, "So far as I know."

"I'll accept that, for now, then," Carrera agreed. "But...so?"

"So you can speak to me," Ochoa said. "I am not your enemy."

"Have you surrendered then?" Carrera asked. "Surrendered unconditionally? Have all of your associates?"

"Surrender is premature," Ochoa said. "We can have peace, however. I propose a permanent cessation to hostilities. I offer that all cartel operatives will be removed from Balboa, that all Balboan operatives be removed from Santander, and that we of the cartels do all in our power to ensure that Balboa is no longer used as a drug thoroughfare."

Carrera told him, simply, "That might have been enough, once. Now? No, not good enough. Too much blood has been spilled. Too much more is threatened."

Elbow on the lunch table, Ochoa raised one hand, palm up. "What then?"

"Your operatives leave Balboa; mine stay in Santander," Carrera said. "You *ensure* no trafficking takes place through Balboa. You turn over all information on the old government's involvement in the trafficking, all well documented.

"I demand ten billion Federated States drachma, within the month. In addition, your people will pay to the legion another fifty million, monthly. You can call it whatever you want. It's tribute all the same. Money paid to us for you to stay alive.

"And don't whine about it. The market share your surviving members will gain from the competition I've eliminated should more than pay that amount. I did you all a favor, really."

Ochoa did sneer now. "That's ridiculous, impossible."

Carrera shrugged and said, "Enjoy your lunch." This caused Guzman to gulp, nervously.

✧ ✧ ✧

"Come," said Carrera to Ochoa, after lunch was finished. "Let's walk and chat." Fernandez, Menshikov, and a half dozen of the guards followed close behind.

They talked of meaningless things on the way, Carrera pointing out the flowers that lined each side of the pathway down. "The prisoners put these in," he said. "They actually have a fair business going in growing flowers for the mainland. Some are even shipped south to the Federated States."

The Santandern, playing along, walked with eyes down, admiring the pretty plants. Then he heard something strange, a sort of a moan. He looked part way up and saw a thick wooden beam sticking up out of the ground. He looked around, eyes still low, and counted seventeen more upright beams.

Then his eyes traveled up the beam. "Oh, my God!" he exclaimed.

In a loose circle, there by the beach, fourteen men and four women hung on rough wooden crosses. The men all showed marks of hideous torture. Through the feet and wrists of each had been driven large spikes. Crusted blood marked their bodies and the wood. The emissary recognized many of his former business associates, and the wives and mistresses of others.

"You know," said Carrera, conversationally, "No one really knows what kills someone who has been crucified. The best theory I've read is that the strain on the diaphragm when the victim hangs by his wrists keeps his chest muscles from emptying his lungs normally. Eventually this tires the diaphragm until the victim suffocates. Of course, with the feet supported—by more spikes, as these are—the victim can push up, at the cost of some *ah, discomfort*, and rest the diaphragm. That way the victim conspires with the killers to draw each life out to its last strength. These . . . might live three days more. Less for the women . . . probably.

"We took these a little less than a month ago. They were turned over to my intelligence people. With some effort, we think they have surrendered everything they ever owned. A lot of pain, then a little period of relief for turning over a few score million in assets. Then more pain until more assets were given up. It must have seemed a good deal to these people at the time. I understand there are computer nerds in the Federated States tearing their hair out because so many of the assets we grabbed they had spent months and years trying to uncover. It was really quite a haul."

Carrera stopped briefly while the Santandern reeled in disgust. He continued, nonchalantly, "I imagine you think that you can better use the money I demand to get to me and mine. It's been tried. Or maybe you think you can hire soldiers to protect you. These thought that. And with a tiny fraction of my force we took them and did . . . this. I control a country's army, you know, while you just have a petty little concern.

"Do you think you might be able to hire mercenaries? They often find it easier to rob the paymaster than to fight for him. No, mercenaries would be more dangerous to you than I am. I have a finite appetite and no interest whatsoever in taking your business from you. Besides, you can't offer them what I can, what they really crave: legitimacy, recognition, traditions, a uniform, a real army to be a part of. I think any you might hire will be second rate, no matter what they charge.

"Professional hit men? They could get to me, I imagine." Carrera turned to Menshikov and asked, "What are your orders if I am assassinated?"

The paratrooper answered, "Sir, to attack the Santandern drug cartels, butcher their followers, then take them, their wives *and* children back to Balboa for crucifixion."

"Will you follow those orders?"

"To the letter, sir."

To the shaking Santandern, who understood English perfectly well, Carrera said, "Perhaps it would not be such a good idea to kill me after all."

Ochoa leaned against a cross briefly, then recoiled in disgust, unconsciously wiping a bloodstained hand on his trouser leg. He risked a sally. "How is it you are better than us? We both kill innocents; we both use torture. What makes you so moral?"

"I never claimed to be more moral than you. As far as the drug trade goes, I really don't care one way or the other, as long as it stays out of Balboa. The only difference is that you failed to understand me; to understand that I would never give in, that no measure could deter me. So all the evil you did was wasted. But I did understand you, and I knew, as I know now, that you would give in. So the lives I took and the pain I inflicted were not wasted. That's the difference. That . . . and that I won, and you lost."

The Santandern took a last look at the writhing bodies of his former compatriots. One of them, *Señor* Escobedo, soundlessly mouthed a cry for help. The emissary turned away. "*Duque* Carrera, I will tell my associates that I believe your offer is fair. My counsel carries weight. I think we can agree to your terms."

"There is one more set of terms," Carrera said.

Ochoa raised an eyebrow.

"Nothing too onerous," Carrera continued, reaching into a pocket to pull out a small typewritten note. "These names popped up on some of the computers we captured. I want them and their families dead."

Ochoa took the note and read alone only the first name before going silent. "Piedad Andalusia, eh? Why her?"

"Because she sides now with the Marxists in Santander, likewise the Progressives in the Federated States, and so can be predicted to side with the Marxists of the Tauran Union at some future and inconvenient time," Carrera answered.

"We can do this," the Santandern agreed.

"I was certain you could."

Ochoa took a last look at the crosses and suppressed the urge to vomit.

Carrera said, "I was sure we could come to an amicable understanding. Now, back to the tent for a drink before your flight?"

As Carrera and the other turned to leave, Menshikov asked what to do about the poor people hanging on their crosses.

Carrera considered, then said, "Kill the women and the accountants, silently. I'd let them go but . . . no, too risky. Still, there's no further reason for them to suffer. Let the others die *naturally*. Bomb *my* people, will they?"

The fact that Balboa was behind the raid did not become widely known for some years, at which point it was far too late to matter. The ACCS crew, if they had ever entertained doubts, had those doubts dispelled when they were individually interrogated by civilian-clad security agents who then swore the crew to secrecy. Shortly after the president of the Federated States' television address, strong young men with good bearing and very little hair began using hints that they had been in Santander for recent bloody missions as devices to attract women in places like Oglethorpe and Wilkes' Folly. Some were believed. Occasionally, so it was reported in various barracks, the technique worked. A few of the Volgans tried the same thing in Balboa, but were not believed.

In the Federated States, counter-drug operational funds for the next three years were severely curtailed as acquisitions from seized assets took a sharp downturn. (Fernandez's methods were much faster if lower tech.) For years to come, rarely would a Drug Interdiction Task Force accountant or computer hacker say the name of Balboa without a snarl. This was one reason why, when Balboa turned over extensive evidence that the old government, in Old Balboa, was deeply involved in the drug trade, that evidence was suppressed.

The fifteen children found at the various targets, such as had not been killed by the attack or released, were brought back to Balboa. Lourdes arranged to place the youngest in good homes. The older ones were to be supported by Carrera himself in a foster home until they were old enough to join the army.

In Santander one voice insisted that the Federated States was not responsible for the attack. This was young Santandern Air Force Captain Hartmann. True to his word, in as sincere a voice and expression as he could muster, Hartmann insisted to one and all that it had been *Balboa* that had raided Santander.

EXCURSUS

"Criminal Justice in the Timocratic Republic of
Balboa: Barbarism at the Bar," Bianca Meister,
from University of Starvation Cove Law Review,
Spring, AC 488

Largely the product of people untrained in the nuances
of the law, the saving graces, the implicit mercies, and
the law's civilizing influences, criminal justice in the
Central Columbian nation of Balboa is itself the greatest crime in the country. Indeed, it is a blight upon the
Family of Man and an insult to the evolution of the
law on two planets over more than four millennia...

In reviewing the Balboan Code of Criminal Justice
one is struck immediately by its almost unremitting
harshness. The least penalty for anything we in the
more enlightened parts of the world would think of
as a common law felony is death by hanging. The
maximum punishments increase in severity from there.
Counterfeiters are hanged, arsonists are burned, rap-
ists impaled, premeditated murderers and traitors are
crucified. Even the lightest of felonies, robbery and

burglary, or lesser forms of nonjustifiable homicide, for example, receive the rope as their reward. And conspiracy law carries this unremitting bloodthirstiness and sadism over to group crimes as well...

In the case of crimes against the person, as opposed to against the state, executions are in preference carried out by either the victims or the victims' nearest kin. They may be, and often are, delegated to the state to perform on behalf of the aggrieved. The law, such as it is, requires that executions be public, and performed in a prominent and accessible spot. This, too, seems to drive the choice of state as executioner.

One of the few instances of mercy permissible within the code is that the victim, if alive, may choose a lesser penalty, for example, hanging for rape, rather than impalement. Even there, hangings come in several varieties and it is the rare criminal who receives the more merciful long drop as opposed to the slow strangle...

The philosophy, if such it may be called, behind this ultradraconian code is nowhere made explicit within that code. Instead, one must delve into the legislative history. This makes it plain that, for example, Balboa—rather, the dictatorship of those who have sold themselves to state's military—believes that deadly force is authorized to any potential immediate victim, or a third party acting in their behalf, to deter or prevent any of the common law felonies. This value judgment being made, they further hold that what the victim, or someone acting on the victim's behalf, may do to prevent a crime, the state may do or permit to deter or avenge.

Also express, within the legislative history, is the value

judgment that man has no natural rights, but rather only those rights which arise within the social compact. Logically enough, given that Balboa does not require but only permits its residents to take on the "burdens" of citizenship, the state also holds that anyone may voluntarily withdraw from the social compact, thereby giving up all rights and losing all protections. Committing a common law felony is considered to be such a renunciation of rights and duties. That this is simply barbaric bothers the Balboan timocrats not a whit . . .

The crime of rape is a peculiarity, as, admittedly, it is around the planet. It is almost always a case of conflicting stories and ambiguous evidence, even when the evidence is clear that intercourse took place. Moreover, because of the tendency to put the victim on trial, more enlightened polities have shielded the victims from having their past sexual conduct introduced at trial, thus somewhat reducing the probability of genuine proof beyond a reasonable doubt being presented at trial. They have, correspondingly, reduced the penalties inflicted. Of course, this was done in goodly part to prevent the murder of the victims of rape.

Balboa is having none of that. They've made the value judgment that it is better that one girl be raped and murdered, and her murderer be put to death, than that ten girls be raped, and better that the victim be put on trial than that an innocent man be put to death.

And they insist upon death. Complete pardon by the victim is not permitted, as the culprit represents not merely an enemy of the people, but a renouncer of the social compact, a threat, and an educational example to be made for the public . . .

✧   ✧   ✧

Besides sparing themselves the expense of caring for many convicted criminals humanely, the effect of Balboa's extraordinary liberality with regards to the death penalty, and limited right to appeal, is that somewhat more money is available (from an admittedly small pot) for the rehabilitation of those convicted of lesser crimes. By and large, so it must be admitted, this rehabilitation seems to work somewhat better than rehabilitation does in most states.

There seem to be three factors at work here. One is that prison sentences in Balboa tend to be comparatively short but, as with everything else in the penal system, comparatively harsh. Rather than, for example, awarding twenty years for larceny, Balboa is more likely to give six to eight, but of penal servitude—hard labor under the sun and under the lash—rather than mere imprisonment. This leaves less time, less energy, and less inclination for incarcerated criminals to treat their incarcerations as postgraduate courses in effective criminal behavior. A second factor is that with so many criminals put to death, there are virtually none left in prison to teach that postgraduate course. Third, while completely ignoring the needs of criminals for psychiatric treatment, Balboa does, in approximately the last third of a criminal sentence, teach at least some of them job skills more useful than making license plates...

There are persistent rumors that incarcerated prisoners are used for biological warfare experimentation...

In any given month, somewhere in the Republic of Balboa, a man or a woman is hanged, or burned, or impaled, or crucified. Some months it is more than

one. And the world seems impotent to put a stop to
it. Economic sanctions do not work, as the Balboa
Transitway and the InterColumbian Highway allow
the government there to retaliate, tit for tat. Military
measures, given the large, well equipped, well led, and
well trained legions of Balboa, are impossible. All that
remains are diplomatic efforts and the disapproval of
the enlightened peoples of the world, and at both of
these the Balboans sneer.

Moreover, such unremitting brutality has the effect
of making the entire people of the nation harsh and
inhuman. For example, when the convicted felon,
Neron Leonardo de Lingero, was crucified, in the
spring of AC 475, a crowd estimated at over one
hundred thousand turned out to jeer. Worse, Mr. de
Lingero had been convicted without the testimony of
a single eyewitness, nor even a body...

Letters to the Editor, University of Starvation Cove Law Review, Fall, AC 488

Dear Sir:

A translation of your article of your last edition, entitled "Criminal Justice in the Timocratic Republic of Balboa: Barbarism at the
Bar," has been published within the Republic
of Balboa. While it had most of its facts right,
there were some glaring omissions I thought
I might acquaint you with. For example, in
discussing the method and mechanism of the
admittedly frightful death of Neron Leonardo
de Lingero, the author, Ms. Meister, failed,
curiously, to discuss Mr. de Lingero's crime.

You see, Mr. de Lingero was convicted of a series of crimes involving Ana-Barbara Encito-Espera, aged eight years. Mr. de Lingero had kidnapped Ana-Barbara from in front of her home. He had then subjected her to a lengthy period of rape, forcible sodomy, and torture, before killing her, and finally cooking and eating her. And, while it is true that there were neither eyewitnesses nor a body, the jury in the case thought the evidence sufficient, said evidence being in the form of video recordings Mr. de Lingero had made of young Ana-Barbara's ordeal, presumably so he could enjoy her suffering after she was gone.

Oh, and it was closer to two hundred thousand people who came to see justice done.

> Very Truly Yours,
> Lourdes Nuñez de Carrera
> Second Vice President
> *Ciudad* Balboa,
> Republic of Balboa

PS: We don't use prisoners for biological warfare experimentation. We don't have an offensive biological warfare program. We do permit a certain number of nonviolent prisoners to volunteer to test *vaccines* developed by your country which your government refuses to permit human testing on. These prisoners are given substantial time off of their sentences. Again, all are volunteers.

CHAPTER TWENTY

Any example of power without the sense of, and acceptance of, responsibility is doomed to disaster.

The elites separate themselves out in space from the ill effects of their ill-conceived programs and inane philosophies. They separate themselves socially and informationally from being reminded or informed. Thus, they award themselves power and influence without any concomitant responsibility. This, however, is not the only way that the separation of power and responsibility can occur.

As the elites separate themselves in space, so do the masses separate themselves in time, voting for the immediately good and pleasurable and leaving it to their heirs, should they have any, to pay the price. The people may vote themselves hefty pension and retiree medical programs from their governments. If they have neither the sense of responsibility to save on their own behalf, nor to bear and raise the children who will work on their behalf, such irresponsible schemes are doomed . . .

In no area is irresponsibility as likely to grow as in matters of sex. Elites, being irresponsible and

especially sexually irresponsible, encourage this sort of irresponsibility on the part of the people...
—Jorge y Marqueli Mendoza, *Historia y Filosofia Moral,* Legionary Press, Balboa, Terra Nova, copyright AC 468

Anno Domini 2525–2526
Anno Condita 471
UEPF *Spirit of Peace,* Lunar Orbit

Maneuvering in zero G, while carrying a cup of coffee, was no mean feat. Fortunately, the cup was sealed and Esmeralda had had some chance to practice. She smiled shyly as she placed the magnetic-bottomed cup into an indentation in the arm of Richard's command chair.

The earl of Care couldn't help but notice how the girl's midnight hair billowed out in a sort of halo framing her face. He thought she was unbearably lovely.

"Thank you, Esma," Richard said warmly. "Any last message from the high admiral?"

Esmeralda leaned close and whispered, "She says, 'Do it. Now.'"

The earl of Care and Captain of the *Peace* sighed. "I was afraid of that. Wish me luck."

"You know I do, Richard," said the Isthmian girl.

They weren't lovers, surprisingly. At least Marguerite was surprised. But Esmeralda was quite young and Richard, in this as in other matters, quite decent. Also, as he'd admitted to Wallenstein when she'd asked, he was for a Class One rather inexperienced.

In time, perhaps.

Richard pressed a button on the chair, close beside

the zero G coffee cup. "High Admiral, this is the captain. The tugs are ready. We're ready. Three-hundred-second countdown to begin maneuver out of the lunar shadow begins in . . . four . . . three . . . two . . . now."

Farther aft in the ship, in the admiral's bridge, Wallenstein fretted far more than Richard did. The big Kurosawa screen on one wall was split into a dozen frames, showing the captain, several different views of the rest of the bridge, forward of the ship, the tugs, the former colonization vessel, *Jean Monnet*, trailing, with its tugs, and certain critical ship's charts.

Marguerite fretted, *I've drilled the boy silly, hand carried him as much as I could, pushed him into the deep water when that seemed a good idea, mentored and nagged and . . . Elder gods, I hope I prepared him well enough.*

The speakers concealed in the walls announced, "two-thirty-seven . . . two-thirty-six . . . two-thirty-five . . ."

Marguerite concentrated on the image of Richard's face. *He's doing pretty well with the whole "confident look" thing. And his voice is steady. The crew seems not too worried. And I'm being an old woman.*

Marguerite felt the ship shudder around her as the tugs took magnetic hold. It wasn't, strictly speaking, necessary to use the tugs. Yet saving reaction mass for emergencies was always wise.

"One-twenty-two . . ."

"Seventy-seven . . . Seventy-six . . ."
"Stations report," Richard ordered, his voice much calmer than he really felt. He *remembered* all the

simulations he had screwed up, and remembered them deep in his bones.

"You're doing fine, Richard," Esmeralda whispered again. She still hadn't left the side of his command chair. He found a considerable comfort in her proximity, more perhaps than he consciously recognized.

"Navigation nominal, reaction mass temperature and pressure optimal... Engineering, ninety-six percent power, captain... Life support, air mix optimal... Medical..."

"Fifty-two... fifty-one..."

"Lunar laser boost station reports ready to push, Captain."

"Forty... thirty-nine... thirty-eight..."

"A little music, Captain?" asked the chief petty officer of the ship.

"Do it, Chief."

Almost immediately the speakers began to blare Verdi's triumphal march from *Aida*.

"Twenty-six... twenty-five..."

I can't believe it, thought Esmeralda. *I can't believe I'm really here... in a starship... going to the world of exile.* She smiled inside. *To be honest, I can't believe I haven't had my heart cut out and my body turned into a stew for the Azteca with all the choicest parts saved and sent back to Count Castro-Nyere.*

I will not fail you, Father, Sister. I remember.

"Take a seat and buckle in, Esma," Richard ordered. "Quickly, please."

She did, pushing off with one arm towards the

rear of the bridge, to an unoccupied seat next to the chief. The chief buckled her in.

"Twelve . . . eleven . . . ten . . . nine . . ."

"This is your first trip, honey," the chief, a capable Class Four, said. "It might be bad or it might be easy; there's no telling in advance."

"I know," Esmeralda answered. "I'm hoping for the best."

"Good girl," the chief said. "I think we'll be okay."

"Six . . . five . . ."

"Tugs report full power, Captain."

"Understood . . ."

"Two . . . one . . .

"Bring us out of orbit," ordered Richard, earl of Care.

The deployment of the sail always gave Marguerite a thrill. This time was no exception. Almost she could hear the snap as gas filled the ring and expanded the thing to pull against the lines.

And the boy's doing well, she mused. *When was the last time I had occasion to be proud of a Class One? Has it ever even happened?*

A portion of the screen on the admiral's bridge suddenly flared, as the lunar laser batteries opened up, giving the *Peace* a slight but perceptible shove. This would continue, and be reinforced by the batteries of the asteroid belt, until distance and attenuation made too little a difference in the light to keep it up. The lunar batteries were multiple, and spaced around that body. These would take turns, firing and shutting down, as rotation masked them.

Wallenstein's eyes turned to the portion of the

screen devoted to the *Jean Monnet*, aft. Already the tugs were moving back, though the *Monnet* wouldn't get under way until the following day.

And she's coming stuffed to the rafters with nearly everything I need to get the Peace Fleet back to Bristol Fashion, plus *enough shuttles and parts for them to keep it supplied from the surface, even with all the ships fully manned. Hah; Martin, you dickhead. That's better than you ever even dreamt of.*

Isla Real, Balboa, Terra Nova

Fernandez knew why he'd spared former High Admiral Martin Robinson's life. *The swine had some skills that were useful.* He wasn't nearly so sure why he hadn't left the former marchioness of Amnesty, Lucretia Arbeit, in the hold to drown as the old *Hildegard Mises* went down without a trace. *Maybe I'm getting soft in my old age.* He considered that for a moment and thought, *Nah, that's not it. Must be a reason, even if I can't think what it was. No matter; it'll come to me. In the meantime . . .*

Wish to hell I knew why Patricio was so determined to get this shuttle working again. Some things he won't share with anybody.

"It would help, sir," Robinson said, head bowed in humility, "if I knew why you wanted the shuttle."

Robinson wore prison stripes, as did Lucretia Arbeit. Both were kept, under guard and in separate cells, under the central hill of the island, just off from the hangar cave wherein sat the rebuilt but still unserviceable shuttle. Their complexions were pallid from lack of sun.

"Never mind," Fernandez barked. "You don't need to know at this point. Just get the dozen men selected for training as able to fly one as you can."

Robinson shrugged. "As you wish, sir. They're already fully capable of preflighting the thing. And they've theoretical understanding of the nuances. I've drilled them into the ground on the inert simulator."

"How's programming on the flight simulator coming?" Fernandez asked.

Again, the former high admiral shrugged. "It's a simulator. By definition, it won't be as good as the real thing. If you could get a replacement flight computer..." Robinson let the thought trail off.

"Working on it." *Which is to say, beating my head against a wall. Patricio's pet senator in the Federated States couldn't help, or wouldn't, which amounts to the same thing. And we can't fix the bastard. Butterfingered damned infantry.*

"No matter how well I train the pilots," Robinson reminded, "the thing still won't fly without the flight computer."

"*Working* on it."

Robinson slumped his shoulders, clasped his hands together in front of himself and bobbed his head briskly three or four times. "Yessir. Sorry, sir."

One of the worst things about torture, thought Fernandez, *is that when it's over—assuming you don't just off the fucker, of course—you've got something less than a human being to deal with. Then again, this one wasn't much of a human being to begin with.*

❖   ❖   ❖

Fernandez, since his own offices were in *Ciudad* Balboa on the mainland, had borrowed a driver and vehicle from a friend once he'd arrived on the island. Since the legion's move to the mainland was still somewhat incomplete, and since full facilities were likewise incomplete and would be for some years, the main military exchange remained on the island, not too far from the *Punta Cocoli* airfield. He had the driver take him there.

There wasn't much he needed, actually, that couldn't have been purchased in the smaller exchanges near the city but, "Since I *am* here, I may as well."

No ID card was required on the island since it was almost entirely military. The few civilians around, mostly in one or another version of the "entertainment" industry, were allowed privileges as a matter of courtesy. Fernandez walked through the main doors and headed for the liquor section. That was one area where the prices and selection beat both the military and civilian facilities of the city hands down.

On the way, Fernandez passed by the bookstore and decided to pick up some reading material. It was one of Carrera's tenets that a major reason that most of the armies of Colombia del Norte stank to the high heavens was that they had far too limited a selection of military reading in their native tongues for effective self education. Legionary Press, a wholly owned subsidiary of *Legiones del Cid*, S. A., made good that lack in Balboa, having translated and printed, so far, about a quarter of Carrera's personal library along with more than a thousand other militarily significant works.

All publications were made available, down to maniple level, by the legion, without cost to the units.

For people who wanted their own copies, however, or wanted, at least, not to have to wait—since the free distribution system was never quite as timely as the "for cost" system—the books were available via the exchange.

Hmmm, Fernandez thought, gazing over the shelves of the "New Editions" section, *already have a copy of* Intelligence in War, *and besides, the author now works in my shop. Ah, I see Marquelí Mendoza has something out under her own name,* Family and State. *I'll get that,* he decided, fingering the book from the shelf and placing it under one arm. *Aha, a new, unabridged edition of* Complete Verse of Rudyard Kipling. *Absolutely got to have that. And . . . what's this?* Memoirs of Belisario Carrera (Abridged). *That might be interesting. And, lastly, since I can't carry any more conveniently, not and have room for a couple of bottles of cognac, I'll get* Poetry of the Great Global War.

That should do for a while.

Fort Cameron, Balboa, Terra Nova

Though Volga had plenty of doctors, product of the Red Tsar's emphasis on quantity, it was the considered opinion of the Twenty-Second, which certainly had enough experience of Marxist medicine, that the legion's medicos were both better trained and *much* better equipped. Thus, the wounded from the operation in Santander, generally speaking, preferred to do their convalescence in Balboa rather than home. There was, however, at least one exception.

✧   ✧   ✧

The Twenty-Second was not only a hard fighting regiment; it was a hard drinking one as well. All the regiments of the legion drank, of course, even if not all of its members did. The combat rations came with a rum ration integral to them. Legionary rum, at 160 proof, was considered pretty vile unless highly diluted. It was especially vile to the Volgans, who much preferred vodka.

A bottle of vodka, imported from home, sat between Samsonov, Pavlov, and Chapayev on a cloth-covered table in an alcove of the Twenty-Second's Officers' Club. Chapayev drank with his left hand. His right shoulder was still immobilized with bandages and a cast.

"I've a list of things we need, Victor," said Samsonov, pushing a file folder over towards the tribune, "and a regimental credit card for you to purchase them and ship them here. Also a list of contacts in case you have any trouble finding what we need. Also, if you are amenable, there is a list of people I'd like you to interview for possible accession into the regiment. If you agree to the last, I can extend your convalescence by half a day per applicant you interview, plus travel time. We *did* have some losses we need to make good."

Chapayev replaced his glass on the table and answered, "No problem comrade col...err...comrade leg...err...sir. I've seven weeks to convalesce. Even with the time I intend to spend on...err...with my wife, there should be *some* occasion for some shopping and even interviewing."

"What's it been now, Victor? Almost two years? That's too long."

"Yes, sir, I agree. I'm hoping she'll come back here with me when I return."

Samsonov nodded. "One hopes she will, Victor. *Duque* Carrera told me he is sending a crew especially to build you a house to raise a family in. 'We need that boy's children,' he said to me. You've made quite a friend there."

Chapayev said, "He's a good commander, isn't he? I owe him for my company, I think." The Volgan's face grew somber then. Slowly and carefully, he added, "I don't know if she is coming back for sure. The last time I got a message . . . you know how the mail is from home, even the electronic mail . . . was before we went to Santander. She didn't seem overly enthusiastic about coming here. Maybe when I show her the drawings of the new house she will change her mind."

Chapayev pulled an architectural drawing from a satchel. It showed a medium size, single-floor bungalow, built on stilts to form a carport under the main house, the house itself stuccoed and roofed with red tiles. Based on the size of the windows, the house looked to be about thirteen or fourteen meters on a side, perhaps one hundred and eighty or so, overall. By Volgan standards, it was palatial.

"No question but it's a better place than she's likely to find at home," Samsonov observed. "You might also mention to her that on your pay here she can afford a maid and cook, and a car if you wish."

"Yes, sir," Chapayev agreed. "That might help. *Duque* Carrera also offered to let me use one of the spare places on his land until my house was complete."

"He told me about how you fought in Santander,"

Samsonov said. "He thinks very highly of your abilities...and your courage under fire. I would cultivate him, were I you."

Chapayev smiled. "Yes, sir. But first, I have to think about how to cultivate my wife. And on that note, I have shopping to do in the city before I catch my plane. Menshikov is driving me to town and the airport."

Pavlov added, "There are a few things I'd like to add to your shopping list, Victor."

"Sure, sir."

"You are going by airship, Victor?" Samsonov asked.

"Yes, sir. The legion paid for round trip fare for one, and one way for another, plus a generous allowance for shipping personal goods."

"Well," said Pavlov, "if the rumors of how much Carrera succeeded in squeezing from the Santanderns are even half correct, the legion is pretty flush, right about now."

Chapayev smiled. "Certainly the combat bonus the *Duque* paid the regiment hasn't hurt."

St. Nicholasburg, Volga, Terra Nova

On Old Earth, the Russians had always been a deeply spiritual people. Not even three generations of the vilest forms of Marxism had ever been able to erase that. Moreover, with Marxism fallen, at the end of the twentieth century, the major churches of old Russia had surged once again to prominence, their adherents knowing that, after all, God had not deserted His people.

The people God may not have deserted, but it certainly came to seem that he had turned his face from the Earth. Thus, when Christianity had become once again a suspect religion, and its enemies had introduced various forms of persecution, the faithful of old Russia had begun to leave for the new world.

Other colonies, in the early days of human settlement of the planet, might call their cities "First Landing" or "Drop Dead" or any of myriad other names. But for the faithful Russ, fleeing religious persecution, there could be no doubt of the name of their first city on Terra Nova. It *had* to be named for their patron saint, Nicholas of Myra.

As the Russians had said, "Even if God dies we'll still have Saint Nicholas."

". . . and," said the speaker overhead, "for those of you on the port side, that's St. Nicholasburg coming up ahead. For those on the starboard, if you look carefully you can see the glow where the Pripyat Nuclear Power Station fulfilled the Red Tsar's Five Year Plan for energy generation in four nanoseconds."

Chapayev had tuned out the purser's voice—at least he thought it was the purser's—as he ticked off the sights to be seen on various legs of the aerial journey. For the neon-glowing St. Nicholasburg, however, he paid attention, closing his wallet and shutting away the picture of his wife that he'd kept with him through the years of separation.

It was a lovely portrait, but not one for general viewing. For one thing, Veronica, the wife, was half, or rather more than that, nude, her breasts—delicate things—on full display. Her skin was creamy and smooth. Cornflower blue eyes stared out, innocent as a new baby's, under midnight bangs that turned into a long cascade down her otherwise bare back. Even after several years of marriage, the image still sent a shiver of desire up the young Volgan's back.

In a way it was better to put away the picture and stare at the town, below. For one thing, Chapayev was reasonably sure of the town. Of the woman in the portrait he was much less so.

The reasons that airships on Old Earth had never, so to speak, taken off was that, despite the advantages in fuel consumption and cargo load, they'd required excessively large and expensive ground crews and been terribly vulnerable to sudden and severe changes in weather, especially when near the ground. On Terra Nova, conversely, which had much less axial tilt to it than had the world of Man's birth, the weather was more predictable and, generally speaking, less severe. The better weather had made airships a better bet, long enough for systems to be developed to reduce the size of the ground crews. The airships had never quite eliminated the need for fixed wing, heavier-than-air craft, but they had proven a more useful supplement to those on New Earth than on Old.

They were still far too vulnerable in war to be used for anything but lifting heavy loads, and then only to and from very safe areas, and along safe routes. In practice, the ACCS was not an exception to these rules.

Chapayev barely noticed the shudder and the metallic _clangs_ as the airship let go half a dozen cables. No more did he notice as the cables were grasped by claws mounted on half a dozen heavy trucks. Even when the trucks carried the cables off to be affixed to the mules—heavy and heavy-duty railway cars—that would take the ship in to the landing pit and hold it steady while the ship winched itself down, the tribune paid no mind.

With the terminal building rising next to his ship, Chapayev laughed at himself. *If I wasn't afraid in Santander, why am I so afraid now?*

Until he'd heard Chapayev's local accent, the taxi driver had been inclined to cheat the young officer. Once he'd heard it, and learned a little of the man's background, it had been hard to get the driver to take even an honest fare.

"I served the motherland, too, sir," the driver had insisted.

"Then take the money as a gift for your family," Chapayev had answered.

Once through the stone-framed doors to the old Tsarist building, converted to apartments, Chapayev was surprised to discover that the elevators actually worked. *Hmmm,* he'd thought, *I wonder if the reds are back.*

The answer to that question could wait. The doors opened and Chapayev walked as quietly as the bundles in his arms would let him. Reaching the door to his and his wife's apartment, he carefully placed his burden down without making a sound. Then he reached into his pocket for the keys. Everything was more difficult because of his bandaged shoulder.

It wasn't the sore shoulder, though, that caused Chapayev's hand to tremble, the key poised just outside the tumbler. It was—

I am afraid. It's been two years. What if . . .

He forced himself to insert the key and slowly to turn it. He tried to keep it quiet. Despite his best efforts the massive but poor quality lock clicked loudly, once, and then again, louder still, as the bolt retracted. Chapayev pushed the door open slightly. It made a creaking sound.

"Darling, is that you?" Veronica's voice made Chapayev's heart leap. He pushed open the door the rest of the way, then turned to drag in the gifts.

As he straightened from moving the bundles into the apartment he looked up and saw his wife standing in a doorway wearing nothing but a shocked expression. "Victor. I didn't know to expect you."

Chapayev looked from Veronica's face down to where a slight bulge told of an early stage of pregnancy. His eyes grew wide with unwelcome understanding. He looked around the cramped apartment for something, anything, to look at other than the bulge in his wife's belly. His eyes stopped on the picture of a man, his own age but somehow soft looking.

Walking over to the picture, Victor picked it up. "Darling?" he asked, holding the picture where Veronica must see it.

Recovering a portion of her composure, she answered, "Well, what did you expect? You left me here alone for months and years on end with nothing to do."

"I sent you every *grivna* I made. I waited for you."

"And so? The more fool you for waiting. The money you sent? A small enough price to pay for the silly, silly love letters I had to write to keep you happy, off with your colonel and your wars." She walked forward, taking the picture away from Chapayev and putting it back in its place of honor. "Leonid here is just the latest. He manages a Columbian ice cream parlor and makes more than you ever did.... And spends it on me, too."

"'Just the latest,'" Chapayev echoed.

"Yes. Just the latest. How do you imagine I kept my job and our apartment here. While you were off playing cowboy with your stupid soldiers, I've had a very fine time, I don't mind telling you. I've screwed half of the city by now. Sometimes, for fun, I even get paid for it. Ask anyone important in St. Nicholasburg where to go for the very best. He'll say 'Veronica Chapayeva. Her husband's off at the wars and she misses him so badly she'll make do with anyone.' Oh, yes, my very dearest. While you were on hands and knees in the mountains I've been on hands and knees—sometimes just knees—right here."

"Slut!"

"So? And what are you? Just a waste of a soldier nobody has any use for anymore, least of all me." Veronica reached for a robe and pulled it on. "So leave me now. I don't need your money anymore. And I *never* needed you." She went to where the bundles lay, pitiful offerings, and proceeded to throw them back out into the hall. In doing so, she turned her back on Chapayev.

Victor saw himself reach under his coat for the knife he had been advised to carry while walking through the city's no longer safe streets. More silently even than he had crept to his wife's door, he crept up behind her now. Like an automaton, with no control over his own actions, his left hand reached for her long, midnight hair and grasped it.

"What do you think you are doing, you cretin?"

Chapayev didn't answer. He just lifted Veronica by her hair and moved the knife to the left side of her neck. She froze as she felt the icy touch.

"Victor, don't?" she pleaded softly.

"Bitch!" he whispered into her ear. Then he drew the knife across her white throat in one smooth movement. Blood, bright and red, spurted from Veronica's throat to splash the wooden floor. Chapayev dropped her body as soon as he felt her go limp. He gathered his bundles, closed the door, and left.

In the real world, Victor found himself still standing in the middle of the living room. Veronica Chapayeva still knelt by his pile of packages, tossing them one by one into the outside hall. He thought about killing her, and decided she wasn't worth dirtying his hands over. *Besides, my shoulder is still such a mess I'd probably make a hash of the job.* He gathered the shreds of his dignity around himself and walked past her and through the door. Before he turned his back on the woman for the last time, Chapayev faced her.

In a voice colder than any Volgan winter, he said, "Veronica, I probably won't be able to stop this month's pay from reaching your account. Consider it a divorce settlement. I also will not go through the trouble of staying here for a divorce. You can do what you like about that. I don't care. Maybe I should hate you. But then, you can't help being what you are...and what you are not. I won't wish you well. Good-bye."

Victor turned and left the bundles where they lay, scattered between apartment, threshold, and corridor. He walked down the stairs and out of Veronica

Chapayeva's life without a backward glance. He didn't trust himself to look at her again.

It wasn't until he was in the relative solitude and safety of a taxi that the young Volgan pulled his coat over his head and, as quietly as possible, began to weep.

UEPF *Spirit of Peace,* Solar System

Richard was being very talkative. Seated at her own mess with the ship's captain, Marguerite suppressed a smile. Watching Richard trying—*painfully* trying—to keep his mouth moving and his eyes off of Esmeralda had become more than amusing.

Except that—dammit!—I've come to care for the both of them. But he's a Class One and she's just a peasant girl I rescued, barely rescued, from slavery. Where do they have a future together in our world? Not even in the computer generated pulp romances they print for the lower classes. Not even on the public television shows.

And anyway, while his face shouts that he's in love, hers is much harder to read. Our class nearly killed the poor thing. I doubt she has much room for love for us. I foresee pain in Richard's future, much pain.

Should I try to help? Hell, no. I'm no kind of matchmaker. I know not the first little thing about romantic love, never had any room for it, what with being at the beck and call of whatever Class One wanted me bent over a desk or down on my knees.

She suppressed a bitter thought. *I wonder what life might have been like if one of them had ever looked at me the way Richard looks at Esmeralda . . .*

She couldn't help sighing at dreams she'd never really been allowed to have.

"High Admiral?" Richard enquired at the sigh.

"Nothing, Captain," Marguerite answered. *Well, why not give them the chance, if only for a bit, to have some of what I never did?*

Wallenstein pushed the plate away from her and stood. Richard began to follow until she gestured him back to his seat.

"I've got a little work to do," she lied. "You finish your dinner, Captain. Esmeralda, please see to the captain's needs."

"Yes, High Admiral," the serving girl said, with a curtsey.

Immediately as the door whooshed shut behind Wallenstein, Richard shut up, turned his reddening face down towards the plate, and commenced eating mechanically.

I can talk with her in public, on the bridge, he fumed. *Why can't I speak with her in private?*

The silence went on for several awkward minutes before Esmeralda asked, "Would you care for some more wine, Captain?"

Richard, in mid chew and not expecting the question, choked . . . literally. He began to choke so badly, in fact, that Esmeralda had to put down the carafe she'd picked up and rush to his side to pound on his back.

His choking ended, but not the sense of embarrassment that made him think, *Why couldn't I have just died?* Muttering something unintelligible, Richard, earl of Care, stood and left the admiral's mess for his own quarters.

Quarters One, Gutierrez Caserne, *Ciudad* Cervantes, Balboa, Terra Nova

None of the planet's three moons were up. The land was illuminated only by the streetlights, whatever light escaped through windows, and the occasional passing motor vehicle. Power for the former there was in plenty, from the half dozen solar power stations that now dotted the nation's northern shore, their greenhouse complexes connected to the mountain top chimneys by sturdy, half buried concrete tunnels. Even at night, with the sun down, heat differential let them continue to produce power.

The softly cooing *antaniae* loved the moonless nights, for those were the vile creatures' best chance to find unguarded prey. Legate Pigna could hear them calling outside, *mnnbt...mnnbt...mnnbt*. He wasn't worried about them, however; he'd already checked the doors and window screens to ensure that the children were safe inside, and the *antaniae* out. Now he sat, portable computer on his lap, continuing his planning.

Every now and again the magnitude and the dangers of the project Legate Pigna had undertaken would get to him and he would being to fret, even to choke up. Three things kept him at his task. One was the burning memory of a wad of paper thrown in his face as if he were an unruly school boy. In itself, perhaps this should not have rankled quite so much as it did. After all, the legion was a rough service, and harsh. He'd chewed out subordinates before, if never quite so viciously as Carrera had inflicted a mass chewing upon his subordinates.

Sitting in his office at his home, sipping a higher end rum, Pigna thought, *But I was one of the bastard's most loyal supporters. I deserved better. I deserved, at a minimum, not to be entrapped with that fucking flypaper report. And he should know better than to wound a man in his pride. If he doesn't, he's not fit to command.*

Deep down, the legate knew that was rationalization. Wounds heal, and his had long since, except when he ripped off the scab to open the wound again. He did that because . . .

Even if I wanted to, I couldn't pull out now. They've got me on video and I have no doubt that that video would go to Fernandez the day, the hour, maybe the second I try to back out. Carrera might forgive me. Fernandez would never give him the chance. I, my family, we'd all disappear.

So much for fear, and so much for honor, or at least the avenging of dishonor. But what ultimately kept Pigna at his task was . . .

And, then too, with the corps commanders, Carrera, his personal staff, and Parilla gone, why shouldn't I become the new commander? I will be first among equals. I'll have the gratitude of the old families. And if I can do that, why not president myself, someday? Why shouldn't I watch out for my own interest?

CHAPTER TWENTY-ONE

Responsibility and authority *will* equal out in the long run. The society that robs the future will have no future. The descendants of the man who places family over society will find no society to shelter them.

The trick, then, is to limit power to those who can, in the aggregate, be expected to use it responsibly. As we have seen, kings and tyrants are, at best, fifty-fifty; elites, oligarchs, and aristocrats are not a whit better; and even popular democracies have no great track record of responsible voting and actions, over the long term.

Geniuses may vote irresponsibly while morons vote wisely, wisdom being more a matter of instinct and experience than raw, native intelligence. Education not only doesn't guarantee responsible exercise of political power, if anything it tends toward the opposite, for the educated—who are too often also the arrogant—fool themselves into thinking they are voting the issues, after sober reflection, when in fact they just vote their emotions and gut instincts. Whatever the airs they may put on, they are, like the rest of mankind, not rational so much as rationalizing.

Just as, in the words of Voltaire, "A rational army would run away," so the act of responsible voting requires at some level an irrational mindset—to vote for the good of the whole over the good of the self—or one that, if really rational, thinks in the long term and understands long-term costs and benefits.

—Jorge y Marqueli Mendoza, *Historia y Filosofia Moral*, Legionary Press, Balboa, Terra Nova, copyright AC 468

Anno Condita 472
Officers' Mess, Fort Cameron, Balboa, Terra Nova

An untouched plate of chorley bread, yellow and smelling buttery, sat on the table in front of Chapayev. Besides the bread was some greenish dip with a dead fly next to the shallow bowl.

Chapayev was in mufti, and unshaven for the past several days. Worse, he had the appearance of a man who had been drinking pretty heavily for all those days. Perhaps worse still, he looked like he didn't care.

Samsonov took one look and thought, *I was afraid of this. On the other hand, I was also afraid he'd bring the little tramp back here and she'd be fucking my officers—just like she did back in Volga—and upsetting my mess.*

The legate took a deep breath, exhaled, and walked to sit at the table where Chapayev sat alone, a half empty glass and a clear bottle directly in front of him, between the table's edge and the bread.

"Victor, what are you doing back so soon?" Samsonov asked.

"It didn't work out, sir," answered Chapayev in a voice totally devoid of emotion.

Samsonov didn't want to ask for details. He could guess at these well enough, anyway. Instead, he just said, "Well, these things happen. I'm sorry, Victor, for what it's worth."

"Yes, sir. So am I. Nothing to be done about it. A corpse would have shown more feeling than the Volgan tribune did. "So . . . I had nothing else to do. After finishing up the interviews and the shopping, I came back here."

"Well, I can't put you back on duty now. You're still convalescing." *And now you have two things to heal from, don't you, son? Too much of a burden to let you bear while still doing your job? Too dangerous to leave you alone to mope? Can't make a decision like this sober, and it's too early to for me to join you in a drink.*

Samsonov continued, "Tell you what, Victor. You look like the very devil. Go to your quarters and sleep a while. Consider that an order. I'll pick you up at eighteen hundred for dinner. There's a restaurant downtown I've been meaning to try. Then we'll get stone blind, paralytic, ossified drunk. Tomorrow I'll decide whether you should resume your duties or finish your leave . . . or maybe something else. We'll see."

Chapayev said barely a word as he ground his way mechanically through his food. Only his glass of vodka held any real interest for him, a glass Samsonov kept constantly refilled from a bottle left at the table by the waiter.

On his fourth large glass, and plainly feeling it, Victor blurted out, "She was pregnant when I got there. Several months."

Samsonov, who knew Chapayev's schedule for the last two years as well as Chapayev did himself, simply said, "Oh. I see."

"No, sir, it was much worse than that." Then Chapayev told his commander all the vile things Veronica had said to him in the St. Nicholasburg apartment the week before. Tears welled in the tribune's eyes.

"Victor . . . there is nothing I can say to you that will make it any better . . . except, maybe, that these things pass . . . the pain, I mean. You are not the first; you will not be the last. And for whatever it is worth to you . . . she's lost more than you have." *The fucking bitch*, Samsonov added silently. *I should offer a bounty for the cunt's life to the next group I send home on leave.*

Pride was stung, too. "What can I tell my company? All this time I've been telling them of my 'peerless' Veronica; the light of my life. How can I face them now? They'll think I'm a fool."

Samsonov sighed. "My friend, every man is a fool sometimes. Especially concerning women. And it wasn't exactly your fault. The regiment called you; you had to go. I'd wager you are not the only one; even in your company. You were just unfortunate . . . or maybe fortunate . . . to have found out."

Samsonov was silent for a moment. "But I do see your problem. Stay with the regiment and risk being laughed at behind your back, or go back to Volga . . ."

"There is nothing left for me there, sir. It's a place where foreigners speak the same language you do, nothing more."

"Yes. Well, I only mentioned it as an option. Or, maybe...?"

Again Samsonov grew quiet, thinking. After a few moments he said, "Victor, I have a requirement to provide several officers, six initially, to become a sort of cadre for 'second formations' at the military schools. I don't know any of the details. *Duque* Carrera already thinks well of you. How about if I call him tomorrow to nominate you for one of those positions?"

"You mean I have to leave the regiment?" Chapayev looked, if possible, even more crushed.

"No, no, I don't think so. I had the impression you would still be part of the regiment, but on detached duty for some years. We have no combat action in the offing, just helping train the legions here. This might be more challenging work. You would, I imagine, be working with boys for the most part."

"Veronica always said she wanted children," Chapayev said, his voice dripping with half drunken bitterness. "I actually did, but it was 'never the right time.' Very well, sir, call Carrera." The tribune shrugged hopelessly. "After all, as low as my life has fallen, what have I got to lose?"

Loma Boracho, Fort Tecumseh, Balboa, Terra Nova

It was a low hill, with a pleasant sea breeze, overlooking the southern terminus of the Transitway. Its name had come from the parties of construction workers, a century previously, who had taken advantage of the breeze for their drunken revels on their infrequent breaks from construction work. Now, it was a training area. Also it was a designated mosquito feeding area. Similarly, it was a howler monkey breeding reservation. The last two designations were unofficial, but real for all that.

With monkeys howling their rage in the distance, and mosquitoes coming in for suicide runs altogether too close, machine gun fire, blanks, rattled in the moist night. Xavier Jimenez listened to the fire, trying to judge its exact direction.

Jimenez keyed his radio to the controller push and asked what the trouble was.

"Monkeys, sir," came the answer. "Stinking monkeys spooked the troops and caused them to go to full stand-to and then to open fire."

"Roger."

Tsk, thought Jimenez. *That will cost you, boys.*

On the hill itself, grumbling headquarters troops cleared their weapons and filed back to the bunkers and bedrolls. Before being spooked, they'd been fully clothed and had their weapons nearby. Now—

"That's right, sweetie-pies," said the regimental sergeant major, his booming voice carrying clearly across the hill. "Off with the boots and uniforms. You spooked once. The price of that in war is a slower reaction the next time. So we're making your reaction slower by having you strip down."

Patricio said in his last training brief that this would be a way to train people to take advantage of surprise, thought Jimenez. *I confess, I have my doubts. Still, worth a try.*

❖   ❖   ❖

There were a number of things, in training for war, that were simply hard as hell to simulate. One of these was to provide an opposing force that was both challenging and realistic when training people for reconnaissance patrolling. Another was giving them a realistic portrayal of surprise, so they would learn to recognize when they'd achieved it and to take advantage of it.

Carrera's last training guidance had addressed both.

"Look," he'd said. "When you send troops out on a recon, in training, you've got a choice of either no realistic probability of them running into opposition, or you have the very unrealistic technique of vectoring an enemy patrol in on them. Or . . ." he hesitated a moment to see if anyone had figured it out. When no one offered a solution, he'd said, "Or, you can have the patrols, for a company say, start around the edge of a rough circle and the objectives be toward the center. That way, there's a *strong* chance of chance contact and they will have to *act* as though there is.

"You've got a similar problem—a little similar, anyway—when you try to train to create and take advantage of surprise. You can choreograph it. You know what? The troops know choreography when they see it. And they don't believe in it. And they don't think, not deep down, that the training was legitimate.

"Or, you can—"

By three in the morning, the defenders—who had had to defend nothing yet—were tired and frustrated. All three moons had gone down, leaving the area plunged into complete blackness, except for the distant glow from Cristobal, across the bay. Worse, they were bootless and stripped down to their skivvies (that was from the first false alert), their weapons' slings were tangled (from the second), and their body armor, their *loricae*, were piled up (from the third false alert). In each case, the speed with which they could react to a real attack had been artificially but realistically slowed. Thus—

Jimenez swatted at a mosquito buzzing his left ear when he heard over the other radio, "Zulu Six Seven, this is X-ray Five One. Fire Target Group Bravo."

"Six Seven, Five One; roger, over . . . shot over . . . splash, over."

Trees were instantly silhouetted as artillery simulators began whistling and exploding all over the hill, from military crest to reverse slope. There was fire, both rifle and machine gun, coming from the hill. Yet it only came from the quarter of the defending troops who were allowed to be fully alert, strung out mostly in observation and listening posts around *Loma Boracho*.

Jimenez saw another explosion flash through the trees, followed by what he thought were probably *antaniae,* winging it upwards to escape the blasting.

Nasty fucking moonbats, he thought.

"Breach One, clear," said the radio. A second explosion followed. "Breach Two, clear."

Jimenez pulled his night vision goggles onto his face and looked northwest. This was the direction from which the Eighth Tercio commander had briefed him that the breach team would blow through the wire. Sure enough, he saw twin files of armed men rising from the jungle floor to dash forward toward the breaches in the hill's perimeter wire.

A crump overhead and just past the position turned into a mortar illumination round. The casing whistled down to impact in the nearby bay. Cursing, "Shit!" Jimenez removed the goggles as *Loma Boracho* lit up almost as brightly as day. Another *crump* from the same direction as the first told that the next round was on the way.

On cue—*as if* on cue, at any rate—evaluators redoubled their throwing artillery simulators, pyrotechnic devices that whistled for several seconds before exploding with a fairly realistic flash and bang. Machine gun fire—still blank, the only live ammunition being used were the mortar illumination rounds—erupted from outside the perimeter.

In the bunkers pandemonium erupted as half naked troops shook themselves out of sleep and struggled to find and free uniforms, boots, rifles, and armor. Evaluators stood by the bunkers to ensure no troop left without being fully dressed and equipped. Men cursed as heads bumped and hands and feet were trod upon.

This was not to say that all the defenders left with their own gear. More than one soldier ended up in clothes too big or too small in the rush. By ones and twos, except where a leader had the presence of mind to organize before moving the defenders began to filter to their perimeter through the trenches.

Under cover of the suppressive fire from the machine guns and smoke from handheld smoke grenades, teams from the Eighth Tercio were already through the wire and beginning to enter the trenches. Here and there evaluators tapped soldiers of the Eighth, making them lie down as casualties. The cry "medic" arose from half a dozen throats.

In their ones and twos the defenders tried to slow down the avalanche of combat power overwhelming their position. It was to no avail. Throwing grenade simulators ahead of them, Eighth Tercio's storming party drove the headquarters troops back and farther back.

Not all of the cries for medical support were simulated; the grenade simulators could cause nasty burns and mild concussions. As the evaluators had rehearsed, an evaluator accompanied the forward elements of both sides, both to assess casualties and to pull unwary soldiers out of the way of the simulators' explosions.

This is fucking great! thought Jimenez. He recollected something Carrera had said in the training brief: *Many senior commanders don't enjoy training their soldiers unless they can maneuver their entire units. I have found that these men typically have fragile egos. The best trainer of combat troops is usually the one who can enjoy the fun his small units are having.*

"Well, I'm having fun, anyway," Jimenez muttered, as another series of explosions, more grenade simulators, moved a prong of Eighth Tercio's attack closer to the center of the *Loma Boracho* position. Jimenez walked forward to oversee the final assault.

Military Academy *Sargento Juan Malvegui, Puerto Lindo*, Balboa, Terra Nova

Two white men, Volgans, in mufti, stood on a spit of land on the west side of the old town's roughly rectangular harbor. A centuries-old stone fort watched over the harbor's mouth. The fort's seaward gun ports were sighted to intersect and interlock with those of another fort across the water on the eastern side. At the bay's mouth was a tree-covered island. It seemed to float on the water. For that matter, people who had stared at the island long enough had been known to say the thing was moving.

Behind and around the two men, more or less surrounding the fort, arose the barracks and classrooms of the academy. Work still continued on some buildings, an irregular pounding of hammers interspersed with a drone of heavy machinery.

Sitnikov, leaning with one hand resting on a verdigris-covered bronze cannon, asked, "Well, Victor, what do you think?"

His companion, Victor Chapayev, nodded. "It is adequate."

Chapayev wore an air of inestimable sadness. Sitnikov knew as much of Chapayev's story as Samsonov had thought he needed to know. He could guess at the rest.

"If the *Duque* is happy with it," Chapayev amended, "who am I to complain?"

"You were with Carrera in Santander, weren't you?"

Chapayev nodded.

"What did you think?"

"He seems decent enough. He's been decent to me. He might have saved my company down there, after I was hit. Probably did, in fact."

"So he seems. Decent, that is. Let me tell you something, though, Victor. Carrera will treat you well right up to the day you cross him. Then, he's no different from the Red Tsar. I've seen it. *Boy*, have I seen it. His goals are not normal."

"You think he's a Marxist?" Chapayev asked.

Sitnikov shook his head. "No . . . not a Marxist. Not a capitalist either. He's . . . I don't know that there's a word for it; but he wants to change this country as much as the Red Tsar ever wanted to change Volga, and to change it as profoundly. But what he wants to change it into . . . I don't know. It's as if he doesn't let it be known so that no one can resist him in achieving his goal.

"The Red Tsars let everyone know what they wanted and applied pressure to force the society into the mold they picked. Carrera doesn't. He seems to be eliminating some things, true, but then he mostly entices people to fit themselves into a mold they can't even see. He's a community organizer, and no one in the community seems to realize they're being organized.

"Think about it, Victor," Sitnikov continued, "to get anywhere, these days, a Balboan must associate with Carrera's army; to become a part of his team. The Red Tsars used the power of the state to force change. Carrera is making the state irrelevant. Balboans who need or want something are getting out of the habit of looking to the government. More and more they turn to Carrera, or rather, the legion. But that is the same thing now. And he's every bit as ruthless as the tsar was."

Sitnikov pulled out a cigarette and lit it. "Despite which, I'll continue to work for him because . . . because he's . . . a terribly good soldier. Do you know how rare that is; in any army, to work for a really good soldier?"

Chapayev said nothing. Sitnikov asked, "Is that why

you are here, too? I asked Samsonov, but he wouldn't tell much of anything except that you were one of his best officers. Still, I had to wonder... why would he let one of his best go? You were back in the *rodina* not long ago, weren't you?"

"I found I didn't belong there anymore." Chapayev cut off that line of conversation.

"Nor any of us, I suspect."

Sitnikov ignored that. He asked, "So is Balboa your home now? Do you even have a home, Victor?"

"I won't know until I find it, will I, sir?"

Sitnikov shrugged. "Would you like to make this your home for a while?" He once again cast his arms out to encompass the school.

"Why not?" Chapayev said with no noticeable enthusiasm.

"Fine. The day before we open this school for the next semester, you are promoted to Tribune III. I believe that makes you one of the dozen or so youngest Tribune IIIs in the country. You will be the assistant to the Balboan legate who commands the school, but you will report to me, as he does. I want you, in particular, to concern yourself with the light infantry training of the cadets."

"How much time will I have for their training?"

"The boys spend two military days a week. Monday through Thursday are for academics. Friday and Saturday are their military training days. Sunday is parade, church, and inspection. By the way, how is your Spanish coming?"

"It needs work."

"You have two months. Make that your first priority."

"Sir."

"I suggest that the best way to learn might be to find yourself a horizontal dictionary," Sitnikov added.

"A *what*?"

Sitnikov shook his head, smiling at Chapayev's innocence. "A *girl*, Victor, go find a girl." Sitnikov cocked his head slightly, musing on something. With a broad smile, he said, "Now that I think about it, Victor, the Castilian, Colonel Muñoz-Infantes, has a very good relationship with us here. I think perhaps you should also become our liaison to him. That will give you a bit more motivation and opportunity to work on your Spanish."

Casa Linda, Balboa, Terra Nova

Lourdes *still* served as Carrera's very private and very confidential secretary, as she had since he'd first hired her, more than a dozen years before.

"The big advantage," he said to her, as she laid the latest consolidated Research, Development, and Procurement Report on his desk, "is that now I don't have to pay you a regular salary."

"Watch out," she answered, "I might go on strike for better working conditions. More sex, for example." She glanced meaningfully from Carrera's office toward their bedroom.

"Why is it," he asked, "that you always get hornier when you're pregnant and stay that way until the baby's a year old?"

"Are you complaining?"

"Oh, not a bit. But you're a lot younger than I am. I foresee the day when I knock you up as the last gasp measure of an old man and you then kill me with your insatiable demands." He sighed. "Can't think of a better way to go."

"You better believe it," she said, turning away from the desk. He was struck, as always, by the fact that, recently pregnant or not, she never lost her shape. Bigger breasts? Yes. *And yum.* A bit displaced in front? Yes, but that didn't last. And from behind she was still the willowy girl he'd married.

"Anything interesting in the report?" he called after her.

"They finished testing on the frontal composite armor for the SPATHA," she answered, without turning. "Likewise the gun. And the global locating system interdictor has some technical problems they need a tactical solution to."

"You're a treasure," Carrera said, just loud enough for her to hear.

"You better believe *that*, too."

Only five people had access to the complete report. There were Carrera and—as a practical matter—Lourdes, plus Fernandez, Grishkin, the Volgan-born chief of *Obras Zorilleras*, and Kuralski. Not even Fernandez's deputy had access. (Though Legate Barletta didn't, in any case, have access to much, his post being more administrative in nature.) This was about as compartmentalized as information ever got. Carrera quickly scanned over the reports from Siegel, in Cochin. Those projects were well on track. The Meg plant at the shipyard on the bay of *Puerto Lindo* was slated to begin full production soon, he was pleased to see. Mortar production was keeping pace with force expansion. *Good . . . very good.* The artillery ammunition plant at Arraijan, not too far from the small arms *fabrica* that produced the F-26 rifle, M-26 light machine gun, and their variants, was experiencing a shortage of brass for shell casings.

Note to Fernandez: Is the brass shortage worldwide? Our screw up in procurement planning? Long term or short? Note to the Ib: Can we substitute?

He did more than just scan the report on the SPATHA, the Self Propelled, Anti-Tank, Heavy Armor project. Balboa didn't have access to the planet's best armored vehicles; those were the purview of the Federated States and the Tauran Union, neither of which was interested in selling to the legion.

And I wouldn't trust a Tauran tank even if they'd sell.

Still, the legion needed *something* that could go toe to toe with a first line Tauran tank, if only to keep the latter from playing too free if—*no, when*—war came.

Hence, the SPATHA, a semi-obsolete Volgan tank, with the turret removed and a fighting compartment built up, a 152mm gun bored out to 160mm slung in the fighting compartment, and enough composite armor added on front to stop even a Gallic or Sachsen 120mm depleted uranium penetrator at knife-fighting range.

And the redundant turrets go out to the Isla Real *to add to its defenses.*

He read first about the armor, a back-engineered composite expressly designed to defeat long rod penetrators. Satisfied with that, he pulled out several photos from an envelope attached to the report. One of these showed a dead pig, strapped into the gunner's station of a tank, with a machine gun driven completely through its body. All the other pigs, so said the report, were likewise killed, if not in so grisly a manner.

So, a hundred pound charge of a plastic explosive, splattered on the turret and detonated, will do that to the crew of the target, will it? Cool.

On the other hand, we still need to build nearly a thousand of the bastards, including for operational floats.

Turning the page to close that section of the report, Carrera skipped ahead several—there were forty-one major sections—to go to the section dealing with GLS Interdiction.

GLS, the Federated States' global locating system, and its Tauran and Volgan competitors (which were incomplete in any case, causing both to rely more or less heavily on the GLS anyway), depended upon timed signals. By comparing the time "stamps" it was given, a receiver could calculate quickly and accurately its location on the surface of the planet, its altitude, and even—if moving—its direction of travel. So dependent had all possible adversaries grown on the GLS system that defeating or sabotaging it was a *major* priority of the legion's R&D establishment.

But, as *Obras Zorrilleras* had discovered, there were some limitations to what could be done.

"It just won't work, sir," the project officer had said to Grishkin, out on the OZ facility on the *Isla Real*. "Not like we planned anyway."

Grishkin muttered, "Why?"

The electronic engineer had pulled a white dome from off a Zion-supplied GLS. Pointing at a series of squared off funnels, the large open ends of which faced outward, he'd said, "It's these little bastards. We can acquire the signals from any eight or ten satellites that are covering an area. We can amplify those signals and delay them. We can send the delayed signals to a directional antenna and bombard an area with false data. But only three of these little devices will be oriented in the right direction to accept a signal. And the machine will ignore them as soon as the data they receive doesn't jibe with what the other horns—they're called feeder horns—are getting. The GLS will still be able to calculate its location from the remaining satellites' time stamps."

Scowling, Grishkin had asked, "Can't we send from more than one location?"

"Yes, sir. And we can totally jam the signals if we can hit the target area from three sides; possibly even two. We *can* make the GLS useless. But we can't fool one into thinking it's somewhere other than where it really is . . . except, maybe, if we are in a very static situation. Even then, though, we won't be able to do anything too fine."

"Better than nothing." Grishkin had shrugged. "What about the other GLS systems, the ones that don't use the encrypted signal?"

"Those, sir, we can fuck with unmercifully. They don't have the nasty little feeder horns to cut out our false transmissions." The engineer had led Grishkin to a different section of the building. A box stood on a table.

Again pointing, the engineer had said, "This is just a prototype, of course. It is intended to be emplaced at some area the enemy is likely to target or move

through. It picks up the unencrypted signals, amplifies
them, delays them, then broadcasts omnidirectionally.
Range: Three to four thousand meters. Unencrypted
GLS is useless within its range unless the jammer's
signals are blocked by something, a building or mountain perhaps."

Considering for a moment, Grishkin had then asked,
"Our own troops won't be able to use the GLS satellites in that case, will they?"

"No, sir, not once the jammer is turned on. Defen-
sively, however, it will still be useful because our men
will be able to use it in a given area *before* the enemy
shows up ... before it's turned on."

The engineer had turned from the jammer and led
Grishkin to a different, larger table.

"This is the most subtle project we have," he'd said.
On the table stood a small remote piloted vehicle,
a Zion-designed Molosar II, built under license in
Balboa. "This doesn't screw with the location of the
receiving set much; it hovers overhead, collects signals
from those satellites that are most nearly overhead,
delays *them,* and shoots them down in a sixty-degree
cone. This convinces a GLS receiver in the cone that
it is much, much lower than it really is."

Grishkin had understood immediately. "It makes
aircraft navigation and artillery fire direction computers think they're much lower! Ha! The planes will fly
too high, the artillery will shoot too far."

"Well ... at least until they catch on," the engineer
had answered with a smirk.

Of course for that, Carrera thought, *we'll have to
have a pretty good idea where the artillery is and*

*where the aircraft will fly through. Hmmm...note to
Training Branch of Cazador Tercio: Troops trained in
maintaining deep hide reconnaissance positions.*

And, thinking about deep hide and reconnaissance...

Carrera pressed a button on the intercom on his
desk. "Lourdes, honey?"

"*Si*, Patricio?"

"I was just thinking about your fringe benefits and
I've decided you have a legitimate grievance. Why
don't you bring your bargaining committee to my
office and we'll see if we can't...ummm...hammer
out something fair."

Unseen by her husband, Lourdes shivered. She was
always so desperately horny after she had a baby. It
was even worse than when she was pregnant. The
strength of her hormone-driven desire was nearly a
physical pain.

"Patricio," she answered in a husky voice, "that is
just *so* tacky. I'll be right up."

CHAPTER TWENTY-TWO

Neither reason nor emotion can be taken in excess.

Reason, in itself and standing alone, is a totally inadequate basis for maintaining a society. This is, indeed, the great flaw of the intellectual—far more so than his obsession with sex, his arrogance, and his selfishness—and why he is as much a danger to society as an asset and an ornament. Reason cannot tell the typical voter that he should not grant himself X largesse from the fisc when the penalty will not be paid until Y generation, a century down the road. That necessary restraint comes from an emotional commitment to future generations, and to the culture, values, and traditions of the society of which the voter is a part.

Indeed, once the practice of robbing the fisc is well established, reason *must* lead the voter to "get mine, before it's all gone."

Alternatively, a completely unreasoning and totally emotional commitment to society and its culture can lead to stagnation, to being surpassed by cultures somewhat more rationally based, and to destruction of that home culture in the general competition.

As with many things, toxicity is in the dose.
—Jorge y Marqueli Mendoza, *Historia y Filosofia Moral*, Legionary Press, Balboa, Terra Nova, copyright AC 468

Anno Condita 472
Pashtia, Terra Nova

It was under three hundred miles from the capital to the land of the tribe of Alena. That was, however, as the crow flew and no crow flew over the Indicus Koh mountains, not unless it carried its own air with it. This high, even the tranzitrees, those green-on-the-outside, red-on-the inside, botanical stores of poison to intelligent life, grew stunted and withered.

And it was cold, so cold. Atop his shaggy mountain pony, so different and so much less comfortable than his accustomed thoroughbreds, Hamilcar Carrera tried like the man he was not yet quite to control his shivering. His breath, and that of the pony, came out in a frozen pine tree in front of his face.

"Iskandr," said Alena, riding beside the boy on his left just as her husband, David Cano, rode to the right. "Iskandr, this is as bad as it gets. Soon we will begin the descent downward."

"I'mmm . . . alllll . . . rrright," the boy ground out. "It's just so . . . fu . . . so cold."

Cano smiled. He knew where the boy had picked up his command of vernacular. Every legionary with whom he'd come in contact had been an instructor. And he'd lived among the legions all his life.

Cano rode to the boy's right because it was his

military duty to shield the little body from any bullet that might come. For his wife, Alena, that duty was religious. As far as Alena was concerned, Hamilcar— Iskandr, to her—was the reincarnation of Alexander, avatar of God, and the man, once grown to manhood, who would lead her tribe to glory again. There was not a man, woman, boy, or girl of Alena's tribe who would have hesitated a nanosecond to lay down his or her life for their Iskandr. And most had not yet even laid eyes on the boy.

No matter, faith saw with the heart, not the eyes, listened with the heart, not with the ears.

Three hundred miles was the distance. On the straight and level, on good, full-sized, horses, it might have taken twelve or fourteen days. Under the circumstances—up, down, winding, bad or no trails, rocks barring what pathways there were, and the need to forage—it had already been six weeks.

They could have flown from the capital to Alena's people. Certainly Carrera had enough markers to call in to arrange for that with the Pashtian Air Force. But, as he'd said, "I don't want anyone to know, to even have a hint, where the boy is, that I could not trust with his life."

And so they rode the distance, spread out in a serrated column with a score of point men forward, backed up by twice that a mile or so behind, a rear guard similarly if inversely composed, and the great mass, one hundred and forty odd warriors and five times that in dependents, in the middle.

The shots that came from ahead weren't a big surprise. No one rode the mountains of Pashtia without expecting to be attacked sometime, somewhere along the route.

On the other hand, the sheer *volume* of fire; that was a surprise. Hamilcar had spent his short life surrounded by arms. He listened to the firing for a few moments, filtering out the much faster rate of his guards' F- and M-26s. He judged, "Five machine guns, maybe a hundred, hundred and twenty rifles."

Cano looked closely at the boy and nodded. "Yes, about that."

Hamilcar looked questioningly at Alena. She was said to be a witch, after all, though in fact she was *probably* just a highly observant and extremely intelligent woman. She closed her eyes and recalled the maps she studied nightly.

"There may be three times that many," Alena announced. "Probably no heavy weapons, not here, not with these tribes."

"Why not?" Cano asked from the other side of Hamilcar.

"Not political," she answered. "Just bandits. Never in the pipeline for the heavy stuff. Poor. Not rich enough to buy for themselves. Rifles and machine guns are probably it . . . well, maybe a few rocket grenade launchers."

As if to punctuate, from the right flank of the column, up high among the rocks, came three loud and echoing *bangs*. The things, rocket-launched grenades, were slow enough for Hamilcar to pick out the smoke trails and follow them to the warheads. None seemed to be coming for him.

While Cano and Alena were still thinking, and fighting their horses for control, Hamilcar began ordering.

"Alena, take charge of the women and children." He pointed at a covered spot not far away. "Take one section for security. Go."

Before Cano could object, the boy ordered him, "Call in the rear guard. Leave some here; your judgment. With the rest, go relieve the point."

The rockets impacted among the people of the column—his people—making Hamilcar's pony begin to roar and start. The boy felt a sudden surge of rage— *they're attacking my people*—and took his gift-rifle from the sling that hung on the saddle. He stood in his stirrups, pointed the muzzle toward the direction from which the rockets had come, and shouted, in the language of his guards, "Follow me!" Then, spurring his pony, he started up the slope.

Lead, follow, or get the fuck out of the way, Cano thought, reaching for his radio to call in the rear guard. *I think the boy can lead.*

Alena froze for a moment, an objection forming in her mouth. But, *No, he is the avatar of God. God will protect him.* She kicked her pony, moving up the column and directing the women and children to go where Hamilcar had ordered them. As she rode, shouting and ordering, she added in, for the men of the column, "Guards! Follow Iskandr!"

One look at the boy, charging the enemy alone but for the few of the company who'd been near him, was enough for the guards. They spurred their own ponies, charging in a ragged line after their god.

Bullets raised little dust-devils at the pony's feet, even as others split the air around boy and beast with malevolent *cracks*. Somewhere behind Hamilcar one of the few guards with him cried out in pain. It only caused him to spur his own pony yet again, to drive it through the kill zone the ambushers had planned.

Firing hand gripped around the F-26, Hamilcar's long-practiced thumb flicked the weapon to high rate automatic, twelve hundred rounds per minute. This would empty the ninety-three round snail drum magazine in under five seconds, but was likely to prove the only way to hit something—or even to get close—from the back of the fast-galloping quadruped.

Horses, being, generally speaking, much more interested in the ancient game of mares and stallions, and having little interest in the affairs of men, were perhaps the very first conscientious objectors. Their objections had—again, generally speaking—been overruled. Being also herd animals, and responsive to imposed, group discipline, horses had long been used to inculcate in men the attitude required to impose discipline on other men.

Hamilcar's mountain pony knew, as soon as its light burden had jerked its head around and applied spurs, that this rider would not be brooked and there was no sense in trying to argue the matter. Indeed, it had already had six weeks to get used to the idea that it was going to do as the little biped directed.

And, ya know, the pony thought as it galloped up the slope, *it could be worse. This one feeds me, gives me treats, keeps me clean, doesn't tire me out too badly, and, best of all, talks to me. So I'll trust it . . . for now.*

I hope it gets me away from all these nasty sounds, though.

Alena

Closing rapidly on the enemy ambush line, Hamilcar saw a man, civilian clad but armed, easing around a boulder to his front. He pointed—it was nothing more precise than that—his F-26 and depressed the trigger. A dozen shots lashed out with a sound like cloth ripping. Every one of them, to the boy's disgust, missed their intended target. On the plus side, however, between the stone chips they sent flying and their own sonic booms, they sent that target, weapon dropped and arms flailing, back behind the boulder.

And then Hamilcar was through the enemy ambush and wheeling his pony around. At a certain point in the wheel he yanked the reins, just hard enough to stop the beast completely. He looked for his previous target and found him, cowering against the boulder. Snapping the rifle to a shoulder firing position, Hamilcar took aim and shot the bandit down without a second thought. He felt nothing except satisfaction.

That's one less rifle aimed at my *people.*

He scanned around quickly. Another of the ambushers, this one with a rocket grenade launcher, stood up from his cover. Trusting his equine to hold still, Hamilcar, both hands on the rifle, fired again to engage the RGL gunner. He didn't miss ... rather, of the seven or eight bullets he sent toward his target, at least one didn't miss. The target spun to the ground, screaming and spraying blood from a ruptured gut.

He could see his guards coming on in two groups, from farther down the slope. First, and closest, just behind him in fact, were those who'd been close enough to hear his command and follow in a group. Farther away, still spread in a long, wide and shallow wedge, were those who had heard Alena order them to his support and defense.

Hamilcar didn't spare either a second thought. Quite ignoring the chance that both of those groups were firing more or less wildly, and so could hit him by mistake, the boy spurred his pony forward once again, this time paralleling the ambush line.

He trusted his pony enough by now to release the reins, counting on his legs alone to control it. With both arms free, he twisted in his saddle to bring his rifle to bear. Still on high rate automatic, he had, at most, another eight or nine bursts before he would have to change magazines.

The pony, a little winded now, moved less quickly than it had when galloping up the slope. This actually provided a somewhat more stable firing platform for the rider, enough so that Hamilcar hit his next target, and the one after, on the first burst he donated to each.

And then his guards were among the ambushers, shooting, hacking and stabbing. Some of the latter began to run, to no avail.

"Kill 'em all!" Hamilcar shouted over the din.

The roughly half of the guard maniple that remained pulled perimeter guard around the women, the children, and the dead and wounded. A cold wind whistled among the boulders, blowing the smoke from the fires generally northward. Other pyres arose in the distance, anywhere from two miles to half a dozen away.

Those were from Hamilcar and the other half of the guard company.

"He doesn't have a radio with him," Alena fretted. "What if he gets in trouble?"

no shook his head. "Of course, it
aid sardonically. "He's your avatar;
ng in your eyes."

Alena caught her husband's doubting to
rbarian," she sniffed. "Iskandr *is* the ava
*And he has already shown four of the seven signs
y which his people would know him.*

There was a low fire burning in the hollow in which
they sat, wrapped in their blankets. The moon, Bellona,
was high in the sky, while Hecate was a mere hint of
light, off to the east. Hamilcar was, for the nonce, a
little boy again. "I didn't know what else to do with
them," he said, apologetically. "We'd killed the men.
Should I have left them to starve, or as the prey for
any other bandits in the area?"

Cano put a hand on the boy's shoulder. "No, no,
Ham. You did the right thing. Or as right a thing as
circumstances allowed.

"On the other hand, have you considered what
you're going to do with them? They're all yours now."

Hamilcar shrugged. "I hadn't given it a lot of
thought. I mean, I'm only ten. But . . . maybe . . ."

"Yes?"

"Well, a lot of the women and girls are pretty.
Couldn't some of the guards use wives . . . or second
wives?"

"That's one set of possibilities. But what about the
kids?"

"I'm not sure," the boy admitted. "Dad sent me with
several mule loads of gold and silver. Already coined,
even. Can I maybe pay some of Alena's people to raise
the kids in fosterage? The languages seem pretty close."

...no laughed and shook his head. "...

...e, wife," the tribune said. "You know
do that the only ones in trouble are the
attacked us."

"But it's been *three days*!"

"You in a hurry to get somewhere?" Cano

"No...but *three days*!"

The tribune's hand swept the skyline. "Relax,
that smoke, a new pyre every few hours? The bo
communicating. To us and everyone else who migh
attack us."

"But *three days*?"

It wasn't until the fifth day that Hamilcar returned,
with the eighty-seven survivors of his guard and their
dead slung across horseback. They didn't return alone.

"What are we supposed to do with over a thousand
prisoners?" Alena asked, making an estimate of the
numbers the avatar of God was bringing in. "Our
little valleys can't use the extra slave labor; they're
just not that fertile."

Cano put his binoculars to his eyes and looked more
closely than his wife could have. "Don't worry," he
said, "they won't eat much. And it's closer to fifteen
hundred. All women and children."

"You mean he killed *all* the men?"

"Anybody who could sprout a beard would be my
guess. I don't see a man among them who isn't one
of ours."

Alena decided to take it philosophically. "He took
them; he must support them. And women are flexible, while children can be brought up properly. It
will be well."

Cano thought silently for several minutes. "You want some advice, Ham, since you're going to be living among the tribe for a while?"

"Please."

"Adopt the lot of them. Then, when you marry a woman or girl off, since she's yours you can be sure she'll be well treated. Same for any little ones you put in fosterage. As for the rest..."

"Yes."

"I'm afraid you're stuck with them. By the way, how did you know which villages to hit?"

Hamilcar sighed. "It wasn't very brave, I suppose, but the ones who fought back hard we broke off from. I figured if they still had weapons and men they probably hadn't had much part in attacking us. The ones where there were no weapons and men, because they had attacked us, we destroyed and looted. It's why I *had* to bring the prisoners in. They had nothing left but their eyes to weep with."

"Good boy," Cano said, once again reaching out to squeeze the kid's shoulder.

Runnistan, Pashtia, Terra Nova

"I had no idea..." Hamilcar's words drifted off in surprise amounting to shock amidst the tremendous amount of fortification in front of them. Sure, he'd seen Cano's and Alena's photo album of the valleys of her people, but those had been pristine. Now?

Bunkers, wire, marked off minefields, machine guns, even a few light armored vehicles sealed the people of the tribe off from any outside contact they didn't want. And it looked as if poisonous progressivines had been cultivated in places to supplement the barbed wire. Or perhaps the wire was just used where the 'vines couldn't be grown thick.

"Your dad sort of adopted them," Cano explained. "Them and, to a lesser extent, the other tribes that formed the Pashtun Scouts during the war here. Add in what they earned and how bloody cheap weapons are . . . and that he passed over to them whatever was too expensive to move once the war was over—mostly over, that is—and the legion pulled out.

"But . . . yeah . . . I didn't expect quite this."

The long column, now much longer by virtue of the prisoners Hamilcar had taken and the animals he had seized, wound through an S-curve in the wire and mines. Heavy, well-built bunkers housing machine guns and light cannon dominated the road. The guns therein didn't traverse to track the column. They couldn't; the men who manned them were atop the bunkers' roofs crying—

"Iskandr, *Iskandr,* ISKANDR!"

Hamilcar, rocking in his saddle, waved back. He nodded shy thanks at the heartfelt welcome. To Cano, however, he said, "It doesn't feel right. I'm not a god."

"You know that and I know that," Cano replied. "What does it hurt what *they* think?"

Alena said, "You are both wrong, too."

A group of young riders, F-26 rifles slung across their backs and lances in their hands, galloped out to meet the point of the column as it emerged from the protective barriers. These men, too, shouted "Iskandr, Iskandr, Iskandr!" The chant continued as the escort party led the column around a steep hillock and into the valley.

"ISKANDR!" came from seven thousand throats as soon as Hamilcar made his appearance on the other side of the hillock. They bore in their arms offerings, simple things like baskets of Terra Novan olives—gray, wrinkled, astringent, and about the size of an Old Earth plum, or loaves of bread, spits of roasted meat on trays, jars of old wine, some gold and silver, usually finely worked, swords and spears and shields . . . whatever the valleys had to offer that might bring a smile to the face of their god. The escort party joined the mass and then, in a wave, every man, woman, and child present went to their knees and then their faces.

"This is wrong," Hamilcar said. "This is *so* wrong."

Alena seemed not to understand. "What is wrong, Iskandr? You are the avatar of God. These are your worshippers."

The boy chewed at his lower lip for a moment, then answered, "My father says that things like this are just appearances, valuable, sometimes, yes. But dangerous, too, because appearances can blind you to reality."

He resumed his chewing for a moment, then suddenly, dismounted from his pony and began to walk toward the nearest of the tribespeople. From those nearest he selected the slightest, a little girl not more than two years old, he thought. Reaching the girl, he saw that she was trembling, as if terribly afraid. Hamilcar shook his head, and took one knee in front of the girl. With his hands he gently lifted her to her feet, then stood up, picking her up in his arms as he did. She carried with her a basket of olives.

"Arise," the boy shouted. "I would not have my own people debase themselves in front of me. I have no need of slaves, but only of free men and women." To emphasize the point he took one of the gray olives from the girl's basket and took a bite through the wrinkled skin.

Slowly, uncertainly, the people began to rise in a wave washing away from where Hamilcar stood. Somewhere in the middle of the crowd, an old woman shouted out, "The fifth sign! The fifth sign!"

"Iskandr, *Iskandr*, ISKANDR, ISKANDR!"

As the crowd began to swirl around Hamilcar, the people vying to lift him to their shoulders, Cano asked of Alana, "What is this 'fifth sign,' witch?"

Alena hesitated to answer, but, after all, David was her husband and practically one of the people, himself. "It is prophecy," she said, finally. "There are seven signs by which we would know Iskandr, seven signs which would tell the great truth. The first was the appearance. I found that when I first laid eyes on him. The second was that, though a boy, he would fight like a great warrior. He's done that. The third and fourth were that he would smite the wicked and show mercy to the helpless and innocent." She pointed at the captives. "He's done that. The fifth was that—" she switched her pointing finger to where Hamilcar was being ported up the slope to the main village—"he would refuse proskynesis. As you can see . . ."

"You mean he would be all the good things of Alexander—"

"Iskandr," she corrected.

"—and none of the bad."

"Precisely."

"And the other two?" Cano asked.

"Those we will have to wait upon."

And from that position Alena would not be budged.

Cano shrugged. Alena was a wonderful wife, but had a will of...well, by comparison, iron was weak.

He tried a different tack. "And what is the great truth you speak of?" he asked.

"It is also prophecy; that he will lead his people, and many others, to crush Old Earth and free it from the tyrants."

There was a distant murmuring as Hamilcar's captives, soon to become his adoptees, were shown to quarters in his palace. Alone but for Cano, his wife, the green-eyed Alena, her father, and her brother, Rachman, the boy rubbed his forehead, asking, "What *is* all this?"

His other hand waved to take in the palace the people of the tribe had constructed, plus many of the furnishings it contained. The palace, while mud brick, was simply huge, dominating the hill upon which it rested, which hill also contained the *hieros*, the shrine to Iskandr Alena's people had taken, piece by piece, from Old Earth and re-established here. The *hieros* was fairly empty now, since better than two thirds of what it had once contained was within the walls of the palace.

"We began building it," said Alena's father, "as soon as my daughter sent word you had come among us. As for the furnishings, some came from here, some from there, and some from the shrine, since almost everything in the *hieros* was already your property."

The witch's father had a bird of sorts, resting on a chainmail brace on the father's arm. At first Hamilcar thought it was a trixie, but on closer examination discovered that the creature was not only considerably smaller than any full grown trixie, it had the head of a raptor, a sort of tiny tyrannosaurus rex, with wings, feathers, and bright emerald green eyes. The proto-bird looked at the boy curiously, but without any obvious malevolence.

"We raise them here," Alena's father said. "Better than any falcon, for those who can train them. They're especially good for killing *antaniae*. This one is for you, once you are taught to keep it."

"I see and . . . I thank you, father of my second mother." Alena flushed with pleasure while Hamilcar's eyes moved away from the creature and travelled to a brace of bronze shields, phalangites' shields, gracing one wall. The things *had* to be nearly three thousand years old.

"It is said," the father added, stroking the bird, "that one of the guards on Old Earth, as we were being sent away, tried to shake down one of our girls, a ten-year-old, for the part of your patrimony she carried. It is also said that they never found the guard's body.

"I believe the tale, since that girl was my great-to-infinity grandmother. Your people have fought for your patrimony without cease, Iskandr. And we have never lost faith."

Hamilcar pretended to nod his thanks, even while thinking, *These folk are nuts. But how can I disappoint them? How do I make them understand that, while there is a God, I am not his avatar or anything else? Do I even try? They've held on to their beliefs for thousands of years. They're not going to change. I'm just a kid with some tricks and knacks.*

Changing the subject, Hamilcar asked, "The clinic

my father had built; the doctors he sent from Balboa, they serve the people?"

"Indeed, yes, Iskandr," Alena's father answered. "Our children grow healthy and strong to serve you. And the—" the father struggled for the word "—the veterinary does work equally as important."

"Good," Hamilcar answered. "Very good. The adoption of the captives, tomorrow; this is all prepared?"

"Yes, Iskandr," Alena answered. She tapped the laptop she'd learned to use in Balboa. "I am not yet finished organizing them by families, but I will be by then. This is important to you?"

"Yes. I don't want to break up families. If one of the men wants to marry one of the women or girls, he is going to have to take the whole group as family."

"Speaking of which," said Rachman, "your twelve wives from among the people have been selected, Iskandr. Would you like to marry them tomorrow, as well, or spread the weddings out? Or do them later, after you've rested from your trials?"

"His father is going to murder us," Cano fumed to Alena, later, in their quarters. "No, forget the father; his *mother* is going to murder us. He can't get married; he's only ten years old. And to twelve girls? No."

"Twelve of *our* girls," Alena answered calmly. "Iskandr may well choose others . . . perhaps from among the captives. And by our laws he may marry. After all, he is not ten; he is twenty-eight hundred."

"That's bullshit," Cano said. "He's ten. And you cannot stick this boy with *one* wife, let alone twelve."

"That is for *Iskandr* to say." She frowned. "But I do hope he won't disappoint the girls chosen for him."

"And what about the game? You know, the one where I got the living shit knocked out of me to win you? *Bushkazi*? You can't put a ten-year-old into that?"

"Of course not," Alena agreed. "Well, not *this* ten-year-old. After all, it would be sacrilege to strike him. No, he is above the game."

She sighed, then sniffed. A small tear crept into her eye. "Poor Iskandr; so much joy he is denied because of what he is. Yet the avatar of God has duties to his people."

Cano shook his head. Sure, the boy was a good kid; everything one might want in a boy, in fact. But Alena and her people were just overboard on the whole subject.

"What about bride price?" he asked.

Alena brushed away her tear. "Bride price?" she asked, incredulously. "Bride price to be a bride of *Iskandr*? That's absurd. The problem is going to be keeping the married women from sending him messages, asking that he buy or trade them out of their marriages."

"Alena," Cano said, "I fell in love with your people when I was leading them in the war. Marrying you was icing...and well worth having the crap knocked out of me playing *bushkazi*. But, I've got to tell you, beloved wife and witch, that you are all *nuts*. Jesus, Redeemer and Savior, *twelve* wives? Don't you people know how the Zhong write the word for trouble? It's a stick drawing of two women under the same roof."

"Well, of *course*," Alena answered. "And if you don't believe it just you *try* taking a second wife. That's one reason why we built Iskandr such a wide roof."

CHAPTER TWENTY-THREE

The key, then, to good and long lasting governance is to reduce the dosage of toxic elements, to drive away and exclude from political power as many of those people who lack the requisite civic virtue as can be positively identified. Implicitly, this requires admitting to political power as many of those who have civic virtue as also can be positively identified.

As we have seen, breeding fails. Wealth? There are many wealthy thieves. Education? The world is full of educated derelicts, utterly self-centered and completely devoid of civic virtue.

Motherhood? Leave aside that sons and daughters vote their parents' interests, and that men vote their wives' and sisters', to boot, thus giving mothers a great deal of indirect political power already. Motherhood indicates an interest in the future, but only for the narrow family, not for society as a whole. Remember that a small number of wealthy and connected Spartan mothers, in the interests of their own narrow gene pool, took control of the property of the society, economically ruining the rest, thus driving them out of membership in the *sistisia*, and ruining thereby both the army and the state.

We must further beware of assigning civic virtue to any calling, be it ever so beneficial to society, that a person does because he simply enjoys it, or derives self-satisfaction from it. A socially beneficial calling, as far as the realm of civic virtue is concerned, exists parallel to those which entail civic virtue.

—Jorge y Marqueli Mendoza, *Historia y Filosofia Moral,* Legionary Press, Balboa, Terra Nova, copyright AC 468

Anno Condita 472
Carrera Family Cemetery, Cochea, Balboa, Terra Nova

Tranzitree wax candles burned in a perimeter around the man. Though the fruit were not deadly to insects, as they were to people, the bugs tended to hate the smell of the things and so tended to stay away.

It still hurt, even if time had attenuated the pain.

Time, thought Patricio Carrera, *is a funny thing. Here it is, only forty odd years since you were born, Linda . . . and centuries, it seems, since you died.*

There had been a time when he would camp out by his late family's graves and drink himself into a coma, usually becoming hysterical sometime in the process. Time had, if not quite healed the wounds, at least reduced the intensity of the pain. Besides, he had other pains to eat away at him, and those he had caused himself.

Carrera sat, back against the tall white marble stele that marked the graves of his slaughtered first family. Next to him was a basket of plum-sized, gray, and

wrinkled Terra Novan olives. He always brought Linda
and the kids a gift offering when he came.

Birds fluttered from branch to branch and insects
chirped in the grass surrounding the candled perimeter.
A steady breeze added a rustling of fallen leaves and
bent the grass under its push. Farther away from the
marker, past where family retainers kept the grass well
trimmed, a gurgling stream—running even though the
dry season and a near torrent now, in the middle of
the wet—added to the music.

Carrera blanked his mind to everything but the
sounds and smells for a moment, then thought, *I
have always loved this place. Partly because you came
from it. But also because it is so quiet and peaceful.
Everything so clean and fresh. As you were.*

*Your mother and father get along well with Lourdes.
Maybe it helps that she's a distant relative. On the
other hand, she tries very hard, too.*

*You know I have more children now, three of
them. Don't worry. No one will ever replace you in
my heart. But they are fine children... I think you
would like them. I tell them about you, too. The oldest, the boy, asks me about you and the babies all
the time. He's been sent away. And even though I
told him it was because he is my designated replacement, I know in my heart that I sent him away for
safety's sake, too.*

*Watch over the boy, if you would. We need him. I
think he's going to be better at this even than I am.*

*Balboa is changing. I wish you could be here to
see it. Just about everyone with a will to work has a
job now. Do you know, the City has the lowest crime
rate of any major city in this hemisphere? Of course,*

there are those who call the punishment the crime.
But I don't care what they think or say.

I never cared what anyone thought but you.

And that's all. I'll be here for a couple of days. I'll
visit. I have to, after all. I've done some really shitty
things I need to talk to you about.

Sadly, Carrera stood up and began to trudge the
half mile back to the house. About halfway there he
heard the steady *whopwhopwhop* of one of the legion's
IM-71 helicopters. He quickened his pace.

Fernandez was waiting at the *Finca* Carrera's front
porch when Carrera arrived. The intel chief was
seated in a white painted, wooden patio chair, under
the eaves, reading a book and intermittently sipping
from a rum and coke that had been brought to him
by Lourdes. He noticed Carrera, afoot, walking up the
gravel road to the house. Before Carrera could even
ask, the intelligence officer sat alert, closed the book
and blurted out, "We have an opportunity, Patricio."

"What's that? Can we talk about it here?"

Fernandez didn't even have to think that one over.
"Best not. Let's walk, shall we?"

"Sure. Let me tell..."

"I already told Lourdes," Fernandez said. "She's
chatting with Linda's mother."

"Fine," Carrera said, turning in place and walking
back toward the cemetery. "Let's talk."

Fernandez stood, closing the book upon a place-
saving finger. He followed Carrera back toward the
cemetery. Once they were out of earshot of the house,
Fernandez said, "The *Charlemagne* is coming. In
about ten days."

Carrera thought for a moment, trying to remember where he'd heard the name before. He halted for a moment, poking his tongue around his molars for a while, while trying to recall. Then it hit him. "The Gallic aircraft carrier?"

"Almost a super carrier," Fernandez corrected. "And she's coming with her full battle group."

Carrera shook his head, doubtfully. "We don't have any reason to think the Taurans are planning to attack in a month."

"Clearly not," Fernandez agreed. "Though I expect the visit is for the air wing to train over our ground. But that wasn't what I meant. I mean that with the second Megalodon-class sub tested and ready for operations now, we have an opportunity to see if we can penetrate the ship's defensive screen to get at it."

"Ohhh. But why tip our hand?"

"I wasn't planning on tipping our hand," Fernandez answered as he kicked a small rock from the roadway. "I thought we could use the second one, with its clicker going, to distract the Gauls while the first one, clicker off, slips in close."

"You talked to Fosa about this?"

"Yes," Fernandez nodded. "He agrees it would be a unique opportunity to test the submarine."

"How are they going to do it?"

"We've got two built," Fernandez answered, "and another that's close enough to completion that we could make it ... mmm ... not seaworthy but at least floatworthy.

"Fosa's got two possible plans. Plan A, he says, is where we'll sail one out of the pens, with its clicker disengaged, and conceal it in some little inlet along

the Shimmering Sea coastline. The almost finished one
will take its place. The other finished one will then sail
to a rendezvous point where it will meet with the one
we hid by the coast. Plan B is we mount a clicker to
the tender we use to shadow them for test dives. Both
subs sail with clickers on, but at a predetermined time
the one with the tender will shut its off, and the tender
will start clicking to simulate the sub's being there."

"Plan B," Carrera said, without hesitation. "If we
used Plan A, and someone spotted the sub and someone
else, say, Tauran Intelligence noticed it wasn't clicking,
the secret would be blown."

"Plan B, then," Fernandez agreed. "The two of them
will then link up at sea and sail to a point outside of
the range of the *Charlemagne*'s escorts and take station,
one to a place above the lowest thermal layer—if there's
more than one—that's still within depth capacity and
one below it. The one with the clicker engaged will be
above. There will probably be only one thermal layer,
mind you, though with the cold current in the Shimmering Sea and the undersea volcanism there may be more.

"At the point where the escorts notice the one above
and come after it, it will break off and head for the
Puerto Lindo sub pens. The other will press on until it
is within engagement range of the carrier and maybe
scoot around a little to make sure they can't detect
it. Then it will come home, too, and we'll move the
floatworthy one back to the assembly plant as if we
discovered some flaw during testing."

Carrera thought as the pair of them continued to
walk. *Possibility one: We don't test beforehand and
when the war comes maybe we surprise the Taurans
and maybe we're the ones who are surprised. Two: We*

test and it's a flop; the Taurans catch us and find out about the Meg class. Three: We test and get away with it.

It's a better than fifty-fifty bet, I think, because we know we're running the test and the Taurans don't.

Ah, but what about the United Earth Peace Fleet? How do we keep them from spotting us? Marguerite hasn't answered the phone in quite some time now. Maybe that's my fault for shutting the communicator up so long. Anyway, there's no way to probe her to *see. And the Yamatan intelligence has dried up. I wonder if she's even still in system.*

He asked Fernandez about the problem of UEPF surveillance.

"I don't think they're watching very closely, Patricio," Fernandez said. "And no, I'm not sure why, and yes, it does bother me. But there should have been something, some kind of reaction, to our operations in La Palma and Santander. For that matter, we've done enough recon flights over Atlantis Base with the Condors that there was a fair chance of visual spotting. But they don't seem to be looking.

"I think it's a good bet."

They walked in silence until reaching the cemetery. There, Carrera nodded and said, "All right. Tell Fosa I authorize him to do it."

"What are you reading?" Carrera asked, really noticing for the first time that Fernandez was carrying a book.

Holding up the thing, front cover toward Carrera, Fernandez said, "*Memoirs of Belisario Carrera, Annotated and Abridged.* Interesting stuff."

"It was right here, you know," Carrera said, sweeping an arm around the clearing.

"What was?"

"The first fight between my multi-great-grandfather-in-law and Old Earth."

"Ohhh. It was here that they killed the slaver, Kotek Annan?"

Carrera pointed at a spot not very far from Linda's memorial. "His head stopped rolling right about there, according to family legends."

Fernandez stopped dead, then opened the book and thumbed back forty or fifty pages. When he found what he was looking for, a description of that first fight, he read the passage and then reread it. Then he furiously skipped chapters to get to the section about the second fight, the one in the city. This he read, too. For a long moment, Fernandez chewed on his lower lip, as if searching for something.

"What happened to the shuttle?" he asked, excitement in his voice. "The one they took out on the ground at the old UN station in *Ciudad* Balboa?"

Carrera shrugged. "Dunno. I imagine the Earthers recovered it. I doubt old Belisario knew how to fly one. And his people were all simple *campesinos*."

"Yeah...maybe. But, give the old boy his due; he was no dummy. Why would he leave the earthpigs with a repairable shuttle? Would you?"

"Now that you mention it, no," Carrera said.

Fernandez smiled broadly. It was so unusual an expression for him that Carrera was slightly shocked.

"Would you happen to know where the *un*abridged memoirs are?" Fernandez asked.

Carrera pointed down the road. "The *original* originals, I'm not sure. But there's a mostly complete copy at my old house a couple of miles down the road. I wouldn't recommend them, though."

"Why's that?"

"Handwritten, and old Belisario's penmanship was not of the best. Likewise, the paper he used was awful...crumbling, now, mostly. I understand that the Ph.D. candidate who did the annotated version used up a lot of research assistant's time trying to preserve them and sucked up a lot of computer time trying to decipher them.

"I was going to try to publish them, myself, back before the war. I finally gave up on the old boy's penmanship."

"Would you mind letting me see the copies?" Fernandez asked.

"Would you mind walking a couple of miles?"

Fernandez shook his head *no*.

"Can you tell me why you're interested?" Carrera asked.

"I'd rather not; not just yet," Fernandez answered, thinking, *Because it's such an outside shot I'd look like a fool if it doesn't pan out.*

Carrera shrugged. "Come on, then."

Puerto Lindo, Balboa, Terra Nova

The new submarine pen was intended to base a naval maniple of nine boats and their crews, any three of which could be presumed to be out on patrol or training at any given time. The concrete overhead was a full three meters in thickness and that on the sides not much less. Nine portals led to the *Puerto Lindo* bay while dual railroad tracks led from the factory, then entered the rear of the pen before descending into the water. With only two Meg-class submarines present, the pen seemed empty and cavernous.

Cavernous it might be, thought Warrant Officer Chu, watching as Meg 3 was railed into the water. *Quiet, however, it is not.*

The boat, about ten meters by forty, moved on four specially modified and linked flatbeds on two straight and parallel sets of track. This was deafening in the confines of the pen. Huge armored doors slid to either side to permit the vessel entry. That added to the screeching of the rails the sounds of machinery and grinding gears. Lastly were the sounds of preparation, by no means soft, though now drowned out by everything else.

Amidst all that noise, the *squish-squish-squish* of the thoroughly soaked Fosa walking up behind Chu and Quijana, the skipper of Number Two, the *Orca*, went completely unnoticed until Fosa slapped palms onto the shoulders of his sub skippers and said—rather, shouted, "I don't believe even the UEPF can see anything with all this shit coming down."

"This place gets twenty-four fucking feet of rain a year, sir," Chu shouted back. "Sometimes more. I don't even know how the *antaniae* can find each other to fuck."

The armored doors ceased moving, much reducing the ambient noise level.

"You think this will work, sir?" Chu asked, in a more conversational volume.

Fosa answered, "I think so. Neither the Taurans nor the UE are likely to know that Number Three is unfinished. I looked at it before they started to rail it over. It looks perfectly complete from the outside. So if they see it come in and another boat leave they'll probably assume that the boat leaving is Number Three, going out for a test cruise. We've got good reason to think the earthpigs can't see down even fifty feet into the water, so when you go past a hundred they'll surely lose you. When the *Orca* goes out to probe the Gauls, that's all they should be looking for, just the one.

"Just in case, though, you boys have full torpedo loads?"

"Yes, sir," Quijana answered.

Chu added, "They finished backfitting my torpedo pods last month, sir. A mix of regular, supercavitating, and light for close-in defense work."

The dark gray nose of Number Three appeared in the portal opened by the armored doors. Even in the dim light, rain could be seen coming down in near solid sheets. The noise picked up again, noticeably.

"We've fooled 'em before," Fosa shouted. "I think we can again. Arrogant folks, don't you know. And it's not like we're really all that important."

While Fosa went to watch the new, unfinished sub being railed into the water, Chu called Quijana aside for a little chat.

"Miguel," he said, "I want you to remember that, to date, the submarine force, such as it is, has a perfect record. The number of dives and the number of surfacings are exactly equal. Don't fuck that up."

Quijana scowled. "You're afraid I'll try to use this as an opportunity to make up for my 'cowardice' aboard the *Trinidad*?"

"Oh, *stop*." Chu shook his head. "You're not a coward, and no, you're not stupid. Still less are you immoral enough to put your boat and crew at risk over a purely personal matter. But..."

"Yes?"

The older man sighed. "Miguel, you've got more talent for submarines than I do. So think I and so thought the Volgans and Yamatans and Zionis who trained us. But you know why you're being the stalking horse while I go in for the test? Because I was afraid that, under pressure, if things go wrong, you might hesitate for just that fraction of a second that might get you all killed. Not hesitate because you're afraid... but hesitate because you're afraid of being afraid... or showing that you are."

At that, Quijana's scowl deepened.

UEPF *Spirit of Brotherhood*, orbiting Terra Nova

Frowning at the distraction, John Battaglia, duke of Pksoi, initialed the electronic tablet showing the daily intelligence report without really reading it. This was understandable; printed, the thing would have run to several hundred pages. What was less understandable was that he barely glanced over even the much shorter summary. If he had, he might have noticed that the intelligence office was unconvinced that—even though a Federates States airship had downed the skimmer from *Harmony*—that it had been the FSC behind the attacks on Santander. He might also have noticed that the Balboan submarine program had apparently launched another boat.

Then again, Battaglia might not have noticed. Those things were trivial and he was already completely taken

up with the coming return of the new high admiral
and his own somewhat precarious political position.

If that twat, Wallenstein, hadn't taken the admiral's
staff with her, there would be people to handle this sort
of trivia for me. Irresponsible bitch! More philosophically, he thought, *Then again, if she were here with the*
admiral's staff I wouldn't have to worry about it at all.

Pushing the report aside, Battaglia raised his eyes
and asked his aide, "What's on the schedule for today?"

"Sir," the aide de camp answered, "a shuttle is
laid on to visit the *Kofi Annan* and the *Mitterand*. If
there's time, the *Margot Tebaf* is also standing by for
a morale raising visit."

The aide managed to keep her tone neutral through
all that. It didn't pay, generally speaking, for Class Twos
to question the wisdom of morale visits by Class Ones.

Unlike Battaglia, the aide *had* read the intelligence
report in its entirety. And, while she had noted that
the wretched little "Republic" of Balboa, below, had
moved a new submarine from the factory to the sea,
she knew—having looked at the specs of the thing—that
there was no way it could pose any threat to her own
fleet. It never even crossed her mind, no more than it
would have Battaglia's, that one tiny little submarine,
stuck down below, could matter in the slightest.

Puerto Lindo, Balboa, Terra Nova

"Engage the clicker," Chu ordered, from his post in
the sail. Almost immediately a small box mounted
to the hull began emitting a regular *clickclickclick*.
It sounded exactly like what one might expect of an

inherently complex naval system, built in—and to the usual standards of—the undeveloped or semi-developed parts of the planet. The sound from the clicker was faint. Chu could only *just* hear it, and then only if he concentrated.

"Take us out."

There was a slight disturbance in the water around the sub's bow, and a marginally more noticeable one aft. The boat eased itself forward, very slowly and aimed directly at the gate. In a control room overlooking the interior of the pen, one of the sailors pressed a button. Immediately, the armored gate—it was as well armored as the rear portal over the rail lines—began sliding open with the expected deluge of sound. Chu's *Meg* passed through the open gate and made its way toward the middle of the bay.

About two thirds of the way to the middle the captain ordered, "Course one-eight-seven. Take us past the island." The boat began a slow veer to port.

There was a single trixie, bright green and red quasi-feathers clear against the blue sky, circling the tree-crowned island as it passed astern to the left. Almost immediately, the waves, which had been practically nonexistent, grew to a height of a couple of feet. A medium yacht would have noticed them; on the *Meg* they had no real effect.

A small yacht, its passengers engaged in fishing just at the mouth of the bay, sheltered behind the small island, saw the sail of the *Meg* pass by about half a mile away. The passengers, sport fisherman from the Federated States, to all appearances, waved at Chu, which wave he returned.

Chu then disappeared into the hull of the *Meg*. A few minutes later, the sail began to sink into the waves.

Fort Muddville, Balboa, Terra Nova

Though built around a large infantry brigade, Janier's command included both air and naval components, as well as some foreign detachments. As such, the brigade staff was a joint-combined staff. As such, each staff section contained officers, warrants, and noncommissioned officers from the other services, and some from other states in the Tauran Union. *Lieutenant de Vaisseau*—Lieutenant of the Line—Surcouf was the Gallic senior naval type on de Villepin's intelligence staff.

Surcouf shook his head, wonderingly.

"What's that?" asked de Villepin.

"Oh, the latest little Balboan submarine just left the pen at *Puerto Lindo*," the lieutenant answered. "A test run, I suppose, since it's brand new. Our people doing observation aboard the yacht just waved it out. I honestly don't know why those people even bother; the things are so outrageously noisy that we could find this one, or any of its siblings, any time we like. Seems like such a waste of money and manpower."

"Think we should dispatch the southern frigate"—there was a frigate at each terminus of the Transitway—"to track it?" de Villepin asked.

Surcouf thought about it for a moment before answering, "No . . . no, sir, I think not. If *Ney* tracks it they'll know they're easily spotted. Then they might actually start thinking about and then fix the problem with the noisemakers they think of as water jets. Better this way, I think. Big surprise for the Balboans if it ever comes to a fight."

"Fair enough," de Villepin agreed. "What's *Charlemagne*'s progress?"

"Four days sailing; then she'll be here."

De Villepin nodded, then said, "It's kind of odd, isn't it, that the locals aren't reacting to the approach of the carrier. It's not like it's a secret. And one would think that it would at least alarm them some, cause some limited mobilization. But nothing. Not even an increase in telephone traffic."

"I agree it's odd, sir. But who can understand these people, anyway?"

Maybe nobody, de Villepin thought. *I wish I could, though*.

SdL *Megalodon*, Shimmering Sea, Terra Nova

The string across the control room was noticeably bowed. The depth meter read six hundred meters. Location was roughly sixty miles out in the Shimmering Sea. The crew was alternately sleeping, or snacking, or playing games at their battle stations, while waiting for the clock to run. A small buoy on a wire linked the *Meg* with the surface, receiving the global locating system signal while Chu and company listened for any code words that would indicate a change in plans.

"Time, Skipper," announced Guillermo Aleman.

"Retrieve the buoy," Chu said.

❖   ❖   ❖

On the surface the captain of the tender that always accompanied test runs noted the time. "They'll be taking off soon," he muttered.

Glancing over his chart, the tender's captain gave the order, "Turn on the clicker simulator. Set course for Point Bravo. Speed, six knots." He smiled, thinking, *Just exactly as if we were still following the sub around.*

It took about three minutes for the small electric motor to bring the buoy back to its station atop the sail, which also closed the tiny doors above it as the buoy settled. The motor itself was contained in and shielded by the sail. It was essentially a silent process.

"Tender's taking off, Skipper," sonar announced. "Heading generally to Point Bravo at . . . call it six knots. She's engaged her clicker."

Chu gave the order, "Ensure the clicker's off. Sailing stations. Boys, let's go link up with *Orca* at the rendezvous point."

Fort Muddville, Balboa, Terra Nova

Surcouf stood in front of a wall-mounted map on which the course of the *Charlemagne* battle group was plotted. There was another plot, too, on the map. This was the plot of the second Balboan submarine which had sortied the night prior. The second plot was on an intercept course with the first. Still a third plot showed the course of the Gallic Navy frigate, the *Michael Ney*. *Ney* was shadowing the sub at a considerable distance. Then again, because of the sub's apparently appalling internal workings, shadowing at a distance was easy.

"Why did you sortie the frigate for this?" de Villepin asked. "I thought you said..."

"Yes, sir," Surcouf interrupted. "I did. But this one"—he tapped the map—"this one is heading for the battle group. I figured that sending the frigate out now would not be suspicious, since we would want to escort the *Charlemagne* in, anyway. But I *am* suspicious. I think they intend to try to get through the screen."

"If they try and we intercept, won't that alert them that they're noisy?"

Surcouf looked worried. "Yes, sir, it would. I'm still thinking about how to warn them off without letting them know they're so easy to track."

De Villepin thought about that briefly, then asked, "How common would it be for the submarine escorting *Charlemagne* to separate itself from the battle group and then try to penetrate the screen?"

Surcouf rocked his head a bit from side to side, thinking. He finally answered, "Not uncommon. Though the submarine with a battle group usually takes point by as much as fifty kilometers, they do—situation permitting—sometimes test their own defenses. Good practice for the submariners, too."

"How hard to vector that escort sub close enough to the Balboan that active sonar would pick both up?"

"Only a little more difficult. A submarine would almost never use active sonar. Surface ships do...at least for some purposes and under some circumstances. *Diamant* is *Charlemagne*'s escort. If they're hunting her, they might well use active..."

De Villepin caught Surcouf's hesitation. "Yes?"

"We also sometimes go to active targeting sonar in the wake of an attack."

De Villepin looked appalled. "I didn't mean we should have the escort sub actually *fire* on the carrier."

"No, no, sir. We do simulated firings. Basically, we shoot a blast of water and air out the torpedo tubes."

"Let's try that, then."

"There is a problem, though, sir," Surcouf mentioned.

"What's that?"

"Well, sir, pinging a submarine with sonar on firing mode, rather than a general search, is rarely done except by prior arrangement. It's *almost* an act of war. It's certainly considered a threat. Submariners start filling torpedo tubes and calculating firing solutions when they get pinged by targeting sonar from a ship or another submarine. They've been known to open fire, even in times of peace, though that is never officially admitted to by the parties concerned. Never."

SdL *Megalodon*, Shimmering Sea, Terra Nova

Sonar heard it even though no one else did. He pressed a button and waited for the computer to do the analysis. When that was done, a matter of a few seconds, he announced in a soft voice, "Captain, *Orca*'s passing two hundred meters above us and twelve hundred meters off of our starboard bow."

"Put it on screen," Chu ordered. Immediately the large plasma screen that was mounted a half dozen meters in front of Chu's command chair lit up with generated images of the *Meg*, centered, and the *Orca*, some distance off. Numbers arrayed around the images gave information on depth, course, and speed. The whole effect of the screen was keystoned, as if to display the ocean not from above but from an angle.

"Helm, follow her once she's eight thousand meters ahead. Maintain this depth."

CHAPTER TWENTY-FOUR

What, then, would be a proper test of civic virtue? Perhaps better said, what range of tests would be proper?

At a bare minimum, such a set of tests must be undertaken voluntarily, at least in practice. It would, presumably, be appropriate to inform the people that there is such a battery of tests. This could be in the form of a draft notice, provided that it is only form and there are no other legal or social costs—not even so much as implied—to failure to report.

The tests themselves should have the following characteristics, if we are to deny the voting franchise to those who lack civic virtue:

They must be dangerous, difficult, and dirty; enough so, at least, to dissuade enough of those who lack civic virtue from undertaking them. They should be useful to society. Lastly, they must train those who have demonstrated sufficient civic virtue to sufficient skill in violence to be able to maintain their rule, for the good of all.

"Sufficient skill" is, of course, a relative matter. A solid basic combat training is adequate for this, when those who lack the vote (because lacking in civic virtue) have no such training. Beyond that, whatever

jobs are required by society should suffice. If what
society needs for the foreseeable future is a mass
of infantry, armor, artillery, and combat engineers,
then that is where the prospective citizen should
go, and those the branches into which he or she
should train. If building roads in the hot sun is more
valuable, that is where they should go, consistent
with the need for roads. Work of any kind, done
primarily in a comfortable building, without danger,
stress, and hardship, should not qualify. Nor should
they be given any real choice in the matter.

> —Jorge y Marqueli Mendoza, *Historia y
> Filosofia Moral*, Legionary Press, Balboa,
> Terra Nova, copyright AC 468

Anno Condita 472
SdL *Megalodon*, Shimmering Sea, Terra Nova

You could cut the stress with a knife, and the Tauran—
really the Gallic—battle group was still nearly twenty
miles away.

From his command chair, mounted on a low dais
overlooking the stations of the crew, to either side of
the sub's bridge and forward, under the main screen,
Chu followed the *Orca*'s progress on an electronic sea
chart. The other sub moved at a speed of twenty-
one knots, so said the display, which speed the *Meg*
matched. This was slow enough for the *Orca* to have
no practically detectable sound of its own, through the
thermal layer that separated the two. Only the clicker
on the sub sounded, as it sailed two hundred meters
up and about eight thousand forward.

Though much progress had been made, over the last few decades, in stealthing surface warships, they were still much noisier than submarines. Even here, below the thermal layer, the noise of the battle group and the frigate moving to meet it were detectable enough for the sonar man, aided by computer, to mark their positions on the screen with a considerable degree of certainty.

"But I still haven't heard *shit* out of the sub that's escorting that battle group, Skipper," sonar announced softly through the boom mike that connected him to the rest of the on-duty crew. The sonar man, Antonio Auletti, thought, *And if that doesn't worry you, it sure as shit worries me. Not that I expect to be able to do much about it. Though it's not, I suppose, as if we were sailing unarmed.*

"Okay," said Chu, "*Orca*'s on her own. Set intercept course for the carrier."

SdL *Orca*, Shimmering Sea, Terra Nova

The torpedo man didn't expect to be used, this cruise, and so sat back in his very comfortable chair—comfortable enough to allow sleeping at battle stations if one cared to put it into its reclined position—with his fingers intertwined behind his head. His control board, in any case, showed nothing but green, fourteen lights for fourteen torpedoes carried external to the pressure hull, just inside the oil-smooth outer fairing.

Seated behind the weapons station, Miguel Yermo, *Orca*'s chief of sonar, could hear the Gallic flotilla much more clearly than could Auletti on the *Meg*.

This was to be expected, as the *Orca* was considerably
closer to the surface and, more importantly, above
the thermal layer under which *Meg* sailed. Sadly for
Yermo, he, too, hadn't the first, faintest clue as to the
location of the submarine presumed to be escorting
Charlemagne. He didn't like that lack of knowledge
any better than did Auletti, presumptively still trailing
his own boat by about eight kilometers.

*And I have to guess at that, because a) my bloody
sonar is primarily oriented forward, b) the towed array
is just that, towed behind us, and c) the* Orca *is not
using its clicker and is as quiet as . . . well . . . as quiet
as if it wasn't even there.*

And . . . what the hell's that? Yermo wrapped one
hand over his headphones and pressed, listening
intently.

"Skipper, I've got sonar contact . . . faint . . . about . . .
a thousand feet down, under the layer . . . bearing . . .
one-seven-seven . . . three to three and a half kilometers
range." Yermo's finger requested the sonar computer
to match the sounds coming off the contact. "She's
moving fast to pass underneath us. I make it an
Amethyst class, Skipper."

"That assumes the recordings the Volgans sold us
are accurate," answered the *Orca*'s captain, a young
man named Quijana with a very fatalistic outlook
on life. Truth be told, Quijana was quite certain he
should have been dead years ago, along with the entire
crew—minus himself, of course—of his first boat, the
Santissima Trinidad. Only luck and a commander who
wanted to save what could be saved had spared him.

"I believe the Volgans, Skipper," Yermo replied.
"And anyway, what other class would it be with a

Gallic fleet? The Pike class isn't due to launch for another two years."

"Fair enough," Quijana agreed. "What's she doing away from her carrier, though?"

The XO of the boat, Dario Garcia, ventured a guess. "Training, Skipper. The Amethyst class is going to try to break through the cordon to get in a position for a shot at the *Charlemagne*. Hell, we're slated to do the same thing next year with *Dos Lindas*."

"Yeah...or maybe they're looking for us."

Garcia thought not. "Skipper, with the clicker going nobody has to *look* for us. They already know where we are."

The exec thought about that for a moment, then said, "But, you know, since we *are* that noisy when we want to be, they really shouldn't be ignoring us like they are. It's odd."

Quijana nodded. "Mark the sub as target seven," he ordered. In a few seconds the screen updated with the designation.

"Skipper," Yermo said, "the frigate that was going to meet the battle group and two of its own escorts are heading toward the sub."

Quijana looked again at the screen and saw the targets designated as "two," "five," and "six" changing course to intercept the submarine labeled as "seven."

"And I'm picking up some noise that suggests one or more helicopters en route, too," Yermo added. "Ummm...Skipper?"

"Yeah, I know. If they're heading toward the Gallic sub they're also heading toward us. Lemme think for a bit."

S806 *Diamant* (Amethyst class), Shimmering Sea, Terra Nova

The control room, though crowded and cramped, was also calm and fully collected. They were a professional crew, with what every man aboard would have agreed was a first-rate captain in command.

"Any sign that the target sub is moving away?" asked the captain of a fresh faced, young deck officer.

"So far nothing, sir," the deck officer replied. "They can't be so ignorant as to believe we don't hear them, can they?"

The captain, medium height and graying at the temples, raised one hand to his jaw and commenced tapping his fingers lightly across thin lips.

"Is it possible they don't hear us—or the escorts or the helicopters—all heading this way?" the captain asked.

The deck officer frowned. "After that burst of speed we put on," he said, "they've got to know we're here. And Intel has said the Balboans bought Volgan and maybe improved that through their Yamatan or Zioni contacts. Volgan may not be of the best, but it's plenty good enough to hear everything but"—the deck officer put out one hand and waggled his fingers—"*maybe* the helicopters off of *Charlemagne*."

"Is it possible they don't know how good our sensors are?" the captain asked.

"Why do you ask, sir?"

"Because Intel also said that every member of a Balboan submarine crew is a graduate of something like our own commando course. That means they're a very determined bunch. And if a very determined bunch is pressing in to engagement range after having been made, that worries me a great deal.

"And then, too, when you think about the rogue nature of the whole Balboan state, an army that owns a country... renting themselves out as mercenaries... their long-standing policy of enmity with everything decent and liberal... uncontrollable... willful... and war is coming, where *Charlemagne* will be a critical asset."

The captain made a sudden decision. "Ready four torpedoes," he said. "Rig for extreme silent running. Bring us back above the thermal. And then bring us into a three-hundred-and-sixty-degree turn."

"Sir?"

"I want to come up on their tail again."

"Sir, they don't carry torpedoes."

"You know, son," the captain said, putting an affectionate hand on his officer's shoulder, "I could believe one research or drug interdiction sub might be built with no weapons. But nobody builds what amounts to a factory to make a class of submarines with no arms. No market for it, you see."

"But Intel—"

"Fuck Intel. They've been wrong before. And they're just the sort to be right about the quasi commando training—that can be *seen*—but utterly wrong about whether that sub is armed, since that's harder to see."

"They could intend for the subs to be commando carriers," the deck officer said, not unreasonably.

"Do you want to bet your life on that?" the captain countered. "The life of the *Charlemagne*?"

"Put that way, sir, no." The deck officer turned from the captain and began to give the orders.

SdL *Megalodon*, Shimmering Sea, Terra Nova

Auletti turned his head over one shoulder and twisted to look directly at Chu. "The frog sub's disappeared, Skipper. No trace."

"Well, *find* it."

Auletti gave his captain one of those looks that as much as said, *Don't be an ass. Sir.*

Chu nodded. "Yeah, right. Belay that."

Aleman suggested, "We might be able to pick them up again if we come up above the thermal, assuming they went above it."

Shaking his head, Chu answered, "Sure, and they might hear us. We're quiet, but you never know. No, we'll maintain course to intercept *Charlemagne*."

SdL *Orca*, Shimmering Sea, Terra Nova

"Lost 'em, Captain," Yermo told Quijana. "I think maybe they went under the layer."

Quijana nodded while thinking, *Man, ever since Pedraz booted me off the* Trinidad *I've felt like a fugitive from the law of averages. And my instructions didn't cover this. What's that frog sub doing? What would I be doing in his shoes?*

"I've got a better signature on that surface disturbance, sir," Yermo said. "It's definitely at least one helicopter...and I've got a *plonk* from a sonar buoy. Active sonar pinging now."

"Don't sweat the buoy," Quijana said. "I doubt they need it for us, with the clicker going. If I had to make a guess, I'd say they're looking for that sub we lost track of." *Of course, that assumes the frog sub is still playing a game with her own battle group. I'm really getting uncomfortable with all this.*

Then again, my mission is to provide cover for the Meg *to get under the fleet. Have I already done that? I could use the underwater phone to find out, but if I do, the frogs will know there's another sub out here. One they hadn't a clue to. That might panic them. Hell, it would panic me. This is—*

Yermo interrupted Quijana's train of thought. "Captain, I've got another *plonk*. High frequency noise but not sonar. One of the helicopters, if there is more than one up there, is talking to the frog sub. And... there goes another *plonk*. Skipper, I'm sure there's more than one helicopter up there."

S806 *Diamant,* Shimmering Sea, Terra Nova

"What the fuck do you mean, 'there's only one sub down there'?" *Diamant's* captain demanded on the helicopter that had dropped the sonobuoy. "I can hear the bastard... Oh, you see us doing a three-sixty *under* the layer, but you can't see them cruising straight above the layer. Oh, you can hear the clicking from the defective water jet? But no active return signal? That's bizarre."

"Could be the material," the deck officer ventured. "The plastic we know makes up the hull might give a poor return signal."

"But *that* poor?" the captain questioned.

"Maybe the sonobuoy's defective," the deck officer offered, reasonably.

"No . . . no, they see us well enough." The captain went back to tapping his lips. He ceased his tapping and put the underwater telephone transceiver back to his head. "Relay to *Charlemagne*," he said. "I want a line of passive sonobuoys dropped in front of that sub. If he doesn't turn back from those it will establish a pretty good case that he intends to intercept the battle group with hostile intent. I also need permission from the admiral to fire if they do pass that line. Tell the admiral I am loading tubes."

SdL *Megalodon*, Shimmering Sea

Now that *I heard,* thought Auletti. "Captain Chu, the Amethyst class is flooding tubes. Location on screen now."

Chu hadn't taken his eyes from the screen lately. He saw the Gallic submarine reappear as his target "Five" (because *Meg*, being under the layer, didn't have as clear a picture of the surface as *Orca* did).

"This shit has just gotten way too serious," was Chu's pronouncement. "Quijana," he whispered, "I think we've already proved our point. You can turn around and go home any time now."

Auletti said, "Sir, the *Orca*'s stopped . . . or maybe just turned off its clicker. I think they must have heard the tubes being flooded."

Chu shook his head. "No, they didn't turn off their clicker. Quijana's the literal sort. His orders were to use his clicker continuously while moving under power. He'll do that right up to the point where it means self destruction . . . and maybe past that point. Maybe he'll be clever and stop for a bit.

"Continue on course for the Gallic battle group."

SdL *Orca*, Shimmering Sea, Terra Nova

"All stop," Quijana ordered, as soon as he was informed that the Gallic submarine was arming itself. The clicker was electronically, although not mechanically, tied in to the drive system, to the extent that it would stop clicking if the jet pumps stopped, or increase or slow its rate of clicking if the sub's speed went up or down.

And now what? They're nuclear, with maybe two or three months' rations aboard. I'm not; I can't replenish my air anything like that long; and we'd all starve long before he does. Fuck.

Garcia walked over to stand next to Quijana's command chair. "If it comes to it, Skipper," the Exec whispered, "The bitch is already in line with our rear tubes. At this range"—the main screen indicated the Gallic sub was less than a kilometer astern—"she'd hardly know what hit her if we use the supercavitating torpedo we've got back there."

"Ten seconds is long enough to press a firing button," Quijana answered.

"Yes, sir," Garcia agreed. "Yes, sir, it is. But if the sub's destroyed, and there's no one to provide guidance to the torpedo, we've got a much better chance."

"You want to start a war, XO?"

"No, sir. But I don't want to die right now, either."

Neither do I, Quijana silently agreed. *But . . .* "I will press on with my Cazador mission, though I be the last man standing."

"Yes, sir," Garcia agreed. "We all went to the school, too."

"The thing that bugs me, Dario," Quijana said, "is

that frog captain. Flooding tubes is not a minor step. Either he's got a crappy attitude or he's got orders to engage. I wish I knew which it was."

"Maybe not," Garcia answered. "Maybe we just make him nervous."

"*We* don't get nervous that easily," Quijana said.

"*We* aren't responsible for guarding a multibillion-drachma nuclear carrier either, Skipper."

"I'm not sure that makes things any better." Quijana considered, and compromised. "Weapons, stand by to fire number fourteen at the Gaul. My command *only*."

"Aye, sir."

S806 *Diamant*, Shimmering Sea, Terra Nova

"The enemy's stopped," the deck officer informed the captain. This was the first time that anyone aboard the *Diamant* had actually referred to the Balboan sub as "the enemy." It was, perhaps, an unfortunate choice of words.

The captain really didn't notice the word choice; he'd long since classified the Balboan as an enemy. He attached no particular emotion to the word.

For the rest of the bridge crew, however, the use of the word went through the men like an electronic shock. Not a one of them, no more so the captain, had ever fired a shot in anger. To actually classify someone as "the enemy" was unheard of outside of a lecture room, a motion picture, or a history book. Indeed, the bureaucrats who actually ran the Tauran Union had a semi-official policy of not considering or permitting anyone to be considered an "enemy."

Tension on the bridge, already high, shot upward.

From a chest pocket the captain took out a hand-kerchief and began dabbing at the sweat building up around his neck, discoloring his uniform collar.

"What now, sir?" the deck officer asked.

"Now we wait. Once the fleet has passed out of range, I'll order our tubes unloaded and allow the Balboan to leave."

"And if he won't wait for that?"

The captain sighed. Yes, he'd long since classified the Balboan as an enemy, yet he still had no great desire to destroy that enemy.

"Pray he does," the captain said.

SdL *Orca*, Shimmering Sea

"We can't sit here forever," Quijana announced, folding the piece of paper on which his orders were written and sliding it into a pocket. "I'm going to try something."

"Skipper?" asked Aleman.

"Start letting the rubbers in the ballast tanks chill. We'll liquefy the ammonia and sink. As we sink I want to use the dive planes to glide."

"But our orders are to use the clicker when we move?"

Quijana smiled. "No, actually, our orders were to use the clicker whenever moving under engine power. We won't be . . . mostly . . . just enough jet to keep us gliding."

The process of boiling the ammonia to expand the "condom" to force water out of the tanks made a little noise, though less than a normal submarine made pumping air in or out. Chilling the ammonia, on the other hand, made virtually none, since the only process used was to cut the flow of power to the heating elements. This cut, they cooled. With them cooling, the ammonia naturally reverted to a liquid state. With that, the "condoms" collapsed under the water pressure, letting the tanks flood. The sub began to sink, in utter silence.

It began to pass through the thermal layer to the ocean level in which rode the *Diamant*. The Gallic sub took no notice. Continuing on downward, through the layer, the *Orca* twisted her dive planes in opposite direction and began to turn back in the direction from which it had come. Because it was natural to drive, fly, or dive forward, it also moved closer to the *Charlemagne*, even as it made its very slow turn. As it did, just before its turn became noticeable, one of its dive planes aligned at right angles, briefly, with the sonar from the hunting helicopter's sonobuoy.

S806 *Diamant*, Shimmering Sea

The captain's face went white and his eyes opened wide at the news from the underwater telephone. "Dear God, she's still closing on the carrier and we didn't hear a thing." The captain was torn with indecision. Still, he was by trade a hunter and a killer, even if that hunting and killing had, so far, been purely theoretical. His indecision lasted but a moment.

"Ping the enemy vessel now. Continuous. Weapons, as soon as you have a firing solution open fire. Kill that sub."

Under the sonar barrage of *Diamant*, closer to the

same ocean level, very powerful, and much more discriminating, *Orca* stood out clearly.

"Target is found, Captain," said sonar.

"Range and bearing to target entered."

Weapons was only a few moments slower in reporting, "Fire control. Firing solution is ready. Torpedoes are ready, one programmed to go direct, the other three to bracket the target and veer inward."

"All tubes in sequence; Shoot!"

"Unit One away. Running straight and normal. Good wire."

SdL *Megalodon*, Shimmering Sea, Terra Nova

Charlemagne was just ahead, five kilometers. They couldn't hear it through the hull, not at this depth, but Auletti had it firm on the sonar. At the current speed of the carrier it would pass almost directly overhead within the next six minutes.

"You sure this is a good test, Skipper?" Aleman asked. His tone of voice made it clear he was dubious.

"Sure," Chu answered, "why not?"

"Because *Orca* drew the escorts away."

"Not all of them. There are enough here for a test and we *did* go right under that Amethyst class's nose."

Aleman nodded. "That's true, I suppose. Even so—"

Auletti interrupted. "Skipper, the frog sub just pinged the *Orca*! Continuous pinging . . . oh, shit, she fired! *Orca*'s returning fire with a supercavitating torpedo! I've got . . . JESUS!" Auletti pulled the headphones from his head and cupped his ears with the pain of multiamplified noise assaulting his eardrums.

S806 *Diamant*, Shimmering Sea, Terra Nova

The supercavitator was much faster than the more conventionally propelled torpedoes launched by the *Diamant*. Flying, for all practical purposes, in a vapor bubble created by a combination of its own speed and the shape of its nose, it closed the five-and-a-half kilometer range to the Gallic sub in just at one minute. Guiding by sonar from the *Orca* and vectoring itself by thrusting out small fins just past the gaseous supercavitation envelope, it reached the *Diamant* and detonated at a point very near and just forward of where the sail met the hull. The resulting shock wave breached that hull, allowing very high pressure water to burst inside.

The captain knew he, his crew, and his boat were dead as soon as he saw the wave of water coming for him. Pressure built up almost instantly to the point of agony. The flooding being more forward than aft, the *Diamant*'s nose sank quickly to point at the ocean floor. Crew, though by this point few, if any, were aware of it or much of anything else, were thrown from their feet and down into the collecting mass of water.

Crew farther back were likewise catapulted from their feet and tossed against bulkheads. One of them, known but to God, managed to get a watertight door shut after of the hull breach. This didn't matter in the slightest as, without control, the submarine continued its plummet into the depths. At a point in time, that depth exceeded the hull's rating. It collapsed. The pressure, thus the temperature, of the air inside shot up so much and so rapidly that it, and anything it surrounded that was combustible, ignited.

The death shriek of the *Diamant* could be heard halfway across the ocean.

SdL *Orca*, Shimmering Sea, Terra Nova

Yermo had had enough warning to remove the headphones from over his ears before the *Orca*'s torpedo exploded. He replaced them immediately after the shudder that ran through sea and ship told him it was safe to do so. Thus, he heard the death of the *Diamant* clearly.

"Poor bastards," he muttered, voicing the thoughts of every man of *Orca*'s crew.

Sympathy, however, was short-lived, mainly because the Gallic sub had gotten off four torpedoes before the *Orca* had fired. With their main guidance platform—*Diamant*, with its greater computational power and better sonar—now gone, the torpedoes were on their own.

"One," said Yermo, "two . . . three . . . four fish in the water, Skipper. Marking them one through four. They're pinging and hunting independently." The sonar man forced a degree of calm into his voice he in no way felt.

"Deceptive countermeasures," ordered Quijana.

The defense station pressed a button to release a small pod from the hull. It began to rise like a cork. Once it was about three hundred feet above the still passively diving sub, the pod let in a minor quantity of sea water, which reacted with a chemical inside to release a massive cloud of bubbles. The pod also generated a major magnetic and electronic signature on the chance that a pursuing torpedo might be MAE-NAD (Magnetic And ElectroNic Anomaly Detector) equipped and proximity fused.

"Two of the fish have locked onto the pod, Skipper," Yermo announced. "I make them as one and four. Two—two and three—are still hunting, and..." Again, Yermo pulled his headphones away from his ears as twin explosions rocked the water and the sub. "I guess they *are* MAENAD equipped."

Yes, Quijana mentally agreed, *since the pod's too small to hit and the bubble cloud too insubstantial. Proximity fused, based off the MAENAD or sonar return. Think clearly, Miguel, think clearly if ever you did.*

Quijana's eyes searched again over the screen mounted forward.

"Right side screen, vertical display," he ordered. After a brief pause for the operations man to enter the command, the right third of the screen changed color from light blue to green. The green also showed the thermal layer the sub had passed through, in a still darker green. Possible thermal layers, caused by volcanism and the cold current that ran through the Shimmering Sea, were marked in a green so light it was almost white. Both screens showed the explosions from the two torpedoes in red, as well as the known tracks of the two still hunting in dotted red lines preceded by torpedo icons. The icons radiated the active sonar pulsing of the hunting torpedoes.

Release another deception pod? Quijana wondered. *On a delay? We only had the two. And what about those surface frigates? They've got to know we took out their Amethyst class.*

D 466 *Portzmoguer*, Gallic Navy, Shimmering Sea

More clearly than any other ship in the battle group, the Gallic frigate *Portzmoguer* heard the engagement below and the death scream of the *Diamant*. The shocker had been that that destruction had been the result of a supercavitating torpedo. Like many another, the captain of the frigate had been extremely skeptical of the notion that the Balboan submarines had been unarmed.

But a supercavitator? Portzmoguer's monarch, Captain Casabianca, shuddered. *We can't hope to outrun one of those, and they're so fast we probably can't even react with countermeasures quickly enough.*

Of course, between ourselves, Horizon, *and* Cotentin *we can* drench *that submarine with more torpedoes than it can hope to dodge.*

Fat lot of good that will do us if she fires first, or even fires last but before we can destroy her. How many, I wonder, of those supercavitators does she carry? Bastard intel shits! Insisting the subs were unarmed!

The captain's musings were interrupted by the admiral's voice coming over the radio. Admiral Duguay sounded furious. His orders were simple. "Sink that submarine."

Already Casabianca could see three more helicopters rotoring in from *Charlemagne*. A quick glance at his own operations board showed that a fourth frigate, *Montcalm*, was joining the hunt, leaving only one to secure the carrier. He thought this questionable policy but, hoping to be an admiral himself, someday, chose to say nothing.

The problem, though, is that we can't hear that sub but it can almost certainly hear us. Fortunately, the carrier is a good distance away.

On the plus side, she's still fairly close underneath. If she'd moved much, we'd have heard those irregularly cut gears again.

SdL *Megalodon*, Shimmering Sea, Terra Nova

Charlemagne was moving slowly ahead and towards the coast. *Meg* had no trouble keeping up with the carrier and being perfectly silent while doing so. Of course the carrier could burst into speed and lose the submarine if it chose to. Range from sub to ship was under two kilometers. Even at the slow headway she was making, and even with somewhat substandard Volgan sonar, *Charlemagne* stood out clear.

In *Meg's* control room, as Quijana had aboard *Orca*, Chu had ordered his main screen split for a vertical display.

Mixed bag, he thought, looking at it. *One of the Gallic torpedoes is searching upward; but the other is gradually spiraling down to where I think Orca's at. Our double hull and the cones that connect the two give pretty good scattering from active sonar, but if the torpedo comes close enough, it will see Quijana. And there's not a lot I can do about that.*

The frustration Chu felt at having a comrade under attack and being helpless to intervene caused a tight knot in the sub skipper's stomach.

I could attack Charlemagne, *and probably draw off her escorts hunting* Orca. *But that would let them know*

we've a sub that can sneak right through their screens.
Ruin the whole point of the exercise, that would. Shit.

SdL *Orca*, Shimmering Sea

The ocean floor below was far deeper than the sub's
even theoretical crush depth. There'd be no escape
in hiding among the clutter of sea bottom.

"The torpedo still hunting us just broke into our
level, Skipper," sonar announced.

Can't go down much; can't stay here.

"Inflate the rubbers, fore and aft," Quijana ordered.
"Just enough for a mild positive buoyancy. I want to
put the thermal layer between us and that torpedo.
Level off just after we pass the thermal."

"Aye, Skipper," helm answered. After a few minutes,
the nose-down angle the sub had taken on reversed
itself as the bow began to ascend. The movement was
so slow that, other than for the reversal, there was
no sense among the crew of ascending.

Another quick glance at the right side of the main
screen showed that the other torpedo, the one that
had gone high, was still patrolling in a spiral and still
actively pinging.

In some ways the screen was a distraction, pre-
senting, as it did, a three-dimensional problem in
two dimensions. Quijana closed his eyes and tried
to imagine the totality of the situation, with frigates hunting above, helicopters dipping above that, a
barrage of sensors having been placed between him
and the carrier, and probably another being dropped
somewhere by now.

If we hadn't taken out the sub, their primary effort would have been protecting the carrier. As is, and with us having dived so low, they probably think the carrier's safe enough. That means their major effort is going to be revenge. Well . . . I suppose I could understand that. The first barrage of sonabuoys was generally south. If they're putting one in now, it's probably north to keep us from heading to port and safety. So we head where? East or west, I think, but which?

West brings us nearer Santander; east there's not a decent port for two hundred miles. But we've got the endurance, easily, for either.

East or west? West or . . .

Yermo's voice was strained, if not shocked. "Skipper, the torpedo found us. Pinging like a bitch and making fifty knots for us. I make it impact in ninety seconds."

"Deception pod," Quijana ordered instantly. "Set for no delay. Dive! All dive!"

Torpedo Number Three, Shimmering Sea

What with the need to pack sonar, both active and passive, propulsive gear and fuel, fuses, MAENAD, controls, and—by no means least—explosive into the torpedo, the room left over for a brain left the thing something of an electronic moron. Even a moron, though, can sometimes be right.

Number three noted the greater sonar return from the pod's bubbles, the simulated engine noise, and the artificial magnetic and electronic signature. It noted them and ignored them. It already had a target and anything that seemed like a better one was likely to be false. Still pinging happily at finding its purpose in life, torpedo three closed the distance to the *Orca*. *Pingpingping. Oh, joy! Oh, happiness!*

SdL *Orca*, Shimmering Sea

"Three's ignoring the pod, Skipper," Yermo said. "And Number Two is heading toward the pod. That brings it toward us."

Weapons' fingers moved over his station in a blur. "I can intercept," he announced.

"Do it!" Quijana ordered.

Weapons' finger lanced down, pressing a button to fire one of the remaining rear-facing torpedoes. A shudder ran through the sub as the torpedo launched itself, breaking through the plastic film that separated its distilled water from the salty sea. This was not a supercavitator, but a more conventional design, capable of, at most, fifty knots.

Weapons kept the torpedo on passive sonar only, with its point of aim set on the constantly pinging Gallic intruder. His hand wrapped around a stick control, not dissimilar to a computer gamer's, with a trigger to fire the wire-laying torpedo should it fail to detonate on its own when close enough to its target. He flipped off a red safety cap over the trigger, then straightened his finger.

Seconds later, Yermo said, "They heard the launch upstairs. We're getting active sonar from one of the ships and...another one has fired. At least two helicopters dipping now and I'm getting *plonks* as something is dropping passive sensors above us.

The sub suddenly lurched with two massive, nearly simultaneous explosions behind it.

"I *got* it!" Weapons exulted.

Quijana looked against at the main screen, now showing the pod, torpedo two aiming for it, and another torpedo just launched from the surface.

"Two has decided to ignore the pod," Yermo said. "I think it's got a lock on us. And . . . another surface ship has launched."

"Bring us down another two hundred," Quijana said.

"We've never tested it that deep, Skipper," Garcia warned. "If we go too much lower we'll hit the critical point for the ammonia. Do that and we can't push out the ballast."

Quijana pointed at the screen and said, "See those. If we don't lose them we're dead anyway."

D 466 *Portzmoguer*, Gallic Navy, Shimmering Sea, Terra Nova

With all the noise going on below, the frigate had only an uncertain idea of where the Balboan submarine really was. It showed the most amazing ability to maneuver without its engines. The captain was fairly sure they were diving and rising, and using that motion to glide with the dive planes.

Could it get as much as a ten or twelve to one glide path ratio? Casabianca wondered. *That could put it two or more kilometers away from our last sighting and with no more sound than comes from breaking through a thermal layer. And that's not much. Twelve to nineteen square kilometers of ocean to hide in, too.*

Maybe more if we didn't have a perfect lock on it to begin with.

Maybe if we blanketed the sea, launch nearly every-thing we have, all at once, we might get it. Fire a pattern of Ulysses rocket launched torpedoes...maintain guidance via digital link to the buoys they leave at the surface and through the wires they drag behind them. We could do that. Of course, one might break its wire and go hunting another but we've plenty of weapons and they've only the one submarine.

And I might suggest that to the admiral, if I had a better idea of where it is or even how deep it is.

SdL *Orca*, Shimmering Sea, Terra Nova

Quijana remembered the groaning of the metal on the various Volgan and Yamatan submarines on which he'd done a portion of his training. *Damned good thing for us the plastic doesn't make anything like that much noise.*

Even so, Quijana looked forward to where one of the crew had strung a piece of string across the control room at waist height. That string was almost touching the deck now. He thought, then, about the ocean pressing in from all sides. He remembered, too, the terrible moments after he'd been booted off the old *Trinidad*, just before it plunged into the side of the Salafi suicide ship in the straits of Nicobar. He could still feel the massive blow transmitted first through the water and quickly followed by the shock wave that came through the air.

Just so you know, God, I really don't want to die. If I ever said I wish I'd gone in with Trinidad, *I*

*didn't mean it. I'm scared and I could use Your help,
by the way.*

Yermo said, "Fish Two seems to have lost us, Skipper. It's started a spiraling search again."

"Keep close track, Sonar," Quijana ordered. "I want to pop back up above the layer *just* as Two drops below."

"Skipper?" Weapons asked.

"Yes?"

"I can try to take Two out with another torpedo."

Forcing down his fear, trying to think clearly, Quijana considered it, deciding, "No, not yet. If it's lost us for now, a launch will let it know where we are. And Two's only the most dangerous enemy out there." Again, he gestured at the screen. "There are at least four more."

D 466 *Portzmoguer*, Gallic Navy, Shimmering Sea, Terra Nova

"Ops," said Captain Casabianca, "review for me what we know and don't know about these subs. There's something I'm missing and it could be important."

Lieutenant of the Line Mortain thought for a moment, summing up his knowledge of the Meg class before saying, "About thirty-six to forty meters long, Captain. Teardrop shaped, X-form tail. Jet propulsors. Fuel cell powered. Crew of seventeen or eighteen, we think. We know now that it's armed, *well* armed. Dual hulled, with a thinner hydrodynamic hull over a much thicker pressure hull. We think—"

"Stop there for a minute," the captain said. "Sonar,

the torpedoes launched by *Diamant* used active sonar. Why couldn't they see the sub?"

The frigate's sonar man, a warrant officer, or "major," in the system of the Gallic Navy, rubbed his face for a moment and said, "We know the hull's plastic, Captain. Maybe it's some new plastic, or an old one with better than normal anechoic tiles."

Casabianca looked a question at Mortain. "No tiles, sir," the latter answered. "Not unless they're putting them on at sea and that—"

"Right. Unlikely." The captain turned his attention back to sonar. "Keep thinking," he said.

The sonar major rubbed at his face for a few moments, then shook his head and whispered, "No, that's a silly thought."

"Tell me this silly thought, major," the captain said.

"Well, sir . . . I read once that it would be possible to build an outer hull that was facetted, like some of those airplanes the Federated States uses. I read that this could cut return sonar down by a factor of one thousand."

"No good, Major," Mortain objected. "The same way we know there are no anechoic tiles we know there's no facetted fairing."

"Yes, sir," the major agreed. "But what if that outer hull is *really* transparent to sonar, and the facets, or something like them, are between the inner and the outer. Maybe they're what hold the two together."

"*Tres elegant,*" Mortain said, almost grudgingly. "And it would account for their invisibility to sonar, from some angles, at least."

"Okay, then, I'll buy that as a possibility," the captain said. "Keep going, Mortain. What else do we know?"

"Sir. We know they have an amazingly quiet method of pumping ballast. I can't imagine what it is."

"Yesss . . . yes," Casabianca agreed. "And that is how they're gliding, correct?"

"I think so, sir," Mortain answered.

"How's your math, Lieutenant?" the captain asked.

Mortain looked both puzzled and somewhat pleased. "Very good, sir. I took prizes in school."

"Excellent," the captain said, rubbing his hands together. "Now take the dimensions of the sub as we know them, and the shape. Plot back to and from known positions. Then figure out for me how big those dive planes are for it to be gliding as much as we know it is. From that, tell me how thick they are."

"Sir?"

"Because if they're big enough, Mortain, I think we might get a sonar return if we were positioned just right . . . or if somebody was. I just might risk an active ping from up here, from all of us if I can talk the admiral into it, to get a lock and fire."

SdL *Megalodon*, Shimmering Sea

Meg still tracked *Charlemagne*, which tracking was pulling them farther and farther from *Orca*'s lonely ordeal. Fortunately, the carrier was both slow moving and zigzagging. On the screen, and barring only the carrier and some of the torpedoes that were still hunting and which, therefore, still had fresh tracks, the other icons had taken on a faded aspect, indicating the lesser degree of certainty as to their locations and other aspects.

Chu shook his head and said, "Okay, enough is enough. We've proved we can get at the best the Taurans have to offer and track them at will without them having a clue. That mission's over. Helm?"

"Aye, Skipper."

"Bring us around one-eighty, drop below the layer, and head for the last known position for *Orca*. Make your speed six knots. Maybe we can get there in time to make a difference."

Chu's exec leaned over and whispered to him, "If they do take out *Orca*, it might be nice to toast that carrier in revenge."

"It's tempting, I agree," Chu answered. "Sadly, it's not our mission. No, that's not strong enough. It would be a *violation* of our mission."

Chu's exec scowled.

"I couldn't agree more," said the captain. "Even so, we can't do it."

"We're not *supposed* to do it. Remember what they say about forgiveness and permission."

SdL *Orca*, Shimmering Sea

Whether the torpedoes were out of juice or had simply gone inactive as a power-saving measure until their passive sensors picked up something interesting, neither Quijana nor Yermo knew. They did know that there were currently no torpedoes in the area actively moving or tracking. Even torpedo two, which had never reacquired the sub, was so far down they considered it more likely than not it was lost.

On the screen, both surface ships and torpedoes

had faded almost out of view. Even the sonobuoys dropped by helicopter and fixed wing craft had gone silent and began to fade. Given the ocean currents and the surface winds, Quijana wouldn't have bet a bottle of not very good beer as to where any of them were now.

"You know, Skipper," Garcia suggested, in a confidential whisper, "we could shut off the clicker and just move off."

"Against orders," Quijana said.

"Maybe not. We proved to them we could be found if we use our engines. They've probably figured out we're using buoyancy differential to glide. We sail off. They sit up there for a week or two and, when they never get our signal, assume we glided away."

Quijana chewed his lower lip uncertainly. "I've got to admit; it's tempting."

"Four knots, Skipper, and we're out of their search area in an hour and a quarter. We can always reestablish our presence by clicking once we get to where we met up with *Meg*, or—better—where Chu shut his clicker off."

It is *tempting*, Quijana thought. *Let me think about the bigger picture. They probably know we had two subs out. They'd have stopped paying attention to* Meg *when it was out on its "test dive" pretending to be the new sub. So they think there's only one here. Does that make sense? Yes, it does; because if they thought there were two of us they wouldn't act so confident once we took out that Amethyst class. No, they'd be shitting bricks right about now. That carrier would have turned away long since.*

We've got the layer between us and them. They're

not going to hear the propulsor jets from up there.
Hell, at four knots, they might not hear them if they
were down here with us.

"All right, XO; leave the clicker off. Four knots,
due east. But keep us bobbing and weaving as if we
were gliding just in case they spot us."

D 466 Portzmoguer, Gallic Navy, Shimmering Sea

Mortain looked embarrassed. "*Mon capitaine*, I am
sorry, but I can't be more exact than to say that the
dive planes are probably both big and fairly thick in
cross section. At least, without my books I can't be
more exact than that. We might pick them up on
active pinging, depending on how they're oriented
when we ping. Or . . . well . . . we might not."

"We have no *mon capitaine* in the Gallic Navy,"
Casabianca corrected. "We have 'my ass' and 'my
God,' but no 'my captain.'"

Mortain looked sheepish. "Yes, sir. Sorry, sir."

The captain rubbed a sweating forehead for a
moment, then said, "Get me the admiral and the other
frigate captains on the horn." Turning to Mortain,
he pointed a finger and added, "And you go figure a
pattern for four frigates to best blanket an area with
active sonar, knowing what we know about the enemy."

CHAPTER TWENTY-FIVE

We must distinguish between such a system and what at first glance would appear to be its antecedents on Old Earth. True, whether in ancient Athens or ancient republican Rome, there appears to have been a close correlation between military service and political power.

That appearance, however, is somewhat deceptive. The true correlation was between wealth and political power. The military power was a symptom of the wealth as the more affluent citizenry were required to provide their own military equipment in accordance with their means; a sort of proto graduated income tax. Other, less wealthy citizens served, but generally speaking had their political power reduced in accordance not with their military-moral contribution, which was always substantial for all but the extremely poor, but with their limited wealth.

Moreover, the ancients practiced true conscription, not the mere reminder we have suggested here. True conscription, fairly and universally applied, can produce decent fighting forces, certainly, but fails to specially identify those who would voluntarily serve society even at cost. Thus, conscript systems fail

to identify civic virtue, the more so as civic virtue
becomes the more rare.

Even so, —

> —Jorge y Marqueli Mendoza, *Historia y
> Filosofia Moral,* Legionary Press, Balboa,
> Terra Nova, copyright AC 468

Anno Condita 479
Headquarters, Tauran Union Security Force-Balboa, Building 59, Fort Muddville, Transitway Area, Balboa

The air in the operations center was thick with anger
and with loss.

Janier's face was pale and drawn. The Gallic Navy
only *had* seven attack submarines, one of those getting long in the tooth, and to lose one of the newest,
the most modern...

If the Navy tries to pin this on me, merde, *I'm
screwed.*

"Are the squids absolutely certain the *Diamant* was
destroyed?" he asked of de Villepin.

De Villepin turned to Surcouf, standing by his
side. The naval officer looked, if anything, even more
distressed than Janier. *Well, I can understand that,*
de Villepin thought. *Boy likely had comrades aboard
the* Diamant. *At least friends of friends. And that was
his service's boat. The question though...*

"No doubt at all, General," Surcouf answered,
distantly, as if awakening from a bad dream. "No
doubt..."

"But...but *how*?"

"They had torpedoes, Volgan-made probably; super-cavitators. We didn't know they had them," Surcouf answered. "I'm not sure how they got them, or when, or where they could have mounted them. But that they have them there is no doubt."

"And they went hunting for the pride of our fleet armed like this? Do the madmen *want* to bring down the entire weight of the Tauran Union on their little brown shoulders? Does this mean war, now?"

De Villepin shook his head. "I don't think so. Other than support to the forces they have hunting guerillas down in La Palma, there's absolutely nothing unusual going on. It's as if the Balboans are unaware that we're hunting their submarine."

"Could it be a rogue submarine, then?" Janier asked.

Surcouf answered, "No. There are two submarines at sea, and while one of them went to intercept the *Charlemagne*, the other is likely off somewhere in the Shimmering Sea, nowhere near the action. No," he repeated, "I think this is just a test of their equipment and ours . . . a test that's gotten out of hand. Badly out of hand."

"I don't think Carrera knows what's happening, just as Surcouf has said," de Villepin finished.

"Who fired first?" the general asked.

"The people I spoke to tried to downplay it," Surcouf answered, "but, based on what they did say and what they didn't, I think we did."

"And they *still* destroyed our ship?"

"Boat," Surcouf corrected, absently. "Yes, we fired first but their torpedo was much, much faster."

"And they're still alive?"

"We think so. The admiral has four frigates hunting

it, plus most of *Charlemagne*'s helicopters. He, at least, believes they're still alive."

"What if we let them go?" Janier asked. "Will we look like fools, being bested by peasants?"

De Villepin said, "I've wondered about that. I don't think we have to worry. Whether Carrera wants a war with us or not—and he very well might—he wants it on his terms, with us as the plain aggressor. He *has* to have that, to ensure the Federated States stays neutral or comes in on his side. A simple sub duel, under questionable circumstances, wouldn't provide that moral cover and might make the FSC think hard about the kind of monster they're letting grow to maturity here, should he advertise the event.

"No, General, I think he'll swear that crew to secrecy and let the whole thing be forgotten. Assuming the crew escapes, of course, and that we say nothing."

"Forget that, sir," Surcouf said. "The . . . the admiral has his blood up. He'll stop hunting that submarine when Hell freezes or the sub's dead."

"We'll see about that," Janier said. "Connect me to the *Charlemagne*."

SdL *Megalodon*, Shimmering Sea, Terra Nova

"We're still in range. Take out the carrier, Chu," the exec said. "That will get those frigates off Quijana's ass, if only to rescue the sailors floundering in the water."

Chu looked down at the deck, isolated from the hull by shock absorbers, the better not to transmit internal noise. *Of course, he's right that it would, but at the cost of blowing our little secret. Then again, does that matter? Carrera only has us, so far as I know anyway, for the purpose of taking out that carrier... well, that one and another and a couple or three from the Zhong. The surprise wouldn't last past our first successful attack anyway. What difference if it's now or in a couple of years? They'll still be shy a carrier. And, hell, in a couple of years the secret of how quiet we really are might be blown anyway.*

Ah, but then there is the timing issue. A carrier sunk now might be the same as a carrier sunk then... as far as the size of the enemy fleet goes... but the timing would be all wrong... could be anyway. I just don't know. I only know...

"We've got our orders, Ibarra, and you have yours. Now shut up and quit pestering me."

"Fuck. I trust that *you'll* be the one delivering the next of kin notices."

"We don't know there'll be a need for any next of kin notices. Now—"

"I know. I know. Shut up and quit pestering you."

Headquarters, Tauran Union Security Force–Balboa, Building 59, Fort Muddville, Transitway Area, Balboa

Whatever it was Admiral Duguay said to Janier over the phone, it was enough to turn the general's face ashen.

Replacing the phone on its receiver, Janier said simply, "He refuses to listen. He says if there's an attack here because he kills that submarine that will be *my* problem. He said other things, too."

"Do we mobilize the troops then?" asked de Villepin.

Still ashen-faced—*What* did *the admiral say to him*, wondered de Villepin—Janier shook his head. "No, no. Let's not let our actions notify the Balboans as to what is going on at sea.

"And now leave me in peace and quiet for the next hour."

D 466 *Portzmoguer*, Gallic Navy, Shimmering Sea

The bridge was hushed. Every man present knew Casabianca was guessing, frankly. They also knew his guess had a few things going for it. He knew where the enemy below could go for succor. He had a pretty good idea of its maximum speed while gliding, as it presumably was. He had a point of origin to trace from.

"East or west," the captain said softly. "One or the other. I chose east. If I'm right, maybe we get him. If I'm wrong..."

"Sir," Mortain said, taking a telephonic radio receiver away from the side of his head, "*Montcalm*, *Horizon*, and *Cotentin* are on station. The admiral says it's your command. Oh, and Captain Bertin of *Montcalm* is bitching about it, too."

"Bertin always bitches," answered Casabianca. The captain turned towards his sonar major. "Major, on Lieutenant Mortain's command. Weapons, stand by. Mortain?"

"Sir?"

"On radio...command...continuous...*Ping!*"

In seconds the major announced, "I've got them."

"Fire!"

BdL *Orca*, Shimmering Sea, Terra Nova

"Skipper," said Yermo to Quijana, "they're boxing us."

Quijana looked up from the deck to the screen toward the boat's bow. It was true enough, with four surface ships taking up position approximately to the four cardinal directions of where *Orca* had been perhaps half an hour ago.

"They don't hear us," Quijana said, uncertainly. "If they did they wouldn't be so far out. They'd—"

The captain's words were cut off as the submarine was suddenly deluged with the sound of four separate sonar emitters all going to continuous *ping*.

Yermo tried to ignore the sounds, listening intently for the much more ominous, "Oh, shit, I've got a surface launch . . . no, two . . . three . . . four. Each ship's fired once."

"Fired what?" Quijana asked.

"The Gallic frigates usually mount Ulysses anti-submarine rockets," Quijana's XO said. "That means they'll be here . . ."

"*Plonk,*" said Yermo, looking straight up. He squeezed a headphone to his ear. "*Plonk, plonk . . . plonk.*"

Do NOT panic, Quijana ordered himself. *Besides, the thing you're most afraid of is being afraid . . . and you don't have much longer for that to happen, now do you, Miguel?*

Aloud, he said, "Friends, we're dead. But we're going to sell ourselves dear. Weapons?"

"Aye"—*gulp*—"aye, sir."

"We've still got two supercavitators?"

"Yes, sir, two."

"Good. Fire one on self-guidance at target three, the other at target...ummm...two. Fire when ready. Once they're away fire two standard torpedoes at targets one and four. Guide those yourself to the extent you can. Stand by to drop guidance on those and guide the close-in defense torpedoes. Helm?!"

"Aye, sir."

"Turn on the clicker. Flank speed ahead."

"The clicker?" the XO, Garcia, looked aghast.

"We're dead anyway," Quijana said. "But the *secret* can be preserved."

The exec started to object, then admitted, also aloud, "Yeah, you're right."

Quijana nodded. His XO then added, "Miguel, I never believed before that old Pedraz booted you off the *Trinidad*. I thought you jumped. I believe it now."

D 466 *Portzmoguer*, Gallic Navy, Shimmering Sea

Mortain went white, not because the counterattack from the Balboan sub was unexpected, but because of the speed of the torpedo coming for his ship. That wasn't unexpected either; it was still shocking. Bending over the sonar screen, he simply couldn't bring himself to credit the way the supercavitator ate up the kilometers.

The "major" running the sonar station whistled and said, "Dear God, I don't think we can escape it."

"Head straight towards it," ordered *Portzmoguer*'s captain.

The helmsman turned his head and eyes in the direction of the captain. "*Towards* it, sir?" He sounded as if he thought that the stupidest order he'd ever heard.

"The things are so noisy they can't use their own passive sonar," the captain explained. "They slow down at a preset point and ping, then adjust and start moving again. If we're not in a position for it to get a bounce from us, there's a fair chance we can lose it altogether. And stop wasting fucking time. Do it! And, Mortain, pass that to the"—the captain looked briefly at his operations board—"pass it to the *Montcalm*."

D 469 *Montcalm*, Gallic Navy, Shimmering Sea, Terra Nova

"Tell that stupid bastard aboard *Portzmoguer* to stuff it," snarled the captain. "Helm, hard away from the torpedo. We'll outrun the bitch! It's got to have limited fuel."

Montcalm heeled over as the helm applied full rudder to turn the ship away from the oncoming torpedo. Men all over the ship either swayed on their feet or fell on their rear ends. Down by the galley a cook, *Matelot breveté*—or ordinary seaman—Dupre, managed both to keep his feet and to keep upright the tray of sandwiches he was bringing to the bridge. The cook was just congratulating himself when the frigate came out of its turn and took off at flank speed. Not expecting this, Dupre slammed his head into a bulkhead and bounced to his arse as the sandwich tray went flying.

Leaving the sandwiches behind, Dupre began to stagger topside to give the bridge crew a piece of his mind. *Imagine the nerve; treating a chef like this. What do they think; that we're an Anglic vessel?*

❖   ❖   ❖

"A stern chase is a long chase," so it was said. It was even true when first said, in the day of sail on Old Earth. But when the chaser has a speed nearly six times greater than the quarry, and the quarry's less than ten kilometers away, a stern chase is likely to be very short indeed. When that quarry has to waste time turning about . . .

Captain Bertin stood over the sonar board, watching the torpedo eat up the distance between the two. *Hmmmf. Maybe that asshole Casablanca was right.* He sighed. *I so hate it when he's right. Why my sister married him, I simply can't fathom.*

Suddenly *Montcalm*'s own sonar major and the captain exclaimed in surprise. The torpedo had stopped. *Perhaps it ran out of fuel. Hah! I'll show that bastard of a brother in law who's right . . .*

The exultant shout coming to Bertin's lips cut off as the torpedo began pinging furiously, only to stop that and commence moving. It rapidly accelerated to a blistering two hundred knots.

Bertin raced topside. If he was going to die he wanted to *see* what would kill him. He didn't have long to wait.

The sea underneath *Montcalm* was suddenly lit by a bright orange flash. The flash itself lasted but a moment before being replaced with a green and black and sea foam circle of Hell, rising to both sides of the ship. Bertin felt his frigate lurch upward from the center. Driven to his knees on the hard steel deck, he felt as much as heard the tortured metal below bending with the force of the blow. Water, moving faster than the ship's upward twist, blew upward along both sides of the hull.

As the pressure underneath was relieved, both by collapse of the cooling explosive gasses and by the movement of water upward to either side of the hull,

Montcalm found itself supported on the two ends by water, and with no support below. The hull, which had so recently been half broken by the upward pressure in the center now found itself unsupported in the center by either water or its own structural strength. It collapsed into the hole thus created, continuing the work of destruction. To add injury to insult, water rushing back into the vacant space met the sundered hull halfway down into the vacuum. This blow was the end; *Montcalm* lifted again and split in two.

Bertin found himself floating, supported by an arm encircling his chest under his own arms. The two ends of his former command floated, points up, a few hundred meters away. Even as Bertin watched, the bow section slipped under the waves.

"Who? What?" he asked, groggily.

"Chef Dupre," came the answer from behind.

"How many got out?"

"Not many, *mon capitaine*. I see only a few heads bobbing in the water. I am taking you to one of the auto-inflating lifeboats."

Automatically, Bertin corrected, "We have no 'mon capitaines' in the navy. We have 'my God' and—"

"And 'my ass,' yes, I know, sir," Dupre finished.

D466 *Portzmoguer*, Shimmering Sea, Terra Nova

"All stop," Casabianca ordered. "Hard port rudder." He, along with every man of the crew, was nudged in the direction of the bow and to the right, as power was cut to the propeller and the ship began a turn.

"Do you really think, Captain...?" Mortain asked.

"I am betting, Lieutenant, that that supercavitator, having been fired from fairly deep, will be too far down..."

"She's passing underneath us," Sonar announced.

"The next few seconds will tell," said Casabianca.

"And she's still going," Sonar amended.

The captain pointed at the weapons station.

"I am tracking, Captain. When she stops to ping..."

"Fire one Ulysses," Casabianca said.

On the foredeck a boxy looking device, partitioned into six sections, two of them empty, rotated to the bearing of the Balboan supercavitator. The box elevated to fifteen degrees, then washed the deck with fire and smoke as its rocket took off, bearing a torpedo to intercept the other.

Casabianca watched the missile *cum* torpedo off, then turned his direction of view over the starboard bow where a brace of helicopters were dropping self-guiding torpedoes ahead of the known location of the enemy sub.

SdL 2, *Orca*, Shimmering Sea, Terra Nova

Quijana could read the forward screen as well as any man aboard. *Orca* now had not only two torpedoes in pursuit, another two had *plonked* in ahead and to either side.

I'd take some satisfaction in the knowledge that we took a lot of killing, he thought, *except that in a few minutes I'm going to be too dead to feel anything. I do take some satisfaction in taking out two for one.*

Hmmm. Confession time? Maybe so.

"Garcia?" he asked.

"Yes, Skipper."

"I've got to clear my soul on this. Pedraz booted me, I didn't jump. But I can't say I was sorry he did. I was relieved."

The exec, Garcia, just nodded. Why not? Any man might feel the same.

"Goodbye, Miguel," the XO said, right at the end.

SdL 1, *Megalodon*, Shimmering Sea, Terra Nova

Chu had the main screen focused in close on the unfolding drama. With all the torpedoes flying around the ocean, in some cases, the supercavitators—literally, it was the only way to distinguish.

About half those torpedoes fired so far had lost their prey to its uniquely stealthy characteristics. These searched the sea in spiral patterns, but too far away to be of much concern to *Meg* and her crew.

Hope surged for a moment as one of *Orca's* small defensive torpedoes took out one of its pursuers. It did so again as one of the Gallic torpedoes destroyed itself and another. Those three, however, were not enough. One of the shots dropped by helicopter found the small submarine, exploding so near the hull that Chu and company couldn't tell the difference between it and a contact hit. Another came in from the rear and likewise detonated. After that it was nothing but breakup noise as the remnants of the *Orca* plunged for the bottom of the ocean.

"Weapons, prepare two shots for the carrier," Chu

said, bitterness in his voice. "Route the fire command to my chair."

"Aye, sir."

Chu's XO, Ibarra, shook his head and placed one hand over the fire controls. "No, Skipper, don't do it."

"Why?"

The exec smiled, sadly, answering, "While it might still have done *Orca* some good, I'd have said, 'Damn the carrier, and every frog aboard.' Now?" The exec shook his head. "Skipper, Miguel never turned off his clicker. Think about that. Even at the very last moment it was 'mission first,' as it should have been. You shoot now, let them know how frigging quiet we *really* are, you throw away a part of what the men aboard *Orca* gave their lives for."

"We'll get 'em, Skipper, never fear," Ibarra said. "But we'll do it at the time that's best for *us*, not for them."

"All right then, we'll wait," Chu agreed. "But we're going to shadow that bitch for a few days, and if war has broken out above and we can tell it has, I'm killing it."

CHAPTER TWENTY-SIX

—though the lessons of ancient Rome, Greece, and Sparta are not perfectly supportive of the timocratic ideals put forth in this work, we should not lose sight of the valid lessons they do have to teach or illustrate. Among these is that only an armed citizenry, and one which is trained to arms, has a hope of maintaining its own political power and freedom in any degree whatsoever, that they can only gain any degree of political power and freedom through either the use or the threat of use of arms, or the withholding of those arms when the state needs them, and that, whatever their stated intent, those who would deprive the people of arms inevitably also deprive them of political power and freedom.

—Jorge y Marqueli Mendoza, *Historia y Filosofia Moral,* Legionary Press, Balboa, Terra Nova, copyright AC 468

Anno Condita 472
Executive Mansion, Hamilton, FD, Federated
States of Columbia, Terra Nova

The Shimmering Sea was, as far as the Federated
States and her Navy were concerned, *their* pond. Oh,
the Taurans could come in and play, but they'd do so—
had *done* so—with an FSN nuclear sub shadowing
them from a distance. Unseen, unheard, the FSS *Oliver
Meredith* had tracked the Gauls long before they'd passed
the island of Cienfuegos. The *Meredith* had recorded
the whole engagement between *Orca* and the Gauls.

That record, digitally sent to Hamilton and reduced
to script, now sat on the desk of the president of the
Federated States, Karl Schumann (Progressive), brought
there by none other than his secretary of war, James
K. Malcolm.

"The Gauls fired first?" was Schumann's only real
question.

"Yes," Malcolm admitted, reluctantly, "but they had
reasons. That sub was attempting to get into a firing
position against their carrier. After being spotted. That
indicated hostile intent."

"That's speculation," Schumann answered calmly.
"Moreover, it's speculation colored by your affection
for the Gauls. Though why you have that affection
after they let us down in Pashtia, I admit I do not
quite understand, James."

Malcolm opened his mouth as if to speak, then
suddenly closed it again and went silent. Though
silent, he thought, *What is it? The fucking spics in
Balboa do a mission and let Schumann take credit for*

*it and he suddenly takes their side? Or is he afraid
they'll reveal the truth after he took credit for it?
Whatever it is, he should be slapping the Balboans
silly and he won't.*

Far worse, from Malcolm's point of view, Schumann
picked up his phone and dialed a number. In French
not quite so good as Malcolm's own, Schumann said,
simply, "About the Balboans, Mr. Ambassador? Tell
your country to back the fuck off."

Sub Pens, *Puerto Lindo,* Balboa, Terra Nova

Fernandez, Fosa, and Carrera, all three, were waiting
inside the concrete pen as Chu climbed out of the
hatch atop the sail and descended the brow to meet
them. Alongside, a crew was in the process of fitting
the new boat, name still undetermined, with diving
planes and torpedo pods.

"What happened?" Carrera asked.

"We penetrated their screen," Chu answered, "but
the frogs killed *Orca.*"

"Was it *Orca* that destroyed the Tauran frigate?"
asked Fosa.

Chu nodded his head, wearily. "Yes, sir, the frigate
and a frog sub we made as being an Amethyst class.
The frog fired first. *Orca* had to fire in self defense. And
later, Miguel only shot up the frigate after a bunch of
them had him boxed in and were salvoing torpedoes
on his ass.

"We hung around shadowing their carrier in case
war broke out. It didn't seem to have happened, so
we came home."

"No," Carrera said, "war didn't break out. I'm not sure why, really."

"I'm sure," said Fernandez. At Carrera's raised eyebrow he added, "I've got my sources, Patricio. Their general, Janier, isn't ready. He even tried to call off the pursuit of *Orca*. And apparently the FSC is not happy with the Gallic 'allies,' either."

Carrera didn't enquire further. Fernandez had his sources. He did say to Chu, "It was still touch and go for a while. There was a Maracaiban fishing trawler about thirty miles from where the Gallic frigate went down. It heard the automatic distress signal and went in to assist. The Gauls sank it before it could get close. Maybe they thought it was a Q ship. Anyway, big stink around the whole of *Colombia Latina*."

"How are they explaining away the lost frigate?" Chu asked.

"They're not. Their story is that it was an unprovoked attack by us. Our story is that it was an unprovoked attack by them to which our sub responded in self defense."

"It was," Chu said.

"I know," Carrera agreed, "but—"

"—but," Fernandez finished, "since you're the only one who can prove that, and since, *officially*, you weren't anywhere near there..."

"It doesn't really matter, anyway," said Carrera. "People who want to believe our story would, even if they had proof of the Gauls' version of events. People who want to believe the Gauls would, even if I had you swear to them on a stack of Bibles that they fired first. There's so much information these days, and so much of it is conflicting, that people have grown jaded and simply believe whatever their prejudices tell them to. Hell, language itself is losing its ability to inform or persuade...or even to communicate."

Chu scratched his head through long-unwashed hair. "Yeah."

He then remembered something he'd been wanting to tell Carrera and Fosa for days. "There at the end, sirs, there's something happened you need to know about."

"What's that?" Fosa asked.

Chu's voice was full of admiration as he said, "Toward the end, *Orca* put on a burst of speed to try to evade some of the torpedoes coming for it."

Fosa shrugged. *Yeah? So?*

"Well...Quijana apparently turned on his clicker when he upped his speed."

This time it was Carrera who shrugged, while Fosa's face was lit by a smile.

Fernandez understood, too, being a man who worked with secrets. "He kept the secret," he explained to Carrera. "He kept it at the cost—certainly the risk—of his life."

Fernandez *ahemed*. "Speaking of secrets, Patricio, if you don't mind, I've got to go look into something in *Ciudad* Balboa."

Headquarters, Tauran Union Security Force–Balboa, Building 59, Fort Muddville, Transitway Area, Balboa

In theory, Legate Pigna was on leave. In fact, he'd gone into the jungle with a fishing pole and a small pack, come out somewhere else without the pole and in disguise, then been picked up and whisked to Janier's headquarters for final coordination. It was the fourteenth meeting concerning the pressing matter of getting rid of Carrera since Pigna had attended the first at the Hotel *Rustico*.

The legate emerged from the unmarked, Tauran Union-owned sedan in the shadows under the arched entrance to the main quadrangle. De Villepin met him there and hustled him through a door that led to stairs that, in turn, led directly to Janier's office suite, bypassing even the general's secretary. This was to the good as de Villepin was beginning to develop some doubts about that one. That she was passing on information to someone, he had no doubt of. But whether that someone was his opposite number, Fernandez, Wallis, the ambassador from the Federated States, or someone in the office of Rocaberti, the rump president, he couldn't say and hadn't been able to discover. It was even vaguely possible that the woman was reporting back to some one or another of the unelected bureaucrats who ran the Tauran Union. Worst of all was the possibility that she was reporting to the Gallic Navy, but de Villepin considered this somewhat unlikely.

A representative of Rocaberti's office was waiting for Pigna when he arrived, as was Arias, the senior of the policemen that still reported to the old president, and another man Pigna didn't know at all but who was introduced as Janier's Staff Judge Advocate, Commandant Boissieu.

At Janier's hand wave, de Villepin began, "The worst part of our little program is that everyone is to a greater or lesser extent infiltrated and compromised.

Thus, anything we may plan or do beyond the simplest is likely to tip our hand well before we are ready. It goes almost without saying—but I will say it, anyway—that if we are discovered beforehand it could be a disaster for everyone.

"Fortunately, our opponents are about as well infiltrated as we are and I can say with considerable confidence that none of Carrera's people know as of yet that we are planning to depose him and Parilla."

"How do you know that, de Villepin?" Janier asked.

"I know it," the intelligence officer replied, "because Fernandez's deputy is on our payroll and *his* secretary *cum* mistress—Barletta's, I mean, not Fernandez's—likewise reports to me. Something of this magnitude, if known, would have sent ripples all through their force. Of ripples, other than those explainable by other events, there has been not a one."

"Nobody knows about my part, outside of ourselves," Pigna insisted. "And I know *this* because I have taken no one into my confidence. Every order has been prepared by myself. Except for a couple of close relatives I will inform only at the end, my men will think they are following Carrera's orders, passed on through me . . . for as long as that illusion holds. Speaking of which . . ."

"I have the team ready to seize Carrera," the policeman said. "All composed of men who hate his very guts; some are veterans of his legions who either left under a cloud or feel cheated in some way. They have been trained by the Gauls as a hostage rescue force. There is little difference between a hostage rescue force and a kidnapping force." The policeman looked directly at Boissieu and asked, "Do you have the warrants?"

The lawyer nodded, replying, "Not only the old ones from the Cosmopolitan Criminal Court, for war crimes and crimes against humanity committed in Pashtia and Sumer, but also new ones from the Global Court of Justice for both men for participation in narcotrafficking."

"That's important," Janier said, "because while the Federated States, even under the Progressives, is fairly unsympathetic to the war crimes issue, they are death on drug running. You will produce evidence of drug running?"

"The best that can be procured," said Arias, "to include extensive samples which will be found on the grounds of Carrera's home and the new presidential palace."

"And the Navy of Gaul will prevent reinforcement from the island," said Janier, "and from the south. One battalion will seal off the road from the interior and another force the road from Cristobal. *If* I am satisfied with the rest of your operational planning." He looked directly at Pigna. "Show me your target list and operational matrix."

With a grin, Pigna withdrew from his lightly soiled pack a very small portable computer drive.

"I am satisfied," said Janier. In fact, though, he was more than satisfied, he was *impressed*. Whatever course Pigna had taken in overthrowing a government had obviously been world class. "But there is one other thing I need you to do." He looked directly at Arias as he said so.

"And that would be, General?"

"One of my subordinates, the Castilian, Muñoz-Infantes, is intensely disloyal, to me, to this command,

and to the Tauran Union. For political reasons I won't bore you with, I can't get rid of him. So I need him kidnapped and killed, and the blame pinned on Carrera's legions."

"That will leave me shorthanded for the other two grabs we must make," Arias objected.

"Nonetheless, it is a condition for my support. I will have one or two people from his unit to help."

"It's pretty dirty, too," said Pigna.

The Gaul shrugged, "So?"

Quarters 39, Clementine Road, Fort Williams, Balboa Transitway Area

Chapayev had become something of a weekly dinner guest at *Coronel* Muñoz-Infantes' residence. It was even perhaps fair to say that he and the Castilian colonel had become friends.

I wish, thought Chapayev, *that as much could be said for his daughter, Maria. She's barely civil and I really don't understand that. I've heard of love at first sight, even—to my cost—experienced it. But hate at first sight? That seems unfair.*

Is it because the coronel *and I talk too much shop over dinner? I like to talk shop. So does he. Where would be the harm in that? And she grew up in the Castilian Army. Surely none of this is over her head.*

"So you were too young for Pashtia, Victor?" Muñoz observed. "I'm surprised your *Duque* didn't bring you over during his campaign there."

"Standing policy, sir," Chapayev replied. Though he'd never found a really suitable "horizontal dictionary," his

Spanish—especially his military Spanish—had gotten quite good through sheer dint of study and practicing with his boys. "The only Volgans from our regiment who were allowed in with the legions were the ones who spoke the language, one of the languages, and had good contacts there. Otherwise...well...there were a lot of hard feelings still and no love lost between us. The less we saw of each other, generally speaking, the better."

"And things with your cadets..." Muñoz began to ask before Maria interrupted him.

"If you'll excuse me, Father, I need to go lie down."

Muñoz gave his daughter a half-dirty look, waved one hand dismissively, and said, "Go then." He stared at her back until she had nearly disappeared around the corner. When the colonel took his eyes away he found that Victor was still staring.

The Volgan coughed with embarrassment. "Sorry, sir, I..."

The Castilian affected not to have noticed Victor's stare. "I apologize for Maria's rudeness. She is a daughter of the regiment, my young friend, but she is also a product of the Tauran Union's educational system. The fact that you are turning young boys into something analogous to soldiers is just beyond the pale to her."

"Ohhh."

"Oh."

Muñoz always took an interest in Victor's job, training the cadets, but was also always very careful to stay far away from his genuine suspicions, that Carrera was training not only future soldiers but current ones, young ones, fanatical ones who would not be counted in the force ratios calculated at Building 59. Even as he avoided that subject, he also took invariable care to drop hints of anything that might be of interest to the legions.

"I'm afraid I'll have to call it a night, Victor," Muñoz said. "We've got some new people coming in and early tomorrow I've a meeting with my quartermaster as to where we're going to billet them. They'll take up at least half a barracks by themselves, but there aren't so many as to take up a whole one. It's really quite awkward; the men don't even speak Spanish."

Runnistan, Pashtia, Terra Nova

"We *are* going to keep this a secret from his parents, right?" asked Cano of his wife, in Spanish to keep it private. She seemed extraordinarily happy. Cano assumed it was because she was doing something for her avatar of God.

The dirt of the *Bushkazi* field where Cano had won his bride, Alena, had been carefully packed down and smoothed. Ringed by torches, crowded with people wearing anything from legionary battle dress to black native costume to Balboan *guayaberas*, an oval opening had been left in which danced a dozen of the tribe's most lovely maidens, to the accompaniment of primitive music from equally primitive musical instruments. In the center of one of the long sides of the oval, on a throne of sorts, flanked by more torches, sat Hamilcar Carrera, watching the show. Hamilcar was young, barely eleven years old. The trees from which the wood for the throne had come were older. Some

of the fittings and jewels of the throne had come
from Old Earth. They were thousands of years old.

Hamilcar kept his thoughts to himself, though his
face said he was enjoying the girls' dance. It was a
wedding dance, though it had not, in living memory,
ever been performed by a dozen girls at once. To one
side of the throne stood his military adjutant, Tribune
David Cano, flanked by Cano's wife, the green-eyed
Alena. Some local notables stood on the other side.
The rear of the throne was ringed by fierce-visaged,
armored and armed Pashtun, facing out while standing. In front was a similar ring, though there the
guards were on single knees, so as not to interfere
with their Iskandr's view.

Alena turned and tilted her head slightly, her emerald eyes laughing. "If you don't tell them, I won't,
husband. But I'd suggest you have a little talk with
his tutors, if you want them to be quiet about it."

Her head tilted the other way. "Still, I don't know
why you would bother. The Carreras are going to know,
eventually. Say, when he shows up back in Balboa in
a few years with a dozen wives in tow."

Cano's chin sunk on his chest. *Ham's mother is
going to kill me.*

"Oh, stop worrying, will you?" Alena insisted, poking
her husband's ribs with her elbow. "It's *years* before
he'll have to go back. By then, Lourdes and the *Duque*
will be grandparents, probably a dozen times over; one
of the factors in our choice for brides for Iskandr is
that the girls had to come from highly fertile mothers
and, in their day, grandmothers. Not a one of these
girls has fewer than sixty first cousins. You think the
Duque or Lourdes will object to *that?*"

"Maybe not," Cano conceded.

"There's something else, too," Alena said. "Something the *Duque* said to me before we left."

"When he asked to speak with you privately?"

"Yes, then. He told me the boy was not who I thought he was—of course I scoffed at that!—but that he really *was* something almost as special. He said he was sending him to us for training, more than anything, and he hoped we would put Iskandr through a regimen to make him grow up very quickly and very well."

"So?"

Alena pointed with her chin toward the oval where a dozen beautiful girls danced with hands in graceful pose and fingers subtly beckoning. "Those were also just about the most grown-up girls we could find, even if one of them is no older than Iskandr. Given that females are more mature than males by something like an order of magnitude, how long do you think those girls will allow him to remain a boy? And, no, I'm not just talking about sex."

"What would you have done," Cano asked, "if Carrera had not, on his own, decided to send the boy here?"

"I'd have brought the girls to him and presided over a wedding by our custom, myself," Alena answered without a moment's delay. "I picked most of them out when we were still in Balboa."

"You are a witch, wife."

"Perhaps," she conceded. "Mostly, though, in this case, I used the Globalnet and had the women here do the legwork."

"No 'perhaps' about it. You know too much. I shall have cross words with your father for having you taught to read."

Alena gave her husband a mysterious smile. "I *do* know something you don't know," she said.

"Surprise me."

"I will," she answered, looking up at him, mystery morphing into radiance, "in about seven months."

Museo Nacional, Ciudad Balboa, Balboa, Terra Nova

Months we've been looking, fumed Fernandez. *Everywhere. Through every literary or physical trace. Even arranging to tear down two buildings in the slum by the old city so I could have a crew search through the dirt. And it was here all the time.* He reached out one hand to touch the thing, reverently, then shook his head. *God, the time wasted!*

The "it" in question was a small black oblong box. Elsewhere, out on the *Isla Real*, was its twin, though that twin was in much worse condition.

"It was donated to the Museum," said the curator, Professor Alfredo Figueredo, "oh, maybe two centuries ago. We've never really had the room, or the funding to expand the room, to put it on display. I'm not even sure what it is, only that it was something that once belonged to Belisario Carrera."

You don't need to know what it is, old man, thought Fernandez, hand still caressing the thing. *It's only important that I know what it is. It's a flight computer for a shuttle and, more importantly, it's the same dimensions, probably the same model, and can probably be fit into the shuttle we captured a few years ago in Pashtia. It looks like it can, anyway.*

We dug through everything. Everything! And then one of my bright boys suggesting checking probate accounts. And that led to a court record of an old estate fight...which led to a branch of a family... which led to another probate record...and to another, and another...to a woman who died rich and childless...and finally, to you.

And you, my lovely little black box, are going to lead us...

Fernandez's eyes turned upward, toward the stars.

Campo de los Sapos, Cristobal, Balboa, Terra Nova

The deployment's first wave was leaving at night. Stars shone down, twinkling off the waves of sea and bay that surrounded the Field of the Frogs on three sides. Loudspeakers placed around the field blared out a marching song, occasionally interrupted by commands from the headquarters, Eighth Tercio, in charge of the movement.

Like the commander of the corps to which they belonged, like the population of the area from which they sprang, the Eighth Tercio, was mostly black. As such, their marching song was "*Cara Morena*," "Dark Face," a glowingly appreciative piece on the girls of the province. They sang it from a dozen departure points, as they boarded a mix of hovercraft, coastal freighters, helicopters and medium cargo aircraft for their deployment to *Jaquelina de Coco* and *Sangre de Dios*, down in *La Palma* Province.

With much less fanfare, a number of Cazador

teams had been shuttled down by submarine, over the past several weeks, from *Puerto Lindo*, just down the coast. They would land on the coast and infiltrate by foot to take up positions well in advance of the general interdiction line—some, in fact, into Santander itself—the better to cover the coming relief in place of the Second Tercio by the Eighth. Those teams would cross into Santander, if for no other reason than to remind the Santandern guerillas that there was no sanctuary for them anywhere.

From loudspeaker and voice the song echoed:

"The hour of deliverance is nearing;
The day of liberation's surely coming;
The era when our *Patria* is sovereign,
No longer underneath the Kosmo boot.

Cara morena, mi chica linda..."

I really don't care for that song, Jimenez thought. *Just doesn't grab me. But what the hell does it matter what I think, if the boys like it.*

Jimenez's driver, Pedro, pulled up next to where he had let off his commander sometime prior. "Legate Higgins"—there were a large number of Anglic names among the black denizens of the province—"wants to know if you've any last minute instructions," Pedro said.

Shaking his head, Jimenez answered, "No. I'm only even here because I'm bitter I can't go along. Just...go back and tell him I wish him and his boys good luck."

"Roger, sir."

I am bitter, too. I liked being a company commander, way back in the day. Now? Commanding a corps, three hundred times bigger than a company, or a maniple, as we say now, is too much like work, and too little like fun. I haven't even gotten to go out on a training exercise in months.

How much worse it would be, Patricio, if you didn't hate both excess paperwork and meetings, I shudder to think.

"Cara morena, mi chica linda..."

Oh, well; could be worse. At least I'll get to visit the boys down there, keep 'em on their toes to the extent the guerillas don't.

Cruz Residence, *Ciudad* Balboa, Balboa, Terra Nova

Though he wasn't precisely sleepy, having slept on the helicopter that had brought him back from Jaquelina de Coco, Cruz had an inner fatigue no ordinary rest could touch. Wearily he trudged up the concrete path to the door of his house. Wearily he turned the knob and opened the screen door. Wearily he dragged himself, his rifle, and his pack inside. Wearily he set them down, and, with exhaustion in his voice, he called out, "Cara?"

He heard footsteps and then saw her, momentarily frozen in the rectangular corridor that led to the bedrooms. He saw his wife's swollen belly initially with mixed feelings. *Let's see... last time was... ummm... match that to girth... yeah, it's mine. Well... assuming.*

For her part, she took one long look at her husband,

framed by light streaming in through the front door, and launched into a very rapid waddle to throw herself into Ricardo's arms. She stood that way, wrapped up, for several minutes before she could manage to get out, "You didn't tell me you were coming home, you bastard."

"Secret," Cruz explained, while running his hands gently over her back. " 'Pain of death' secret. They *just* got another tercio sufficiently trained to take over from the Second. We couldn't say a thing until they had taken over by more than fifty percent. And I couldn't send you our code phrase because there were no computers out in the *jungla* and my last scrap of writing paper had gone to a 'We deeply regret' letter for one of my privates."

His hand wandered from her back to her belly. "Why didn't you tell me about this?"

"I wasn't sure until just after you left for La Palma, and I didn't want you to worry about me when you had more immediate things to worry about."

He nodded. The explanation made sense. For Cara, anyway.

"Did we win?" she asked.

"What's a win?" he half answered. "We drove the guerillas and druggies out of La Palma. But they'll be back if we let down our guard."

He grasped her shoulders in his hands and pushed her back far enough to look down into her face. "Hey, I've got some good news. At least I think it's good news."

"And that would be?"

"New assignment for us. We're going back to the island so I can be First Centurion of the tercio-training maniple. Promotion, more money, and—since most of the troops have moved back to the mainland—the standard house out there for a senior centurion is what they used to put senior tribunes and junior legates in. Also"—he glanced down at her stomach—"the legion still has most of its medical capability there."

Cara's eyes lit up at that. "Oooo . . . shiny." *And I won't have to worry about you being killed all the time, either. A nice safe training billet would be just the thing.*

She immediately got suspicious. She'd learned long since that nothing too very good and nothing too very bad lasted for too very long.

"How long?"

He shrugged, shaking his head. "Till we go to the island? A few weeks. How long will we be there? Sorry, don't know, love. Everything's in flux. But a year, at least, I think I can guarantee. Maybe two or three years."

"Oh, that would be wonderful," she whispered, laying her head against her man's chest.

Individual Combat Training Center, Eighth Legion, *Isla Real,* Balboa, Terra Nova

Esteban Escobar, late of the *Frente Nacional Liberacion Santandereño*, shivered in the early morning fog and the salty sea breeze. His thin physical training uniform was no help at all. And somehow the gravel underfoot was sharp enough to hurt his feet, even through his shoes.

Even if he'd been more warmly clothed, or the air had been warmer, the former guerilla might still have shivered. The corporals, sergeants, optios, and centurions he'd met so far might have made any man shiver.

Beasts in human form, was Esteban's learned judgment. *Was that ferret-faced bastard, Fernandez, doing me a favor when he pulled a couple of strings to let me enlist?*

Well, that's not fair. He did get the judge to dismiss the charges against me, and without even a hearing. That, at least, was a favor. Though, then again, I might have gotten credit for time served while I was being held in Fernandez's headquarters. In which case . . .

The fog was too thick to see the source of the command, "Maniple . . . Atten . . . SHUN."

Thought forgotten, Esteban stiffened to attention, head and eyes locked to the front. He heard the command, "Open ranks . . . MARCH!" and automatically took two steps forward to allow the squad behind to take a single step.

Esteban heard the leaders of the other three squads in his platoon give the command, "Parade . . . REST." His own first squad remained at attention. Keen ears heard the sharp gravel crunching under booted feet, somewhere off the right. He couldn't turn to see, but assumed that was the new first centurion they'd been warned about, inspecting the troops.

Vicious bastard they say he is, too.

Someone, the top of his head being at about the level of Esteban's chin, stepped in front of him and faced sharply to the left.

"I don't fucking believe it."

Esteban looked down, slightly, and his previous blank expression was replaced by a very nervous smile. "Hello," he said, lamely. "Ummm, Centurion."

Ricardo Cruz put the tip of his centurion's stick, his sole badge of rank, under Esteban's chin and pushed upward until his head was back in the proper position.

"I will someday want to know the rest of your story, Private Escobar," Cruz said, sternly. "But it can wait. In the interim, do try"—for punctuation, Cruz tapped his stick twice, hard, against Escobar's chest—"*do*"—tap—"try"—tap—"to remember how to stand at the position of attention."

"Yes, Centurion. Sorry, Centurion."

"And shut up."

Batería Pedro el Cholo, *Isla Real*, Balboa, Terra Nova

The bronze plaque by the rolled-open steel doors proclaimed the battery was named for an Indian, a man without surname, who had been a follower of Belisario Carrera in his war of independence from Old Earth. Each of the eight batteries ringing the island was named for a different character from that long-ago conflict. Jorge and Marqueli Mendoza had a common ancestor among those so honored, while Marqueli had yet another.

The battery's armament consisted of two triple six-inch turrets, themselves removed from one of the cruisers scrapped by Carrera as not needed for naval efforts. The turrets sat atop artificial hills, the sodded and tree-planted dirt surmounting thick hollow cones of concrete. Behind the twin hills for the two turrets, various ammunition bunkers, twelve of them, were situated to either side of a rail line, a spur running from the ring that encircled the island about three kilometers inland from the coast. Eight of those twelve bunkers were on the coast side, with their large steel loading doors facing toward the central massif, Hill 287. Short rail lines ran right from the main spur into the ammunition bunkers. The turrets themselves, while capable of all-round traverse, were oriented primarily to sea. Unseen, underground and connected by tunnels, were concrete headquarters, the fire direction center, and quarters and mess facilities for the battery's troops.

Sig Siegel was there, watching, as a railroad car bearing a shipping container was gently pushed through the doors. With Siegel were the Cochinese girl, Han, now free and his freely employed administrative assistant and translator, as well as a couple of hundred other Cochinese Sig had purchased from the highly corrupt chief of a reeducation camp.

"Han?" Siegel said, once the flatcar was inside.

"Right, boss," the tiny girl answered, then walked to the railroad car and scampered up the side. In their own tongue she addressed the workers, daintily.

"All right you dicklessclapriddenpussies, get the cables and shackles on this thing and get it into the air so we can get rid of the railroad car. Once it's been hauled off, and the doors are closed, then you fuckfacedrefugeesfromthevendorsoffatlittleboys are going to lower it, open it, and reassemble the big gun you disassembled back in Prey Nokor. You will then fix the gun on the railway mounting in the big metal box. Don't try to pretend ignorance. *You* semengarglers took the things apart and packaged them up. Now if you backpassagewhoreswhodon'tevenknowenoughto-chargeextraforaswallow can do that before dinnertime,

I *might,* and the operative word is 'might,' tell our gracious and beloved boss"—she turned and gave Sig a blinding smile—"that you deserve to eat real food tonight.

"What? What? I could have sworn I told you shit-eatingtrollops to get moving..."

Oh, Han, Sig thought, smiling broadly, himself, *wherever have you been all my life?*

Casa Linda, Balboa, Terra Nova

All my life, I suppose, Carrera thought, with a sigh, his eyes glancing back and forth from the printout on his lap to the map on the wall, *all my life I've wanted to lead a lot of men in a great, desperate battle. And in this particular case, that battle—the final one, not the one to toss out the Taurans—looks like a losing proposition.*

The figures don't lie. On my eastern flank, all those coastal ports along the Mar Furioso—*little enough, individually, but collectively enough to support an army—mean I'm going to be facing a corps or two—Zhong or Tauran, but most likely Zhong—and I'll have nothing left to face them with. Everybody else will be committed.*

And recruiting is about maxed out. I can finish building the force, and financing it, but that's it. No more. In any case, a regiment or two of men would stand out like a sore thumb in a area full of refugee camps loaded with women and children.

Kuralski's plan of moving the civilians, mostly women and kids, out of Ciudad *Balboa to provide a*

block is a clever one . . . maybe cowardly, but clever.
The invaders will have to feed those civilians, and a
half million mouths to be fed, at a distance from the
ports, makes the logistic problem insurmountable.

For a couple of weeks, until whoever it is forces
the civilians to move nearer the ports. Which guerillas
could interfere with, maybe even defeat, as long as
the guerillas could blend in. Which, being men, they
won't be able to.

Women. I've got women troops but no women
combatants to speak of. And even if I wanted to raise
a tercio *of women fighters, who would train them?*
Who would . . . hmmm.

He put down the printout and stood. Rocking his
head from side to side, muttering—thinking out loud,
really—he walked up the stairs to his office. There,
he used the secure phone to dial Parilla's office.

"Raul? Patricio. I've had a kind of an odd thought.
I think it might be useful. See, I want to raise a regiment of women, and, to train those women, a regiment
of gays . . . no, I'm not crazy . . . yes, I've thought about
it enough . . . trust me . . . yes, I know it might cause a
rift with the Church . . ."

Cathedral of Santa Maria, *Ciudad* Cervantes, Balboa

"Pull over there," Pigna said to the driver of his command vehicle, a mottled-green painted, one-quarter
ton, open top and sides, four-wheel drive job made
by a factory in Volga. The factory was partly owned
by the legion, with a local subsidiary to make spare

parts. Eventually, it was intended that the parts manu-
factory would begin assembling entire vehicles. The
troops called them "mulas," or mules.

"By the church, sir?"

"Yes, right by the church."

The driver shrugged, turned on his directional signal,
motioned with his hand for the trucks following to keep
on going, and turned the wheel. He eased through
traffic, in itself no mean feat in the busy square in the
middle of the city, made worse by the passing convoy
on its way to Fort Cameron. The square was, in fact,
the same square where a gringo, Patrick Hennessey,
had once shot a number of Moslems, precipitating
the wars that followed.

Once the mule stopped, parallel to the curb, Pigna
got out and walked the dozen or so steps across the
wide concrete sidewalk to the cathedral's main door.
This he pulled open, then entered. Even as the door
opened he could hear the choir at practice, singing
something he didn't recognize but which sounded
vaguely Gregorian.

The interior was dark, lit only by early morning light
filtering through stained glass windows. The legate took
a few moments to let his eyes adjust. Once he could
see well enough, he dipped the three middle fingers
of his right hand in the holy water font, used his
thumb to spread the liquid out, and crossed himself.

He then walked to a rear pew, genuflected, and
knelt. With his hands folded together, Pigna began to
pray nervously for the success of the coup he intended
to launch in a very few weeks. He began, *Thank You,
God, that that bastard, Jimenez, will be down in La
Palma visiting his troops. Thank You, too, that . . .*

CHAPTER TWENTY-SEVEN

But then *why* just a military test? There are so many things of value to society, so many of which are difficult and even dangerous. And where would we be without mothers and motherhood? How impossible a life without the farmers' produce? Civilized life without dentistry is unimaginable, without entertainment so dull as not to be worth living.

And so what? We wouldn't be here without air, either. Shall it vote? By mass or by volume? Or would by molecule be more fair and just? We need meat and bread. Shall the cows and buds of chorley vote?

People pay taxes. Why should they not have a say? Because if paying taxes is sufficient, and not a cover for some other status, like being a warm body with a temperature around 98.6, then logically those who pay more should vote more. And yet where is the civic virtue in wealth?

—Jorge y Marqueli Mendoza, *Historia y Filosofia Moral*, Legionary Press, Balboa, Terra Nova, copyright AC 468

AC 472
Estado Mayor, Ciudad Balboa, Balboa,
Terra Nova

Though the sun was long down, two of the three
moons long up, and the *antaniae* crying *mnnbt, mnnbt,
mnnbt* in the brush that edged the complex walls,
a light still shone from the window of Fernandez's
administrative office. With his wife long dead and
daughter murdered by a terrorist's bomb, Fernandez
had no real life outside the legion. He didn't really
feel the lack of that, though he missed his wife and
especially his daughter terribly. This was the single
best explanation, more than patriotism and more
than dedication to the profession, that he worked
such long hours, often sleeping on a the couch of
the waiting room.

His men and women, likewise, took their cue from
their chief. In a sense they had to, given the sheer
workload and the relatively small numbers of people
able to do the job. The expansion, of late, hadn't helped
any. Thus, it was no great surprise when Fernandez's
deputy, Legate Barletta, knocked, despite the late hour.

I don't know how I get into these things, Barletta had
thought to himself as he'd walked nervously down the
corridor leading to Fernandez's administrative office. He
was certain his chief would be there, because he wasn't
in his "secure office" down below. *Yes I do, I acquired
a little too much gambling debt, mostly entertaining my
secretary, the bitch. That led to doing a couple of favors
for money, which led to some more of each, which led*

to . . . ah, to hell with it. I'm here, now, and I'm stuck. But shit, Omar's my friend.

Reaching Fernandez's outer door, Barletta turned the knob and walked in to the waiting area. There he removed a pistol from under his uniform tunic with his right hand, while his left sought out a smallish cylinder contained in the tunic's left hip pocket. The cylinder went smoothly onto the end of the pistol's muzzle, quite despite Barletta's trembling hand.

But then again, friend or not, he'd have me down under that fucking Arab's care in a heartbeat if he knew I'd been turned. So, friend or not, it's him or me.

Barletta walked the couple of steps to the inner door, then knocked with his left hand.

Fernandez recognized the knock. He said, "Come in," then looked up, nodded a greeting, and turned his attention back to a small metallic or plastic box that sat atop his wooden desk. Barletta's hands were clasped behind his back, but that wasn't anything particularly unusual.

"What's that, Chief?" Barletta asked. Since the deputy wasn't cleared for this particular piece of information, Fernandez just shook his head in negation. That could have meant anything from, "you don't need to know" to "I don't know." Barletta was used to that. He waited silently for a few moments until he was certain that the intelligence chief's full attention was back on the box.

"I'm sorry for this, Chief," Barletta said, taking aim at Fernandez's chest. The deputy sounded sincerely sorry and also very nervous.

"What?" Fernandez asked, looking up.

Fernandez was short, thus the difference between a

pistol aimed at his heart and one aimed at the box was
minimal. He didn't think much of his own importance—
and there he was quite wrong—but did think the box
was important. As Barletta squeezed the trigger, Fernandez grabbed the box and spun around in his chair
to his left, placing his body between it and the weapon.

The move was quick, taking Barletta by surprise,
enough so that—added to his case of nerves, his first
coughing shot went wide of his aim, taking Fernandez
in the right side of his back, the bullet passing though
the lung on that side, driving blood, phlegm, and tissue
out of his chest. The energy transferred set Fernandez
to spinning, so that the next two shots went though his
spine, in one case, and his gut, in the next. Arms flop-
ping limply back, he was thrown chest forward to the
floor, his body falling over the black box.

Nervous almost to the point of hysteria now, Barletta dropped the pistol and ran off through the office
door, through the waiting room, and into the corridor.
From there he forced himself back to a brisk walk,
and began to move to the stairs that led down and to
the front entrance where his secretary was supposed
to be waiting with the car running.

National (Parilla's) Presidential Palace, *Ciudad* Balboa, Balboa, Terra Nova

The police van was the same model as some of those
used by the legion. It was no longer obviously a police
vehicle, however, having been given a paint job in legionary colors by one of Balboa's many highly talented body
and paint workers. It was also the same model as that

used by the guard on Parilla's palace for the ch
of the guard, which was rather a less formal exerc
in Balboa than it was in, say, Anglia.

In any case, the nine men in the van weren't interested in formality. Nor was the guard on the gate
interested in much but that they looked right, their
identification cards looked right, their uniforms were
legionary, and the van wasn't inherently suspicious. He
passed them through with a smile and a wave.

Only when past the gate did this portion of the
hostage rescue team remove their heavier arms from
bags sitting at their feet. Magazines were quickly loaded
into the side wells of submachine guns and then the
bolts were jacked. There were suppressors already
screwed onto the muzzles. The weapons were the
same Pound submachine guns as used by the close-in
presidential guard, in lieu of the more common F-26
assault rifle that was standard legion issue.

The team had opted for the unsubtle. As soon as
the van stopped in front of the palace, the side sliding door popped open and a half dozen men stepped
out. These walked purposefully toward the two guards
on the front entrance and shot them down without
warning. The only sounds made were the coughing of
the submachine guns and the gurgling death rattles
of the guards.

Though the "rescue" team had plastic explosive in
case the door needed blasting, and a police locksmith,
in fact the door was open. They'd had and studied
the floor plans exhaustively, but assumed, not unreasonably, that at this time of night Parilla would most
likely be in bed with his wife. Two men remained
on the door, after pulling the guards' bodies inside.

The other four raced upstairs, soft-soled, high-grip shoes making little more noise than would a cat on the marble steps.

Parilla's door was open as well. As silently as possible, the chief of the kidnappers turned the knob and gave it a slight push, letting it continue to swing open on its own.

Then came the rush, the sudden throwing on of the lights, and a piercing scream from Parilla's wife.

One of the attackers cuffed her into silence, while another stroked the folding metal butt of his submachine gun across the president's chin. Parilla, stunned into silence, was quickly turned over and cuffed. The chief of the team then said, *"Presidente* Parilla, you are under arrest, by order of the legitimate president of the Republic, for election fraud, war crimes, crimes against humanity, and narcotrafficking." The man then spoke a code word into a small radio.

"Get him to the helicopter pad."

Casa Linda, Balboa, Terra Nova

Nine policemen sufficed to take down the president. It was thought, not without reason, that Carrera would make a harder target. More than twice as many men, and three vans, plus the only other helicopter still under Rocaberti's control, were assigned to his capture and evacuation.

Of course, the *casa* was considerably less hard a target that it once had been, what with Hamilcar's Pashtun Guards gone, and security the responsibility of rotating sections from the Mechanized Legion at

Lago Sombrero. Moreover, most of the original staff had moved out and moved on as they'd found wives or better housing elsewhere. Perhaps worst of all, with Sergeant Major McNamara living elsewhere with his young bride and growing brood of children, there was no one single person charged with security and paranoid enough to see it done properly.

Though McNamara and Artemisia were still very frequent guests at the place.

The children, Lourdes' and Artemisia's both, were playing upstairs, minus only Lourdes' youngest, Little Linda, who was not only too young to really be willfully difficult but also on the "Lourdes Diet," and would be for some time yet. The others had been impossible at dinner—they always were when they got together—and had been sent away early. In theory, this meant they hadn't eaten much. In practice, it meant the cook smuggled dinner in to them.

Mac leaned back in his chair, stretched, and belched. "Damned fine feed, Miss Lourdes. My compliments to t'e chef." As if to punctuate that, the sergeant major broke of a piece of chorley bread, dipped it in some "Joan of Arc" sauce, and popped it into his mouth, chewing gustily. "Could use a little more 'Satan Triumphant,' though," Mac said. "Just a tad, not enough to take the skin off the tongue."

Artemisia shot him a dirty look, not over the belch, but over the sheer volume of food he'd managed to tuck away. "It just isn't right. I have to diet, exercise, and practically kill myself after I have a baby, and this tall bastard can eat enough for ten men and stay slim. It's not *fair.*"

"High metabolism," the sergeant major answered, in Spanish. "And you must admit, love, that this has its advantages in an old man."

"*Some* advantage," Arti agreed, "though *I* end up paying the price for that in the form of a distended abdomen, and eventual rigid dieting."

"Good wit' t'e bad; good wit' t'e bad. It's pretty good, still, ain't it?"

"As a matter of fact . . ."

Lourdes sighed. "If you two are going back to teenage games, I've had a metal plate installed between the headboard and the wall in the number one guest room, so you can pound away. Alternatively, we can move a mattress down to the concrete floor in the basement, though I shudder to think of the damage to the foundations of the house."

"I'm getting a little old for t'at, high metabolism or no," Mac said.

"Not so old," Arti corrected. "Not yet, anyway."

"Time," announced Moises Rocaberti, nephew to the soon to be full president and younger brother to that Rocaberti who had been shot for cowardice years before, in Sumer.

Moises was, his uncle thought, a happy choice. He was, indeed all the Rocabertis were, effectively barred from higher office in the legion by Carrera. Given that, and given a military bent, the younger Rocaberti had joined his uncle's police force. He was bright, handsome, ruthless, loyal to his blood, and had—best of all—an abiding hatred of Carrera and Parilla, which hatred had festered in the long years since his older brother's execution.

"What are you going to do after we take down the prick?" his driver asked of Moises as he started the first of three vans parked in the nearby town of Bejuco, Balboa.

"Fuck his wife in all three holes and then turn her over to you bastards."

"Works for me. Especially if the rest of us get to fuck the former Miss Balboa." He started the car.

"Nah. She's off limits, Mrs. Artemisia Calderon-Jimenez de McNamara. Too many people care about her. And neither she nor her husband have ever harmed anybody. But Carrera's tall, skinny whore? She's getting stuffed. To punish her bastard gringo husband. Those were my uncle's orders."

Though it really wasn't needed, indeed it was wasteful competition with the air conditioning, there was a fire blazing in the fireplace. The light from that reflected off the living room's mirrors, and then again from the ancient sword hung over the mantle.

"So this fucker," Carrera told Lourdes and Arti, pointing at McNamara with the glass of scotch in his hand, "jumps in the back of one of my squad's tracks and proceeds to spend the day with them. Observing. Teaching. The next day it was different squad, and then a different squad after that. For nine days."

He sighed. "If every sergeant major in the Federated States Army was like that, they'd be unbeatable."

McNamara, embarrassed, sipped at his own drink, then said, "It ain't t'e sergeant majors t'at won't do it. It's t'e system t'at keeps t'em chained to a desk. T'at, and t'e spare parts t'eory of personnel management."

"You didn't let the system chain you," Carrera said.

"I was so freakin' senior, t'ey couldn't make me do anyt'ing. Hell, t'ey tried to make me division sergeant major and I told 'em to stuff it. Hard to control someone who got no ambition for anything t'ey can give."

Outside, *Jinfeng* the trixie gave off a loud warning screech.

"Even so . . . what the fuck was that?"

"Now!" Moises Rocaberti ordered, lowering his submachine gun and firing a burst into the bird whose screeching head stuck up above one of the bushes flanking the main entrance. Immediately four of his men, standing under windows, propelled two more through those windows and into the house. The distant sound of crashing glass told of similar maneuvers around the back. Two men standing by Moises pulled back the door knocker—a welded steel battering ram—and slammed it into the door, once—*cachang*—twice—*cachang*—thrice . . . and the door burst open.

By twos a mass of men flooded through the door, each careful to avoid the cooling bodies of guards silently slain when the attackers had first left the first van. This mass split off, some turning into the living room, some ascending the steps, and some racing for the back part of the house.

Resistance was over before it could be said to have begun.

Lourdes screamed.

"Shut up, whore!" Moises ordered, his gaze lingering for a moment on Lourdes' milk-swollen breasts. "Patricio Carrera, aka, Patrick Hennessey, you are under arrest for . . . hmmm . . . do we have the evidence?"

"Outside in the van," one of the policemen reported. "I didn't see the point of bothering to bring it into the house."

"Very good. You are under arrest for war crimes, crimes against humanity, election fraud, and narcotrafficking. All over the country forces are moving to get rid of your people. You're finished."

"Piece of shit!" Carrera twisted in the arms of the men cuffing him and received a cuff in turn for his troubles.

To two other of his men the younger Rocaberti said, "Escort the *puta* upstairs. Make sure her kids are accounted for." He pointed at Artemisia and said, "And take this one to a different room."

"Fuck you, you bastard," Arti sneered. Moises slapped her to the floor. That was too much for McNamara. He'd been standing with his hands up, in front of the fireplace. He turned immediately and grabbed the old sword Lourdes had purchased for Carrera. Before he could well turn around, one of the police fired a burst into his midsection, tossing him forward and into the fireplace.

Lourdes pulled away from the hands gripping her and ran to pull Mac away from the fire, kneeling on the floor and keening besides him.

"Never mind, Lourdes," Mac said, weakly. "This is a better end than any I'd hoped for."

What can I DO? Her eyes pleaded.

Whatever you must, his own answered back. *Anything*. Then McNamara closed his eyes. He could feel the life pouring out of him. "Take care of Arti for me, Miss Lourdes," he said, at the end.

"Get this twat upstairs," Moises repeated. "And carry

the new widow off, too." To Lourdes he added, "Get into something more comfortable and easier to get out of."

Fort Cameron, Balboa, Terra Nova

In his analysis of the problem, Pigna had come to the conclusion that there was only one force really capable of intervening in the city. All the others—barring only the troops in the jungles of La Palma—would take from hours to days to mobilize and move against his Seventh Legion. The troops in the jungle would take even longer.

But the Volgans . . . they're the only real threat to my operations. They're here; they're trained; they're organized. Let them loose and my legion would collapse like a house of cards as soon as any of them came to understand what is happening, beyond the handful I brought into the plan last night. Most of them are just following orders to secure the city and do certain things that they think come from Carrera.

Got to neutralize the Volgans.

With that in mind, he got out of his mule and walked the fifty odd concrete steps to the Volgan commander's quarters, the two moons cancelling out his shadow. He mounted the stairs and knocked. A somewhat plump Volgan woman answered the door, then turned and called something in a language he assumed was Russian. The man he recognized as Samsonov came to the door quickly.

"Legate Samsonov," Pigna began.

"Legate Pigna."

"I just wanted to let you know I've received orders from Carrera to do some very odd things in the city.

My legion is already moving, by vehicle and on foot, to secure certain vital assets and critical facilities."

"War with the Taurans?" Samsonov asked. The prospect didn't seem to worry him overmuch.

"No," Pigna shook his head in negation. "At least I don't think so. Frankly, I'm not sure what Carrera has in mind. Though he insisted we break out and issue our basic load of ammunition."

"Damned strange. I would have expected him to have told me."

Pigna shrugged. "He did say that this was a test of readiness, so perhaps that's why you were not informed."

"Maybe. I hope no blood is spilled by mistake because people were not informed."

"Oh, I understand that he or someone will be speaking tomorrow morning. It should be all right."

Casa Linda, Balboa, Terra Nova

Lourdes never noticed that her knees were covered in McNamara's blood. Perhaps she avoided looking down instinctively. Instead, she paced frantically about the room she shared with Patricio. She heard her children and Arti's crying in the room next door. She went to the adjoining door and opened it, only to be met by a grim-faced guard who pointed her back to her own room. Behind that guard, two others were laying Artemisia down on one of the children's single beds.

What am I going to do? What am I going to do?
"Anything" Mac's eyes told me. Anything. What is "anything"?

Calm, Lourdes, calm. You have to think clearly if

ever you did. For your own sake, for your husband's, for your children: Think.

She picked up the phone. *Dead. They must have cut the lines. Aha: My mobile* ... She grabbed the phone and flipped it open ... *is dead. Has no signal, anyway. They must have taken control of the wireless system. Damn it! Think, Lourdes, think.*

Who is behind this? Not the legions, or not most of them. But maybe some. Who can I trust? Not the police. Who ... who ... the Volgans! But how do I get to them?

Quarters 39, Fort Williams, Balboa

So far as he was aware, Colonel Muñoz-Infantes didn't have a single reason to worry about much of anything. Oh, yes, that skinny frog, Janier, had it in for him, but no more than he, the Castilian, had it in for the frog and the Tauran Union. Yes, he was passing information to the other side, but that was an old Tauran tradition, and something the bureaucrats who ran the place would be loath to curtail. Besides, he *was* Castilian, and the frogs had no real authority over him. This phenomenon was one of the reasons that the Tauran Union was so militarily ineffective, even though its individual armies were generally quite capable in battle when allowed to be. Though there were rumors, persistent rumors, of a change to this that would create a unified armed forces with a unified chain of command and legal code.

"I can't see that happening, though," the colonel told Victor Chapayev. "We're Taurans; we all hate each other, deep down. I mean ... maybe if we had an outside enemy threatening us. Maybe."

Maria, the colonel's daughter, hadn't yet stalked off as she usually did. Instead she sat quietly on a chair opposite her father and Victor. Her father had had a very long and not particularly pleasant chat with her on the subjects of rudeness, honor, and the duties owed to one's father and one's guests. She still thought that the work Victor was engaged in was vile, even if he seemed nice enough.

"On the other hand," the colonel continued, "we've got an inside enemy— the bureaucrats of the TU—and that hasn't brought us together."

"The Tauran Union is *not* the enemy, Father," Maria said, heat in her voice. "It's all that's kept us at peace since the Great Global War."

"So say the schools that propagandized you since you were a girl," her father answered, calmly. "Personally, I think it was a combination of Federated States occupation troops and the external threat of the Red Tsar that kept us from each others' throats and that the TU was a beneficiary of that but had absolutely nothing to do with causation."

Best not to take sides, Victor, Chapayev told himself, *though the colonel is clearly right.*

"And then there's the corruption that permeates . . ."

"I'll get it, Father," Maria said, rising to answer a knock at the door. *Anything to cut off another of these TU rows,* she thought.

"No, never mind," Muñoz-Infantes insisted, likewise rising. "I'll get it. It's probably business anyway."

He walked to the door and undid the latch. As soon as he had, the door swung open *hard*, knocking the colonel to the floor. Victor stood and Maria screamed. Both stopped, the one in caution and the other in deer-in-the-headlights panic when presented with an armed group of men in Castilian battle dress pushing into the living room, and the muzzles of pistols pointed in their direction.

"Colonel Muñoz-Infantes," said one of the *pistoleros*, "you are under arrest for..."

At that, Maria fainted.

The colonel was being dragged down the walkway when Maria came to. Chapayev made sure she was all right, then reached under his uniform tunic to take his service pistol in hand.

"What are you doing?" she asked.

"Didn't you notice that those men were in your country's uniform but had the local accent? That was no legitimate arrest."

"Bu...but *why*?"

"That I don't know, but I do know your father's been a good friend to me and I'm not going to see him dragged off by fakes." Victor looked around and ordered, "Get into the kitchen, behind the refrigerator. I'm going to go get your father."

"But there were three of them, and there's only one of you."

"There are probably four of them. So? Trust me; they're toast." Chapayev stood and ran for the side door.

Casa Linda, Balboa, Terra Nova

I get to the Volgans by killing at least one of my guards, Lourdes thought, then amended, *No, be honest. I get to them by killing the one who obviously intends to rape me. But...how?*

She looked around the bedroom. *Patricio keeps a pistol under the mattress, but it will make noise . . . a LOT of noise. That will put an end to any escape. Knives? No . . . no, no knives here. But . . . aha!*

She kept a small desk in the bedroom, since by common, if unspoken, agreement with her husband that room was hers and he was just an invited guest. And on the desk was a large brass letter opener with an onyx handle.

I can't kill for beans with this, she thought, *unless I can get it into his heart or his brain. And I'm not sure I'm strong enough to push it through the muscles on his chest. So brain it will have to be.*

She suddenly felt nauseated at the thought of the thin, dull point driving through eye and bone. And then she considered how she was going get him into a position to drive the blow home. That made her more nauseated still.

But still . . . "Anything," Mac said. And . . . if this is what I think it is Patricio is a dead man and my girls orphans—assuming they're allowed to live—unless I act. So . . . "anything." Forgive me, Patricio.

Quickly, Lourdes began to undress. As she tugged at her clothing with one hand, the other took up the letter opener. *Now where to put this? What piece of furniture am I going to defile?*

Santa Clara Temporary Detention Facility, Dahlgren Naval Station, Balboa, Terra Nova

The facility had been a school once, with the classrooms built atop a hill and the gymnasium down at the base, both connected by a covered walkway. Later on, after it had lost that function and been abandoned, it had served as a training facility for city fighting for the very first incarnation of the *Legion del Cid*. This function it had lost once better facilities were built. Now the upper level school served as temporary barracks while the lower level held Parilla. The helicopter bearing a bound Carrera from his home touched down by the upper level. President Rocaberti was waiting to meet it when it landed, along with a couple of his larger and beefier presidential guards.

"*Duque* Carrera," Rocaberti sneered as Patricio was tossed at his feet. "How very pleasant to meet you again in this way."

"Fuck you, fat boy," Carrera answered.

"Fuck me? No, I don't think so. I did tell me nephew, Moises, to fuck your wife, though. He's a good lad, and obedient to his clan patriarch. By now your skinny, working class bitch, Lourdes, should be on all fours making the choo choo."

Turning to the guards, Rocaberti ordered, "Beat the foreign swine."

Quarters 39, Fort Williams, Balboa

He knew he would need an advantageous position. To that purpose, Chapayev first ran parallel to the road leading away from the house. His uniform was the legion's dark pixilated tiger stripes. Against the light beige house this would have stood out in the moons' glow. Against a background of jungle, it would be considerably less noticeable, essentially invisible, in fact.

About twenty meters past the house, he cut left, aiming himself toward the vehicle into the trunk of which
the colonel's captors were attempting to stuff him.

Right, he thought as he padded across the soft grass,
legitimate police don't stuff a prisoner into a trunk.

His pistol was lining up on the head of the captor
nearest him when Victor thought, *I need* one *prisoner,
but only one.* His finger stroked the trigger lightly, his
pistol's muzzle flashed, and a man's head exploded in
red mist and spraying bone. Chapayev rolled then,
dropping from the view of the other two men as they
turned to face the threat, for the moment forgetting
Muñoz-Infantes. They, however, were looking in the
wrong place. Victor was already almost behind them.
He fired again, three rounds into the one, and then
again, a single round, center of mass, into the other.
Then he was on his feet, running again to stand next
to a shocked driver. This one had time only to open
his mouth is a surprised "O" before Victor put a single
round through his head, just under his left eye.

He returned around to the back and began helping
the colonel out of the trunk. "Maria! Call out the guard!"

"No!" the colonel said. "One of those people was
mine!" His voice was rife with bewildered hurt. "One
of my own men. Who could believe it?"

"Then we'll take you to the military academy. You'll
be safe there."

"But those are just chi—" Muñoz began to object.
"Ah. Yes, of course. And we must take Maria as well."

"Of course. Are you up to helping me move the
bodies inside?"

"Sure," the colonel answered, "if you can get these
handcuffs off of me."

Victor knelt on the bloody ground and began searching bodies until he found the key to the cuffs. "Thanks," the colonel said, once he was free. He then went and grabbed a corpse by the feet.

From the post golf course, helicopters began lifting. It was too dark to see in any detail, certainly too dark to make out the uniforms of the troops riding inside. Even so Muñoz knew his equipment and knew his own organization.

"Those are the frogs who got settled on us a little bit ago," the colonel said, as he dragged the corpse towards the house, a dark and wet looking trail staining the concrete behind it. "Where are they going?"

Victor's burden was moaning slightly. He paid the wounded man no attention as his eyes followed the navigational lights for a few moments. He answered, "They're going to the bridge over the Gatun River."

Muñoz dropped the legs of the body he'd been dragging. "To cut off troop movement, south to north?"

"That would be my guess."

"Then we're not going to the Academy; we're going to my headquarters. Maria!"

"Father?" asked the daughter, now standing framed by light in the doorway.

"Don't call out the guard, but *bring me my pistol!* And get my *escopeta* for yourself to guard Victor's prisoner."

Casa Linda, Balboa, Terra Nova

"I trust the prisoner has complied with her orders," Moises Rocaberti said to the guard on Lourdes' bedroom door.

"I wouldn't know about that, sir," the guard replied. "I haven't looked. Willing to wait my turn, sir, don't you see?"

Moises nodded and unconsciously licked his lips. "Don't disturb me, then, until I send for you."

"Yes, sir."

Lourdes chewed at her lip, nervously, nervous, in fact, about seeming nervous.

Don't be silly, Lourdes, she told herself. *There's no sense in trying to pretend you're anything you're not. The most this swine expects is that I'll give myself to him in fear for myself and my children. For that, I should seem terrified and disgusted. If I actually am, so much the better.*

She saw and heard the doorknob turn and unconsciously moved one arm across her chest to cover her nipples and the wet circles their leaking had made in the sheer and short camisole she'd donned. Below, she wore a black thong. Her doffed clothing was tossed on the desk. She had travel clothes secreted under the bed.

She caught a glimpse of a guard's short hair, his face turned away, as the door opened halfway and the chief of her captors slid in sideways. He closed the door behind him, one handed, then half turned and slid a bolt closed.

With one arm crossed across her breasts Lourdes' other hand slid down to cover her crotch.

This suited Rocaberti perfectly as he hung his submachine gun on the doorknob by its sling. With both her hands occupied she had none to defend herself when he walked to stand directly in front of her and slapped her across the face, hard enough to hurt, to bring tears to her eyes and a quiver to her lip, but not hard enough to make her cry out. However, when her hand moved of its own accord to her insulted cheek, her arm moved away from her nipples. Rocaberti's own hands then moved, insect-quick, his fingers clamping painfully on both of those, then twisting. This made her cry out with pain, the more so as they were tender from nursing her youngest.

The next she knew his hand was entwined in her hair, forcing her down to her knees. His other hand fumbled with the fly of his trousers. As his penis shot out against her face he twisted her hair again, saying, "Suck it, whore."

She forced a smile to her face, looked up, and said, somewhat unconvincingly, "I like it rough, you know. And I'm really superb. 'The best,' my husband says, and he should know. You should sit. I guarantee you won't be able to stand once I start. He never can."

Moises was a little taken aback, perhaps even shocked. *She's a good actress,* he thought, *but she can't hide that she's afraid.*

Lourdes stood then and pulled his hand from her hair. She led him by that hand to the chair and pushed him lightly into it.

It isn't sex, she told herself, as she dropped again to her knees and began undoing her captor's trousers. *It isn't sex-it isn't sex-it isn't sex . . .*

She was still telling herself that as she bent her head and took him into her mouth.

But if he comes in my mouth it will be, she thought, several minutes later, her head moving on autopilot.

The thought made her gag even more than the pressure on the back of her throat did. *And that I'd rather die than.* She pulled her head off and began to stand.

"What do you think you're doing, bitch?"

"I want to fuck," she answered, grabbing him with her left hand and placing first one knee then the other on the chair cushion. She hadn't even remotely gotten in the mood for sex with him, but she had gotten enough used to what she'd been doing that her voice sounded almost sincere.

Lourdes must have placed the right knee badly because it slipped off, causing her to fall sideways. She caught herself with that hand on the floor. She recovered after a moment and began to resume her straddle, her left hand guiding his penis as if to enter her. Her shin, in one case, and thigh, in the other, confined and restrained his arms.

"Hah! You really are a whore. I should have known." Half mad with desire to rut, Rocaberti had eyes only for the glistening head of his penis, and the nether lips approaching it.

And then the woman's right hand was full of something brassy and bright, which was the last thing young Rocaberti saw before it plunged through his eyeball, cracked the bone behind the eye, and was then spun like a pestle, Lourdes twisting the letter opener furiously to turn a good sized chunk of his brain to bloody froth.

"I belong to *Patricio*, you son of a bitch," she whispered into a corpse's ear. Then she looked at the blood again and proceeded to vomit on the corpse, the vile smelling puke running out through her fingers to mix with dripping blood.

✧   ✧   ✧

Lourdes was dressed in denims and leather. She had a bottle of Thymoline mouthwash in one hand and a stubby firearm slung across her shoulder when she opened the door to the adjacent room holding Artemisia and their children. She was furiously swishing the solution as she placed one finger over her lips to command silence, before beckoning for Arti to come and bring the children. She spat the solution out onto the floor and began calling out, "Oh, God...oh, God...Faster...Oh, God," even while she pushed and prodded the others toward the door that led to the balcony.

Arti's eyes flew wide when she saw the corpse with the exposed penis and an onyx letter opener handle sticking straight out from under his forehead. A rivulet of blood ran down one cheek. She didn't ask about that, but did ask, in an urgent whisper, "What about Mac?"

"They sent him to the hospital," Lourdes whispered back. *Plenty of time later to tell her the truth. I hope.* "Oh...oh, Jesus...Fuck me, Moises, fuck me!"

"Hurry on ahead," she ordered Arti, still whispering. "Head to the boat. It's straight downhill. Follow the path."

"Can you run the boat?" Arti asked.

"I can push the button to start it and turn the wheel to steer it. Now go."

"What about you?"

"I have to ummm...to come...Ahhh...aiii...—go, dammit!—aiiii...ahhhh...ahhhh..." Lourdes waited until she heard footsteps on the walkway behind the house before letting out a soul searing scream of utter, and utterly fake, pleasure. Then she followed. It wasn't until she had the boat well out to sea that Lourdes told Artemisia she was a widow. Indeed, they were almost far enough out that attentive people on land wouldn't hear the scream.

Estado Mayor, Ciudad Balboa, Balboa, Terra Nova

Warrant Officer Achmed al Mahamda's job was, frankly, torturer in chief, even though the title he held was merely "Senior Interrogator." Most of the time, in fact, he really didn't have to resort to torture, though he always made the threat or promise to do so plain enough. An immigrant from Sumer, and former senior interrogator with the late dictator of that country's secret police, he got more results than any three of Fernandez's other interrogators, and did so much more quickly and reliably. "It's a shitty job," he admitted, "but someone has to do it."

In relation to his job, he took the private elevator from the sub-basement, where interrogations and, it must be admitted, the occasional killings were done, directly up to the waiting room outside Fernandez's personal office. As soon as he stepped out of the elevator, he sniffed something odd but still familiar.

Gunpowder? Here? "Legate?" he called out.

Mahamda walked briskly into Fernandez's office, took one look at the body on the floor, and rushed over. Though unconscious and ghastly pale, he saw that the chief of intelligence was at least still breathing. The red froth oozing from his chest said as much.

On autopilot from his own otherwise none too impressive basic training in the Sumeri armed forces, Mahamda went through the drill: *Clear the airway, Stop the bleeding, Treat for shock, Protect the . . . Screw that for now.*

He picked up the phone with bloodied hands and discovered it was dead. *Shit. Now what? Maybe . . .*

The internal intercom was not dead. In practiced Spanish Mahamda said to the guard room, "I want an ambulance here ten minutes ago! If you can't get one, get something—anything!—that will fly or roll. And I need a medic and four men with a stretcher in Legate Fernandez's office five minutes ago. Move!"

Only then did he rifle the desk, such part of it as wasn't locked, and come up with something non-air permeable. This he slapped over the exit wound that seemed to be frothing the most.

Fernandez's eyes opened. They were glazed and unfocused.

"Who did this?" Mahamda asked.

"Bar . . . B . . . Barlet . . . Barletta."

"We'll get him," Mahamda said.

"S . . . Screw him. Save the black box."

CHAPTER TWENTY-EIGHT

In the final analysis, then, everything else appears to have been tried and nothing has ever worked very well for very long. That the system we propose is unlikely to work well in perpetuity does not strike us as a sufficiently good argument to prefer systems that work, if indeed they work at all, for a very short time only.

The objection that such a system has "never been done before" strikes us as extremely unpersuasive, given that the usual and typical font for such an objection can be heard, regularly, insisting that the only problem with Tsarist-Marxism is that "it's just never been done right."

We should prefer a system proven to be rotten, wrong in conception, wrong *ab initio*, false in its logic and false in its premises to one that is unproven but promising? In Heaven's name, why? To make the Cosmopolitan Progressives happy? To set things up for the arrogant global and interplanetary elites to control the planets? There can be no worse reasons.

—Jorge y Marqueli Mendoza, *Historia y Filosofia Moral,* Legionary Press, Balboa, Terra Nova, copyright AC 468

Punta Gorgona Naval Station, Balboa, Terra Nova

"Hang on!" Lourdes shouted over the *thrum* of the engine. She throttled down to nothing, letting momentum carry her craft forward while aiming the bow of the boat toward the dock but away from the five patrol boats tied up to it. She wasn't very good with the boat, no experience, after all, but that didn't matter. All that mattered was that she hit the former and avoid the latter.

Artemisia didn't move except to clutch the children tighter to her. She hadn't moved, to speak of, since the tears had dried perhaps an hour before. Her lips still whispered, "Mac... Mac... Mac," with some regularity.

A sailor on one of the boats, the stern said "San Agustin," shouted and waved for them to veer off. Lourdes was having none of it. Instead, she ducked down seconds before the yacht crashed into the dock, crumpling its own bow and splitting the pole and frame of the other. Lourdes and her passengers were thrown forward.

The sailor, still shouting imprecations, jumped from his own patrol boat to the yacht's deck. "Lady, are you out of your fucking mind?" The sailor then noticed she had a submachine gun slung over one shoulder and amended, "If you'll pardon my language, ma'am."

Lourdes stood straight and answered, "Possibly. To both. My name is Lourdes Carrera. I am *Duque* Carrera's wife. I need to see your senior man present and I need your help."

In the dim white light of two moons, one of them now setting, and the yellow light of streetlamps, the sailor peered at this strange woman's face.

"By God, you *are* the *Duque*'s wife." He turned away, toward a small building just off the dock, and shouted, "Chief! Chief Castro!"

"I've got the five boats, yes, Mrs. Carrera," the chief said, once Lourdes had explained as much as she knew. His was a face burned dark by the wave-reflected sun and deeply seamed with a life of wind, and storm, and squinting against the elements. "But I've only got the crew coming off and the crew going on duty. And they're not even full strength. It's one of the downsides of being a militia." The chief shrugged apologetically.

"Can you run a boat on half a crew?" Lourdes asked.

"Well...yeah...if we're not going to fight anybody," Castro admitted.

"All right then." Lourdes turned to Artemisia. "Arti," she said, "I need you to take your children and mine to..." she leaned forward and whispered something in the black woman's ear, "and from there to wait. If what I am planning works, come back. If not, run to Hamilcar's...people...in Pashtia." She leaned forward again and whispered something else, a set of five numbers and the name of a bank, which she made Arti repeat back to her. "That will allow you and them to live well if it comes to that."

Turning back to the chief, she said, "I need you to take me to the coast, nearest where the road to Fort Cameron touches it. And I need a car to meet me there and take me to the fort."

The chief considered. "I've got a brother-in-law who bought a taxi with a legion loan. I can get him to meet us."

"The phones are out," Lourdes objected.

"His taxi has a radio and I know his frequency."

"Then let's do it."

Castro inhaled deeply and let out an equally deep sigh. "Yes . . . all right . . . let's. And, madam, if you've never been on a boat that can do better than seventy kilometers an hour, let me tell you that you are in for the ride of your life."

From the boat shack a voice called out, "Hey, Chief? Something's wrong with the television. There ain't no TV at all."

Television Studio, *Canal* Seven, *Ciudad* Balboa, Terra Nova

There were lights lit in the windows of the building. Under streetlights, trucks were rolling past, carrying troops to stations all around the city. Others, three of them, were stopped outside the TV station, disgorging troops. The second in command of those troops, Centurion Garza, walked up to the commander, Signifer Garza, and said, "This just doesn't make sense, Signifer. Orders in the middle of the night to take over the TV and radio stations, and to shut down the phones? Others to collect up the Senate? And no rumors preceding those orders? All in the *Duque*'s name? Sir, we never do *anything* without at least some rumors in advance. Never. We're just that kind of force.

"I could see it if we were going to attack the Taurans without warning," the centurion continued. "But we've been expressly warned *not* to attack the Taurans. It just doesn't make sense."

The signifer shrugged. He was a youngish kid, just

out of OCS, and without even a close combat badge to his name. Truth to tell, he was a little in awe of his centurion. "I don't know, Centurion Garza," the kid said. "I just know we—Seventh Legion, I mean—got orders to secure the town. We're doing that."

A look of nervous and apprehensive puzzlement crossed the centurion's face. He leaned forward and lowered his voice, as he spoke to his younger cousin "Manuel," he said, "this stinks and if I were you I'd start looking around to find the source of the stench."

"All right," the signifer agreed, "just as soon as we shut down the station. Which, now that you mention it, stinks, too."

Bridge of the Colombias, Balboa, Terra Nova

The lieutenant of the Gallic Twentieth *Infanterie Mécanisée*, out of Fort Muddville, was doing what lieutenants do; running around like a headless chicken trying to put each combat vehicle in his platoon into exactly the right position. On the other side of the bridge a different platoon was doing the same. The company's third platoon was on the other side of the broad water, acting as a combat outpost of sorts.

Centurion Garza wasn't the only one puzzled by the ongoing events. A grizzled Gallic noncom told the lieutenant, "Sir, I don't like this a bit. There's a coup going on; we all understand that. But we got orders to move and secure this bridge long before that started. So we're in on it; the general is, anyway."

"Logical, so far, *Adjudant*," the lieutenant agreed, momentarily ceasing his useless clucking about.

"Well, sir, there's nobody around us—nobody friendly, I mean. There's a heavy division to the east of us that is definitely not friendly, and at least two Balboan infantry divisions—legions, I mean—behind us, and maybe closer to five, not including their Tenth Artillery Legion."

"Yes, so?"

"If that coup doesn't work, sir, we're at the bottom of an artillery funnel."

The lieutenant looked momentarily nonplused. "What do you recommend, then, *Adjudant*?"

"For starters, sir, let me worry about setting up this blocking position. Meanwhile, you should get over the map and get on the radio and figure out a way for us to get the hell out of here if things turn to shit."

"As my father, the general, often said, *Adjudant*, the good officer listens carefully to his sergeants' mess."

"Wise man, your father."

BdL *San Agustin*, Chepo River, Balboa

The boat was anchored as close to the bank as it could go without grounding itself. Chief Castro, not content with getting Lourdes to the coast, had motored upriver to bring her nearly a third of the way to Fort Cameron and the Volgan Tercio. He'd have gone farther still but for two factors: This was as close as the road got, because a bridge crossed the river here and the bridge itself was built on pylons too close together to permit the width of the patrol boat to pass. Overhead, just off of the abutment, a single flashlight signaled three times.

"Is this wise?" Lourdes asked, with only the lightest nervous tremor in her voice. "How do you know it's your brother-in-law driving the taxi?" Automatically, she had ducked all but her head low behind the frame of the boat's cockpit.

"We both went to Cazador School," the boat's skipper explained, flashing a light of his own three times as well. "Though he's infantry, the poor benighted bastard. That's a common recognition signal we agreed to over the radio."

"Oh. Okay. And now."

"And now we're going over the side. Let me go first and help you down."

Lourdes waited until the chief had splashed over the side and called out to her.

For a moment she didn't know what to do. She'd never exited a boat except by dock or by dive. And diving in this jungle-shrouded blackness, into the muddy river, seemed like one of those really bad ideas.

Castro understood her problem instinctively. "Lie down on the gunwale . . . the top of the side wall, and slide your legs and rear over," he ordered. "I'll catch your legs and help you down."

"Oh, okay." She did as directed, except that she almost screamed when the chief lowered her and the chill water went up to her breasts. Under the circumstances, she didn't complain that Castro had had to get a pretty good grip on her rear end, at one point, to keep her from going in sideways.

Not that I didn't appreciate the opportunity, the chief thought to himself.

"Come on," he told her, tugging her through the water and up the muddy bank. The chief stopped only once, to step on and smash an *antania's* head that made a lunge for Lourdes' booted ankle.

Quick introductions were made at the taxi. Then Lourdes, Castro, and the brother-in-law, Reyes, sped up the road to the south, heading for Fort Cameron.

Headquarters, Tauran Union Security Force–Balboa, Building 59, Fort Muddville, Transitway Area, Balboa

Having furiously bullied his way past guards and functionaries, Ambassador Wallis burst into Janier's office without warning or escort. "Janier, you frog bastard," he said, most undiplomatically, "what the fuck do you think you're doing?"

The TU's ambassador to the Republic of Balboa was likewise present, in itself something suspicious. He attempted to rise and object before Wallis' pointed finger pinned him morally to his chair. "And you, shut up."

Janier smiled, knowingly and condescendingly. "I, Mr. Ambassador? Why, *I* am doing nothing really. Though there seems to be a bit of trouble downtown. I've sent a few troops to secure our interests, of course. Naturally one would when faced with an unplanned emergency."

Surcouf walked in through another door and announced, "*Charlemagne* reports air interdiction patrols between the *Isla Real* and the mainland are up, General. Likewise, de Villepin said to inform you that the Bridge of the Columbias is sealed off, as is the Gatun River Bridge. He also said to pass on to you that 'Williams' is apparently a failure. No details."

Janier scowled. "*Merde!*"

Without another word, Ambassador Wallis turned and stormed out to make a report to his government.

Building 232, Fort Williams, Balboa Transitway Area, Terra Nova

Chapayev drove the captured vehicle at breakneck speed, squealing tires at each turn. Muñoz didn't object. Indeed, his only comment was "Faster, Victor, faster!" right up until the thing appeared ready to career right into the battalion's headquarters. At that point the cry became, "Stop, Victor, STOP!"

The auto did, with a few feet to spare and smoke pouring from the tires.

Muñoz-Infantes was neither a particularly small man nor a weak one. Once he got out of the car and pulled a corpse from the trunk, he effortlessly dragged that corpse by the scruff of its clothed neck. It was the body of the one man among his recent assailants that the colonel recognized from his own organization. He was still holding the leaking corpse when the sergeant of the guard, jerked awake by the shriek of brake pads, came out of the guard shack under the headquarters.

"*Coronel* Muñoz," the sergeant greeted, while standing to attention and sketching out a salute. "If you don't mind my asking, sir, what are you doing here? I was told you had been kidnapped by locals and that we had received a demand for ransom." The sergeant's eyes moved down to the body. "Local . . . ummm . . . kidnapper?" he asked.

The colonel released his grip on the corpse, which

flopped bonelessly to the concrete. "Summon my staff and company commanders and—"

"They're all already here, sir," the sergeant interrupted. His finger jabbed upwards, in the general direction of the battalion conference room. "The XO called them all in when we got the report."

"Fine. Have someone see to this corpse." Muñoz used a booted foot to flip the body over onto its back. "Do you recognize him?" he asked.

"By sight, sir. I don't know his name." The sergeant of the guard scratched at his head for a moment and then answered, "I think he worked in the S-2 shop, sir. Odd..."

"What's odd, Sergeant?"

"It was the S-2 who told us you had been kidnapped."

"I see." Muñoz stormed off in the direction of the stairs that led upward. On the way he muttered, "I smell those bastards Janier and de Villepin."

"What are you going to do, sir?" Chapayev asked, following close behind.

Muñoz pulled out and checked the load on his pistol. "Shoot my S-2 and lead my battalion against the stinking frogs. Then ask the Balboans to take on my battalion, on spec, so to speak."

"I don't know if they will," Victor said. "But...maybe."

"I think it likely," the colonel assured him. "But there's also something I want you to do."

"Sir?"

"I'm going to send a detail to relieve Maria of the prisoner. I want you to go with them and after they do, to take Maria to the Academy at *Puerto Lindo*. Will you do this?"

"Yes, sir. Of course, sir."

Fort Cameron, Balboa, Terra Nova

The Volgan gate guard had been uncertain about letting the taxi in. It was Lourdes who had the clout to talk him into calling for the staff duty officer. That man, a junior tribune, had arrived quickly from Samsonov's headquarters to show them the way. He recognized Lourdes from the pre-Santander raid dinner, though she couldn't pull up a memory of him from the sea of faces of that night. The taxi followed the Volgan staff duty vehicle, passing it when it parked to deposit Lourdes right at the front door. Samsonov, alerted by the staff duty officer, was waiting to greet her.

"You've got to help us," Lourdes exclaimed, as soon as she saw the Volgan commander.

"Shit," Samsonov said as soon as she had explained. In turn, he explained, in his slow and strained Spanish, "This is ... touchy ... umm ... touchier than you may know, Mrs. Carrera. We not part of ... regular Balboan forces. Not sure what Federated States do ... if *Volgan* regiment intervene. Not like we ... best of friends or anything, you know. We could end up doing ... more harm ... than good.

"Worse ... not sure we legally ... can ... intervene. Or what Volgan Republic do. Most men ... still Volgan citizens.

"And this thing ... this coup ... very advanced. Have word now other president, not Parilla, going to speak tomorrow morning, nine A.M. Shit."

"Can I speak to those who aren't Volgan citizens?" she asked. "Please, Legate. Please. I have to save my husband."

"You speak," Samsonov agreed, then, after a minute's reflection, shouted out something in Russian to the staff duty officer, waiting outside his office.

"Give twenty minutes," the Volgan said. "Then I bring you to mess."

The faces that met her at the mess were stony. She looked at them and was just certain they wouldn't listen to her, that they just didn't care. In fact, she was wrong. The problem wasn't that they wouldn't listen, or didn't want to help, but that Samsonov was the father of the regiment and, without knowing which way he would go, the officers and *praporchiki* didn't want to open their great Volgan hearts to a hopeless cause.

Still, whatever Lourdes thought, she gave it her best. As she passed men sitting in the small officer's mess, she greeted those she knew by name or sight. A name spoken here, where she knew it, a warm touch on a shoulder where she didn't. She had a feeling that whatever Samsonov had said to his staff duty, it had included at least a truncated version of recent events. They'd had that version, she could sense from their faces and somewhat shamed expressions.

No sense in repeating what they know, she thought, so she didn't. Instead, taking a position next to Samsonov at the head table, she reminded them of all they owed Carrera. She spoke of what she knew of the raid on Santander and how he had saved one of their companies. She explained that, no matter what the politicians might promise them, they could have no faith in those promises. She moved them, she could see, but not enough. Finally, she walked over

to where Menshikov, one time translator and aide to
Carrera, stood.

"Miro," she said, giving him the nickname he
would have had had he been born Balboan but with
the equivalent first name, Vladimiro. Menshikov had
been promoted to Tribune II and had taken command of Chapayev's company. "Miro, where would
you be now, if not for my husband?"

Menshikov couldn't answer. He hung his head in
shame, thinking, *In a dead end job in a dead end
country ... that or really dead and probably unburied
in Santander.*

Samsonov, sitting at a table with his face cupped in
his hands, looked thoroughly miserable. Then, briefly,
his face lit up as he seemed to have an idea. *Sure.
Why not. Fuck 'em.*

He lifted his chin from his hands and spoke, "You
know, gentlemen, this is really a mercenary organization. All through history, regiments like ours have
been noted for their lack of discipline, their almost
democratic structure. I really don't know what I
could personally do if, say, Menshikov here decided
to take his company and help Carrera against my
orders. Or even if *a maximum* of one other platoon
decided to go with him ... oh, say, yours, Chekoy.
Why, if even one of your tank sections elected to
disobey orders and go with them—Dzhugashvili, are
you paying attention?—it would only further the
point. Why, in an undisciplined organization like
ours, I wouldn't be surprised if my own operations
officer decided to take the lead." Samsonov looked
pointedly at that man, Rostov. "And, of course, you
would need to have the cooperation of one of the

antiaircraft boys in case the Taurans decided to try to stop you from the air."

"But if you gentlemen decided to disobey orders, and take Mrs. Carrera to the nearest television station, and capture and hold that station while she broadcast an appeal for help from the legions, the rest of the regiment could hardly be held to blame. But, of course, you couldn't do any serious planning for such an eventuality with me sitting watch over you. Besides, it is quite impossible for you to do such a thing, undisciplined as you no doubt are, before the president speaks at zero nine hundred, sharp."

Samsonov consulted his watch. "Oh, my," he said. "I have summary punishment to administer in just a few minutes. My wife's cat is going to be given extra duty and have his rations docked for failure to catch a mouse that's been pestering us. So I must be hurrying along to take care of my administrative duties. Good day to you, gentlemen."

Lourdes didn't understand a word that was spoken, as it was all in Volgan. But as soon as Samsonov left, Menshikov let out an "Urrah!" Officers clustered around him and Lourdes, smiling and laughing. The ones mentioned by name by Samsonov, or implied by their commander's name, smiled more ferociously than the others.

Television Studio, *Canal* Seven, *Ciudad* Balboa, Terra Nova

Lourdes hadn't ridden in an armored vehicle since Artemisia's wedding. Then she had been afraid of soiling her dress. Now she just wanted the damned thing to move and to hell with her clothing. Menshikov had put her in his own Ocelot, ordering her to keep inside until further notice. Occasionally she heard gunfire, barely audible over the engine's roar. Twice she had seen the turret turn and a shower of smoking, stinking cartridge cases pour onto the floor of the track. Finally the truck came to a stop, jarring her in its suddenness. The back doors opened. Menshikov again told her to stay put until further notice. Then he, with his RTO, dismounted.

The Volgans had discussed whether or not to demand surrender from any Balboans who might be guarding the TV station. They had decided there just wasn't time. "If we knew who was in on this and who was duped," Menshikov said, "we could ask for surrenders. As is, we just can't know and can't take the chance."

This, since the Garzas and their men were guarding the studio in all innocence, was the stuff of tragedy.

Assaulted suddenly and unexpectedly by three tanks, thirteen Ocelots, two rapid-firing, four-barreled rolling antiaircraft guns and sixty or so dismounted infantry, the platoon of the Seventh Tercio hadn't lasted long. They might not have fought at all except that the Volgans who dismounted were all white and wore somewhat unfamiliar uniforms. They looked, if anything, Tauran. The Balboans hadn't even had the chance to call for help, it was over so quickly. Then again, they hadn't had even the possibility of being attacked mentioned to them. Nonetheless, after tank guns, lighter cannon, and explosives had blasted out windows and walls to let shrieking Volgans in, the men under the two

Garzas, such as remained standing, had given a fair accounting of themselves. Not all the bodies carried out of the studio were Balboan, in the end.

Shortly after he had left her, Menshikov returned to the Ocelot. "Mrs. Carrera, it's over. Come now, quickly."

Lourdes dismounted and saw a few Volgans being treated for minor wounds. A couple of others were plainly dead. Others still were dragging Balboan bodies out of the way, perhaps twenty or so of them. Lourdes began to cry as a squad of Volgans clustered around her to shield her from even the chance of fire.

Menshikov led Lourdes upstairs. A number of civilian-clad Balboan television workers were cowering on the floor when they arrived in the studio.

"On your feet, all of you!" Menshikov shouted. "Who's in charge!"

A wide-eyed man, fortyish, identified himself timidly as the station chief.

"I want your hairdresser and makeup man," Menshikov said. "I want anybody necessary to run this studio. And I want any file shots you have of any of the projects to help the people Carrera and Parilla have started." Menshikov pointed towards Lourdes. "She's going to make a speech and if I think for a minute you're not doing everything you can to make it perfect, I'll hang you by your balls 'til they drop off. Clear?"

The studio chief's eyes grew wider still. He nodded emphatically, but said, "But the president of the Republic—well, President Rocaberti, anyway—is supposed to speak soon."

"Not over this fucking channel, he's not. Now move!"

The studio head began to issue orders to his people.

Old Presidential Palace, *Ciudad* Balboa, Terra Nova

The president leaned back in his chair while camera makeup was applied to his face. His mental rehearsal of his coming speech was interrupted by an aide.

"Mr. President, we have received a report of shooting, a lot of shooting, over by the Channel Seven studio."

Without moving from his position the president asked, "Did you investigate?"

"Yes, sir. I tried calling the studio but the phones were out. Over the satellite link, when I was able to use that, they said some drunken soldiers were firing their guns into the air in celebration. The person I spoke to seemed very nervous, though."

"Well, send someone to investigate."

"Yes, sir."

Makeup job finished, the president turned to face into the waiting cameras. Television workers huddled over monitors behind the cameras. He began to speak:

"Citizens, countrymen, it is my sad duty to—"

"What the hell?" shouted the man who was overseeing Channel Seven's monitor. He pushed his chair back as if struck. The president's eyes opened wide to see Lourdes' face on the screen. She looked very sad.

Forgetting where he was, the president shouted, "Get that damned bitch off the air." The man leaning back in his chair just shook his head helplessly. "No way," he answered. "It's originating at the Channel Seven studio. I can't control it from here."

The president turned to the Seventh Legion commander. "Then shut the studio down."

"Too late, I think," answered Pigna.

"Not too late to limit the damage," Rocaberti insisted. "Send a full regiment, if that's what it takes."

Nodding, Pigna left to issue the necessary orders.

Looking into the camera, Lourdes began to speak.

"Most of you won't know me. I'm Lourdes Carrera, *Duque* Carrera's wife. I've come to talk to you today about two men. One of these I love like a father. The other is my husband, Patricio Carrera."

"As much as I love them, I must tell you I know these men love all of you more than they love me. How do I know this? I know the heart of the man I share my bed with. I know how much time my husband gives to me . . . and how much he gives to you.

"You know too, in your hearts. Think back a dozen or so years. Where were we? Our economy was bankrupt by a hostile foreign power. Our unemployment was almost universal. Our cities were in ruin and chaos. Crime and the Federated States ruled our streets. Many . . . too, too many, of our best young men were killed or crippled by an unprovoked invasion.

"And who caused that invasion? Don't bother to blame the Federated States; they acted in their own interest, as they always do. Do not blame the shark for being a shark, he knows no other way. Blame instead the man who would speak to you on the other channels. Blame too those selfish, immoral advisors and helpers who abetted him in his scheme to reintroduce colonialism to Balboa.

"Now, of course, the scars of that time are healed.

Crime is almost gone from our country. Our people are back to work. More fine young men have risen to take the place of those fallen in battle. Our cities are clean and safe. The future has never looked brighter for us.

"Despite troubles, you are happier than you have ever been. At least, those of you who have always been shut out by the oligarchs are happier. Plainly the oligarchs themselves were displeased with your new prosperity. They feared that if you weren't starving, you might be thinking . . . thinking of them and the stranglehold they wish to have over your lives.

"How many of you have jobs now better than any you ever dreamed of? Better places to live? How many have children in free schools? How many of your children have been treated in clinics without charge? How many have sons and daughters being trained even now for the bright future ahead? Even for those who don't have these things yet, you have at the least the hope of them . . . a hope you never had before.

"And who gave you back these things? Do not look to Rocaberti or his coconspirators. They would have you all groveling in the dirt—you, your children, your children's children—through eternity if they could.

"Only two men had the vision and the love to help you to these things: Raul Parilla and Patricio Carrera, my husband. Please join me in prayer for them, wherever they are, if they are even still alive. For, you see, last night evil, wicked men came and took them away from you. I, myself, barely escaped with my children, mine and Patricio's, and my life."

Lourdes paused to shed a tear. "I . . . I had to kill a man to bring you this word.

"But do not just take my word for what these two great men have done for you. Look for yourselves."

Lourdes' voice continued, but her face was replaced with a series of shots of newly built schools, clinics treating children, and factories full of busy, smiling, often sweating workers.

From outside the studio came the sounds of more heavy gunfire as the presidentially ordered "investigation" reached the Volgans' perimeter. On screen, before a nation, Lourdes visibly shuddered, but continued even so, "They accuse my husband and General Parilla of running drugs. I know, and you know, that could not be the case. Yes, they take money from the Santanderns, a lot of money, all of which they use for your good. But the operative word is *take*. They give us money because they're afraid of *Presidente* Parilla and my husband. No one in the world has fought harder against the drug lords than has Patricio Carrera. Listen to the words of this foreign born officer. Foreign born he may be, but he is Balboan by blood given if not by blood received." The Camera panned to show Menshikov sitting next to Lourdes.

Still speaking, she asked, "Tribune Menshikov, would you please tell the people where you were and what you were doing on the first night you were in battle with *Duque* Carrera?"

"Why, we were in Santander, Mrs. Carrera," Menshikov said, "fighting to put an end to the terror the Santandern drug chiefs had inflicted on Balboa..."

As Lourdes and then Menshikov spoke, all over the city units of the Seventh Legion began turning themselves, and command of themselves, over to local forces, even as those local forces grew with reservists and militiamen showing up armed and accoutered for battle. Before noon, the first elements of Third Legion were crossing the demarcation line that had separated out Rocaberti's Old City from the rest of Balboa, killing all who resisted and stood in their path.

Headquarters, Tauran Union Security Force–Balboa, Building 59, Fort Muddville, Transitway Area, Balboa

Janier's face was ashen, in stark contrast to the blue and gold of his unofficial dress uniform. "What went wrong?" he asked, of nobody in particular.

"Two things," de Villepin said, his voice low with worry, "Muñoz and the woman. We might have succeeded if either of those had gone right, the woman kept incommunicado and the Castilian kidnapped and killed, with the other side being blamed for it. As is..."

"Can we extract the two companies of commandos at the Gatun River?" Janier asked.

De Villepin shook his head in negation. "When he wants to move fast, Muñoz plainly can. The commandos are trapped and the pickup zones we could have used for helicopter extraction are under heavy mortar fire. And, after we tried to have him kidnapped, I doubt he'll be in a reasonable mood."

"Don't you have a contact there?" the general asked.

"The Castilian shot him."

"*Merde!* What about the Twentieth Mechanized?"

"They're clear for now," de Villepin said. "I can't for say how long that will be the case. The Balboans are swarming like ants. I think we should pull them back while we can."

"Any sign the Balboans are crossing into the Transitway Area?"

De Villepin shook his head again. "Not 'crossing,' no. But..."

"Go on."

"Their Tenth Artillery Legion, which, as near as we can tell has something approaching two hundred guns, heavy mortars, and rocket launchers, is taking up positions from which they can level this post."

"Why haven't they opened fire, do you think?" Janier asked.

De Villepin laughed. "Because their commander hasn't given them the word to. And is still alive, so far as they know. If he were dead, or gave the word..."

Officer's Mess, Santiago Air Force Base, Santiago, Santander, 16 January, 0920 hrs

Lieutenant San Martin looked at Captain Hartmann incredulously. "You were giving us the straight word? I don't believe it. I *can't* believe it."

Hartmann, San Martin, and most of the pilots of their squadron were listening raptly to the Global News Network's rebroadcast of Lourdes' speech. When Menshikov began to speak, however, all eyes turned to Hartmann. He tried to, but couldn't look smug. *That bastard,* thought Hartmann. *He was Balboan all along. Working for them, anyway. And he convinced me to lie, by telling the truth...by lying.*

Everyone present thought Hartmann's laugh was

in self-congratulation. He didn't try to disabuse them of the notion.

Hamilton, FD, Federated States, Terra Nova

Karl Schumann, the president of the Federated States, was livid. *Those miserable fucking spics,* he thought initially, then with more immediate practicality, *How do I squirm out of this one?*

By the time the first reporter was put through to the White House, the president of the Federated States had his answer. "Well, Dan, you see, it was like this. We and the Balboans both had good cause to hit the drug lords. But they just weren't able to stand up to Santander if the Santanderns retaliated. So they did the job, with our tacit support. And we took the 'blame' because Santander can't hope to hurt us."

A more objective reporter might have pointed out that "tacit support" really means no active opposition, even if one didn't oppose because one didn't know. However, with an election year coming up, few, if any, of the press would have done anything to hurt *their* candidate, not when he was expected to run against a "rabid" conservative Federalist.

Presidential Palace, *Ciudad* Balboa, Terra Nova

There was firing—all small arms, so far—around the perimeter of the old city enclave. That was the two companies of civil police still loyal to the Rocabertis. They had the advantage of fighting from buildings

but neither the arms nor the training to do so with
any long-term prospects for success. From the old
Palace, the firing seemed to be growing ever closer.

"It's too late, Mr. President," Pigna said, upon his
return. "None of my units will listen and the few
officers I brought into the plot late have either turned
or been shot. We've got to get out of here, now. It's
all over. We've lost."

At the word, "lost," Barletta, who was present now,
put his head in his hands with despair. *Can a man
have made a greater mistake?* he asked himself.

"No," said the president. "The Taurans will help
us. They must. Has there been any word from their
general or their ambassador?" he asked.

An aide answered, hesitantly, "It seems that the
Castilian battalion at Fort Williams has defected and
is currently engaged in battling some of the TU commandos at Gatun River. The mechanized troops at the
Bridge of the Colombias are probably going to be
pulling back to Fort Muddville. And General Janier
reports that the *Charlemagne* is pulling back to the
docks at the Dahlgren Naval station and recovering
its aircraft."

The president hesitated. "Fine. We'll go now. But
send the orders to where Carrera and Parilla are
being held. I want them and any other prisoners we
hold all shot within the hour. They'll not live to laugh
over our failure."

"By sea or by land?" Pigna asked. "Forget that,
stupid question. With the Frog carrier pulling back,
the other side owns the sea."

"Yes," Rocaberti agreed. "Our only chance of survival
is to get to the Taurans. If we can do that, it's even

possible that the Federated States might intervene and force them to give us back this much."

Pigna said nothing, but shook his head.

Rocaberti looked dismally around his ornate office. It was hard, *hard*, leaving his life, the remnants of his power, and his chance for revenge behind. The rump president waited until the order to kill Carrera and Parilla was transmitted, then left his office for his limousine and safety among the Taurans. Pigna and the chief of the city's police, along with some few others, followed.

Santa Clara Temporary Detention Facility, Dahlgren Naval Station, Balboa, Terra Nova

Tribune Rojas, older than most, which explained much, and fatter, which explained even more, was one of the policemen who had remained loyal to the oligarchs when Parilla had won election to the presidency. He looked at a piece of paper slipped into his hand by an underling manning the radio. He looked at it again, crossed himself, and said, aloud, "Pablo, this is wrong on so many levels I don't know where to begin."

"Sir?" asked the radio operator, Pablo, who had passed on the message.

"They want me to kill Parilla and Carrera in cold blood. I can't do that. Turn them over in answer to a legitimate extradition order? Sure. Just shoot them like dogs? No."

"Then what, sir?"

"Then . . . I'm going to try to cut us a deal."

"A deal?"

"Sure. Why not? He and Parilla are both men of their word. But . . . ummm . . . Pablo, do we still have the guards who worked the two over?"

"Yes, sir."

"Good. Go get a few men and arrest that crew. They might make an adequate sacrificial offering. And after that, see if you can raise someone at the *Estado Mayor* to let them know we have their chiefs. Meanwhile, I'm going to see about getting someone's word of honor."

Three Hundred meters north of the Bridge of the Colombias, Balboa, Terra Nova

"I don't understand it," Rocaberti said. "Janier gave me his word that there would be soldiers here to provide us a safe haven and escort if things went to crap. But . . ." He shrugged, eloquently, while gazing in the general direction of a Tauran Union fighting vehicle, legging it trippingly for the demarcation line between the Transitway Area and Balboa proper.

Suddenly the street around the convoy seemed full of soldiers, in the pixilated tiger stripes of the legion, all armed and looking decidedly dangerous. Their bayoneted rifles aimed steadily at heads and torsos, engines and tires. Perhaps just for emphasis, still other legionaries aimed rocket grenade launchers, or RGLs, at armored limousines.

The forwardmost of the vehicles in the convoy, not Rocaberti's, attempted to run. An RGL armed legionary fired, his rocket impacting on the front windshield. The armor was useless against the directed explosive.

That vehicle veered left, crashed into another, and stopped dead, blocking the road.

As the rump president and his staff and collaborators were hustled out and bound with duct tape, three IM-71 helicopters in legion colors beat through the air overhead, heading in the general direction of Dahlgren Naval Station and Santa Clara.

Santa Clara Temporary Detention Facility, Dahlgren Naval Station, Balboa, Terra Nova

Tribune Rojas was waiting with Carrera and Parilla. Only Parilla was standing, as Carrera's beating had been long and thorough. His face was a swollen, mottled ruin, nose twisted to one side, one ear half detached where a boot had scoured it. His lips were split and a couple of teeth had gone missing.

Volgan infantry poured off the rapidly opened clamshell doors at the backs of three legion helicopters. Their bayonets were fixed and there was blood in their eyes. Parilla moved directly in front of Rojas, who was trying his best not to soil his trousers.

"Leave this one and his men alone," Parilla shouted. "There are two bound prisoners in the lower level. Bring them to me *alive.*"

Lourdes had followed on the heels of the infantry. One look at Carrera, lying on a stretcher, had her sprinting for his side and throwing herself over him, sobbing and wailing at the damage done to the man she loved.

"What have they done to you, Patricio, my very dearest?"

"Nozink...goo...I t'ink," he got out through bloody, swollen lips. "Lon' tahm wit' t'e den'is' for me, nu."

"Thank God, at least you're still alive." She had her arms around Carrera's body, her face pressed against his neck. Carrera, too, had his arms around her, but was too weak to hold very tightly. He assumed she didn't kiss him because his lips were such a ruin.

"Roca'er'i tol' me 'ee ha' somewhu 'ape you. I swear 'ee'll pay, Lour'es."

She hesitated a moment, collecting her thoughts, then backed off to look in his eyes. "I wasn't raped, Patricio." *Which is the truth if not the whole truth.* "I'm fine." *Also something less than the truth.*

Carrera twisted his head. "Rau'?"

"Here, Patricio," Parilla answered.

"Don' le' anywhu execu'e t'e bas'ar's, please? No' ye'."

"Of course, my friend."

Carrera stirred again. "Lour'es, wha' abou' Mac?"

"He...he died, Patricio. And Linda's trixie, *Jinfeng,* too, was killed for trying to give us warning."

After that, Carrera couldn't speak for a very long time. When he did, it was to say, "Ah'm goin' to crucify t'em all."

Academia Militar Sergento Juan Malvegui, *Puerto Lindo*, Balboa, Terra Nova

Maria Muñoz had asked Chapayev to bring her to the school chapel as soon as they'd arrived from Fort Williams. She wanted to pray for her father and his men, she'd told him. Now, while he waited in a pew in the back, she, on her knees, talked with her God.

And, Heavenly Father, the girl prayed, after taking care of familial and regimental duties, *please forgive me for being a vile, rude, nasty bitch to Victor Chapayev. He saved my father, and quite possibly myself, and I promise to be a* much *nicer girl to him than I've ever been in the past.* She crossed herself and began to stand, but then went back to her knees again.

Which is not to say, O Lord, that I won't have to come here and beg forgiveness for myself for some of the very *nice things I intend to do for him. First, though . . .*

Ciudad Balboa Beach, Balboa, Terra Nova

The conspirators had been tried by the full Senate. For the main ones, the ones about whom there could be no doubt of their guilt, the trial hadn't taken long. The sentences had been something of a surprise.

Rocaberti was first in the procession, a wooden timber over his shoulder and iron chains about his ankles. Behind him came his own two rump vice-presidents, Pigna, his chief of police for the old city, Barletta, the entire set of teams who had captured Carrera and Parilla—such as could be taken alive, the one survivor of those who had tried to grab Muñoz-Infantes, and about three score of the remnants of Rocaberti's police force, excepting only those Rojas had bargained for. Armed men, legionaries, not Volgans, marched to either side. Closer in, still other legionaries used cattle prods liberally.

Along the beach nearly one hundred stout posts had been driven into the sand and wedged in securely. The posts had U-shaped, steel fixtures attached. Unsurprisingly, these were of a shape and size to accommodate the beams carried by the condemned.

Pigna was almost unique in the party in that he didn't weep along the short march from the prison to the beach. For this reason, Carrera, seated on a wheelchair, pointed to him and said, "This traitor first."

Pigna was seized, stripped down to shorts, and his arms were bound together at the wrists. His beam was placed in the U-shaped fixture. Then he was hoisted up, his bound hands hooked over the upright, and allowed to drop. This hurt, but not enough to raise a cry. Indeed, he said not a word until his ankles were pulled into position and first steel spike was driven through into the wood below.

After that, Pigna cried more than had most of the others. At least until their turns came to be hooked over and nailed up.

The TV cameras caught all of it.

Rocaberti's turn came last. "Why?" was all the ex-president could come up with.

Carrera had healed enough, and had enough dental work done, to speak easily.

"You know," he said, to Rocaberti, "I don't think your nephew ever got to rape my wife. She killed him, you see. That much is certain. And she denies having been raped. Now, is it possible he raped her beforehand and that she's lying about it? Sure; it's possible. And that's one reason why you're going up on that cross, just in *case* she needs to feel thoroughly avenged. As important, I want anyone who might even *think* about siding with the TU to realize that they can't be relied upon at all and that the penalty for doing so is *extreme*. Lastly, I just hate your guts. "Take him."

Casa Linda, Balboa, Terra Nova

Lourdes watched the televised crucifixion dry-eyed and unsympathetic. She'd changed a lot in the last month, so much so that she hardly recognized herself. These people had threatened her and hers, nearly killed her husband, nearly raped herself. They *had* killed someone her husband looked up to almost as if a father. Other innocents, too, not least the Garzas and their men, deserved their revenge. Those men could hang there and die by inches over days and that was just fine with Lourdes de Carrera.

Artemisia was staying at the *casa*. "I just can't go home yet, Lourdes," she'd said. "Not until I can look at something of Mac's without breaking down." Of course, she was welcome to stay forever, if she liked.

Someone, Lourdes hadn't a clue as to who, had rearranged Moises Rocaberti's corpse before anyone could see that he'd been partially undressed. Whoever it was, Lourdes thanked that person, silently. *It would never do for Patricio to think anything had happened to me for which he would blame himself. Better to hold it inside.*

For that matter, oral sex was the only kind she would give her husband now. *I told him it was because I didn't want to damage his setting bones. And that's true ... as far as it goes. Mostly, though, I want to wash the taste of that bastard's cock out of my mouth. And that is going to take a lot of washing.*

Her reveries were interrupted by Arti. "Lourdes, that satellite call to Pashtia went through. Ham's on the line."

She rushed for the phone.

Ham spoke first, in a voice on the edge of puberty and cracking on about every fifth word. "Mom, what the hell is going on back home?"

"We had a coup attempt," she answered, "but we came through it all right."

"Do you need me to come home?"

"No," she answered, "but there is something you can do for me."

"Anything, Mother."

"I've discovered we can't trust people. I'd never have believed that before, but it's true. I need some guards, maybe two hundred of them."

"You want me to send some of my people to you?"

"Could you? Please? As trustworthy as you can find."

"Well . . ." the boy hesitated, then continued, "these people take blood and marriage ties pretty seriously. Would two hundred sons-in-law and nephews and cousins-in-law do?"

"Where would you . . . WHAT?"

"I'll have to ask my wives for their recommendations, of course . . . Mom? Mom, are you there? Mmmooommm?"

EPILOGUE

I

UEPF *Spirit of Peace*, Rift Point, Terra Novan side

The rift was fixed in space. The planet, however, moved. That's what made timing a rift jump tricky. Pass the rift too early and a ship could end up chasing a receding planet even while trying to slow down, and having a harder time slowing down because the lasers on the far end were running away, hence more attenuated. Come too late and spend a year or two swinging around the local sun, and *then* having to chase a receding planet.

Wallenstein—rather Richard, earl of Care, acting under her instruction—had timed it rather well. *Peace* would assume orbit around the new world in just about seven months. Already they were in communication with the fleet, though there was a not inconsiderable time lag—just under eight hours—between messages. This would shorten as the ship closed on the planet and the planet continued in its orbit.

Not that every message took that long. Not long after *Peace* came out of the rift, Wallenstein ordered a tightbeam opened with UEPF *Dag Hammarskjöld*, Captain Bruce Shi (Class One), count of Wuxi and knight commander of the Order of the Sun, commanding.

"Captain Wallenstein," Shi began, with a small nod of his head. Raising his head and eyes, Shi looked more carefully. "Ah, *Admiral* Wallenstein. Let me be the first this side of the rift to offer my congratulations, Marguerite."

"Thanks, Bruce. From you, that means something." Wallenstein gave Shi the smile she normally reserved for former lovers, still on good terms.

"Honestly, Marguerite, I wasn't sure I'd ever see you again...in this turn of the wheel. You convinced the Consensus, then?"

"I convinced the SecGen," she answered. "*He* convinced the Consensus...or enough of it. But Bruce... things are getting really bad at home. Bad in ways... well, you might not believe me without seeing for yourself."

"More areas reverted?" he asked.

"That, yes, but..."

"But?" he prodded.

"Let me tell you a little bit about the *Ara Pacis* and the Burning Man..."

Richard, earl of Care, was burning up inside. *And I know why,* he thought, *I know the exact cause. She's brown and petite and hourglass-shaped, with a face like an angel and a disposition so different from the Class One women I've known that she shines their superior in every way that matters.*

Of formal education she has not much, though once

she learned to read she began picking things up at an amazing rate. Surrounded by mostly classes above Four, her Anglic has gotten to be something no Class One would have to be ashamed of back home. And such an adorable accent!

Elder gods, she terrifies me. What if I approached her? She couldn't reject me by law and custom but it would be meaningless for her to accept me unless I gave her the freedom to reject me in advance. And if I did that she might reject me. She's no cause to have any love for my class.

It was too far away to see the new world with the naked eye, but Esmeralda could see the bright dot of the sun of this system from the observation deck.

Just a few more months, Richard told me, until I'll be able to see Terra Nova. I can hardly imagine; a place where Man is free of the uppers that tyrannize poor Earth.

Richard, she sighed. *What am I going to do about Richard? He loves me, I think. And, though I hate his class, I can't hate him . . . nor even, maybe especially, the high admiral. What am I going to do? If I become his lover, as he plainly wants to ask me to become, could I then do what I must? Should I push to become his lover so that I will be in a better position to do what I must? God, I don't know.*

I only know that my sister who took my place a few days before the high admiral freed me . . . took my place to have her heart cut out on their filthy altar, made me swear revenge.

She thought upon it long, weighing advantages and disadvantages, conflicting duties and responsibilities.

Finally, still undecided, she stood and began walking the ship's corridors, in the direction of the captain's cabin.

II

Ammunition Supply Point, Legionary Base *Lago Sombrero*, Balboa, Terra Nova

All three moons were up, Bellona, Hecate, and Eris. They bathed the world beneath them in a bright and, because of their spacing, virtually shadowless light.

Under those moons, just outside the door of bunker number twenty-three, a huge meter-thick assemblage of old and very, very strong concrete, *Duque* Patricio Carrera gazed up into the night sky. Though trees blocked his view of the ground to the south, he knew he could see the airstrip if he wanted by just climbing to the earthen, treed roof of the bunker. He didn't bother; he already knew exactly what it looked like.

Carrera's title, *Duque*, was a military title rather than a title of nobility. It signified that he was the commander of the *Legion del Cid*, the originally mercenary, or more technically, auxiliary force that had been raised in the Republic of Balboa, adopted by Balboa, and which had adopted Balboa in return. Ultimately, the title derived from the Latin "*Dux Bellorum*," Commander of Wars. The legion took many of its traditions from ancient Rome on Old Earth.

A set of night vision goggles hung by their straps from Carrera's neck. The goggles rested high on his chest, itself covered with the peculiar custom-made, slant-pocketed, pixilated tiger-striped camouflage that the *Duque* had selected for his legions' jungle wear. Between the two was the legion's silk and liquid metal *lorica*.

Above goggles, *lorica*, uniform, and chest was a salt-and-pepper haired, deeply tanned face, with striking eyes, a narrow, aquiline nose, and more wrinkles than Carrera's years should have accounted for.

The sky was clear, unusually for Balboa's wet season. Mosquitoes droned in Carrera's ears. From farther off the nighttime cries of the *antaniae* came softly, muffled by the surrounding jungle. *Mnnbt . . . mnnbt . . . mnnbt.* As with the mosquitoes, Carrera likewise ignored the moonbats. Besides, they were fairly harmless except to children, the physically disabled, and the feeble minded. Cowardly creatures, they were.

Carrera stole a quick glance at his watch—forty minutes past midnight. He stood in the small area defined by the bunker's door, the berm of concrete-revetted earth that was designed to protect the contents of the bunker from either an accidental explosion or a near miss from a deliberate attack, and the two angled projections from the door to the access road. In this little trapezoid, hands clenched behind his back, Carrera paced out his frustrations and anxieties.

"*Duque*?"

Carrera turned to his driver, just emerging from the shelter of the bunker. Without another word Warrant Officer Jamie Soult handed his commander a cup of coffee, black and bitter. It was an old routine. "Sir, how do you *know* they're coming?" Soult asked.

Soult, tall, slender, and rather large-nosed, had been with Carrera in two armies, over as many decades.

He was more a son or a younger brother than a subordinate. Even so, the term that best described the relationship was probably "friend."

The corners of Carrera's mouth twitched in something that vaguely resembled a smile. "Jamie, I know they're coming," he said, "even if I don't know which units or in what precise strength, because they think they've no choice. I *made* them think they have no choice."

In point of fact, Carrera actually did have a pretty good idea of who was coming, the units and the strength. After all, his enemies in the Tauran Union only *had* so many airborne units of the requisite quality.

Anglian paras or Gallic, he thought. *Sachsen, just possibly. But I don't think so. Probably Gauls.*

Over the hill that separated the ammunition supply point, or ASP, from the rest of the base, blocked from Carrera's view by the thick, intervening trees, was the bulk of the cadre of the First Legion. At current mobilization levels, this amounted to the cadres, the very *senior* cadres, of two of the mechanized tercios, or regiments, of the legion, supplemented by a small number of select reservists. In terms of strength, these made up roughly the equivalent of six fairly small companies.

Mostly dug-in in a ring around the base; the reinforced cadres were there as bait. Good bait, however, ought not resemble bait too much. Therefore, some of them actively patrolled the perimeter. This patrolling had an additional and vital purpose. The one thing Carrera feared—not just here but in half a dozen places around the republic—was that the Taurans would find out that something beyond the obvious was waiting for them at *Lago Sombrero* . . . or at the airport...or at Fort Williams...or at any of half a dozen spots where, in fact, a major ambush or surprise attack *was* waiting for them.

Aerial reconnaissance wouldn't tell them enough. He had flown over the base himself that very day and there wasn't a sign of any special reception. Even the United Earth Peace Fleet, orbiting overhead and de facto allied with the Tauran Union, was unlikely to see what Carrera wanted to remain unseen and unsuspected. He had some measure of the capabilities of the UEPF. In this case, though, he believed he'd met and matched those capabilities.

Still, the Taurans might send in a ground team, scouts or pathfinders, to check things out before their main invasion force dropped down on the Balboans. That *ground* team might just stumble onto something· Carrera wanted kept secret. Hence, the patrols.

Carrera didn't expect the patrols to necessarily catch or stop a ground recon team. Rather, he thought that they should make one as concerned with personal survival as with finding out anything important.

"Nothing's perfect," the *Duque* said, *sotto voce*.

Around the airfield proper, four Volgan-built self propelled air defense guns stood; one at each end of the strip and two to the sides where the Inter-Colombian Highway bisected the strip. Sandbagged in on three sides, the guns were unmanned. Still, their radar was turned on. Other, simpler air defense guns stood manned by solitary Balboan soldiers. These were in the open; they had to be manned to be credible. More bait.

Within a radius of fifty or sixty miles of the base

more than twelve thousand reservists and militia of the First Legion (Mechanized) waited in their homes or clubs with pounding hearts and with their issue rifles at hand for the call to report to their units at *Lago Sombrero*. Some of the legion's wheeled vehicles had already been dispersed to pickup points to bring the reservists in a hurry when called. Still others had their private vehicles and pickup rosters. Some would go to pre-planned pickup zones to await helicopters, assuming any survived the initial Tauran onslaught. Busses from what Carrera liked to think of, and hoped was the case, as the "hidden reserve" would take still more.

All this was known to both the Taurans and the UEPF. Indeed, it was knowable, in broad terms, to anyone who cared to study. Without the threat of those reservists, and hundreds of thousands more like them, waiting for the trumpet's call, the Taurans would probably never have jumped.

Not everything was known, though. Carrera would have bet—in fact *was* betting—that six secrets had been kept. Inside the ammunition bunkers was one of those six real secrets. Hidden away, as they had been for the last three days, roughly eleven hundred young Balboan troops waited, unknown to anyone outside of a very small circle. They were little more than boys, most of them; the average age was just under sixteen.

The boys had been painstakingly smuggled in from their military academy just after the most recent outbreak of tension between the Tauran Union and Balboa. They had found in the bunkers a complete set of all the equipment needed for them to form a mechanized cohort, a very *big* cohort.

✧   ✧   ✧

"But it's as perfect as I can make it." Carrera turned and left his post outside the bunker, going inside to speak with the commander of the hidden force.

Once out of possible observation, Carrera lit a cigarette. The smoke drifted up and hovered about the ceiling of the bunker. "Rogachev, are you ready?"

Unseen by the light-blinded Carrera, former Volgan Army Major, and current legionary Tribune III, Constantine Rogachev nodded in the affirmative. Rogachev was a typical, even a stereotypical Volgan; a short, stocky, hairy bear. Above his round head and light blue eyes was a thatch of blond bright enough to gleam in the flash from Carrera's lighter.

"We're as ready as we're going to be, sir," the Volgan answered. "All of the vehicles that are going to start are topped off with full fuel tanks. The ammo is loaded. My cadre knows its mission . . . well, the mission is simple enough. Let the Taurans land. Pop out of these shitty bunkers. Get in formation. Drive off their close air support, and crush them with armor.

"The only thing that has me worried is the traffic jam we'll have trying to get out of this place and into formation." Rogachev shrugged ruefully. "Couldn't really rehearse *that*. If the Taurans notice us, or the UEPF does, and a couple of thousand tons of steel moving is very noticeable, sir, they could destroy us before we're properly deployed."

"I know the risk, Legate. There is nothing to be done about it except get your air defense systems out first, before anyone really notices."

Rogachev nodded briskly. "Yes, sir. We know that's the plan." He chuckled, apparently at himself. "Maybe

I'm nervous about it because that's all that could go wrong. A soldier has to worry about something, after all."

Carrera laughed a little. "Indeed we do. Fine. I'm going back out. I suggest you get your boys into their tracks now. It can't be too much longer." Carrera threw his cigarette to the ground and stepped on the glowing ash.

Outside again in Balboa's thick, even stifling air, Carrera did climb to the top of the earth-covered bunker. He lifted his night vision goggles to his face before turning them on, lest their green glow betray him to a possible sniper. He then scanned the sky through the grainy, green image.

Was that a flash? he wondered, looking toward the west. *Maybe.*

From this position he could even see part of the airstrip itself, one spot where an air defense gun's radar dish spun on its axis. Even if its radar picked up something, there was no one on board to see and report it.

Carrera's question of a moment before was answered. He saw the first impact of a homing missile—*Radar Homing? Contrast Imaging? Terminally guided? Who knows?*—as the SP air defense gun disappeared in a great flash. The echoes of other explosions told of similar bombs hitting elsewhere around the field. Each concussive blast was felt in the form of rippling internal organs at least as far away as the bunker.

Carrera hated that feeling. Even so, he looked up and smiled. *If you were planning a long war,* he mused, *these bunkers would be the better target. But you're not; you're planning for a very short one. Amazing how often such plans fail to quite work out.*

Overhead the screech and sonic crack of the jets was nearly loud enough to drown out rational thought. In Carrera's view, one of the barracks expanded and crumpled from a direct hit by an aerially delivered bomb. Vainly, a lone and very brave Balboan gunner fired his air defense gun into the sky. Carrera could see his tracers rising in the black night and then more as another gun joined him. He made a mental note to check the boys' names for later—Carrera assumed they would be posthumous—awards.

The Balboans' tracers didn't rise for long. What Carrera had almost seen a few moments before was the shadow of a Federated States of Columbia-built aerial side-firing gunship. This now poured down a stream of fire.

Like something from a science fiction movie, thought Carrera. The defenders' guns went silent, both of them. *And gunships. Hmmm. So it'll be the Anglian paras, not the Gauls'. They're the only ones outside of the FSC that have gunships. That's a pity,* he thought, and meant it. *I'd hoped they'd stay out of this.*

The air shook as more fighter-bombers raked over the legionary base. Down came regular unguided— dumb—bombs, twenty millimeter cannon shells, rockets, cluster bombs. Had there been any serious opposition on the ground around the airstrip these might well have broken it, even though well dug-in troops were not terribly vulnerable to air attack.

Joining the air armada now came a flight of half a dozen helicopter gunships, presumably flying out of the Tauran-held Transitway Area, or perhaps even from something at sea.

Hmmm... more proof of Anglians.

The helicopter gunships didn't carry anything like the airplanes' firepower. They made up for that lack, however, in the attention to detail they could apply to a mission. By the glow of the burning buildings, Carrera could make out the gunships' track as they shot down legionaries attempting to flee from them.

Holding a fist in front of his chest, Carrera spoke out loud to himself. "Now," he commanded to no one who could hear. "Now! Report that the area is clear enough to jump."

Carrera's order, or prayer, or wish was quickly rewarded. Under the bright moonlight, he saw the outlines of the first of twenty-four medium and fourteen large cargo transports and troop carriers approaching the *Lago Sombrero* airfield. Coming in low, Carrera thought maybe just over one hundred and twenty meters, these planes began disgorging their loads—over fifteen hundred Paras of the Royal Anglian Airborne Regiment. At that altitude the Paras didn't even bother with reserve chutes. If their main parachutes failed there wouldn't be time to open the reserves anyway.

I wonder what friends I have up there, jumping to their deaths.

The first of the medium transports made its pass over the airfield and surrounding cleared area in about forty seconds. Then, duty discharged, it turned to head for home. Others, in a long double trail behind it, were still dropping troops. Hundreds of these were already on the ground struggling to free themselves from their parachutes and harnesses. When Carrera was sure that enough had landed to guarantee the others would also land despite any danger, he shouted down to Soult, "Jamey, radio silence off. Get on the horn to fire the caltrops. Tell Rogachev to roll."

The boys must have felt the shuddering bombs even deep down in their concrete hides. Carrera heard song, boyish voices supplemented by older ones, coming from the now opening vault doors:

"A young tribe stands up, ready to fight.
Raise the eagles higher, *mis compadres*.
We feel inside the time is right,
La época de los soldados jóvenes.

High, from His Heaven,
    the God of battles calls us.
Ahead, in ranks, march the ghosts
    of our slain.
And in our hearts no fear of falling.
Legion, *Patria*, through the steel rain!"

Carrera looked skyward, past the incoming transports, and whispered, "Enjoy the show, Marguerite."

GLOSSARY

AdC	Aide de Camp, an assistant to a senior officer.
Ala	Plural: Alae. Latin: Wing, as in wing of cavalry. Air Wing in the legion. Similar to Tercio, qv.
Amid	Arabic: Brigadier General.
Antania	Plural: Antaniae, septic mouthed winged reptilians, possibly genengineered by the Noahs, AKA Moonbats.
BdL	Barco de la legion, Ship of the legion.
Bellona	Moon of Terra Nova.
Bolshiberry	A fruit-bearing vine, believed to have been genengineered by the Noahs. The fruit is intensely poisonous to intelligent life.
Cazador	Spanish: Hunter. Similar to Chasseur, Jaeger and Ranger. Light Infantry, especially selected and trained. Also a combat leader selection course within the *Legion del Cid*.

Chorley   A grain of Terra Nova, apparently not native to Old Earth.

Classis   Latin: Fleet or Naval Squadron.

Cohort   Battalion, though in the legion these are large battalions.

Conex   Metal shipping container, generally 8' × 8' × 20' or 40'.

Consensus   When capitalized, the governing council of Old Earth, formerly the United Nations Security Council.

Corona Civilis Latin: Civic Crown. One of approximately thirty-seven awards available in the legion for specific and noteworthy events. The Civic Crown is given for saving the life of a soldier on the battlefield at risk of one's own.

Dustoff   Medical evacuation, typically by air.

Eris   Moon of Terra Nova.

Escopeta   Spanish: Shotgun.

Estado Mayor   Spanish: General Staff and, by extension, the building which houses it.

FSD   Federated States Drachma. Unit of money equivalent in value to 4.2 grams of silver.

Hecate   Moon of Terra Nova.

Hieros   Shrine or temple.

Huánuco   A plant of Terra Nova from which an alkaloid substance is refined.

I	Roman number one. Chief Operations Officer, his office, and his staff section.
Ia	Operations officer dealing mostly with fire and maneuver, his office and his section, S- or G-3.
Ib	Logistics Officer, his office and his section, S- or G-4.
Ic	Intelligence Officer, his office and his section, S- or G-2.
II	Adjutant, Personnel Officer, his office and his section, S- or G-1.
Ikhwan	Arabic: Brotherhood.
Jaguar	Volgan built tank in legionary service.
Jaguar II	Improved Jaguar.
Jizyah	Special tax levied against non-Moslems living in Moslem lands.
Karez	Underground aqueduct system.
Keffiyah	Folded cloth Arab headdress.
Klick	Kilometer. Note: Democracy ends where the metric system begins.
Kosmo	Cosmopolitan Progressive. Similar to Tranzi on Old Earth.
Liwa	Arabic: Major General.
Lorica	Lightweight silk and liquid metal torso armor used by the legion.
LZ	Landing Zone, a place where helicopters drop off troops and equipment.

Maniple   Company.

Makkah al   Arabic: New Mecca.
  Jedidah

Mañana sera   Balboan politico-military song.
  mejor   Spanish: Tomorrow will be better.

MRL   Multiple Rocket Launcher.

Mujahadin   Arabic: Holy Warriors (singular: muja-
                     had).

Mukhabarat   Arabic: Secret Police.

Mullah   Holy man, sometimes holy, sometimes
                     not.

Na'ib 'Dabit   Arabic: Sergeant Major.

Naik   Corporal.

Naquib   Arabic: Captain.

NGO   Nongovernmental Organization.

Noahs   Aliens that seeded Terra Nova with
                     life, some from Old Earth, some pos-
                     sibly from other planets, some possibly
                     genetically engineered, in the dim mists
                     of prehistory. No definitive trace has
                     ever been found of them.

Ocelot   Volgan-built light armored vehicle
                     mounting a 100mm gun and capable
                     of carrying a squad of infantry in the
                     back.

Meg   Coastal Defense Submarine under
                     development by the legion.

PMC   Precious metal certificate. High denomination legionary investment vehicle.

Progressivine   A fruit-bearing vine found on Terra Nova. Believed to have been genengineered by the Noahs. The fruit is intensely poisonous to intelligent life.

Push   As in "tactical push." Radio frequency or frequency hopping sequence, so called from the action of pushing the button that activates the transmitter.

PZ   Pickup Zone. A place where helicopters pick up troops, equipment, and supplies to move them somewhere else.

RGL   Rocket Grenade Launcher.

RTO   Radio-Telephone Operator.

Satan Triumphant   A hot pepper of Terra Nova, generally unfit for human consumption, though sometimes used in food preservation and refinable into a blister agent for chemical warfare.

Sayidi   Arabic form of respectful address, "Sir."

SPATHA   Self Propelled Anti-Tank Heavy Armor. A legionary tank destroyer, under development.

SPLAD   Self Propelled Laser Air Defense. A developed legionary antiaircraft system.

Subadar   Major.

Surah   A chapter in the Koran, of which there are 114.

Tercio   Spanish: Regiment.

Tranzitree   A fruit-bearing tree, believed to have been genengineered by the Noahs. The fruit is intensely poisonous to intelligent life.

Trixie   A species of archaeopteryx brought to Terra Nova by the Noahs.

Yakamov   A type of helicopter produced in Volga. It has no tail rotor.

LEGIONARY RANK EQUIVALENTS

Dux, Duque: indefinite rank, depending on position it can indicate anything from a Major General to a Field Marshall. Duque usually indicates the senior commander on the field.

Legate III: Brigadier General or Major General. Per the contract between the *Legion del Cid* and the Federated States of Columbia, a Legate III, when his unit is in service to the Federated States, is entitled to the standing and courtesies of a Lieutenant General. Typically commands a deployed legion, when a separate legion is deployed, the air *ala* or the naval *classis*, or serves as an executive for a deployed corps.

Legate II: Colonel, typically commands a tercio in the rear or serves on staff if deployed.

Legate I: Lieutenant Colonel, typically commands a cohort or serves on staff.

Tribune III: Major, serves on staff or sometimes, if permitted to continue in command, commands a maniple.

Tribune II: Captain, typically commands a maniple.

Tribune I: First Lieutenant, typically serves as second in command of a maniple, commands a specialty platoon within the cohort's combat support maniple, or serves on staff.

Signifer: Second Lieutenant or Ensign, leads a platoon. Signifer is a temporary rank, and signifers are not considered part of the officer corps of the legions except as a matter of courtesy.

Sergeant Major: Sergeant Major with no necessary indication of level.

First Centurion: Senior noncommissioned officer of a maniple.

Senior Centurion: Master Sergeant but almost always the senior man within a platoon.

Centurion, J.G.: Sergeant First Class, sometimes commands a platoon but is usually the second in command.

Optio: Staff Sergeant, typically the second in command of a platoon.

Sergeant: Sergeant, typically leads a squad.

Corporal: Corporal, typically leads a team or crew or serves as second in command of a squad.

Legionario, or **Legionary**, or **Legionnaire**: private
through specialist.

Note that, in addition, under legion regulations adopted
in the Anno Condita 471, a soldier may elect to take
what is called "Triarius Status." This locks the soldier
into whatever rank he may be, but allows pay raises
for longevity to continue. It is one way the legion
has used to flatten the rank pyramid in the interests
of reducing careerism. Thus, one may sometimes
hear or read of a "Triarius Tribune III," typically a
major-equivalent who has decided, with legion accord,
that his highest and best use is in a particular staff
slot or commanding a particular maniple. Given that
the legion—with fewer than three percent officers,
including signifers—has the smallest officer corps of
any significant military formation on Terra Nova, and
a very flat promotion pyramid, the Triarius system
seems, perhaps, overkill. Since adoption, regulations
permit but do not require Triarius status legionaries
to be promoted one rank upon retirement.

The following is an excerpt from:

THE AMAZON LEGION

TOM KRATMAN

Available from Baen Books
April 2011
hardcover

CHAPTER ONE

...a failure, but not a waste.
—LTC (Ret.) John Baynes, *Morale*

A phone was ringing somewhere. People—women and children mostly—screamed. Others, men and women both, shouted. Their voices were distant, as if they came from the mouth of a tunnel. Runaway freight trains, having jumped their tracks and taken off into low ballistic flight, crashed into scrap metal yards, one after another. Over that was the sound of jet engines straining and helicopter rotors beating at the air.

With a barely suppressed shriek of her own, Maria Fuentes sat bolt upright in her trembling bed, her hand going automatically to her mouth to stifle the sound. As her eyes adjusted to the small light streaming in through her bedroom window, she realized that she wasn't asleep any longer.

"It was a..." she began to say. She stopped, mid-sentence, when she realized that she could still hear the trains, the crashes, the screams.

"Mierda!" she exclaimed, as she threw off the light covers. "Not a nightmare. Shit. Oh, *shit.*" Maria felt nausea rising, mostly fed by sudden unexpected fear.

The phone, which had stopped ringing, began again as Maria raced for her baby's—Alma's—room. She stopped and picked it up.

"Sergeant Fuentes."

"Maria? Cristina." Centurion Cristina Zamora was Maria's reserve platoon leader. "Alert posture Henrique. No drill." Zamora's voice was strained, nervous. Maria couldn't remember ever having heard Cristina's voice as anything but perfectly calm before. Not ever. She felt a fluttering in the pit of her stomach. *Zamora's upset? We're so fucked.*

"*Not* a drill?" she asked, pointlessly.

"No, Maria, not a drill. Alert posture Henrique."

"Henrique? Okay, I understand." *"Henrique." Call up all the reservists, but only those militia who can be quickly and conveniently assembled.* "I guess time's more important than numbers, huh?"

"They don't tell me these things, Maria. Later."

The phone's tone changed, telling Maria that Zamora had hung up.

Maria's phone was already programmed with the necessary numbers to conduct an alert. She scanned through until she found the number for her assistant, Marta Bugatti. She pressed that button, then the button for "speaker." She placed the phone on her bed and, while the phone was ringing, pulled out her legion-issue foot locker. A couple of flicks of the retainers and the top popped open. She was pulling her tiger-striped, pixilated battle dress trousers on when the ringing stopped and a deep voice—deep for a woman, anyway—answered, "Bugatti here, Maria."

"Marta. Alert. 'Henrique.' No shit."

"Oh, *really?* I would never have guessed!"

Unseen by Maria, a mile and a half from Maria's small apartment, Bugatti shook her head in general disgust and then held her own telephone receiver towards the nearest window. On her own end, Maria could easily make out the sound of chattering machine guns.

Marta's voice returned in a moment. "So what fucking else is fucking new? I'll take care of it. I'll—" Marta's phone went dead.

"Marta? *Marta?*" Maria pounded her own phone on the foot locker's plastic edge in frustration mixed with fear. "Shit. Dead." She closed the cell and tossed it on the bed. She thought, *Okay, Marta. You're a bitch . . . sometimes. But you're a lovable bitch and you're* my *bitch besides. I'll trust you.*

Maria pulled on her boots, green nylon and black leather, tucked her trousers into them, and then speed laced them shut. She wound the ends of the laces around her legs and tied them to hold the trousers in place. From her locker she took her battle dress jacket. She was buttoning this as she started again for her daughter's bedroom.

She started, then stopped short at Alma's door. *My God, I am going to have to leave her, then fight; maybe die, too, and leave her forever.*

Suddenly Maria felt even more ill. *How can I leave my baby?* Just as suddenly, she felt even worse. *How can I abandon my friends, my sisters, my troops?*

Bad mother; bad friend. Responsible parent; irresponsible soldier? Hero? Coward? None of those words mean a damn thing. Whatever I do, it's going to be because I'm more afraid of not doing it than of not doing the other. I'm going to be a coward in some way, no matter what.

Had she been a different person, *any* different

person, she might just have stood there, indecisive, until it was all over. But Maria wasn't just *anybody*. The powers that be had selected her very carefully, then trained her more carefully still. They had even organized her unit very carefully, paying more than usual attention to the needs of single military mothers. With or without Maria, Alma would be all right. She knew that. But without her, her troops—her friends—might not. She had no choice, really. She'd made the decision years before.

I have to go.

Alma was still sleeping soundly in her little bed when her mother entered. Maria smiled as her sight took in her daughter's few dozen pounds and few little feet of soft lines, dark lashes and curly hair. Maria marveled that not only was Alma hers, but that the baby wasn't awake and screaming.

I could never hope to sleep with artillery flying anywhere nearby, not even in training. What makes it so easy for a kid?

Maria looked out the window from Alma's bedroom. She couldn't see much but the street they lived on, and not all of that. Streetlights illuminated the scene. So far as she could see none of Terra Nova's moons had any noticeable part in that. Then the streetlights began to flicker out, leaving nothing but the moons' light.

Below the apartment, people were running in the streets, most of them tugging on uniforms. Just about everybody was carrying a rifle, machine gun, or rocket launcher. A number of those who weren't armed seemed to be trying to hold back someone who was. Somebody's mother, wife, or maybe girlfriend was crying for him to come back. Maria couldn't see where anyone did turn back though.

Returning to her own room, Maria continued pulling gear from the locker. Out came load-bearing equipment, her helmet, her silk and liquid-metal *lorica,* the legion's standard body armor. Her centurion's baton she picked up for a moment, then replaced it in the locker. Last came her modified F-26 "Zion" rifle.

She held the rifle in her hands for a moment, drawing some small comfort from its heft and weight. Then she slapped a drum magazine in, turned the key on the back to put pressure on the spring, and jacked a round home.

I hope Alma stays asleep. She hates to see me in helmet and body armor.

Fully clothed and armed, Maria slung her rifle across her back, walked back to the baby's bedroom, then picked her up in her arms.

Alma almost woke up then, sucking air in with three gasping "uh . . . uh . . . uhs." The mother waited a minute or two, holding her, stroking her hair and saying, "Don't worry, baby. Everything will be all right, baby. Don't worry, love. Mama's here." The child snuggled her soft hair into an armored shoulder and fell back, sound asleep.

Once Alma had fallen asleep again, it was out the door and down three flights of stairs. Maria didn't bother with locking the door behind her; crime hadn't been much of a problem in this part of the city for some time; current invasion excepted, of course.

Lance Corporal Lydia Porras, of the *Tercio Amazona's* Dependant Care Maniple, affectionately called "the Fairy Godmothers," careened her van through the streets, barely missing men as they hurried to their duties in the dark. The Fairy Godmothers were not actually part of the *Tercio Amazona*, but seconded to it from a regiment of elderly and late enlistees.

Though Porras was in uniform, her vehicle was plainly civilian, both in color and design. Otherwise, it would certainly have been fired on by any one of the dozens of helicopters that swooped in from time to time to shoot at the soldiers in the streets.

Porras made a sharp left-hand turn onto Maria's fast-emptying street. She jerked the wheel left again to pull up to the apartment building, then slammed on the brakes to bring the van to a screeching halt. Porras killed the lights and listened for a moment for the sounds of one of the fearsome attack helicopters the Taurans had in such abundance. There was nothing or, at least, nothing she could hear over the rattle and *crump* of artillery.

Porras prayed, "*Santa Maria, Madre de Dios,* take pity on an old woman who has borne children. Take pity on children too young to die. Most importantly, Our Lady of Victory, grant it to us."

Porras crossed herself and stepped out of the van. As she did so, Maria and Alma appeared in the doorway. Porras took Alma from her mother's arms—well, pulled, actually; the mother didn't want to let go—and placed the girl gently, sitting up, in one of the seats of the van, taking the extra moment to buckle the child in. There were a couple of other children there, too. One of the others, an older girl, turned sideways in her sleep to throw an arm around Alma. Porras smiled for the first time that night. *Kids can be so sweet.*

When one is young and alone and the call comes to fight, it really helps to know someone is going to take care of the kids. That was Porras's job. She was a nice old biddy. Gray haired, wrinkled; but her eyes shone bright and her posture was immaculate. She had not volunteered for service until she had turned sixty-two years old, with grown children and grandchildren of her own. She'd gone to geriatric basic training then, and then volunteered for assignment to the unit.

Old, Porras might have been. Steady, calm and reliable she was too. She was also a surprisingly good shot. Even so, Porras couldn't hope to do what Maria and the others did; she was simply too old. Still, she certainly made it easier for them to do their jobs.

Alma loved her. So did Maria.

Filled with inexpressible feelings of pity, love, and fear, the old woman looked at Maria carefully, as if for the last time. *Pretty girl*, she thought, eyes glancing over Maria's five feet two inches of height, healthy figure, straight nose and large, well-spaced eyes. She placed a hand gently along the younger woman's sculpted chin, saying, "Go with God, child. And be careful. I'll guard your daughter with my life."

Then, eyes clouding with tears, Lydia Porras jumped back into the van, slammed the door, and pulled away amidst screeching, smoking tires.

For Maria it was *so* hard to watch that van pull away.

Maria Fuentes's hands trembled. She was frightened, damned frightened, and she had reason to be. Her country's enemy had one hundred times Balboa's own population; three or four times that ratio in disparity of wealth. Between their regular and reserve forces they had more people under arms than the entire population of her country. Weapons? Except for small arms and a couple of tricks there was no comparison. Technology? Sister, Balboa wasn't even in the race.

But it's not hopeless, she told herself, forcing her hands to steady down. *We have some things going for us, too. Our weapons are generally decent and reliable. We have a better doctrine for battle and a much better one for training. We have damned good leaders.*

And this is our *country. We have no place else to go.*

Tougher to measure were some *softer* factors: Heart, soul, a pretty good knowledge of their own country, and the fact that the enemy was arrogant—and might, with luck, sometime show all the stupidity arrogance entails.

Besides, the Taurans *did* have some place else they called home. And if they didn't mind much making others bleed, they didn't much like bleeding themselves.

Maria thought, *If we're going to make them bleed, we'll have to bleed some ourselves.*

She looked up at the sky and, with the streetlights gone, saw the thin crescents of two moons, Bellona and Hecate. *Yeah, they've got more night vision capability than we do; they'd hit us at a time with minimal illumination.*

She turned away from the direction in which Porras had taken Alma and, her mind on bleeding, faced in the direction she would have to go. She took the rifle from across her back and, weapon in hand, began jogging.

Left, right, left, right.

From the apartment building it was about a mile to the assembly point, the "hide." This was a small restaurant in Balboa City owned by one of the other squad leaders in Maria's maniple.

Left, right, left, right.

It is not, repeat *not,* fun to run, or even jog, in a tropical environment, when you've got forty-five pounds of combat equipment and ammunition dragging you down. It wasn't fun for a man. For women it was worse. Maria knew it would become even worse than that after she picked up the rest of the ammunition hidden at the restaurant.

Left, right, left, right.

Maria heard the steady *whop-whop-whop* of a helicopter coming closer. Her army had more than a few helicopters, but none of them sounded like this one. She began to look around at her surroundings, desperately seeking someplace she could hide.

"Hey, Johanson, look left. Single grunt. Take 'im?"

"Yeah, sure, why the hell not?"

The helicopter tilted left as its tail swung around to the right, bringing its weapons to bear. The target ducked and disappeared from view.

"Fire a couple of bursts. See if you can spook him out."

"Roger."

In the recessed doorway in which she'd taken shelter, Maria pressed herself against a wall to try to blend in with the shadow. Her heart was thumping so loud in her chest that she was sure even the helicopter's crew would be able to hear it.

Suddenly the shadow disappeared as the street was lit by the strobe of several dozen heavy machine-gun rounds being fired. Against her will, Maria screamed. Again the helicopter fired and she pressed her hand to her mouth and bit down.

More than the sound, it was those solid streams of tracers lighting up the landscape that terrified her. She just tried to make herself smaller, even as she bit down on two fingers again so as not to hear herself scream out loud.

"Fuck it, Jo. If he's still around, he'll be wanting to change his pants before reporting to his unit. Call it a 'Mission accomplished.' We got shit to do. Let's go look for easier meat."

"Roger. Don't like hanging around one place too long, either." The chopper tilted right as Johanson flew it up and away from where Maria's trembling form crouched unseen.

In combat, fatigue and fear are "mutually reinforcing and essentially interchangeable." So Maria had been told in training. Her training cadre had even done their best to show her, and her sisters, how that worked. *Nothing* could have fully prepared her for the reality. She felt so weak from the terror of that helicopter that it took an effort of will just to start moving again. Once she did, though, it got better. She was even able to start thinking and stop just reacting.

Left, right, left, right.

Maria thought, *The Taurans may be stupid, but they're not that stupid. They know we have to assemble to defend ourselves. I wonder what they . . .*

The Tauran sniper should have had a spotter, and preferably a man for security. Under the circumstances, the desperate need to destroy the Balboans' leadership before they could fully mobilize their not inconsiderable force of reservists and militia, spotters and guards had been dispensed with. His spotter, indeed, was also alone, someplace a mile or so to the west.

Alone, on flat roof overlooking one of the enemy capital's major thoroughfares, the sniper carefully rotated the focus ring on his rifle's scope as he tracked his target down the street. He'd begun to squeeze the trigger once, when the target was in an open space. But the target had disappeared behind a small truck before the rifle had fired. The sniper relaxed the pressure on the trigger, waiting patiently.

Ah. There he was again. The sniper gently slid the rifle over to bring it to bear on the target. He began to squeeze the trigger once again. "Keep your damned head still, asshole. Stop swinging like some *bitch*," the sniper whispered. The trigger depressed....

KAZINGG!

The bullet passed by Maria's head so closely she felt the wind of its passage. *Sniper!*

Even as her mind put a name to the threat, her body was diving behind the nearest auto. In falling, Maria scraped her right elbow on the concrete hard enough to rip her uniform and tear the skin beneath. She ignored it, except to think, in some distant part of her mind, *My God, Centurion Garcia would kick my ass if he ever saw me do a dive like that.*

Her body armor, tougher stuff, protected her breasts, as aramid fiber knee cups protected her knees. Her heart, which hadn't ceased pounding since her brush with the helicopter, began to race: *thumpthumpthump-thumpthumpthumpthump*.

"Shit! Shit! *Shit!*" Maria cursed, even as she crawled

to put the engine block and the right front tire of the car between her and where she thought the bullet had come from. It was better than nothing.

Unless, of course, the bullet didn't come from where I thought. In that case, I'm probably toast.

She rolled over to her back, then slithered her posterior around. Trying to make the smallest target possible, Maria sidled her back to get her head flat behind one of the car's tires.

Another bullet sent a cloud of broken safety glass raining down on her. Another and she heard a bullet ring off of the engine block then pass through the sheet metal of the body just over her head. Maria began to pray quietly.

Her back hunched against the tire, Maria looked to her left. The next nearest car was better than twenty-five meters away. She didn't think there was any way she could make it before the sniper put a bullet in her. She knew, too, that he wouldn't be picky, this time, going for a headshot. *He'll put one through my guts then shoot me in the head as I lie there on the asphalt. The lorica's good for shrapnel and light rounds, not heavy, full caliber bullets. I'm pinned, but good. Worse, if all else fails he'll probably eventually go for the gas tank. Then it's going to be fricasseed Fuentes.*

She began to pray a bit more fervently, whispering, "Our Father, who art in Heaven, hallowed be Thy name. Thy Kingdom come . . ."

Next to the main door to Maria's maniple's headquarters there was a hand-painted sign. She'd seen it a thousand times. The sign showed a duck trying to eat a frog, the frog's legs sticking out of the duck's mouth. The duck couldn't eat the frog, though, because the frog's front feet were wrapped around the duck's throat, choking it, blocking its windpipe and gullet.

The caption on the sign said, "Never give up!"

She stopped praying to think, *Okay. Never give up.*

Maria took the drum magazine from her F-26 rifle, then tapped it against her thigh to make sure all the cartridges were well seated. She then replaced it in the magazine well. The magazine made a click as it seated, soft enough but seeming loud to her. Her finger flicked on the rifle's integral night sight. Maria took one deep breath, crossed herself and prepared to get up and shoot back. She was NOT going to burn without a fight.

Even as her body tensed, she thought, *If they could think of putting snipers on the roofs to block our mobilization, why couldn't we have put people on the roofs to block the snipers? Or, at least, to keep the bastards busy?*

"Quietly, Pablo," the old man whispered with authority. "Don't let the ammunition drag on the steps, boy."

"*Si, Abuelo.*" The grandson looked overhead, past where a lightly built shed protected the stairwell that ran through the building from the frequent rain. He could see only one moon, and that a thin and weak one. Perhaps another was up; from where he was, Pablo couldn't tell. In any case, he couldn't imagine even the remotest possibility that anyone would or could hear anything over the ceaseless drumming of the artillery, the screaming of the jets, and the *whoosh* of light air defense missiles trying—usually in vain—to bring down an aircraft. Still, orders from his grandfather, more importantly orders from Legion Corporal (Med. Ret.) Vladimiro Serrasin, were not to be ignored. The old man was a veteran not only of the terrorist war, but even of the invasion by the Federated States, many years before. He was the boy's hero.

The boy, himself a junior cadet with a slot waiting at one of the military schools, clutched the bandoleer tight to his chest.

"There, Pablo. See him?" The old man pointed to a soldier, enemy presumably, lying down on the sloping roof with his rifle aimed through a large open chink in the wall surrounding the roof.

"This one is good," *Abuelo* gave as his professional judgment. He had a tone of approval in his voice the boy found incongruous at best. "Good fieldcraft. From the ground only his target would have a chance to spot him. If he is as good a shot, that wouldn't be a problem for him."

Abuelo got on one arthritic knee, the rough gravel of the roof digging into it. Instead of showing a wince, a mild sneer crossed the old man's face. The light machine gun he bore in his arms—an older and more primitive arm than the fancy F- and M-26s the legion carried nowadays—went to his shoulder in a motion so smooth it was obviously long-practiced. The old man leaned into the shed that shielded the stairwell to the roof from rain. He took aim on the indistinct shape on the opposite roof. The old man inhaled, let the breath out, and began to squeeze....

Maria crossed herself quickly, then twisted up to one knee to bring her rifle to bear on the building from which she thought the fire had come. Even as she did so, a long, long burst of machine gun fire came from her left rear. She hadn't been expecting it. The surprise ruined her aim. Her bullets hit the building opposite, but that was all.

She did *not* wet herself.

From the other side of the street came a scream that might have been heartbreaking if it hadn't also been so satisfying. The machine gun fired again and the screaming stopped.

Mildly faint and more than a little nauseated, she slid down to rest her back once again against the tire.

As Maria sighed her relief, she heard a laugh from overhead. Then an old man's voice called out to her, "I once was young and brave and strong."

Maria answered, loudly as she could, her voice still breaking with terror, "And I'm so now . . . Come on . . . and try."

Then a young boy—he sounded all of thirteen or fourteen—shouted to the world, "But I'll be strongest, by and by."

"Go on, girl," said the old man. "We can see for about three blocks. It's clear that far, anyway."

Maria shouted out, "Thanks," then got unsteadily to her feet. Thankful to be alive and substantially unhurt, she resumed her jog again for the restaurant.

—end excerpt—

from *The Amazon Legion*
available in hardcover,
April 2011, from Baen Books

Here's a sneak peek at:

EXILED

Clan of the Claw
Book One

a new shared-world
fantasy series written by

Harry Turtledove, S.M. Stirling,
and **John Ringo & Jody Lynn Nye**

ENJOY!

Available from Baen Books
August 2011
hardcover

The Mrem Go West

HARRY TURTLEDOVE

RANTAN TAGGAH STARED NORTH ACROSS THE ARMS OF
the sea—the New Water, the Clan of the Claw called
it. His lips narrowed, so that the tips—well, more
than the tips—of his fangs showed. Like the rest of
his clansmates, the war leader called the New Water
other things, too: things as foul as he could think of.
An angry growl rumbled, down deep in his throat.
The New Water was much too likely to mean death,
not only for him but for all the Clan of the Claw,
which meant for all the Mrem trapped south of it.

A fly landed on the tuft atop one of his upstanding
ears. The ear twitched, but the fly didn't leave. He
scratched his ear, shooting just the tips of his claws
from their sheaths. The fly buzzed away. His ear
twitched again, as if reminding it not to come back.

High above the salt-smelling water, a sea bird circled,
hunting. No, not a bird: the long, drooping tail said it
was a flying Liskash. The leatherwing folded its wings
and plummeted, striking the sea like a spearpoint. A

moment later, it flew off again, a fish writhing in its toothy jaws.

Where one hunter had luck, others might hope for more. That was a rule everywhere and for everything and everyone: leatherwings and birds, mammals and meat-eating Liskash, Liskash nobles and Mrem. A second flyer dove at the water, visions of a full belly doubtless dancing in its narrow skull.

Something reared up out of the sea to greet it— something far bigger, far fiercer, far toothier. That enormous mouth opened and closed. Rantan Taggah stood too far away to hear the crunch of breaking bones with his body's ears, but it was sickeningly loud in the ears of his mind. A leatherwing was far from enough to sate something that size, but snacks were always welcome.

"Aedonniss!" Rantan Taggah muttered. "What were you thinking when you made those horrible things?"

The sky god didn't answer. Rantan Taggah hadn't expected him to. Aedonniss looked for his folk to take care of themselves and not waste his time. He was a hard god...but then, it was a hard world, and getting harder all the time.

Mrem who'd lived by the Old Water spoke of the savage reptilian monsters in the sea when they came inland to trade or to raid. Like any other inlander, Rantan Taggah listened to the tales. Why not? They were an entertaining way to make time lope by. Just because you listened to a story didn't mean you had to believe it. He'd discounted most of that the seaside Mrem claimed.

Now, though, he'd had the chance to see the ocean monsters for himself. The really alarming thing was how little the talespinners exaggerated.

He snarled. No, the *really* alarming thing was that he'd had the chance to see the ocean monsters for himself. He hadn't gone traveling. On the contrary—the ocean had come to him.

Some few Mrem priestesses and learned males had always claimed the great depression by whose southern edge the Clan of the Claw dwelt was an ancient seabottom. With a great part of the world's water tied up in sheets of ice, land advanced while the sea retreated. Now the glaciers were melting, shrinking, as if ensorceled; and, as the world warmed, water in the oceans piled higher and deeper.

Piled higher and deeper...and sometimes spilled. For as long as the Mrem could remember (and, surely, for longer than that), the Quaxo Hills to the east had held against the Old Water, held it out of the Hollow Lands. Rantan Taggah, now a male in his prime, had just been coming out of kithood when the Quaxo Hills held no more.

Now the Hollow Lands were vanished from maps and charts. Now the hunting clans and townsMrem who'd lived there were either fugitives from their homes or, most of them, vanished beneath waters Aedonniss only knew how many bowshots deep.

Rantan Taggah snarled again. Few of the Mrem had much use for water or for travel across it under any circumstances. And that said nothing of the reptilian horrors like the one he'd seen, creatures that preyed on anything they could reach. The Clan of the Claw—and the handful of survivors from the drowned Hollow Lands—would not, could not, rejoin their kind by sailing across the New Water.

The only trouble with that was, the Clan of the Claw

couldn't stay where it was, either. Rantan Taggah turned away from the New Water and toward the south: toward the Warm Lands, the lands where the Liskash flourished best. The pupils in his emerald eyes widened from slits almost to circles, as if he were confronting his folk's foes in truth, not merely in thought.

His clan was rich, as these things went. Peering south, he saw broad herds of horned bundor and krelprep and shambling hamsticorns. The Clan of the Claw did not lack for meat or milk or leather or hair and wool.

But one clan, alone (or as near as made no difference), could not hope to stand against the Liskash nobles and the weaker but still dangerous reptiles the nobles could gather to fight at their side (or rather, under their feet). Not for nothing did the Mrem picture the demons who opposed Aedonniss as being formed in the image of the Liskash. Maybe it was the other way around: maybe the Liskash looked like demons. Priestesses and savants argued about that, too. Savants, of course, would argue about anything. It was part of what made them savants.

There were times when Rantan Taggah enjoyed arguing as much as anybody else—more than most males. What the Clan of the Claw had to do now, though, was not a matter for argument. He didn't think so, anyhow. But he was only too certain plenty of other males—and females, too—would be ready, even eager, to argue with him about that.

—end excerpt—

from _EXILED: Clan of the Claw Book One_
available in hardcover,
August 2011, from Baen Books